ALSO BY JAMES D MCCALLISTER

NOVELS

King's Highway

Fellow Traveler

Let the Glory Pass Away

Dogs of Parsons Hollow

Down in Dixiana (2019)

Dixiana Darling (2020)

Reconstruction of the Fables (2020)

Mansion of High Ghosts (2021)

STORIES

The Year They Canceled Christmas

Fables of the Reconstruction (2020)

The Night I Prayed to Elvis (2021)

DIXIANA

OMNIBUS EDITION

BOOK 1:
DIRT SURFER

BOOK 2:
BLACK BLADE

BOOK 3:
DOUBTLESS THE SEA

JAMES D. MCCALLISTER

MHP
Mind Harvest Press
COLUMBIA, SC

This is a work of fiction. Names, characters, businesses, places, events and incidents are either the products of the author's imagination or used in a fictitious manner. Any resemblance to actual persons, living or dead, or actual events is purely coincidental.

ISBN: 978-1-946052-14-8 (ppbk); 978-1-946052-24-7 (ebook)

Library of Congress: 2019904268

Cover Design by Marc Cardwell (marccardwell.com)

"The Dixiana" drawing by Patrick Mahoney / Totally Mundo Productions

"Waltz Across Texas" Lyrics ©Ernest Tubb Music, Inc.

For more information:

Mind Harvest Press
COLUMBIA, SC

Mind Harvest Press
PO Box 50552
Columbia SC 29250-0552
www.mindharvestpress.com
www.jamesdmccallister.com

CONTENTS

BOOK ONE: DIRT SURFER

BOOK TWO: BLACK BLADE

BOOK THREE: DOUBTLESS THE SEA

For Jenn

BOOK ONE

Dirt Surfer

Death-day greetings are the sweetest
  Let trumpets roar when a man dies
  And rockets fly up, he has found his fortune.

— ROBINSON JEFFERS, 'SUICIDE'S STONE'

It's meaning we need to coax into our lives.

— TERRENCE MCKENNA

ROY E. PETTUS

With the curvature of the Earth in evidence and a scrim of fading daylight bending around the edges of your vision, this epic vista, observed from the cockpit of your hobby aircraft, fills you with dread instead of wonder.

You're in trouble. You don't fly at night.

The pair of hands on the yoke of the Piper PA-46-500TP Meridian—an aircraft you've coveted and now own and that hums and purrs along at 10,000 feet—belong to you. As per your training, your eyes sweep the visible sky and horizon in ten-degree wedges, a few seconds per wedge all while wishing to have made a few more night landings.

The eyes, burning.

Your hands, sweating.

Twilight, fast approaching.

Aside from losing the light you're piloting fine, and this despite suffering one of your anxiety spells. You've had them since you were a little boy. Mostly under control. Until earlier in the day, upon discovering your life is a lie.

As your wife shrieked on the tarmac: *Roy, you ain't in the right frame of mind for flying.*

And here, about to attempt a landing. At dusk.

Nah. Go ahead, call it nighttime. And with landings already being a weak area for you. For many other pilots, too. Seasoned and otherwise. Piloting—it can be tricky.

Face it. She's right. You're in no condition to fly.

A LEATHERY, mustachioed father figure, Captain C. W. Gracern, an ex-military flier from whom you'd taken your first lessons two years ago, had emphasized every pilot's goal: returning the aircraft to the ground.

"Every comfortable landing succeeds from an approach that's stable, tracking the runway centerline down the glide path to touchdown. Everybody slapping each other on the back, and it's Miller time, and another few hours logged. Best-case scenario."

Prayerful, he held his hands in front of an outdoorsman's weathered, tan face. "Worst case?"

You and the others sensed a pall settle over the classroom. But nobody spoke.

Gracern smiled. Nodded. "Damn straight—we don't wanna say it aloud."

The teacher had ambled around the desk and leaned his stubby body on the edge. "During the all-important approach, if a pilot's lax in achieving and maintaining stability early enough, if at all, he's courting trouble. Hoping and wishing for critical details to fall into place on their own—is that how we want to fly?"

"No." The breathy syllable had escaped your lips.

Gracern, winking at you. "Right. Thinking it'll magically come together, and that bird'll find itself back on the earth again? Yeah; no. I can already picture the NTSB team preparing to scour the accident site.

"So listen. Stabilize early. Remain alert for deviations, however minor, from the desired course, glide path, and speed. You need more stability? Adjust—with a light touch, now—the power and-or flight control inputs."

At the time, none of his words held quite as much weight—you hadn't yet piloted. But they do now.

As though reading your mind, he said, "You want a real world example? Watch the big planes. See how they do it." The instructor hooked a thick old man's thumb out the window of the community college where you took the flying classes: "A jetliner pilot's goal is minimal rolling and pitching, all dependent upon external conditions. Their engines? They ain't throttling. Or they better not be, anyway. Not with all those souls onboard, those fliers under our heroic pilot's care and control. Settle that bird into ground effect, and then? Home again."

The class breathed a sigh of relief. You realized you'd been gripping the sides of the desk.

Ground effect, now you understood what he meant: that glorious floating sensation as your wings draw toward the blessed earth below, and the return to safety.

You'll know the feeling soon. No magical thinking—you're Roy E. Pettus. A captain of your aircraft, and your life.

Complete awareness.

Total control.

Except for the explosive situation you left on the ground—the shrieked accusations, the threats of recrimination. Her weak-sauce denials—the phrase 'red-handed' comes to mind—continued to echo inside your cans during what should have been a routine flight. Your life, it occurs to you, may not be 'routine' again for quite some time.

◉❂◎

EXPECTING an imminent return to the tangible bedrock awaiting the touch of your wide, sport-sandaled chunks of feet, you grasp and cling to the bound leather stick. Maybe pray. A little.

You wipe a damp hand on your khaki cargo shorts and grab the radio to signal for the airfield lights using an on-off automatic radio sequence. At a low volume airstrip such as podunk Edgewater County, lying a hundred-fifty miles due north of Sedge Island where you and your wife live, no tower crew anticipates your landing.

Key 1-2-3-4-5. Flick the sequence with your thumb. Easy peasy.

But the lights, which ought to be ahead of you, are nowhere in sight.

Without the airfield landing lights, and with your limited flying time at night, you need to get wheels down.

On the ground.

The Mercedes would have eaten alive the concrete of the freeway. But you didn't drive, and here you are. You had to fly, didn't you? To get away from her fast.

The airfield beacon—there, you see it. Flicking the thumb sequence again, you wait.

No landing lights.

Calm down; it's not as though you're in bumpy weather or having trouble like in a movie; this isn't a modern version of *Airport 1975*.

You flick the sequence again, with deliberation.

Nothing.

Cruising now across the fall line, high above Edgewater County here in the uppermost of the state's midsection, your dusty old hometown sits off to the right, closer to the river. You can see the lighted town green, its trapezoid shape and big oak trees, the courthouse, the highway bypass skirting downtown. Soft, amber street lamps illuminate the neighborhoods. But no landing lights.

A different beacon jumps out at you: the neon sign glowing orange outside The Dixiana, your granddaddy's honkytonk.

Home.

At least you're not over water. Whatever happens, you won't end up being remembered as the JFK, Jr., of Edgewater County. Calm winds, a clear September sky—clear as 9/11.

But now, the sun, gone.

And no landing field lights.

You, Roy E. Pettus, need wheels down. And fast.

☀

An extravagance, the aircraft.

You're not wealthy, not by the standards of the day. No, you're only flush. A billion, that's what's cool. You're only a million. A few million. Not rich. Cash rich and without liens of significance, with wealth compounding more wealth and the stock market hitting new highs every month, your ass sits in high cotton.

But not like, rich-rich.

Still, enough you could afford the Meridian. Deserving a rich man's toy like this. Had outgrown your first plane, a used Piper Cub that rattled like a death trap. Had outgrown it in more ways than your flying hours, had deserved the finer appointments and details of the Meridian, as befitting the size of your wallet.

Now, a few of the swells you know from the hanger are big big money. Carry themselves that way. But in the hanger, where you all have flying time, you dwell among peers regardless of fortune.

Tin cans with wings, as you and your buddies in the airfield lounge call your personal pleasure aircraft arrayed along the tarmac and under the sheds. You and the boys gather to shoot the shit either before or after flying, the way the stiffs congregate on tennis courts and golf courses and in the many exclusive clubhouses found in a magical land like Sedge Island. You dig your hobby, big-time, but flying also makes you claustrophobic, a little breathless. Not as much anymore. Not since you got in your hours and began flying your own plane, and in those moments feel like the captain of the planet, not at all anxious.

Until this flight.

Brutal. Horrifying. You are in no shape to fly.

You're airborne not simply to escape your wife, Creedence.

On your way.

To attend to your dying grandfather.

At last.

Don't be like that. How cruel.

But you can't help it. Pushing ninety, both Mama Runelle and your grand-daddy. It worried you, having old-timers of such vintage on your sheet. A miracle they still lived on their own. No broken hips, no major illnesses or injuries, but still frail. Why you built them a house with an upstairs is a mystery—they don't need the room.

Lord knew you wondered what kept them going. Him, in particular.

The hell you wondered—you knew he wouldn't be happy unless he croaked sitting outside on that bench beside the entrance to that honkytonk of his, the wretched old dump you couldn't stand to think about getting near.

But yeah, this fresh crisis came at a bad time, no doubt. As far as the implo-sion of the marriage goes, the catastrophe loomed so fresh you literally flew away from the last confrontation, which had come earlier today like a black swan event in the markets. In the context of the day so far, the news of your grandfather's purported heart attack at The Dixiana, or wherever it had happened, came inopportune and unwelcome, while also long overdue—if he wa'n't careful, the old fart might find himself in triple digits.

Into overtime.

Another ten years? Forget it—the codger still smokes, for god sakes.

IF HE DIES, as you thought upon hearing the news which rippled into your thoughts through the brackish marsh water of betrayal surrounding your marriage like the ugly stalking snout of a gator, maybe you can let go of some of that Edgewater County energy you've always been certain has held you back all this time in some obscure fashion.

You didn't know such release would involve losing Creedence, too. Did ya.

The twanging strains of a hundred old country songs about betrayal and heartbreak earworm their way into the soft gray meat of your mind. You rued enduring such music during your youth at the honkytonk. Every syrupy melody, every minor key lament, all overlaid and reverberating like a hollow soundtrack to a simmering cauldron of gut-sick disappointment at how your life has turned out, at least on the relationship side of the coin.

For all your successes, you still haven't shaken off the past. Not that marrying a hometown girl, a childhood crush, helped in that regard. You owned the house on Sedge Island and loved that selfsame beautiful wife, and what's more, had cashed out at forty-seven. Your net worth in stock and assets, brushing up against eight figures.

But you feel held back, still.

From what?

Your grandparents still alive here in the almost-upstate. Perceiving their energy tugging at you.

You thought by now they'd be dead, and The Dixiana would be closed, and you'd sell the house you built them a decade ago across from the more modest ranch house in which you grew up, and for a sick, sick profit. Dump the houses and the land, every square inch, all the way over to the pecan orchard and into the backland toward the river. Donate every lick of the proceeds to charity, like Creedence's animal rights groups, or maybe the old alcoholic's home in Edgewater County.

Now there, an idea—wouldn't that constitute spiritual recompense for the decades of drunks your granddaddy's tavern had served, including your wife's dead brother, the pitiful sot?

Spiritual recompense. You don't even know what the words mean.

⊙❋◉

COMING AROUND for another attempt at landing, you twinge as you recall a fantasy you'd had of trying to goose matters along: you considered hiding in their bedroom closet, waiting to pop out in a black robe and holding a scythe. You know, a cartoon-ish Mr. Death like in the Monty Python skit—there's a man at the door, something about the reaping.

Well well, a voice chastises. It's here now, isn't it?

You awful grandson, you.

True. You'd felt so guilty over feeling this way you'd built them a house, more house than they needed, a situation not unlike you and your childless wife down on the island. A coldly tiled, pale stucco mansion compared to the warm, classic Victorian you'd insisted on constructing for the folks.

Back in the woods.

Like you want for yourself, in many ways.

Just not there in Edgewater County.

The voice in your head, a phantom, could have belonged in meatspace to Dobbs Vandegrift, a homie and oldschool hombre from whom you received the call about Rabbit. Dobbs, one of your oldest friends, in this case calling to break bad news. When you heard his voice, you already knew a momentous event at hand, because neither of you spoke anymore. A significant example, years ago now, had been when he'd called to bemoan receiving a postcard from Creedence's brother Devin, the no-good drunk who'd made an avocation of disappearing on his family, at last for real.

The postcard had read: Tell 'em it's for keeps this time. That it's close, getting real close. Love to you all. After eight years had gone by, you and Creedence had him declared dead.

Devin. He always had this dramatic schtick about dying young, and had come close: drunken falls, fights, a car wreck in which his girlfriend Libby had been killed, also leaving Dobbs paralyzed. Awful stuff.

Maybe Devin made the reality of all that death stuff. All his gloomy obsessions. And the drinking, Olympian in scale. What would Dr. Phil say about all this self-destructiveness?

Problem is, your wife still suffers over him, the asshole—Devin, not some television shrink. She writes letters to him, still. Saddest shit you ever heard. Problem the deuce is that, for you, Devin remains in your heart as one of your best childhood friends.

Creedence. Her grief over Devin didn't matter to you anymore—y'all are finished. That's the main problem. Change has come upon you, in an awful wave. Faithlessness trumps heart attack.

Wait—did it? A debate above your pay grade. Back in college, you'd dropped out of Philosophy class after only a week. Too much intangible bullcrud.

In any case, your life as it'd been, dwelling in the quiet violence of your wife's disinterest, has been bad enough, wondering where her heart and head had gone.

Which is complete crap. You woke up this morning thinking everything fine—that's the god's truth right there, boy. You hadn't a clue. Not a clue. You had dreamed of a white pyramid on a hill. You had thought it was your recurring dream of the mountain bald like Max Patch, but in this dream, as you got closer on what felt like an epic hike through lush green forests, what you kept glimpsing turned out to be a pyramid. Blue-white. You felt the presence of magic. Shimmering energetic magic, and in the dream your feet had lifted off the ground, and you'd levitated.

You'd awakened in a state of grace. It wasn't to last. Not after reading all those emails between your wife and the lover for whom her rhetoric indicated she intended to leave you.

⊙✳◎

ON APPROACH AGAIN, the lights from the Sugeree Nuclear Station along the river, for reasons of national security a no-fly zone, fall away. Looking again for the airstrip beacon, turning turning turning, green-white-green-white. Your glasses, forgotten in the fight with Creedence at the hanger and now this, this, this, the landing strip lights still cold and dark.

Beacons all around, these last fifty miles: Columbia Metro, Van Loan Field, McNabb National Guard Base, and farther east the AFB, but all those fallen behind you now, and only Edgewater County ahead.

Flicking the thumb switch sequence on the mic again, and again.

What you wouldn't give now for one of those guys from back at the airport on Sedge Island, eh? Older dudes, retirees who'd worked for airlines or as mechanics on the airplanes themselves or who'd been pilots, a couple claiming to have now forgotten more about flying than they still knew. What you wouldn't give to have one of those old coots to ask what to do now.

Fried from the last battle with your wife and the revelations that'd come out of her mouth, gut-punching facts you already knew, but damn if it didn't feel all the worse hearing her confirmations, you can't think straight. From what you read, this, no mere fling. This crap sounds like love.

Now, this hurts, enough to make a man like you forget his goddamn glasses, which you hate wearing anyway because of the new bifocals; a grim reminder how at your age you're more than halfway to the end: the eyes, the bad hearing in one ear, a dick not always a stiff and pulsing flagpole every morning before you rise, which is after Creedence because she's up and at it these days, and hoo-boy, don't you know why now.

Writing little love letters.

Maybe you can't see the airfield lights which now flare blue and bright as ground-fallen stars, because of the smeary tears on the lenses not of the missing glasses but of your eyes themselves, crossed and burning and red— you've been crying ever since you took off from Sedge Island. Half-blind over it all. That's your problem. Besides needing the fudging airstrip lights to come on.

As though a wish being granted, on the second approach you flick the sequence and the blue lights appear clear as crystal. Your self-confidence comes roaring back, and you take that hunk of tin and put it wheels down.

On the ground.

Relief.

As for whom you'll call for a ride, wellsir, you are not one to Uber. Who lives nearby? 'Tis a shitty part of the county here, way outside town near the airstrip; this is Pirkle country, and with that in mind you rationalize reaching out to Trudy, your granddaddy's right-hand gal at The Dixiana.

Face it: you'd be calling her no matter what. Trudy, an old love. One about whom you still dream. Jerk off to, even. Not that you'll call about such personal matters. It had been one of those let-us-never-speak-of-it-again situations between you.

Trudy: Not only your first lay, but the first woman in whom you believed you felt love. Such as a sixteen-year-old neophyte can know what love is, especially with a redneck barmaid from the honkytonk. A few years older than you, she's now well over the crest of fifty.

Trudy. She had been the go-code to begin a race you hadn't run. Not until Creedence, years later.

Was it all circular? *Today's also the day I'm to come to terms with Trudy Pirkle? Now?*

In a word? WTF.

The idea of seeing her produces a bracing chill down your conflicted spine.

Trudy.

Concentrating on your flying, you approach with no lack of landing indicators or directional confusion: inexorable, your destination, looming ahead in the middle distance.

Wheels-down you might now find yourself, son. But face the facts: you're lost, still.

Fumbling with the iPhone you kept turned off while airborne, you discover a number of missed calls—from Dobbs again, Creedence, and from your grandmother, a fragile voice calling you darling, and telling you hurrying is no longer necessary; your grandfather has passed away.

You curse and stomp your feet; you do not fail at life this way. And yet you have.

Trudy. Trudy will make this all okay.

If only your eyes weren't so blurry, you could better punch in the number to The Dixiana, which to make some boneheaded personal point you don't keep saved in your stupid, powerful mobile device connecting you to the whole of human knowledge.

Pitiful, Pettus.

You disappoint yourself—a web search to find out what's now an important phone number? You'd better get it saved in your contacts—it's the one belonging to your latest business venture, a recent acquisition: the decrepit, third-rate Edgewater County honkytonk you'll now own. Lucky freaking you.

'GOOCH' WIMMEL AND 'RABBIT' PETTUS

By the time Bill Wimmel hobbled down the flight of steps, supporting himself on the track of the AmeriPro Premiere Series stair-lift his disabled second-in-command, Dobbs, used to ascend to the second-story offices of the *Edgewater Advocate*, the publisher and editor of the paper for the last two decades had managed to forget his purpose in the world.

Out on the sidewalk, he squinted through the monuments and trees on the town green. His stomach rumbled at the smell of the chicken broasting before the lunch rush, from kitchens in both The Dixiana and Manny's on the Green. The Dixiana didn't enjoy a lucrative lunch trade anymore. At one time diners had come from all over the county and beyond—not for the honkytonk, but the barbecue. As late as ten years ago, even the President of the You-Knighted States picked up a to-go basket. Glory days.

Gooch, a childhood nickname that'd stuck, sighed with rank sentiment—there Rabbit Pettus still stood in front of the honkytonk. Smoking, spitting, hitching up his pants. Seeing the man, older than dirt but still on his feet, brought everything back.

Most everything, anyway. Involved Rabbit and The Dixiana. That's all Bill knew.

His reporting task.

Purpose in life.

Immediate assignment.

However one perceived the present moment, Bill Wimmel slip-streamed through the hours and days grasping with a tenuous fingertip grip on the where and how and why of his duties. It had become a problem, his mental acuity, but so far no one else had noticed. Thank god.

He'd fake his way through. As before, so ahead.

Saluting Sheriff Oakley passing by in his unmarked cruiser, Bill shuffled by the salon and tattoo parlor and jaywalked toward the angled parking spaces along the green, most of which were empty, especially this time of the day. His knees crackling like a bowl of Rice Krispies, Bill caught sight of the columned, granite old bank building where the Edgewater Ladies' Munificence Society held their meetings, and more of the story he was chasing down today came back to him:

The mural. The damned mural, again. At least it was a story that, in these times of renewed sensitivity about the Confederate flag, had some steam behind it.

Feeling outside himself, the old reporter ambled over and stood alongside the even older tavern owner, the men crafting for themselves small talk for which resplendent Carolina mornings on the green in downtown Tillman Falls were created. Innocuous and casual, the conversation included a rumination on the grueling, humid summer now ending; progress on the nuclear plant expansion; who was and wasn't running against Hill Hampton for mayor next year; the special race for the new seat on the expanded town council the Reverend Roosevelt Nixon seemed destined to win, which was fine with Rabbit Pettus; how the fighting Southeastern University Redtails looked so far this season, about which Bill Wimmel couldn't give two poops, whether we're talking football or any sport; lastly, activities in the back rooms over at Pike's Bait & Pawn, which far as Gooch knew involved typical vice and licentiousness, which Pettus knew with intimacy from the years when hosting the county's criminal cognoscenti upstairs at The Dixiana.

No news in any of it.

Blather.

Nothing of any use to a newspaperman like Bill Wimmel. Small talk made him feel enervated and useless, like after watching too much TV.

No, only raillery from old man Reynolds Pettus, or else gossipy BS that rolled off his soft-voiced tongue with no useful mention of the mural; the mural, but more to the point, Rabbit's response to the proposal to restore the artwork.

Fifty years old last year. That's what people kept arguing. Historic.

Jiminy Cricket—that's what he came to see about. The ELMS meeting to propose funding a successor mural. To replace the offensive one. On the side of the honkytonk.

Gooch, forgetting the mural question and instead asking Rabbit if he had childhood memories of the Sunbury School Fire, which the old man said he didn't; and also that Gooch had asked him that just yesterday. Reminded

Gooch that the Pettuses had come here from West Virginia coal mining country when he was a teenager, not long before he joined the army to get away from his daddy.

"Folks talked about the fire back then," sounding like far, more of an upcountry accent, still, despite his long life here in Tillman Falls. "Can't be time for another article about that mess."

"Anniversary coming up."

Dry. "Coulda swore y'all just had yourself one."

His faulty memory again, dang it. "No—I'm thinking about a book project."

"About the far?"

Shrugging. The idea wouldn't fully form. "About this'n that. A county history."

"You better narrow it down. You'll have yourself a mess of stories to sort out."

"Lord knows that's the truth."

For some reason, both men enjoyed a hearty and knowing laugh. If only every emotion Gooch experienced didn't feel forced and false, he might feel less unsure of himself. Perhaps the humor to which he reacted would become apparent.

BESIDES THE ACTUAL disturbing news of the world, like Ferguson and the ebola scare and going to war with Russia over Ukraine or Syria or both, the local stories of note unfolded in a fashion outrageous yet mundane: Bomb threats called into the local high school every other week. A teenage boy, covered in blood and showing up at school, confessing to the counselor in the front office that he had fatally stabbed his grandmother and grandfather over an issue of money for a videogame purchase. A young woman from a few counties over, high on meth in the parking lot of a church, gouged out her own eyes. Vandals apprehended digging up graves with the intention of mining fine jewelry to pawn or otherwise fence. A pair of deputies and a Department of Natural Resources agent decided to follow up on "outstanding warrants" late one night by kicking in the door of a little old black woman's house, and when she emerged from her bedroom holding an air rifle, shot her to death; the cops, cleared of wrongdoing, but when the family filed a civil suit the county settled out of court, the third such case in a decade. Two prepubescent boys facing life-long disfigurement and pain lay in the Augusta burn center after playing with matches and a bottle of rubbing alcohol. An area judge, convicted of sentencing teens to jail time over minor infractions in exchange for kickbacks from mysterious elements lobbying on behalf of the private prison complex. A pair of high school seniors reported seeing an enormous, man-sized bird crouching in the national forest near the crossroads called Red Mound; the boys claimed the creature, glimpsed at dusk during a quail hunting excursion from which they were returning, took off with a flapping of wings as large as "fifteen or twenty feet." Not the first local giant bird sighting. They happened every few decades. Probably on dope, those boys.

But in this era of almost-daily shooting events carrying high body counts like evil, liturgical public mega-rituals, none of these modest items presented as novel. None close to breakout, wire story material. Only another day in Edgewater County, USA. "I have always felt that whatever the Divine Providence permitted to occur," as the great nineteenth century editor Charles A. Dana once said, "I was not too proud to report."

Now, you get a Sunbury School Fire, or an event like San Bernardino or Sandy Hook? Here would be juicy news into which partial plates could be sunk.

The biggest such story of late, one of the first local items to crawl across the worldwide wires since the Coy Wando murders a few decades ago—not that anything would top Coy Wando's depraved child-killings—involved a woman, Sheba Lynn Swampscott, 56, who in the course of shacking up with two men in a Mayfield Acres mobile home, had murdered one with a shot from a handgun. Gun violence a common enough occurrence nationwide, true, but the angle here resulted from her stated grievance, that he wouldn't stop playing a particular Pink Floyd album. Gracious, but the "hits" Dobbs Vandegrift, junior editor-in-chief and web guru, said the paper had gotten on its online edition over it. Dobbs knew all about the complicated tech world leaving folks like Gooch behind, all these gadgets and hoodoo. Dobbs even had "his own cloud," whatever that meant. Mercy, it sounded like being touched by angels, all this internet connectivity.

Gooch sat amazed as he read comments on the Swampscott story coming in from all over the world. "Bless its little heart, but South Carolina does it again," John Stewart crowed with glee later that night on live global TV. "Good girl!" Fame was Edgewater County's, if only for a news cycle.

About the Pink Floyd kerfuffle, everyone seemed to want to know the same question: not about the victim's injuries or the perp herself, but rather, which record? The album with the prism on a black background? Or the one with the man on fire? Foolishness. Myopia. What did it matter? Wasn't the fact that a person had come unhinged enough to kill another human being over playing a record sufficient fodder for discussion, and about more than irrelevant details? Who cared which record? People losing the thread. Burying the lede.

The succinct saying, a truism explicating this idea, sat right on the tip of his tongue, but wouldn't form. Dang it.

Rock music, too much for Gooch. All those wailing guitars and thudding, bombastic drums. Playing an obnoxious record on repeat might have driven him to kill too, come to think of it.

Hell, he'd never cared for country music either, not after the whole Outlaw trend back in the 70s, when The Dixiana had started going downhill. Greasy-headed, pill-popping Waylon Jennings. Dope-smoking Willie. You could keep all that. Give Gooch the Chet Atkins-era material. Lush production. Melodies, plaintive and memorable. Human voices. Little short stories about failed romance, longing, poverty, faith. Country music—real country music. The kind you still heard played inside these walls.

The wall, the mural, and the meeting—that's why Gooch was standing outside The Dixiana. Check.

◎◉◎

A STEP-VAN RUMBLED down Common Street and backfired, the shot heard round the green. Gooch's loafers cleared the gritty sidewalk, and he farted with involuntary suddenness.

The Mexican driver, in paint-spattered coveralls, stared straight ahead and zoomed around the corner north toward the bypass, clattering ladders echoing in his wake. KA-pow, a second backfire, echoing back from the wall containing the mural.

Rabbit cussed and spat and wrenched his shoulder around like he'd suffered a bee sting. "Great God almighty," his voice but a wheeze. "Thought somebody decided to take me out."

"Same here. When you're a newspaperman long as I've been, one earns himself many enemies."

"Don't doubt that one bit."

His eyes found a nearby war monument, a squat, obsidian obelisk placed in tribute to a variety of twentieth and early twenty-first century international altercations. "You ought to know what it feels like to get shot at."

"Them Germans did their best. Took a few potshots at my ass. Damn straight about that." Checking his watch. "Reckon Burnie'll be along soon."

"Surprised he's not here already."

"Ain't that the truth."

In the old days Bill would wait for a meeting like this across the green at Lucinda's Lunch. How her coffee had been so right. So consistent. A cube of sugar, a dash of half & half. Delightful.

Bill, damn near believing he could still see the old Lucinda's sign instead of the fresh paint of the sandblasted Manny's on the Green logo, wishing he could walk over and eat one more time. Get that coffee. Sit at his favorite table and write or interview or politick, or read the *New York Times* and the Columbia paper. Imagining the Bunn coffee machine and the angle of its stainless steel boxy body, how it sat behind the counter warming its handled round pots, black for regular and orange for decaf. The comfort of the pies, the meat-and-three blue plate specials, the Friday night buffets featuring fried catfish bites and greasy fresh-cooked collard greens; the sense that, whatever happened, it'd all be okay.

The world without the old diner across the way?

A pervasive malaise, an encroaching lack of permanence and continuity in the ongoing, presumptive thousand-year epoch of American peace and prosperity, what with reality playing out more on a smartphone near you than the streets of the cities and towns. With citizens mesmerized into sedation and unperturbed by the building wave of tumultuous social and cultural change looming in the distance, as Gooch had railed in a recent editorial column the younger and more socially savvy Dobbs had talked him out of printing, community engagement, civil discourse and interpersonal relations were all crumbling into vacuous tit-for-tat sniping in online comment sections, useless rhetoric better suited to the schoolyard than the public square.

Nothing about life felt all right. Not close to the old standards anymore. Whether in the world at large, or within Gooch's own head and heart.

His insides quivered all along his ribcage.

He realized he had wandered into the street.

Rabbit called to him. "Going somewheres?"

His hard leather soles crunching, Gooch wandered back. Felt a touch dizzy. "Guess it's not quite time. For the meeting."

"Look like one of them pickers coming in here with the Chinese eyes going on. You smoking dope, now? Like all them crunchy granolas out in Colorado?"

Bill, not knowing how to answer. Taking a breather, sitting on the bench, Rabbit's bench. Sweating. Another hot day. Autumn couldn't get here soon enough.

Cigarette dangling from the corner of his mouth, Rabbit gripped his own left wrist as though it hurt. "Boy, you look peaked."

Fanning himself and checking his Blackberry for email—spam, a good bit of gay porn spam today—it occurred that Gooch already knew Rabbit's news, which really wasn't news: the man didn't give two shits about history, whether the damn mural, or the war he went off and fought seventy years ago.

Rabbit managed to give at least one shit: when he could tell folks were set on stirring a pot that, at this late date in such matters, needn't be disturbed. Back then, 1963, Burnie Sykes had been the one who wanted the mural put on the building, about the same time they raised the naval jack atop the State House dome down in Columbia, a flag no boy in gray had ever flown on any battlefield. The politicians, and Burnie, both swore with hand upon heart their gestures weren't over the colored students being let into Southeastern University. It went without saying, however, that integration of the state school hadn't gone over well with the more entrenched class structure conjoined to a vision, and version, of the past no longer tenable.

Hadn't been tenable back in 1963, either. That'd been the point of integration.

Painting that old General Reb mascot, though, with his confederate battle flag flapping behind him? That told the black children of Edgewater County, perhaps dreaming of matriculating to Southeastern and bettering their lives through higher education, nothing about history, only that they'd better remember who and what still reigned here in the modern age. As a layperson, Gooch, long in favor of the mural's removal. But he didn't let that change the way he wrote and reported the issue. Trained in objectivity, objective he'd remain.

"Should've heard what that grandbaby of Burnie's done last night." Rabbit, offhand and untroubled through a dry belch. "Stinker pulled a fast one on old Uncle Rabbit."

"Do tell." Wimmel, wondering if he ought to note the coming information. As a reporter, such action dwelled inside him as a first instinct, but of late if he didn't take extensive notes he'd forget minor details—who he was, where he was, what he was doing, and why. A wee problem. "But I can probably surmise."

Rabbit described Button's subterfuge, a 'comedy' routine she'd talked him and Jasper Glasscock, who ran the open mic night on Thursdays at The Dixiana, into letting her do, which Rabbit said she kept describing as her "tight twenty."

"Do what, now?"

"Some show-biz bullcrap."

This, a phrase Gooch had to write down: The flip-top notebook appeared in hand, the reporter muttering and scribbling as fast as pen would pull. A lightbulb. "Twenty minutes of decent jokes." So relieved he thought he'd weep. "I get it, I get it."

"Damn, son. You ain't right." Rabbit, suspicious and squinting against the brilliant Carolina sunshine of late summer. "And this ain't no interview."

"I can almost guess—the reactors."

"Said she was thinking about becoming a 'consciousness comedian,' whatever that means. Hey—what you writing down?"

"'Tight twenty.' Haven't heard that."

"You writing it down again?"

"Oh—no." He regained control of the interview. "It's a—wait. A conscientious comedienne? Like a conscientious objector?"

"Hell if I know. The point is, she lied through her teeth. That little squirt."

"Who?"

"Burnie's grandbaby."

Gooch's mind raced. He'd been getting so forgetful. Burnham Sykes's grandbaby. Burnie's grandbaby. Button. "Oh—the one working for the governor."

Rabbit gave Gooch the once over. "Son, you need another cuppa joe this morning? We talking bout Button. Not the other'n."

Okay. Not Thim Sykes, the governor's aide-de-camp, of late advising the Reverend Nixon in his town council candidacy. Not the political consultant, Thim; the younger sibling, the hippie, the flake—Button. The one they'd just been talking about, as Gooch castigated himself. "I'm with you. Sure, sure. Button."

"They don't understand nothing. Young'uns. There's got to be jobs. But she got up there and started hollering about them new reactors like they was the devil."

Now Gooch felt up to speed. Ever since the reactor construction announcement, a national story and the most positive jobs news the county had seen in ages, Button Sykes had been agitating against the expansion at the Sugeree Nuclear Station. "Not to mention all the electricity."

Rabbit, scoffing and spitting. "They don't know shit. Young'uns."

"They'll find out."

"Damn straight they will. Less they want to end up bumfuzzled."

Gooch, musing to himself and chuckling at not only what Rabbit meant—bumfuzzled was a catchall term for him—but also regarding who 'they' were. Damn if he hadn't misplaced the beginning of the conversation.

Again.

Happened sometimes. His old bean could only hold so much new information—that's what he kept telling himself. Wasn't but into his early 60s. Way too early for Alzheimer's. Too young. Look at Reynolds Pettus standing next to him—eighty-eight and strong and spry as the oaks providing shade in the courthouse plaza.

Gooch concentrated: Button. The reactor. There we go.

Or, wait—the mural. Reactor, or mural?

"Ain't like there wasn't one there already." The Sugeree River Nuclear Station, a 1950s construction contemporaneous with the opening of The Dixiana, had been pumping out electricity ever since. "And the hydro-dam before that."

"It can't be denied."

"She gets idears all up in that noggin of hers. Little hippie doper."

"Mercy—don't I know it."

"Ain't changed. Still smokes grass. Smell it all over her when she come to work."

"These kids. I tell you what."

Rabbit shrugged. "I was always thankful Roy never got into that mess. Or, who knows, he might've anyway. Don't take much to fool an old man. Which I always was to him." As Rabbit launched into a fond reminiscence about his successful, beloved grandson, Gooch grunted, his mind itching to wander.

About once a week submissions from Button Sykes arrived over the transom at the *Edgewater Advocate*, letters he'd declined to publish but for the first one or two printed out of deference to her grandfather Burnie. The way Rabbit, he supposed, had by giving the little freak the job of running the PA at The Dixiana. As well as allowing Button up on stage, it sounded like, to make her nuclear-reactor protest.

All very interesting.

He supposed.

Far as Gooch Wimmel knew, Button Sykes was the only person in Edgewater County who didn't want the power company to build the new reactor. Plenty, on the other hand, would love to see the mural gone. Now that was a topic that seemed worth debating.

In fact, the mural situation represented the primary topic of discussion at the biweekly meeting of the influential ELMS about to convene, and constituted what Bill hoped might become the biggest story to hit the town in years. Folks held superstitions about the mural relating to the success of Redtails teams the university fielded in various sports; other than minor-league versions of baseball and hockey squads, and the occasional PGA or LPGA tournament down on one of the sea islands, South Carolina enjoyed no actual professional sports teams. Men like Jez Rembert, a local underground economy entrepreneur, often seen on football Saturdays making a pilgrimage to the mural and placing hand over heart before General Reb, a gesture of respect said to energize the luck surrounding the squad. You didn't want to mess with tradition. Rabbit, wise and deferential, knowing to leave well enough alone.

So here, as Gooch understood it, was Rabbit's compromise—no restoration. Too contentious an image, this he understood and mostly agreed with, and always had. Let it fade away with him, he said. Let it stand as a teaching tool, fading not into further glory, but ignominy. That's what Rabbit planned to say to the ELMS around their long and storied and burnished conference table, candlelit and dripping with money and atmosphere and authority as their civic-minded presence and pedigree commanded.

In truth? Gooch already had his story. He'd type it up, print it tomorrow. The way of his world. For now, he enjoyed hanging out in the sunshine. The news would get to writing itself. Eventually.

⊙✸⊙

BEFORE LONG, Burnie Sykes got dropped off by the granddaughter in question. So short you couldn't see her behind the steering wheel, Button, waving a curt karate chop to the men and speeding away in her silver, muddy, four-wheel-drive Subaru Baja, an SUV-pickup hybrid, squat and stubby like the woman's own body.

Bill shouted about getting a statement regarding the comedy-routine protest, which had turned heads, or so he'd heard from somewhere, somewhere, he knew not where. In response, he got only a lungful of her exhaust.

Who told Gooch about her onstage protest, anyway? It had slipped his mind.

Rabbit did. Not five minutes ago.

Jesus, boy. Pull yourself together.

After hobbling inside the dim bar and helping himself to a draught PBR, first of the day, Burnie, swaying on bad hips, came back out onto The Dixiana's front porch to join the other codgers with hands stuffed into their pockets.

Wasting no time, Burnie launched into his best friend Rabbit over the mural, and for a time Bill stood watching like at a tennis match as the men grumbled and groused to one another about their respective positions.

"But think about history. We need to talk them women into paying to repaint it as it stands." Gooch noted how Burnie said this in a manner more pleading than angered, slurping his foamy draft beer and wiping his mouth on a flannel sleeve. "Think how much it means to Redtails fans here, and all over the state. The country. The world."

Rabbit squeezed his eyes. Grunted. Seemed preoccupied. Worked his sore left shoulder around.

"Well?" Burnham Sykes lolled slack-jawed and bleary-eyed, as though he were trying to shake off a bad dream. "You gonna give them what-for?"

"I don't give a good god-durn, to tell the truth. Let the wind blow it all away, for all I care."

Burnie screwed up his mouth and sucked his dentures and said, "Mm-mm-mm. Mighty sad."

"But what's sad is, a bunch of busybodies—trying to—" Belch. "Tell me what to do with my brick wall. Damn straight I'm gonna tell them what's what."

"That's more like it." Burnie, mumbling and cursing. "I tell you, it's hubris," with a denture whistle on the 'S'. "Hubris, plain and simple."

"Might as well be standing around a bubbling cauldron, them ELMS's."

Gooch couldn't let it stand. "Now, boys. The ELMS do a lot of good for this community. Worth hearing them out."

Burnham, stomping his foot and disagreeing in a manner as vituperative as possible with his weak old-man's breath, which as Bill observed with a poetic flourish sounded like the wind on a high, lonesome mountaintop.

Burnie found his breath, and with it came a full measure of roiling, dyspeptic disapproval concerning the ELMS and every woman in the damnable coven. Questioning their charter to exist at all much less lead, which in execution went way in the damn hell past what you expected from a gaggle of puffed-up old geese with long noses, in his words. It took place because every last one had too much time and money on their manicured hands. *Lousy with hubris-s-s*, he kept repeating, what with their call for Rabbit to remove the mural and allow them to commission an image more modern and agreeable and less, far less divisive greeting motorists coming from the northern part of the county into downtown Tillman Falls.

Rabbit belched and cussed. "But Burnie—they ain't wrong. Maybe it ought," sounding like *ort*, "to be took down. Like maybe this whole dump. Don't nobody give a shit but Jasper and Trudy. Roy ain't never gonna want nothing to do with it. Ain't none of it mean what it used to. Not even to me."

"I give a shit." Burnie, gripping his mug of PBR close. "Damn if I don't."

"You can drink cheaper buying at the IGA, boy," a line familiar from many such afternoons sitting outside at The Dixiana. "Or run over yonder to see old N'awlins. Drink his high priced rotgut."

"Sooner drink muddy water out of the Sugeree. Or paint thinner."

Gooch watched Burnie hack and cough and swirl the dregs in the cracked and chipped stein. To say Burnham Sykes hated 'N'awlins,' which was what he and Rabbit called Manny Theodore, a New Orleans ex-pat who'd bought Lucinda's diner and turned into a juke joint right there on the beloved common green of Tillman Falls, an understatement. Manny and Neecie put on a hell of a vinegar-based barbecue lunch buffet, though. Had to admit that.

It didn't help matters with folks like Burnham Sykes, one of the townsfolk responsible for painting the mural in the first place, that Bernice Theodore, Manny's wife and business partner, had been the one leading the charge against the mural. "Ain't even lived here five blamed minutes."

But she was no interloper or carpetbagger in terms of town politics. Her place on the ELMS, earned both through the co-ownership of their restaurant, but also a civil rights legacy: her mother had conducted a famous sit-in at the mill, pressing the company about the hiring of Negro women, which at the time represented a high percentage of the working-age population in this region of the state. The argument had been sound—she and many other young women offered labor-ready workers for what had traditionally been a man's game, the struggle coming fraught with as much gender and class issues as racial ones, though considering the times, an angle also playing into the situation.

Burnham, bitter: "Damn so-and-so's from across the bridge are taking over."

Rabbit cleared a frog out of his throat. "I like Manny. He's all right. Blows a mean sax, he does."

Burnie, a crusty old dog—worse'n Rabbit Pettus ever was—offered a stream of racially charged invective that all but burned Bill's ears. Clinging to the old ways. But even hardcore race-baiters like Sykes had learned to tone down the rhetoric even among supposedly safe ears, which by any modern standard oughtn't to have been the town's principal journalist. These men thought of Bill like a fellow gentleman of the town, however, not a reporter per se.

At their age, what useful secrets could they carry and protect? Likely few. Their power, now at a low ebb.

Gooch's power and influence waned, too. His reporter's instincts told him to get used to it.

⟐

BURNIE, despite only having had the first of the day, seemed unsteady on his feet. Rabbit feeding him PBR all afternoon didn't help. But Burnie had had a rough time of it—losing his son Buddy, all the failed businesses. A onetime county big-shot, now reduced to slobbering and drinking and watching the light fall on the town green every day, all day long.

The way Gooch himself felt, he had to admit, from his second-floor office across the way, eating his sorry bag lunch and smelling the hair chemicals from the downstairs salon. Only, his melancholy watchfulness came without the drinking. Never touched it.

This old newshound was getting forgetful as a drunk. That much for sure.

"Well—let's go, so we can get on back." Rabbit rubbed his wrist and coughed through a fresh Pall Mall he'd sparked into life off his scarred and scratched Zippo. "Burnie, you gonna hold down the fort whilst I go and deal with these busybodies? Fridge and Idahlia is back yonder doing the lunch prep." Rabbit took himself a good long look at the facade of his old honkytonk. "And Trudy'll be along any minute to get the bar opened up."

Burnie said he reckoned he could manage. "Don't nobody need your crusty old ass, Pettus. This dump could run itself."

"Try to keep from draining the keg this time. My back's too tender to change it today."

Gooch, trailing behind, called over his shoulder. "Yeah, Burnie. Try not to drink the man dry."

The old drunk cussed him sideways, a nasal twang carrying down the block. Told Gooch he could shove his sorry little snot-rag of a paper up his puckered ass sideways.

Rabbit, still a robust, broad-shouldered man despite being stooped with age, shuffled across Congress Street toward the old bank building on the next block. It had been built as the Farmer's & Merchant's Bank of South Carolina, later becoming the Palmetto State Bank. It failed following a Depression-era robbery, its lost deposits among the first FDIC claims ever fulfilled. Why he carried all this useless ancient trivia but lost track of the last five minutes, this reporter couldn't say.

Bill scurried alongside as Rabbit strode across the town green, with its small patch of azaleas and trees. Like almost everything else in downtown Tillman Falls—Burnham Sykes, Bill Wimmel, and Reynolds Pettus included—the monuments and sidewalks seemed grimy and worn-down.

Rabbit Pettus stopped in the street. Looked back at the building he owned, a cornerstone of the town for decades. He made a gesture in its direction, the sign of the cross three times with his thumb. Muttering under his breath.

"What's all that, Rabbit?"

"Nothing I should've let you see. But you won't remember anyway, will you, son?"

Gooch winked and waved his reporter's Moleskine. "Nothing gets past Gooch Wimmel." He put the notebook back into his satchel without noting Rabbit's Catholic-like blessing of the honkytonk.

On the block opposite the newspaper offices sat the imposing gray granite columns of the ELMS headquarters. After its life as a pre-Depression financial institution and later the district Masonic lodge, for the last two decades the iconic downtown building had served as home base for the county's longest standing philanthropic organization. Elegant, candlelit and still as a mortuary, Bill always found the conference room inside calming, the air seeming to vibrate with legitimacy and power.

"For all I know?" Rabbit rubbed out his cigarette on a lamppost and put it in the green wire trashcan, rusty and caked with years of grunge. "They're liable to cut off my crooked redneck prick in there."

"Who knows what secrets and occult rituals have gone on behind these doors."

Rabbit shot Gooch a glare. "What's that supposed to mean?"

"Well, look at today—'executive session'," a posted notice read. "That means I'll have to wait out here. Dang it."

"Oh. Ain't gonna take me long to say what I got to say. Back in a jiffy." The thud of the big door shutting behind Rabbit Pettus resonated in old Gooch's brittle ribs.

He tingled; sensed the approach of news. A story, breaking like a wave on the sandy shores of Myrtle Beach. The future, arriving heralded, fully-formed. And making now more now than now had ever been.

A story about what, though? Now? What they hell did that mean?

Wait—what was he doing over here across the green?

Maybe about the time Gooch's fabled news arrived, this time a real doozy, it'd all come back to him. Again. He'd wait out the confusion, find his way back. He always did.

CREEDENCE

Creedence, crumpled out by the pool on a chaise lounge and watching the sun sink into the marsh like Roy Earl had said he wanted them to do together more often, worried herself to pieces about him flying the plane all upset like he was. Torn in two, like a character in some stupid pop song about a love triangle.

She made him fly away from her. With what she done.

Leaving that computer open.

Like she wanted him to find out.

Oh, no. It kept rushing over her in a hot wave. Making her tremble, head to toe. How keeping the secret about her lover felt like it was making her have stomach cancer. Seed-pods kept falling out of the tall tupelo next to the clay-tiled roof of the faux Spanish Colonial Revival house on the marsh Roy loved so much for its price more than the house itself, with its little entrance palazzo and gurgling fountain, its charm, its woodsy yard of mossy live oaks and the one tupelo, the pool, the gourmet kitchen in which she barely fixed anything beyond the kitty-cat breakfasts and lunches and suppers.

Creedence, thinking about what had gone through her husband's mind while reading what he had. How Roy must hate her, now.

What a mess—she didn't want to hurt no one. Just wanted to feel appreci-ated. It would be fine if it were Roy loving her again. How messed up she was to think she could get his attention by letting another man have her the way she had Estes. Only way to feel less messed up was to have a drink. Calm down. Sort it all out one more time. Fix it.

"But I don't love him," had been the last she'd yelled at Roy Earl on the tarmac of the airport. And she didn't. What he'd read in the messages had been schoolgirl nonsense.

A crush that got out of hand. That's all.

"And we only did it once," she added, a blatant fib, but in the moment a necessary attempt to downplay as much as confirm the awful truth. "He—he tricked me into it."

"Will you give me a freaking break," spots of color in his cheeks nearly purple with blood pressure. "You lie!"

More lies, to herself: about how she still wanted her lover. Estes made her feel good, before she felt bad. It was fair. To get what she wanted. Roy had wronged her. She could swear that he had. Somehow.

The assertions rang hollow.

Or did they?

How being with Estes, despite his youth and supposed inexperience compared to a man like her husband, had been like out of a girl's fantasy of how IT could be. Finally. A spark, an explosion; the angle just so and just different enough that some magic place got touched by him, by the way he pulled her legs up and held her calves against his brown shoulders and moved ever so progressively faster. Building up energy and friction in her body. And if he didn't get her there on the first try, a recovery time like nobody's business.

But two husbands so far, she pouted, and neither getting her where she needed to go. This twenty-nine-year-old half Indian, half Puerto Rican boy—that's what Estes was, after all; her boy-toy—made her come like no other. It made little sense. In a way, she reckoned, it felt like what she'd always fantasized the sex would be with her unrequited love Billy Steeple, though with his death that door now long closed, and closed forever.

Still—she'd gotten icky about it all. Had been from the git-go. Knew it was wrong. Deep down.

Done it all anyway.

She never did have good sense.

So in the wake of this disaster, she'd kept Facebook closed tonight sitting home in their fruitshake mansion, as she thought of the house at 626 Albermarle Way, tucked back on the opposite side of the island from the megaresidences along the point. Here, in her neighborhood, lived the merely rich versus the superrich.

Were they all as lonely and bloated with gas as she was tonight? Her stomach, twisting like rotten snakes. Nerves.

She needed a drink.

After fixing herself a tall one, she shuffled back through the outdoor kitchen, its stainless steel tinted golden in the dying light of the late summer's day, where only a week before he'd grilled marinated prime-cut steaks and roasted ears of white summer corn so sweet you'd have sworn he sugared it. With Roy gone to attend to his ill grandparent, and her left to putter around in this spotless and airless home, Creedence Rucker-Pettus (this time she'd held onto her maiden name as an identity anchor) thought she'd perform her little ritual, a letter to her brother, who ought to be her last link to her childhood family, missing now for over a decade. An all-but unrepentant drunk, he'd come home the last time to bury their mother Eileen, had seemed sober and ready to get on with a healthy second act of his misspent life. But like a good drunk will do to you, Devin piled into the car one Sunday afternoon only to vanish yet again. This time for good.

At first she actually mailed the letters to Devin's last known address in Colorado, but after Roy hired a private investigator to search for her brother, and the PI had come up empty—said, the Commerce City apartment's been rented out to someone else, the girlfriend out here got a call saying he was on his way but he never arrived, with all other trails cold as a snowy mountaintop —Creedence quit sending them. Then, stopped writing altogether.

One day, she decided to try again. She missed her brother. Missed the innocence of their childhood together. Creedence, continuing writing the letters on her laptop as a kind of self-directed therapy. She'd read a blog post about journaling, realized she'd already been doing it in the form of the old letters.

It also helped keep Devin alive, she thought. Nobody really knew for sure he was dead. Sure seemed that way, though.

All done so carefully, her letter writing, the way Roy Earl handled his business affairs there in his pristine home office, a glassed-in corner overlooking the lush side-yard rather than the marsh. He kept his expansive, beveled-glass-topped desk with nothing on it save his own Macbook Air. The rest was space, he told her, usable space, because the emptiness inside the container was the source of the energy, one of his little sayings that went over her head.

Empty was empty. It held no power.

Empty had been Devin's life. And she supposed that it was now over, but the authorities to whom they'd turned, both official and otherwise, had all been quick to write off another alcoholic who'd succumbed somewhere. Alone. Broken. And sad.

Alone. She couldn't imagine it; she'd never been on her own. Not for a second.

And when Roy had become distant, that's when Estes happened. Exploded inside her body and her whole life, she now realized, like a bomb.

❋

Roy Earl and Creedence. How they fell in love, back when Devin had been home the last time, and she'd been going through the nasty breakup with Dusty, her first and far more foolish attempt at matrimony. And where it'd all led now. All this success. All this plenty and wealth.

Right. All an empty space for which she had no use, could sense no power —not in the relationship, not at the breakfast or dinner table, nor in the classroom pursuing a degree she'd never finished and now never would, nor in the bedroom. Sometimes. Not often enough.

The second marriage, ruined. How she'd told herself that part didn't matter much; but how unloved she felt. He'd been so grateful and giving at first. How it had ebbed away.

Hot tears leapt from the sides of her eyes like escapees from the top floor of a burning tenement building, splattering to their meaningless and minuscule deaths on her freckled, pink thighs below her white shorts. Her ankles and shins, dirty from the airfield hanger when she staggered over and braced herself against a greasy barrel of fuel. Gasping for breath, hearing her husband taxi away. She'd fallen against a filthy tool locker, went boo-hoo-hoo until she almost puked on the shoulder of Mr. Nawalinski's lime-green golf shirt.

But once Roy had taken off, she's recovered enough to check her phone to see if Estes texted, which he had, which gave her an icy stab of anticipation— like seeing a note from him always did.

GF I want it so bad
girl I cant stand it
u r thottest ever
<3 :P

She assumed he meant 'the hottest' and not 'thottest,' whatever that could mean. A forty-year-old, she'd learned, had little reason to believe she knew all the slang of the younger gen.

Estes, he had no idea what'd happened. Poor baby.

Roy Earl might go and kill him—but at least her husband left the island.

To attend to sick Uncle Rabbit. Mercy, what timing.

What had she wrought.

She read the text again. Thought about the oral sex. Estes, sometimes going so long on her clitty that it hurt, and she had to push him away.

Using the emoji, awkward, a practice that Roy railed against—emoticons, tweeting, texting, social media, he considered all of it base and childish, unless of course when used to promote business interests. And here, she'd proven him right. The heart. The :P, normally a sign of mild insult or jest, here in the context of Estes and Creedence's secret love affair, a signal between the two that the other party wished to engage in oral sex.

That stuff, mm-mm-good, but only him on her. She irritated him more each time she demurred on a reciprocal act, but look, it'd never been her thing. Not to be nit-picky and snobby.

As well she resisted a few of the more odd contortions he expected, trying to get her up on her hands and squatting backwards facing the wrong way, which hurt her lower back and knees and made her say, I like it on top of you the right way, it's the only way I can come; please, sweet loverman, and where do you get these crazy ideas. Or from behind, easiest on her back.

Was she aging? Was that the issue here?

A moment of clarity. Aging? She was still squeezing zits. And figuring out what she wanted—from her husband. From life. All this splendor didn't seem to be it, for either of them.

Roy. He caused this. His ignoring her. The time to nurture had come for them, an early retirement and freedom, and all he did was open another coffee shop. Get a hobby she couldn't stand. Unfulfilled, he'd done it all on purpose; but now she'd shown him, boy. Hadn't she.

Disgust, flooding into her the way endorphins did during an orgasm. Anti-endorphins. Her stomach-snakes, knotting and twisting and writhing. A hot fart tore at her asshole, already sore from Estes poking his in middle finger while tonguing her.

BACK HOME AFTER being dropped off by Mr. Nawalinski, who reassured her it would "all blow over between her and the Royster," and how he and his wife of many decades standing had "been through it all, it ain't pretty, but ya work it out somehow," and with this in mind, Creedence ignored the text. Didn't want to think about Estes. Told herself it was over, and her marriage was worth saving and the shortcomings could be fixed; and how taking a lover, a younger man who had no assets and no future and nothing but a penis that felt good inside her, and a stroke that brought her to orgasm from intercourse in a way other men had barely managed to do, all this was folly and a lark and indicative of a weak mind and heart.

These words, what her mother Eileen would no doubt say, if only she were here. Creedence, glad her smothering mother was and had remained dead for the last decade, but then who had she to talk to now? Only Devin. In one-sided letters.

Now almost full dark, with squawking herons and the low *oong-ka-choonk* of the reed-hidden brown bitterns calling across the marsh, and frogs bellowing and cicadas buzzing in the last summer air, which felt thick with Carolina low country humidity, and indeed smelled marshy, Creedence mixed herself another V&T, took a half a Xanax and began yet another letter to her brother, the missing sot and a son of a gun. If only he were still alive, her precious life connection, she often wondered if her world might be better and complete. She'd thought it possible, too, when he was still alive and had taken steps. Only to be rebuffed.

To be forsaken by him. More than once.

Still, she wrote, trying to keep alive her only relative, if only in the imagination:

```
E. DEVIN RUCKER
1111 Purgatory Way
Hades, SC 29666


    Dearest Darling Devin:


Oh, how I done gone and done it now.
    Roy Earl probably hates me. I have effed up his
life, and my life, by doing something no good
person goes and does. I will let you think about
what all that could be, and will say it was
something I did to Dusty too, now that I let
myself consider it.
    Which is starting to make it seem like I'm the
one with the problem, rather than the men I keep
marrying.
    Shit. That doesn't feel too good to type.
    Well you know, with Dusty there was more to what
all I done. Much as I have told you about it these
last few years, as you know all well and good.
    I still can't believe you didn't beat him that
night at Mama's, the last Christmas we had
together. But you didn't. I thought you were so
much better, then.
    You could have knocked me over with a feather
when you just up and took off like you did. Lord,
how many times have I written to you now. Like it
will make you feel guilty for having done so, I
guess. For making me wonder like you have all this
time. Ack. I hate going down this road again.
    I stopped hearing from Millie a while back. She
kept up hope for some time, you know, but she
seemed to understand you much better than I did.
She said, this is what drunks do, which is an
```

excuse I think you might have made to me as well along the way.

All right, now I am getting mad again, which is silly considering you are so gone that you must be dead. I guess I hold on and keep on fussing like this because I had written you off once and you came back, and I suppose it could happen again.

That's called hope, I just heard your nasty old voice whispering in my ear.

Poor Roy Earl. What did I do to him?

Maybe if I explain this to you by steps, it will make sense to me. It happened this way. I met Estes after Roy decided to open the new Beanery here on Sedge Island, which seemed ridiculous to me because that was like going back to where he started, in Columbia, as you well know. Getting back to his roots, he said. He'd wanted to grow the Carolina Beanery into a franchise, not the fruitshake stand. But that is what seemed to take off. Now, Roy Earl wants to beat the big boys at their own game. Thinks he's gonna face off with Starbucks. Show those boys how it's done. How things ought to be.

I still think he only wanted to have a coffee shop cause it was like the opposite of his granddaddy's bar, you know? In any case, he's so full of himself.

"Past is prologue," he keeps saying.

I can't half stand him no more. Mercy.

Honestly? I thought, and think, he's going nuts.

Whatever it was all about, why he wanted to go and do the same stuff all over again was and is beyond me, and buster I am here to tell you that if he had not gone and opened a new business here around the corner from our house, surely none of this mess would have happened! It was the time for us to find each other, finally. Cause we hadn't yet. Not really. The whole time we were — are — married, it's been like, he's off opening another Spotted Banana™ every five minutes.

Oh, but it takes so much more than five minutes, Devin.

I'm so alone. That's why my boytoy happened. Alone in this big ol' house on the marsh. I don't have nothing. I've got to have something that's mine. I mean more mine than the kitties, but for other reasons — they are looking to me. Me. And if I help them all, I will be serving some purpose.

Which I don't have. Not really.

So that's why I took and got myself a boytoy. To have a sense of me outside of all this. Otherwise, I'm just Roy's wife. Not myself. His wife. And that's not enough!

Is it? I don't rightly know. I only know I don't want to cry no more.

You remember how Mama would wail and holler till she got her way? How she would have these gales of grief (ooh that sounds good, like poetry or song lyrics!) until she twisted reality to her liking? Of course you do. You don't never forget no spectacle like that. Well anyway, I tried that with Roy. To get out of this thing I done. It wasn't all an act. The shame I felt at my husband having read what I wrote and knowing in his mind what I had been doing was considerable. Like a big weight on my chest.

Blackness inside me. A soul tribulation.

Oh, shit. I have so much regret about you, and about all this. All this could have changed so much for you. If only you'd stayed. Roy could've set you up with a good job at one of his businesses, and all would be fine and good and right.

Hell, forget working for Roy. Just getting Mama and Daddy's house like we done, that would've given you enough money to live for a good while. A nice big old house back home in Chilton (I know, I know), and paid for, and yours. Well, ours. You could've sold it. Lord knows I did, finally.

Actually, Roy made me sell it. Said there wasn't no reason to pay taxes on a house we were keeping for a dead man who wasn't coming back.

Mercy, but Roy E. Pettus was mad at you, Devin, when you up and left again. I don't know why I

keep coming back to that, not now, not in the face
of the awful things I have wrought. I guess cause
I just feel like I have lost everything, now.

And for what. For what?

I feel as dumb as you were for throwing away
your whole life on a bottle of booze, what had
caused you all your problems in the first place.
Me, it's trying to figure out who to let stick his
peterpiper inside, and what I get out of it.

I'm tired, Devin. I'm sick and tired.

Some people might even think I drink half as bad
as you used to, which is twice as much as anyone
ever drank.

But with me, it ain't so over the top. I'm not
like you. I can drink, or not. I just like it, so
I choose the drink.

I reckon that, at forty, I won't have to worry
about it none too long. From what Mama told me,
you don't have too many urges, not after a certain
point. Course, it might be different with me,
since I didn't have no children of my own. You
know all that mess already, though, don't you? Me
and Roy Earl didn't try again after the one
miscarriage, which made for two total if you are
keeping score, ha-ha. Too busy anyway.

'Ain't in the cards for us, maybe?' he kept
saying. I don't know, big D. Maybe my body didn't
want to make one with either one of them. I know
that's what I used to think about Dusty.

Mercy. I dee-clare, as Mama used to say, bless
her heart. I do think I have had enough of this.

It's all so embarrassing, too. I have been
banished, prohibited from seeing my in-laws, even
at this time of family grief. Poor Mr. Rabbit. And
what must Roy be saying about me to Mama Runelle,
and whoever else. Shit shit shit.

I should scoot by the coffee shop and see if Mr.
Manager is working. And what a safe idea that
would be, considering how Roy Earl is half a state
away now in his peter-Piper airplane.

Oh, that sounds mean — is all this just me being
mean to him? For what? For why? For being himself.

```
     I am so confused, Devin. I wish you were here.
Drunk or sober, you always did have an answer for
me. It might not have been right, or what I wanted
to hear, but it was an answer.
     You remember what Daddy used to say? Always try
something, Creedence, even if it's wrong. Well,
boy, I tried something wrong this time, didn't I?
I think I did. I think I effed up, maybe even
bigger than when I didn't get with Billy, bigger
than marrying Dusty.
     Oh, Devin. What a mess this is. Would that you
could help me. Could hear me. But you can't, and
that's that.

Until we meet again,
   CCR
```

Devin lost, her folks dead, a vast emptiness rushed into her like a black wave.

If she left Roy, what would she have? Not have-have as in stuff, but in life?

A kid she was seeing, who was still talking about being in a band as an actual viable living? Over ten years younger than her? Who had plugs in his ears?

Who would surely get tired of doing it to her saggy old ass at any moment?

No. He had said he loved me.

But what could a kid know about love?

Shuddering, Creedence saved her document as DEVIN LETTER SEPT 12 2015 and put it in the folder the way Roy Earl had set it up for her, with the important folders like LETTERS TO DEVIN right there on her desktop. Organizing the folders, one of many small and large favors her husband had done for her.

Not enough to stop her from snapping shut that laptop, though, and going to rinse off and fix her face. Sprucing up to take the golf cart down the walking paths to the plaza, with the outparcel on which her husband's latest business venture sits, his beloved coffee shop. To see Estes again.

Roy wasn't even here—no one to catch them, now.

Are you really going to keep on with this? With Uncle Rabbit laying dead up in Edgewater County?

One more time, she promised, having herself another stiff cocktail for the road, her third since starting the letter. The lime fizz tickled her nose and the liquor graced her throat, sluicing down into pipes gone numb, quieting the terror that she'd ruined her life for no good reason other than hot sex.

One more time. That's it.

She gathered the cat bowls and cracked open cans and gave Doodlebug, her overweight little white kitty-boy with ginger highlights on his nose and whiskers and which she had lured away from his owners a few houses over, an extra scoop of his low calorie, high fiber special food that didn't seem to help his tum-tum get smaller.

Another drink, and she re-persuaded herself how one more time with Estes would be okay. And that'd be it. Time to get responsible about this mess. Finally. Get her story straight, get Roy to settle down about it and convince him it was a mix-up, a misunderstanding. One more time, and afterwards, the whole mess evaporating like the water in the kitty cat dishes she discovered, horrified, she had forgotten to refill now for several days running.

ROY, CREEDENCE, AND TRUDY

Once on the ground in Edgewater County and with the aircraft secured for the time being, you realize how much your legs have been shaking. How close to making panty-fudge you were up there.

One thing Creedence had gotten right today had been her admonition about you being in shape to aviate. But who was she to talk? Your wife, in a fit of shame at being found out, suffered what seemed both a classic hangover accompanied by a mental breakdown, as good an explanation as any for what she'd done.

Clomping around in a pair of wedges—fucking wedges had come back into style—and a sack-like printed summer dress, a beachy housedress like she wore twenty-four seven since moving here onto the island, the shoes made her TOWER over you, rather than besting your own modest height by an inch. How in the last few years she'd become not-so deferential on the height issue, and before long you were entering the dining rooms of fine restaurants, choice joints like Beau Monde, accompanied by a goddamn amazon. How often you had lied and said you were five-ten when you're only brushing five-eight, an extra imaginary two inches of self confidence.

God, how you despise liars.

Shouting, weeping, waving her arms, pleading, with the roar of aircraft engines reverberating all around the large sheet metal sides of the individual storage hanger bays: "I should go with you. Please—please. God forgive me. I shouldn't have said what I said earlier. I'm sorry. I'm sorry. It's not like it sounded. I—I didn't do nothing with him."

"I read what you a-holes wrote to each other."

"It's not like what, what I said was real. It wasn't happening. It was a schoolgirl fantasy. We shared a hug or two. In the coffee shop parking lot. Please. Please. Oh my god. It's not true. It's not true. I didn't do what you think."

No spinning this. You had read what she'd written. Reiterated this.

"No," a bleat. "No, no."

You cursed her, vicious and profane, and you never swore.

Creedence flashed a look like, it's worse than I thought. "Gobbledygook," she wept.

Again: you told her in explicit terms to F-U. And flipped her off. A double-eagle.

She came rushing out after you, clip-clopping, her bright dress fluttering in the humid breeze flowing in from the island's southern tip. "Wait, let me come —I'll finally fly with you."

Despite the momentous gesture on her part—she'd never set foot on either of your aircraft, and would have shit herself if she knew what you'd paid for the Piper Meridian—you shoved her, stumbling over the wedges, back inside to the lounge of the hanger where on many afternoons you spend hours hanging out, haha, with all your flying buddies.

"You'll be hearing from my boys at Verbrick, Adger and Hagood," attorneys and gentlemen all, guys who had frequented your original coffee shop back in Columbia during their law school days, cats who'd always had your legal back, "as soon as I can get the papers drawn up."

Inside, as she hyperventilated stricken and suffused with awful regret, you explained you'd sooner forgive Sherman for the ransacking of Columbia than her for what she's wrought. You said this in your way, which wasn't terribly articulate, but still forthright and colorful. "I don't think I can look at your damn freckled face for more one blessed second."

"But I love him too, damn you." Creedence, hollering about heart-stricken Rabbit Pettus, a side issue that ought to be the main act. "He's like my own granddaddy."

"I know who you love. I read all about it."

Boo-hoo-hoo, hands grasping like claws. "It ain't true."

You had called to the faces of the other guys standing there watching it all unfold, mouths agape. The stories they would later tell their own wives! "Free lattes for a month to the man who gets her home safe."

Her face, flushed and feral, betrayed the turmoil simmering behind feigned nonchalance. "Roy, honey, it's a misunderstanding. You're wrong."

"I've never been more right."

Breaking down: "Don't leave me behind."

"You did it to yourself."

You slammed the door to the hanger in her face and hot-footed it over to your plane. You fired the engine and watched as your unfaithful, long-legged frecklefaced wife, in your eyes still gamine and coltish as the day you fell in love with her, waved her arms and shrieked ragged, weepy Creedence-speak. When she drank too much, episodes of babbling and sobbing reduced her to incoherence.

Ron Nawalinski, one of your fellow hobby-pilots and kings among men, led her back into the hanger office, giving you a furtive, all's-under-control wave. Before she arrived, you had told your fellow Piper enthusiast everything. "Ouch," all he could say. "Yikes."

Drunk and crying.

A frequent condition.

The drinking. That's what had caused this. The booze.

A real SHTF moment—your granddaddy, a drinker and a bar owner, a place you were forced to inhabit against your will and the toilets of which you scrubbed, and now your wife, changed by alcohol and nothing like the girl you'd married, carrying on her brother's sorry trade in pernicious dissolution. You've no idea how much longer you can go on with it all.

Then again, here you have an easy out. Thanks to Creedence screwing the Carolina Beanery Sedge Island assistant manager. Check.

Change is upon you; death has come both for your forebear, and your marriage.

You mustn't complain (because who'd listen?); but, you've been so bored and empty, with no purpose in life anymore, that of late you've wished and prayed for change.

Unexpected change.

Momentous change.

Well-well. Nice wishing, dill-hole.

SHE TRIED TO TELL YOU.

You remember now with clarity and shock an evening you went out to the gourmet pizza place a block off the tourist-trap wharf area on the harbor side of the island.

"I wish we'd ordered a different pizza." She held a half-eaten slice of mushroom medley with two cheeses—gouda, and what the menu called "razor-shaved two-year aged Grana Padano"—drooping and limp in her hand, its point only but nibbled. "Or—another one."

"You mean a different kind? Or a second pie?"

"Both. No—a different one."

"What's wrong with this one?"

"It's not very exciting, is all."

"You could've gotten anything you wanted." You cut your eyes over toward the server, a rangy surfer boy with an Adam's apple bigger than your dick. At your direct eye contact he snapped to and started over, just as you had them all trained, even people who didn't know you. "I'm-a betting you still can."

"Can I?"

"What's stopping you?"

This had been her moment of decision, you now understand, and about more than pizza—she had folded her hands in her lap. Had looked off out the window at the parking lot of the locally owned, high-class pizza joint; a hell of a writeup on Yelp you had posted, oh yes. "Maybe I will, then."

"Have at it. Order yourself a personal size, babygirl. Or a bigger one—we'll take it with us for leftovers."

The server, nodding and chill, an island vibe, probably baked like the muffins and scones over at your coffee shop a few shopping plazas away. "Everything to y'all's liking? Pizza hitting the spot?"

"My wife wants to order another—"

"No, honey. Another time."

"Suit yourself." You flick your fingers at the server, who knows who you are—one of the island's merchant class, the owners, the job creators—and duly withdraws.

She ate the mushroom pizza but without vigor. Superficial small talk followed about the cats and vet visits and litter boxes and flea treatments, all of which was fine, but you could have stood to discuss flying or coffee or whether to franchise out the Beanery like you kept considering.

Subtext. You now perceive much subtext in the language.

Different.

Bigger.

You get it.

Nawalinski had called it: *Ouch.*

⊙⊛⊙

BUT HOW YOU ended up living at the beach? That debate, yeah, what a battle, until you at last fell wanking to the floor and agreed to Creedence's girlhood dream of living on the seashore. How you, by agreeing to Sedge Island rather than your desire to put down fresh roots in the upcountry—either in South Carolina itself, or ideally somewheres like, you don't know, say, in the western North Carolina 'hills' where you often fantasize about buying land tucked back in a holler, with cool breezes, less humidity, lots of trees and solitude—did nothing to make you feel you've reached any actualized, resonant life goal.

What reward in residing on the Island, as you keep asking, if it's not floating your boat? It's why you opened the freaking new coffee shop. It's why you took up flying. Bored out of your mind down yonder.

After cashing out—wait, all right, 'selling out'; whatever, dude—the Spotted Banana Fruitshake Company™ brand and stores to an enormous food service conglomerate, you could have done whatever you wished. But you agreed to what she wanted. It seemed like a sweet gesture—what a husband did for his wife.

At least you pouted and kvetched until she accepted a marsh-side home rather than oceanfront, which you did not want and never really enjoyed the beach, not since *Jaws*, which you remember so well from the Palmetto Grande there on the green in Tillman Falls, a few months after seeing Karen Black for the first time in *Airport 1975*, with *Jaws* and the disaster flick du jour both representing keystone prepubescent intellectual and adenoidal experiences.

Plus, a recurring dream of a giant wave crashing. Not for years now, but that one, yeah, it still stuck to your ribs. You're afraid of the sea. You never said it to anyone in your life. Especially not your wife.

Marshside stinks, but it's peaceful and you get the sunsets, you said. She remained unconvinced.

You argued for the sunsets. "Think of us holding hands out there, enjoying ourselves a cold one and then a hot one inside later," you said on the deck while checking out the house, magnificent in every way, the deal a no-brainer —in the bad economy, they'd get a palace for the cost of a mere mansion. "Won't that be awesome?"

"I reckon." Your wife, holding herself with those bony elbows sticking out. "It's some house, though. I got to say. This dream place."

"We can get it, if we want it. Today, girl. What you think?"

"I don't want to decide right now—let's wait."

Waiting. Your least favorite concept. "For what? This ain't what you want?"

She reckoned-so again, as you recall.

It took another couple of visits and days for her to make up her mind. All of which you spent thinking, but but but, I keep dreaming about the mountains.

Hell. We'll do both. Selling out had made all things possible.

Yeah: the suits came calling when the fruitshake stands had grown three dozen strong, a number of which you still owned outright save for the ones franchised out to longtime trusted managers, with all of it going to the boundless pockets of ConParAgCorp, reps of which sought you out with tenacity before you finally took meetings regarding the valuation and selling price of your company. ConParAgCorp owned many food service delivery platforms and formats, including familiar brands ringing food courts and airports throughout the land. "Proper stewards of all you've built," had been the mantra from the reps.

"We can trust them with our fruitshakes, boys," is how you finished up your quiet and reasonable speech about knowing when to hold, and when to cash in them chips. "We can leave our brand in good corporate hands with ConParAgCorp."

That had been your pitch to the partners, nodding and going over the numbers and thinking, sweet deal, even sweeter with the ConParAgPro stock options. Yep. Heard what the reps had to say, how they'd work hard to ensure the integrity and healthfulness of the brand; what these corporate cats brought to the table had been like in *There Will Be Blood* when the fellas from Standard Oil show up and offer to make the plucky but viciously misanthropic prospector Plainview "a millionaire from one minute to the next."

It had happened to you.

What people dream about.

Cash.

Except, by the time of your deal? You already were, in paper and cash, a millionaire, if barely. But still. A couple dozen successful small businesses can do it for a frugal redneck boy from Edgewater County. A further cash-out, the big enchilada, well, it'd only make folks back home that much more proud of your ass. Wouldn't it.

✸❋◉

AFTER THE AIRFIELD manager whom you've rousted out of his comfortable nearby home helps you get the plane squared away under an open shed along the field where local pleasure craft are stored, you get someone on the horn at The Dixiana.

But it's not Trudy, rather a female voice that sounds like some stoner dumbass, albeit one who's at least capable of mumbling out Trudy's cell number. You listen, ruing the accursed twang of country music blaring in the background. Not even the old bastard laid up half-dead was enough to silence that twangy, useless hillbilly crap.

On another level: it sounded busy. A crowd at the honkytonk? You hoped they had enough staff to handle it until Pa-paw got back on his feet. You wouldn't have a clue how to run a craphole like that broken down old Dixiana.

The stoner, mumbling: "Roy Earl. I'm like, so, so sorry—"

Having extracted your information, you hang up. You need a ride, not sentiment.

Besides—if he doesn't live, you'll never have to think about any of it again. The shitty music. the stupid honkytonk.

This notion feels like relief; felt like wind beneath the wings. Which is like totally in your wheelhouse type-deal, far as aphorisms go.

Trudy answers in a froggy drawl that's but a shadow of her soft girl-voice that'd once moaned in your ear, cooing and showing you how to make love, where to put it and how fast to do it and how to eat pussy and everything else a boy needed to know about getting laid.

"Oh, sugar. What a durn mess."

Feeling like a child, you inquire if she'll come and fetch you from the airstrip.

Taken aback. "Wait—you flew into Edgewater County Airfield?"

You tell her yes.

"Flew on what?"

In your Piper Meridian.

"Flew yourself? In your own plane?"

"Yep."

The notion seems to take her breath away. "If that don't beat all."

You resist a ridiculous impulse to sing to her, *I like pleasure spiked with pain and music is my aeroplane*, a nonsense lyrical fragment that drops into your head, but you're on the verge of bawling and trying your hardest not to. Not to Trudy on the phone. Not after all this time.

Oh, how you want to spike her—not with pain, only pink pulsating pleasure, the memories of which loom as visceral and damp as if the charged couplings, fraught with milestone and meaning to you, had occurred only last week.

You'd dig a spite fuck to take revenge on your wife, yeah. But you also want Trudy for Trudy, if that makes any sense.

"I was fixing to head back over to the bar, so I reckon I can come scoop you up."

"Working? Tonight? The dump ought to be closed."

"Yeah, I'm working. Soon as I can get back there."

"Sounded busy."

"I'll be shit."

"Who the hell you got covering? Sounded like a female Cheech & Chong impersonator."

"She's fine. But I need to get moving."

"Why the hell's it open?"

Trudy tells you they all asked Miss Runelle what to do, and your granny had said, "'You little shit-asses better have my husband's place of business open tonight like normal, 'cause y'all are acting like he done died already','" as Trudy mimics Mama Runelle saying. "Which at the time. He—he—he hadn't." A volcanic, bubbling sound like haw-haw-haw.

"Hadn't—? Oh, no."

"Roy Earl—don't tell me you ain't heard yet."

Your reply tilts hard toward what you call negatory territory.

"Sugar—I didn't want to be the one to tell you." She bawls some more.

Your Granddaddy's dead. With no goodbye, either from you or for you.

It sinks in.

You FAILED, Roy E. Pettus. FAILURE, in gaudy color-streaked neon letters like on The Dixiana sign.

Failed. At everything.

Even this basic human function.

Now you grant to yourself the luxury of weeping, but not for him, rather for her—Creedence, Trudy, your now-widowed grandmother. Pick one.

Which you do, picking Creedence.

You howl with catharsis, echoing across the empty tarmac of the deserted, darkened rural airstrip.

For real.

Not an act.

Like your guts have been ripped out.

That old bastard. Dying on you like this.

Trudy Pirkle soothes you. Trudy, whom you haven't screwed in thirty years, but would do so in a heartbeat tonight if only she would allow you, says, "Sweet Roy Earl. Hang tight—Trudy's coming for to get you."

Nobody calls you Roy Earl anymore, reserved only for Edgewater County folk and the few oldschool friends you still have. The ones who really counted, however—Devin Rucker, Creedence's brother, missing and presumed dead for years now; Billy, another close college friend, a suicide by his own hand; and Libby Meade, Devin's girlfriend, killed by a drunk driver while they were still all in school—were all gone. Only Dobbs Vandegrift remained from that circle. The rest? Ghosts.

Trudy Pirkle, though? Real and alive.

Fluttering in your gut. Tingling teenage lust. An echo, anyway.

Good grief.

"Thanks," in a strained gurgle. "Appreciate that."

A CRAPPY BEATER of a rusty red late 90s Ford Taurus rolls into the airfield off Windwright Road. You make eye contact with its pilot.

Trudy.

Pulling up beside the front gate by the highway where you've been waiting, she puts it in park. Gets out.

Seeing a crooked, familiar smile, you're hurtled back thirty years.

Trudy, older. But still Trudy.

Zing.

A senior when you'd been a freshman at Marion Sims High, you hadn't paid her much attention, other than to note the cute freckled face and long legs of an unapproachable upperclassman. Pirkles tended to run with what today you'd call a 'downmarket' clique of folks compared to your circle of friends. What few you had.

A Pirkle lineage came identifiable to anyone with a modicum of Edgewater County experience under their belt: a strange family of blue-eyed, bird-beaked gangly bipeds, Pirkles sported spindly, osteal frames and big feet and crystal blue eyes, genetics here having run not wild, but rather consistent. Trudy, a feminine version, one where the pieces-parts came together in an appealing package: Trudy, with legs from here to Charleston, whom you first got to know on one of your afternoons spent cleaning the toilets in that crud-hole honkytonk. Your Pa-paw's new bartender. A girl this time.

The hug, awkward, lingering, causes literal heat lightning to flash on the far horizon across the flat airfield. So long since your bodies have touched. A tingle to cut through all the confusion and grief flooding in at every turn.

"Dang it all."

"I'm-a tell you what," she says. Shakes her hair, which seems flatter and thinner—back in the 80s she had a perm blonde curls that had dangled in your face as she rode you like a rodeo steer. "This beats all."

"Can't believe we're standing here. At this moment."

Trying to sound tough, a tough Southern shitkicking woman who don't take no guff. "Shit, I been worrying about him keeling over for long as I can remember. You'd think I wouldn't be so broke up about it."

"I hear you."

Nothing tough about her. She gushes, hard.

Another hug. Nodding and patting her on the back. "It won't sink in."

That voice against your ear: "No."

A shiver down your leg, you push back and give her the once-over. Still got it, but looking her age, a little stooped. A bit weary, crispy around the edges— the bar life. Dark smudges under her eyes. Fine lines. But her body much the same. The concept of sinking in takes on a different meaning in your mind, a lascivious one.

The earlier events of the day wash over and through you, hot despair and anger and confusion. "Man—it's worse than you even know."

Her hand, warm, on your forearm. "Sugar, what else is wrong?"

"I'll try to explain. Let's warp out of orbit."

◌◌◌

IN THE TAURUS, whose floorboard beneath your Keens sits littered with crumpled candy wrappers and crushed cans and other assorted trash and with the interior smelling of stale tobacco, Trudy carries you down Windwright to the west side highway and downtown, a road of which you feature fond memories, and only looks different now because of the sheer proliferation of political yard signs.

Many of them have names that sound right for Edgewater County—Macklin, Hinnant, Bagley, Busby, and Lawhorn standing for offices like Judge and Comptroller and Coroner and Court Clerk—but still others betray the more polyglot nature of modern-day suburban South Carolina: Gegenschatz, Frangopoulis, Vanesh Rupam, Nalusa Falaya, and Rebekah Rivkin, a Yankee sounding name if there'd ever been one. Probably looked and sounded like one of the mob wives in *Goodfellas*—as do an entire class of wealthy snowbird ladies down on Sedge Island.

As for the ethnic names, though, in truth Tillman Falls, thanks to the nuclear plant and proximity to the state capitol, t'was always a cosmopolitan community: you had fixated for a year or more on an exotic olive-skinned beauty named Natasha Prothro from Delaware, for one—way way out of your league, which wasn't even a league—and then you had folks like Dickie Giuffrida, one of your nemeses. Rednecks, blacks, Mexicans, even a few Germans—former POWs, had settled here after being incarcerated nearby during WW2—populated the rolling hills and sandy pine barrens of Edgewater County. America, that ever-changing smoothie-sucking inter-flux of human social interaction.

Highfalutin ideas pop in your mind out of nowhere, feeling as though coming from the future somehow, a voice that is not yours. Not exactly.

Goosebumps.

But what the west side highway makes you think about is one crazy day, getting to follow your Uncle Burnie Sykes home from a car auction on the other side of Camden, well over thirty miles away. It'd been that time he'd found a low mileage, clean Impala for a steal and wanted to take it back and sell on his car lot, which'd been only one of his numerous businesses.

"I ever tell you the story about the time when I was a kid, and Burnie Sykes let me drive a car home from Beauchamp County? On the highway? Like, following him?"

"Nuh-uh," blowing snot into a wad of stiff tissue and signaling to merge onto the highway.

Shaking your head. "Letting me drive like that. Wa'n't but thirteen."

"Burnie was a crazy old coot back then, too, I reckon. You musta been scared."

"At first. Then, it was cool as heck. Especially when it was over. We pulled onto that car lot of his, and I felt relieved. Also about a foot taller—none of my friends had driven yet. You should've seen my boy Devin's face. Street cred."

"Musta seemed all kinds of awesome."

"That it did. That it did."

"Lucky y'all didn't get pulled."

"That's what my granddaddy said." A pall settles in the car. "But Burnie, he didn't seem too worried. That's how I think of them both, him and old Rabbit. They never seemed scared of nothing."

This pine-barren part of the county, dusty and poor, sat as a wedge between developed Tillman Falls and the national forest to the farther west, and to your squinting peepers hasn't much changed. Uncle Burnie used to bring you here to watch the model airplane club. Its miniature launches and landings occurred on the far end of the runway when real planes weren't taking off or landing, a rare event anyway at such a tiny, rural county airstrip.

There, the old CME church looking as ramshackle as you recall; here, Gesthemane Holiness, the snakehandlers, much spruced up with a new brick sanctuary and the crisp white lines you admire in the clean, asphalted parking lot, recent and fresh; a no-frills SMALL ENGINE REPAIR business still in operation, with its selection of refurbished lawnmowers chained together in front of a cinderblock building with a garage bay that in your early childhood had been an Esso station; Mr. Vincent's ACE Hardware, still holding off the looming shadow of the big boxes, which hadn't made it this far north on the freeway; a peeling, faded billboard for a landscaping company called Sonrise to Sonset Lawn Care and featuring a prominent Jesus fish; the old Sky-Vue Drive-In property, which closed when you were a kid, standing unrecognizable, razed and barren; a couple of ethnic grocers—the standalone El Mercadito Popular, and the more upmarket-looking Tienda Viviana, situated in a newish, three-unit strip alongside an ABC liquor store and a payday lender next to a decrepit strip property new in your childhood, now crumbling and home to a storefront church called the Received Word Ministry and a dingy electronics repair shop with the blank gray cabinets of unwanted projection TVs lined up in front of the unoccupied retail space separating religion from entertainment. Only a few new trailer parks you don't remember, and the Spanish-language Rent-To-Own and other business signage, make Windwright Road seem at all different.

Rent to own, eh? You do not rent. You can buy it all.

Hell, you could probably buy the airport.

For cash.

On the spot.

For your last car purchase? The BMW? Wrote a check.

You'll never forget the look on the salesman's face, cutting off his low-or-no interest financing spiel. "You can offer a deal for cash in hand, right?" That, your only question. "Right?"

Flustered. "I'll talk to my—my boss."

"You do that."

Dude had wary wonder in his eyes. Who the hell pays cash, that's what his face said. Thought you a drug dealer, maybe.

But, what criminal writes a check?

You ponder: What is money, anyway? Who determines its worth?

What is worth?

What is value?

What the hell is money?

⊛⊛⊛

You stood there at the car auction in the hot sun. Blazing, dusty, South Carolina in summer. The ground was sandy and weedy; you found a seashell. It happened in this part of the state here on the fall line, where eons ago brine and foam had once lapped. The Impala, its tires brown with dirt, a deep candy-apple red finish with a black vinyl hardtop. All it needed was a wash. You wished you were sixteen, and had a license, and could drive.

"Right pretty, ain't she?"

So shy in those days you could barely speak above a whisper. "Yes, sir."

"Do what, now?"

"I said, it sure is."

"Agreed. That's a mover, right there. Lemme go get the skinny."

Your Uncle Burnie went hustling across the noisy auto yard full of car seekers to confer with a colleague, another man around his age—both ancient, or so it seemed.

He came back and asked, "Boy, you think you can drive this car back home?"

"By myself?"

"No, I mean following right behind me."

Uncle Burnie's car auction buddy, spitting tobacco juice into the sandy midlands earth. "It's not but a straight shot down 217. You ain't even gonna stop at no lights but once or twice. Up and down them hills and across the river and home free."

"We know the way home," Burnie said. "Don't we, Roy Earl?"

"Sure do."

You asked if it were a stick shift, or automatic. Your uncle, actually your grand-father's best friend and not an uncle, said au-to-matic. "Put her in D and go."

More juice into the dirt. "Burnham, he ever drove a car before?"

"Shoot, yeah. Ain't you, Roy."

"Sure," your voice cracking. You fixated on the sweat stains under the car auctioneer's plaid button down shirt. "I can drive good as you want."

"I know you can. Your granddaddy told me you'd been driving Runelle's T-Bird around the yard."

Your stomach went cold. "He—did?"

"Ain't that right?"

"Yes, sir."

Busted. He winked. "Got to practice somehow."

While she was out with Letty Glasscock getting their hair done, you had taken the keys to Mama Runelle's big green boat, a 1977 Thunderbird LTD in which you would later take your driver's test, and you would practice by going up and down the long driveway on your grandparents land between the row of crepe myrtles to either side. Such golden memories—you and Devin and Dobbs messing around and pushing boundaries, adolescent glory, also without a care or worry in the world. At least not that you let on to either one of those best pals. But that day, you felt caught in a major no-no.

"So—you up for it?"

You worried how much of this made for a trick, a set-up to expose and punish you for driving the T-Bird. "Yes, sir," you finally said.

You waited. Uncle Burnie and the man got the paperwork squared away.

Getting out of the auction lot you just about backed it into a telephone pole, the two old men waving their arms and yelling. Once on the road and following the Buick you rolled down the window, turned on the radio and looked for WABA, but its signal was too faint way over here in Beauchamp County. You settled for a country station out of Camden.

It all seemed so grown up you couldn't stand yourself.

At the stop signs, he'd wait until clear enough for both of you to go, waving you forward. You stepped on the brakes a little too hard. You pushed the gas down too much, revving the engine.

Waylon Jennings singing about the same old tunes and how we need to change, one of the few country songs on The Dixiana jukebox you halfway liked. That was also about the time you started working at the honkytonk for your granddaddy. Scrubbing the urinal trough. Mopping up after the kitchen help like a common workhouse slave. But paying you, at least.

You couldn't wait to leave this place.

But the day of the drive, for a brief shining moment, you felt so badass, never more than crossing the bridge into Edgewater County and passing by Pike's Bait & Pawn and the biker bar, at that time called Fast Traxx but of late the more wry Ape Hangers, as well the filling stations and the Hollow Bone barbecue hut. At last you both pulled into Uncle Burnie's used car and mobile home lot, at the time a mini-empire with his appliance store downtown and a trailer park he had developed across the bridge in Easton.

Not that Burnham Sykes and Thurmond Pike were rivals; far from it. Uncle Burnie'd been the one who had gotten the ridiculous prop monster truck for Pike, who'd emblazoned it with his bright yellow logo. He also paid a welder to create an oversized wallet chain to hang from the bumper to the mirror on the passenger side, as authentic an Edgewater County touch, you thought, as there'd ever been.

You stood in the sun with your Uncle Burnie. He patted you on the arm. "You done good, Roy Earl. Here."

He handed you money, a twenty dollar bill. "What's this for?"

"You was working for me today. Don't never work for no one without getting paid."

You told him you understood.

Your gut clenches and you wish you were thirteen again; and you'd do it all different this time, except for how well you drove that Impala home behind Uncle Burnie in his shark-blue Buick Riviera. The afternoon had passed in a golden string of moments of perfection and awestruck amazement, teetering, you perceived, upon sudden and newfound maturity that wouldn't blossom in reality for so long that, in retrospect, if someone had said you'd be in your 40s, and worth eight figures, but still trying to figure out who you really freaking were? You'd have been shocked by the notion.

Chagrined.

Mortified.

You always figured, I'll be who I am when Granddaddy and Mee-maw pass on, and damn if they hadn't lived longer than you had expected.

As Trudy drives you into town, you beat your thigh with a hard fist. No more tears in front of her. On the phone had been egregious enough. You're a man, now. Not the boy she fucked and forgot. You will show her how powerful you have grown. You will show them all.

How stupid—you flying the plane home. Absent traffic, the whole process ended up taking longer than driving. Now safely here in Edgewater County, sure, but you've got to be carted around like a nine-year-old.

By Trudy, no less.

The other woman who also once broke your heart.

What—you trying to make this all worse than it needs to be?

Or what?

And yet: all crackled with symmetry and synchronicity, and nothing seemed like an accident, but all that notion did was make the situation seem that much worse: if the plan you or a future you or God or whoever set out had come to a kind of fruition, a plan to bring you down low, about low as you can go, then you hoped somebody somewhere was happy, because it'd sure worked.

As you approach the town proper, pawn shops, liquor stores, check cashing seem the order of the day. Meanwhile in the car, you pour out the whole sorry mess. Your grandfather—your father, basically—is lying dead, but as Trudy passes by Munn E. Greene's Pawn World, a west side competitor to Thurmond Pike over closer to the freeway and the river, all you can talk about is Creedence being unfaithful.

Trudy, listening and cutting her gaze sidelong, uh-huh, uh-huh uh-huh; her big pretty eyes now scrunched up crinkled and bloody from all the cigarette smoke, hers and the customers, she's endured through the decades.

"An employee, of all things." That's what you keep harping on. "A millennial."

The subtext, thick. The regret you feel at having said it this way is enormous.

"Well, dang. I'm in shock. I thought Creedence was a—was a—"

"A what?"

"A good girl."

Your look must be withering. She apologizes. You say, just a helluva day.

Collapsing into your own footprint at the speed of gravity, and despite not being hit by a jetliner, the tears flow there in the bucket seat of her Taurus.

Trudy goes, "Oh boy, hon."

Your salty rain shower's over, fast. The way it goes with dudes. Over and done.

You manage a weak smile, note a couple of bandaids around her fingers, and other little nicks. Her nails, then as now, short and unadorned. She used to wear a particular ring on her finger, but it's not there. It'd been cheap sterling costume jewelry—a dragonfly, its small metal wings wrapping around her index finger. Now, no rings of any sort.

Pulsing lust for her, throbbing inside with every heartbeat.

A spite-fuck? Is that what you want right now?

Memories rush back: that fateful weekend Rabbit and Runelle had gone to Texas for her brother's funeral, your great uncle Hollis that you never met. Had left you alone for the first time in your life, to help keep an eye on The Dixiana through the weekend, which you did, its smoky redneck clientele hollering and hooting, the offensive country music blaring on the jukebox, the same terrible Garth Brooks song like three times, accompanied by idiots drunken enough to believe themselves capable singers, not to mention the bluegrass on Saturday afternoon you had to suffer through. The beer, rivers and lakes of beer under your sneakers. Ruing the memory of the fuss Runelle had put up not about you staying behind, rather your having said you didn't want to go with them. Saying, you couldn't because of the marching band competition, an event you had to cover for the school paper. A project tied to a grade.

Lies.

What had come of your perfidy?

Heartache.

Punishment.

But first:

The miracle of Trudy.

Your first time. Her naked flesh, hot and damp, lying pressed to yours. Your flesh, sticking together. Your tumescence, plunging within her body. Fantasy made real.

But truthfully? You were both drunk, and in some respects the details have always remained vague: Fumbling around in her bedroom in the dark, screwing and coming, all in about four or five minutes. You barely remember it.

The hell you say—you can recall every caress. Every kiss. Every thrust. Because she did it with you again, too. And again; again. As many times as you wanted, or were able. Glorious. A thousand-petal lotus blossom opening inside your chest. But withering, almost as soon as it began to thrive.

❀❀❀

IN MR. RABBIT's absence there in the late spring of 1986, the staff of mostly young people had begun whooping it up even before closing time. But not stealing liquor—Trudy, keeping a tab and making everyone pay up.

The eldest bartender, a scabby old coot named Chester, had gone on home. Rabbit or no Rabbit, a slow Saturday anyway, and Trudy, volunteering to shut her down. At last, only you and Trudy there, and thirty-odd years later the sound of the lock turning in the front door still reverberates in your ears.

Clunk.

You had earlier gotten a call from Pa-paw and Mee-maw, who'd stopped at a payphone to check on you and the honkytonk and the house and the dogs and all was fine, except that it wasn't busier. But then the old rascal said, if it was busy y'all couldn't handle it without him, laughing his *nyuck-nyuck* and coughing out the Pall Mall phlegm like he always did, even when you were little. Then, Mee-maw wanting to make sure you had eat good for dinner. And for the next few days you should go to Lucinda's and the Congress Street Grille to eat your lunch and dinner, where it had been prearranged for the proprietors to feed you without charge. All spelled out standing on the front porch before they left. Your grandparents, a real trip.

Once the rest of the staff had gone—your grandfather had deputized you to keep an eye on things, a task intended to empower you but that only seemed annoying—Trudy's flirting intensified. Before it had seemed mean spirited, like she'd been making fun of you, a kid, from her high perch as an all-but grownup.

She let you drink a beer.

Shoot—who did she think she was. You had been behind this bar pulling draught beer since you were ten years old. You didn't much care for it, but Trudy didn't need to know that.

Y'all drank a couple, and another, along with a shot of some German crap that tasted like licorice cough syrup, cold and thick and shocking: your first Jäegermeister. Sitting at the bar with Trudy, who chatted and joked with you like you were another adult and not a kid. Slapping your knee and forearm. Reminding you how much cuter you were now than then. Like it had happened overnight.

"Sometimes you look at somebody you know, but it's like you ain't never seen them."

"I know what you mean."

You told her you remembered the first time you saw her, at a football game when you were in eighth grade. You left off that part. She thought it was all so sweet.

Being pulled into the musty stockroom lined with cases of beer and bottles of liquor. Away from the front windows, the bar lit up by the fluorescent fixtures in the ceiling that stayed off during business hours, what you called the cleaning lights that illuminated the grunge in the crevices and the dust on all the frames with the autographed 8x10s, most of which were country music stars, but also other entertainers like the wrestler Gorgeous George, whom your grandfather always told you had been in his heyday such a big personality he held as much influence over performers as Elvis Presley and Little Richard as did other musicians. A few glossies of movie actors like Warren Oates, who had visited the bar when shooting a movie in the South in the 70s called *Cockfighter*, other stars Burnie or Rabbit admired from westerns and war pictures, the bread and butter of televised entertainments for men their age.

"You're cute." Trudy, good and drunk. "Did I say that already?"

"No."

"Remember how you used to be chubby?"

"I guess."

"You grew out of it."

All you could do was shrug, grateful the dim overhead bulb in the stockroom full of liquor mini-bottles and cases of PBR and Bud Longnecks would help hide your blazing cheeks.

"I bet you got a girlfriend. Don't ya."

You shook your head.

"So then. If I were to want to give you a little kiss, I wouldn't be stepping on no little girl's toes." Her fingers, tickling the buttons of your Southeastern Redtails polo shirt, the modern version of General Reb embroidered on the breast pocket. "Would I?"

Shaking your head.

Draping her arms around you. Taller, she had to lean down, her cute curly hair dangling and tickling your cheeks. So close you could smell beer on her breath. A whiff of nicotine. A grownup mouth.

The lips, meeting. Electric.

You stood there, her mouth on yours. Clueless. Quivering.

Getting hard.

She went Mmmm and began: Tongues, slow and languid. Trudy, leading as though on the dance floor.

The kissing part seemed to go on a long time, and included tight hugging with the result an erection of such rigidity it felt painful.

"I got my house to myself tonight too."

"You do?"

"Uh-huh. You want me to help you with this?"

She grabbed hold of the pulsing shaft, jutting to the side of your zipper. You drew in your breath. Came close to exploding already from the brief grip she'd exerted. Voice cracking. "I ain't done anything before."

Saying nothing. But galvanized. Making you do another shot of the licorice stuff.

Making sure the bar was locked up and secure. You, running around with a hard-on, checking all the doors and flipping off the neon sign outside.

Riding in a pickup she drove back then, a Dodge Lil' Red Express that one of her boyfriends, she told you, had customized with racing stripes, that had a four-barrel small block engine she further told you was modified from a police car engine. Both of you drinking PBR cans she'd grabbed out of the bar cooler, she warned you not to spill on the upholstery, which had been recently cleaned.

Leaning over at a deserted four-way stop to kiss you some more.

After that, flashes and flash-frames:

Naked in her bed. Sliding inside her. A miracle of sensation. Coming fast. Intense, but a disappointment. Her laughing and saying, mercy, honey. "Slow down."

Shamefaced, you told her you had not done it before. And that you now loved her.

She burst out laughing. "I could tell it was your first time. It was —nice, sugar."

Rolling over and covering your face with a meaty forearm and wrenching the sheet across your body, your primary emotion one of awkwardness and embarrassment. Horrifying.

And yet how right it seemed: Of course pudgy doofus Roy Earl couldn't even do it right.

Aw, she'd said. "Come here, angel. Let's get you going again."

Stroking your face, your body you'd always felt had been so ugly, your penis, and the balls, too.

Wait—she was playing with the balls! Was that right?

Either way, you became harder than you'd ever been before, the alcohol wearing off and then Trudy showing you how to do things.

All night. You both slept, some, but you had managed to come off a few more times. You were sixteen. The stuff of beautiful boyhood dreams made real.

When you awoke, you found it wasn't over.

After daybreak Trudy rolled over, groaned, and stretched a long arm across your midsection; she found there another flagpole. You had awakened and looked over at her leg poking out of the sheet and it had sprung right up.

She opened her eyes, mascara-stained, a hint of the makeup left you'd kissed away. "Well—good morning," through a froggy hangover throat. "Dang, boy."

You were still feeling out of your body, out of your mind, out of time—you woke up next to a woman. A beautiful one, who'd made love to you. "Top o' the morning, Miss Trudy."

"Mmm." Ignoring your dragon breath Trudy leaned in and kissed you closed mouth a few times, more like pecks. A rustling of sheets and the tousled head disappeared. You thought she was going down there to tickle you.

Not exactly.

Trudy, taking her time, like eating an ice cream cone. And if you thought your mind had been blown before, now the explosive, gratifying reality of her attention to your sore member sent you heavenward again, and perhaps beyond. You hollered loud enough to make one of her Def Leppard posters fall off the wall.

Her lips, puffy. "My turn now. Okay?"

"Oh-kay."

Your head still dizzy with endorphins, you'd have done anything she asked. She wiggled into position, leaning back against the headboard. Totally unsure about how and what to do, you slid downward. Down there.

The details, compelling. Her scent, an intoxication like nothing you'd ever experienced—and not until Creedence would it again feel this way. You set to work, probing and exploring, her scent rushing to a vital pulsing secret center of your brain.

"Right there," holding your head in place. "Oh, sugar—don't stop."

You swirled and licked and tickled. Arching her back and with her feet on your shoulders Trudy came in a gusher. Stunned and soaked, you fell back and went, whoa.

"Keep on," she pled.

"Oh—I—"

She grabbed your head, pushed your tongue back down onto her clit. Another torrent. Again. And again, her long legs drawing up and toes curling next to your ears. She screamed, after which set seemed ready for you to ease off, which you did, tongue swollen and aching.

Covering her scarlet face framed by stringy hair, she became suffused with afterglow giggles. "Shoulda warned you—I get the girly squirts like nobody's business."

Dripping, you couldn't help but ask: "Is that—is it—normal?"

"It is for me. I reckon."

You didn't know from girly squirts—or now you did—but either way, your red and sore cock had become rigid again, and you rose to slide inside her for the fifth or sixth time in eight hours. Primal urges overcame you. You took Trudy, giving her your all but for only a minute or two, like the first time. Sore as heck, it almost hurt.

Worse? It'd hurt for years, that last time inside her.

But in the moment, it had been beautiful. Trudy had held you close, cooing and wiping your face with a towel, chuckling at your empty, hung-over stomach that growled like mad.

She traced a fingertip up and down your belly, giving you chills. "You so fine," sounding like a black girl. "No way I would believe you were only sixteen."

"We do our best," you said. "We try."

"'We'?"

"The royal 'we'."

"I get it." She put her hand on the royal we, squeezed. Heaven. "We."

How Trudy had rolled over, groaning; the sheets a tangled damp wreck. Her feet brushed against your shins, soles rough from working behind the bar.

When it all went wrong.

"Shit, shit," she said. "If your grandmama and granddaddy knew I had done this—?" Terror flashed across her face. "Great God almighty."

She'd run and slammed the door to the bathroom, calling, "You can use it after me. But we got to get you out of here."

"I should get home, anyway. I got to feed the dogs."

"Oh, hale, boy—them dogs is starving to death by now. Another reason he'll kill me."

You called out to her that the dogs would be fine. Heard the toilet flush.

As you got up to get dressed, you pondered: had Trudy Pirkle peed on you? What was all that? Back then, no Google to consult. It'd be years before you would hear about female ejaculation. Sheltered little fucker.

Ejaculation.

And then it hit—you could have impregnated one of Rabbit's bartenders, a redneck girl from out in the sticks near Red Mound. A Pirkle.

What about the film in health class? The rubbers?

You idiot.

This did not fit in with your rubric, that of thorough planning, a lesson you picked up: three moves ahead, like in chess. Sticking your dick inside Trudy Pirkle without a condom—her letting you, for that matter—did not constitute planning.

Nothing along those lines had come of it, though, and you'd never made love with her again. Not with Trudy all freaked out at being found out by Mr. Rabbit or Mama Runelle. That morning, however, as you got the dogs fed and you showered and walked around the empty house and felt on your own for the first time ever, you thought you might be in love with Trudy Pirkle. And how you couldn't wait to tell her. But you never got the chance.

For the first few weeks afterward at the bar, Trudy, giving you the cold shoulder. So goddamned confusing. That's when you had told your Pa-paw you didn't want to work for him anymore. That you were going to get a job with Mr. Sortwell at the Palmetto Grande. He understood, encouraged you. Never knew about the Trudy part, though.

You have never gotten over her.

You glance over at your driver, a sexy as hell tomboy, still. Other than the eyes, she hasn't changed much. Maybe some parts sagging. But fudge it.

You want her so bad.

In your grief over all the terrible threads of your life, you crave those brief, youthful moments of discovery with Trudy. Joining her body with yours had been cosmic, so much that for years you hadn't bothered to try to get sex with another woman.

Years.

And here she sits again. Inches from you. Your elbows, touching on the armrest. Trudy.

BUTTON SYKES AND HOWDY SHULL

Having penetrated the subtleties with sufficient proficiency but to no beneficial effect, once again Button Sykes carried her grimoire, a text filled by page after page of ritual and sigil and incantation, to the riverside park for disposal in the cradle of nature. Setting her intention to one of release and finality, she brought along a purple Bic lighter to spark the cursed notebook aflame. Here in solitude, she hoped dispelling the book's magnetized energies into ashes and dust would harm the fewest other human beings.

Done with it all.

Yeah. Magicking, it had run its course.

Except for the powwow Uncle Rabbit taught her. Which she considered trying on her own aching back. He cautioned, however, that this sort of hex magic involving symbols and semantics—performed in this case to heal oneself—represented the most difficult to pull off. Powwow, he said, must at some essential level be about service to others.

Eh—not another discipline. She'd been through so many. A depth of esoteric knowledge, true, but master of no worlds.

As the epigraph on the first page of her grimoire advised in her own spidery scrawl, with words courtesy of Blake:

> *If you have formed a circle to go into,*
> *Go into it yourself and see how you would do.*

How she had done: No workings seemed to fluoresce as they should; her myriad approaches and attempts at placing her size-five feet on either side of a dividing line between two worlds only attracted the stink of failure rather than mastery of the subtle energies. She'd been stuck for months working on fully entering the astral plane through lucid dreaming, and with precious little success. Dweller upon no thresholds.

But escaping misfortunes, avoiding a hundred ills, with good tidings ahead, yeah: Button felt safe and remained on her Way to a state of superior immortality. When the time came of full manifestation, she would evade death by stepping into another life. How it worked; the alchemist's true goal.

Still, she'd heeded the warnings found in every esoteric text she'd studied, from the *Picatrix* to the theosophists and Crowley and beyond—that, the practice of so-called white magic still retained enormous capacity to attract malicious actors alongside ostensibly benevolent ones. But maybe not enough heeding, yo.

A truism: what magic has done, it should also be able to undo.

But for whatever inscrutable reason, at the last minute—like the time before, and before that, a few weeks ago when she'd first seen the face of a simian-like entity peeking in through the purple veil of her morning meditation, a little Pazuzu sneaking in from an unguarded seam, a demon but more on the impish side—she'd left the handwritten softcover notebook in her Subaru parked in the small gravel lot of the Sugeree Riverside Trail Loop. Secluded and scenic not far below the old mill, the concrete walking path along the sloping, stony riverbank a few miles outside Tillman Falls had been a perfect place to study and practice ritual. She said to herself, the grimoire survives another attempt on its life.

Like it possesses a will of its own.

She shuddered: The banishing ceremony may have lost its punch. Her defenses, weakening.

Magicking—it had only led to more self-doubt.

Retain the grimoire; but keep it closed. Go back to the Eastern stuff, the Taoism, the Confucianism. Completing the elixir pill, the ultimate melding of sense and essence, body and mind, spirit and energy. Culmination of this sacred process, working the bellows of heaven and earth, taking up the apothecary scale of fire and water, had seemed so close. But in a fit of impatience, she ditched it all to win back the heart of Heather Ponderview by any means necessary— through spellcraft and sigil and ceremony. She couldn't talk about it further. Shhhh.

Suffering a bout of self-consciousness, and perhaps a tumble backward into a kind of paranoia the writer Robert Anton Wilson called Chapel Perilous, a period of uncertainty about what was and wasn't real and out of which a psychonaut emerged either paranoid or comfortably skeptical, she kept thinking she ought to burn her book of workings and rituals, cobbled together from quite a few obscure texts from deep in the antiquity of occult letters.

But like, enough already. Enough with the magicking and turning the Tarot cards and walking around trees a dozen times repeating incantations. It was time to get real. Time to enact some grass-roots activism, some down-home realpolitik, some agitation, some preaching on matters earthly rather than ethereal.

Time for tangible matters.

Wasn't it?

Deciding it better to not-know than to stand waiting for some all-encompassing answer of answers likely to never arrive, Button beep-beeped the door lock, shoved in the ear buds and entered the park gate to begin her power walk, long-ass dreads shaking snakelike and bouncing against her back and buttocks, an off-tempo counterpoint rhythm to that of her footsteps as the concrete trail descended through old-growth trees toward the riverside. In her fireplug of a physicalized form, as she thought of the body now whittled down from its traditional stoutness, she felt pride—a dangerous emotion. For once, admiring the sight of her naked self in the mirror rather than repulsed. Liking herself, for almost the first time in her life.

A reason to walk beside this river of forgetfulness, its waters like that of the Lethe rather than the Sugeree; motivation to walk harder, to bolster her commitment to good health.

Daily.

Commitment.

As with her numerous other practices. Whichever ones she planned to keep on practicing.

Some magicking worked, but to what ultimate result she knew not. As Sylvan Muldoon advised in his seminal 1929 text Projection of the Astral Body: throw away reason and try experiment.

What had worked, or seemed to? Her beloved and unrequited college paramour Heather Ponderview, once again in reasonable proximity, a fondest wish conjured. Heather had moved back to the East Coast, only a state away, once again living at her rich father's mountaintop estate near the North Carolina and Tennessee border. Deep woods; snakelike roads leading around curves and up grades until the population density fell below that of the Sasquatch who probably lived in those hollows.

They'd camped there as college-age lovers. Twenty years ago.

The ache—the dreadful ache in her gut, in her side. Heartbreak, no joking matter.

Button performed an entire working, a year's time and energetic investment, to get Heather back. A move three thousand miles closer had to represent a sign the needle was moving.

But at what cost? The possible attraction of Archonic influence, like the little creep poking its snout into her meditation?

See? More bullshit. She had to try for something real. Lest she start to think she might actually be nuts. Or sick. Or something.

❁❋❁

SHUT THAT FUCKING nuclear plant down. There we go. That's what she would do. Its wicked, ever-present plume of steam floated omnipresent not far downstream from the concrete path, a remote county park where Button exercised her way through the waterside woods. While not a practicing Christian, Button made the sign of the cross with her thumb and forefinger three times in the direction of the nuclear plant, a hex of protection the old man taught her.

And so now what did they have in mind?

Oh, yeah.

Building more reactors.

Wait—what?

You heard that right. Hah. Hah. Hah—madness, that's what.

Now she knew, at least. Knew for sure.

Not that the power plant was killing—she could take that part as-read. No. What she knew. For sure. Was this: She'd found a purpose, one different from the last ten years spent as caretaker to family members suffering degrees of decrepitude and disease.

Unfair to herself—this service, it is a sacred duty. Reminds herself of this daily, she does.

And before that, her dying father's brutal slog through terminal cancer, a fatal traverse engendering horrific suffering and indignity. Which meant that everyone in the house suffered. For him, and with him.

After he finally passed away in '12, Button had taken time to go back to something of her old routine prior to the horrible year of his decline and death: trips down to Columbia to the hipster coffee shops there around the campus, strolling among Southeastern University's storied buildings, old and new, that sprawled across that part of the city, journaling and sketching and storyboarding little mind-movies, and wondering if she shouldn't have finished her degree closer to home like her family had wanted instead of transferring to Foothills State, that crunchy granola school, as her grandfather called it, in the mountains of North Carolina. All problems and issues had flowed from that decision.

Hadn't they?

Button, refusing to enter the mental palace of ancient recriminations about having decided this or that or the other thing, deep in a receding past; not this morning here by the shimmering and gurgling river, on the walking path by the old mill along the lovely stretch before the canal area downstream, and the nuclear station beyond. Where the profane reign of the devil unleashed on Earth, in all due radioactive splendor, glowed on unabated.

⊛✳◉

THEY TALKED about the post 9/11 world; what Button Sykes wanted to discuss was the post-Fukushima world. What had happened over there? The Fukushima Daiichi tsunami and subsequent, ongoing nuclear disaster. Years since the tsunami, now. Didn't hear much about the crisis, except in alternative media.

But then, much had occurred in the atomic age that rarely got discussed: what had happened to all the radiation released during the era of above ground atomic testing? Where did it go?

When did rates of lung cancer worldwide increase? Maybe it wasn't cigarette smoking—well, it had to be cigarette smoking. She'd heard the tobacco companies encouraged the use of irradiated fertilizers, and this was behind all the lung cancer, not so much the smoking part.

But she couldn't go down that road; she'd known so much cancer—her father, others. They all lived near the nuclear station. It was epidemic; it was obvious.

Thank god she'd been working out hard for a year or two now, otherwise she might attribute her weight loss to disease, a tumor consuming more than its share of resources, sucking her dead like the growth in her father's neck and chest.

No, that wouldn't happen to her; in control. Mental discipline.

You had to be careful. You couldn't think about 'cancer'; you shouldn't say the word, or let the idea take hold in your mind, lest you manifest this into reality inside your own body. The way so many were manifesting diseases, their fleshy vessels reflecting the state of the planet, of Gaia herself who so suffered the depredations and profane incursions of its principal controlling species swarming antlike, inventing ever more complex technologies that produced ever more refined and toxic wastes, and all of it so unnatural, with nowhere to go, so removed from the natural balance: the four elements. An equipoise that'd been perfect before womankind had existed. And would be so again. After her demise.

The concept of mental discipline applied to other maladies besides cancer, which itself represented many other diseases, an umbrella term. Any way you cut it, the mind could be held responsible; similarly, the mind could also stay in control of matters. Keep the body healthy. You had due diligence in terms of diet and physical activity and other aspects of human physicality, but mental fitness a crucial, foundational building block of any one person's health and general state of reality.

Be worth thinking herself into cancer. Hah. Just to help make the point.

For all your mental discipline, you get some silly-ass thoughts sometimes, GF.

But her thinking regarding the knowledge to which she'd been led, it went far beyond nuke plant radiation. If she went all the way with what she believed—that she'd been chosen for transformation and spiritual growth by angels who visited her during her deep meditations and sang their songs she decoded into true gospel—no one would listen. It would be all-too-much, as the Beatles sang, in revealing these truths about reality as she now understood them. They'd dismiss her as a whackadoodle.

Worse: They'd put her away.

Again. Like at sixteen when she'd received a diagnosis of 'defiance syndrome' and found herself committed to a behavioral facility full of junkies and the mentally ill.

Actual whackadoodles. How she'd hated her father over that.

Had wished him dead.

A stab of panic.

Can't go there.

Forget everything else. At least with the no-nukes proaction, she had plenty of compatriots around the world. Not that the PTB—the Powers That Be—held any truck with allowing truthtelling activists, however guided by angels they might be, to reach enough hearts and minds to the point that anything of substance would change and humanity would move on from this destructive cycle instead of perpetuating it. They who controlled the language controlled history, offered their version of the truth. A tough row to hoe for an insignificant woman like her, in a place like Edgewater County.

A WELL-LIGHTED PATH in the woods, paid for by taxpayer dollars. Call boxes every tenth lamppost, in case of emergency. If this nice tree-canopied riverfront trail had been placed in a SimCity town, its virtual residents would have been gratified the mayor had built it. Would have used the living crap out of it. Why so few in Edgewater County seemed to care about this quite real path, Button couldn't say. Too close to the creepy abandoned mill building, an enormous red-brick rectangle once the heart of the county's economy and now left to crumble in ignominy, maybe? Too far from the main drag? Still, a fine and wholesome idea. Its construction advocated and partially funded by the ELMS, among other civic organizations and government bodies.

Button, halfway done with her power-walk and certain she was alone by the river, chose a shady, level spot to do yoga stretches. Despite forsaking magicking, she still felt compelled to perform her daily lower banishing ritual, which she'd modified from its traditional roots in a variety of personal ways, also consult with a particular tree, one with whom she had a working relationship, on the aim and direction of her plans to protest construction of the new nuclear reactors.

Next, she practiced a few minutes of conscious, yogic breathing and light meditation, only afterwards finishing the walk. Going for the burn and the sweat, all while thinking ahead to another attempt that night with lucid dreaming, about which she'd been doing research.

As for the physical exercise, her perpetual chubbiness had dissipated like never before in her whole life, and this time with relative ease. She hadn't been this skinny since her freshman semesters back in the mid-naughty 90s at Southeastern, before transferring up to Foothills State, and the beginning of the Heather Epoch.

During the misbegotten year wandering SEU's sprawling campus in downtown Columbia, she did manage to lose a quarter of her body weight, prompted in part by academic stress as well as a fit of body-image horror alongside a veritable army of leggy Southern sorority queens. They didn't look that different from the cruelly gorgeous and poised sister she'd grown up with, so the contrast between Button and them shouldn't have been, like, a total revelation and all. It made sense anyway to put down the junk food. Took up running from her dorm on campus to the State House and back again, weaving in and out of men in business attire and tourists taking photos of the Confederate monument or the copper dome, adorned at the time by its little rebel flag rubbed right in everyone's nose.

Of course in those days, her weight loss came courtesy an occasional starvation attempt through forced vomiting.

But hey, not like actual bulimia or anorexia, which Button knew all about and fully understood, a level of conscious choice involved in making herself puke up a pizza or a grinder from the Sub Station, none of which she did anymore. Not for years. Little dumbass she'd been.

Such a lengthy and bumpy traverse to find her correct and true course, a meaningful path. She could measure the period in fucking decades, now. Took forever to find this lighted way—Goddess knew it did. Hadn't trod it in school, her path, nor anyplace else she'd gone before returning home to become caretaker to ailing family members.

Now? Different.

Clear.

A state of ascendant consciousness. Higher than high. Which on top of actually being high, felt high indeed.

⊙❋⊙

How'd she know about the path being correct?

Easy: her future self, an entity Button called Walfredo, whom she understood represented another aspect of the embodiment of consciousness manifesting here in this physically incarnated third-dimensional state, had visited numerous times. Had offered assurance about her correct thinking in opposing two more cold-fire spewing reactors along the placid river and lakeside to the south.

An encouragement almost beyond emotion, warming her across her shoulders. A glowing feeling. A hand resting on her shoulder.

Sweat trickled down into her butt-crack and made her do a skipping stutter-step she wished she could have seen. Funnier than her failed comedy stunt last night. This much for certain.

⊙❋⊙

How her misguided attempt at educating the Dixiana open mic audience went over:

Lanky old Trudy, as much a fixture as any other aspect of the old honky-tonk, and an authority figure with a no-nonsense management style that struck fear into all who dared cross her, mounted the stage. The crowd, bustling, quieted.

"Look here. We got a special treat tonight—I know y'all'r here to hear some pickin', and all. Right?"

Hooting and hollering came the response.

"And I am, too." She cleared her throat. "But first, we got ourselves something—different. Y'all put them hands together for our own Button Sykes." Trudy, squinting, consulted a blue index card. "Um. The Wicked High-larity of Button Sykes, y'all."

A reasonably robust response—polite, but far from sustained. Jasper Glasscock, with a sour and impatient expression and a limited edition Lester Flatt D-28 Martin guitar resting on his big gut, watched from the bottom of the wooden stairs off to the side as Trudy, with a vibration of disapproval and mistrust, gestured toward Button.

She jogged up the stage steps and over to the center mic like a game show host, Trudy scampering out of the way. "Right on right on right on—I sure appreciate y'all letting me lay my tight twenty on The Dixiana audience tonight."

Silence; a shuffling of feet and chairs and clinking of beer bottles. Conversations bubbled back into murmuring audibility.

Working her fist and stalking the stage, she wound herself up. "So, like, I went away for a long time, but since I came back to Tillman Falls, I've been running front of house here, yo." Scattered applause. "I guess those of you who come out to these gigs know this. Yeah—I see a lotta familiar faces out there. And so maybe you trust me enough to lay this here comedy-rap on y'all. Yeah," doing beat-box on her chest with the mic. "All right! All right!"

Her rap rang hollow—the energy hadn't risen to meet hers. Thrown off her game by the silence, she nonetheless pressed onward.

Normally she spoke in a halting manner belying her inner thoughtfulness, while well illustrating to anyone who knew her an undeniably robust history of experimentation with various psychotropic substances both synthetic and otherwise. Onstage, however, her words, born of conviction as well as thoroughgoing rehearsal at home, came tumbling out. After working on the routine, she'd opened her circle and cast a spell for loquacity. Just to be sure.

"But I ain't up here to do that kinda comedy. I appreciate it, y'all, but this here ain't that kinda routine."

"Get to the routine, then," a voice called out. "Cause you suck."

"All right already, keep your panties dry. I got something here that don't just lay on the floor, it wiggles around in your head and teaches ya some stuff, too."

At 'wiggles around' a chorus of hooting and catcalls drowned out the rest of her statement.

"This might come as news to lots of you. But our survival as a species is threatened. Yeah—I'm talking about the disaster of Fukushima."

Silence fell.

"It's an ELE—extinction level event. Containment is a myth; cold shutdown is a myth; cooling is a myth because there's no way to measure cooling when nobody knows where the nuclear fuel is. Waste processing is a myth. Cleanup is a myth."

Rabbit had come inside. A smoky, backlit silhouette standing still as a cigar store Indian, he watched her through the coming and going of the musicians and drunks. He raised a gnarled hand up to his face, drew on his Pall Mall.

She gulped and continued. "But what I want to talk about now isn't ten thousand miles away, it's right here on our river. My little routine, with these funny voices and this foolishness, is about the Sugeree River Station. Yeah. And those new reactors they're building, and how there's no way in HELL WE OUGHT TO ALLOW ANOTHER DAMNED POISON-SPEWING PIECE OF LUCIFERIAN ARCHITECTURE NEXT TO OUR BLESSED RIVER—!"

With the microphone feeding back, the audience had heard enough. A chorus of boos.

"We want tunes!"

"Fuck that shit! Music!"

They chanted and stomped their collective feet. "Music, music, music."

Trudy rushed back and grabbed Button by the shoulders, who continued to spout anti-nukes rhetoric. "This's a post-Fukushima world now, y'all," the last words she shouted, grabbing at the mic stand. "And we gotta get real..."

During the walk of shame back to the soundboard platform through a crowd still roiling with disdain, Button caught Rabbit's eye. Shaking his head, he pitched his butt outside and lumbered over to the last booth, his traditional spot in the back corner, with its direct eye-line to the stage, and where he'd receive petitioners and well-wishers throughout the evening.

As Trudy bade the room to settle down, Button threw on a set of cans and ran sound for Jasper's open mic night, which proceeded with him doing his usual schtick, with no further mention of her perfidious act of consciousness-raising performance art.

In fact, no one asked her for more info about the reactors or Fukushima or anything relating to her activism; not a single Dixiana patron came over to discuss her concerns at all. They were all as bad as that shriveled up old raisin Bill Wimmel at the paper, who deigned to run one out of maybe every twenty columns she submitted on issues of pressing local concern.

What would it take for folks around here to listen? To wake up? A miracle.

FORGET the stand-up at The Dixiana.

Forget all this materialist nonsense. Another world awaited. A higher one.

In Button's state of near-ascended consciousness, the sunlight shimmered on the water and the energy danced around the edges of all the trees and plants and the rocks in the river. Colors popped with a vibrancy no retina-display Apple product screen could duplicate. The air and the sounds of the chirping and chipping wrens and mockingbirds accompanied her power-walk, and she knew what she knew.

Swimming in consciousness.

And purpose.

Stretching her arms to the life-giving sun, she recited to the morning air:

"Change the body, change the mind. Change the mind, change the body. Change the mind and feel it in the body. Change the body and feel it in the mind. Change the mind, change the world. There is only information and change. Energy is controlled by information."

She had changed her mind, all right. And felt it in the body. No doubt. At times, she believed herself as powerful as the Sugeree River Station.

Sure, along with its penchant for spewing cancer-causing radiation into the environment, the plant existed to light warm, comfortable childhood homes and provide jobs. Literal power, like one found in the damn sun itself—the font of all life and existence and reality as we understand it at this vibration of physicality—but also, ya know, producing highly dangerous waste materials. Dangerous as crap.

Yeah.

You hated to tell people the truth. All so comfortable.

All that power flowin'.

Hardest part from her end? You can't wake up a person who's pretending to be asleep. But the truth pulsed and existed inside everyone. One only had to peer within long enough to find it. Hard to get across, as Dylan sang.

How could anyone ignore the reports about Fukushima, the ones found online, in alternative media?

Because nobody on the regular TV said anything anymore about Fukushima.

Button understood this not from watching mainstream television news herself, but rather that her aging parent and grandparent spent much of their time doing so. At home as here on the walking trail, Button kept buds, a nice set of non-tangle Etymotic Research 4PTs, a used pair she bought on eBay for a hundred bucks, plugged into ear-holes with the tunes spinning. Blaring. Shutting out the babble—from the TV, as well as her people.

Bless their hearts.

How many folks in Edgewater County—and downstream—died from cancer-related illnesses every year? And this, only one of several similar facilities in the region. Like the bomb plant down along the Savannah River, the SRNS had been positioned over the enormous Southeastern Coastal Plain aquifer. Glad everyone's so sure no Cesium or Strontium has leached down into that vital source of fresh water, serving tens of millions.

Button fretted and stewed. Told herself *Don't-Worry*.

Walfredo brushed by her, warming her shoulders. Her archangel, her future self, telling her she would get where she needed to be. She sighed with relief.

BUT WAIT.

If Walfredo were merely another iteration of herself, and communicating from a point in the future of this continuum, could the Button of right now send a message back? To herself, at times of great strife and uncertainty?

A message saying it would be all right?

That everything was *already* all right?

Maybe.

She dredged up memories, a few grim occasions when during a crisis she'd felt such comfort. More than a few—a laundry list. Decades ago. When Heather had quit the Phish scene, ditched her, alone. Other low moments having to do with bad sex, or sketchy drugs. Sketchy peeps; or the po-po.

Sitting in the back seat of an Indiana cop car, arrested on tour for weed and shrooms. As a recalcitrant, withdrawn teenager, she sneaked off to a Grateful Dead concert against her father's wishes, afterwards finding herself committed to the psych ward over her impertinence.

Her first involuntary institutionalization. Later, her road family, like Heather before, had abandoned her during the Phish Fall Tour 2000 nitrous oxide episode, and she woke under sizzling fluorescent lights with faces staring down at her. The hospital; afterwards, with her friend, the actress Maddy Durango, who supervised Button's detox, an unusual course of treatment. Lucky she had good friends willing to do her a solid.

Glowing within, projecting herself BACK into some of those awful times when she most needed a friend; when she needed rescue. Putting herself again in those desperate, troubled shoes, as least as much as she remembered how it felt to be those earlier versions of herself. Making like Walfredo and saying, it will be all right. You will get through this. Whatever it happens to be, you will survive.

⊛❋⊛

FEELING SPENT by all the additional glowing from her elevated heart rate, Button slowed down and spun away from the recent Phish show she'd been digging—*Randall's Island NY 7-13-2014 Set 2*—and put on a playlist of 80s and 90s tunes she admired, almost all by women. Particular favs were the Cocteau Twins, Elizabeth Fraser's siren-like wails expressing deep-dive emotions Button could only dream of unleashing. Memories of adolescence. Pre-rebellion. Innocence. Crushes. Heartbreaks. Early onset computer geekery. Curiosity not about the opposite sex, but the same. Movies. Screenplays. A golden age after Thim had gone off to college, and for the first time Button had had space. Still the same weirdo, though. Socially graceless miscreant skulks about to a Walkman soundtrack, in those days cassette mixes, dominated also by Kate Bush, Alanis Morissette, and The Cranberries. Dolores O'Riordan's lilt was another voice giving definition to Button's teen angst in a manner that stuck to her ribs even to this day.

Traversing Memory Lane came with squishy ground, unsure footing. That period had ended with her locked up for being crazy. Hah. Nostalgia offered many perils.

She picked up the pace, the knobby bundle of dreads swish-swishing. The riverfront path, maybe three km altogether, made for a decent huff of a power-walk. Twice around, anyway, to get enough distance.

But only so long as the wind blew toward the chicken processing plant across the river in Easton—hard to enjoy the workout with the stench of factory farming in one's nose and mouth. Bad energy, of a more immediate and measurably tangible sort than radiation's slow, invisible, insidious march into the environment.

As a particular track began, Button fumbled with the iPod, spastic, saying no no, not Natalie Merchant, and certainly not 'The Letter,' that two minute mournful ditty about a brief love affair, and a letter never sent; too late, though, and at hearing the first bars, a wave of grief over Heather Ponderview rushed hard into her gut.

Loss.

Yearning.

No magic. The letter Button would write? A bitter epistle.

Skipping the song. There—Alanis Morrisette. Better. Harmless fluff.

How had twenty years got behind her? A stab of panic at the notion of aging. Castigating herself for allowing the vibration.

Time, meaningless.

Twenty years later, and I'm still upside down.

Was she losing her shit, now? About this whole cancer kick?

Nuclear reactor kick, rather?

Sure sure, kid. We know you miss your dad. We know he suffered. That's what they all thought. An overreaction to the death of her Pa. Sure.

Hell no.

They didn't know squat about suffering. About loss—of dignity, of life itself. She'd tell them, though. If they wanted.

No—nobody needed the pictures she had in her head. Images that kept her up at night even years after he'd passed away, at last free of his suffering. He'd been blind at the end, his eyes swollen shut. And mute for so long before, thanks to the feeding tube. Unable to take the communion of life that is food.

Never take anything that seems ordinary for granted, he'd scribbled to her in the little spiral notebook he used in his last, silent months, after the surgeries to remove the throat tumor and the course of purportedly curative radiation, and the feeding tube and breathing apparatus that'd replaced the swollen tissues of his mouth and throat. *Going outside for a walk. Eating a sandwich. You dont know how good it is till you cant do it any more.* He'd written this while hanging his head, the machines humming and wheezing and green mucus running down a tube, and holding one of his swollen eyes open with one free hand so he could see well enough to write.

Was her ire about the new reactors really about her father's suffering?

Shit yeah. If need be.

If somebody needed to make it personal, sure. This cancer epidemic going down before everyone's eyes. Everybody too damn matter of fact about it all. Including the docs.

How many victims had Button herself known?

As she rounded the far end of the beige concrete walkway snaking through the gum and cypress trees, the faces drifted through her mind like the chicken feathers often seen floating across the river and through the woods along the path. Could smell the death there, from that meat processor. She'd been veggie since the Phish tour days. Vegan, now. For ages. For health reasons, sure. Had to maintain the vessel, yo. For spiritual purposes as well.

But the nuke plant—that she didn't need to smell, or see. Invisible death. A feeling about it. A sense of assurance that went beyond feeling.

As in. She'd get some terrible tumor, too.

Wouldn't she—sure. She'd resigned herself. After all her youthful drinking and drugging—and that godforsaken plant, and her genes, and the general toxic environment in which almost everybody lived—it was coming no matter what precautions she took.

But she reminded herself, wiping sweat that rolled down from through a soaked tie-dyed cotton bandana holding back kinky, ginger-red dreads, how we create reality with our thoughts, and she pulled her mind back to One, back to nothing, and then back to the key thought she held onto and cultivated daily: health. Health. Health.

Health.

Not cancer.

She'd done an inventory on so many levels. Knew growing up here, coupled with her substance abuse, made the odds of a long and disease-free life unlikely. She could fight it—we all could, she thought—but making the alternative reality, that of HEALTH, foremost in her mind seemed the way to go. The eating and exercise, sure, but the mindfulness created the external reality.

Button walked faster. Visualized a white glow not from the nuclear reactor, but from another realm, and manifesting inside her short, wide body—the glow of HEALTH.

She walked.

Chanted.

Felt present; felt gratitude. Truly, a marvelous time to've chosen to incarnate, during this temporal epoch of signs and wonders, however illusory and ephemeral the whole game.

❃❀❃

But the faces returned.

Two girls from her own class back in high school who didn't live to see graduation, and two more who only made it into their early twenties—an outbreak of leukemia, as though it'd been catching. Her own father. Who'd run the damn plant. Been smart, and proud.

The powerman—her dad held the keys to the kingdom, like an alchemist.

family. Always asking about her grandfather; had been kind during Daddy's illness and the funeral. Hill Hampton would allow her activism. Surely.

But if need be, she'd press Becky LaFreniere to back her up. Becky—so much more sophisticated than most on town council and in the ELMS, the two centers of power in Edgewater County—would take Button's side. Hell, the damned square in front of the courthouse was named for Becky's family. She'd throw weight around, help Button get her free speech tent idea done.

Becky L, wise and progressive-leaning. She'd gone and lived in New York for a time trying to make it on the boards, but failing at mastery of the cruel and difficult trade of the thespian. Not if she were back here in the EC running the Fine Arts Center, with its local theater productions and other events. She didn't even perform in the shows. Failed at all those silly adolescent dreams of making it, at least by traditional standards.

Like Button.

Movies. Novels. She planned to take on the world. She'd show them. Et cetera.

Foolishness, as her father and grandfather had always deemed her aspirations. She supposed her forebears had either been right, or else she simply believed them. Couldn't help it. She burned, even today, with the sense she had a story to tell.

Face to face. One on one. On the town green.

HER MOST COMPELLING ACCOMPLISHMENT, achieved while still a student? A short documentary about Otilya Duckett, a civil rights pioneer who'd paved the way for other young women of color by staging an eight-hour job interview sit-in at the offices of the huge mill by the river; and, a narrative screenplay called *Mohammed's Radio* that had received an A, as well a research paper in Film Studies entitled "What a Sucker You Must Think I Am: The Femme Fatale Archetype in the Work of Jacques Tourneur." These had been the highlights of her media arts collegiate career, along with one A+ American Lit term paper analyzing Toni Morrison's novel *Paradise*. Button called this one "They Shoot the White Girl First: Race, Class, Gender and the Reproduction of Trauma." The title, and much of the paper's content, had come courtesy of Heather's input.

Whenever she felt enervation welling up as though from a bracing, deep spring, Button reminded herself she'd gotten out of South Carolina and lived a marvelous, magical and eccentric life touring the country several times over following jamband heroes Phish, with their never-repeated setlists and prog-rock quirk and heavy psychedelic drug scene rocking and rolling in the parking lots. Didn't that count for some worldliness chips?

As for her current charge in life, she believed in the tenet of knowledge equaling power. Yeah. Her info booth plan, a benevolent act. Personal engagement. Use social media, they'd tell her. Make youtube videos. But no. Taking it to the streets. Bringing it to the green. To the faces and bodies here in meatspace. Agitate for a county-wide strike to halt the construction. Strike. Strike. Strike. Strike at the money-engine. The only way to wake them up.

Make a difference.

In the life.

Of her hometown.

As a kid she'd had one thought—to get far away from Edgewater County. But now Button Sykes said to herself, Maybe the universe wants this. Wants me here. And it's not to write or take care of my mother and grandfather; rather, to get these nukes shut down. The environment had been her issue ever since high school; inevitable she'd pursue such ends in her adult life.

The time seemed right: A flock of geese, honking, flying in a V above the river. The trees, leaning toward her, eager to hear what she had to say. Her intuition beamed YES into her soul, in golden neon letters glowing behind her eyelids. YES.

◉❂◉

AS SHE MADE the turn on the verdant and shaded concrete back uphill to the gravel parking area, Button switched from the Genius playlist fraught with emotional triggers back to recent live Phish. Enough of the merciless wallowing and yearning for the time when childhood innocence still seemed possible. Distasteful.

Faulkner had been wrong—the past was the past.

Never thought she'd feel wistful about the EC, and those childhood days. But she did. Pre-heartbreak era, in retrospect, anyway, seemed awfully sunny, a well-tended, benign, sheltered world on the oak tree-lined grid of old Southern homes east of Common Street, ground zero of the Edgewater County bourgeoisie. With streets named for either flowering trees or perennial South Carolina heroes like town father after-the-fact Pitchfork Ben Tillman, the Reconstruction-era former governor and senator and whiskey-peddler—you also had Calhoun, Hampton, Marion, and Simms—the thoroughfares sat lined by a remarkable number of antebellum homes that escaped becoming kindling and cinders at the hands of Sherman's troops.

No Sykes Street, however. Not now, not ever.

Her grandfather might once have made a candidate for the honor, back when he'd been one of the driving forces in the county's business community. Had lost it all. Miracle they still owned the house, as he often noted, with its wraparound verandas and high ceilings and creaking hardwoods, nooks and crannies and fresh ghosts, more Southern gothic with each passing season.

The nest egg money, Thim kept Button informed, dwindled with each season, a stash her father left for Thim to disburse. Despite at one time enjoying a modicum of money-energy at his own disposal, her grandfather long ago lost what he might have carried into his golden years, this due to circumstances she didn't quite understand, and that seemed beyond his capacity to describe. "Just be glad you got a roof over our heads, still," all he would ever say about his decline.

The glory days of Burnham Sykes as a mover and shaker in Edgewater County lay decades in the past. That he still lived at all seemed a minor miracle. Or maybe a curse.

At least the family had sired a powerful personality and player in gorgeous, poised, intelligent Thim. Like her boss, Governor Sandy Three-Rivers, Button's sister appeared only a step away or two from power-brokering in Washington rather than Columbia.

Button often asked Thim for extra money, always so awkward and stupid and unnecessary. Why didn't Thim herself check to see if all was well with Button and their mother and grandfather? Why did she make Button have to prostrate herself and petition for help that, in her imagination, one gave to one's family without being asked?

Had she not done so herself?

Had she not given?

Heal me. Button, at her lowest, had asked the universe this favor. "Heal me and, in gratitude, I will serve." And Sisyphean though it may seem, she served.

Her bargain worked: since the day of the pledge, she hadn't touched a pharmie or a drink or any powders.

As for the service? She lived it, everyday and every day. Her mother. Her grandfather. Dutiful. Without either of them, as she rationalized, no Button. No existence. No resistance to serving. No opportunity to question—no time. An ongoing process.

Longer than anyone could imagine.

Yeah—her spirit had been at this game a long time, or so she'd understood; this time, either despite or because of all the trials and grief and heartache, her soul seemed close to maturity, and the agreements she had with her fellow travelers, forged eons ago and in other realms to enact their physicalized dramas together seemed to progress in a healthy and meaningful fashion. Her near-ascendancy demonstrated this reality. Check it, yo.

Conclusion: she first incarnated who knew how long ago in the anthropocene, possibly an Atlantean or Lemurian soul, here choosing to re-incarnate itself to help raise the overall vibration towards higher consciousness.

With this in mind, it became clear she had a huge contribution to make. Not making a movie or writing a book or any of that adolescent nonsense on which she'd spent far too much time concentrating on outcome and achievement (though far too little, admittedly, to accomplish any goals); nor, perhaps, caring for her forebears. No. She had more to offer. Change would soon break over her like a wave regarding her family obligations, though, and afterwards? Her larger service would become clear, even if at this moment in Right Now it still loomed murky and ill-defined.

The power plant protest deal?

Sure. On an intuitive level, it felt right.

Her spirit guides whispered, yes, go on, forge ahead, and so on and thus and such and yes yes yes; she bloomed inside with the warm glow of assurance oh-so much like being in love—like being suffused with light and love, the way she twinkled when she thought of Heather, and the time they spent as friends and onetime lovers.

Button pulled out her earbuds and recited from memory a snatch of sonnet courtesy none other than Giordano Bruno, hermetic heretic and martyr. She projected through the trees and across the river like a trained Shakespearean actor, words used as part of an incantation to manifest Heather in body:

"Render thyself, O Goddess, unto pity! Open, O lady, the portals of thine eyes, and look on me in thou wouldst give me death!"

◉❀◉

NEARING a final incline and the park entrance, Button grooved to a spirited Cocteau Twins track, "Carolyn's Fingers," and considered the tormented yearning her everlasting, if unrequited, bond with Heather instilled. Oh sure, on some days? Not so acute anymore. Not so bad.

Other days? Agony. Heather Ponderview had seemed to be Button's Person, her soulmate and companion and guide and partner.

Truth, but obscured and occulted.

For whatever reason.

Nah. Getting over her. At last.

But then...

Popping back up in Button's time-stream, as happened back in the late spring with an email saying how, after many years away, Heather had moved back to North Carolina to live on the family estate, a baroque and moneyed place Button visited while in college, in the mountains near the border with Tennessee. Despite being sole heir, the whole of the Ponderview Trucking fortune, diverse and considerable, left to her alone, Heather intimated her life had been in the crapper; how it'd been time to start over; and the way forward involved the notion of home. Dial it all back to zero. Pass go again. Etc, etc, as she had written.

Like me landing back here, Button replied. A homegirl. How weird is that?

—Come see me. Not now. One day soon.
   —Sure, thatd be sweet. Soon.
   —Our story continues! 😃

Welling with emotion, Button stopped herself from replying:

Yes—it is my fondest wish to be with you again, to hold you, to breathe you into my body, to merge with you and fulfill what seems my destiny, all-encompassing and inexorable.

Instead, she responded with only a simple emoticon, a bright big-smiley face upon which she concentrated, infusing the image with warmth and love, fifteen years' worth, projecting it onto the pixels and bits that formed the symbol. She held onto the idea of love between her and Heather growing wings and taking flight, a phoenix of remarkable resilience and power. Gave the idea tactile plasticity, an image held in her mind with an enormous amount of discipline and stillness. Button powered up her green-glowing heart chakra, and hit send.

Months passing, though, and she had yet to receive an invitation.

She embraced patience. A new tangent began from the instant of their reconnection, a reality filament leading who knew where. It would all work out.

Button, getting a last burst of pep, dashed on stubby but toned legs up to the parking area. The land beyond turned more hilly and belonged, still, to the same farmers, mostly, who'd owned the riverside country for as long as anyone could remember.

Her beloved silver Subaru Baja sat forlorn and lonesome, tires and underbody splatter-stained with Edgewater County river clay the color of the terra cotta Italian shingles on Mayor Hampton's mansion down the block from the Sykes house. The vehicle, bought new by her father a dozen years ago when she first moved back home and got the library job in Columbia, had been christened 'Piper,' a Phish reference.

Some jerk had traced WASH ME, YO in the grime on the passenger window.

Her senses on edge, fully present, she whipped her dreads around.

Deserted as usual. Pine trees, cicadas buzzing. Late summer heat and stillness.

Must've happened last night at work. Probably Trudy.

Button, spinning out of the trailhead parking lot in Piper and bidding her river path and all the trees and flowers and animals and rocks fare-thee-well, but only for now.

◈◈◈

SHE MANEUVERED THE SUBARU, running rough and in need of a tune-up and the wash, around the bend on the highway. Here loomed the stolid and crumbling red-brick edifice of the abandoned Gray-Peele textile mill, an aging industrial structure that, in more progressive urban towns, would have been rehabbed and gentrified into condos or lofts, or facilities like the State Museum down in Columbia, appropriate enough considering that particular factory's designation as one of the first electric mills in the world.

Here, though, the old heart of Edgewater capitalistic endeavor stood behind a sagging, high cyclone fence going to rust, the structure taking up its space on what ought to be land in the process of reclamation by the woods and the river itself. The Great Flood of 1910 had shut down the first-generation mill after inundating the surrounding village, but afterwards it'd come back strong for most of the rest of the twentieth century. But now it stood here abandoned, a pockmarked, graffiti-tagged shell surrounded by the poorest neighborhood in an overall impoverished county.

If only a master came along to make use of the space inside the vessel.

The mill village of houses through which she now drove, most occupied if sitting dilapidated and weedy and downmarket, had been built farther upland than the original community. With the distinctive hilly yards containing smooth, ancient stones jutting up from the lawns, the area existed in modern times as a crummy neighborhood that, in a larger town like over in Columbia, would by now have become gentrified into pastel hued, yuppie-renovated bungalow mini-fiefdoms. Here, though, it remained only a poor and crumbling non-community, the antithesis of Button's street on Whaley Way.

Then again, crummy it had been even when the mill operated and the village bustled. Capitalism's dirty little not-so secret—the servitude of the underclass necessary to grease its wicked mechanisms. Some said slavery hadn't truly ended, had only been repackaged. Mill villages. The company store. Scrip instead of cash. Child labor. Dangerous conditions. But once improvements come, they pull the plug and take the jobs overseas. Profit over people. Go, capitalism. During the textile strikes in 1934, human beings were shot and killed outside the mill, the river clay soaking with the blood of patriots. Who knew what spirits hung around by the river.

Turning onto the main road and shifting into third, she drew in her breath at a seeming manifestation—she tooted the horn at legacy town nut-ball Howdy Shull, walking his crazy floppy-armed walk beside the culvert, a route that turned into Common Street and led right into downtown.

Howdy—the real dweller of the threshold around here. One foot planted in this reality, the other in one of his own apparent fabrication.

As she pulled alongside, Howdy seemed to acknowledge her, but kept his face turned away. Muttering to himself, a green plastic two-liter Canada Dry bottle clutched under his arm like a football, babbling about this'n that—meet Howdy Shull, a tragic legacy figure of the community.

Liquor inside the bottle, she felt certain. Spirits indeed. Howdy and his sister, a retired college professor, lived a few blocks away in another of the old mansion-style places, one rotting in Gothic, weedy splendor befitting its eccentric inhabitants.

Howdy never looked at Button, or anyone else. Often, if he passed her downtown, while she sat out front of The Dixiana hitting her vape or while chilling on the green, he'd fall silent. Nothing more eerie, Button noted, than a silent Howdy Shull, who under typical circumstances kept an obscure monologue going nonstop.

"Howdy, Howdy," she shouted out the passenger window. With no traffic behind, she slowed and kept pace beside him. "Yo."

"Howdy! Howdy!" He answered like a caged parrot. "Yo. Yo."

"What's new, buddy?"

Howdy worked his arm, marching along with a stern expression. Ginger ale sloshed in his soda bottle. His eyes, red-rimmed, danced and sparkled and spun. "The Egyptians held that everything which is a result dwells in the cause of itself and turns to the cause as the lotus to the sun."

Intrigued. "Good stuff, Howdy. I agree completely."

He made eye contact, brief. She beamed a happy vibration.

Slipping back into his running monologue, his deep Old South brogue sounded almost English in inflection: "From where or from whom did Imhotep acquire his vast knowledge of astronomy and the art of stone masonry? And perhaps more intriguing still, what was the real purpose of his Step Pyramid Complex at Saqqara? Is there embedded in it an encoded message? And if so, what is its substance? And from whom?"

"You got me."

"We are being called to explore the totality itself as an interface between insight and beauty."

She kept an eye on the rearview. "Are we, now."

Howdy turned all the way toward her, a creepy, drooping half-lidded leer, head bobbing along with his loping gait, his nose swollen and red and full of blackheads. "I need something. From you."

She gestured for him to step away, pulled over and turned on her hazards. "What is it you need?"

He leaned on the door into the cab. "I need you to take me."

A chill down her spine. "Take you where?"

"To the house of the second birth."

"To your house? You want a ride back to town?"

Agitated, exasperated, he flung his free arm around in an arc. Drool ran from the corner of his mouth. "No no no no."

"Where's the house of the second birth?"

Subject change. "Gas—you have any?"

"Why do you? Need gas?"

He made direct eye contact for perhaps the first time in many such encounters through the years: "This story—it never ends."

"So I've been. Led to believe. Care to elucidate?"

Button, shocked: He did.

"Throughout history, humans have been interacting with the quantum cycle via bio-electricity. Our conversations with other dreamers have led to a summoning of hyper-Vedic consciousness. It is time to take purpose to the next level. Eons from now, as the world guides us we warriors will self-actualize like never before."

"You're sure about this."

"Soon will occur an unveiling of potential the likes of which the quantum matrix has never seen."

"Howdy: did you incarnate now? Like I did? Because of this momentous—um—next level—um—happening? And why now? And why us?"

"The photon belt—we entered it in 1972."

"We did?"

"The sacred seventh sun of the seven sisters encircling sacred Alcyone, our sun's sacred sun-sister. Sister. Sisters. Sacred. Sister. Ten-thousand years of dark, two thousand of light, add it up times two times two and you have the Great Year, here we are."

"We are?"

"Sisters. The seventh. That's us."

BOOM. She'd read about the Pleiadians, from a star cluster forming the 'eye' of the bull in Taurus. Their supposed message. Their star-seeding of intelligence and evolution here on Earth. Only days ago, she'd been flipping through a book at home in her growing and voluminous collection of esoteric literature.

As such, Howdy mentioning this made for a synchronicity. They happened all the time, with greater and greater frequency. She'd read sync described as consciousness noticing itself absent the normal duality. Something mysterious, yet seeming to underlie the totality of reality, expressing itself, poking its head up from the surface of the sea of awareness. Like seeing the wind blowing the leaves of a tree—you perceive the movement, which results from motion and energy, but coming courtesy of a medium you can't see, like what they call the aether.

Button, familiar with the Pleiadians. Now this seventh sun stuff, photon belts and Alcyone, she'd have to look into it. But still, here she had the town crazy, verbalizing much that she believed and thought about—quantum realities within reality, hidden truths from ancient times, that type-deal. Maybe he'd tapped into her own unconscious or subconscious—maybe Howdy's circuits, fueled by Canada Dry, were wide open to everyone's vibration and thoughts. Who knew?

Button, her mind, like, blown. "I need links, bro. Tell me more."

At this inquiry he shook her off, laughing no, no, no with mocking disdain. Working his arm and picking up his pace, he drifted back into a more pedantic and specific mode of discourse about Imhotep and Egyptian architecture and sacred geometry, a hot trend these days, at least if you read certain New Age-y websites and blogs, which Button did, often getting sucked into clickbait like *Did a 1974 Jerry Garcia Guitar Solo Usher in the Aquarian Age?* and *7 Signs your 7 Chakras are Blocked* and *Ten Facts They Don't Want You to Know About Human History* and *Russia's Nuclear Nightmare Flows Down Radioactive River.*

Of course! Howdy, only spouting internet nonsense. Nothing cosmic about his discourse, just good memorization skills. Her intuition told her this.

Still. That shit had felt fo-real, yo.

Only when the movement in the rearview of an approaching vehicle caught her eye, a big rig coming from the Wal-mart distribution center over in Easton, the biggest employer in the county, did she put the Subaru back into gear and continue on, passing him and watching as Howdy loped on toward town. She'd have given him a ride, especially since they lived so close together. But no way did she want Howdy Shull in the car, even with the intriguing little speech he made.

Random. Weird. Or maybe perfect. Just exactly perfect.

TOWN MYTHOLOGY HELD that Caughman Howard Shull, now in his early 60s and once a respected student and budding attorney with political ambitions to follow in the steps of his father—Judge Shull, a robed and wise Edgewater County powerbroker of his day, which meant he turned cards and crooked his elbow upstairs in the onetime private party rooms of The Dixiana—got dosed while away at college with a powerful, unknown drug. Howdy, never returning from what must have been an epic trip.

Jasper said the oldtimers called what happened to Howdy "getting slipped a Black-Eyed Katy—in his case, a permanent one."

"Excuse me?" Button explained how 'Black-Eyed Katy' was also the name of a Phish jam. "Are you sure? That's what they called it?"

"Pretty durn sure."

"Not 'slipping a mickey?'"

"There's that, too. A Black-Eyed Katy would be worse."

"How?"

"Look at Howdy."

Another fascinating synchronicity. For the last few years, her life had been fraught with sync.

"Someone else told me," Button probed on her first night running sound for Jasper's open mic when they'd been playing getting to know you, "Howdy was part of government experiments. Like, MK-Ultra or whatever."

Jasper, shaking his bald head. His voice came faraway as he perched on a stool behind the soundboard beside her, staying focused on tuning his beloved Martin while Button got acquainted with the lighting board, trying out different combinations of colors on the low, empty stage against the back wall of The Dixiana. "That's all bullcrud. We was in law school together. Howdy, a 3L when I started, he was a real star—bound for glory, a sharp litigator and a smooth operator. He didn't know who I was, and if he did, he would've looked down his nose at this farm boy from over near the river.

"Then one day," Jasper finally looked at her, "Howdy was just gone. They said he suffered a 'nervous breakdown.' Whatever happened, he's walked the streets ever since. After his mama died, his sister moved back home to Whaley Way to take care of him."

"That's like—totally sad."

"It's a damned shame. Folks'll make fun of him, and I tell them to go stuff it. He's a human being like all of us."

Ever since his drug incident Howdy had loped the streets of Tillman Falls, not unlike a corporeal version of Agatha of Aberdeen, an infamous local ghost said to haunt the Forest Knoll Garden cemetery behind The Dixiana. Button often watched for Agatha while standing out back of the honkytonk getting tweaked most nights she worked, except last night when she choose verbal eloquence over relaxation. She'd wanted to remain sharp for the folderol, as it happened, that became of her fake tight twenty.

HER HEADSPACE NOW?

Honestly?

Honestly?

Righteous.

For a desiccated mummy of a lonely hag of a failed writer-slash-filmmaker, stuck in Edgewater County like a curse? Sure. At least as a music lover, she could say she worked the board at a legendary room. Not that many notable acts playing now. For the last few years, Jasper Glasscock's open mic had been the big draw. Tribute bands covering country tunes classic and otherwise.

Driving through town, she noted without interest a small crowd gathered outside the marbled columns of the ELMS headquarters. Up the hill toward Whaley Way, Button vibrated with warmth and happiness and confidence, as though a major notion had come upon her, and scarcely hearing the wailing of a siren approaching from behind.

Time to check in with Heather Ponderview.

It'd been a couple months, now, since the previous texts; since her lost love had moved back to NC. So close, yet so far. Button, letting her mental discipline slide, playing sad pop songs while hot needy tears sneaked out, weeping born of desire rather than the detachment she practiced on her path to becoming a Taoist meditation master. Or whatever she was. Now that she'd forsaken the magicking.

In weak moments, Button questioned what she'd learned, or accomplished, only to encounter reminders from the big U of how far she'd come in the consciousness game. No talks with God necessary to know this, only cultivating her three treasures—energy, vitality, spirit—to form the Golden Elixir, ineffable but permeating in its Universal influence.

❂❄❂

AT LEAST WHEN feeling unaccomplished or feckless, now with a concrete goal in pursuit. No Sancho Panza at her side, but a windmill in her sights—she envisioned a row of wind turbines gracing the top of the ridge along the northern half of the county, where the river ran swift through a narrow channel and the bluffs sat way up high. Eighty to a hundred feet below, whitewater tumbled across vitreous crags of granite, a stony traverse whereupon the infamous Class of '77 Tragedy occurred.

Wind power. Along the ridge.

And solar—shimmering arrays on every rooftop.

Anything but nukes.

Button, a stakeholder by rights; an actor, however, by choice. Seeing in her mind a particular outcome. Holding the image until it acquired mass and plasticity, until 'real.' One of the secrets. Hard to hold an image big as wanting to make a pair of nuclear reactors disappear. A tough task. Big dreams. Easier to picture Heather Ponderview's face, the curls of her hair dangling, leaning in to kiss Button 'hello' when next they met.

Soon. It had to be soon.

Why the rush? Patience. Patience and tenacity would make it all come true.

GOOCH

The ambulance carrying Rabbit Pettus had pulled away, and it didn't look good. Gooch Wimmel, collecting himself, heard his own voice breaking with urgency into his digital recorder:

"He fell down. He said, 'kiss my foot' to the ELMS proposal... and just toppled over like a mighty tree, felled in the forest. God help Reynolds Pettus." He wouldn't be printing that last part.

Composing the lead-story for Friday's edition of the *Edgewater Advocate* left little time for sentiment. If he'd had half a mind about him anymore, he'd have already prepared an obit for town figures like Rabbit, like they did at the big city papers and TV cable news outlets, where Gooch pictured filing cabinets bulging with the dossiers of aging and at-risk celebrities, from Kirk Douglas to Lindsay Lohan to the one Durango twin, the wild one who might check out anytime while on some gossip-rag vice binge. That's how important a man like Rabbit Pettus was to Tillman Falls, and his grand old honkytonk.

But the standard obit would be left up to the family. What family Rabbit had at hand. The reporting and remembering and honoring would be Gooch's journalistic task.

He hustled across the grassy green as fast as his spindly sticks would carry him. He could shine at this big story, sure. And perhaps afterwards they'd get rid of him, and Porter Bucknam would let Dobbs run the whole show, and there'd be a more efficient house of the fourth estate operating in Tillman Falls. One more big byline first, boys. If you please.

He stopped to rest on the bench across from the paper, a shady spot, and hit RECORD. "Biggest town death of the new century," holding the slender metal device about a foot from his downturned mouth. "There aren't many here in Edgewater County who don't have a tall tale or two about the legendary Rabbit Pettus. And so, here's a few of them."

He clicked off the trusty Olympus DVR. The most interesting stories about men like Reynolds and Burnham the reporter knew well, but those you couldn't print.

For the rest of the day he planned to wear out the shoe leather, do interviews, nail down the legend and see it to print. Stake out a spot over at their house, catch well-wishers coming and going. Rabbit Pettus deserved a sidebar along with his obit. A special section, even—photos, that Dobbs would have to handle. Stories, colorful and meaningful, from folks who loved and knew the man well? Gooch would gather them.

He imagined the headline:

The Dixiana's Reynolds Elder 'Rabbit' Pettus, Dead at Eighty-Something

Sinking in—not even a birthdate at hand.

Shoe leather? That didn't half cover it. Gooch didn't even have the basic facts down. Maybe it's because even a sober journalist like him didn't expect men like Reynolds Pettus, giants of the earth as described in the myths and legends of old, to die.

What kind of talk was that? He should lie down on the bench and die himself.

Nonsense. He'd talk to Burnie's granddaughters, both sure to know specifics; Jasper Glasscock would have plenty to say; as would many. In a fit of grandiosity, Gooch got the notion he'd turn his recorded interviews into segments suitable for airing on WABA, or up-sold, he thought the term was, to NPR. Or, what did they call it now? Podcasting. Bill Wimmel, podcasting from high above downtown Tillman Falls; his eye, all-seeing, contemplating and reporting on the turmoil of his fellow beings far below.

How Bill loved the soothing voices of the newsreaders on NPR. He wished he could be one. He daydreamed often about doing more glamorous work than being the owner—check that, former owner, now just editor-in-chief—of a dying small-town paper. The press runs were pitiful, the revenue worse. He could hardly look at Porter Bucknam, the new owner and publisher still keeping his distance from the day-to-day, as had been their agreement, in the eye. The man still possessed his higher faculties.

Envy.

Then there was Dobbs, looking on with that sardonic, wheelchair-bound gaze of his. Judgmental little queer.

A snide, hectoring voice—his mother's: *Takes one to know one.*

Shut up, Gooch warned her. Or himself, rather.

Moments before he'd been engaged in consoling Burnham Sykes, beside himself over the collapse of Rabbit, and since hustled into the back of Timmy Truesdale's patrol car so Dr. Boykin could check over the distraught man. Sykes, Wimmel noted, had been less demonstrative than deflated, shaking like the paint-mixer at the Ace Hardware store and reeking of beer, a sharp, sour smell like after you wake up from a screaming blue bender.

He smelled like the bar itself, Bill Wimmel thought.

Hell—that had been true of Burnham and Rabbit, both.

An angle, a hook. He died smelling like the cheap beer he sold, and the cigarettes he sucked on to the last bitter moment, firing one up inside the ELMS conference room and bellowing at them all that the mural was his to restore or destroy as he saw fit. Of course it'd been the impertinent smoking that precipitated a mini-riot of shouting before the mural proposal provoked his ultimate collapse.

Another possible angle: blame the atmosphere of rancor during the meeting. No spinning the truth, though: it'd been Rabbit himself who'd swept into the ELMS conference room with bluster and attitude. Not to mention the mysterious, frosty cloud of tension simmering between Bernice Theodore and Rebecca LaFreniere, who, despite solidarity on the mural issue, snapped at one another like bitter rivals over procedural issues.

All this mortality and newsmaking made Gooch consider his own pending retirement. He assumed, though, that with his exit from the stage of productive adult life, the paper would fold, and he couldn't abide the thought. Papers were folding like poker players without the courage to call a bluff.

The *Advocate* would continue as long as he—no; Porter Bucknam, with all his journalism experience as a former editor of the *Columbia Record*—sustained the endeavor, which never made much money, anyway. Enough to keep going. A commitment of the heart, and the soul; a civic duty, being the town journalist.

About Rabbit, who'd gone pale and inert and likely dead though they said he still had a pulse and so there was hope, how many would weep? Not all, Gooch predicted. Neither the Pastor Mires nor the Reverend Nixons of the community, who always deplored having a tavern like The Dixiana in such a cornerstone position in the town.

The issue of the day, however—the mural—now tabled. Out of respect.

The grand but fading Fightin' General Reb cartoon on the side of the building had long loomed as an established point of contention. Controversy over the mural's depiction of the antiquated Confederate flag waving rooster mascot of Southeastern University—sleek and modernized to exclude the stars, the bars, and the gray military togs formerly worn by the bird—felt moldy and all-but forgotten in the shadow of the ongoing, occasional hoo-haw over removing the Confederate naval jack flying on top of the State House, a battle simmering, and occasionally boiling over, for decades. Common Street in Tillman Falls only thirty miles away as the crow flies, but lying far from downtown Columbia in other ways. Not to mention The Dixiana being a private business, and free to display artwork of its choosing.

The divisive, wretched shank of linen had finally been removed from the state capitol building about ten years ago, but in a bargain many felt made for an enormous eff-you, as Bill thought of the profane sentiment: placing a fresh Confederate Army Battle Flag behind the DAR Civil War monument at the front of the capitol, in a spot yet more prominent than atop the more ceremonial and symbolic place above the burnished copper dome. At least this time they hoisted an historically accurate banner.

Throughout the same period, some wanted the General Reb mural designated as a landmark and preserved; others demanded its removal, including Gooch himself, in an editorial he wrote a few years ago that had gotten his car vandalized. He said if Southeastern University removed the stars and bars motif from its mascots and logos, time for Tillman Falls to do the same.

Ad revenue to the *Advocate* dropped by fifty percent.

He'd been strong-armed into the editorial by Rebecca LaFreniere and Roosevelt Nixon. That'd been the season before being approached by Bucknam. The asking price of the paper, adjusted down to meet his realistic offer.

Gooch wondered if anyone noticed how he kept forgetting he'd sold the publishing company. He always remembered eventually. Didn't he?

⊛⊛⊙

SPEAKING OF CURRENT EVENTS, and he hadn't been, but boy, could he: Gooch was convinced—or persuaded; was persuaded a better word? He used to always know the better word—that Roosevelt Nixon and Rebecca LaFreniere were doing the Filthy McNasty, and oh what a scandal that would make, especially here in election season, and the race for the open council seat on the line. Becky already possessed political power in town; the square wasn't named LaFreniere for nothing.

But then, Gooch saw how their confederation—alleged—could have more to do with politics than some old queen's lurid, imaginary fantasies like out of a bodice-ripping, trashy romance novel. Besides, the racial element, even in a place like Edgewater County, no longer held much steam. The fading away of miscegenation laws had brought into the foreground of everyday cultural behavior nothing but what had already existed, if often forced by bigotry into the unfortunate shadows.

Still: Gooch, titillated by the thought of a huge dark cock inside LaFreniere, in her ass, her mouth. Enormous. Nixon, at least six-four, hands big as catcher's mitts and sporting a chocolate baseball bat, throbbing, glistening, twitching, exploding with jism thick and ropy and covering Gooch's entire body.

Shaking out of a trance, he found himself standing by the side of the road, all the way down near the high school ballfields.

But—how?

Clarity: Instead of going to get in his car and do interviews like he'd planned, he had wandered halfway out of town, and, how much time had passed?

An hour. More.

Drenched in sweat.

Confused.

Wait—Roosevelt Nixon, didn't he have a press conference that afternoon? One that Gooch needed to cover?

What on earth was he doing here?

With a half-mast hard-on?

On the roadside for all to see?

Too many questions. Too much was happening. Cars where passing. One or two tooted the horn. Gooch, a well-known figure.

Winded, he sat down on the bus stop bench by the entrance to the high school sports complex. Behind him stood a polished granite monument, large and square and inscribed with names upon names, set back from the road and commemorating the scores of victims of the Sunbury School Fire, an infamous, seventy-year-old tragedy that'd influenced building code improvements the world over. The school had been back in the woods, with the modern commemoration placed nearer the highway for ease of access.

Thinking of all those dead children made his insides quiver.

He allowed his unfocused gaze to drift away from the names on the plaque and over at the empty dugouts and dropped into a lengthy reverie about a boyhood period of playing baseball—not here, but down in Augusta, where he'd lived while his father worked for the paper there. Gooch had come back here as a young man of fifteen. His key people, though, all buried in Georgia.

He wasn't even from Edgewater County.

And yet, he felt so compelled to document the place he considered his home. Not as a journalist, rather through a great novel, one chronicling the history of the county.

The fire. Maybe the Sunbury School tragedy might present a jumping-off point. Or offer a central event around which all other narrative matters revolved.

Time, short. If he wanted to write his novel.

Novel.

Newspaper.

Stories, both.

Wait—hadn't he somewhere to be? He had to write up the story about the mural. The mural.

The mural—right?

What was it?

Oh.

Rabbit—the heart attack. The hospital. "You're supposed to be going to the dad-blamed hospital. Damn you."

WINDED AND PANICKING—ANOTHER half-hour had gone by during the baseball reverie, or so it seemed—Gooch hurried his flabby old self back down Common Street to The Dixiana's open front entrance, where a few townsfolk and a couple of the black kitchen workers milled around, shaking their heads. Etna Dixmont wept and prayed, rocking, on the wooden bench that ran along below the dark-tinted front window. Stooped and gray and still wrapped by her barbecue-stained apron, Etna had worked at the honkytonk since before Gooch had settled here. A long time.

Family—she wept because Mr. Rabbit, as these folks all called him, loomed large in their lives.

The patriarch.

Gooch, getting all tingly: he had found his hook for the obit.

After wetting his thumb and flipping his notebook over to a fresh page, he scribbled with mad abandon until a rough lede took shape.

"Thank you, Jesus." And meaning it.

Other employees had by now been called, including a tear-stained Trudy Pirkle, who paced back-and-forth smoking and shaking like she needed a bracer. The cook, a lumbering black man with thick, horn-rimmed glasses everybody called Fridge, cried in silence, fat tears running down his face and dripping onto his stained size 4x Carolina Panthers jersey. Civilian clothes. Gooch didn't think he'd ever seen Fridge out of his cook's whites.

"What the hell we supposed to do, Gooch?" Trudy, in a gravelly smoker's voice made more hoarse by her sorrow. "Open up? Or—I don't know which way to turn."

"You need to call Miss Runelle." Fridge, impatient and annoyed. "She the one we need to talk to about what we expected to do, here. I told Trudy, Mr. Gooch, to go and call. But she won't."

"Oh, you did not." Trudy and Fridge, whose real name was Frankie Washington, bickered like brother and sister; they'd both been at The Dixiana for as long as Gooch could remember. "Besides—she's at the hospital." Trudy sucked in her breath, held back a sob. "Where I ought to be."

Gooch, comforting her. Fridge, shuffling his feet and wiping his eyes.

"Well I c'ain't go broast chicken with Mr. Rabbit laying up yonder in that hospital," Fridge fretted. "I'm frustrated, yo, that you want to just go on like ain't nothing bad happening."

A good question: Rabbit Pettus lay dying, and they would open The Dixiana for the early bird special? Like normal?

But then, Gooch felt like himself for the first time in hours. Thought himself capable and wise and seasoned, like the reporter and editor and publisher he'd been for forty goddamned years, going all the way back to Atlanta, where he'd covered the blessed crime beat—in Atlanta. Seasoned didn't half cover it.

He spoke up. "I'll tell y'all this much: I bet you a dime to a dollar that what Rabbit Pettus would want to see is this place open tonight. As will lots of folks once the word gets out. You might ought to call in Nathan too, honey," Nathan being the weekend night bartender. "I know I wouldn't mind raising one to our friend later. But for now, let me get to the hospital."

"Nathan quit last week. There ain't no one else to call to help." Trudy cried harder, but it passed. She nodded and said, okay.

"Besides—maybe Rabbit'll make it through. That man's got an iron constitution."

"Don't I know it, sugar. We got to pull ourselves together." She hugged it out with Fridge. "There's always Button. She can help."

Gooch cringed—not the hippie Sykes girl, his most persistent LTE submitter. "Good luck with all that."

From inside the bar, the house phone, ringing.

After Trudy told Fridge to answer the call: "Where was you walking back from just now? You're soaked through and through."

"Long story." Gooch mopped his brow. Asked if Roy Earl notified yet.

"I called his wife." Trudy, chin quivering. "I reckon she had the sense to tell him."

Gooch, noting the inflection, the disdain, which in a curious reporter's mind raised all manner of questions about the relationships here.

"Here's hoping he's on his way."

"That high-strung little Rucker thing he married, she must've shrieked my ear half off." Trudy scoffed and sparked a cigarette off her Zippo, snapping it shut like she was slapping Roy Earl's disloyal spouse clean across the face. An aside. "I couldn't half believe it when he got with that freckle-face little turd. Could you?"

Bill, shrugging and absorbing the subtext, which pointed to a story this reporter had never gotten wind of—what had gone on between Roy Earl and Trudy? And, when might it have occurred? Roy, gone for decades, it seemed.

❂❊❂

Gooch, popping over into the Advocate offices. He bounded up the creaky wooden staircase to check email and the *Drudge Report*, grab himself a cup of gulped, refreshing water from the cooler. Darting out the back door, he tromped down the metal fire stairs fast as he dared. Jamming his Volvo into gear for the drive over to the hospital, he peeled out of the sandy rear parking lot and trash-alley serving several other businesses on the block. Saluting the glimmering glass and steel cube of the county administration building, he roared out of downtown half-blinded by reflected sunlight.

On the short drive to wherever he was going, the reporter prepared himself by musing about a figure such as Rabbit, his role in the life and history of the town, and how change, like death, could be good. A paradox of life—balancing the senses of grievous loss and positive change. Gooch had only lost his mother, really. His longest-term relationship, besides Dobbs Vandegrift, he supposed.

Gooch hoped Runelle would be strong. She was a robust woman—not fat, tall and big-boned, though—but she'd slowed down in the last year or two, as he noted when seeing her in the IGA or at the post office. She and Henny Sykes, Burnie's wife, both strapping farm girls.

Burnham Sykes, too, would need strength. Devastated time and again by loss—wife Henny, his son to cancer, and now, a best friend in Rabbit Pettus— who knew if this wouldn't finish him off, too.

Rabbit told Gooch that since Henny died, he'd made an effort at spending more time at home with Runelle. Not only to comfort his wife, he said, but because Henny's death reminded him of all the nights in his life when he hadn't been home—and for all he put Runelle through, the half of which she didn't even know.

The stuff she did know? It was bad enough. There'd been dalliances, but none to the point of abject public humiliation. It wasn't as though Rabbit was screwing Letty Glasscock on the town green, though there had been Eileen Rucker, back when she'd been a Bevins and not a Rucker.

And then there'd been Trudy—her loyalty and affection for Rabbit had at times seemed less like daughter-father than of another, perhaps more scandalous character.

As for Mama Runelle, Gooch suspected that she'd been more upset at some shady deals in which Rabbit got mixed up through the years than the occasional meaningless indiscretion with a sex-worker. No doubt, if Runelle felt suspicious of her husband's endeavors, it'd have been justified; ugly stuff went on. Way worse than running girls out of the honkytonk.

Rabbit had a longtime bartender, Duwayne Driggers, who turned out to be running crack, coke, meth, whatever he could get his hands on. He dealt through a black dude, a face for the operation, across the river in Easton—a black face to suit the demographic of neighborhood, long one of the poorest pockets of a poor county. And when Rabbit found out, you know what he did? He let it keep on. So long as Duwayne coughed up a decent cut, that is. The way of commerce.

Duwayne got busted, eventually, but it wasn't by the DEA or anybody like that. Local cops. Rabbit told Sheriff Oakley that it was the damnedest thing he'd ever seen, that boy dealing drugs right under his nose. When Duwayne started singing that Rabbit knew all about it, the next morning the perp was found dead in custody of what the coroner called a rare heart issue exacerbated by the suspect's substance abuse, of which his blood screen demonstrated a high concentration of toxins. Case closed.

Passing the hospital, Gooch mulled the writing of a secret history of Tillman Falls, documenting the many shenanigans within the walls of The Dixiana, and in modern times at Pike's Bait & Pawn.

Not that he'd do that.

Around here, certain folks conducted wicked, secret rituals.

Who have always been invested in their activities remaining concealed. Like, forever.

Gooch tried not to think about all he knew. His forgetfulness, a passing phase, might work to his advantage. Might keep him alive. A county tell-all could cause him to suffer a previously undetected heart ailment.

By the time Gooch realized he'd been thinking too hard about Edgewater County's shadow history, he had missed his turn and ended up all the way at the end of the bypass in Chilton, with its colorful fast-food eateries and gas stations and motels clustered around the interstate interchange. He swung around in the Applebee's parking lot and headed back to the hospital entrance he'd passed. Forcing himself to remember the task at hand.

On the front steps, he ran into no less than the mayor himself, Hill Hampton, accompanied by an aide-de-camp, a young man in seersucker and a bowtie, and who tended to prattle in the mayor's ear behind a cupped hand.

The sudden presence of the town's principal newsgatherer caused the political power team to break into suspicious, sunny smiles.

"Mr. Mayor—you hear the news yet?"

"What, that Rebecca LaFreniere or Roosevelt Nixon done moved into my office?"

Gooch winked. "No, sir—about Rabbit Pettus."

His bright blue eyes bulged. Breathless. "What'd they decide about the mural."

"Nothing. He suffered," consulting his notebook, "what the EMT's seemed to think was a cardiac event of some magnitude."

Genuine sadness colored the Mayor's response. "Well—I'll be doggone." When one attained the age of men like Hampton and Wimmel, one understood what such news could portend. Not to mention Rabbit being a full generation older than them both. Hand over heart, the mayor leaned against the brick column and repeated himself, this time with a more profane variation on 'doggone.'

"It's a big story, all right," Gooch said.

Hampton snapped into leadership mode, dismissing his underling—Gooch couldn't recall the kid's name—and grabbing the newspaperman by a brittle elbow to drag him inside the hospital, saying they'd buttonhole somebody to cough up an official update on Reynolds Pettus's condition.

Gooch, scurrying alongside the robust car salesman-cum-politician, drew in his breath as nettlesome, sharp pains flared in his groin, a niggling annoyance that either came and went and was nothing, or else bothered him daily and seemed to be worsening; he couldn't recall which.

Both men stopped in their tracks in the lobby by the security desk when Runelle Pettus herself, stooped and shuffling along in her gardening clothes and a pair of Crocs, appeared walking down the hallway. Mama Runelle was attended by a voluptuous hospital counselor named Carlotta Maldonado, who wrote a twice-monthly self help column for the paper that leaned at times a little New-Agey for the *Advocate*'s more conservative readers.

"Ma'am," the administrator pleaded, "please let me get you a ride home."

"Don't need no ride."

"I insist."

"Let me explain something, prissy—I drove myself when y'all called. I'll drive myself home now, too."

"But—"

"Don't you 'but' me, little girl. Let me guess—y'all's lawyer is worried I'm too upset to drive, and if something happens, I'm gonna take and sue. Well, I ain't. So pull your drawers out of your crack and let me know when the funeral home has the body."

There it is—the Rabbit has died.

Hill Hampton, his voice hushed. "Mama Runelle—from all of us at Hampton Motors, and City Hall, let me be the first and most sincere to say to you—"

"Mayor. Gooch. Lord have mercy, don't start with all that mess already." The tall woman, a sweater pulled tight around her still-broad shoulders, complained about the ungodly cold temperature in the hospital. "At least there ain't much chance of the body turning, not laying here in this meat locker."

Hampton clasped his freckled paws in supplication. "The entire town is grieving right with your family."

"Really, now." Gooch watched as Runelle Pettus, who suffered no fools, scalded Mayor Hill Hampton with a cutting glance. "That'll be news to him, and to me."

"Have you talked to Roy Earl?"

"He's up in the durn air, flying his plane home. I'll have to tell him when he lands." Sudden shock in her eyes. "My poor sweet grandbaby. In that god-durn little airplane of his."

Gooch, interjecting. "Trudy's confused about what she should do."

"What she should do?"

"About the honkytonk."

Runelle leaned on the security desk. Pulled her sweater tight with a gnarled claw with dirt under the nails—she'd been gardening. "I called her right before I run up on y'all. The last thing he said was to make sure The Dixiana was open tonight."

Gooch, excited as could be. "May I quote you on those last words?"

Runelle, with a pitying look, said he could print what he liked, but also, no, her 'Rennie' as she called Rabbit, had not regained consciousness. "I only said that for her feelings."

The Mayor, getting it. "Trudy Pirkle's gonna be a hot mess."

"Now, if you'll excuse me, gentlemen, I've got that nitwit at the funeral home to deal with, and go look in my husband's lockbox for the papers. The papers, the papers," she repeated while raising her arms, the drooping sweater sleeves flapping like angel wings. "The all-important papers."

Gooch thumbed his recorder, his tiny red eye glowing. "But I wonder if you wouldn't give me an actual quote about your husband, rest his soul, for the paper. We're doing a special article about him, ma'am—a special section, in fact."

"Bill, boy—I already told you, write what you want." Runelle, over her substantial shoulder as she headed for the doors. "I'm slap in the middle of a chores list long as your arm. Mercy. Mercy, me."

"I'd love to get some thoughts from you," Gooch hollered. "May I pop over later?"

"If you take a notion," going out into the blazing sunlight and seemingly untroubled by the death of her husband.

Gooch thrust the recorder toward the Mayor's substantial maw. "My angle's gonna be, 'biggest Edgewater County death this century.' Any comments?"

Hampton grunted. Gooch knew the Mayor had butted heads with Rabbit through the years, but then again, he'd also sold him a few cars along the way, and on the flip side had drunk a river of Rabbit's cold draught beer.

"Well, dang—he was Tillman Falls, that old Rabbit. But wait, that's not the quote. 'For many of us, the idea of a Tillman Falls without The Dixiana, and

Rabbit Pettus, sitting there on the corner of the green—well. You just can't imagine it.' Can you?"

"What will we remember most about Reynolds Pettus?"

Hampton's gaze landed on the sign on the wall indicating nuclear medicine, surgery and the cafeteria. "He got along real good with everybody. That he was a real good man. Easygoing. Fought in the big war. Didn't take no guff. There you go—didn't take no guff."

The Mayor, not known for his verbal skills; as in the past, the published quotes would be massaged into a more elegant form. "'Didn't take any guff,'" he edited aloud. "Perfect. Those greatest gen guys—not many left."

"Getting on a long time ago, that mess."

Bill agreed it was. "Ain't nothing but black and white movies, now."

Wait—when was now?

Where was here?

What were they talking about?

Bill's head felt dizzy at the thought of parsing the discussion. He'd have to surf crests of ambiguity to glean meaning. Like he resorted to doing so often these days.

"You ought to go to the bar tonight, if it's open. When word gets around, you'll have plenty of folks full of all kinds-a pull quotes."

"Pull quotes? About what?"

Hampton narrowed his eyes. "About Mr. Rabbit, beau."

A white-hot exclamation point of relief appeared above Bill's head. "I was also getting comments regarding Rev. Nixon's campaign," at which the Mayor snorted and chuckled.

"He ain't had his press conference yet, has he?"

Gooch, panicking—he hadn't a clue. "I don't—know."

"What?"

"I mean—no." Gooch had zero memory of a press conference. He wasn't that far gone. "He hasn't."

"Didn't think so. That man's got a helluva nerve. Gonna get some attention."

Gooch, his intuition blooming with warmth alongside a flare of pain. "Care to share?"

"Better coming from his lips." Hampton snickered. "On the record? That part of the county deserves all due representation on council. I support the will of the voters."

"Anyway—too many stories in my head today. Jasper's next on my list about Rabbit. But yes," ruing the thought and only wanting to go have a decaf mocha and a nap, perhaps resting his weary head on the lap of Dobbs Vandegrift as Dobbs stroked Bill's white wiry hair, a fantasy he'd had for eight horrible years now, that came to him in dreams both waking and asleep. "I will be newsgathering later at The Dixiana."

"I'll swing by and pay my respects by having a snort or three. What she told Trudy was close enough to the truth. The bar being open is how Rabbit would want it."

⊙❋⊙

GOOCH LEFT the hospital parking lot and drove around for a spell collecting his thoughts and noting ideas about his book, his novel, his history of all things Edgewater. He ended up back downtown. He circled the green several times, trying to figure out why so many people were hanging outside The Dixiana on an otherwise ordinary afternoon.

After pulling over and watching everyone's body language it came to him about Rabbit having died. He remembered the entire scene at the hospital, and furthermore, the way his stomach was growling suspected a number of hours had passed—the whole day? He'd gathered no news, no quotes, no facts.

Putting the car back into gear and needing to pee, he drove on down toward the river, cutting through on a bumpy two-lane through fields of younger fruit trees, then older ones on the farmland the Glasscocks sold off, onto River Ridge Road and toward the Pettus house. All keeping in mind his mission: Rabbit's obit.

A triumph—Gooch hadn't felt this together in ages.

He went by the turnoff to the Glasscock land. Letty, a retired baker and caterer whom Gooch had a crush on back in the seventies when he'd still been pretending to find women attractive, still retained a few acres of what used to be a large working farm. She'd be a good person to talk to about the Sunbury School Fire. When she was but a toddler, four members of the Glasscock family, including her mother and all three older sisters, perished in the fire. Who knew what she remembered, though. Too young.

If he ever got around to that novel.

Who knew what anyone remembered? What did it matter?

And where was he going, again?

On River Ridge Road? At this time of the evening?

Runelle—the widow.

Rabbit Pettus.

Gooch closed his eyes and saw a subhead to match his enormous headline from earlier:

BIGGEST EDGEWATER DEATH THIS CENTURY

There, the wooded, secluded Pettus property, the entrance framed by two enormous crepe myrtles and many more lining the lengthy driveway. Dust floated in the twilit air; another vehicle, perhaps more than one, had passed through not long before. Gooch hoped nobody from the Columbia paper had already beaten him to the story. He'd show them who still knew how to report the news.

ROY AND TRUDY

Earlier today, around lunch, you left for your power walk around the island before you discovered the emails between your wife and Estes. Striding in blithe ignorance, your love handles bouncing in time with your footfalls, your worst problem a little toe gone arthritic after a number of bedpost incidents in the old, cramped duplex in Columbia, the original home away from home for you.

Beautiful day on the island, uncharacteristically cool with low humidity, one of those early fall days where the light glimmers before you dreamlike, bright and surreal and magical.

Self-Actualized and Complete. Not a care in the world.

Thinking about opening another Beanery, not far away, the mainland, near the Southeastern University satellite campus in a new plaza, a dude-bro buddy of yours the developer. No-brainer; plenty of money on the mainland there in the sprawling retirement developments; Plainview, your movie hero, tapping a gusher and blowing gold all over the place.

On the way out of the yard and onto the black asphalt of the island walking loop that snaked for miles upon miles you noticed one cat, Rafael, a ginger tom, watching from inside the patio door. You remember this moment and wonder if the animal, one of your favorites out of the multitude Creedence has amassed, could sense in its keen feline perception the ripple of darkness approaching to shred the lives of the two humans to whom it looked for care. When you consider the idea, you decide that it's ridiculous. That you are projecting onto the innocent animal your higher-order human bullshit. That you are a silly person. With foolish ideas.

Fooled, all right.

Exercise has never been your thing, but admit to enjoying the walks: the relative solitude, for one. But also the feelings of pride in the well-to-do marsh-front community, in considering your own business success, and that of the country itself. Children played and dogs barked and colorful banners hung in the warm Carolina air from porch overhangs: America in action, a goddamned Norman Rockwell magazine cover you helped make, and that, despite its problems and failings, still best represented both the answer and the solution to all that troubled humanity and the world, the idea of itself forever and in permanent perpetuity drive the engine of the general culture and economy, as America had for lo these many decades now since the end of W-W-the deuce and all your granddaddy's secret shenanigans therein.

Forevermore, America, the new Atlantis; of this one could be certain.

Shoot, beau—look around at Sedge Island. Nothing wrong with the economy here. You'd know; you are among the pacesetters. The landed gentry. The merchant class. Well earned, you might add. Nobody'd given you diddley.

Earned.

Worth repeating.

You walked, feeling great. Cranked up the workout playlist, an eclectic mix of stuff like you'd have them playing in one of your businesses—modern rock, classic cuts, a Dead jam or two. You aren't some snob, nothing too eclectic. Classic rock to you is Badfinger or Blue Öyster Cult., comfortable and satisfied knowing you were a person of, by, and for your particular time, which was Right Now, you breathed in deep and basked in the sunlight, stretching a quad on one of the waist-high stop signs designed to manage pedestrian and bicycle traffic at cross streets. A bona fide member of the community, you. Sitting on the neighborhood association and Chamber of Commerce, well liked both here and in prior neighborhoods and as part of similar bodies going all the way back to Tillman Falls; money, money, money sticking out of every hole; and with a mate who epitomized everything you'd ever wanted in a woman: sexy, caring, pretty, kind. Ever since the day ten years ago that Creedence kissed you for the first time—or rather, let you kiss her, to be honest—you've felt as though you won the lottery romance-wise. Hell, lottery-wise, too. But not without awareness or gratitude—you always remember to feel grateful for the largesse, material and other-wise.

Until this morning.

"You're the first one," you told Creedence. Not sexually, you explained. The first love. The great love. It had been that way since you met her, as kids. "You."

"For me, too," or she had said. "I never thought that way about Dusty, even though he was. You know. The first. My first love in the physical—"

"I remember."

Creedence, married during her 20s to a low-class doofus, stuck in Edgewater County. More of a doofus than you, anyway, chubby Roy Earl Pettus, which is saying something. "Dusty was like the boy who didn't grow up. I needed me a real man."

This morning, you had still believed you were that right man.

She had seemed furtive and distant.

You had been bored and flying a lot. Or, working on getting the CBSI up and running. Or closing the complicated deal on cashing out the Spotted Banana chain.

Okay, okay.

Right about the turnaround you waved to an Island cop, Phil, who resides in your pocket, who knows you to be an upstanding, wealthy citizen he's paid to serve and protect. Phil all but gave you a snap-to salute, the way you like it from your managers. Like Estes, the kid she's screwing. Which at the time, no clue.

Not a clue.

Idiot.

Back home, your workout tank and shorts damp and boxer briefs wedged in your crack, you'd found her laptop sitting there open. Heard her downstairs trying to break up a cat fight. Saw she was in the middle of chatting.

With your assistant manager, Estes Patel.

That fact alone—a member of the merchant class lowering herself to a sexual assignation with a prol like Patel—rang an atonal and clangorous bell.

You scrolled back in their conversation and read.

In disbelief.

In anger.

In pain.

Right about then you got a strange prickling sensation at the back of your neck, and you thought about old man Rabbit, and a story Jasper Glasscock had hinted about one time, that your grandmother and Burnham Sykes had had a fling way back in the ancient past. How the notion had made you sick to your stomach.

You heard the landline, faraway, a muted electronic pealing. All outside lines blocked but a few key relatives back home. Like your grandparents.

Next, the muffled sound of Creedence answering. And hollering, oh, shoot. "Shoot shoot shoot. I'll go and get him. I'm so sorry, Mama Runelle."

Before she could speak, she saw it on your face.

Saw the laptop.

You grabbed her by the arms. "Honey—you're hurting me. You're—"

"I know everything," you had shouted, an inch away from her puffy face. "You hear me?"

Creedence, already known as the pale princess, blanching and ghostly. Blue eyes bulging with fear. Shaking her head. Trying to smile. "Nuh-uh. No."

"Everything."

Creedence, grabbing that Macbook and slamming it shut so hard she must have broken the screen. Sputtering and playing dumb and denying, denying. Whispering. "You're misinterpreting. You don't understand—"

"The last thing you were writing was about you couldn't wait for him to be —to be—inside you again." Choking off.

She belched like she would puke. "Oh—honey. Oh—my god."

Her eructation, smelling of booze. Last night's, today's, who knew anymore with her. Your heart rate, already elevated, racing.

You hadn't seen her look this bad since she'd had her brother Devin, missing for years now, declared dead.

You had been upset as well; Creedence's brother had once been a friend, a good one, too, albeit with problems. After the fatal car accident that took the life of his girlfriend Libby, Devin Rucker had drifted away into a nightmare of substance abuse and psychosis through which no one—friend or professional —had ever penetrated. Devin, a lost cause even while still alive.

Close to vomiting, you planned to Ctrl-C and Ctrl-V all of it into a text file you will name Infidelity Evidence 2015 and forward to the boys at the law firm. Shoving by her, you went to grab the laptop.

"I'm sorry." She howled this over and over, you in your damp workout duds and breathing like you'd run a race, and her in her floppy pajama pants and fuzzy slippers like always, both struggling over the Macbook. "I'm sorry, it's true it's true it's true," she screamed. "But it's also Rabbit."

"What—you're screwing my grandfather, too?"

She broke down into wet, hollow sobbing. "No. He's—he's—"

Every hair on your body standing up, you gathered yourself to ask what she meant.

That he's in the hospital; they think it's a heart attack or a stroke. "Mama Runelle said he's asking for you."

In a fog, and with terrible and yawning regret, you raged at her. She crouched against the wall. How unfair for this all to happen. The price you paid for being awesome. Forget all the anger management aphorisms you were supposed to deploy. You had only gone to two sessions. It hadn't been court mandated, only a suggestion from one of your managers, a trustworthy worker whom you ran off on account of being a rage monkey, and suggested to you for fear of your health.

Afterwards, you were hot all over, no relief or release. Into the bedroom, locked the door. Changed. Avoided your reflection in the mirror. Unable to look at your own genitals, puckered and shrunken. Brushed your teeth.

Back in the family room, your sweet wife moved toward you with a crazy look, smiling and saying, now, now, now, and you had shoved her—hard; she fell against the wall—and told her to go kiss a duck. You hustled outside to haul ass to the Sedge Island airport so you could get home to attend to your grandfather before he passed away. You would deal with her in due time.

⊙⊛⊚

AROUND THE BEND where it changes from the highway to Common Street you're pleased to see the iconic tilted ice cream cone sign of a defunct fast food drive-in called Zippy's, home of chili dogs and greasy baskets of fries, although you preferred Hermie's dogs. Now it's a car dealership that kept the name and the neon sign, incongruous yet memorable enough, you suppose. OUR DEALS ARE SWEET painted across the windows where you once stood waiting on a milkshake.

You always preferred the Congress Street Grille's burgers, anyway. Hell, you even preferred the Hollow Bone's barbecue to what your Pa-paw served at The Dixiana, a controversial statement even he didn't muster much guff to dispute, but then the Hollow Bone had burned down not long after you left for college.

Your stomach growls.

You lust for Trudy.

The enormity.

It all hits you sitting in Trudy's car and your granddaddy being dead and your wife out of love with you and in bed with another man. Not even a man —a boy. You are nutted anew. You got to get this dead grandfather shit squared away so you can get back down there and murder yourself an assistant GM. Do it OJ–style.

Or, pay somebody. Clean. Make it look like a robbery.

That's how much your heartache burns. Murderous is your state of mind.

Trudy produces a pack of Winstons. Starts to fish one out.

Is she kidding? In the car with you?

"Dear?"

Tucking the smoke into the corner of her mouth and pushing in the ashtray lighter, all of which takes you back to boyhood afternoons riding in the truck with Pa-paw. "What, sugar?"

"I'm a nonsmoker."

Reluctant, she understands and puts it away. "I feel ya."

"Appreciate it."

"Tough day, is all."

The lighter pops out, breaking the mood.

Now Trudy looks broken and old. Not sexy. Not the same. Also pissed at you for not letting her puff.

Yeah. Smoking.

One aspect you've always hated about that fucking Dixiana—AMONG MANY a cavernous and thunderous God-voice intones—is the cigarette stench, and your grandfather's wretched smoking you'd suffer driving around in his truck or the various Pettus sedans. Breathing that crap. Coupled with the early years when you had swabbed the deck at the honkytonk, and had barista'd at the coffee shop you'd eventually own, where the smoking came with the territory, seemed pervasive and endemic to the culture at hand, it's likely you'll die of lung cancer. Yeah. And without ever having touched one of the filth sticks of leaves wrapped in paper people inhaled like demented fiends.

After you bought the coffee shop—Maxine's Koffee Klatch, a Southeastern University college ghetto fixture since 1972, and which you would transform at no small financial peril into the Carolina Beanery Café—one of the first changes you instituted had been to enact your own first-in-the-city restaurant smoking ban. This had been in early 90s South Carolina, as you remind your-self, far behind the rest of the country (as usual), and few talking about a smoking ordinance in hospitality businesses. Not before you came on strong, anyway.

Alas, you found no support from fellow business owners in the bar-heavy district.

A brash young upstart, you said you'd show them: running for and winning a seat on the Downtown Business Alliance board, where you shot your mouth off the way you'd seen your grandfather do at ELMS and town council meetings.

Much resistance; a battle in the media. But you spurred a larger movement, became a progressive figurehead in your neighborhood and a talking head on TV, all of which contributed to the success of your business venture. Your grandfather had never been shy about telling you how proud he was of you, even if he thought you was wrong to tell people they couldn't smoke where and when they damn well pleased.

"Damn if y'all ain't religious fanatics, you nonsmokers. I tell ya what."

"Just trying to stay healthy, Pa-paw. Keep my people on their feet."

"You can't save them, boy. Try as you might. You can only save yourself."

❖❖❖

"Hold on here for a sec."

Trudy has pulled up to the flashing red light at the turnoff take to River Ridge Road, and your childhood home thereon.

"Run us into downtown first."

Puts on the signal—left. "You need to be with Mama Runelle."

"Check; but I wanna see the old dump. Please."

"Ain't nothing to see. Ain't nothing different."

You huff and puff. Accustomed to getting your way. "Be that as it may."

"Do what?"

"Just take me there."

"But why?"

"I got my reasons."

Trudy sits waiting.

"Please," you repeat, unable to articulate any specific reasons. Headlamps are coming up in the mirrors. "Do it."

Agreeing, Trudy clicks over the blinker to the right and drives on through Whaley Way, by all the old houses with the wraparound porches, and the archives and the library and the oaks and elms with their great limbs soaring and sheltering the wide streets of this antebellum neighborhood that survived the destruction wrought during the Civil War.

The new-ish courthouse complex rising above the trees, built in the late 80s, makes for a modernist glass and steel cube welcoming the motorist from the west into downtown, but to your mind the building looms silvery and artificial, feels out of place. The old Rexall drug store, its original signage faded and peeling on the bricked side of the building, is now a cell phone provider; brand, T-Mobile. They built a KFC where an old Gulf station used to be. The marquee under the smiling cartoon Colonel Sanders icon reads

8 PEICE with 4 FREE BISQUIT

You wonder if they did any remediation of petroleum wastes on the site. You imagine crunching into a greasy Extra Crispy breast that leaves a brackish hint of antifreeze aftertaste at the back of your teeth.

"That's a good deal right there." Trudy pats you on the knee. "I ain't eat all day."

Your stomach, roiling with nausea. Tasting the black oil. "Me neither."

"Drive-through's open."

"Are you serious? Shoot no, girl."

Trudy goes huh. "Good enough for me."

"That makes one of us."

At seeing the power lines and the poles and the phone lines and the TV cable strung along all the roads, you experience further revulsion. A need to bend someone's ear about getting a streetscaping initiative underway. No wonder this place feels dead. Had they never seen that Crumb cartoon 'A Short History of America'? Where it all changes over from messy nature to civilized and managed orderliness? You dig all the other progress depicted in the comic strip, except for those ugly power lines and power poles and old-fashioned streetlights, and the downmarket single-use retail strip mall depicted in the last panel on the left. No no no. Needs one more panel to show how cool it can be again when you don't have the infrastructure hanging everywhere and looking all sloppy.

"Damn, y'all."

"What now?"

"Get these lines buried. Spruce it up. Tillman Falls needs a makeover."

"You sound like your Uncle Burnie."

This makes you smile. "He raised me almost as much as my folks did. It takes a village, et cetera."

Trudy, coming up on the cemetery. Almost there. "I seen where they did that over in Columbia. It looked real pretty after they got done with it."

Damn straight, you tell her. Buried lines. A water feature or two. Planters, refreshed seasonally, hanging from new street lamps. Decorative pavers delineating crosswalks. ADA compliant sidewalks and curbing. Twinkling LED lights in the trees, year-round. You describe all this.

"Sounds real pretty—but expensive."

"Pish-posh. There's money, public and private, for such endeavors. You just have to find out who's flush, and put the screws to them until they come off the dime."

Puffing out your chest, you boast how you led the initiative to streetscape the Old Market, the neighborhood where you got your start owning the first coffee shop; you led the fight to change the zoning laws to encourage mixed-use development, to encourage grants to local small businesses. To beautify and improve. You elide your efforts to enact a smoking ban indoors.

But outdoors? A vision you'd had for the Old Market. Streetscaped. Water features. Growth. Home number two to you, that neighborhood, where you lived for years like a perpetual college student, or what felt like being a college student, down there in the university ghetto amongst them all. But different. As a business owner, not a kid with no responsibility except going to class and partying. A stakeholder. Invested. Like, emotionally and literally and all? With real and tangible money, whatever it is, on the table? Damn straight.

The sickly glow of the neon Dixiana sign. Sputtering, half burned out. A travesty. Looks horrible. As does the mural, and the rest of downtown.

And yet, viable: The green sits surrounded by vehicles, every angled spot filled with motorcycles, pickups and beaters. The honkytonk appears alive with activity: shitkickers and drunks out on the sidewalk, beers in hand, milling, a regular crowd. News about your Pa-paw has gotten around.

"Pull over in front of the square, in the yellow zone."

"What's wrong?"

"Just gimme a sec."

Trudy, fretting. "I should be in there."

"You'll be back to work in a jiffy."

"Roy Earl." She's hushed and spooked. "I got to tell you something—I think he knew. He knew. He told me that not two weeks ago. 'Trudy-girl, the day I drop dead, you got to do one thing for me, and that's make sure this old barn is open that night. So all will seem right with the world'." Catching a sudden sob, forestalling it. "And so it is."

You reach across and grab her bony wrist. "He couldn't have run this place all these years without you."

Trudy needs to cry, now, but you aren't intimates anymore and never were in that way, and it feels awkward, and so you don't move to further comfort her, not beyond patting her on the bony, freckled forearm. You hop out. Give her tears the space they need to evaporate.

You stand on the green with your back to your grandfather's honkytonk, the music from inside thumping, a bluegrass combo tearing it up. You take in your hometown, empty your mind of the present and revel in the past. You start at the marquee of the Palmetto Grande, the old movie theatre two blocks away, your original escape from the doldrums and pine barrens of Edgewater County, from your grandfather's nasty honkytonk and your grandmother's cloying kitchen and the empty pecan grove in which you'd wander for hours lost in rumination, wondering why it was you'd been so cursed as to be alone, so alone, in the world, or so chubby, or too shy, or whatever deficiency you felt. The movies were another escape from that ruinous self awareness, at least until you developed the fortitude and resources to control and shape your destiny by doing what you loved, which involved selling yogurt and fruit-shakes and coffee and moneychanging, your only real job now.

It's a particular thrill seeing the refurbished movie theater marquee, even if dark. That this space is now the Fine Arts Center seems much better than sitting empty and abandoned like the last time you saw it, a few years ago. The sight of the Grande takes you further back than sliding your beyond-hard teenage dick into twenty-year-old Trudy Pirkle in her smelly old ramshackle house that stunk of cat pee, an odor you'd associate with sex for all your days, in both a good and bad way. The Palmetto reminds you of Karen Black piloting a giant airplane to safety. Karen Black, the ideal woman whom you revered and coveted, but could never possess.

But it's not *Airport 1975* or *Five Easy Pieces* or *Day of the Locust* or any of the DVDs on your shelf at home on Sedge Island that occupy your mind, no; it's another movie, one in black and white about a dying American town, with a tumbleweed and the sound of wind rushing on the soundtrack, a slow pan around to see what's become of Tillman Falls, and Ben Johnson is dead and you have to choke back a raging and bilious red tide of emotion.

The Palmetto's resurrection seems a bright spot in an otherwise blighted-looking place: A payday advance joint, a cellphone outlet and smartphone repair business that looked beyond low-rent, a thrift store where once had been the wig shop, a beauty supply store with windows papered by posters of gorgeous black women. A salon where Mr. Halsey's used to be, with the ridiculous moniker 'Head Trauma'—really? Da-fuck that mean?—and next to that a tattooing and piercing place, lit up and open for business. Another late night trade.

Tattoos?

Here?

Da-fuck?

You turn to address the corner now held down by a joint called Manny's on the Green. No longer Lucinda's. No more beloved meat-and-three plates from the home-style restaurant at which you ate so many times you wanted to FREAKING DIE.

In other words? Good.

In fact, good riddance to everything about Lucinda's, everything but the Oreo pudding she used to feature on the buffet every Sunday, the one meal at Lucinda's you looked forward to because of that Oreo pudding. You ate so much as a kid it made you fat, and if you tasted it now you think you'd projectile vomit, because God knows what's in Oreos and commercial vanilla pudding and all that refined sugar.

As for Lucinda's, nothing pleases you more than the fact that Lucinda is gone and in her stead you find the tasteful signage of Manny's on the Green, with classy blue-tinted window under-lighting, and from inside you can also hear music, more rhythm and blues than country—indeed, the kind of place your grandfather called a juke joint, like the private clubs tucked around the county.

You nod to a shadowy figure standing and smoking in front of Manny's, a black man in khakis and a tight muscle-T and white Chuck Taylors all but glowing on his feet. He acknowledges you with his cancer stick, a tiny red dot that rises and falls.

All you can think: gotta get these power lines buried. Gotta get some streetscaping going round he-ah! The future's here, we are it, we are on our own.

What all will you want to do with this place, now yours? An entire block in this little Southern town.

The mind reels.

You've been considering becoming a developer anyway, what with all your fruitshake largesse lying fallow but for the pathetic interest it brought in—you had most in CDs rather than invested in stocks, which nobody could understand. But in development, as you learned during your time in civic leadership, one looked to local government largesse first for investment opportunities, way before anybody spent dollar one of their own money.

For a real world example, look no further than your own ledger: through facade grants and other tax incentives, Sedge Island had practically given you the money to revamp the building that housed the Beanery, the CBSI, your shiny new baby.

With your own money, though, you don't need gubmint taxpayer dollah dollah bills. You could develop the living god-durn mess outta this podunk place on your own. Complete autonomy to do as you will.

Couldn't you?

One way or another. Yeah.

A warm glow suffuses throughout your chest as you consider The Dixiana, its fate never in your grasp. The neon sign, a work of art and beauty itself, intricate and ornate and from another time and place, so distinctive in its lettering, but so sad and in disrepair—that'd be the first to come down. Rabbit had told you before what it would cost to fix. That it wasn't worth doing.

In fact, some tubes had been burned out for as long as you can remember. Occasionally you see the sign in dreams, but in that context the signage always glowed new and bright and perfect.

You've never quite understood this dream-image, any more than the recurring mountain bald on which you spun like Julie Andrews, a place in the dreams that always feels like freedom. One afternoon a few years ago you finally saw and experienced such a view, a moment of triumph that in retrospect had presaged the dissolution of the marriage.

But you can't think about Creedence, any more than you can hike back up to Max Patch and redo that stupid day, the drama of which had been chicken-feed compared to earlier today. You have a granddaddy to bury.

The throaty engine of Trudy's Taurus revs—once, twice. You get the message.

MANNY THEODORE

Manny T, smoking, stand his ass on the sidewalk out front his club, knowing his babygirl watching him from the doorway. He gonna be in trouble for sneaking and puffing. Supposed to be done quit.

She disappointed. "Daddy."

Stubbing it out, tossing the butt into the wire wastebasket by one of the old iron lampposts that need painting. "You ain't helping shut down the line?" The buffet ended at nine.

"Wasn't nothing for me to do."

"Bullcrud."

"Go on and check for yourself. Ahmad say he don't need me."

"Ahmad ain't the boss."

Sounding distant, dry and wise. Like her mama. "He boss enough to see how much work's left. And whether he need help."

She got him there. "You can stand here and watch me smoke, I reckon."

"Please don't smoke another one."

"I promise I'm-a quit again soon."

"Your promises ain't worth much."

"All right, now. You watch your mouth, talking to your daddy like that."

Past nine now, she ought to be home. But Manny also feel Lillyanne should be at the club much as she want or he need her. That as a family member, and at her age—on the cusp of young womanhood, and impressionable—she needed to have her ass taught what work all about. To want shit, and work for it. That how you get anywhere in life. Work your ass off, try to keep a taste here and there for y'self. Get somewhere.

Manny didn't have her messing around the bar or the stage, no; he wanted her to learn the kitchen and the food service end. Not out of sexism; because food where the money is. And in the bar too, yeah. Big time, if you work it right. Time enough later. Bad enough to have his innocent girl-woman exposed as she was to the music business, and the trade that come along with it. But trade it has been for Manny.

Man, and wo-man, need to earn they way in the world. Way he'd been muh-fucken taught. Way he teach it, and the main person he had to teach: his babygirl.

He show so little of what inside to her. You can't. Not with a young'un. He know how it seem—cold and hard and ungiving. He believe himself to be giving everything to her though. Showing how to be this way, because when you wasn't this way, you was like her no-good uncle Ahmad.

Manny got his anger shit under control. Katrina had been God's way of showing him the way and the light and that the time of maturing had come upon him, and to temper his raging emotional ways; his survival from the storm and the aftermath a sign God's plan included not an angry man, but a coolheaded and always on top of his shit muh-fuh who blow a god-damn mean saxophone, who know food and liquor. Who know how to treat his ladies, and with his babygirl, how to get ready to be a grownup and take care of herself.

"Never understood how a woodwind player—oh, never mind." All judgmental and weary, she change the subject. "Sad about Mister Rabbit."

"Me too, babygirl."

"Look at all them folks over yonder outside The Dixiana."

"Don't say 'yonder' and 'folks.' Sound like a little redneck."

"Yes, sir."

Manny fight the urge to light another'n up. "Pettus welcomed us here. Despite a dumb rebel flag painted all up on the wall, he repent his own muh-fucken racism. His ass embrace love, not hate."

"You sure? Mama say he sure didn't want to paint over that cracker flag."

"Sure as I'm standing here. Good man. Look you in the eye, shake your hand firm. Give you a squeeze right on the forearm."

With a slant to her words. "He must go to church."

"Now, far as I know he wa'n't no religious man. But that don't mean you can't live a straight and righteous life. Do right by your fellow man. Like he done with us."

"That ain't what the preacher say."

Manny snort like a bull. He don't give a rip what Reverend Nixon say. But he don't put it so harsh to the babygirl. "Go on inside now," Manny say. "We got to pray hard for Mister Rabbit muh-fucken soul tonight."

"Already done it."

Lillyanne say it all smartass the way kids do, which he let slide cause of the subject. Told her to pray again at bedtime.

And to get that homework squared away, and listened to her say yes-sir in a downmouthed voice that rub him wrong, but he let it go cause it one of the big anger management lessons they taught him. Let shit go. Do it do it do it, he say. Manny hard on himself too, but everybody be taking selfies too often to consider anyone else's part in the play.

He said it again, and again. Hard on himself. A mantra. Once a muh-fuh done shot dope and then got straight, muh-fucker keep stoked a flame of e-ternal vigilance. Or he shoot up again.

"Daddy?"

"What." He waited.

"You ought to go to church with me more often."

"Done told you before. Grandmama drug me there sufficient back in the day."

"The Reverend-Doctor Nixon's a wise man. He don't just talk about the Bible."

"Sure he is, with his pedi-degrees and all."

"He says they not telling us the truth about Egypt. And the past. And history in general."

"I can believe it."

"Not just what it was, history. But when it was."

Manny shake his head. "All above my pay grade. But Daddy got wisdom for ya, too. If ya'd listen."

"You the one who needs to listen, with your stink-ass cigarettes." She brave enough to confront, but not to wait for the retort. Inside she go, door-bells jangling on the old metal-frame glass door, all original, heavy, they used to build shit to last but not no more.

Manny laugh. She growing up. Testing him.

The thought also made feel kicked in the gut, her growing up. Hard world awaited.

⊛⊛⊙

N'AWLINS, as the dead redneck across the street liked to call him, done got himself a mess of old muh-fucken rules. But it had all gotten them where they asses was, and he didn't care if he had to remind Neecie and his babygirl and Ahmad's ass, he didn't mind and that was part of the charge and he under-stood this. He didn't do it angry no more. Not after the storm blew them here, and not anymore because anger hurt your heart, your own insides. Anger be a vibration, he read on the internet, that made you sick. Along with everyone around you.

Wanting another cigarette, but instead Manny ease down onto the iron bench out front and gawk over at the shitkickers lifting they longnecks to the dead old one, and next thing he think is, I wonder who gonna keep that place going, because as Rabbit himself said, the two clubs of their'n worked good together. This could be a music town for tourists, because now and then some already came to the honkytonk. Said he wanted more than anything to put on a music festival, a bad-ass event unlike the po-face little street carnivals the ELMS stage like May Day in the spring and Harvest Holiday in the fall. Said it would put this dried-up old town back on the map.

Or: promote concerts at Becky L's Fine Arts Center. Another good idea. Jazz down yonder, cracker country over cross the way, and R&B and smooth soul at Manny's.

Manny wasn't sure the town had ever been on anybody's map, but coming from a place New Orleans he could get down with tourism money talk. Could get on board with that shit. Used to live by it, in the glory days before the junk had got him, and he had lost everything. Doing like Coltrane and Yardbird, honking on horns and poking in needles. But all a long-ass time before anybody got blowed away by no Hurricane Katrina. Before Neecie, even. Way-ass before babygirl. Thank the lord.

But this idea, it keep percolating in his head: He knows already some tourists come to see The Dixiana cause of all the country legends who played there and whose pictures hang on the walls. Manny had at least some of his pictures here he collected back home, till the storm come and washed shit away. And Rabbit was right; folks would come if they knew about this place, but also if it had more to offer, and that's why the old coot had liked Manny's on the Green so much.

Rabbit Pettus a forward looking dude, even on his last muh-fucken legs, and durn if Manny don't get a tingle down his own leg. You want to keep on till your last damn day and then drop like that old redneck. None of this nursing home shit. Nuh-uh.

Well, maybe not fall down in the street—in a nice crib, not downtown, out in the country like Manny used to dream about, and dick-deep in some tight trim, blowing a mean solo while some sugarmamas shaking their booty at Manny onstage. That how his ass want to go. While he know he still alive.

Lillyanne Theodore, his precious only little babygirl, she score the highest goddurn marks in her school during the last round of standardized testing, before Katrina had forced them from their home and life. Lillyanne might go her ass to Princeton, Harvard, anywhere. A smart little girl, black or not, could go far. Hell, back in 2008 they even talked about Condoleeza Rice running for vice-president, if not the top slot itself. (Sister or not, no one from the Bush administration would ever get Manny Theodore's vote, not after that Katrina bullshit and everything else.) Nowadays a black woman of ambition and intellectual vigor can own her shit.

Still hard to believe. Like with Obama sitting in there. He ain't no thang, though.

Manny know he provide a good home, and give his young'un a nurturing and comfortable environment in which to grow, thrive, and become the woman she gonna become. This his legacy, the creation of a new history where an entire old one had been wiped away, clean and abrupt and cruel. New Orleans had plumb sunk—the poor parts, anyway—but the world kept turning and new days piled up and the old people faded away. Manny understand about time, and the great cycle of reality, the importance of sending a child into the world who gonna do more and go farther than his ass ever dream. Who destined for it. This is his muh-fucken vision for his daughter. His mission in life.

He smoke the fuck outta another menthol 100, because who the man here and the daddy and all, but damn if he don't wanna be a genuine brotherman, now. Not lie no more to his daughter about smoking. Not that ya can hide the smell of it.

Manny feel guilt at the back of his head about other shit than smoking another'n against a thirteen-year-old girl's wishes, though. And she right about one thing: his wind ain't what it used to be. Halfway through a set he sometimes ain't got enough breath to blow the tenor with power. That don't feel good.

Everything else working good as shit though.

Word on that.

Ask Manny wife. If ya wanna know.

Or, ask his sidemeat. She know, too. The girlfriend understand it every which way.

But his little fling on the green ain't nothing to do with his babygirl, other than keeping it secret from her and from Neecie. That some high-wire shit there. Girl sit next to his muh-fucken old lady on the damn ELMS, and the proximity—the danger—give hitting the pussy another sheen, Manny here to tell you. Da-yum.

Manny got out his phone, which he had switched to silent when he came out here, because he want solitude to smoke and think and look out on his town. Tillman Falls his in a way New Orleans could never be and never was, either before or after the storm, and that's why he thought God had led him here the way He had.

Led him to all sorts-a shit. No lie, no doubt.

Including Becky L.

And there it was—a text. A booty call.

BAM.

What ya gonna do. Ever since he turned fifty, Manny'd been a hot-dicked horndog ball of fire, but mercy never had he got with a woman—pick ya a color or creed, yo—like Rebecca LaFreniere. God-damn.

What he supposed to do—say no?

And with that text he would do it tonight, soon as he go back inside and tell his wife Neecie he going out to do politicking on behalf of Roosevelt Nixon, which make her so happy Manny getting involved the way she done with the ELMS. He don't feel guilty. If asked, he say, shit, girl. You getting in with them old hens caused this mess.

Next, he reckoned to get hisself involved with Becky and her Fine Arts center. Maybe Manny could act in them plays they put on in the Palmetto. Give them an excuse. To rehearse. Heh.

Had to admit they got classy shit at the Edgewater County Fine Arts Center, and a good complement to Manny's, and in his redneck honkytonk way, what Rabbit had too. Muh-fucker had the coolest sign Manny ever seen, all that neon, a big bad DIXIANA logo from way back before mofos knew what a phat logo all about. That, and Manny's place, and the theater all make Tillman Falls a bad-ass little district, like one block of a cool-ass town, but surrounded by a whole lotta nothing going on.

But ya know ya know, that work talk. Tonight, he gonna relax and hit the backside of that LaFreniere pussy, soon as she done with some errand. And then, late late night, go into his home gym and get in a workout. Maybe watch a blu-ray, while working on the pads on the alto which done started sticking. Ain't gotta get up early tomorrow.

A good life Manny got himself. Better than they'd ever have in the ward. A life he run on his own terms. Till his old lady bring down the hammer one day, he figure it go on long as possible. It work out, and Manny get away with the shit he pulling. He always did before. Why not again?

BUTTON, THIM, AND TINKY

As Button stripped off her damp workout wear, skintight Lycra gear in neon colors that made her look like a tennis ball, or used to before she started losing weight, her mother hollered from the hallway:

"Button-Button—where you?"

"In here, Mama."

"Button? Button? Button?"

Calling again, this time with more force. "A moment, please."

"Chowtime, yep? Chowtime?"

Under her breath. "Keep your. Support hose—uh—on. Would you?"

Button, stilling herself. Standing in a sports bra and granny panties. Preparing to get in the shower. Maybe think about Heather Ponderview, rub out a good one, redirect the energy into charging up a new sigil she'd been coaxing into existence through many iterations and refinements across several pages in one of her magickal notebooks.

Not the principal grimoire, however, still in worrisome existence and not going anywhere. She had tucked it back into its place of rest, another book among hundreds scattered throughout the corner upstairs bedroom facing the trees of the backyard, with good light through two windows and perfect for a reader and writer. Not that she could get to her desk, covered as it was by paper and books.

But first, naked and covered in goosebumps from the cold AC vent under her desk, to compose a hey-now, catchup email on a laptop she sat propped onto her thighs; lay the seeds of the impending reunion certain to manifest soon.

Pausing, first, to bow before her altar, with its totems and candles and the sigil, a symbol crafted with a sharpie through many drafts on a page torn from the handwritten grimoire and intended to 'work' a particular energetic transaction. You couldn't talk about the specifics. Spoiled the magic.

At her mother's voice, however, Button put the lengthy, heartfelt note she'd been writing in her mind on hold. Hadn't been the first time she'd bailed on emailing Heather—most of the others she'd started over the last two months had gone into the Trash bin instead.

"A few minutes, Mom."

Hopeful. "Chowtime?"

"And turn the air up, please." Recalcitrant scamps, her charges. Her forebears, jacking around with the thermostat the second Button left the house. "It's freezing. In this dump."

Her responsibility, these people. Annoying but sacred, yo.

Button, stretching her calves amidst the stacks of books in her cluttered childhood room, the disarray a sign not of scattered mental processes but deep intelligence, thumbed a text to her sister, working at the governor's mansion in Columbia.

Thim had not called in over a week; she deserved an update, of which there was none, other than to remind that Button existed here, keeping the household managed and everyone fed and watered.

Hey—got a sec? No biggie

Only seconds later came the Thim ringtone, a blaring obnoxious electronic klaxon. (Heather Ponderview's ringtone, not that she'd call, was the fanfare known in the Phish world as the "Tweezer Reprise," no higher compliment from one phan to another.) The alarm suited Thim, who never called to chat. Always conflict based.

Thim, alarmed. "Granddad's fallen again. Hasn't he."

"No, and you didn't have to call. It's nothing. That's why I texted. Just. Checking. Ya know. On ya."

"Are you kidding? Get to the freaking point."

"There's not one. Just wanted—ya know—to chat."

"Well, get to it."

"Nice to hear. From you. Too."

"Button—for god's sake. I'm busy."

Thim, always so impatient with her sister's halting cadence. It was as fast as her processor would go. She'd been quite an experimenter, back in the day, in college and on Phish tour. A dirt surfer, all spun out on the lot for weeks at a stretch.

Her crazy Phish dance? When the band and the groove and the crowd were dialed in? A frenetic, grabbing-at-flies hand jive accompanied by little side-to-side foot circles, for as long as the jams lasted. This band's music could make the magic even in the absence of drugs; four shamans to an extended tribe.

Let them think about her what they would. She preferred to think of her careful diction and zoned-out demeanor—yah; she knows it's how she comes across, and so what?—as an indicator of innate and considered thoughtfulness rather than drug burnout; 'sides, no drug-drugs in years now. Only the herb. Sure, she'd sometimes forget how one of her spun out, choppy sentences began. Did it matter? Long as she got to the end?

"What is it you need, again?"

Button, sighing. "I was. Checking in. Checking on, on you. It's—nothing."

Flabbergasted. "Everyone's fine?"

"Of course. They are."

Sweat running down her body, now she stood and grabbed the toe box of her running shoe, stretched out her tight quads. Button described the conditions at home as nominal—her mother in the usual state of half-trance in front of the TV, grandfather half in the bag, and lucky to not be in the liver ward somewhere. "Situation normal."

"We've got to get him sober." Tsk-tsk-tsk. "Of all people, you ought to understand."

"You can't. Make a person not drink. They have to—want to—"

"He's ninety," imperious and impatient. "He can be forced to do what we wish."

Boy, did that attitude fit in with her boss's smug, right-wing politics. "'We?' Who is we? Where are you? Not here, sis."

This only angered her, but rather than castigate Button further Thim barked, "Hold, please." Muffled voices and rustling. "May I put you on speaker?"

Button said. She guessed. Thim could. Do so. "Why not."

"Button Sykes? The Button Sykes?"

The voice sounded grating and familiar—oh, no.

The Governor. Of. The State. A tea-bagger, no less.

Button halfway despised her right-wing ass, except for not wanting to despise anyone or anything alive on the planet right now—but yo, dog, the salty bitch keeps threatening to cut all arts funding and resists meaningful ethics reform and fills up appointment posts with political cronies often far from qualified to run their agencies. "Yes, ma'am?"

"Mercy, Button, but I'm honored to talk you. Uh-huh. Thim here's spoken so often of your dutiful devotion to family—which is, as you know, one of the principal planks of my party's platform—that I finally just had to hear your voice."

Button, saying she appreciated hearing from the governor.

"You should get a darn medal. A statue there in Tillman Falls for all that you, and caregivers like you everywhere, do for your loved ones. Bless your hearts."

"Bless your heart. Isn't necessarily. A positive thing. Madame Governor."

"Pardon moi?"

"Just saying, Madame—"

"Button, please: call me Sandy. Just on the phone, never in public." She went haw-haw-haw. "But seriously. I admire you so. Take care of your granddaddy. And your mama—an immigrant. A legal immigrant," adding this with breathy awe. "Bless their hearts. Every one of you."

"I'm not. An immigrant. We were born here."

"Oh, that's right," sounding testy. "But still."

Button, polite. "Governor Sandy. Let me ask you something. I was going. To ask just you, Thim. But since you're both—on the—on the horn—"

Thim, brittle and fake-cheerful. "Just get to your question, honey. Governor Three-Rivers has a full slate today."

Button took an extra long pause. "I'm preparing. To do some. Civic organizing."

"*Wuuuhnderful,*" the governor sang. "Do tell."

"I wanted to. Ask you both. What you thought. About my hair."

"Your hair?"

Thim, incredulous. "Button—"

"If y'all thought. I should. Get rid of. My dreadlocks."

"Honey, your what?"

Thim interjected: "Governor, my sister has that horrid Bob Marley hair."

"Bob Farley? I don't know who that is. But I know this much: your hair's an extension of you, and you ought to make it pretty. That's what folks like."

"One supposes you could get away with salon-class dreads," Thim said with disdain. "Passé, in a fashion sense. Semi-acceptable, but only in the spirit of inclusion. Except for the cultural appropriation faux pas. I mean, really: dreadlocks on a person of Asian heritage? It's really a touch offensive to African-Americans. Don't you think?"

"Oh, hush with that PC mess, little snowflake." The Governor, rasping with vocal fry. "Miss Button? Here's my advice: Lose them dreads—L-O-O-S-E them awful things. This's South Carolina, and if you want ordinary folks on your side, you need to look like them. Now, like your smartypants sister said, we got a meeting to get ourselves to. Buh-bye, sugar," squeaking in that cute, aw-shucks way the pundits and right wing-leaning public found so persuasive. "It's a great day to be a South Carolinian."

Three-Rivers, bound for the Senate—the U. S. Senate. They even talked about vice president.

Of the nation.

Which left Thim destined as the Lee Atwater of the twenty-first century, and made Button want to vomit blood.

Despite Thim's personal feelings on issues of social justice, the push-polling Button's power-hungry sister had engineered in the last election made their opponents, both in primary and general and regardless of party, sound like godless homosexuals conducting black masses on Sunday morning instead of the church services at which they all trolled for votes. Button couldn't have been more ashamed of a family member if she'd had Dahmer or Manson or Dick Cheney for a sibling.

Wasn't fully partisan, this feeling. She despised all politicians. They all reported to the same master, that of mammon.

Thim, having put Button back on the private line. "What is this really about? You need money?"

"Nah."

"Do they need *anything* of substance from me?"

"No, Thim. Everything's okay." Button, clearing the tickle in her throat troubling her for weeks now; twisting and trying to pop her upper back, which had been bothering her, a pain sluicing down from clavicle into tender ribs. Late summer ragweed or other nettlesome plant, putting off spores or pollen or other particulate matter, that's what was wrong in the throat. Working out too hard, that caused the back issues. "Like I said. Checking on you. You're my sister. I love you."

Thim, duly grateful for the concern, concluded in her clipped and professional manner she'd see Button and their mutual forebears as soon as her ruthless, unforgiving and ambitious schedule would allow.

BUTTON, sitting on the edge of the bed, her nipples two hard nubbins aching to be kissed. Button, accessing her third eye, the energy rippling along the crown of her skull not unlike the first creeping high from two bong rips of killer kush from Colorado, like she'd had when she went out for the monumental Phish shows last year, an epic special treat, some of the best the band had played in years. Closing her ordinary eyes and seeing a purple pulse of energy, the chakra of her higher mind. Willing into being a notion of patience. All good things in all good times type-deal. Pulsing with this thought. Sending it to her mother, whose face she visualized.

This image, held there in her mind's eye.

Floating.

Mouth moving, but nothing coming out.

As though her mother's face actually there behind Button's eyelids. Backlit by the purple fire of intelligence. Of consciousness itself. Patience—patience and quiet, Button's message to her mother.

"Button-Button!" Tinky Sykes tumbled through the unlocked bedroom door with a crash, rattling the transom of the old doorframe. "Chowtime?"

Button, covering herself. "Will you. Give me a moment. Please."

Her mother, in housecoat and slippers, hair kinky and wild and black despite her age, smiled and held out her hands in supplication. "Chowtime. Ya know."

"Like, duh. I'm on it."

"Good-good. I go downstairs and wait."

As opposed to what? "Duh."

Looking her daughter up and down. "You naked."

"I'm fixing to shower."

"You skinny."

Button thanked her for the compliment.

"You shower. You stink-stink."

"You've no idea. How bad. I need this shower."

Her beaming smile, a polite and formal bow, returned by Button. Tinky Sykes backed out of her youngest daughter's bedroom. A routine.

Button, composing herself. Trying to return to the stillness and the glow, but saying, why bother. Going cough-cough and clearing her throat, which felt dry, like sandpaper.

Not drinking enough water. Kept trying to talk Trudy and Rabbit into putting an R/O system in at the bar, like Button had had done there in the Sykes house. Get that fluoride, and other toxins, out of her system. Critical. All life, originating from water. The original essential earthbound element of the life-experiment. Too much to go into.

But decalcifying the pineal gland—the third eye, suppressed in modern times by all sorts of means and for many reasons; too much to go into, redux— this was essential to effective higher consciousness functioning. Getting off the fluoride though? Super-essential. But too-too much to go into.

Her side, cramping. A stitch.

She hadn't stretched. You couldn't skip stretching, not after a hella power walk like today's.

Or rather, a physical manifestation of the burning desire to write to Heather.

Button took a moment to flex and bend. Felt the little pine cone inside her forehead squirming. Put out a thought-message, on repeat, to Heather:

I miss you. I miss you. I miss you.

◔❂◔

THIS ONE TIME? At an outdoor summer tour show?

Heather and Button, happy and high and in love with the music, cooked up a plot to communicate with the band by decorating a beachball using a beloved keepsake black chisel-point El Marko magic marker Heather had had since grade school and here wished to expend the last of its fading ink in this most important and sacred of purposes, a method of transmitting messages of adoration to Trey and the boys unimpeded by mediators, assuming they seat-surfed close enough to toss it onstage rather than letting the upraised hands of destiny, the general admission throng thousands strong clustered in front of the stage, determine whether their letter in beachball form ended up at the feet of their musical idols.

Phish: these nerdy dudes of prep-school privilege who met at Goddard College in Vermont when Button had been but a toddler; four doofuses and stoners who, instead of of geeks holing themselves for days on end up playing D&D or video games, practiced their instruments. Developed their chops, both technically and compositionally, refining the art of improvised musicianship to such a point they'd transmogrified into a cohesion union of four indisputable virtuosi, living embodiments of that Malcolm Gladwell, ten-thousand hours to mastery rubric, and here manifested to profitable artistic, business and socio-logical fruition. Phish. Amazing. The undisputed jam-band champs, at least once Jerry died.

To this end, Heather and Button schemed to tell Vermont's prog-rock favorite sons how they felt: how grateful, how excited, how happy, how fulfilled. In the campground near a legendary outdoor venue north of DC called Merriweather Post Pavilion, both stinky dirt surfers took turns writing their thoughts and symbols with deliberation and care on the taut vinyl of the inflated children's water toy. Afterwards, they let the air out for stowage and concealed carriage into the concert grounds, where they'd again take turns blowing it up, sitting there on the grass of the steep lawn. Sisters, on a mission.

"What is that?" Heather, scrunching up her nose at an odd symbol Button had drawn, like an upside-down question mark crossed with a cross. "It's familiar."

"I think it's an old heavy metal thing? I saw it painted on this big rock back home in the woods. Where school kids go to like, fuck and hang out. Party. That type-deal."

Heather's eyes grew wide: "Not Black Sabbath."

Button shook her head. "No—that 'Don't Fear the Reaper' bunch."

She relaxed. "Oh yeah—Blue Öyster Cult. But, why?"

"I dunno. Just some silly thing. They'll recognize it and think, ha ha." She didn't know why, really. But being of Gen X age, the musicians often covered music from the 70s and would see the symbol and chuckle. "They'll get it. Whatever 'it' is."

"Maybe."

"We'll find out next All Hallow's Eve. Eh?"

On Halloween the band always covered a classic rock album "Right! Then we'll know they got your message. Whatever it is."

But only one problem: Rain.

The El Marko love they'd inscribed became smeary like heartbroken mascara, all their thoughts and prayers melting into black tears of nonsense that stained their hands as though they were press operators in the basement of some newspaper building. They tossed it anyway, this despite admonitions and insults from the crowd of people all around in the sold-out, jammed pavilion of the amphitheater into which they'd weaseled their way like the show veterans they were.

No luck. The beachball caromed off the corner of Page McConnell's grand piano, falling into the security pit where it bounced off the rail and under the stage and disappeared forever.

The action did have one effect: McConnell, startled by the object hurled at him from the swirling mass of gray and black and white, hit a wrong chord, a terrible clam that caused bandleader Trey to scowl and shake his head at the audience.

Epic fail.

Heather at the set break, laughing and holding up her blackened fingers, looking as though she'd gotten booked down at the station, which would happen for real later that tour on what Button would forever think of as the ill-fated Fort Benjamin Harrison Gambit.

"That didn't work."

"Oh, well."

"Maybe paper airplanes next time?"

Heather, troubled. "Suddenly seems like an ego thing. The beachball."

"They already know we love them. Don't they?"

"Of course they do."

Button and Heather, hugging it out and dancing their asses off during the second set, which had been sick, totally sick, only four songs including a forty-minute 'Tweezer' that completely melted everyone's faces, the hallmark of a jammed-out frame, an all-timer. Beach ball didn't work, but by the end, they'd both forgotten, anyway. Or Button had.

How many more pure and innocent shows were there after that one? Without Heather, or with her, for that matter? Over the winter, they'd both gotten into the pharmies hard and heavy, but then Heather finished her degree and said, that's it, no more Phish, no more Button, see-ya. The beginning of the dark times.

❀✿❀

Relaxed and damp in her fuzzy robe downstairs, Button put together her mother's lunch, checked on the crock pot of black bean soup she'd put on this morning, and did prep work for dinner later by assembling a bowl of salad, everything but the avocado she'd slice right before serving to preserve its bright color. She'd meant to make the black beans last night, but after Rabbit grumbling at her about profaning the stage of his god-durned beloved Dixiana with that nuclear station claptrap, and getting home at one-thirty, she hadn't had it in her to chop onion and green pepper and garlic and cilantro. Full of self-doubt about disrupting the open-mic night. With her political ranting.

Eh. No second guessing. Only onward.

Oh, how he'd gone on and on with such pity and disappointment, though. That he'd been in the war, the great big one. and if it wasn't for the nuclear part, both in ending the war and fueling industry and providing power, there wouldn't never have been a Dixiana stage to care about profaning, nor a world in which a smart-assed little half-chink, as he liked to goad her when her grandfather wasn't around the bar (which wasn't often), could have a decent life and never work too hard for a living.

Now that, Button thought, had been an insult. If she retained any self-consciousness at all, and thanks to her daily Tao consultation and other consciousness and ego-mitigating work she didn't feel she did, it came when someone asked what she did, which was running front of house at a decrepit old honkytonk, a music hall more about the drinking and cigarette smoking than the songs, now. Taking care of Tinky Sykes, her mom, that'd been her true vocation, at least since her dad died.

Of cancer.

After working all those years at the plant.

"Here we are, mom-mom." Button, as happy a voice as she could muster, putting down the bowl of oats with honey and cinnamon and the tea and slices of fruit, apples and grapes.

Her mother, however, always wanting rice, rice, rice, which Button refused to honor: Tinky Sykes may have been called Thanh Thi Trinh and had been a poor farm girl from the Thua Thien-Hue province of Vietnam, a fertile farming region sprayed during the war with a certain notorious mixture of 2,4 dichlorophenoxy acetic acid and 2,4,5 trichlorophenoxyacetic acid more cheerfully and famously known as Agent Orange, but this was America and it was getting on into the second decade of a new century, and we didn't eat rice for breakfast. They'd put on a new war or two to ring in the new era, but Vietnam had been a long long time ago, which was how her dad always wanted it. Never mind that the war killed him anyway, and this without ever being wounded in combat. No rice. If that made sense, and if it didn't, Button didn't give a rip. Fruit and whole grains other than rice—oatmeal.

Buddy Sykes brought home a troubled relationship with the war. His pal

Lucky Latham from over near Red Mound made it home too, but left their friend Ronnie Pettus over there, which seemed to have affected them both in a manner acute.

Once, when Button and Thim, already a snooty little asshole, had been prepubescent schoolgirls, their father picked them up one afternoon and taken them for a side trip. It had surprised Button to see Mr. Latham, who worked at the IGA as the produce manager, sitting in the front seat of the car, a boxy Buick.

"We got to run ourselves a quick errand, me and Lucky." Her father, crinkling the ruddy skin around his blue eyes, both traits which he'd given her, but coupled with her Asian features always made for a striking combination that hadn't often been called beautiful or even pretty.

"Where?" Thim demanded. "For what?"

"We need to run on over by the cemetery, and while we do, I want y'all to sit right here in the car and get started on your homework."

"Dad-da," Thim screeched, her face pinched. "But I don't want to."

"I don't wanna, neither." Button, echoing her big sister, because back then, Thim could do no wrong in her eyes. "Nuh-uh. Go home."

"Too bad, little angels." Her daddy, driving on over and turning into Forest Knoll Garden cemetery, scene of the action for ghosts and more ghosts, it seemed. "We'll get you home to Mom-mom soon enough."

"We old codgers won't be gone over yonder too long," Mr. Latham said in his country drawl, the thickest Edgewater County had to offer. "It's something we got to do, though. Your daddy and me."

"Yes sir," Button's daddy added with a solemn sigh. "Yes sir, it is." He clapped Lucky on the bony, middle-aged shoulder, both seeming froggy in their throats and wet-eyed in a way that Button never remembered seeing her father look.

Button and Thim both sat in silence and watched, but only Thim had been able to spy what was going on—Button, too short to see over the brick wall running along Common Street.

"They have their arms around each other!" Thim whispered. "And Mr. Lucky, he looks like he's crying."

"I want to go home," Button remembered saying. "I'm scared."

"Well, I'm not. But this is weird. Oh, my—I think Daddy is crying, too. Aw."

Button, going *boohoo*.

"Something's wrong. Something's really wrong." Thim gripped Button's tiny arm and snarled, the older sister's principal method of communication to her diminutive sibling. "I'm going to sort this out."

Button, remembering how Thim had blown the horn, and the men raced back with red faces, annoyed but not yelling at them. A silent drive home, first dropping Lucky Latham off at the IGA where he worked.

Later, when she'd been older, Button asked her father about that particular day. He explained it had been the anniversary of Ronnie Ed Pettus dying over in Vietnam, how he and Lucky always paid tribute in the cemetery. It'd also been the first time she remembered seeing The Dixiana sign, and the mural on the side of the building, noticing because both men seemed to give the rooster a little wave as they passed. She assumed her father's reticence about discussing Vietnam and the war had to do with Ronnie Ed. Only later was she told that the reasons were more about national security issues than sentiment. That, and personal shame. A complicated story.

She'd always and forevermore associated The Dixiana with that first instance of consideration regarding death and loss, and the implications of being alive and then not, so maybe getting fired from the honkytonk, as she expected Rabbit would do today, had been in the cards all along: being stuck here in Tillman Falls felt like death for some time now, even before she'd left the first time, as a teenager going off to college.

Perhaps leaving The Dixiana would be like a resurrection. If only she didn't have her mother, and Grandpa Burnie, Button, at her still-young age, could decide how she wanted to live the rest of her life.

Hell, maybe she'd go out on tour again—that'd been the peak of her music-loving life, not working at the ramshackle old Dixiana, and not being the care-taker to the sick and the old and the dying. Phish tour—the first access to higher consciousness and sensing the high vibration of life as well as the nadir, dwelling deep down in puddles of muck. The thick strawberry goo of oblivion. A long time ago, now. Could one go home again?

◐ ✾ ◑

Button, dishes in the washer, trotted back upstairs and checked her phone to see a missed call: Trudy.

What the hell—Uncle Rabbit firing her through his sergeant-at-arms? Undignified.

Trudy?

Really?

But hadn't the whole deal been undignified? From the start? Her being given the easy job and a steady, if small, paycheck by her granddad's best friend didn't feel terribly dignified, ever. Felt like a handout. A favor.

Truth? She didn't want to get fired for having made her big anti-nuke speech from the stage last night. The Dixiana gig had been the most she'd ever done professionally with her media degree.

"What up, dog?" Button greeted Trudy. "I'm canned? Or what?"

Trudy's voice came thin and constricted, like when pretty much anything from the smallest issue to the biggest bullshit went awry, like how she sounded over the constant brouhaha about the old mural. "Oh, sugar—it's Mr. Rabbit. He's done had a heart thingie. Or a thrombo. Or something—"

Button sputtered a series of stupid questions. "Where is he—is he—okay?"

Trudy, suffering menopause hot flashes and rampaging emotional tears and drinking too much, in Button's opinion, here devolved into mewling and weepy despair. "They carted him off to the *hos-hos*-hospital," heaving for air.

Rabbit Pettus, a heart attack? At his age? Bad. How surprised she'd be if he lived.

"What do you? Need me to do? Wait—" Gripped by another facet. "Where's my granddad?"

"Somebody gave Burnie a ride to the hospital." Grandpa Burnie drank away his days at the bar, catching a ride into town with Button on her way to the walking path. "He's all right, sugar."

"Good. Now: what about you?"

"I'm going over yonder to sit in the waiting room with Mama Runelle. Look here—you go and get the bar ready to open. When Mr. Rabbit wakes up and sees me sitting there grinning, first thing he's gonna ask is, Trudy Pirkle, who the hell's over at The Dixiana? Won't he?"

Button said, um. "Sounds like Uncle Rabbit."

"You durn right. We got to open tonight, or he'll kick all our asses when he wakes up. So come in soon as you can. Help Fridge get the kitchen fired up."

Button, thinking all this irrational, but going along. "He doesn't need my help."

"You got to watch that nitwit every second. Be my eyes, girl. Cut my limes and lemons."

"I'll be. Your eyes, ears. And fruit knife."

"That's what I want to hear."

Button, only half joking, but unable to resist: "I didn't give. Him. A heart attack. By getting up and profaning his? Ya know. Music venue. With my politics. Did I?"

"Maybe you did. You little asshole. Now go and get my—get his place open for business." Breaking down again. "Lord, say a prayer for Mr. Rabbit. And for Mama Runelle, and sweet Roy Earl too, girl."

"Sure. Thing. Trudy."

Button, hanging up. If only prayer, as they all thought of their mystical practice, worked that way. A version of it can, but it neither originates nor illumines from without. But, oh—plenty of ways to influence one's personal and external reality. Methods not up for public discussion. Those who talk don't know, et cetera.

Muttering to herself. "Yeah—you tend bar. Sling liquor. Right. That's what. You should be doing. With your non-using life."

Now her gut turned to stone: wait. If Rabbit died, the ramifications, duh, went way beyond her getting fired. What was to become of the honkytonk? The honkytonk she had to run tonight?

She could picture the subhead on Bill Wimmel's story about Uncle Rabbit's demise: End of an Era. The thought made her soul clench with sadness. And loss.

Pulling on a pair of baggy jeans and slipping her size-five feet into worn Birkenstocks, last she chose a favored royal-blue Phish concert T she'd snagged in Colorado with artwork spoofing Creature from the Black Lagoon. Button breathed in a measured, conscious rhythm, endeavoring to stay detached and centered.

A car door slammed downstairs, followed by her grandfather's aggrieved voice—he would be heartbroken; his best friend, dying.

She smiled and chanted that all is normal, death is natural, all will be well, after which Button Sykes went to get her people, and Mr. Rabbit's honkytonk, straightened out, squared away, and fully Awake.

CHRISTY BEAUDOCK AND
HIS DADDY

Christy, he thinks:

Daddy and me is off on the wrong foot tonight, boy. Whoo-wee.

"Christy," Christy's Daddy calls from the kitchen. It ain't far down the little hallway to the back bedroom which ought to be his, but is Christy's cause he had to have more room to lay his big old body down. "Get your fat ass in here."

Christy, he don't pay his Daddy much mind. He's on one of his bender type-deals. And Christy has his games to keep to. It's his routine, and it's comfortable and it's safe—these are the feelings that wash over Christy when he's alone with his games, and the world, his Daddy-world, is shut out.

"Christy."

Christy, he snorts and picks at one of his zits and keeps on with the stick in his hands, the beloved flight simulator game—it's called White Hat Aviator, played like you were the POV of a pilot. This game speaks to him in a way all the soldier and zombie and war ones do not. Soaring through the pixilated CGI sky. Freedom. Never been on no plane though.

The day his Daddy brung home the console, Christy, yeah, his life got better. His Daddy had got the game console from an n-word, he said, who owed him money in a business deal. Another of his deals. Christy already had a PC that he'd gotten the same way, same story. Always the same with his Daddy.

Christy, thinking he should get some real flight simulator software. Learn to fly for real. This game console stuff, as he'd read in an online forum dedicated to the platform, was for sissies when it came to flight simulation. He would check out the latest software, maybe find it on piratebay.com. Lucky his Daddy liked to look at TV so much, so at least they had cable and an internet line. Christy don't know what he'd do without a pipe to connect to the net.

But his Daddy, he had gone mental if he thought Christy, at fifteen now, don't know what the money-mess all is about. Not that the doper hid it.

Christy, he thinks to himself that his Daddy would be a better Daddy if he tried hiding his rock and meth and oxy ways. And dealing ways. Like Christy a big blonde curlyheaded monkey at the zoo that don't know what them zookeepers keep talking about.

His Daddy, he ain't got good sense. No; he don't.

Christy, trying to figure a way out.

Sorta.

Not so much anymore, not after his Daddy come home with the game console. His granny, with all her money, never got him a gift like that, not even at Christmastime which she didn't seem to celebrate no way. This present had come out of nowhere. Just appeared in Christy's sweaty palms. He had been wanting one. That was for durn sure. Wanting it hard. Hard as he could. Shutting his eyes and thinking about them games. Wishing.

And dang if it hadn't come to him.

A wish come true. Wasn't no denying it.

There it was.

Console.

In his freaking room.

Christy, he wants to think it's like magic. That he made this small miracle happen. But he knows it's what they call coincidence. Magic ain't real.

"CHRISTY—COME on, now. I got to lay a rap on you bout some shit."

Lord help me. This is gonna be some mess of his. Sighing and ducking his head, he goes down the hallway.

Smoking and twitchy—whoo-wee, what a surprise—Daddy sits across the table looking all walleyed and pooch-mouthed, the way he always does when he's in over his head with some mess. When he's up to some crap. Christy's Daddy, his big bottom lip is all sticking out, and Christy thinks it ought to have a hook hanging out of it like a crappie caught in the river.

He reckons what he wants to say out of that stinking butthole of a mouth of his. It's like Christy, he can see green vapors coming out. As though his Daddy a wastehead, meth-mouthed dragon. "Christy. Look here."

"Daddy, I sure wish you'd quit bothering me." Christy, in his mealy mouthed way, sounding so small compared to his bulk. Like a little girl, they taunted him. Christy not only got a girl's name, he sounds like one. That's what they said, following him around and telling him he smelled bad. And that his skin looked pink like a baby bunny rabbit, and his wiry golden hair and cleft lip and pointing out his appearance all the time, making him flush and look pinker than normal and everyone going *haw-haw*, a weirdo albino. And calling him dumb-dumb.

Which he isn't. It's his secret that he ain't so dumb. Which they was all gonna find out one day soon.

"Christy." Stubbing out his cigarette and leaning forward. "You not gonna believe this shit. I—I found out today I got to pay taxes. Five thousand dollars in taxes," and taking another drink of that pisswater rotgut that makes the devil come up inside him. That he drinks more of when the right drugs ain't around. His Daddy laughs all high and silly, snot blowing out of his nose. Wiping his sleeve across. Cussing under his breath. "And I don't know where I'm gonna get it."

Christy, he shakes his head. "Well, I can't do nothing about it."

"You gonna help me get it, is what."

"No I ain't."

"You ain't even heard how yet!"

"Don't care." Christy fixes himself some cereal-supper and goes to sit on the couch and watch TV.

He thinks:

Wait—I read somewhere that you ought to not do that: you ought not to read nor watch TV while you eat food, cause food is sacred and should be worthy of your full concentration. And you ought to bless it and feel thankful and making so it fills your body with something besides itself, if that makes any sense.

Christy's not sure it does, but turns off the TV anyway. *Boy, but I'm glad to have cereal and milk to eat,* comes his blessing of the cereal. He cups his hands together over it; his palms feel warm. Thinks, *I am grateful.*

"What the fuck you doing over there, dumbass?"

"Fixing to eat my cereal."

"Look like you was praying over it."

"So what if I was?"

"Don't start none of that in this house. You hear me?"

"I wasn't praying over no durn bowl of cereal."

"Better not be. Religion's like dope that don't give you no buzz. Stupid. But anyways, this five thousand dollars. I got to talk this out."

So while he talks his mess through, Christy, he sits eating cereal and trying not to read the *Edgewater Advocate* sitting on the coffee table amidst some of Daddy's dope mess, beer cans and cigarette butts. It don't take long for him to finish eating anyway, though, and he picks up the paper and glances through, cause smart people keep up with what's going on. Least that's what the teachers have always taught Christy.

He can't half see, though. The words, all blurry. He reckons he needs glasses. That's what his Daddy ought to be getting money for. But it wasn't worth even bringing up. Christy's Daddy, he don't believe in doctors no more than he did praying.

Christy, he turns to the **OPINION** page and reads an editorial about rezoning parts of Common Street from res to commercial, which ain't too interesting, nor is a letter from some weirdo named Button, like some fairy tale character's name, complaining bout the nuclear plant, or some such mess.

Before a few weeks ago, Christy hadn't never give that plant no thought. It was just there. Thinks now, though: after we learned about radiation in science class, since then I ain't quit thinking about how all that stays inside the buildings and don't get into the river. And all of us, somehow. If something's invisible, how can you tell?

Christy asked the science teacher Mr. Bates in the hallway about how all that radiation don't get all in us, but he said if it wasn't safe, they wouldn't put it nowhere near people. Mr. Bates would know. It made Christy relax.

"Christy."

"WHAT, Daddy?"

"I got to get that money. Somehow or another."

Christy explains how he ain't no dummy. "It ain't April."

"So what?"

"That's when taxes is due. And so, I know you don't owe nobody taxes on nothing. Not right now, anyway."

Christy's Daddy does his that's-bullcrud face. Licks his lips. "What—you learnt that in school?"

Christy didn't care for admitting when he had learned from other people. Felt more comfortable believing he had always known stuff. But the truth: "From looking at the durn newspaper."

Christy's Daddy don't like the way this is going. "It ain't nothing but lies. Like that shitrag you poking through. If it was me, I'd wipe my ass with it before I'd read it."

"The news ain't lies."

"The shit it ain't. On TV, at least. You can guarantee it." He waves his fingers all around like a crazy person. "They put stuff in there you can't see, messages and crap, that make you do stuff." He gets all wound up. Lights a cigarette, drinks down his liquor. "Makes you buy shit. And more shit. And—and—and fill your durn head up with bullshit. Like drugs is bad and will mess you up. That ain't true—it ain't the drugs what do it. It's them secret fucken signals, Christy." Tapping his temple with his cigarette hand. "They messing with all our heads."

Christy, he gets bored with this talk. "For somebody so afraid of it, you sure look at TV a lot."

"Lies. Nothing but lies."

Christy thinks, *Huh. Daddy ain't nothing but lies himself. Like I can't see that. Like I ain't been lied to by him. I figured that out when I was twelve. And after Granny told me some stuff. I can't. Quite make sense of yet.*

Stuff about my missing momma.

Christy, he feels the only thing ain't lies is the game console. Christy, his life changed. It got better. But that's the only time he would say it about his Daddy and all his mess. "Them taxes—there's your durn lie."

"You don't know jack-shit bout grownup shit like taxes," slurring his Ss like one of them drunks over across the river in Easton. "Sides, they got other kinds," chewing his cuticles and drinking his nasty rotgut. "Taxes you pay other times of the durn year. It's—it's property taxes."

"On what?"

"On the trailer."

"We pay rent on this trailer. We don't own it. You only pay property taxes on—"

Christy's Daddy, he whacks Christy upside the head. Swinging so hard he almost falls off his chair; his hand glances off Christy's blonde curls.

Used to hurt when he whacked Christy. Yes it did. Not no more. Christy's Daddy, he's so small and meth-weak: on the down-cycle, chewing the insides of his cheeks and sweating and scratching and twitching and picking black bloody boogers out of his scaly nose.

"Nuh-uh—don't start no mess with me."

"You hush that smart mouth of your'n."

Christy, so hot inside. Not like when he imagines naked girls. A different heat. Christy, from here on out, he don't mean a word he says. "I'm real sorry."

"Yeah—me too. The day your fat ass was borned."

"I know. I'm sorry." And durn if most of the time Christy ain't sorry for real.

"You ought to be."

Christy, he's being a smart-ass, but his Daddy don't realize it. What a surprise. "I'm so so sorry, Daddy."

Now, he says. "About them taxes."

Christy, he wants to tell him, *I might only be fifteen, a kid, but I know the money you want ain't for no durn taxes. Daddy, you don't do nothing but trade money with people—at places like The Dixiana, and the Pot O'Gold out on the west side highway, and Ape Hangers, the biker bar not far from the Bait & Pawn; in houses and in cars and trucks out at the truck stop, and who knows where else. You don't pay no more taxes than the man in the moon.* That's the way Christy's Granny would put it.

CHRISTY'S GRANNY, she'll sit there and shake her head. Says she never could do nothing with his Daddy, and is thankful to have her girls who live with her in the big house over in Red Mound, all these young girls she finds and helps to get on their feet again from troubles and whatnot.

Christy's Daddy, though, he calls her—his own mama—a whore and a viper. Says if he didn't need her to help him with Christy's fat dumb ass, he wouldn't have nothing to do with her.

"Bitch's lucky I don't break her damn neck." He said this other night, and Christy started to go over and do that to his Daddy. "Her and every one of them trashy whores of her'n."

"You better quit talking about granny like that."

"And you, fat boy, best watch your ass around women. If they turn on you, they'll kill you soon as look at you. Suck you dry, first. And I don't mean in a good way."

Christy, his thoughts unbridled:

When? What time's it gonna be? When I decide to hurt him for real?

Maybe soon.

Next time he hits me.

Might as well—I'm gonna live with Granny instead of him. Take care of her. She's old and can't hardly get around. Needs somebody to take care of her. And there, I can play games and be left alone totally. Except for her, and what I could do with her.

For her. I mean. She can't do nothing. She's old.

The point is she needs somebody—me. Because she can't do like she wants. At her age. Which is like, fifty.

Why he don't seem to think it matters, I got no clue. I ain't no trash. I'm gonna go live with Granny. Saying it over and over. Sounds like a song. A stupid song in Christy's head.

⊙❀⊙

CHRISTY, he decides to play along. Play a different kind of game while he fixes another bowl of cereal, this time blessing it only with his thoughts and not his hands. "What you want me to do about them taxes?"

Drinks the bourbon. Smokes and nods. At least Christy's Daddy ain't on pills right now—he seems halfway awake. "You're gonna help me. For once. If you wasn't so fat, you could get you a good job, for one."

Christy tells him, I got school and that's more important than some job so's he can get money for his stupid fake-ass taxes.

"You ought to do like me and quit that school." He smokes and taps his temple. "All that mess gets inside your head. Make you into a robot."

"It don't make you no robot. It teaches you stuff."

"You don't know shit. Fat face."

Daddy picks on Christy like everyone at the school. Calls him some of the same names. It don't matter. It don't bother Christy none. Not like it used to.

Or so he keeps telling himself. To keep from hurting his Daddy.

Christy, he's breathing hard anyway. Getting up the gut to tell him, I want to live with granny. But Christy, he's scared, all sudden-like. Cold jelly inside his big jiggly stomach.

He tries to say the words, but it's like in them dreams when you're trying to yell out, but can't. Something's stopping Christy. It's like an invisible PRESENCE that stalks him in his dreams, his recurring dream when it comes over him like this. Cold jelly again, but throughout the body, and he can feel the PRESENCE and it is evil and in the dreams it gets inside him.

One time in a dream he could levitate, like the PRESENCE got inside him and lifted his big fat body up and his feet went off the floor of his room. Terrified and trying to scream, but can't.

Like now, in making your wishes known to the real Presence in the room, the god-awful presence of Daddy. His back, bumping up against the ceiling of the room in that dream, and the trailer started rocking and fell away and the PRESENCE was gone and Christy, he was flying under his own power. Flying up and away.

Flying. He wants to be flying right now, on the simulator—it's on pause back in his room. Christy, he only came in here to get cereal, and a glass of water, which in this trailer comes out the tap yellow, like pisswater.

"You never done nothing bout the nasty water coming out the pipes."

"I'm gonna do something bout that." Christy's Daddy, sucking on a cigarette with that fisheye face of his. "Damn if I ain't. That ain't right."

Mayfield Acres. It's got about twenty trailers stacked in the pine trees outside Tillman Falls going toward Red Mound where the Indians is buried, where it's all scrubby and sandy and it's all poor people. But Christy, he says to himself, he says, it ain't on no dirt road or nothing. Mayfield Acres ain't that bad.

But he also knows there ain't no landlord you can call. Not less you ain't paid up, and then they come round for the money. Two black men run the trailer park. They're bad-asses.

"Yeah. Daddy, I'm-a talk to landlords for you."

"No, you ain't."

"Somebody got to. You're afraid of them."

"Smart to know who I ought to be afraid of."

But he don't want to talk about the water. Nope. His Daddy's got another idea. And when he tells Christy? It makes him sick to his stomach, much worse than the yellow water out the grungy old taps in this trailer.

THEY BEEN LIVING HERE three years, since Christy, he was twelve. Wasn't but a 36 waist back then, now a 48 and way taller than his Daddy.

Christy, he's-a gonna beat ass one of these nights when he gets like this, all drunk up and full of dumb ideas about where he will get the money to make up for what he lost gambling, or the money he lost turning over a brick of marijuana, as his Daddy finally confesses.

Christy don't want to go back to his flight simulator. Nope. He's gotta hear this shit.

"I feel like I owe you a straight talk, son." His Daddy, pouring an inch of bourbon into another glass. And handing it to Christy!?

"You're a man. Look at you, now."

Sniffing the liquor, Christy, he's all like, I dunno. "You sure?"

Daddy starts to blubber—what?! "You drink this, son, instead of that mess oozing outta them taps." It's a mealymouthed voice like Christy ain't never heard, pouting and whining. "I'm-a tell them buttholes what I think about this trailer and the water."

Christy, thinking his Daddy done lost it totally, takes himself a sip. It's tiny. The booze stings and stinks and tastes like brown Listerine.

"That's the good stuff there." Christy, forging rapport, repeats a line from a movie.

"You bet it is, son."

Christy, he says funny stuff to people sometimes. To make them like him. Nobody does though. Not even his Daddy. Unless he gets pitiful like this.

This is important, his Daddy says, because he ain't got no one else to talk to. "Mama left so long ago, and never looked back," Daddy says. "Left our asses to fend."

Granny told Christy the truth, though. That his Daddy's lying. That Mama went to jail for breaking into people's houses. Later, a black girl also in the jail stabbed Christy's Mama over money she owed for cigarettes.

"Your poor sweet mama," his Granny said. "She didn't deserve that."

Christy asked. "How much time that judge give her?"

"It wasn't but for three years. She would've got out," Granny said, all breaking down, "in another six months. When that black little shit-ass stabbed her."

"What'd they do to the black girl?"

His Granny, scoffing and saying nothing had happened—the little n-word was already doing life for murder. Christy reckoned to Granny that since the killer was in for life, what else could they do to her? Granny had screamed out they could kill that black-assed bitch in the electric chair, that's what. For icing

Christy's mama and leaving Granny alone, stuck with Christy and Christy's Daddy.

That had made Christy cry, finding out what happened to his mama. And how Daddy wasn't nothing but a liar. Granny said he was protecting Christy, but Daddy ain't never protected him from shit, y'all. Daddy's bitch-ass self, worthless.

I'm-a make his sorry ass sorry for all this mess. I'm-a find out why mama was breaking into houses instead of taking care of me. Instead of putting his paychecks in the bank, and fixing suppers like people supposed to. Why.

Why.

Why?

Right?!

Wouldn't y'all ask these questions, y'all?

It all becomes clear as a dang bell—clear as Luzianne iced tea—when Daddy, that scrawny shit, tells Christy what he's got in mind to get this money. And this what Dr. Phil would call a bonding moment, like he ought to be telling Christy how to mess with a girl, y'all.

Instead, he's going all like, "What we ought to pull is a stickup, you and me. We go over into Beauchamp County, hit one of them juke joints like the Monkey's Uncle. Wait outside for last call, and their drunk asses coming out to their cars, and roll in there jacked and hollering. Easy money."

Christy takes another sip of his bourbon. It does something this time—it hits the stomach fast. The cold jiggling jelly turns warm—different from the girl-warm, and way different from the snapping-Daddy's-neck hot that comes over Christy sometimes like sickness. His voice is more present, now. It comes out BIG. "I ain't pulling no strong-arm robbery for you, Daddy. You made mama break into them houses, but YOU CAN'T MAKE ME DO NOTHING."

"And then's there the Gas Chief," his Daddy says, ignoring Christy—the big voice didn't work? It would have to get bigger. "One of them towelheads they keep bringing here done took over. There ain't no real jobs no more, and you can't own nothing cause of motherfuckers coming off the boat and over the borders and buying it all up—but who's giving them the damn money? O-bummer, that's who. You think I could go into a bank—a white man—and get money? Shit. Man, I tell you what, the world ain't right no more. We ought to take the money from them. My boy over yonder, he says he knows for a fact that on a busy weekend day? Them shit-asses bringing in three, four thousand dollars."

"Thought you needed five thousand dollars."

"Close enough."

Christy thinks about them people—they're from Iraq. They come over thanks to some Christian thing—they were Christians back over there. Lillyanne Theodore told Christy all this. She said her daddy knows everything going on in Tillman Falls—he owns that place on the corner that used to be Lucinda's diner.

Christy marvels: she's so beautiful. Not Lucinda—Lillyanne.

"And what you gonna do is drive, son. That's why I been saying I should teach you, soon. So you can be the driver on some jobs we pull together. Don't that sound good?"

"Daddy, we ain't even got a car, though. You're so full of it."

His Daddy, cussing, rears back to hit Christy again.

But before he can, and with a cold fire dancing in Christy's stomach like he ain't never felt—a fire like courage—he draws back and knocks his Daddy end over Sunday across the kitchen.

Christy's Daddy, lying crumpled against the cabinets, drools and sputters and says hold on, now.

Rough and rowdy like a wrestler, Christy, he picks up his Daddy. Squeezes him.

"Damn, son. Let me down."

Squeezing harder. "I ain't robbing no Gas Chief."

Christy's Daddy's eyes bug out. His voice ain't nothing but a wheeze. "All right—all right, boy."

Christy puts him down. He tells his Daddy he don't give two craps about this plan to pull jobs.

"I need me five thousand dollars, and I gotta get it. You know why, son?"

"Cause you gonna make me steal it for you?"

"No—because I done prayed for it to happen." He pours himself another drink. "Yeah, I keep picturing it in my head."

Christy sits dumbfounded.

His Daddy busts out laughing. Drinks some more. "Fooled ya."

"Don't joke about praying."

"Look here, now," rubbing his neck and cussing Christy for knocking him sideways. "Hear me out on this."

The plan: Christy will go over tomorrow to the Gas Chief, and he'll play the video games and watch the comings and goings, as his Daddy keeps putting it. "And the times when money is dropped."

From all that lingo, Christy can tell his Daddy's been watching TV or movies about boneheads pulling a heist, and he can tell because his Daddy ain't got the good sense to come up with no plan like himself. It's like Granny always says: He ain't got the sense God give a turnip.

But Christy, much smarter than anyone knew, with no plans on robbing anybody; playing along for one secret reason, to make possible the opportunity to talk to Aisha Jubouri, the daughter of the man and woman who own the station.

Unlike with Lillyanne Theodore, Christy, he thinks he might have a chance with the new girl: Aisha doesn't go to the school with everyone else, and so she don't know Christy is Special Ed. With her, he's got a chance at friendship, and maybe love. Christy, he's heard folks talk about love for as long as he can remember, and durn if he ain't ready to feel what it is. Because what's inside now is a big, fat nothing.

ROY AND MAMA RUNELLE

With the loud Taurus engine modified from its factory settings by Trudy's troglodyte biker husband thrumming under your nuts, Trudy, roaring down good old River Ridge Road. The farther you get from The Dixiana, the better you feel.

You speed by the lonely WABA radio tower with its red eye, the tower you saw so well only a short while ago from your tin can, frantic, thumbing your microphone switch and peering, desperate, for those landing lights.

The tiny cinderblock radio station has been supplanted by a two-story brick structure next to the original building, with two stations, an FM and an AM version, now broadcasting. Progress. Good. You've had satellite radio for years, available to you across a broad platform of devices. You don't know from FM and AM anymore.

"Does anybody still listen to WABA? Or any radio station?"

"Rabbit got us satellite at the bar. Got it at home, too. I got hooked."

"Surprised he agreed to put it in. Can't neither one of them stand anything to do with computers."

"We got a PC in the office, finally."

"You got a POS?"

She snickered. "A piece of shit? Yeah, I know a few."

"Hardy har. A point-of-sale system."

"Still regular old cash registers. I replace them pretty regular. Don't hold up worth nothing. Not like them old ones when I started there. They recognize my face at the Office Depot in Dentsville."

"I remember them well, those registers. Learning to change the receipt tape."

"Expect you do."

"Remember it all well. Too well."

A heavy silence. Trudy, drumming her long nails on the steering wheel.

The turn off; all the trees and greenery nearby cut way back. Looked like a power-company special, whole sides of mature trees hacked away from the lines. Had to be done. Too bad they couldn't get these lines buried.

A sign reading END STATE MAINTENANCE, knocked over into weeds growing high and deep. "*Fudge.*"

Your sugary expletive causes Trudy to scream and slam on the brakes at the dirt road leading to the Pettus driveway. "What on earth—?"

"You telling me some drunk redneck hit that this far off the road?"

"I seen stranger things in Edgewater County. Damn, boy—you like to scared the mess out of me."

Around the long curve she pulls into the driveway framed by crepe myrtles standing taller than such trees had any right to; many moons ago, since before your time, the Glasscock driveway had been planted the same. Mama Runelle always said she and Letty got themselves into a competition with one another.

She turns right into the new yard instead of left toward the old house set back in the overgrowth, which still doesn't feel right. A glimpse of the original Pettus house inspires a vision of the wood paneling and the metal decorative peacock above the console television where your earliest socialization occurred; those myriad afternoons and evenings absorbing every frame of the *Star Treks* and *Losts in Space* and *Gilligan's Heroes* and *Hogan's Island* and *Green Petticoat Junction Acres*, and the game shows, *The Price is Matched* and *Right Game* and *Wheel of Jeopardy*, and your scattered mind begins racing with undisciplined thought-patterns characterized by misremembered TV show titles:

You are panicking.

Cars—vehicles—conveyances parked every which way. Cars and cars.

Shit-fire: Walking into a mob scene. You can't imagine what you to say to your poor bereaved Mee-maw. Can't predict her condition.

"You all right? You're breathing hard."

"I'm okay. All catching up with me."

"I know, sugar."

Trudy pulls under the big magnolia against which you'd sit and read comics and later books, novels and history and everything you could get your hands on, and you look with pride at the glow from the high-pressure sodium streetlamp illuminating the well-tended yard of the house you built for the grandparents—for your grandmother. A Queen Anne Victorian, elegant and classic and eternal, all while being less than six years old.

Why'd you build it?

Easy. One day you looked at all the money you had. Thought for all the rancor between you and your granddaddy, how his hardworking example had inspired the greatness you'd achieved. How you had to give back, at last, to the elderly couple saddled with raising their orphaned, pink cheeked grandbaby. The house, a keeper painted in a class-act battleship gray and burgundy wine motif the paint consultant had called Night Dream. In this artificial light, however, the palette appears a ghastly ochre and black, like a Halloween-deco-rated haunted mansion ready a month too early.

☼☀◉

Your hug with Trudy in the vehicle-filled yard of your childhood home lingers. She pulls away, but you hold on.

In a fevered trance, you kiss the side of her neck.

A nascent hard-on forms against your thigh.

Against Trudy.

"Whoa, whoa, whoa," sounding stricken and pushing you away. "I got a man at home waiting for me. He might not be worth a damn, but I can't come home having kissed nobody, neither."

A cold rush of reality. "I don't—that was—I'm mixed up."

"Baby." Gentle, taking your hand. "I know you're all messed up. Can't imagine. Now go see your grandmother. I got to get back to work."

"Thanks for the ride."

"You really got your own plane?" You notice a certain hard and shim-mering curiosity in Trudy's eyes.

You tell her, yup. "A Piper Meridian."

"Dang." She gets faraway. "Rabbit always said—says—how good you done in life. I've always been so happy for you."

Wait—the way she says 'happy,' it's like a tell: An energetic reaction seems to crackle in the air. *Is she expressing regret*?

Trudy, sneaking a quick peck on the cheek. "Call me tomorrow. Or just come down to the bar—I'll have it open around lunchtime."

"Jesus—I understand about tonight. But dang, close the bar tomorrow."

"I can't, hon. It's Saturday. Rabbit would—"

"My granddaddy's dead," you say, direct and cocksure. You're in Mr. Owner mode now, the first of what will be myriad instances of you telling someone all about who is in charge now, the initial moment of realizing:

You are the new owner of The Dixiana.

"I don't care what day of the week it is."

"But Saturday's when we make our nut."

You can hear your Pa-paw saying it—it's drilled into your head, too, but didn't always translate to your own businesses. Weekday lunchtime made the fruitshake nut. You do not know from Saturday being the big day. "Still. I'm ordering you not to open."

"Ordering? Is that right."

"Asking, then. A wreath on the door. What's happened to everybody's sense of Southern decorum?"

Her arms, folded. A different energy. Defiance.

Okay, then. "You remember when old Dubya came that time to get barbecue?"

She looks at you like, yeah, right; I forgot when the President stopped in. "Duh."

"I'm the decider."

"I get it." Trudy, stiffening and cooling like a sudden frost of crystallized freezer burn growing in an old tub of generic IGA ice cream, that brand your grandmother always buys. "Respect, and all? But I'm gonna go and open anyway, hon. It's what we do."

"We."

"We all need the money, Roy Earl. We can't miss a Saturday shift."

For now, you stop yourself from saying what you'd like. Does not compute, this attitude. You get what you want; you call the shots.

Money. Plenty of money.

Your leg, twitching. Itching to put that girl in her place.

But it ain't the time.

Instead: "Hey—so open, then. If you think it's what he'd want."

"Besides, Burnie Sykes wouldn't have anywhere to go if I don't." Trudy says this with a wearied air suggesting Burnie's wellbeing may be the least of it all rather than a true motivation. "Open for lunch tomorrow. Like normal."

"I'm sure he's real broken up."

"Button says he ain't right in the head, anyway. Not since losing his wife and son so close together."

You tell her you're sorry to hear it. "Pa-paw being gone won't help matters."

A lump forms in your throat. Reality settles around your neck and shoulders. You grab her hand, squeeze. She squeezes back.

Trudy drives away in a cloud of glowing dust, puttering back down the long driveway, the giant crepe myrtles illuminated in red from receding Taurus taillights. Realizing how she only wants to get to the honkytonk and keep it running and profitable gives you a fresh jolt of excitement, seeing this non-owner employee demonstrating such commitment and zeal toward the enterprise.

Trudy. She will be of use to you.

And Button? Button Sykes? Now there's a name you've not heard in a long,

long time, not to go all Obi-Wan on everybody. A little freak, as you recall. Who knew what to expect from her now.

⚙

HESITATING IN THE YARD, you listen with horror at the babble of voices inside, like a bustling house party underway. If you felt reluctant to face your bereaved grandmother, navigating a crowd of strangers makes you want to vanish in a puff of logic. Feeling foolish and discombobulated, you wish you could take a pill to escape. Or drink a few beers. But that's never the answer to anything.

Now you must go and see people.

Among the many vehicles sits a customized three-wheel Harley you suspect must belong to Thurmond Pike, pawn shop, motorbike and bait and tackle entrepreneur, peer of Rabbit's there in the county. With a onetime acne ravaged face and a stooped but broad posture, you've always called him Buke, because he looked to you so much like Bukowski. You've forever marveled at the ability of crusty, grotesque redneck, who always seemed old the way your grandparents did, to enjoy such a parade—a bevy—of attractive women at his side. You always had to try hard to get them to look sideways at you, and you're not so terrible. Maybe all in how one carries oneself. That's what you've read. Confidence.

Or, could be it's motorcycle related. Who the fudge knows.

As you take your first step onto the porch, it all comes rushing into high relief against the deepening Edgewater County nighttime, and back lit by the yellow porch light is the pawnbroker himself, hunched over and leathery, coming out the door.

True to form, and causing you to swoon with a sense of time having stopped, Thurmond Pike has a woman on his arm half his age. She's overweight and dressed as though going out to a bar rather than a visitation, but with a lovely face, if made up in a garish fashion, with hair frosted and teased.

"Is that Roy Earl? Come here, son." Thurmond, grumbling and raising his stubby, thick wrestler's arms—that's what he had always looked like to you as well: one of those wrestlers you'd sit and watch with Rabbit. He loved that wrestling on Saturday afternoons. "Your grandmama's fit to be tied you ain't here yet."

You tell him your preference would have been to get here sooner.

Your eyes find those of the woman, whose own are spilling over with tears, a lipsticked mouth downturned and quivering. "Hey, Roy Earl—I'm so sorry, too."

The eyes. The shape of the chin. The voice, low and sexy, even back when they'd been fourteen. Fifty or sixty pounds heavier, but it was her: Chesnee.

Chesnee Campobello.

Holy moly.

In the flowering of your adolescence you suffered middle school crushes on many others besides Chesnee—Shelby Fordham, Jessamine Deliesseline, Margaret Tuggle, Natasha Prothro and the voluptuous Bev Mabry, with whom you had slow danced and thought you would have a heart attack, and a hard-on, at the touch and heat of your bodies as KISS's 'Beth' played and you swayed on a darkened gymnasium floor with colored lights pointed into the stands, huge pastel circles, and everyone's swaying bodies but hazy silhouettes and Bev Mabry's curved flesh pressed close; Bev, who after the dance talked to you on the phone sometimes, and seemed to like you, but moved away later that summer. Never to hear from her again. Action item: search social media for Bev Mabry.

But Chesnee, the only one with whom you came close to having a relationship. First kisses. The hints of more to come than kissing.

Your first love.

But forestalled.

And now with Buke?

With that scaly old reptile Thurmond Pike? Who'd been just as scaly back when you both were kids?

Your heart has stopped. You stammer and stutter and trip over a welcome mat. "Chesnee?"

Demure, she shrugs and pulls Pike closer. "It's Mrs. Pike, these days. But otherwise, same Chesnee."

The blood, it drains from your head. You steady yourself. Chesnee, all grown up and paired with nasty old Buke, standing here with his chinos and white socks showing over polished Frye Engineer motorcycle boots, and the ridiculous swept back pompadour he's had for fifty years as shiny and black as the boots; you've always imagined the entirety of the man's body filmed by a perpetual sheen of motorcycle grease wedged into every wrinkle and crack. An ogre. "That's—wow. Congratulations. To both of you."

"We had us a good run together—so far, anyway." Buke spits tobacco juice over into Runelle's flower bed full of pansies. "It ain't all no pony ride at the fair."

"Oh, you hush up." Chesnee, giving him a peck. "Roy—you're so slim and tall."

"Thanks," as your face heats up. Your words come thick and strange. "Get a lot of walking in. You both look great."

"Shit, Roy Earl. You ain't got to stand there and lie to a man's face, boy." Deep, phlegmatic laughter bubbles up, amusement in which you try to join, but it all feels as forced as you're sure you sound.

More pleasantries and condolences; an exhortation to get on inside.

At that Thurmond cranks the hog, louder than shit, more than you remember from your youth spent seeing him roaring along the river road, test driving a motorcycle some schmuck's trying to unload on him. Those were the times you didn't see the ever-present chiquita on the back—when he was wheeling and dealing.

Chesnee probably works in the pawn shop with him, you think with pity. Maybe she test-drives the bikes. What a life. Oh well—she had her chance with you. Didn't she?

◉❀◎

AFTER THEY DEPART you marvel at the smorgasbord arrayed around on every surface of Runelle's already cluttered kitchen and the breakfast table, and as you see when you peek around the corner, on the big dining room table, too— the Southern way of support for the bereaved. Food, plentiful food.

At last you sneak into the packed family room to find your dear old grand-mama. You hold one another and cry, and all the people fall hushed to watch the moment there among fishing trophies and bric-à-brac and pictures of young Runelle, when she had been Runelle Kittery and later Mama Runelle; there, the framed publicity photo of Mama Runelle and the Dixiana Darlings, her in her little dress and cowboy hat, and had sung sad country songs on the Dixiana stage. The wall of record albums, almost floor to ceiling. Thousands. Your Pa-paw's collection.

"I'm so glad you made it all right, son."

"Me too, Mee-maw." Your pet name for her, the one only you used. They all called her Mama, but to you she was Mee-maw. "Took me way too long."

The assemblage begins to converse again, moves around and goes into other rooms to eat themselves some of the food they'd all brought. The actual wake wouldn't be for a few days—you have decided nothing about that yet, and yes, surprise surprise, it is you who'll be deciding—but for a death the stature of Rabbit Pettus, you supposed the general grieving of the community had had to start here tonight. You'd let it go on. For a smidgen longer.

Easing your frail grandmother back into her chair, you make your way around the expansive family room, around the L-shaped couch and into the foyer and back around again through the dining room. Alice Faith Westmore-land, one of the ELMS, glances at your T-shirt and shorts and Keens like you are way way way underdressed.

In a similarly judgmental vein, all you can think is how your grandparents are stuck watching bulky, ancient, late 90s Sony flatscreens you'd bought them in '99, a trio of sets in sizes appropriate for the kitchen, bedroom, and the big daddy taking up a ridiculous number of cubic feet on its boxy stand in the corner.

As you endure small talk and platitudes, your eyes drift over to the wall full of your granddaddy's records, all neat and organized on the special built-ins you'd had custom made to accommodate the enormous collection.

The tears come, hot and sudden. You kneel at her feet.

"Son." Your grandmother, who is for all intents and purposes your mother, speaks with a quaver in her voice. "I can't hardly believe this."

"Mee-maw, so sorry I didn't get to see him."

"I know you got here fast as you could."

"Yep—I flew."

"See? You couldn't do nothing else. Nobody could. When it's time, it's time."

A raw moan emerges from deep inside her, awful and alien coming from formerly strong grandparents not prone to showing such raw emotion. "Oh, mercy me."

Your guts, twisting.

She sees your distress. Comforts you. It is what she has always done, from the moment of your birth but more so upon the loss of your mother, when you were but a swaddled toddler, still.

You recall a period in which you hated your mom for having died. For having left you. A woman you'd never known. Not really.

And if you allow yourself, you may feel contempt for your grandfather now, too. For leaving you with all this mess on your hands. For leaving you a grandmother to care for, and an estate to settle, all on top of your marriage falling apart.

Your timing is bad, you son of a bitch.

You collect yourself and try to cajole all these extraneous meat-bodies out of your family home. You must speak with your grandmother.

Alone.

In fact, you're desperate to let it all tumble out—how you might stay in Edgewater County for reasons other than needing to attend funerals and begin the process of liquidating your grandfather's saloon.

Project number one. Poor Trudy. No idea what's coming.

One thought settles:

How quickly can I get all this wrapped up—the divorce; sell the house on the Island; unload all possessions but the hobby aircraft; and otherwise go hike the Appalachian Trail? Build a cabin in the woods? Take the money and run?

Soon.

Real soon.

Mama Runelle, your Mee-maw, stroking your face. She seems a little shorter than you, which you don't understand—you swore the woman used to be taller. "Where's my darling Creedence?"

"She couldn't come. With me."

"Couldn't come?"

"She's—indisposed."

"What did she have to do? Something terribly important, I hope?"

"She doesn't like to fly. We had a big fight about it," trying not to cry. "Nobody was thinking straight."

"Well, darling," assuming your grief is for Pa-paw. Which it is. "She'll drive up tomorrow."

⊛⊛⊛

YOU EMBARK upon more small talk, giving the well-wishers the grownup, generic persona you present to customers from behind the coffee bar or the fruitshake counter: easy banter, aphorisms, your go-to, fill-in responses to generalized questions from Alice Faith like, "How are things down there on the Island? We heard you and Colette," how non-family types would remember Creedence, a nickname, from school, "had moved into a magnificent home on the marsh."

"A million-dollar view—million-dollar house, too, come to think of it."

"You've done so well. An Edgewater County favorite son to be sure, Roy Earl Pettus."

Alice Faith, from old money. She could understand not having to work anymore, or ever, for that matter—the Westmorelands, long the cream of Edgewater County blue-blood authenticity and respectability and cold cash.

Your cousin Mervin, two years older, and his wife and twin boys stand huddled in the corner. You go over and can smell booze on him. Notice how she looks miserable, and the boys, Dale and DJ—yes; Dale and Dale Jr, twins, and despite your childhood history of loving NASCAR, this naming convention, with its obsessive fandom and obtuseness about what ought to be suitable monikers for a pair of healthy American boys with long futures ahead of them, makes your skin crawl—have noses buried in iPads, and you wonder how these poor white trash cousins of yours earn enough to keep their children in up-to-date tech.

White trash.

Dude—listen to you. Wasn't like you didn't dig NASCAR for a time, mainly to be contrary to your grandfather and Uncle Burnie, neither of whom cared for auto racing. Too noisy and pointless, they both said.

⊛⊛⊛

SURE, you were into racing for a season or two, before adolescence set in. You loved movies more, but kept trying here and there to branch out into something more normal. NASCAR. This one time you watched an exciting Final

Four tournament and were 'into' college basketball for a while; and yeah, you had to pretend to love Redtails football. Ephemeral interests gained in the service of fitting into some crowd or group, in your case. No one need know but you.

Knowing how much you adored movies, one Christmas Uncle Burnie surprised you with a special gift he'd picked up at an antiques show at one of the malls in Greenville—a one-sheet, as posters are known in the exhibition trade.

Uncle Burnie and his wife Henny had all kinds of money, and would take day trips to different towns to shop at stores and buy exotic treasures not found in Tillman Falls, none of which your grandparents seemed to have any interest in doing. They liked to sit there. Old. Burnie, he always seemed younger than your Granddaddy, somehow—spry rather than creaky.

"There was a man at that show selling movie posters, Roy Earl. I thought of you."

"You did?" Excited by the large kraft-paper wrapped rectangle, you hoped for a Star Wars-related item.

"Open it, darling," your Mee-maw had prompted.

But having gotten over your car-racing dalliance, you deflated at what you found inside. Despite thanking your Uncle Burnie for the poster of a B-movie called Thunder in Carolina and promising to hang it on your wall, you hated the gift. By then you were almost thirteen, and the whole racing deal had become kinda downmarket for your tastes, if you didn't yet have such a term at your disposal. But you weren't so spoiled and self-absorbed not to feign a little surprise.

"Son, they filmed part of this over yonder at Darlington—how about that? I remember when it played at the Palmetto. Before your time."

"Before his time," your grandfather intoned from his recliner in the corner of the living room in the old house. "Back when movies were movies."

Pa-paw didn't care about the movie poster, not flipping through a stack of records Burnie brought for him. Rabbit Pettus, then as now, had so many records it became part of your reasoning for building them the new house. He wasn't faking nothing about loving records.

⊛⊛⊛

"Heard you flew in your own dang plane." Mervin, pulling you out of your fugue state and into a man-hug that leaves you reeling both from the force of his grip as the sour stench of beer leeching out of your cousin's pores. "If that's not the beatin'-est thing I ever did hear."

"It's not that big a deal, bro."

"You granddaddy said you had money, now. I reckon if having your own plane's not a sign, ain't nothing is."

Their eyes shine at you, Mervin's more than his wife Carla Mae's. You hardly know her. Married for a while now, far as you can recall. Maybe longer than you and Creedence. Had they been together at your wedding? Hell, you don't remember. You hadn't gone to theirs. Didn't matter. "It's not like a G-4."

"What's that?" Carla Mae asks.

"A Learjet."

"You ain't got that much money, then. I reckon."

You start to correct her; yes, yes, you fucking do.

But instead it's a self-deprecating, no'm, I do not have Learjet money. Which is true enough. You could get one, sure. Just wouldn't be any bucks left-over to buy jet-juice. Or to eat. Flush, remember. Not rich. Rich-rich, anyway.

Pastor Duson Mire arrives; you cannot believe the man's still ambulatory, nor the hour, pushing nine o'clock, at which folks keeping showing up.

The ladies of the church have kept Mire fed; his suit seems too small, the sleeves too short on the jacket.

"I want to pray with you," he says to your grandmother. "Let us pray."

"Reverend, here's my grandson, Roy Earl. 'Roy.' He likes 'Roy,' now."

"Roy Earl. Bless your soul."

"Like she says. Roy's sufficient." You shake his hand and try to lead him away from your Mee-maw, who can't possibly wish to pray in front of all these people. "Wait—didn't you people used to stand outside my granddaddy's bar and shout hateful rhetoric?"

"I have only ever done the lord's work, and followed His calling, son. Like coming here tonight to minister to you."

"Exactly." Runelle brings us back to the moment at hand. "My prayer, Reverend. If you please."

"Now, Mee-maw. No need to go overboard here. I don't think anybody's prayed around here since—"

A glance cuts you off; she locks hard old eyes with yours. A tiny shake of her head. "Roy Earl Pettus—you show respect for Pastor Mire, just as he has shown for us."

You scan the faces of the rest of the guests, with arms folded and sour lemonsucking faces and realize, or remember, that despite the lack of religious faith in your own household, a place like Edgewater County expected these rituals. It's all you can do to keep from going into hell-no mode.

Deep breath. "Sure. Let's say a prayer for my granddaddy."

The rotund Reverend Mire leads the Jesus Christ-centric prayer for the sanctity of dear old Reynolds Pettus's unredeemed soul.

Meanwhile, you say 'ohm' or 'aum,' as Guernsey, the granola gal manager of SBFC Myrtle Beach #1, taught you about meditation the summer you opened in that market. Jamband tunes on the boombox. Good times. Big money from that location, at Broadway on the Beach, huge ass retail and entertainment complex. The Spotted Banana™ had a good view of the Hard Rock Cafe, its golden pyramid of a building next to the complex on a prime outparcel facing the King's Highway bypass. You had gotten high looking at that pyramid, there in the parking lot with this hippy manager, keeping one eye peeled for the security patrol and the other on her tanned legs and sandaled feet. Had thought yourselves growing close, you and Guernsey Swinton, a free spirit who glowed with good health and youth and red-eyed hippie chill. Only married two years, you'd fooled around once or twice before coming to your senses and firing her. You were off to open another Banana, anyway. The last time you got stoned with any regularity, those days.

Poor Guernsey—how she'd wished she could've seen Garcia play, a badge of honor you're always gratified to pull out, because with your buzzed short fuzzy hair and your totally nonhippie bearing, with the bossman routine and your Tevas or Keens on your pink man-feet, and cargo shorts and plain black T-shirts and a jocular but brusque, tough-but-fair management style, nobody you hire thinks you're the least bit hip. At first.

Not that you've been a hippie, ever. You'd seen the Grateful Dead twice with friends more into it than you, but honestly, you dug the songs more than the long jams; had never done acid, only pretended to take it at that first Dead show, with Devin and Libby and the rest. Big chicken that you were.

Your interest, you often claimed, lay in sports like Redtails football, much as the next Southeastern U alum, anyway. Nothing like the old days. Before you hooked up with Creedence, you'd been big into tailgating and going to the games.

Not anymore. All too much—the noise and giant scoreboard flashing color and light and the cannons and the fanfare and the 89,727 screaming Redtails fans, and the rivers of alcohol, and the weird vibe after the game: trash everywhere, hooting and hollering and a massive traffic jam full of vehicles driven by how many people who'd been drinking? Forget it. Last season two people lost their lives outside the stadium, one run over by a drunk driver and the other beaten to death in an altercation between rival fans when a raucous Georgia crowd had shown up on a blazing hot Saturday afternoon. Demented tribalism. Faux battlefield conflict. Yawn.

It helped that Creedence hadn't given a shit about football. Had hated it.

Once you started flying, you didn't need a hobby like watching a field full of oversized, under-brained nitwits banging into each other and grunting apelike and making millions of dollars. That ain't working. That's getting your head bashed in.

Is money worth all that? Now that you've acquired as much cheddar as you could ever have needed—depending on how nice a plane you want to upgrade to—you aren't sure. Money can't cheat death. Can't make your wife true to you again. Useless numbers in somebody else's computer.

You note that Mama Runelle has on lipstick. You can't remember the last time you've seen your grandmother with make-up on, perhaps that Christmas Eve two years ago when a phalanx of Kitterys came for dinner, the first time such had occurred in many a holiday season. After someone held a long overdue family reunion the previous summer, several long-lost family pledged to stay in touch, visit at holidays and so forth, and there, it happened. You dig it when people say what they're gonna do, then freaking do it. That is how you make your bacon. That is how you get rich. Say what you'll do, do what you say.

For example: You missed the reunion because you were opening the SBFC Asheville #1, one of the last stores you'd founded. Creedence told you choosing to open this location over a proposed second store on St. Simon's Island in Georgia seemed weird and dumb; she always chose beach over mountains, as you had scoffed into her face.

Boy, she'd said all that and more the day you announced plans for the Carolina Beanery Sedge Island. That you would build the coffee shop empire that'd been your dream. The smoothie stands, trademarked or not, successful or otherwise, had been somebody else's deal—you'd taken over a failing college ghetto business called the Spotted Banana and made it into a power-house brand, sure. But smoothies, fruitshakes, no; those hadn't been in your blood, not like good coffee.

It'd been the moment you went into the Main Street Bijou over in Columbia to see an art movie for the first time, and the fragrant medium roast hit you in the lobby alongside the popcorn, and milling among the sophisticated South-eastern University and downtown Columbia types, you felt like another person; you smelled the coffee and watched the art movie in a foreign language and felt grownup and so apart from Edgewater County and The Dixiana and your grandparents and you said, coffee is my future.

The next morning before class—you were a freshman at Southeastern, living with Dobbs and Devin in the suites down from the student union—you had coffee and a danish for breakfast. Before you'd always eaten a pack of crackers and a Pepsi or Mountain Dew like you'd watch your Granddaddy eat every day, though it had served as his lunch instead of breakfast. Granddaddy, never seemed worried about food. Simple tastes and habits—the cigarettes more important than the grub.

Didn't drink coffee, either. You weren't sure you ever served him a cup of your fine brew from custom-roasted beans. And now you'll never get the chance.

⊕❋◉

Rebecca LaFreniere and other members of the Edgewater Ladies Munificence Society, the premiere women's activism and philanthropy group in the county, a set of determined individuals whose influence could be felt in the city hall and all across the tri-county area, arrive in a flurry of covered dishes and make their presence known in the main room by shooing away other more ordinary attendees and well-wishers. The ELMS, as you well know from growing up here, exist as master charity event planners, festival organizers and fund drive specialists; the causes they support, as you recall, make up a varied lot, and here reiterated to you by 'Becky L' as she asks everyone to call her, a kind of personal rebranding, it seems; Becky, a hip hip lady compared to the cotton-topped crones in the ELMS you remember from your childhood. She moved to New York, took a stab at pro acting on the legit stage. Ended up back here. Happens.

Besides being the secretary to her powerful civic organization, Becky L serves as director of the Fine Arts Center, negotiating the local arts waters lapping at her long, alabaster neck and keeping herself in the game, at least on the community theatre level. As for the ELMS, their good works, as she says, extend to the stray animal spay and neuter program begun by Creedence's late, tenderhearted mother, Eileen Rucker; Alice Faith's bake and yard sales to support female victims of domestic abuse; Becky, overseeing grants given to historical preservation projects; and Letty Glasscock from across the pecan orchard, with a senior citizen's and poor kid's literacy program, and et cetera, et cetera until every molecule of oxygen in any particular roomful of ELMS became transformed into warm carbon dioxide. Not to mention the danger of having a checkbook lightened by their entreaties.

A hush falls at the arrival of Ruth DeKalb, accompanied by a little weasel of a gladhander named Cole Breedlove. While the matronly and formal DeKalb speaks in hushed and comforting tones to Mama Runelle, Breedlove introduces himself to you as a deacon in Mire's church, but looking way young. Oleaginous and suspicious, he's got a robot-eyed glare often seen in religious fundamentalists, cops and politicians, a 'tell' making such brittle reeds ripe for exploitation by the right bossman in the right frame of mind.

"Your family is in my prayers—but then, the whole county's in my prayers every night, what with this crazyman we got for president," Breedlove says, holding onto your handshake. The flesh of his palm, warm and gooey. "A few extra for the Pettuses, though. Bless your hearts."

Bless our hearts? Fudge you, a-hole. "Appreciate it, beau."

"Let's pray right now." Breedlove, in a breathy rush. "If we could. Everyone—?"

"Whoa whoa whoa," waving your arms. "We did CYA on that already."

Breedlove's already glassy eyes dampen. "But, I've already called out to the Lord."

You pity him—he doesn't realize who the eff's in charge. Um. Hello. "Relax, pal. It's chill."

"It's fine, son." Pastor Mire pulls Breedlove aside. "Mr. Pettus is upset."

Rolling your eyes at the backs of the evangelicals, you whisper to Becky L, "Who's the *grande dame?*"

DeKalb's son had been governor, Rebecca whispers back, and exists as a sort of ELMS éminence grise, at her age one seen in public only on the most significant of occasions. "The mother of a governor doesn't go out calling—you go to her," all explained in LaFreniere's aristocratic drawl, one of those thick dialects preserved from antiquity and sound almost British in their inflection. "So this is quite the honor."

"Why, I just got chills. Respect."

She winks, sly and flirtatious. "In a small town like this? Indeed—a sign of deep respect. From all of us."

The rest of the room falling away, the totality of this attractive, mature, poised and professional female becomes apparent. After what your wife's pulled, you are allowed to suffer sudden lust for LaFreniere, a grownup compared to your drunken wench back down there on the island. Tall, with a fashionable, short hairdo, and a sleek power suit and killer Manolos on tasteful, French pedicured feet, Rebecca's scent, subtle and spicy-sweet, damn near overwhelms you.

Becky, whom you recall being a few grades behind you, had been gawky, bespectacled, a rich girl and an arts weirdo. You used to sit in the other room listening to your grandparents talk about the LaFrenieres, who they said thought their shit didn't stink. And the DeKalbs, too, come to think of it.

"The ELMS—y'all still in business?"

You note with interest how Becky L, speaking in whispered confidence, grips your forearm. Her hands, pale and long. A heat emanating from her flesh into yours. "'Business'? We're a 501C/6. Nonprofit."

"Really, now. All those paid-wristband town festivals?"

A hint of irritation. A removal of the hand. "Our charitable work remains an open secret."

Knowing smirk: "I'll bet it is."

Why you're blowing your shot with her for the sake of snark, you haven't a clue. Other than indulging in superiority to all those old-school town mothers. Or over hearing your grandparents complain about them so much that it sunk in, you reckon.

You suffer a vision—of moving back for the duration. Setting them all on a course of modernity. Startles you, this notion. But you hold it for a moment. Can almost make the image tangible. See yourself sitting outside the honky-tonk on the town green. You and the other codgers. Waving your hand across your field of view, ripples of your energy changing the reality of all you survey.

You, taking a wrecking ball to the entire block—no, the whole county. On hiatus for retooling.

You, rolling paint over the mural.

You, deciding.

A legit outbreak of chicken-skin erupts along your forearms.

"The ELMS—no offense, but it feels like a relic. Maybe time for the old forms to fall away." Nodding. "And replaced by shinier, newer Gen-X versions."

Frost. "We have much to discuss, Roy Earl. Your grandfather—well. Now's not the time."

You ask, what about your Pa-paw?

"Before he fell ill, he'd come from a contentious meeting. Over the fate of the mural on The Dixiana."

Before you blurt, no worries, that effing thing's so gone, you realize: she doesn't know how you feel.

Meaning: you retain the strategic advantage. To what end, you know not. But advantage you possess.

You could change her world with a word—they want it as gone as you do. But you're so irritated by this frisson of well-wishing, all this hullabaloo and rigmarole, you refuse to throw anyone a bone regardless of Dubya-style 'strate-gery.' You will let them dangle about the mural. Let them wonder. Just to amuse yourself. "Give you my thoughts on that another time. Like the honky-tonk itself, that piece of public art's in the lifeblood of the town. Have to handle it with tweezers."

"You've had such a shock. To be continued." A final squeeze on the fore-arm, and she's off to speak with the former governor's mother. "And otherwise —it's so so wonderful to see you again."

Watching Becky L sashay around the gathering, you're like, she's hot to trot. You stood here running down her 501C/6, and withheld a money shot about the dreaded mural, but still she squeezed that arm.

My, my, my.

Okay, Creedence Rucker. We'll see who lands on his feet out of all this drama. Forget Trudy Pirkle, that redneck skank—here's prime time. And here, too, LaFreniere family money.

Jesus, did you move fast—it'd all come apart only this afternoon. Time was strange. Moved funny sometimes. Seems like it had been ages ago.

But now? Irons, blackening in a stoked fire. All but squared away. BOOM.

And, yeah. Money. Becky and you, a formidable team. It's as though you can sense an impression left by her fingers still vibrating on your skin. It assuages the pain and hurt over your wife. You can see the future, envision it, and it's bright, not blighted. You need shades, bro. Hells yeah, you do.

RIDING this burst of self-righteous esteem and mad, compulsive optimism, you puff yourself up and work the room, avoiding Breedlove and Duson Mire. Surprised a man of the cloth could go so many decades free of scandal. Church must use a canny accountant.

Letty Glasscock, who has arrived and given you a quick hug, expounds empathetic and warm and comforting in your ear, an aunt-like presence to you. Letty, you barely recognize her; growing up she'd been a typical southern lady, all makeup and hairdo and having had two children and a husband, but now, in the wake of a divorce and with an empty nest but for her younger brother Jasper, a woman who'd discovered in her late 60s both her inner lesbian, and an expertise in matters like organic gardening. You'd discussed various aspects of all this the last time you were home for Thanksgiving, and the Glasscock siblings had come from their house on the other side of the pecan orchard to break bread. With a shaggy gray haircut, a sassy attitude, and from her outfit—loose work pants, a dusty long-sleeve T-shirt, and beaten-to-shit green Crocs that'd seen better gardening days, you knew Letty had settled with grace and don't-give-a-fuck into this truer persona, a realer her than had ever been, and you are both glad to see her—she's genuine and warm—as well as envious of this late-life comfort in her own skin. You'll get there one day.

At your and Letty Glasscock's insistence, time for the pity-party to end, and people start to leave. You get asked three times how long it took to fly from the coast. Like Superman.

You watch the parade of farewells from across the room, noting how your grandmother looks healthy, glowing and alive. Grateful for the attention, you surmise. You haven't paid her much for the last decade or two, what with your time occupied by conquering the fruitshake economy in such a grandly profitable fashion.

SEEING off yet another vehicle of departing consolers, you cringe at one last set of headlamps coming down the driveway and think, I cannot do this; I will not survive this process. Maybe it didn't matter, all things reconsidered.

But it's only Letty Glasscock's brother Jasper, older, heavier, balder, but no less Jasper. Unsteady, you note, as he gets out of his Accord in a rumpled seer-sucker suit over a kelly green polo shirt.

"Jasper."

He squints against the mustardy porch light. "That you, Roy Earl?"

"It is me."

You suffer through another round of condolences, compliments on your weight, and the fact of you having flown your own plane in earlier, soon as you heard the news.

"Soon as I heard the news," you confirm yet again.

"Well, that's something. Hopping into your own aircraft."

"Everybody seems to think so." Sour-sweet funk; Jasper, drunk. He better lay off those Ss.

"I appreciate you coming by."

"Well—your mama. Your grandmama, rather. She called me earlier. Said to come on by. Bring the will and read it tonight."

"Tonight? Jesus, he hasn't even been embalmed yet. It can wait."

Smacks his lips. Seems slow, in low gear. "Well. She said tonight. So—I pulled my copy. I went to the office, and I pulled it. Then I came over—"

"She's not in charge, bub. Hate to be blunt. Tomorrow morning instead. At your office. Still downtown, right?"

"Yeah. But, Runelle. She told me—"

"Dude." You are about to come out of your skin at his slo-mo routine. "I love ya, buddy, and appreciate this. It's late. I'm wrung out. She's wrung out. Christ—"

Your heart nearly stops—more lights from down the drive. You are in hell. "So look, get your ass back across the pecan orchard before I grab one of Rabbit's shotguns. And I ain't saying that to be folksy, bro. Seriously—I got problems."

And one more: more headlamps. Gooch Wimmel, sliding to a stop in his modest royal blue Ford Focus. Bumbling out and over toward you like a tottering old man.

All of them. All of them here seem old. It's like that down on the island, too.

A voice like Morgan Freeman narrating a Serious Documentary: *Your hair's going gray too, Roy Earl Pettus. Don't kid yourself.*

But these codgers—mercy. Dried up old prunes, like the prunes they must eat, and reminds you how, on this horrible long day starting with horror and inconvenience and shock and more inconvenience and a near-death experience of believing the landing lights weren't popping on at the airfield, you've not crapped. Nobody wants to hear about your coiled, serpent-like inner pipes, but as regular as you are, this stoppage represents a last wrinkle and a layer of conflict in this complicated, melodrama that's become your formerly happy life, here transformed into a slapstick comedy of errors, suffused with such raw emotion born of frustration and inconvenience that your physical molecules have been affected. Oh—and bereavement for the dead. That's in there, too.

"Roy Earl," Bill Wimmel says. "I'm so sorry. It's so late. I fell asleep."

The stodgy decorum of these country mice. More condolences? At this hour? "No worries, pal. We just got the house emptied."

Jasper, nodding. "Gooch."

"Jasper. How you been?"

"Partly to fair. You believe this mess?"

"Biggest Edgewater County death in—in—"

"That's what you said this afternoon. You remember following Runelle here this afternoon. Don't you?"

"Oh, sure," Gooch says, looking terrified. "I hadn't—I didn't—I didn't get a quote from Roy Earl, though."

Jasper, skeptical, making eye contact and shooting you a wink you grapple with decoding. "Okay, then."

Giving them both your best Nicholson smile, all malevolence and glee at the thought of bashing their two white-headed noggins together and dragging their bodies back around the house for fertilizer to throw into Runelle's flower beds full of fall pansies, you say, "Guys, this is a big day and a big night and all that, but right now I need to go—" You feel self-conscious at revealing you need to take a massive dump, and this knowing no decent fellow human would begrudge another such urgency. "—get some rest. And so does Mee-maw."

"Thing is," Gooch says, doing a flustered little dance of anxiety, "I need to put Reynolds's obit to bed first thing. And the arrangements—I need this information. It needs to be right. It—the church. And all. For the—so the—people will want—want to know."

You observe, dry, how your granddaddy never stood on ceremony, and certainly never set foot in a church. "Service'll be at the funeral home, I reckon. I'll pick out some songs. Shit—pictures. I'll see if I can get help on this."

Enraged, you think of your wife, and your leg twitches—you would delegate the photos chore to her. If she were here. You're a strong leader not because you do it all yourself (though you do), you also know how to delegate —except, in this case, you can't delegate to a team member who isn't present and accounted for. "I'll get organized in the A-M and call with the deets. Surely for a death of this grandeur and size you can hold the edition a few minutes."

"Well, look-a-here..." Jasper says slo-o-owly. "Runelle. She said. He told her. He always told her. That everything was laid out. In the will."

Now that sounded like good solid foresight and planning. "Tremendous."

Gooch, exasperated, a little hotfoot dance. "Can we find out? I need to pee."

Peeing, shitting, you have had enough with the scatology, but now your own bowels roil from all the snacking and gorging on the desserts folks have provided.

"Why didn't you say so. Come inside," but you don't feel welcoming, and still think all this foolishness can wait. "You go and pee, now."

Runelle calls out from the screen door. "Are you men coming for this little ceremony, or do I have to go into the yard and get eaten alive by mosquitos? And Gooch Wimmel, what on earth are you doing here again?"

Sheepish, he shrugs. "Still getting the story down."

"Mercy," shaking her head. "Lord help me."

⊛⊛⊛

THE READING, concluded. "Well—that's it," Jasper says.

You're tickled. "This is stupendous."

The elderly people sitting around the dining room table, overloaded with cakes and pies and bread and food—how had the well-wishers prepared it all so fast? The man had been dead barely eight hours—each looked a different shade of chagrined, but you, prodigal son, pace around all but squirming with delight:

Your granddaddy has thrown everyone for a loop and slapped down a damned control grid on his afterlife by declaring there'll be no public remembrance or memorial, only that all due effort—and a certain amount of money, set aside and bequeathed for the purpose—should be expended to inaugurate an annual music festival. His final wish, this, bringing the stage and the back porch of The Dixiana, where bluegrass legends had once picked and country sirens like your own grandmother had crooned, to the town green. You heard the speech a million times.

"Shit, ain't nothing changed around here." Your Mee-maw, yawning. "The ELMS ain't no more gonna let another town festival go on than my husband would give up them cigarettes of his."

"Oh, no? Leave them to me."

Gooch, scribbling with fury. "Rabbit Pettus Memorial Bluegrass Festival? When? How? Where?"

"Stop writing."

The old reporter puts down his pen, though with reluctance.

"And no more questions. All this festival talk is off the record. No publicity at all."

Gooch, coming to terms: "Color me confused."

"When the time's right, my event PR gal will issue a press release."

"But, Roy Earl—what about—a service? None?"

You go over it in your mind. Cremation, check. No memorial; stage a festival instead. With your experience at event planning, consider it all done,

done-r, and done-est. Obstacles you may encounter, well, these are but stepping stones to success.

"None, Gooch. It was his decision before; it's my decision, now. My show around here. Well—my and my Mee-maw."

"No, son. Your Pa-paw wrote his will knowing you will be the one to decide everything. He assumed I wouldn't be here, son."

"Why's that, Mee-maw?"

"Rennie, he was always so worried about losing me. As though I was going anywhere."

"Everybody thought you were gonna up and run off." Jasper, beaming. "And become a big-time radio star on the Grand Ole Opry stage."

"It's true," Gooch added. "Or so the legend holds."

"Wasn't neither one of you around for all that. Or I should say, you was both too young to know nothing about country music, and singers. And honkytonks. But I did like to sing," she says, smiling, "and would still now, but my throat's too dry all the time."

You slap your hands together, making them all jump. "Here's the news: Rabbit Pettus's ashes will be scattered in a private family ceremony, at the river bluff where he loved to fish, and we'll go ahead and say, and say—Sunday? Monday?" You look to your grandmama for confirmation.

"Anytime but Monday, son," in her quavery, old lady's voice. "Monday's when I get my hair done."

"Check. So, Mr. Wimmel, you may put that in the paper about the ashes being scattered, but please emphasize private and family only. I'll see that a few select folks will be there—Jasper, you of course. The right people. The best people."

"Appreciate the thought."

"Maybe, if you could, you'll sing one for him—you're the mainstay at the old honkytonk, anyway. Ain't ya?" Listen to the patois creeping in—you're like Zelig. Easier that way, right? "The living embodiment of the honkytonk man himself."

Jasper, blushing. "I expect I could do that for Mr. Reynolds Pettus, who gives me his stage once a week." Jasper asks if you want to run down to The Dixiana with him, where he ought to sing one for the old boy tonight, too.

You politely decline—if you went in there tonight, the stink of the place would make you puke, that's the God's truth right there. But you only say, it'd be too much. A hand over your heart: "I couldn't take the memories."

Mama Runelle chimes in, hurrying it all along. "And I'm about finished with hubbub and chitchat, gentleman. So if you would—"

A last series of goodbyes. Gooch, asking if he should come and cover the ceremony for the Rabbit Pettus special page he had in mind, and you say, of course, of course, you could give two fudges. But otherwise, **Private** and **Family Only** at that dad-blamed river bluff.

You check your iPhone for the forecast, see sunny and mild and a warming trend through the weekend—the dreaded Edgewater County Indian summer. "Let's say eleven on Sunday, before it gets too damn humid in this fetid swamp."

Gooch nods. "Yes, Lord—I can't stand this muggy late-summer heat like I used to. I wish I lived someplace cooler. Like up in the mountains."

Chicken-skin again. An idea that's so often gripped you. Verbalized. Boo-yow. "You and me both, dude."

⊛⊛⊛

At last, the house empty but for you and your Mee-maw. Both exhausted.

Midnight.

A new day.

A fresh frame.

A hand on her elbow, the old bag of bones leans against your shoulder as you assist her into the bedroom. An unfamiliar sensation. Never had this strong old hunk of hickory from back in the depression leaned on you.

For anything.

"Mee-maw? You holding together all right?"

"Her husband died, and she took to bed."

You say: do what, now?

"I'm fine, son. I'm tired. Your granddaddy was tired, too. He just wouldn't own up to it."

"Till it caught up with him."

"It does us all. Doesn't it?"

"Nothing you need worry about tonight, Mama Runelle."

She said, reckon not.

And went to bed, but not before telling you to hush up that smart mouth, and call her by her right name, which to you is not Mama, but Mee-maw. As you know.

Ready to collapse into a heap of broken, tangled tinker toys, you drift into the silent living room, sit down in his chair and listen to the ticking of the house. Being among your grandfather's possessions—the album collection, the fishing mementoes, the old pictures of Runelle onstage at the honkytonk, the portrait of him in his Army uniform and her looking impossibly young and beautiful walking down Main Street in Columbia, a brief time they had lived there after the war, and before the decampment for North Dakota, of all places —a sense of your own history sweeps into the room, high and sweet like sticking your nose into one of those cartons of Neapolitan ice cream Mama

Runelle always keeps on hand for you, which you dare not find and give into emotional impulse eating.

Instead, you submit to having one last cloudburst of reluctant but cleansing, super-heated tears, a raging torrent that sweeps you into a tortured half-sleep on the couch in the Great Room of the beautiful house you built for your grandparents. A gift; your contribution for all they'd done. What a fuss they had put up. You'd have thought them insulted.

Drifting off, you foreswear any further feckless weeping, over either Rabbit Pettus or your faithless wife. Tomorrow, day one of year zero. For all, yourself included.

JASPER GLASSCOCK

The microphone fed back on Jasper at the first words out of his mouth, which came echoey and sibilant. All Burnie's grandbaby had done was turn the board on, and then run back over to the bar to keep serving the beer to the crowd who'd gathered, older men that Jasper rarely saw in the club anymore, except for the few of them who were pickers like him. Who come out on open mic night and did their three songs for the twelve people in the audience.

Not tonight. Everybody and his brother come out tonight.

Even Jez Rembert and his crew, all of whom gave Jasper the creeps. Snakes and reptiles, them boys. Like Rembert's daddy J. W., a summanabitch if they ever was one. Hadn't kept Jasper from doing the occasional favor for one or the other'n, usually in a legal sense. Dealing with this'n that.

His legal work wasn't anything near as interesting as getting up and making music for, and with, other likeminded folks. To Jasper, the vibrations of his guitar strings and vocal cords, and words he wrote like poetry—hell, songs was poetry, including his—constituted the truest human currency. The reason for the season.

"Can y'all hear me—?" More feedback. "Shit-fire."

He stepped back from the mic and adjusted the tuning on his beloved Martin, blocked the glare of the magenta spotlight that most impeded his view of the bar area way across the room and up on the riser. Button, he could see her punching numbers into the old cash register with fingers that seemed uncertain, and which seemed to deliver results unexpected. She spun around in a circle with her hands pressed against the sides of a tie-dye doo-rag holding back her dreads. Then got real calm as Trudy hustled from the other end of the bar. Red-faced. Yelling at Button.

Jasper felt woozy. Shouldn't have driven over like this. Late.

"Button?" He cupped his hands, shouting over the din. "This here's a hot mic you give me."

Over the buzzing of the crowd around the bar, many with hands in the air waving money, she yelled back an unintelligible response. Go deal with it yourself, her body language seemed to say. A frenzy of activity roiled in what was often a sleepy, all but empty honkytonk.

Except when the Columbia people drove up from the capital city. Button had talked Rabbit into booking in a few up and coming rock bands from down there, and some of that crowd had started coming to the open mic nights. Pickers from Charlotte and Asheville too, sometimes. Jasper tried to tell them all how old school it felt, how authentic. Really, this old Dixiana had been more lively of late than in quite a few years. And here Rabbit had to go and die right in the middle of the renaissance.

Jasper grunted his way offstage and over to the board. Potted down his mic, adjusted the monitor, which you couldn't do without somebody to run sound. All this trouble, only one song or two for old Rabbit. Had to be done.

Back onstage, he test-test-tested, now feedback-free. As Jasper made his remarks to the crowd, the attention of which was difficult to maintain, Trudy and Button conferred in an animated and frantic manner over the cash register. Their raised voices carried over Jasper's words of condolence for the Pettus family.

"Ladies?" He called out, getting more feedback. "Please."

The crowd, fallen silent; Trudy: "—so I'm only gone for a durn hour and this's what you do to me, Sykes?"

"Hey." Button, holding out her arms in a gesture of peace and conciliation. "I did. The best. I could, yo."

"Hush," someone shouted. "Jasper's talking at y'all."

"Yeah—you two squawking hens shut your holes." Jezmund Rembert, big as a bull on its hind legs but still babyfaced and with the same fine blonde mullet he'd had since forever, called from his end of the bar. He doffed his fedora. Looming, threatening. Lord, but Jasper hated to see Jez coming.

His boys, too, a bunch of hard ass dopers who didn't never roll up in here, not normally. Fellas he knew would beat somebody's ass—if not worse—like it wasn't nothing. Well, they wouldn't do it in here, not with Rabbit Pettus standing over them all.

Now, though? All bets might be off.

Trudy, a dragon. "I'll thank you not to tell me a damn thing I ought'n to do, son. You think I won't kick you out fast as—fast as—Mr. Rabbit—" She choked off.

Jezmund the redneck gangster called for attention over the hushed assemblage, every head pivoted his way. All his boys wore the fedoras, as though they thought themselves one of the street gangs in The Warriors: the Fedora Fellas. They hung out in Columbia, in the Old Market near the campus of Southeastern. Lot of bars there. Lot of people to deal white powders and pills to down near that university. "I ain't trying to stir no shit. Jasper's up yonder trying to talk about Mr. Reynolds Pettus, RIP. Now you of all people ought to know enough manners to hush. This is South Carolina. A member of the tribe passed on today. Respect."

"All right, all right." Trudy, wiping her dagger-eyes, which she held on Jezmund until drifting over to the guitar picker onstage. "Go on, sugar."

"Ladies, gentlemen—thank you." The room of thirty or forty fell into the silence of a rapt theatre audience. "Now look, I'm not gonna do my whole act tonight for y'all, especially since we done it last night. But thought maybe it'd be a good way for me to feel like I was making a tribute worthy of the man we lost today. Because of music. The music. He loved. We ought to play one or two."

He belched, hot and wet and stinging his stumbling, inarticulate throat. Way too much to drink today. "Old Rabbit Pettus, he loved his music. He loved this old honkytonk. So the more music we make in here, the more he'll keep on living. But it's getting late, and out of respect for his family, I think we ought to close this old place down soon, let the staff go home and grieve. And the rest of us get on with our grieving, which will be about more than right now, and today."

A murmuring swept through the crowd. All this talk of grief, unseemly and weak to these mostly-men. Acknowledgement, Jasper knew, involved the idea that no matter who you were, or what your general condition, the days were countable.

Jasper strummed an intro to the first song, which he explained came from a country songwriter and singer everybody loved, a million-seller, a number one hit recording by Merle Haggard and it's called "Sing Me Back Home."

The tune went over good, everybody dabbing at their eyes. The tune, about a prisoner making one last request, that of hearing a gospel song he'd once found in a moment of grace, pinned down the attention of the room. Jasper, choking up himself. Button and Trudy, behind the bar, hugging and sobbing.

"Sing me back home, a song I used to hear... make my old memories, come alive... one last time, before I die."

Following the Haggard came an old spiritual, "And We Bid You Goodnight," which continued the theme of endings, a tune that Jasper often did anyway at the open mics, including last night.

But first, a last speech, this one more cogent. "His loss and life, remember, was filled not with illness and pain, and he did not fade away—earlier today he stood in the room where you all stand. No. Instead, Rabbit Pettus, collapsing onto the cracked concrete outside. Just like that. Bless his durn old tired heart."

A chorus of approval, and the raising of glasses.

Jasper, his emotions running wild—at one time the man had been like a father to him, back when he was a boy and his own crusty old farmer of a daddy had seemed so old—struggled through the song: The thought of the open mics ending, and of The Dixiana going away, and of Rabbit dying, all but overwhelming.

But he made it through, only cutting short by one round the song's "goodnight, goodnight, goodnight" repeating *ritardando* ending. It was all he could do not to go crashing right into "Will the Circle Be Unbroken," but he didn't think he had anybody to come and sing along.

A last cheer, and Jasper put his guitar away.

He came offstage shaking hands and saying, "I know it, I know it," to everyone's comments about the enormity of Rabbit's death, which seemed, even to the assholes like Rembert who despised old man Pettus like his daddy J. W. always had, a momentous event indeed in the history of the town of Tillman Falls, South Carolina.

Jasper went to help Trudy and Button Sykes cajole all the weepy drunks out of the bar. Probably the best night The Dixiana had had in a long-ass time, he suspected.

Fridge, Rabbit's longtime kitchen manager, could be heard in the back, mopping and sobbing and cussing. Button went over to turn off the PA and soundboard gear. Trudy started wiping down the bar top like she did on any regular night. If Rabbit ever came in the next day to a sticky bar, there would be hell to pay.

She sighed. "I guess we ought to cancel Calico Bonnet."

Button's head popped up from under the soundboard where she'd been switching off the juice.

Jasper got a catch in his throat. "You closing her down tomorrow?"

Trudy got an oh-shit look. "Tonight was tonight. But tomorrow—it ain't up to me."

He'd been looking forward to the act, a Gram Parsons tribute band out of Georgia. "Want me to call? I know their manager pretty good."

Trudy, coughing back a sob. "I reckon."

"It's no trouble."

Playing off her grief by sucking on a cig like her life depended on it, she keyed open the steel-gray, punch button National cash register, vintage even back on the first day she'd started work thirty years ago, and began counting down the drawer. "Yeah. That'd be a big help."

"Sure thing. You tell me what else I can do, now."

"I will, sugar." She caught Jasper's eye in the old Stroh's Lager mirror above the register. "Check on Roy Earl for me. If you would."

"Will do. He seemed tired, earlier. But okay."

"That's good. He's on my mind."

Roy Earl was on everyone's mind. Who knew what that boy would do about the club. Sure didn't need to keep it open for the money.

Jasper tried not to dwell on it. Or the provisions in Rabbit's will about the music festival he'd always wanted to have out front on the green. Over Jasper's pay grade, all that. Long as he got to play on the main stage, of course.

He carried his guitar case around the corner to where he liked to park on open mic nights, around back. Nipped his flask. Regarded General Reb's slitted, predatory eyes, glaring flinty down upon him from the wall.

Roy Earl—or somebody—would be sure to repaint that old mural, the one everyone rode by and touched for luck on game days. Jasper wondered why Rabbit hadn't done it by now—times had changed. It had some juju about it, the mural, going beyond the usual 'heritage' polemic most wavers of the old Confederate battle flag purported to promote. Nothing but paint on brick to him, not much else. Lord, but people got their drawers in a bunch over symbols, didn't they?

RABBIT PETTUS

Was it gonna be worse every day, now? This pain in the arm and across your back wasn't nothing but bumfuzzled, durn old bursitis, and putting on the icy hot was good enough and there wasn't nothing else to try.

Not even powwow. Nothing your grandmother taught you all those years ago—eighty years, it was beyond belief—would keep you alive much longer. They hardest hex to make, the toughest powwow to pull off, was the hex wielded to heal yourself.

Much easier, though you would have a hard time convincing most people, is making work with the spirit partners in wherever you're living, who keep up their end of a bargain and will keep you out of their nasty crosshairs. Even crazed, vengeful spirits like Agatha of Aberdeen were open to bargains, and you did it, long ago—a deal to keep her fiery ways away from your honkytonk and your home, in exchange the tending of her grave—and durn if the magic hadn't kept fresh for you for a good long time.

But all good things, they come to an end. In any case, you could not do powwow on yourself and expect much of a result, though a powerful and disciplined application of the principles could do some good. No doubt.

For a younger practitioner, maybe. Your faith in it all is weak. As is your heart, which you know deep down.

And if that harpy of a songbird Runelle didn't quit pestering you to get over to Dr. Wise, which if ever was a wrong name for someone then it was that one, you thought you might just about shit.

You wasn't gonna take no pills. Couldn't stand that mess no more'n you ever had, getting drunk like them wastrels done sitting there in his place every night but Sunday since nineteen and fifty-three.

Jesus. Your mind reeled at the time done passed.

You flashed back and forward both at the same time.

Time didn't make no sense.

It's a hoax. That's what your dead son Ronnie tells you in the dreams. You still have the war dreams, sometimes. But for the last forty-something years, more often it's been Ronnie Ed. Coming to visit. And telling you that time is a hoax. Whatever that means.

⊙❋◎

ALL YOU CAN SAY IS that you's good and sick of listening to Burnie's blather. Sick of them all, but especially those busybodies, those ELMS—and you'd have them know that for years you'd wanted to paint over that wall, and only hadn't because of its power to several men here in Edgewater County who believe Southeastern Redtails football success hinges upon the existence of the mural, and furthermore, the exact and precise mural in its current state.

If the mural went away, you couldn't protect your family from reprisal.

Why the hard men of Edgewater County ascribed such mystical hooey to a bunch of paint on a brick wall you couldn't say. Hadn't been painted with good intentions in mind, that much for sure. Over fifty years ago, now. More. Touched it up in 1980 when rumors went around that Gov. Reagan was coming on his campaign. Didn't happen, and the mural ain't been repainted since.

You can't believe what year it is, or how old you is, but after a certain point you don't do as much counting. Or maybe don't allow the mind to linger on such matters, and for obvious reasons. But Thurmond, Rembert, Burnie, Jasper, the others who frequented Pike's Bait & Pawn had imbued the mural with powers and qualities.

Some people said Howdy Shull had cast a spell on the wall back when he was a teenager. Jasper had heard more crazy stories about Howdy than he could remember, none of them true.

In any case, many believed the mural held what you might call luck-energy —a familiar sight, the men filing out of The Dixiana as the team on TV came running into the stadium over in Columbia, charging across the field to their bombastic theme music; touching the mural, one by one. Touching General Reb on the peeling paint of his red feathers and gray Confederate uniform of distinction. Muttering their liturgies.

Wasn't always about the team winning, per se—money changing hands over these contests, real money, and sometimes better for the team to lose so the gamblers could win big. Another part of it all that never much made sense to you, but there your redneck ass was, throwing in and betting like the rest. Not that you'd ever own up to your wife about the wagering. No sir.

⊚ ❂ ◎

Which doesn't go over well.

Shouting. Pissy attitudes. "What we want to see."

It rankled him.

The arm, hurting.

Out on the street, the damnedest thing: in front of your eyes stands The Dixiana, your place, your honkytonk, your stage you built so your beautiful wife could be happy and sing her songs, but it's become a crystal cathedral, and Burnie, he's out there waving at you; and Trudy Pirkle, a glowing saint behind the bar.

All the sound now echoing and faraway. Light, blinding light.

Cars passing, color-streaking across your vision, and the altar before you seems in motion, myriad intricate clockwork parts in perfect harmony and purple crackling lightning all around, shapes and whorls that are like people's faces, you realize, all calling for you and cheering as though you, for once, are the country music singer.

And moving closer to the stage, the stage where you've no business, and this despite being the owner of the club, because you've got no voice, no ear. Could only strum a guitar, and not very well.

But the stage approaching, and all these rascals, people you don't know from Adam, all happy as can be and stomping their feet and dancing, you realize, all around the edges of your vision, infinitely and exponentially expanding far as your old dog's eyes will carry, and you realize it looks like a science-fiction movie, all shimmering and blue and green lasers, like in one of your grandbaby's movies he looks at, that Star Wars mess. Four doors from which to choose, but everyone making it clear which one was his. Wa'n't sure whether it was a trick, a ruse, feels like a dream, you can't make a wrong choice, even if you did you'd wake up.

And then on the other side of the door you choose it seems you're in the Palmetto Grande sitting beside Roy Earl, looking at him so excited he is bouncing in his seat, and he's telling you about the movie you will see, and the ones coming later. That was your grandbaby's childhood obsession, those movies. Now you didn't know whether he still loved them, only that you're in the truck riding with him along River Ridge Road and he's talking about the movies, but you're moving back through your crystal cathedral of blue lasers again, and people are cheering you on and urging you to hurry.

As the walls melt, the entity you've become finds itself on the town green. No; floating above the green, watching as people scurry around and an ambulance comes, and the cheering audience and the doors and the theater, along with it Roy Earl, are falling away.

Where you are is back in North Dakota, and it is the spring of 1948 and you are watching as Runelle, a willowy reed with that mane of dark hair and those lips and those eyes struts across the muddy barnyard in her elegant pumps and dress she made you drive into Fargo to buy, carrying her guitar, ready to sing to the hayseeds. Said, if you would keep us out here in this hell, then you will get me clothes, and the guitar, and you did.

The barn dances, all there had been to do there on the outskirts of Oakes, North Dakota, four miles from the town and on this cockamamie idea of being a wheat farmer that one of your buddies put in your head on the way back from overseas, and as you float away from Runelle, she disappears inside the barn like she hasn't noticed her handsome man Rabbit waving and calling to her as he rushes back from the flat farmland you'd called home until returning to Edgewater County.

How she broke the news: "I'm taking Ronnie, and we're going back home," she'd said. "You are welcome to come with us, if you like. But we're going."

"Well-sir," you had said. "Reckon I'll get to packing it up."

Which you did, breaking the lease on the farm and heading back home, a place to which you said you'd never come, not after going overseas and seeing what you had: not only the death and blood and horror, but that the world worked different in other places. Different from South Carolina, but also from them West Virginia hollers full of coal minors where you'd growed up before coming south. Back home from the war, you liked the sound of North Dakota and all the open space. No more being hemmed in, that's what you said. You didn't know having a kid and wife would be hemming enough, and would be no matter where you ended up.

So you came home to Edgewater County, and when she didn't seem all that happy there—Runelle had grown up in West Columbia, right on State Street, and had gone to college in Charleston, and was a city girl through and through—you opened The Dixiana so she'd have a place to sing. That fixed it.

Singing and playing country music—that seemed to make her happy. She looked so different when she played and sang. You loved her so. She took up the guitar while living there in North Dakota, when there'd been nothing do, particularly all winter long. How you'd sit watching for the light of Oakes to emerge through the gloom of the blizzard, the only way to tell the snow was finally letting up. Sitting there, warm and cozy but isolated, Runelle strumming the guitar and you both making love to stay even more warm, and that next autumn Ronnie coming along.

How can you be there again, as you were flying away from the barn?

Ronnie knows.

Ronnie's right there with you.

"Daddy," he says, standing there in his uniform. "I missed you."

"Lord, but we been missing you, son."

"All right, then. It's all right. Look at us now."

"Who'd a thunk it."

"There we go, Daddy. It's all good."

"You want to know what all you missed? With your boy, Roy Earl? He's something."

Laughing at you, the way Ronnie used to; it'd make you want to smack him.

"Lemme show how you leave all that behind. Lemme tell you all about the letting go. Besides—he'll fill me in later. He'll tell me himself—I've been waiting for him, too."

So young and slender, your boy. Lord, but he lost even more weight once he went into the army. He looked like a different boy, the way Roy Earl had the last time you'd seen him, when he seemed in his forties to have lost his baby fat. Ronnie, he ain't changed, and when you see he's holding up this mirror—it's a magic mirror, the surface rippling like water—you see that your own face is young, your Adam's apple bobbing on the front of your skinny neck and your eyes alight, and you have on your own uniforms, one after the other: football, army, overalls, and the shirts and slacks you'd wear the rest of your life, but your face remaining the same, smiling at yourself, and the light all white and brilliant and filling up the space where the mirror and had been, and you go into the light.

You, Rennie; you, Rabbit. You, yourself.

And it feels so good, like never before. You wonder how, after all the time of being alive, you could have missed this wonderful sensation.

Only the thought of the money you hid in the old house—a lot of it—nags at you from the other world. You never told a soul, always meant for Roy to have it later. It might never be found. Oh, well. Money wa'n't real no way. Not the way everything else was.

Not real like this new place you're going seems to be. Realer than real, it is. More than anything that's come before. Now this you never expected about being dead.

BOOK TWO

Black Blade

But who can give soul to an image, life to stone, metal, wood or wax?
And who can make children of Abraham come out of stones? Truly this
secret is not known to the thick-witted worker... and no one has such
powers but he who has cohabited with the elements, vanquished nature,
mounted higher than the heavens, elevating himself above the angels to
the archetype itself, with whom he then becomes co-operator and can
do all things.

— CORNELIUS AGRIPPA

ROY EARL PETTUS

A threadbare old robe of Mee-maw's cinched around your pudge-bod, you preen on the back deck with the steaming first o'the day halfway to your lips, staring into a newly fenced square in the backyard in which sits an enormous white dog.

Like, bigger than crap, beau.

Big as a pony.

Panting. Whining and pawing at the gate.

"Cujo? Really?"

The beast snorts and shakes its prodigious head. Saliva sprays in graceful, slo-mo arcs like a money shot from a 70s John Holmes porno epic. As though taking care of Mama Runelle won't be enough of a burden. A freaking, freakish dog.

"This beats all I ever seen."

The dog, panting, draws your gaze into the uncanny valley of its unnerving, intelligent eyes. Smacks black, fleshy jowls. Ropy saliva oozes. Disgusting.

You ask the animal from where on earth it came; it answers only by flopping down by the gate, head between paws with a sigh, and here you have a huge white bear about to nap.

What must it go through in kibble? Nothing new when it came to industrial-grade sacks of kibble, not for this old hand at pushing a loaded cart at the pet superstore, coupons fluttering in your wake like ticker-tape. With a dozen cats cooped up in your marsh mansion, feeding the dog would be far from your first rodeo with these matters.

Not to mention how y'all had had mutts back here in the woods, an old hound dog named Buster Brown, a ragamuffin poodle called Benji, a couple of others. Living in the country, they'd sometimes wander up to the house from people dumping them along what used to be a rather lonesome stretch of highway. Rabbit said he'd never turn any dog away, but would just as soon not have animals. He'd seen too many suffering overseas during the war, and didn't want much to do with dogs and cats and all that mess.

You remember how you told Devin and Dobbs that story, and afterwards, they'd speculated soldiers had had to eat dog meat to survive. The image made you sick and sad inside, like you feel anyway about this shit pile you've stepped into with your slut-wife and dead Pa-paw.

Damn—Pa-paw's dead. It hadn't seemed possible.

You try not to panic. Your lovely Sedge Island home, filled with felines, remains your responsibility. For all you know your wife has run off with an assistant GM forever, and you may have to deal with the cats yourself.

And now a dog.

Your Mee-maw has come out on the deck holding her coffee and a skinny cigarette she's already got smoldering. Seems so frail, you're afraid she'll break. Your nerves are toast.

"His name's Rico."

You stare into the dog; the dog stares back.

"It looks like a goddamn polar bear."

"*Gro-o-oan,*" Rico rumbles from deep in his mighty chest.

"Go and tell him good morning, son. He's the sweetest dog you ever seen. Acts like a puppy. When his hips ain't hurting him."

Sounded like vet expenses in your future, but you keep such a remark to yourself. As you approach, his ears go all square and boxy, the deep brown eyes staring right through you. Growling. Low, but there.

"He's scared—talk to him. That's his worried face."

"He don't—doesn't—need to be afraid of me."

"How's he supposed to know?"

"I wouldn't hurt a fly. I love—animals," but you almost choke on the words. You do love them, but now fraught with layers of nonsense from Creedence back home.

"When Rabbit took him in, he had been beat."

A slow burn. "Who the hell beats a dog?"

"It don't matter."

"Rico: who's a good boy?"

Rico's pensive expression drops, the dog ears no longer boxy. That panting, dripping, smiling-eyed dog look of happiness and wonder. Another deep groan.

You unlock the sliding bolt of the gate. Cautious, tail wagging languid, the graceful, unhurried stroke of a great whale. Hips swaying, the comes over and offers a heartfelt display of unearned trust: Rico leans heavy against your legs, gazes upward. You scratch his fuzzy ears.

"He's got bad joints." Runelle, sucking her dentures. "You get that with big dogs."

"What is this thing?"

"Great Pyrenees."

"Really, now." Grief travels the length of your arm, settles in the middle of your chest. Rico goes to the ground and rolls on his side, looking askance, the eyes so large and brown and human, in their way. "Good boy. Who's a good boy," your voice breaking.

The dog arches its back, its penis pink and distended. More groaning.

"He's wound up."

"He misses his pappy." Your grandmother wails, now, weeping as hard as an old woman can into her crumpled coffee-stained napkin. "And he's so old, too. I swear—everything got old on us, Lord. Mercy, me."

Choking back your own grief, a quick rub of Rico's belly and you go to her, sitting and consoling and talking till you both get cried out. In your case, crying for Rabbit gets Creedence off your mind. Layers and levels.

A process.

Maybe he died now as a favor to you—a distraction before you could do anything rash regarding your wife and her lover. Like you still wanted to. At least it sounded like the dog wouldn't be on your balance sheet for long. One less thing, sooner rather than later.

Despite not having a relationship with the dog, the thought of your Papaw's dog following him into heaven hurts your heart. You're sensitive about animals, but most people don't know this about you. Maybe not even your wife.

⚙✳⚙

WHILE YOUR GRANDMOTHER fries pig sausage and a pair of fresh eggs from Letty Glasscock's chickens over on the other side of the pecan orchard, you phone the funeral home; you call other people about crap not worth recounting, like your broker with a few portfolio adjustments to suggest. Good clean fun. Money stuff. It takes your mind off the real problems.

Leaves you empty though. Money, an obstacle you've overcome, but to hear your broker tell it, you need more:

"I'm gonna make you so much fucking cheese-whiz, pal." Your guy barks this all bright and fresh as a new copper penny straight out of the Philadelphia mint.

He's been pitching hedge funds. "You sound mighty confident."

Rodney Cowan's office is in Charleston. He's ten years younger, a good-looking gym rat with greased hair and teeth and a diamond-stud earring, his blazing energy and sparkle like he grew up watching *Jerry Maguire* on a loop and said, CRUISE IS GOD, and I will imprint this persona upon myself. *"How could I not be confident? Bro: I love this game."*

You began investing while y'all lived on the peninsula, after you opened Charleston #1 and soon thereafter #2, over in a Mount Pleasant outdoor mall by the main road onto the Isle of Palms, and Christ the Jesus did you move fruitshake that first summer season. When you had the idea to try other college neighborhoods like Columbia's Old Market where you'd begun, Creedence, pushing you instead to expand to Charleston. And not wrong about tourism. Cruise ships docked near the slave market, and the antebellum mansions and ghosts of the well-preserved colonial port had made the city in modern times into one of the top travel destinations in the world. Let the fruitshakes flow.

Wanting to move there had also been for selfish reasons though, not only business acumen. Charleston, Charleston, Charleston, she'd begged; her dream from childhood to live there, she said.

And so you delivered for your bride, moving right downtown in a two-bedroom top floor condo you paid far too much per square foot to rent, but could afford. Enviable harbor and city views, the church spire, South of Broad architecture, the freighters chugging in from overseas loaded down with sneakers and Christmas decorations and cat toys and gewgaws and doodads. A musky, swampy smell. Charleston.

Not that you had time for horizon gazing. Expanding the Spotted Banana™ brand reach into the Carolina low country had taken its share of sweat equity by its mastermind, but at least the financing had been a snap. Your credit, awesome, your core businesses profitable and primed for further growth. Cash on hand.

Damn if it all hadn't worked out in spades, short and long term, and motherfudge it all but did you NOT enjoy living in Charleston, neither as a port-city tourist trap, nor college town. You couldn't abide that sickening Old South bourgeois air of privilege and entitlement. Plus, because of your upcountry pedigree, you'd have a tough time becoming in charge of anything meaningful in Chucktown re: civic affairs.

In those days of drinking and partying, you found other like-minded professionals and entrepreneurs with whom to socialize, which you went along with but didn't much enjoy. Creedence reveled in the flitting from cocktail party to happy hour to lavish dinners taken out because, hell, she'd been cooped up in Edgewater County her whole life. Partying on the peninsula seemed big time compared to a night on the town in Tillman Falls—the Pizza Hut, maybe, or a barbecue basket from the Hollow Bone, followed by a few sweating longneck Buds at The Dixiana. Plus, living downtown, you could walk everywhere. Get lit, stumble home, check out the view, have a screw, sell fruitshake all the live long day. Three years went by like that.

You suppose it wasn't so terrible, those days. Not now.

You worked most of the time, saving the partying for the nighttime. And she had school, the three semesters she attended C of C trying to finish the graphic arts degree she'd abandoned after only a year at Southeastern. Now, she said, she'd get back on a degree track at thirty, after she'd restarted her life alongside you. Moving on after a decade of her failed and unfulfilling life there in Edgewater County with first husband, Dusty, a sub-human, three fifths of a person to you. With whom she had no contact and made no kids, thank god. Dusty.

Wait—you said Dusty lives "there" in Edgewater County. No. There is now "here" for you. Dusty is "here" in the EC. As are you, my boy.

There is here, and here? *It's there.*

Whoa, dude. For a second, like, you saw yourself? Across the room? Holding your phone and gripping your coffee cup with the other hand? Some real David Lynch crap going on.

Maybe it's the coffee, some of the worst you've ever experienced, this swill that your grandparents drink. No wonder the old coot croaked, because yeah, this coffee is killing you, too. You examine a generic label on the can from the IGA that yields, yeah, you say it to yourself: hot brown water with the flavor notes mainly of the chlorine in the city water Runelle and Rabbit drink out of the pipes now instead of the original well. You were surprised to learn they'd connected to water and sewer once it had come all the way down River Ridge Road, thanks, you knew, to the couple of sandy subdivisions carved out of former pine barrens with names like Falcon Forest and Edgewater Downs. You'd never have believed the county would run sewer this far out on River Ridge. But here it lay. Maybe it's the coffee, some of the worst you've ever experienced, this swill that your grandparents drink. No wonder the old coot croaked, because yeah, this coffee is killing you, too. You examine a generic label on the can from the IGA that yields, yeah, you say it to yourself: hot brown water with the flavor notes mainly of the chlorine in the city water Runelle and Rabbit drink out of the pipes now instead of the original well. You were surprised to learn they'd connected to water and sewer once it had come all the way down River Ridge Road, thanks, you knew, to the couple of sandy subdivisions carved out of former pine barrens with names like Falcon Forest and Edgewater Downs. You'd never have believed the county would run sewer this far out on River Ridge. But here it lay. This used to be so far out in the boonies, your grandfather always said, that the chickens had eyes the size of saucers from interbreeding with owls for lack of roosters.

Where would growth end? How much money would Rodney make you today? Money, it could go on growing forever, that was the magic. But to what end? Who would buy all the houses you saw being built—you? If they kept on building in this part of the county, it wouldn't be the country anymore. They won't quit until there are condos like yours in Charleston, but on the high bluffs over the Sugeree River where the Tragedy of '77 kids died. A historic site. A selling point.

◌❀◍

AFTER A BRIEF CONVO with Karlaney Funeral Home, you check in and debrief with Sharolyn, your manager at the Beanery Sedge Island, dealing with the workplace fallout from that whole sordid mess. You go back outside on the deck so as not to let Mama Runelle hear what's sure to include cursing and awkward euphemisms.

"Sharolyn: you are not in the middle of any drama. Sort of. But not."

A gale of concern. "What on earth, Mr. Roy? What going on with—them?"

That Creedence of yours, literally fucking you over. Maybe right now—a morning screw like you so love, her red hair dancing on his chest instead of yours as she rocks herself to sweet release.

Your wife.

But you can't think about it. And yet the hard truth flashes through your mind, and the anger changes on a dime into a chasm of abject, gut-kicked heartbreak.

You pull yourself together, hold your voice steady. You're the leader. Reiterating: "You aren't in the middle of a blamed thing, other than shouldering responsibility for the Beanery. And, helping me figure out whether we're promoting from within, or putting out for résumés to see who replaces —replaces—"

"Estes?"

"See how easy it'll be to replace him? I've already forgotten his name."

"What about Miss Creedence?"

Simmering. You maintain. Barely. "What. About. Her."

"She come by last night and—and—"

"And what?"

"And said she'd make the deposits in the morning. Herself."

"Did she, now. Did she."

"Like y'all would do sometimes. She said. So what could I say."

Your head, hot like the charcoal briquets in your granddaddy's grill made from a rusted, flame-licked 55-gallon drum, that you used to tend during the epic Sunday afternoon cookouts and hootenannies at the Pettus spread back in the woods. One Christmas when you finally had extra money, you bought your Pa-paw a Weber Genesis E-330 propane model grill, that first holiday season after buying the coffee shop from Maxine. He cussed you for doing it. The first of many times, and over many gifts.

"That witch is trying to poison my ever loving soul. But look, I'll get to the bottom of this deposit stuff. Leave that to me."

Sharolyn says, "Yes sir," in a voice that trembles, as though waiting for chastisement. "I swear I didn't have no clue what's been going on."

"Check. But look. From here on out, Creedence—Mrs. Pettus—is not allowed to handle monies. Deposits need to be made, but it's not important enough for her to do. It's beneath her. Understand?"

"It didn't seem right. But what I can say? She's your wife."

Walking it all back. "I didn't say it wasn't right; I said she shouldn't have to do such a menial task."

"I think I understand."

You both know the truth—Creedence has taken the money. For what, though?

A few minutes grind by as you think it through, and when you realize what's happened: she's pitying the little fucker. Some of what she'd written in those heart wrecking, profane messages, like how she only wished she could share more with him. That she hated a musician of Estes's talent had to suffer as a coffee slave for a non-creative type like Roy Pettus. That she knew how such suffering felt.

How he—you—keep her on such a short leash financially, emotionally, whole bit. Control it all. You monster.

Your manager wonders aloud if she should quit, and in that moment you consider letting her.

Yeah—close the damn place. Make poor Creedence happy.

But you don't shutter a successful business concern, one with positive cash flow. You have people counting on you. For money. To live. Including your manager, whose life and career you uprooted from the mainland to come and work for you.

"Having dispelled energy by voicing the wrong idea—quitting—do you feel better?"

"I'd rather not quit this job, Mr. Pettus. Truth be told."

Moving on. "Got a new assistant GM in mind?"

Sharolyn, going *urm*. "Plenty folks out there looking for a paycheck."

"No duh. We want known-knowns. Go-getters."

"Good luck with all that. But I'll poke around."

You ponder and weigh. Take a deep breath. "Well, look. I don't want you to think you can set up your own fiefdom there. The CBSI is my show, still. But if you know someone who knows coffee, who knows money, who knows people, who reflects your standards of behavior and commitment, then you have my tacit authorization to hire."

"For real?"

"Shoot, yes." You lower your voice. "Gonna have my hands full."

"I know, sweetie—I mean, Roy."

"Appreciate it."

"We're all so sorry about your granddaddy."

Back inside you sip your coffee, smile at your grandmother as she sets the plate of sausage and eggs down, the toast, the apple butter and real butter you haven't tasted in ages. You put Sharolyn on speaker and butter the toast, your mouth watering and stomach growling as though you haven't eaten in a month. And you realize you haven't, not really. Never a proper, balanced meal at all yesterday, only endless snacking from the pile of sympathy food.

Chewing and sipping with relish, you get back to the unpleasant business: "You recovered all his keys and passcode card?" Sounding like his coffee shop and cafe were a classified and secured government lab. "Right?"

"He gave them up. Yes sir."

"Call the locksmith. Change everyone's keys anyway, would you?"

"For real?"

"Indulge me."

Sharolyn muttered that she'd get right on it.

"There's a nice bonus in all this extra rigmarole. For persevering. You're chipping away at it in my stead, girlfriend. You know that?" You wink at Meemaw, whom you notice watching and listening.

"I appreciate that, Roy."

"And I appreciate you. You'll see how much."

Sharolyn, sounding more skeptical than grateful, rings off.

"Why in the hell did you open that thing?" Runelle, stiff and ancient, lowers herself into the chair across from you. Sunlight streams in, her wild and flyaway white hair back-lit like the glimmering corona of a saint. "Do you know Creedence called me boohooing over it?"

"Over opening a new Beanery?" You choke on a sizzling hot sausage link, the skin of which bursts with a spray of hot pig-juice between your teeth in a manner no fake-sausage soy tube could ever match. "But why not? There's no risk. It's a safe investment. More dynamic than letting the money sit. I'm a job-creator."

"Darling, how much more money do you need?"

You wouldn't mind upgrading the plane. Again. And buying land in the mountains on which to retire. Hide away when the shit comes down. That type-deal.

Any of which you can already do.

All right, what about a boat? A real boat, like Creedence talks about in her hinting manner. The rich lady on a boat. The ongoing costs of ownership—hell, fuel alone—is enough to warrant needing to trademark another brand and sell it off to some big corporation. Forget it. You have not given a shit about going on the sea since seeing Jaws on opening night at the Palmetto when you were six-year-old—and who the hell takes a little kid to a movie like that? You don't go in the ocean over your knees.

You've never told Mee-maw that. She'd laugh at you. Only a movie. But sharks, quite real. No fucking boats, not even a skiff to tool around in the marshes. Who gave a crap, you would ask. Any old nitwit can get a boat and bob in the numerous island waterways. Swat mosquitoes. Dig pluff mud out of the grooves of your sport sandals like dog mess.

Flying, now that was a noble pursuit.

But Creedence? No, she wouldn't set foot on your aircraft. Insulting. Insulting as hell.

"I don't need any at all. I needed something to do, I reckon."

"Nothing wrong with that."

You ask what your wife said.

Mama Runelle waves it away, butters her own toast with her bony fingers, hands bent by arthritis into claws. She must never play guitar anymore. This you know without being told. "That she couldn't understand why you were spending money and time on that. That you'd already done it. Oh, also that you claimed you wanted to do something different—something with her, she said. That that's what you promised her when they come and made you the offer on your company. You would have time for each other."

You search your memory—you'd promised a pursuit with her, hadn't you. And all you had done was choose an expensive and dangerous hobby she can't stand, and open the same coffee shop you started with twenty years ago, only in a place where you can get away with charging twice as much as in the Old Market. These weren't college kids on a budget, well-to-do snowbirds and retirees and the nouveau riche like you, fruitshake boy, as you call yourself in low moments like these, when you have to acknowledge to your grandmother you do remember saying that. That you were both drunk on celebratory wine and had headaches the next day, but you do remember.

"I told her it was all going to be different."

"Life's feeling that way for me," she says. "Mercy."

"Ain't that the truth."

You eat breakfast with your grandmother. You perceive a vast emptiness in the house. His absence like a presence. If that makes any sense. You make an executive decision to smear extra butter and preserves on yet another piece of toast and chew every bite with presence and aplomb. It tastes like greasy cardboard.

FLIPPING THROUGH THE PAPER—NOT the *Edgewater Advocate*, rather the *Columbia Record* from down in the capital, once the 'big' paper, but now as thin as the *Advocate*, and worse for wear with regard to copyediting; mainstream journalism, withering on the vine.

One day you watched a YouTube compilation of local newscasters from around the country all reading what sounded like the same script, puff piece after puff piece, all coming from some anonymous and central voice. Scary stuff. Another reason to keep the TV off.

It's been so long since you looked at an actual dead tree newspaper that the pages in your hands seem oily and cumbersome, musty and brittle and worst of all, an ephemeral relic of a rapid and receding past. You have desktops and laptops and a pair each of iPads and iPad Minis, dedicated devices kept in upstairs and downstairs bathrooms, and the ever-present iPhone, yeah, for the streaming of your news-feeds. Paper. One day the surviving historians will look back and think, how crude and destructive.

Oh, what news there be: The top story today a murder-suicide on University Terrace, the kind of heinous act that includes the two children as well as the dead mom and dad. Throat-slitting with steak knives. Dad, a former award-winning physics professor working on theories of quantum mechanics and a diagnosed paranoid schizophrenic, had been in and out of institutions, medicated for years. This, a known fact in the man's family and circles. It had worried the wife, an anonymous family friend said. Bill had gone off his medication.

"But still," a neighbor reported. "Nobody thought him capable of this level of violence."

You suck your teeth and rattle the page. "God-dog, that's raw."

Mama Runelle knows to what you're reacting. "Don't that mess beat all?"

Now you're downright sick inside at what the story forces you to consider: since the moment you saw the light glowing from the screen of Creedence's laptop (a Macbook Air) and it sunk in what you were reading, you've had thoughts of shooting her, and then yourself. Not a joke.

"Who'd do such a thing," catching in your throat. "Kids and all."

"Better not to even ask. Because there ain't no good answer, son."

"Everybody's got a reason for doing what they do, I reckon."

"P'shaw."

"Well, look: don't ask me questions I can't answer, and then when I try to come up with one, sit there and give me that irritating old 'p'shaw' of yours."

"I'll give you more'n a p'shaw if you don't watch that smart mouth."

As though twelve again, you feel self-conscious and fat. The contentious adolescent years to come, when sniping occurred on a daily basis, incoming from both directions. A wide gulf between teenager and grandparent. "Yes'm."

Your mind, spun; the hot greasy country breakfast now rubbery and tasteless in your mouth, golden buttery eggs you continue to eat out of courtesy. You salivate at the notion of whipping up a Bluesberry MegaMonster with ginseng, B vitamins and added protein, a healthy meal in a cup.

Ha—Bluesberry. You had all sorts of cleverness going.

How's that working out for ya? Being clever? Gangbusters.

More than that:

Wish you could go back to those days when it had been only the Beanery, and the first Spotted Banana™, before you'd hit on the 'fruitshake' tag. When you had gotten hold of the girl of your dreams, Creedence. Against all odds. Against time itself. And after that miracle, all else had seemed a breeze. Still did.

Now that the money itself made money, was Mama Runelle right? You can do anything you wish with your time. Including finding more ways of spending it with your wife—time, not money.

What have you been thinking?

Because the marriage didn't feel right anymore. Because Creedence withdrew from you.

That's the real reason you started flying and opened the Carolina Beanery Sedge Island. You are the one who needs fulfilling. You are the one shut out.

That's what you tell yourself, anyway, but choose not to verbalize it to your grandmother. You clean up the breakfast dishes and consider all the food and the desserts folks brought last night and think, there are only two of you.

Who will eat all this food, you ask?

Your grandmother answers by saying she'll be damned if she knows.

"There a Food Not Bombs chapter here? Or some other treehuggers?"

"A do-what?"

"A philanthropic activist group who feed the poor."

"You know what? Burnie's grandbaby tried to start up something like that. Right there on the town green."

"And what happened?"

"Council voted it down. Rennie and Burnie both tried to tell her, there ain't no way there'll be black and Mexican trash lined up around that green being served food they can get themselves, if they'd only set their lazy-assed minds to it. Besides, don't you think one of them tenderhearted ELMS would've done that by now? If somebody was of a mind to allow it here in Tillman Falls? God knows there's enough of them that'd line their asses up for a free meal. Shit," she says, wiping her mouth and coughing. Sipping her brown coffee. "Put out fried chicken and you'd empty half the churches. But you could ask her."

"Who?"

"Button. Burnie's grandbaby."

"That chubby little mutant?"

"Roy—hush your mouth. She's sweet as can be."

Button, what a disaster compared to her sister, Thim, who came of age a slender Asian reed of a hottie. A little red-haired, freckle-faced freak with too much weight on her, thick glasses, silent most of the time, these are your memories of Button—unattractive, monosyllabic, possibly autistic. God only knows what she's like now. "Sorry. I'll try to be nicer."

◎◈◎

Mama Runelle rises to police the dishes, but you protesteth, demanding that you'll take care of it. This attitude precipitates an argument, one you lose.

Watching her stoop and bend and rinse off plates, you top off both your terrible cups of coffee. After she fixes hers with cream and sugar and sits back down, you try to get her to talk about the past.

"Tell me some stories."

"Stories about what?"

Tight-lipped as ever, both of them. A generational thing. "Never got how a couple of Carolina crackers just up and moved to freaking North Dakota."

"Lord. It's so long ago now. Almost like it wa'n't real." She works her lips, seeming to chew on the memories. "Oh, your granddaddy had this friend from the war, Ed Schulein. Had to think of his name. Talked Rennie into it. But there was another reason."

You wait. Raise your cup, along with the eyebrows.

"It was because of the Germans billeted here."

"Germans?"

She explains how in 1945 they made a German POW camp right there in Edgewater County, over by the airfield in a barracks that at the start of the war had been used for housing for pilots in training. That they made the POWs work in the fields and factories here as part of their wartime imprisonment, though she noted how it wasn't slavery, they got paid, and fed, and well treated. Makes a big deal about that part.

But despite their relative comfort and courteous disposition, she also remembers the German boys getting into trouble for carving little swastikas into the tomatoes they were picking, a reminder how the war was still going on. That they were the enemy. "All that went on right over yonder on Mr. Glasscock's farm. Believe it or not."

"Pa-paw must've hated them fellas. To pick up and move to North Dakota to get away from them."

"Like I said, he had his reasons. Couldn't stand the thought of POWs being here, living nearby." Faraway; reliving those days. "He got back and seen them men marching in their gray outfits, or being driven around on buses through the middle of town and down this here very road. They put them down at Camp Jackson, and in Myrtle Beach, and Aiken, and other places all over the state. Well," lighting another of her slender cigs. "Your granddaddy half lost his mind over it. Got all panicky. I thought he was having a heart attack, or a fit, or god knew what."

"He was different. When he came back."

A shadow across her face. "I don't think I seen your granddaddy cry but two or three times his whole life. That was one. Over them damn POWs."

Dang. "Brought the war home for him, I reckon."

"He had guarded them overseas, too, Roy. That was his job right as the war was ending—guarding boys they'd captured."

"Really?"

"You didn't know?"

"He never even told me that much." You get a sharp taste in your mouth, a bitter seed from a slice of orange you've been sucking. "No war stories. No going upstairs at the bar. No this. No that."

"Well—" She smiles all sad and weary. "He didn't want to burden you."

"Did he burden you?"

"No, son. I don't know what all happened. Any more than you do."

"At least we know it had to do with captured POWs."

"Lord, yes. He had such a hard time getting over the war. I wished we hadn't had to fight it. But then, I never would've gotten with him."

"You might've anyway. You and Granddaddy."

"Makes your head feel funny to think about how things could've gone."

"Don't I know it."

You watch as your grandmother's eyes fill with tears. "War or not, I sure am glad I did. A good man—he was a good man." Her voice, suffused with the weight and distance of the years. "He was such a gentleman. A bit of a hillbilly, but a gentleman."

How nervewracking to be so close to death, with so much of one's existence fading into the deep past rather than stretching ahead, unknown but filled with promise. Your life, it still feels fresh, somehow, your memories close at hand, all like yesterday. Most of it, anyway.

But at Mee-maw's age? Certain death.

Sooner.

Soon.

You? You never think about death. Not in your mid-to-late 40s.

You?

You're at your peak.

Sure, plenty of dude-bros croaked at all ages including yours, but you? Hah! You've gotten your pear-shaped bod whittled down. Stopped with the fast food, an indulgence that kept on the flab, as did quaffing your own fruit-shakes like the Peanut Butter Bunker Buster, with a yield measured at nearly a thousand megatons, er, calories. Creedence, buying the free-range eggs and the grass fed beef. Steaming stuff. Putting a piece of fruit in your lunch pail instead of a cookie. Cutting back on the constant grilling, also going from charcoal to gas, much better for you in that outdoor kitchen of yours down on the Island.

Hah. No home there. Not anymore.

You want to go burn the fucker down.

No, pay some cat to do it—an expert; a pro.

⊛⊛⊛

THE BOYS at the hanger would have a line on a hit man, but you'll have to be careful; a couple are retired LEOs.

Wait—those are the guys who would know.

How to commit a crime.

Wouldn't they.

Among the lot of seasoned and moneyed male specimens of American humanity, they presented themselves as experts and masters of most everything, a collective of Yodas sitting around, which you are well on your way to being as well: a tribal elder. Hell, thanks to your money you already are, only younger. Less seasoned. And less moneyed than a few. Sedge Island, a rich boy's playground. And not overrun with criminals.

What puts you off arson and murder, however, is the memory of Mickey Rourke in Body Heat, which your twelve-year-old self screened at the Palmetto Grande. How the hot young actor, mannered as could be imagined, flicked his finger against his lip and said, With any good crime, counselor, there's fifty ways you can fuck up. And if you think of twenty-five of em, you're a genius.

But you, fruitshake boy? You ain't no genius.

You squelch this horrible and unproductive line of thinking not because of getting caught, rather over the collateral loss, and the additional pain to Creedence herself.

The kitties.

Your kitties, belonging to the two of you. As you imagine the suffering and dying of the cats you like, which to be honest includes most, your tortured heart clenches with shame.

Ridiculous emotionalism. Where, your precious mental discipline?

And what little left now collapses. Tears well up. Your chest tight and hollow, you hold them back.

"Mee-maw," a wet croak. But you can't go on your voice breaking like back when you were trying to tell her who had been picking on you at baseball practice. How it had been Cecil Waugh again, but you couldn't get out the words without bawling. "Help me."

"What is it, my precious angel," the loving grandmother voice. "Tell Mee-maw."

"My heart's been tore out already, even before granddaddy. It's Creedence —she don't love me anymore. Creedence. It's—" You collapse in grief, holding your grandmother tight, too tight.

"You hurting my neck, honey."

You loosen up. Pull yourself together best you can. "None of that's your business, though. Is it. How selfish of me."

"Well, darling—it's not selfish. But you're right. It's none of my business, but if it has to do with your happiness, then I reckon it is. But let's not talk about it. We got to figure things out."

You nod and say, don't you know it, y'all got plenty of pie plates already spinning, and so on. That it's never too early to get the plan together. That you need to set your mind to work. To have a purpose.

Here's one: Now is the time for you to be strong for your grandmother, who is your mother, or has been. And in the spirit and memory of that stalwart old son of a bitch who raised your pink, chubby, spoiled little ass into the man you've become:

A doer.

A master.

Puttering with the dishes against your wishes, she asks, "When they gonna be done with him. With his ashes." Difficult for her to say aloud.

"Tomorrow morning. That when you want to do it?"

"Tomorrow, next day. He ain't going to get no more dead, is he?"

"I reckon not."

"But we don't wanna wait too long." She's so old and frail. Still tall and birdlike, but stooped. Thin—too thin. Her age stands in high relief on her lined face. She won't be here much longer, either. Will she.

Will any of us?

You aren't sure if you can stomach living much longer yourself. It's too soon to tell. Mercy, but is it too-soon, like that time you cracked wise on a clear-skied September the 11th about what a beautiful day to fly a plane into a building.

◌◉◌

AND SO YOU busy yourself with thoughts of what you'll say at the scattering. And what you will do with your granddaddy's honkytonk. Which means, Trudy.

"I guess I need to get up with Ms. Pirkle about what's to happen. Don't I."

"It's—too much for me to think about."

"You mean, about what we're gonna do?"

"No, honey—what you're going to do. He didn't leave The Dixiana to me.

He left it to his only grandbaby. You'll be the one who's left, soon. The only one."

You get ice in your gut.

You will be one alone motherfucker.

Won't you.

Running the fucking Dixiana.

Holy mother of scrambled eggs.

But the wheels, a-turning: The first thing you'll do?

Ideas.

The hair on your arms stands up. Making your mark on the whole enterprise.

You go to the cabinet where your Granddaddy keeps the spare keys, something he shows you every time you come home, 'just in case,' as he always said. And yeah, they're still hanging the way you remember them, on gold screw-in hooks with peeling Avery labels scotch-taped and marked in your grandmother's careful script.

With trembling fingers, you thread onto your keyring the one marked DIX FRONT DOOR, a deteriorating shank of scalloped metal on which you're counting to unlock the honkytonk; the door to your future, and everyone else's in your immediate sphere of influence. Lucky them; it's a bubble of awesome that now, surely, has nowhere to go but up.

CREEDENCE

tupid, stupid, stupid. All she could think. So careless.

Prone.

Kitchen floor.

Kitty kibble under her back, hard little rocks.

She'd come stumbling through their bowls, earlier, making a mess. Needed to lie down for a spell. Staring up at the light fixtures and the pots and pans hanging down and crying over her kitties, whom she thought she'd never see again—several of them were getting on in years.

Roy planned to banish her.

She could hear it in his voice.

Earlier, she had had a couple more drinks at home, went to break it off with Estes, but instead loved him for all he was worth. In bed together, his cock flopped across her thigh still twitching and dribbling spunk, her boytoy reiterated how he knew the whole deal offered them a sticky, complicated wicket.

Said he didn't care; he loved her.

"But shit, girl," punctuated by a fretful whine. "We got a prob."

Son, you don't even know. "Like what?"

Tracing his fingers along the swell of her freckled hip. "This is hot, and all? But compared to your old man, I'm broke. Compared to anybody."

"What does money got to do with it?"

"Nothing." But his face said, something.

Cruel to not tell him. A jolt of adrenaline. "Roy found out."

Estes, freezing in mid-caress. Fully present. "Holy. Shit. Holy—holy shit."

"We can't go on."

A different shock. "Aw, yo—don't say that."

She began to cry.

To comfort her he had started fucking again, this time like he meant it. And not like only sex for fun—a love-fuck.

Slow and patient and gazing into her eyes. "Don't cry, Mrs. Pettus—I mean, Creedence."

A problem.

Afterwards she slugged back an iced tea glass full of cheap white wine at Estes's crappy apartment but stopped for a real bracer at the Swank Palanquin, a high-end tourist bar on the way back home. After ordering a double G&T she ducked into the bathroom and washed herself. Squeezed and grunted to make sure his spoogie spurted back out, a habit from when she'd been hiding it from Roy, who's not even on the island.

Maybe never coming back.

Terrified at the thought.

She scrubbed her tender genitals with the rough brown lavatory paper, her labia still swollen and swampy with the dregs of a hard-fought orgasm. Guilt had kept her from coming until the second time, when there was no one and nothing but the Moment and it came and it went, ebbing and transcendent and this was what life was all about?

For about twenty seconds worth of afterglow?

Followed by emptiness?

And fear?

After freshening up she ordered a drink, make it a double, then saw she'd already had one waiting. Drank it down, whoosh, like Roy slugging bottled water after one of his walks, the power-walks she never felt like taking alongside him.

Dropping a twenty, Creedence stagger-stepped toward the front entrance.

The female bartender, Abbie or Andie or Ashley or whatever, hollered after her. "Mrs. Pettus—this is too much."

"Keep it, sweetie. I got plenty."

Creedence lunged for the door handle but missed, her momentum carrying her forward into the tempered glass. She bonked her elbow, sharp. "*Fudge*," like Roy would put it. Every head in the bar turned. "That hurt."

Back in the BMW, she only had a half mile on the Cross Island Express before reaching her neighborhood. No prob.

Her vision, doubling. At the guard gate, unmanned but requiring a code she had to punch in six times to get right, she bumped up and over the curb into the neighborhood.

Once on her and Roy's street, however, she grazed and toppled one of the clean, blue herbie kurbies they had issued residents at the beginning of the year. About the same time, the brilliant, pulsing blue beams of the cop car popped on behind her.

Panic.

No, she'd talk her way out. They all knew Roy. She'd skate—they had money.

The island cop, looking about twenty minutes out of high school, gave her the once-over. "Mrs. Pettus?"

See, he already knew who she was. "What seems to be the problem?"

"Looked like that trash can might have jumped out at you?"

She relaxed. "There ya go. I tell ya," laughing and flirty, gesturing with a scolding index finger. "Those things, they're dangerous. I ought to—I'll make a speech at the next homeowner's association—*hup*." Damn hiccups. "Association meeting."

"Roger that. But—I'm concerned over this driving I observed just now."

Now she focused her vision, and sure enough the dude was one of the young cops who frequent Roy's coffee shop; his nameplate read Webhannet. He had short buzzed black hair, tight muscles under his Kevlar, eyes probing hers the way cops do. Young. So young, and beautiful not unlike Estes, but in this case a regular old whiteboy.

Maybe she could screw this kid to get out of the roadside stop. What did it matter now? She needed this over and done. She needed a fucking drink. "Y'all still enjoying all that free coffee from my husband?"

Webhannet sighed. "You had anything to drink tonight, ma'am? Besides coffee?"

"White wine—only two glasses. And, I didn't even finish the second one," her Ss sounding like Sylvester the Cat. "Look. My phone, it beeped and distracted me when I—brushed by that trash can." Fumbling with the door locks, motioning to let her get out. "Lemme go and pick it up."

"Just stay in the vehicle, please." She watched in the mirror as the handsome, fit police officer, his slender hips rolling, went back to his cruiser. She saw him making a call.

He came back. "Okie-dokie. You're a lucky lady tonight."

Her spirits had soured. She worried about having downed that stiff drink. In the rearview she glimpsed a sunken-eyed mess. Worse, she still had bedhead from doing the deed with Estes. "I hope you ain't being sarcastic."

"Hardly. I just got off the phone with Mr. Pettus."

"You got Roy on the phone?"

"Mm-hm."

She smarted off about how her husband wasn't her keeper.

"I'm not supposed to do this. Real unorthodox. But Mr. Roy, he asked me to always keep an eye out for you. To help him keep you safe. Which is my charge for everyone here on the island already. An honor, in fact."

"Don't do me no favors." Glum, sounding like the Edgewater County girl she still was at heart. "Okay, beau?"

"I could lose my posting here with the island police force for calling him. But because I know the kind of community leader he is—and who you are—I thought I'd give us a chance to work this out."

Amazing. But it's no wonder. She's seen how these young guys look up to her husband. The thin blue line, Roy calls them. Creedence has wondered if Roy shouldn't have chosen a job that required a uniform, or gone into the army, the way he looked up to these assholes. "I don't think it's up to the two of you to decide nothing about me."

Troubled. "Look: Let's forget you said that. And I don't wanna be the guy with the badge and all, but I'm in charge here. So here's how it's gonna go. He's asked me to see you home, and I'm going to get you there. Your car'll be towed, but you can retrieve it tomorrow. That's gonna be a couple hundred dollars, plus a ticket for too fast for conditions. And I'm real sorry about that part. But hey, you get to go home tonight. Instead of to the Sedge Island drunk tank." His voice turned stern and frosty. "Doesn't that sound like it's worth a slight attitude adjustment on your part, ma'am?

Rather than feeling gratitude, Creedence, thinking she should question the propriety of this arrangement. Annoyed that Roy E. Pettus can tell the po-po what he wants done. She was so tired of him and his pompous ass. Roy, he had asked for Estes. Asked for it, he did.

She belched vodka and prevented herself, somehow, from smarting off. "I reckon I ought to thank you."

Webhannet nodded, avoiding her gaze. He spoke into his mic for dispatch to send the impound tow truck. "Mr. Roy said he'd talk to you later. And that he wished you had your phone and wondered where you were. Where you'd been." His words, stilted, as though he'd been coached to say it all that way.

Roy's little puppet, from all the way up in Edgewater County. Disgusting.

"I'm right where he knows me to be, which is here, at home."

"I'm sure he'd be glad to hear from you. At some point."

She thanked him for his gentle suggestions. Got her purse and other junk together to be carried the three moss-shrouded blocks to her home on the marsh.

❁❖◉

Roy, on becoming good buddies with the cops: he had learned this from being in business back in the Old Market, the college neighborhood near Southeastern U, where you had muggers and grifters and date rape and binge drinking, and needed decent beat cops to help keep a lid on it all.

Now, Creedence had become the thing needing a lid.

A volcano, in fact.

Especially with her lover.

Who, like he said, could provide nothing. A self-aware kid.

Contrasted with Roy Earl Pettus, Estes was kinda like all dick and no wherewithal, and that was a dead effing end for real, girlfriend. Creedence, she might as well have stayed married to Dusty Wallis and lived in their little manufactured house there in Chilton, half a mile from her mother's house. She didn't have squat in her name. A household allowance. Wow.

Inside the beautiful home, all stucco and Ludowici Spanish roof tiles and open square footage, so much more room than the two of them needed (but that the cats adored), Creedence sat in the hollow family room on the sofa looking at her iPhone, its battery icon into the red, where it had been sitting since this morning. She hadn't forgotten it, had left the device behind on purpose: After Roy had read the emails, she'd become convinced that he was watching her every move. Had programmed her phone to keep its lens and microphone trained on her. Even now she regarded it as an interloper, that phone. Threw a dishrag over it there on the kitchen counter, her palatial dream kitchen in which she rarely bothered cooking a decent meal anymore.

As the phone vibrated and rang with its brittle electronic generic ringtone, which she wanted to change but couldn't figure out how, Creedence all but shit herself. Pulled the dishtowel away with two shaking fingers.

Her husband calling; the loving and dutiful man she'd coldcockled, whatever that old fashioned word for a spouse's betrayal of her vows. She slid the bar on the face of the smartphone and answered in a shaking, contrite cadence. "Guess I'm sorry. Again."

"I already told you—don't say you're sorry anymore. Ever. About anything."

"But I am."

"Won't help. Not a bit." His words, dripping with a flat malevolence she'd never imagined coming from her sweet Roy Earl Pettus, who above all was an easygoing good guy, even when some shit would come down, like when the Old Market in Columbia would flood during summer rain showers and he would spring into neighborhood leader mode. She recalled his lighthearted attitude while putting out the orange cones the city had given him, and helping other merchants lay sandbags, all with a smile on his face and a joke on his lips, or using one of his silly voices.

This voice, not so silly; this one sounded to Creedence like a judge leveling the ultimate sentence: death. "Let's be glad you didn't wreck the car. Or hurt yourself. Or anyone else who might've been in the car with you."

"There wasn't nobody," in the most tiny and pitiful voice she can muster. "Just me. By myself. And missing you."

"Bull doody."

Creedence, shamefaced and grieving; yes, grieving tears over losing him. Pleading anew. "Please don't cast me out for this. For my sins. I'm—sorry."

Roy Earl, letting loose with a stream of cusswords, actual ones instead of his little substitutions, a torrent that almost curled her already kinky red hair. Telling her she could drink with, and fuck, whoever she wished, now. That she could go to Hades.

And yeah: Also that he's not coming back. That if he came back now, he wasn't sure he be able to keep from 'unleashing holy hell' upon her, language never used, and reminding all too much of being beaten by Dusty. Also, that she could come up for Rabbit's memorial, but not to speak to him or look into his eyes, and to think long and hard about facing Mama Runelle, too. That Mama Runelle's also upset with her.

"Hell, give Phil Webhannet a blowjob, why don't you? He deserves it for letting you off the hook. Driving drunk? You could've killed an innocent person. You fucking piece of Edgewater County trash."

Creedence, a cold bucket of viscous, mortifying whale oil sluicing over her head and into her soul, and none to do with his insults and anger: *"You told Mama Runelle what I done?"*

Chuckling, making his voice sound like that stupid movie character, that Daniel Day Lewis oilman turning into the devil, or whatever that mess had been. "Of course I did. And you know something else? I told her I'm staying up here. Right? I'm not coming back. I'm not coming back at all. I'm taking the money, sufficient to get away not only from you, but from all people. I'll come back to get my things. But that's the only goddamned fucking goddamned reason."

"Don't talk like that. This is a big misunderstanding. I—I love you."

"Rucker? I'm gonna bury you underground."

"Oh, Roy—please—"

"Will you go and fuck yourself this time, instead of my assistant manager? Mercy. Mercy."

Anguished. Broken. But maybe a break in the frost? A chance? "Oh lord, I miss you," she waits for him to say, sounding like a brokenhearted baby; they'd cry together.

She continues waiting.

Cold and flat, his words finally come tinged with the steel of what he calls the 'black blade' he pulls out on an employee who's done wrong. An employee like Estes. And it ain't pretty, no sir, when he's like this. Part of what makes him a good businessman and boss, he always says. But scary. "Now. Seeing as how I'm not returning anytime soon, I'll need you to act in my place. I want you to—"

"Like, how?"

"That's what I'm trying to tell you." An interval of silence.

"Well?"

"I want an assurance I won't be interrupted again."

Now her turn to sit in stony silence.

"That's better. Now. You are to go to the Beanery tomorrow and see Mr. Patel, where you will deliver a message: that he's released from his position. And you're to do it in front of the other employees; and you're to do so without a reason, which the law does not require of you under at-will employment like we have in this two-bit state. Also, you're to perform this function in a way leaving the rhetorical door open for you to admit to everyone, in your own way, words and manner, that you got him fired. Do you understand these instructions?"

"Please," is all she can say. She's the only one crying. Not him. "Don't."

"And afterwards? The both of you fuck, and suck, all everything you need to do to one another, and I hope you screw yourselves to fucking oblivion—"

"Stop. We ain't done nothing but one time. And, it was real quick. Baby, it wasn't no good and I was drunk and I don't even remember it. Please. He don't—he ain't—he ain't nothing next to you."

"Creedence." Roy says this emotionless but for what sounds like pity. "I read what you motherfuckers wrote to each other—you're having a goddamn love affair with this little shit. I read every word. So go and fuck him all day. You can't spin this but damn if you ain't trying, you little Karl Rove. You should go into politics."

She ain't got a clue what the hell he's talking about—that political stuff he goes on and on about sometimes. She's so confused and broke up nothing makes any sense. Creedence murmurs, mumbles, begs.

He keeps his smart-assy routine going. "What's your Southern strategy? Huh? Shaving your pussy for him? That little—little—towel-head."

Hushed. Shit's extreme. Roy gets steamed when he hears people use racial or ethnic put-downs—to him, all are as bad as the big-bomb n-word, and she swore it spun her mind around to hear him use such a term. "I don't think I ever heard you talk like that before."

Her hubby, tubby hubby she used to call him, cries out as if in pain. Says her name, anguished. "I'm not—I don't—I ain't been myself. For a while. I reckon you can just probably guess why. Can't you."

Of course; but, as she starts to comfort him, Creedence realizes he's hung up on her.

For the best—her battery, now but a sliver of red left on the meter.

"Now I'm gonna lose both of you." Blubbering into the dead phone, she went huh-huh-huh and said how much she missed him, and thinking there'd never been a time he would have rung off without saying those magic and special words she'd found with him, after the awful years with Dusty. Huh-huh-huh, until nothing left.

Only then does she head into the kitchen and grab a cold beer out of the fridge—just to hold it against her hot forehead, as Creedence explains to herself. Opens it, and like always with the first sip, even on a shameful evening hung over from the afternoon drunk and getting out of a DUI and while cheating on your husband with his assistant GM, she sighs and feels better. Drinks long and cool. Down it goes. Yum.

Thinks of Devin; thinks of all he went through.

But drinks anyway.

What has she left? Whom?

A text from Estes offers another solution, and temporary relief.

She responded by calling. He said, look, if this thing works out, no way I can work at the Beanery. That he went in after she left his place and gave Sharolyn Montine, Roy's GM, the resignation.

Well, that solves that issue. Gets her out of the punishment. Ha.

"And so, if he's not there right now, and I'm not working for him anymore? We can hang out even more. Right?"

"I don't know. It's—he's leaving me."

"Like I said. Get it? Like, starting tonight."

The guilt rushes over her like an awful sexual-sinful wave of desire and shame. But she says all right, all right—now she's lost Roy Earl, and Creedence has no choice but to say yes. No parents, no brother. No one else. All dead. Like she said, she can't lose both—she's never not had someone. Ain't gonna start now.

Estes reminds her that his band, Meatbody, would play later at the Sand-flea, a nasty-ass Sedge Island music club. Rap metal, some derivation. Not a fan of loverboy's little band, which cut an EP at a studio in Charleston that had cost them a buttload. At least to hear Estes tell it. It finally occurred to her one day he was hinting around about money.

That night, while Roy farted around on the computer, she had shoved in her earbuds and listened to the Meatbody album, entitled *Harvester of Likes*:

1. Clickbait Billyclub
2. Keeping Me Fed
3. Red-Flag Waving
4. Numeric Nomad
5. Liquor and Grunt
6. Black Iron Prison
7. Where Notifications Lead

Seven and done—thank god. The lyrics, rapped over a plodding, distorted guitar and bass drone, addressed concerns about technology. She hated the music and the band, loved the boy.

Did she, though?

Creedence, finishing her beer and steady as a rock, says she'll meet him there; that she'll cheer and dance and be his biggest fan. And how she'll talk to Sharolyn, smooth it all over. Explain that all the drama's over Roy Earl's granddaddy dying, and how this will shift the focus away from their mess. She hoped.

Creedence, going to get another cold beer, which is what her body wants more than another deep dicking by her lover. Or her husband. She'd fuck the Bud man instead, or maybe that little spear-carrying dandy on the Beefeater gin bottle. Sounded like a strategy.

Until she reconsidered what Estes said, and remembered how good it was that afternoon. After getting drunk she decided, I've fucked up this much already. Why stop now?

CHRISTY AND HIS DADDY

Now if they's another wrong foot to get off on, it's not sleeping worth a durn, and when Christy gets up for school, he bangs around in his room, bonking his elbows, eyeing the game console. Ain't got no patience with nothing. Dreamed all night about flying—but in the dream he didn't need no plane or video game.

Well, it started as a game, dreaming about sitting in his chair, his big recliner they had pulled off the side of the road and sprayed Febreze all over. Flying for real with the wind on his face, his eyes watering, trying to see across the expanse of sky that'd replaced his room in the trailer.

A giant glass cube, off in the distance. Trying to swim through the air toward it.

No, not glass, ice—a giant sweating ice cube there in a lush green jungle that couldn't be Edgewater County. Christy, afraid he didn't know how to land, awoke right as he hit the top of the cube, hitting it hard and his plane had disappeared and running to try and slow down, his feet sliding every which way and the edge coming up and a steep drop-off—

Boom. Awake. Christy's dreams—they sometimes seem more real than reality.

Christy, though, he ain't scared. Wants to keep flying. But on the game console. Not in some dream.

He's already moved up from the little single engines, the Piper Cubs and whatnot, to the jets. Christy's getting good, and he ain't always been able to get good at any particular thing. School ain't worth nothing, but it's what normal people do and Christy thinks, he wants to be normal.

He don't understand why he can't live with his granny. She tells Christy she's a pillar of Edgewater County, with her big creepy old house tucked away back in the boggy blackwater swamps over along the national forest out beyond Red Mound. Which makes Christy wonder why he can't be there with her.

Cause of his daddy. That's why. Easy enough to figure out. Now that Christy ain't no little kid no more.

⊙❋⊙

IN THE KITCHEN it smells bad, and Christy frowns and squints at the shape on the couch which is his daddy all curled up, passed out, the sunlight streaming down on him. Same every day.

Christy thinks he'll be quiet as he can be, which ain't much, and not wake his Daddy's ass up, cause that ain't gonna do a thing but make him start up again about his five thousand dollar foolishness, and the filling station plan, and Christy wasn't having none of it. Aisha, so mysterious and sweet hanging out there with her father. He wasn't gonna mix up a dark-eyed beauty like her into no cock-up robbery bullcrud.

His Daddy must've gone out of his damn mind.

Christy knows this and shakes his head, and says, he says to himself, rehearsing-like:

Granny, I don't care about them girls you take care of, and I don't need as much room as I seem like I would. Please let me come and live in Red Mound with you.

Christy thinks he might not go back to school after the Christmas break, when he'll be sixteen—his birthday falls on December 30, way too close to Christmas to be the least bit special and which he had gotten used to by now. Christy's pretty sure how, with the internet, and even going into the library down on Common Street, he could teach himself what he needed to know. He proved it overnight by finding and downloading the latest release of X-Plane, the world's top-rated flight simulator, which when he had installed it and booted the program at first seemed like the hardest thing he ever tried, dude. Right?! Flying is harder than shooting.

So, yeah. Someone could learn other knowledge from teh good old inter-nets. School made for too much rigmarole, and people making fun, and many other distractions.

Like the girls.

It drove Christy crazy to be around all those girls he kept loving but could not go with because he's just too big. And sometimes the teachers would take him aside and remind him about hygiene and grooming, and Christy would say, well dang, I washed, or tried to. It's hard to get clean, mainly because he's so big. Especially when he messes around too long, because on some mornings, his peepee hard-on won't go down. The thought of dealing with his Daddy was enough today to keep his mind occupied, though, and a long way from thinking about getting with girls.

◉◈◉

CHRISTY'S DADDY, he moans and rolls over. Smacks his lips.

Christy squints and sees green foam caked in the corners of his Daddy's mouth. For real?!

Sneaking on tiptoes, imagining he looks like Elmer Fudd creeping up on Bugs Bunny's rabbit hole, Christy, all bright and excited inside despite his empty stomach. There's cereal again, he reckons, or maybe Pop-tarts, if Daddy hadn't eaten them, before the bus comes by on the highway out front of Mayfield Acres.

Maybe his Daddy's fixing to die.

Nope. Groggy, but alive.

"Wipe your mouth," Christy says. His voice, deeper than usual. His throat's full of snot, like always. "You making me sick."

"You got any beans?" Christy's Daddy says. That's slang for pills. "I got to get up. I got shit to do," but he sounds like he's drifting back off again. "Beans," he repeats, and his nose whistles.

Christy don't feel nothing for his Daddy like he knows a person is supposed to for their own daddy. Fact is, Christy thinks his Daddy ain't worth nothing.

Christy thinks:

Heck. I'm all grown up, pretty much. That's the way I feel this morning. Like somebody who knows how to decide what he wants to do, and what he don't want to do. Maybe I don't need to mess with school today—I didn't do my homework anyway.

Maybe another project.

Christy goes back down the hall, his shoulders stooped and he hears his Granny's voice saying, Christy, stand up straight, stand up straight, but he never does because he's always tallest. Looking down on them rather than being like them. Always wanting to be one of them.

Be with them.

But always something kept him apart from the others. Christy, he's either too big, or smells funny; his cleft lip, his pink skin and wild yellow-blonde hair, all of it makes him different even if he wasn't also tall and broad as a barn, like his Daddy says. Or, the wheezy high voice, it don't suit him good, only gives the bullies in the regular classes another thing about Christy to pick at.

He's wheezy because Christy sure could use another of them inhalers he got that time. It cleared up his lungs for a while. Daddy keeps saying he's gonna see about a refill. Sure.

He never does, though. Ain't worth a damn.

He don't care about you, Christy. He only cares about himself. Christy's own Granny—his Daddy's own Mama—had said it, and he hears this in her voice instead of his own.

But he's always been like that, Granny says in her croaky old smoker's voice, putting out her cigarette and tending to her makeup or to fixing up the girls she helps. Runaways and wastrels, she calls them. Tells them how to be women, and how to get ahead and how to paint their faces and put on hose and shoes and little see-through outfits. They're always so so so beautiful, but they girls are grownup and furthermore belong to his Granny, so Christy don't fall in love with them the way he does the girls his age, like Lillyanne and Aisha at the Gas Chief.

Aisha.

Yeah, Christy loves her best. She's the one this year, Christy is certain. That's why he don't want Daddy messing around with their gas station, and coming from Iraq, don't he think they done had enough troubles already?!

Something got to happen.

Before he wakes up all the way.

By the time Christy comes back with a pillow, the big thick one he puts under his back to help him sleep, his Daddy has passed out flat on his back, snoozing away.

Dang if that don't make it all easier and quicker.

⊛⊛⊛

WHEN IT'S OVER, or at least Christy's almost sure it's over, he lays his head on his Daddy's bony chest, listening.

Quiet.

Watching for movement, Christy inspects his Daddy's body. The skin, turning gray and blue in patches. Swears he can see the blue getting darker in spots right before his eyes. It's so still and quiet in the trailer, and Christy is so focused on watching his Daddy's inert body change color he feels as though outside his own body, observing the scene from a far corner.

"Daddy." Christy, wheezing. "Look over here, now."

Nothing.

Christy, sitting and filling up the recliner so when he moves the slightest bit, its springs shriek and creak. Reaches over with his big tree-trunk leg and fat toes inside dirty white socks with holes. He pokes his Daddy in the brittle skinny ribs, rocking his torso back and forth.

Nada.

For real?

He gets a steak knife. Sticks into the flesh of his daddy's forearm. Pushes harder. The knife breaks the skin. Blood oozes, slow and thick.

Now Christy's scared.

He ain't got no way to get over to his Granny's. It was while he held the pillow over his Daddy's face with all his weight bearing down, hard as he could, and doing his high whining like when he's excited or trying to trick his Granny into giving him money that Christy heard the school bus come. The bus would have at least gotten him part of the way.

Maybe he'd go downtown and walk around. Ain't gonna be nobody down there, not on a morning like this. Everybody else would be in school, and there wasn't no businesses down there to speak of, not really, not like when you go out to the mall or the big new plaza with the movie theaters down below the lake country. There's stores with new signs, bright colors and red bricks in the sidewalks, and it's safe. They show a commercial for the lake country and you can see with your own peepers how it's all white people smiling, so you know it's chill and safe there. It's like Christy's Daddy says, with them blacks putting in that restaurant they way they done it's all going to hell, now, all them moving in from across the river to get away from the Mexicans. "It ain't never gonna be safe no more. Just you watch."

Christy don't see the world the same way as either the commercial or his Daddy. And, as though Christy's Daddy's world is a safe space right now?! Meanness ain't got nothing to do with what people look like, their skin or hair or whatever. Christy's Daddy seems set on making his own danger, and he's whiter than snow.

Christy hears all that bullcrud and worse from Granny, who uses the N-word and cusses like nobody's ever heard, but that's the way she is, and like she says, people respect her. She's a pillar of Edgewater County.

Christy didn't understand much as he'd like about how it all worked, but he's seen the way visitors treat her—men Christy doesn't know, who he figures must be ones his Granny's marrying the girls off to, or however it worked. They kowtow and act all syrupy and nice. That's how she is with them, too.

"The Mayor himself, when he comes," she told Christy one night, when she had been drinking like his Daddy does, and Christy didn't like that but you don't tell your Granny what to do and what not to do, "his ass comes to see me. Not them little skinny biddies I got running around. You know what that says about your old Granny, boy?"

She had waved her drink at Christy, and he didn't-yet-did sort of know, if nothing else from the selfsame look of satisfaction and accomplishment on her made-up, wrinkled face and in her voice, in her gestures, even in the clinking of the ice in her glass, which sounded to Christy like success. He didn't like drinking before, but after last night and the way the whiskey made him cold and calm in his stomach, he thought, well, I'll be danged but I bet that's why I had the courage to put this dog down today.

A dog. That's what Christy had done. You had to put them down. Because his Daddy had been suffering. And causing suffering. The Bible, Christy was almost certain, says you're supposed to take care of people who suffer. And so he done it. Jesus had turned the water into liquor last night, and it had given Christy strength and clarity and will.

The will to act.

Before he started whining and fretting again about how he was gonna get all the way from this side of the county to his Granny's he also says, says to himself, shit, I guess I will have to bury this dog I put down, somehow.

Bury it. Or leave the body somewhere. The county dump. His Daddy did drugs. He didn't wake up. Nobody's gonna care.

Or will they? Will they know? And Christy, how will he accomplish this without a car?

Now Christy gets scared. He takes his cereal and goes into his room to start another tutorial training flight on the new software, and maybe think about how he could get his hands on another RAM chip, because already he could see it would be a memory hog, that software.

A plan—think all this crap through. Wait. Make sure-sure his dog-Daddy was dead. And then, bury his skinny ass out in the woods. Christy, being smarter than anyone knew, would figure it out. Right? Right!?

MANNY AND HIS FOLKS

Manny wake up with Neecie tracing one of them razor nails of her'n in his curly chest hair, and on up to his throat. Play all around Manny lips, tickling his mustache.

Shee-yit, y'all. His dingus, rolling over all a-twitching.

Morning time with the old lady.

Right on. Right on.

Besides, Becky LaFreniere, she ain't done jack last night. Just to 'talk.' All he ended up doing with his hard-on was hitting the free weights downstairs and listening to that fuckhole Ahmad watch a damn movie. Told him to turn the shit down before he wake up Lillyanne.

Ahmad know Manny whip ass if he don't snap-to. But he work hard in that kitchen, hard as Manny make him, anyway, so Manny guess his brother-in-law could sprawl out looking bugeyed at the big TV. He say, movies ain't as good except on the HD set in the family room. He right. But still. Long as he keep that volume turned down. Tell ya what.

Oh, lord—his wife could throw down. Under the sheet Manny dick now harder than the concrete pad his ass pour out back last week to put up a hoop, a regulation decent hoop like they had at the boys club in the projects.

Neecie—she know what get him going.

"God-durn, boy," grabbing hold. "Mama surprised baby got anything left."

Uh-oh. "What-cha mean, sugarbooty?"

"After all them workouts."

"Oh—right on, right on."

"All them weights, and them smoothies?" Light as a butterfly, tickling with them nails, edging and teasing and hot-dog. "They doing you good. Ain't they."

Damn thing throb so bad it hurt. But what with her rap? Shit seem all subtext-y, and shit.

She pause in mid-stroke, knuckle right under the head, bumping a wee little bit—and hoo boy. Their asses married a long time. She know what he like.

His old lady ask what the magic word is.

Manny tell her 'come.'

She go mm-hm.

"Well, go on."

Neecie all like, "Go on? Who you think in charge here?"

"Nah, mama. Slide down on it slow like you do."

"I ain't wake up with no wet pussy. Earn it, son."

He ain't get what she mean by that—she the one start up.

"You ain't got time for more than a quickie anyway. Do ya?"

"I have my meeting."

"On Thursday?"

"Yesterday's calamity threw us off the agenda."

He got it. After old Rabbit croak, Manny reckon they ain't bother getting to either the mural or the whole n'other agenda he was sure them ELMS had going.

Hell—she going down there to sit next to Manny sidemeat. With all that ELMS shit.

Woof. The danger, it make Manny scared.

At first.

Which make his dick hard.

Harder.

From the time he was a little dude, Manny always dig keeping secrets. Secrets made him feel like he got one up on everyone else. Even his wife, who he trust. Or some shit. He ain't know.

Shit yeah—it all a game. That all it is. Secrets is fun, y'all. Powerful fun.

Shit, but he love to fuck. Ain't no secret there. "Right on, girl," he say all dry and flat. "Go on with your bad, horny-ass self."

That the Manny way. He don't give them much. He keep that shit close. Keep his fire stoked. Keep that dick hard. So, he ain't all that sweet to them. It part of the game. He stare out at the backyard which need cutting. Manny still ain't used to having this big yard, not after growing up in the Ward. He sigh.

Manny, he don't know why he fuck around on her like he always do. She bout durn near the best piece of ass he ever got himself. Him poaching them sidemeats ain't nothing but man shit. That all it was. Don't mean nothing untoward in terms of the family life.

Manny get brought back down to earth: Neecie dig one of her long-ass nails into the tender spot—not hard, but hard enough.

"Hey-ho! Go on, now."

"Oops."

"Best get your freak on, before you bite it off."

"I might still." Gripping it like a baseball bat. "Twist this knob right off."

Dang. Manny can't figure on what to do with that. "Word."

Maybe Manny shitting too close to the kettle on the stove.

Maybe?

He ain't got good sense.

Manny, a muh-fucken moth fluttering in his gut. Like shit fixing to go down. Her face ain't right.

"What wrong, baby?"

She slap that dick back against Manny flat stomach.

"What up?"

Neecie roll off and jiggle across the room. The big ass of hers look so fine, and Manny still so hot he want to lick that hole and slip it in back there; he might be in middle-age, but dang if his shit ain't hard as a brick.

She get back from pissing in the lavatory they fixed like they always wanted, a marble bathroom both could stand in and a garden tub and separate shower like they never had in the city, not in them shotgun houses they lived in so long. Holding onto his pole, Manny beam at her: "Baby—let's fuck."

Sour and skeptical: "We ain't done it the morning since I don't know when."

"Ain't nothing wrong with it. We ain't old."

Neecie have her hair pulled back and robe on, cinching that shit tight, with a look like she ain't gonna fuck nobody. She gonna kill 'em instead. "You like doing my ass? Do you?"

"What you think?" Manny display his hard-on. "Yo."

"Love my ass?"

"Bitch, you know I do. Now come on and—"

"Then why you fucking around on me, Manny?"

Half-mast shit now. Drawing up. "Ain't know what you mean."

"How many does this make, now?"

"C'mon, now. It ain't like that."

And worse, she say? One of her sisters in the ELMS. That part she c'ain't get at all. "Betrayal twice over. Twice over."

"Aw—what, now? Get on with y'self. You imagining it all."

Her anger break, and she slam the bathroom door and start bawling.

Now his shit finish going on down, the second hard-on of the day, not to be. Manny say to himself, wellsir, this ain't good. That current secret of yours don't got no damn power now, do it? Or rather, not the kind Manny got in mind.

⚙ ✴ ⚙

"Girlfriend, you better say, hup hup. The day getting away from ya."

Manny, in his robe and with his wife's juice still slick on his thighs, stand in his babygirl's room shaking like a muh-fucker, but he got a smile on his face stretched out tight like the Joker. He don't know what else but to keep the damn routine. "You best have got that homework done like I said, too."

"Dang. I was just having the best dream." Lillyanne pull the covers over her head and feign snoring, which make Manny laugh, laugh for real and for relief, because his ass been cut down to size, now.

He feel like crying, but keep that wicked smile stretched cross his face. "Get up, now, dreamgirl." He reach under the floral-print comforter. "Gimme them foots."

"All right all right all right. Shit, Daddy—"

"Yo, yo." Manny head go all hot. "Watch that mouth."

"Yes, sir," she say from under the sheet. "I'm sorry."

"You best be. You too pretty to cuss."

Going out the door, he hear her whisper: "Bullshit."

All good. Part of the parent game, with a babygirl her age. A different girl-game.

Downstairs, a shape on the couch catch Manny eye.

Ahmad. His ass, passed out in the family room. Even in the bright morning light from outside, Manny see a faint glow from the wall showing that the flatscreen still on.

Manny seethe and cuss. He warn Ahmad the last time he'd hit the bottle he only had so much high ground before the liquor would drown him. Ahmad might be his own family, but if the boy slid far enough, in Ahmad's case the bottom meant the crack pipe, or the needle. And ain't no fucking way on god's green earth Manny Theodore going to let that go on in the same house as Lillyanne.

He grab Ahmad up by the front of his stained and stink-ass T-shirt from under yesterday's chef whites. "Get up off my couch, slim-shady."

"God-dog, Manny—!" Ahmad tumble off onto one knee, coughing and sputtering and hacking. "Scare shit outta me."

"You puke on my carpet and I'll kick the shit out of ya."

"Lay off, now. Ease up." Ahmad pull himself back onto the sectional sofa. "I musta pass out looking at that movie."

"What I tell you about this? What you drink? When you come home? And look at that screen—" The disc menu, frozen in place with bright white letters in the movie logo. "If my muh-fucken plasma screen got burn-in, I'm-a whup your crack-sucking ass."

Manny hear thumps at the top of the stairs, in this clean, modern crib like they asses could never have afforded back home in the city. He make his voice so low it feel like an engine running in his throat full of sex and phlegm and now fear, he got to admit. Fear of his wife. "You my flesh and blood, but only cause of Neecie. And the chance I'm giving you, to run my kitchen, is a good solid foundation for a man that need one bad. I don't mind giving you that chance. But a chance all it is."

"Ain't nothing in life a sure thing. Is it?"

Ignoring him. "Neecie? She might be your sister, but after all the mess you pulled on her and the rest, I'm surprised she give two shits about you. Think you on a short leash with me? Keep on. She say, let him live in this house till he get his shit wired straight. Till he save up money. And then be on his way. And I say, well, I c'ain't turn away family. But it been a long ass time now, n-word. S'all I'm saying to ya this fine morning."

"I know it." Ahmad pick up his trash and shuffle toward the patio door to go to his room over the detached garage in the back, what had been a work-shop for the dude who own this place, before Manny and Neecie buy it off the bank with the Katrina insurance money. "I'm-a quit with this drinking shit."

Manny glare at Ahmad holding two empty Bud Lights, which he know sure as shit come out the cooler at work. Bet money he didn't write a damn one down, either. Manny don't care about a couple beers, not long as you work hard. But write muh-fucken inventory shit down. That how you keep a good bar trade going. Play straight, keep up the numbers. Pay off the man when you got to. But keep an accounting, no matter what.

Well—another reason Manny worry about Ahmad drinking them beers, is because his ass ain't got no business drinking nothing. No more'n Manny does, which is why he don't. "You drink a beer here, a beer there—you know where it lead, brotherman."

"I c'ain't tell you how much it mean for you to bring me here with y'all. I should-a come when I first had the chance, after them levees broke." Ahmad, all pitiful. "I'm-a do better. Damn if I ain't."

Heard it all before. "When I want bullshit, I'll pull that string hanging off the back of your neck. Till then, save it." Manny, seething like his old angry self; Ahmad trying to rationalize like addicts do as familiar a tune as a TV show theme Manny ass done watched a thousand times. "Just get on in your muh-fucken little crib with your bad-example self before Lillyanne see you sprawled out every which way."

Ahmad snatch up his work shoes. "When I get my shit together, like my own HD screen, I ain't trouble y'all no more."

"If I see burn-in, your ass is buying me a new one for all up in here."

"Manny—yo, dog."

"Bet. Watch if I don't."

Ahmad hang his head and close the sliding door behind him. His ass need to mow the grass, next. That the next little conversation Manny could look forward to having with his bro-in-law. That, and you better keep off the bottle before you hit that rock again, dumbass.

Broken record shit.

Manny wave the remote with a flourish and the cycling menu for *BloodGun* disappear, the white title fading into the soft gray of the blank screen. Manny toss the remote onto the couch where Ahmad lay all night, hurry into the kitchen and clean up before his wife and daughter get downstairs.

He worry Neecie might boot him out for real, this time. And Manny, he don't want that. Like he said: his ass love her ass. Manny got to fix this. And fix them women some pancakes.

Slopping eggs and milk and flour in the glass bowl with the big whisk, Manny pour batter on the griddle, six silver-dollar size cakes, and microwave the grade-B maple syrup for his baby and his babygirl. His gut so tight, he ain't want no bread for breakfast.

Maybe Becky LaFreniere was a piece of pussy too far.

Shit a goddamn shit, but his ass in real trouble now. If getting caught with sidemeat like Becky L wasn't so destructive to the family, it might be, Manny don't know, halfway exciting and shit.

GOOCH, ROOSEVELT NIXON, AND BURNIE SYKES

The Reverend Roosevelt Nixon, broad of chest and shoulder and tall as a one of the legacy oaks arrayed around the courthouse plaza in the background, ran a massive hand across a shaved bullet-shaped head, tugged at a soul patch, touched a fingertip to the diamond stud glimmering in one ear. Smiled, bigger than life. Waved. Nodded. Pointed. A politician, preparing to preach from a make-do podium, nothing more impressive than a music stand sitting on two concrete blocks. The blocks, necessary for the stand holding his speech to reach to the politician's height, said to be six-six, if not six-seven. Gooch, a good reporter, needed to nail that figure down.

The setting hardly befitted a figure, he thought, of Nixon's status. Maybe if Nixon one day became Mayor, he'd rent a flatbed truck like Hill Hampton from which to give his orations and exhortations.

Wimmel noted in shorthand that the scholar-preacher turned politician 'loomed,' then thought better of using the term. That was editorializing. Facts only, please. He 'appeared' before them all. That was about as fancy as allowed. Even that sounded like a hallucination or magic trick. A little flowery —that's what Gooch's high school editor Mr. Bingham would have said.

From the NIXON signs everywhere alone, the journalist G. Wimmel felt dizzied and uncertain of his place in the timeline of what all had been going on. Didn't Rabbit Pettus die? This, the first question his mind asked upon awakening. He checked his notes from the day before, notes by which he managed to keep living. Yep. Dead. Big story.

Seeing the NIXON yard sign across the way first thing this morning, however, had startled him into confusion. He stumbled over to his reading desk near the other window, bumbling the lamp into life. Gooch snatched at an appointment book.

September. 2015. Right now.

The year had given him pause, but only until he saw his shriveled up gray-headed self in the bathroom mirror and fought his way back from a place of cottony confusion. He remembered about Roosevelt Nixon, and how it was 'present day' as they say in the movies, present and accounted for and stooped over the toilet waiting for a decent stream and when it finally streamed, it only dribbled. Also stung and hurt, deep inside his pelvis.

Going back to the appointment book, seeing what he had to do today, Gooch remembered again that Rabbit died. Now, he recalled about the Nixon presser on the green. Nixon signs, but not 1972. All seemed right.

To tell the truth, covering the campaign for the open seat on council here on the lovely town green, everyone milling around and with the tiniest hint of fall in the air, made Gooch feel as though his pieces were all in good order. He couldn't wait to listen to the speech and write the story. 'Twas what he lived for.

Not much drama here though. Nixon, running unopposed for the seat created for the newly annexed Easton area, a deal brokered by local U. S. Congress-critter Mauldin Saugus, one of the longest serving and most powerful African-American pols in the whole country. When Saugus got involved, everyone, even the white folks, fell into line. Cole Breedlove, along with a swamp rat *Duck Dynasty* devotee named York Durden, had both made noise about running against Nixon for the technically-open seat, but got talked out of it by some cooler heads, or who knew—back-room persuasion came in many forms. The way of the game. He wished he were able to see it all as scandalous, but an old journo like him? Hell. SOP.

The Reverend-Doctor Nixon smiled and waved and pressed the flesh with the crowd of a few dozen gathered near the thirty-inch miniature statue of Pitchfork Ben Tillman. The effigy sat perched atop a pedestal much more grand than such a diminutive monument deserved, a trapezoid of polished red granite glimmering in the sun and worthy of an Egyptian temple or cenotaph.

Gooch had been reading about such matters in a book he'd checked out of the library called *Civilization X: Egypt in 39,000 BCE*, a tome concerning itself with theories regarding an ancient high civilization, that the pyramids were much older than orthodox Egyptologists would ever admit, yadda yadda. The evidence, the author contended, was found in what have to be precision machine-tooled hunks of granite.

Yes: red granite like that of the Tillman pedestal. Stone in the case of the Egyptians which couldn't have been tooled by hand with copper chisels and other crude construction implements, a demonstrable fact. Many fragments of rock at megalithic sites the world over contained clear evidence of machine-tooling marks, for one example, that could only have been made by enormous circular saws powered through means unclear. Again, obvious facts that mainstream Egyptologists and historians and archeologists seemed reluctant for whatever agenda or reason to accept. All Gooch had wanted to do was a little research regarding the Reverend's academic background, had gone down a side road.

Research on his historical novel caused him to go down various internet rabbit holes. That's right—a novel; the one tracing the history of Edgewater County back further and further, he found, all the way to the native peoples who would have lived in the area. And now he'd been led into theoretical Egyptian prehistory. The journey of all of humanity. Writing, a peculiar beast of a process to wrangle; research, a pillowy berth prone to tangential traipsing through internet link after internet link of supposed interest, but of no clear relevance. Maybe it would all come into focus.

The granite. The Egyptians. Nixon.

All running through his cluttered head.

Sunlight, glinting off tiny flecks of crystal imbedded in the granite.

Mesmerizing.

The minuscule Tillman statue, small because it'd been the maquette produced by the sculptor before the casting of the oversized, iconic version that stood guard over the front steps of the Capitol in Columbia; the model, a gift from the sculptor to the township. Assuming the town would put this crude proposed version of the finished statue in its archives, the artist discovered it instead bronzed and placed in its position of honor near other town monuments. Incensed, he termed the townspeople coarse, uneducated hillbillies who didn't know the difference between a finished objet d'art and a piece of preparatory pseudo-art never meant to be seen and displayed in such a manner. Still, the mini-Tillman stood in its place of reverence. The number one question from visitors to the town involved the size of the Tillman statue. A close number two? The location of the nonexistent 'falls,' which hadn't run with regularity for seventy years.

Statues. Sculptors whose names Gooch ought to know, but lost in the cobwebby recesses of his mind a jumble, like the frisson of would-be voters milling around, mostly African-Americans, but also a number of middle-aged whites wearing Birkenstocks and looking more like lake country than the poor part of the county Nixon would represent.

The reason for Gooch's presence here—potential voters. Nixon. Campaign event.

Wait—or was it the George Wallace visit today?

You old fool, a rational voice said. *That was 1968. Years and years ago.*

When Gooch had been a young buck political reporter writing a story on a Wallace campaign stop here on this same town green, it'd been well attended, at least far as he remembered. Wallace had carried South Carolina for his so-called American Independent party. At least the Governor could say he'd succeeded here, no mean feat for any candidate. Was that the same year Wallace got shot and paralyzed? Gooch hadn't a clue.

⊛⚙⊚

THE REVEREND-DOCTOR ROOSEVELT NIXON of the Calvary Full Gospel Church of the Holy Redeemer, ready to read from prepared remarks handed to Gooch by one of Nixon's sons. Skimming, Gooch saw a substantial message about good governance, along with one bombshell he couldn't wait to hear roll off the Rev's mellifluous tongue.

His wife Constance stood alongside their four boys aged twelve to twenty-two, all young men themselves now, the lot of them coifed and dressed to an impeccable, Sunday morning sheen. Nixon's campaign advisor, a severe looking white gentleman whose name escaped Gooch, had been recommended to Nixon by Thim Sykes from the Governor's staff, stood off to one side, focused and lasered on the back of his candidate's head. Constance appeared proud and stalwart and dignified. The eldest son, almost as tall as his father but nowhere near as broad of shoulder, stood with a countenance so serious that he appeared angry; he clutched a large family bible under his arm. Gooch wrote it all down, his pen streaking with urgency across the notebook page.

The damnable Blackberry, a relic he refused to give up, buzzing in his pocket. He fumbled and dropped both pen and notebook. Gooch gathered himself and read a text from his second-in-command, Dobbs Vandegrift, whose message read

Getting Good Shots From Window—Perfect Angle! :)

The old reporter craned his neck around with a pop and saw his protege waving from the second story of the Advocate building, above the hair salon and tattoo parlor down the block, the gold-flecked gilt lettering of its dynamic masthead logo glinting back from the window next to Gooch's savior and friend.

Despite being wheelchair bound, Dobbs Vandegrift gained access to the upper floor where the editorial offices were located by the motorized stair-lift. The machine carried him up and down the wall, a grinding vibration that seemed to shake the old brick building to its foundation. A dedicated office wheelchair sat waiting at the top, always at the ready for when the lift arrived. Nothing Gooch wouldn't have done for that boy, who held the future of the paper in his capable hands.

The future.

The campaign.

The reason for the season.

Egypt—Nixon himself had some advanced degrees dealing with history and Egyptology and such. That's why Gooch had been reading that alternative archeology book, which he'd come across by chance in the county library. Now it all came together. Not research for his historical novel about Edgewater County—Nixon had been talking about Egypt in an interview Gooch had done last week. Fussing and cussing, he bent down and grabbed up his notebook right as the Reverend-Doctor began to speak.

In a tasteful gray suit likely purchased from a big-and-tall store, the Reverend's skin shone from his bald head, with what little hair that remained having been shaved in a twice-weekly ritual down at the barber shop—the black folks's barber shop, where Gooch was sure most of the vital community politicking and campaign research was done—on the main drag across the Sugeree River in Easton.

But Easton was no longer Easton, except among the lips of the people who lived there; since the annexation the previous year, unincorporated, rural Easton was now part of the Tillman Falls city limits. This had been achieved through a complicated series of political and legal maneuvers including a ballot referendum during the last town election. Upon passage, the measure called for a narrow strip of land along and across the river included in the annexation to make the two areas 'contiguous'—a stretch—so that its residents could be added to the municipal tax rolls and call themselves Tillman Fallsians.

Change, as Bill reported, came to the heretofore mostly African-American population of Easton in the form of police protection and city services; the promise of curbside trash collection had been the kicker for many residents, old folks who'd had a belly full of hauling crap for the whole of their lives to the Edgewater County dump ten miles away. The trash collection hadn't started yet, but the Mayor and the Town Council kept promising, and Bill reporting the statement that all promises would be made good and true "after the first of the year."

Besides: the bedroom-community nonresidents trickling into the area on that side of the river, in new low-priced subdivisions not far off the interstate— because the land was still cheap! because houses weren't selling, yet developers still cleared land for lots and built new ones!—wouldn't sit still long without their God-given right to municipal refuse collection. These were sophisticated folks, many of whom worked in Columbia, a thirty or forty-minute trip upon the gleaming hardtop of the highway that snaked along between the river and the railway, modernity superimposed upon an ancient commercial corridor whose roots as a trail predated its use by Europeans.

Gooch, irritated, stood scribbling into his reporters' notebook—he'd been in such a bluster to get downtown for the almost-forgotten press conference he'd dropped his digital recorder on the driveway, and the damned cheap piece of Chinese crap had splintered into no less than four pieces, useless. Worse, all prior Rabbit quotes gathered now lost forever. A setback.

Lost, like half the events of any given moment. Gooch remembered that his memory wasn't what it used to be, resulting in many slip-ups in both copy and on the business side of the paper going way beyond his broken DVR, and he knew Dobbs Vandegrift knew, though neither had discussed the difficulties with memory Gooch experienced.

He shoved worries out of his mind, focusing only on the aspect of the memory loss and not its consequences; he attributed the problems to marijuana smoked with a fellow cub reporter back in the late 60s, a devil weed that put him so much in touch with his realest self it gave him what they now called a panic attack. Last dope he'd smoked. Bill Wimmel, too invested in not getting in touch with any true selves. By necessity.

❖

THE REVEREND NEEDED NO MICROPHONE; the voice that issued forth from his great chest, Bill thought to himself as though writing the novel he'd always dreamed of writing, was as thick and strong as the rolls of flesh on the back of the huge neck spilling over Nixon's starched collar. As he orated he brushed lint from the lapel of his suit, which bore the two hallmarks of any good, smart politician in South Carolina, or anywhere else in America: a ubiquitous, waving Old Glory pin, and below that, a small cross of gold.

The assemblage, three dozen strong and most being members of his church, applauded and cheered their spiritual leader. The average age of the throng was sixty-five if it was a day. This wasn't a church event, though: This was political, and Bill Wimmel stood ready to report the Reverend's big announcement, which was now anything but a surprise:

"My brothers and sisters," the Reverend Nixon campaigned in his *basso profundo* cadence, "I stand before you today not as a member of my church, a member of my race, a citizen of Easton township across the river, or even as a man of faith, but instead only as the thing that binds us on this earthly plane in a manner heartfelt, deep, and important: As an American.

"An American," he repeated after a pause, tapping the music stand for emphasis. "One of us; one of you."

"Praise be," someone called, followed by a few "Amens." A child's voice rang out, "One of us!"

Wimmel scrawled notes in his spiky shorthand, the pen dancing across the steno paper with little regard for the lines upon it. His shorthand came courtesy of his youthful reporting years away working the Atlanta crime beat. This had also been when he mastered the impassive, grave, and most important of all, objective expression on his lined and craggy face.

"And so it is in the spirit of this great nation I stand here to discuss a key new plank of my candidacy for the town council of Tillman Falls, South Carolina, to represent the citizens across that bridge, across that body of God's water—the lifeblood that flows through His veins, and our veins." He gestured east toward the unseen Sugeree, and the Lance Corporal Lawrence Lautenschlager Memorial Bridge spanning a mile above the river's terminus at the hydro-nuclear station. "Now that we have received official sanction and been welcomed into the bosom of this fine township upon whose soil my two feet now stand, it is critical—critical," he thundered, an index finger pointing off into the middle distance, "that the newest citizens of this municipality have their say, their opportunity to be heard, their opportunity to be counted."

Applause. Who could argue.

"Now, I know what some of you may be thinking." He glanced at Gooch, winked. "We are taught to come unto each other with humility; yes. And it is not out of hubris I come before you today, nor is it my position to come as a theocrat, governing from the word of God." He paused, working his eyebrows. "But as a representative of all citizens. As Americans," he called out to a fresh swell of approval. "So stand with me, assured I have prayed for guidance how best to apply my abilities and knowledge for the betterment of my community, of my brothers and sisters throughout our new unified township. And it is thus I have been moved by the Creator to do works both within and without the church. Though, the church is never far away, now, is it?"

"NO," seemed the consensus of the crowd.

"And so, I declare I am a human being capable to represent all of you, present and otherwise; I am the conduit through which your voices, often neglected and frequently silenced, will at long last be heard!"

Applause bubbled up again. Gooch thought the earlier swell had more *oomph*.

The Reverend smiled and nodded his head with a beatific expression of confidence and conviction. He held up his hands for quiet, but the applause persisted. A woman Gooch recognized as Nixon's aunt blurted, "Tell truth!"

Gooch saw that Burnie Sykes had appeared around the edges of the crowd, peering and squinting. Sykes, the burst veins in his cheeks the color of pickled beet juice, spat off to the side into the grass of the town square. Cussed and shook his jowly head.

"Surprised to see you out and about, Burnie," Gooch whispered. "You holding up?"

"Well, I can't just set on my butt and ponder all day." He glanced back over his shoulder at The Dixiana, a wreath of bereavement on its closed front door. "If I'd knowed Trudy would button the old girl up like this, I might've stayed at home. What time she gonna open, anyway?"

Gooch leaned over, spoke in a low voice. "Later, maybe. Yesterday was too much for her—I could tell she was barely holding it together."

Scolding, hissy voices shushed them. Burnie, his hand trembling, grumbled and waved them off. "I know this much. That sum-bitch would want the bar open. Ain't gonna make no money closed."

"—as well it must be clear, perfectly clear, that I seek office not for personal glory, personal aggrandizement, or other such trappings in which men and women find themselves entangled and spiritually undermined, but instead to continue the work and toil of those who've come before, have had their blood spilled and their bodies torn in the fight for justice, the battle for equanimity, the war between the souls of men who would hate, and men who would love and honor the glory of God's will, and the beauty of His divine gifts to us all as human beings. This is the core and basis of leadership, this understanding of the high vibration of love."

The Reverend, interrupted by a more subdued and reverent chorus of praise-be's and hallelujah's and ah-men's, which he acknowledged with a knowing nod of his enormous round head. He raised a hand in the air with the meaty fingers held together as though taking a sacred oath, the appendage appearing as wide and substantial as the Bible itself.

Nixon smiled and continued, now more in the cadence in which he held forth from his pulpit: "I stand before you to provide a voice for the downtrodden, a language that speaks for the people who have had no one to speak for them, to sing a song of *puh*-raise and-*uh* faith. To shout out from the hilltops and uh-cross that river for a justice that no man who dares to forsake the Creator can imagine, much less deserves. That no woman who turns a blind eye to the Lord will know. And that no child who lives in the shadow of inequality, injustice, impairment, intolerance, and internecine political gamesmanship can rise above without resorting to the hate and the fear which I decry by my very existence!"

The last syllable boomed out and reverberated among the buildings surrounding the green, seemed to vibrate the ground of LaFreniere Square and the oaks standing tall and proud and protective over a brick plaza put in years ago as the first step in a general streetscaping scheme that, owing to the continued soft world economy, had yet to reach phase two.

"And it is thus I pledge to govern, and to fight—as a man of God, a man of the people, and a man of my country, yes sir: my country as much as it is any man's. Any man's," Nixon repeated, his tone now lowered to a more conversational level. "And so I stand before you as your servant—I ask not for obeisance, nor for deference, but for your support." Nodding, making eye contact, resting a hand on the shoulder of his youngest child. "I ask for your vote— your sacred and civic permission to lead."

Something about the Reverend speaking in a measured and downright quiet tone seemed to grip the assembled listeners. The crowd, including Wimmel, leaned forward and appeared in a collective state of holding its breath. All except Burnham Sykes, whose face remained as pinched as if he'd bitten into the world's bitterest persimmon.

The Reverend Nixon placed his fingertips on the sharp, black metal of the music stand. "And so, I stand here today, a humble servant of my flock and my Lord, not simply to promote my candidacy, but to call for a new day, a new hour of fellowship, a new bridge to the twenty-first century much grander than the one that stretches across that river."

He gestured back at the undersized Ben Tillman stature, covered in green oxidization and pigeon-poop, got around to what he must surely have known would be, if not the lede itself, a highly emphasized aspect of the newspaper account describing his campaign rally. "As the mayor and the town council and finally the voting citizenhood themselves all decided, it is a new day in Tillman Falls, and in what was the Easton community. Together, we're a part of a whole that is more than it once was—a new construct. A bond forged among a people who heretofore *had* no bond beyond that of mere proximity. As such," he explicated here with a gravity of confidence that indicated a coming tide-swell of immutable truth, "it is in my view we should—we must—find a name for this new municipality, a name which reflects not the future not the past, of new traditions not old-UH," he slipped back into preacher cadence, "of a name that reflects a new mission instead of old suspicion, between peoples of all colors, black and white, brown and yellow— "

"Sounds like a tour of my unmentionables drawer," Burnham said in a full voice. Gooch, startled into embarrassed amusement by Burnham's childish, irreverent bon mot snorted like a schoolboy trying not to laugh at a classmate's contumacious misdeed. A few folks nearby turned to shush.

"—all of us, who are all God's children, and we deserve a place that is ours, one and all, a place we can call by a name we have chosen ourselves!" Roosevelt held his arms wide. "Yea-YUH."

Women waved hats and handkerchiefs in front of their faces. Men stomped their feet and shouted out declarations of faith and hope, a cacophonous demonstration that lasted only until the speaker, with but a subtle gesture of his large hand, quieted them down one last time. "And so we must find this name, not in the ledgers of the past, not in the name of a man who spent his life fighting against the rising tide of a new paradigm, this Pitchfork Ben Till-man, but in a new name that befits all the people, and the new day upon us as a community, unified, codified, and municipal-ized."

A minor roar; many gnarled fists raised to the sky.

"Yes: once duly elected, my first order of business will be to initiate a referendum on this issue, on the name of our new home, a name to which all may glance with pride: I propose that this township be called New Falls City, and I will work to make this change, not just to have an arbitrary new name for this place we all call home, but as a symbol of the age of equality and opportunity that's upon us. God bless you all—praise be to Jesus, our Lord, and God Bless America..."

His last words, lost in the enthusiastic trilling of the voices of his followers.

As Bill Wimmel wrote *IT'LL NEVER FLY*, quite pointedly not in his reporter's shorthand, a voice rang out: Burnie.

"Why don't y'all bunch of dang black-assed fools get outta my town square with all this mess." Burnham Sykes had gone downright feral, rheumy eyes wide and watering. "You ought to get on back across that damn river, and stay there."

Voices declaimed, in aggrieved and suggestive tones, that Burnham should hold his water. Or else, to go to Hades with his epithets and intolerant drivel. "Hate speech, hate speech!" a teenage girl shrieked.

Burnie scoffed and p-shaw'd and waved a palsied hand in disgust. Gooch watched him hobble away, going around the Korea-Vietnam-Grenada-Panama-Gulf War I slab of a monument on the west side of the green and in the direction of The Dixiana.

Sykes stopped and shook his cane with menace. "Ain't nobody gonna vote to change the god-durn name of this here town."

"You'll see, my brother," Roosevelt called out as his adherents and family swarmed around him. "You'll see the light of the new day soon."

"Heck of an agenda," Gooch hollered over the heads of Nixon's admirers. "Any further comments?"

"Are you complimenting me on style, or content?"

"Oh, both, both, to be sure." Gooch smiled and clasped the reverend's enormous hand. "You display courage, sir, a trait worthy of admiration. And courage is something nobody can buy."

"Neither with votes nor money." Nixon, a hand on his enormous belly. "The false-fake courageous are nothing of the sort—they are frauds and fiends."

"Heard that." Gooch, note-taking with mad abandon.

Nixon, a smirk. "Let us be frank, Mr. Wimmel. I consider you a fair man. You seeming to hold your position as a member of the fourth estate with an oath not unlike that of the physician: First, do no harm. Indeed. But, please: I can see it in your eyes. You think this is a fool's errand, don't you?"

"Far from it, Reverend. Far from it. I figure that, all things considered, and

wifi, oh-my. In any case, I will minister to them both. I've known Roy Earl for many, many years."

"Rabbit always said he had a good head on his shoulders, that grandson of his. He seems to be hanging tough."

"Roy Earl is a man of strength and character."

"How about a quote?"

"About Roy Earl?"

No, Gooch says. About Reynolds. Now who was getting senile? Who cared what Nixon thought about Rabbit's grandson.

"I knew the man more by reputation than personally, Bill. And I know his grandson. But not him. Forgive me."

"No problem. I understand."

Gooch, frustrated—no politician in history had turned down the chance for a quote in the paper. At this rate, Nixon won't make much of a politician—the Rabbit Tribute would have been perfect for getting his name in the paper. That's politics: the flapping of gum before men like good old Gooch.

Politicians. Vapid blatherers going "listen to me, look at me" like perpetual three-year-olds upon whom great adulation and much doting had occurred from the time of birth. Bill, a little sick of covering small town politics. A little sick of himself. When he remembered to be.

The crowd dispersing, he trudged over toward his building. The Dixiana sign caught his eye. Burnham Sykes sat, alone, on the hard bench out front, resting his hands on his cane and chin on top of his hands. Nodding off. Probably drunk already, based on that display earlier. "Lucky that crowd didn't beat the crap out of him with their own canes and walkers," Gooch said to no one.

He felt bad, but at least for now another Samaritan would have to help the old fellow through his time of grief instead of this tired old queen: News waited to be reported, and plenty of it. He needed to get the Reynolds Elder Pettus obit squared away, as he tried to think with dispassion about his old friend's notice, the information for which he'd need to talk over with Miss Runelle and Roy Earl, whom he assumed had heard by now and would, these hours later, be well on his way to Edgewater County.

Or that been yesterday?

It had. A public memorial, tomorrow.

Or—the next day?

Remember, Bill exhorted himself.

Remember.

Dobbs.

Dobbs will know. Thank god for Dobbs.

ROY AND CREEDENCE

On the way downtown in your granddaddy's rattling, nicotine-stinking F-150, you're dialed into WABA-AM, classic country, the volume turned down low—just as your grandfather left the setting of his radio. You suffer a swelling, nay, a surfeit of nostalgia. His presence here lingers, as does your childhood, lurking in every direction.

But you could do without the country music. Your taste? Yours? You? Blasting heavy rock tunes from a CD player he probably never used, one of your go-to's like The Who.

CD player. Listen to you. On your phone may be found your favorite Who album, *Quadrophenia*, along with digital rips of fifty other LPs of personal significance and specific tastes. You'd first heard the Who's second rock opera on an LP your Uncle Burnie had given you from his downtown electronics store's cut-out bin not long before he closed the business in the late 70s.

You plug in your bluetooth buds and turn off the tinny WABA signal, Waylon and Willie, enough already. Pete Townshend's pained and plaintive warbling suits this mood best depicted as melancholy. Burdened. Confused.

How you have always rued missing the giants of rock who passed before you came of age, legends and myths forever out of reach. Moonie and Bonzo and Hendrix and Lennon and Morrison, all dead before you even knew who they were. Their eternal absence, frozen in time as youthful icons worshipped like once the gods of old, colors your fandom like an angst-y itch you can never scratch.

Except with the Grateful Dead back in your college days, in the presence of living legends. For sure. Not that dropping major bread on a rock concert could ever be the answer to your problems. Particularly at modern ticket prices. The remnants of the Dead put on big sold-out anniversary shows in Chicago earlier in the summer. Crazy prices on the aftermarket for the best seats. You were like, yeah, I can pay it. But Jerry's been dead twenty years. Forget it.

As you motor on a ridiculous zigzag pattern along back and side roads, a feint to put off going to The Dixiana, you struggle with ignoring Creedence's mess. Talk about putting crap into boxes, compartmentalizing. File it away. A gray box with a question mark—what would become of the marriage.

For now, the agenda is to meet Trudy. Look over the honkytonk. And discuss the future.

What future?

Everyone looking to you for answers. Hoping you'll care for them.

Maybe not Mama Runelle—she seems no worse for wear, isn't depending on you for squat, really. And you've barely spoken to anyone today, so who the hell's looking for answers?

You?

Yeah. You.

But what's sending you upriver are those brutal, boxy, out-of-date TV sets sitting in accusatory decrepitude. You, sir, will go nucking futs trapped in Edgewater County trying to watch HD content squeezed onto 4:3 monitors. Relics of a dead century. Every aspect of your life needed updating, if not upgrading. With certain parts requiring removal. These sets offered a problem immediate but manageable. Check.

❂❂❂

By the time 'Drowned' crescendoes and climaxes into the swirling sea-sound effects sprinkled throughout the Who's classic concept album, you've bypassed downtown altogether and merged onto the west side highway toward the national forest and Newberry County and the upcountry beyond. Toward no-man's-land, a still-unsettled part of the county much too far from the major highways to attract subdivisions.

What is this random nonsense? You don't just drive around. You move with purpose.

What's your action item?

TVs.

They—she—must have updated screens. Up-to-date sets throughout the Victorian. Today.

More important than Trudy. And completing a walk-through at The Dixiana. The thought turns your stomach, in fact.

The highway deserted, you steer with one insouciant finger to cut a wide, smooth U-town right in the middle of the freaking road, like you own this stretch of asphalt. Haul ass and passing downtown yet again, you head instead toward Chilton, and the burgeoning commercial corridor closer to the lake country.

In the electronics section of the massive, crystal cathedral of a big box anchoring the latest development south of Tillman Falls and one exit nearer Columbia and thus choked with housing developments, you flag down a pair of blue-vested employees to help haul the new sets you've chosen to the front for checkout. They snapped-to once you switched your money clip, thick, deliberate, from one pocket to the other, a deft move designed to demonstrate wherewithal, along with the implied will to wield it.

Underlining this idea, a stage whisper: "Let's play make a deal. If you dudes could get these televisions squared away in my truck outside, there's five bucks in it for you both."

"What you whispering for, beau?"

"For real. We a'ight, yo."

One of them maneuvers the lead cart with the big set past freestanding displays of on-sale ladies lingerie, a titillating obstacle, while his partner and you managed a cart burdened with the two smaller video display units. You're out the door under two-K for the three sets. Extended warranties, whole shebang. A no-brainer. Chicken feed. The improvement to your grandmother's life, as well your own, in the interim at least? Immeasurable. "I just figured y'all weren't supposed to collect tips."

They both shrug. "Ain't no one ever offered."

You can tell from their furtive expressions it's a no-no, but dang if they don't want that money. You will finesse the hand-off.

The mock innocence and sincerity of the two charm you, and once squared away, you decide you'll give them a sawbuck each instead of a five-spot. Watch their faces then, yo.

And in the future? If needed, you'll be able to call on these two faceless characters at will. They'll never forget you and your gratuity. The guy handing out bills. A mythic quality to such generosity in these troubled times.

The last restaurant trade show you'd attended had made clear how all not well on the economic landscape. The show itself, a shadow of its former self. Fewer vendors and entrepreneurs. Not good. Grimaces passing for smiles on the sallow, pitted faces of hungry sales reps, slavering like starving dogs.

You, though? An outlier. Fat with cheddar. So you'll spread it around. Buy some TVs.

A restless throng of both hard goods and grocery-store shoppers trying to merge their carts from two directions congeals into one seething, impatient mass, being crawled over by toddlers and prepubescents and sullen teens and infants, squalling infants, swaddled in carriers or propped on shoulders and dripping fluids onto shopping cart child seats. This group, writhing like a petri dish biology experiment, reminds you on a symbolic level of hitting the Sedge Island toll plaza at rush hour on the Friday of a long holiday weekend.

You snort, sigh and decry. "What a cluster-fudge."

"Word to that." The bored black kid on the lead cart, scratching behind a cornrow jangling with beads like Bo Derek, looks high. Halfway want to hit him up. You used to enjoy getting stoned, in less responsible times.

You muster halfhearted small talk with the clerks, their smiley face buttons and name tags reading Tucker and Rodrigo hanging crooked on sagging, threadbare blue vests. Such a quality badge—raised lettering, thick plastic, heavy-duty clasp, a workhorse badge—would look good on the breasts of the college girlies working the industrial blenders at a Spotted Banana™ Fruit-shake Company® store somewhere near you.

The boys discuss the ins and outs of streaming using Apple TV or Roku; the various services offered thereon like Amazon Prime versus Netflix, Hulu Plus, Vudu, Crackle, dozens more; a whispered assessment of their mega-corporation's own branded streaming service, to which they display only a modicum of loyalty.

You note how the boys debate these matters with a precision befitting science students in a lab, a fine discernment regarding fees and offerings on the various 'channels' as they appear to consider these digital content delivery platforms, all customizable in a manner beyond the imagination of a Gen-X boy who once sat on his grandparents' living room floor turning a knob through four channels not even on all the time, like the middle of the night, which people now regard as prime time for binging entire seasons of beloved TV series all in one compulsive glurt, like an all-you-can-eat media buffet. You are still getting used to this way of consuming content, the myriad choices at your disposal often overwhelming.

As such, you reminisce about the old days, the lack of choice, waiting for broadcasts of favorite movies on Friday night on ABC, suffering through commercials, later freaking out because of tape and DVD and being able to 'hold movies' in your hands, and the dudes are like, no duh, old dude. "Every-body got DVDs and Blu-rays now."

"But streaming, yeah. That's what it's gonna be from now on, eh, guys?"

"Yeah. I'd get me an Apple TV."

"Do y'all sell Apple products here?"

"Naw."

"Guess it'll have to wait."

Rodrigo, chuckling at your naiveté. "Naw, naw. All these TVs got wi-fi ready chips, dog. You might think about upgrading your router if you ain't done so in a while. Check your bandwidth limits and shit. But yeah—these bitches internet-ready, yo."

"These sets are for my grandparents," a cold chill settling inside. "They don't know from wi-fi."

"Word. You got to set it up for them, then. That way they can watch all them old people shows. My grandmama love to sit looking at the same shit she did back in the day."

"I'll pay someone to do it."

"You want us to come and do it for ya?"

You give them both the once-over. Not on your life. "That's cool. In the no-thanks sense. Nothing personal."

"I feel ya."

The line, creeping. You keep looking at all the bargain-hunting shoppers, their carts overloaded with more crap than you could dream up if you tried. Weird, colorful crap. We beat the Axis back in World War II, your grandfather's war, and saved the world and made it safe for everyone to die choking on little bits of plastic, ever smaller and smaller, broken down by the oceans and killing all the plankton, the first link in the food chain, and so winning the war had solved nothing, only perpetuated more self-destructive behavior. Not two weeks ago, you and Creedence had screened a documentary about the oceans filling up with plastic, though come to think of it she had passed out snoring on the couch, smelling of ethanol despite denying that she'd had any liquor that night. You wondered where she stashed it.

Look at them all, your fellow line dwellers. Every one of them fat and having reproduced. Chunky fleshy legs and arms, everywhere in sight. Chubby distressed sets of women's feet, flat and dirty, in rubber flip-flops and grimy threadbare house slippers and white sneakers on the Mexican ones, housekeepers like yours down on the island. Get thee to the pedicurist. Creedence's late mother, the prim and proper Eileen Rucker, had despised the flip-flop era, the idea of casual footwear taken to a distressing extreme. "Everyone dresses these days as though on their way to the seashore. Young people, I do not want to see your grubby little toes."

Stuck in the line, still two carts back from the register, your stomach clenches at the energy of the incipient commerce roiling around you, building, ready to strike; the money in your pocket, coiled and tense like threatened snakes.

Filthy, all this.

"Problem, fellas: I can't commit to the purchase of these sets after all."

The associates are like, aw, naw, naw. Rodrigo, the most incensed: "You playing?"

"Just can't do it. Not today."

Much grumbling. "These is some nice TVs."

"Be that as it may, but I'm in an emotional crisis right now."

"Them new TVs make you feel all better, I bet." Tucker's sincerity, touching.

"You'd think so. But I'm not making the purchase. That's that."

You apologize further and slip the boys the tip anyway, ask them to put the sets back into floor stock. Not only are you not buying new sets, you're not into facing down the backbreaking chore of hauling off the old TVs to the dump, because that's all you can do with the standard def models. Nobody wants 'em. Not even poor folks. Not with sets at these prices, cheaper still after they start rolling out 4K models. You'll pick up sets like these for pocket change. You'll wait.

Yeah, the economy of Edgewater County could live without your extravagant television set binge, designed only to see the look of surprise and gratitude on your grandmother's face. To show her how grown you've become, how much money you have. As though building an entire house under their feet hadn't already instilled this intended sense of awe and loyalty and fulfillment.

But you still feel inadequate. Even after the house-building episode.

More TVs wasn't gonna cut it, beau. Maybe you could buy your bereaved Mee-maw a hobby aircraft.

⊙⊛◉

BACK IN THE TRUCK, you peel steel-belted radial out of that vast parking lot and signal to get on the highway to Tillman Falls, the plumes of the nuclear station dancing along the distant tree line to the east. Talk yourself out of a chicken sandwich and fries from the KFC.

Grilled sandwich. Not fried.

If you get one.

Hell—why not.

Another U-turn. Rocking the tunes. The Who. Damn, your granddaddy had hated your Who tapes. Said it all sounded fruity as hell. That the drummer sounded like he was beating the drums with sledgehammers. A bunch of junk. You touch the tiny control on your buds and crank it louder.

Belching grease, you arrive at The Dixiana with a tickle in your side, an unpleasant gurgling that's a precursor of lower GI distress. What's wrong with you, eating that food?

"But chicken sam-mich taste good." Your Mee-maw's reasoning. The kind that had kept you chubby through adolescence.

You nose the F-150 into one of the angled spaces along the green and hop out, tooting and feeling like an idiot over that foolishness on display at the Wal-mart.

You're stopped in your tracks by the front grill—a plume of wispy smoke or steam. There, and then not. An acrid odor, like scorched rubber.

"Awesome. A truck problem. Ain't got time for this, yo."

A throaty rumbling grows from the mural side on Common Street: Sure enough, it's as familiar an Edgewater County sight as the water tower or the old confederate monument on the north side of the green, as recognizable as the nuclear station and its plume, the trees in the pecan orchard or the marquee of the Palmetto Grande, or the neon Dixiana sign itself: Thurmond Pike, rolling through on a used motorbike he's considering buying to resell at the Bait & Pawn. Stooped and taciturn, his dyed-black hairline may have receded, but he still test drove the bikes personally.

Tested Chesnee Campobello personally.

Gag.

"Thurmond," you call out to him with a cupped hand. *"Looks like a wiener!"*

He waves a lazy hand but doesn't pull over to speak, thank god.

Maybe you'll buy a motorcycle. Take Chesnee out for a ride yourself sometime.

A zany breakout character on the hit sitcom playing only in your head say, he say, "You be tripping, bro!" Studio audience howls, hoots, catcalls your dumb ass.

You will your smallish gut not to pork out again despite indulgences like a fast-food lunch, ease down onto the bench outside your granddaddy's honky-tonk and crossing your legs and sitting like the old men in your life have been doing for as long as you have memories. Your guts twist not over an old heartbreak like Chesnee Campobello, but because of how much you miss your Creedence. How you can't freaking believe it's all come to this. What all she's done.

Was doing, for all you know.

You'd told her yesterday you didn't care. Gave her a license to go on with it. Not that she acted like she wanted to.

Yeah—you allow yourself to remember the ferocity of her grief and fear over having been found out. Your own anger. The wounding words you wielded.

The pitiful pleading.

The pathetic contrition.

The sickening lies.

You read the messages. Knew the truth. Keystrokes on a screen, they didn't lie.

At the thought of FB you're gripped by an automatic urge to stab a finger at the iPhone and scroll through notes and posts and whatnot, but your mind dwells elsewhere, three hours away in the North Carolina mountains: The approach to Max Patch had been where the marriage had begun to crumble. This you have defined for yourself. And yet the mountaintop remains a vaunted and magical place, one to which you have the sense you will soon return.

❀

AFTER TWO YEARS on Sedge Island, with a vast and torpid emptiness filling you from stem to stern, gazing from within the four corners of the California king bed where you both lie, watching egrets and ospreys making their own living out along the reeds of the salty tidal plain, you insisted that you solve your disenchantment and boredom with all your financial success by dragging your wife on a hiking trip. The mountains. If you couldn't live there, you'd insist on it becoming the go-to vacation spot.

"But we already live in a freaking vacation spot—that was the idea," showing how she didn't share one whit of interest in this presumptive hiking enterprise.

"Nature. Fresh air. Quiet. It's quiet here, but it's not quiet enough. It's natural—*but not natural enough*. Somehow."

Agreeing in part, she complained about the landscapers taking care of the common areas throughout the exclusive housing development. "They use the blowers too much. It's the stupidest shit I ever seen. Blowers got to be the dumbest waste of fossil fuels I can imagine. If raking and burning them in a barrel was good enough for Daddy, it ought to be good enough for them Mexican boys."

What a moron she could be. As though the Point Egret homeowner's covenant allowed for 55-gallon barrels all charred around the edges like the ones in which your granddaddy used to incinerate trash beside the storage shed behind the old house. "Blowers keep my parking lot sparkling clean. All I can tell you."

Giving you dead-eyes: "Well, they get on my nerves."

Enough of this. "Let's get into this hiking deal. Take a sojourn up in them-thar hills."

"Why?"

"Something different?"

"We barely go and walk on the beach."

"It's because we've done it to death."

She scoffed and mumbled.

You clasped your hands, prayerful. "Here's what we do—we Google around. Look for nice places. Rustic cabins. Tucked way back."

"But what if I don't wanna get tucked way back?"

"We stay in Asheville, then. Drive into the national forests for day-hikes, but crash in a plush bed. Grab ourselves fine-dining vegetarian breakfast served by a dude with hairwraps—no, dreadlocks all bundled up in one of those knit caps—and rope sandals. It'll be so authentically chill, we won't know what to do with ourselves."

She shrugged; her look of my-give-a-crap-seems-broken. Hunched shoulders of nonchalant disinterest made your flesh tighten and body temperature rise in a manner nonsexual and irritating.

You hadn't been hiking since Boy Scouts when you were fourteen, and of late the idea of returning to a condition of outdoorsmanship had consumed your imagination. The casual camping you did as a kid with Dobbs and Devin had been more fun that the Scouting trips, but they'd still been memorable. Perhaps you only wanted to recreate the innocence you felt in those North Carolina mountains, away from the oppressive smothering laid on you by your grandmother.

You couldn't seem to explain it to Creedence, although after enough stomping around and cutting, hurtful asides about entombing you inside this godforsaken, humid tourist trap terrarium, she caved on the hiking idea. Browbeaten, more like it, but you'd take agreement wherever you could mine it.

"Want to know what you gotta do?" Rabbit had asked one day while you sat fishing next to him from the bluff, your Keds stained by the red Carolina river clay. "To get by in life?"

"What, Pa-paw?" as you called him. You were bored with life then, too. You didn't much like fishing, but you loved sitting there overlooking the river. And sometimes, your granddaddy would take and pronounce some bit of wisdom to you in his backwater Socratic method there by the fishing hole. "What do you do? You mean, make money?"

"You work and endure and provide; you serve. But what I'm warning you about, is that you must learn to grieve." He cast his Winchester Fancy 2644, an ornate brass fishing reel over forty years old. It had belonged to his father as well. It spun all-but silent as he cast out and down into the Sugeree.

You remember a coldness sluicing into your guts. He was gonna talk about death. Your voice shook. "What do I need to know?"

Faraway. "You sure as shit gonna grieve, boy. You grieve like a son of a gun. About different things, in different ways." He found your eyes, and Pa-paw almost never made direct eye contact with you, or anyone. Not for long, anyway. "Things you done. Things done to you. Things you seen. People you lose."

You recall asking, in your childlike way, if steps could be taken to gird for these eventualities.

"Sometimes it's all gonna come at once, it seems like. Like, you get into a rut and don't do nothing but grieve. But it passes. And gets better."

"It does?"

"It has to."

"Does it?"

Yes-sir, 'Punkin,' which is what he called you, but only when no one else could hear. "If it don't, and all you do is grieve, you ain't gonna get to the next step in life. You accept that it happens. It's a test. And passing the test is letting the grief go."

You didn't ask what all he meant, but already at that tender age you understood it must have to do with the death of his own son, your father. This moment made you want to never suffer grief. To get away with not having it.

Also instilled a sense of avoiding having kids of your own. You might have to grieve for them, and them surely for you, one day. Try to break the cycle.

A little secret—you were glad when they told Creedence how, after yet another miscarriage and the bleeding and the pain, it seemed clear a pregnancy to term didn't represent a healthy and viable choice. Yeah. Good on that. Even if you didn't say so aloud. At the time there had been tears, though yours flowed more out of pity than your own grief.

Grief?

Fuck that noise.

The same summer Rabbit made that speech, you and your friends camped down in what you called the Glade, upriver from the clay fishing bank Rabbit so loved, and to where you will later scatter his ashes. In the backland sloping down toward the river, meadows once cleared long ago so that sheep and cows could graze, the Glade looked like a storybook idyll: a dense stand of weeping willow and river birch and one stout oak with mighty arms stretching out around which the rest clustered in seeming deference, this rich and grassy river-fed copse felt and looked in its isolation as though from a different place, a different time. Secluded and unspoiled. No power lines, no bridges, no railroad tracks, no cars, no roads; you couldn't see the nuclear plumes or the blinking radio tower at WABA, only the river and the sky and the trees on the other shore. And yet, this slice of heaven lay only a few miles out of town, near to the houses along River Ridge Road including your own, as you'd discovered on peregrinations into the backland as a bored kid stuck being raised by two old people. You could make a Super8 version of Lord of the Rings back there. Or Lord of the Flies, for that matter.

To this day, The Glade—who named it that? Dobbs?—still symbolized oasis and escape. The seclusion from the world lent precedent and context and history to your adult desire to settle in the mountains, way back in a hollow away from everyone and everything and which she shot down but-good, instead dragging you down to the lowcountry to perspire and swat mosquitos and pump termite poison into the ground and wash the dang salt off the cars every fifteen freaking minutes.

With your hiking idea, you sought a measure of recompense. Actually, you knew she'd never camp, and you can't say you were up for sleeping on the ground either. But a day hike? Damn straight. It's what you both needed. Your instincts, never wrong.

⊛

You needed to seek hiking advice. You could Google around all day, but always better to ask someone you trust. One of the seasoned cats at the hanger, for instance.

Your boys. Your crew. Your peers.

"Day-hike." You specified this to Ron Nawalinski, who'd told you he once did the entire A-T, albeit decades ago. Camping vacations in the Smokies for years afterward. An expert. "No big whoop type-deal."

"Ye-*eah*, ye-*eah*"; Nawalinski's thinking mantra. "North Cackalackie day-hike. Got a pen?"

These old dudes, Cal Luchok and Colonel Hodges Ringholder and a few other guys, are all transplanted yankees, which fits with the image of Sedge Island as a sunbelt retirement destination for the well-heeled. None of them sport Southern accents like the codgers who used to run their mouths at Mr. Halsey's barber shop, with you or Timmy Latham or Dobbs or Devin sitting there waiting to get your heads cut and listening to the old-men's stories, opinions, and told jokes you didn't quite get. These guys all hail from places along the northeastern mega-urban power and wealth corridor, and that's how Nawalinski sounds.

Cracking a cold Aquafina out of the lounge fridge, you talked the idea through with the old-timers. This made for a change from the usual amateur aviation *schtuff* comprising your airfield bull sessions. "Nothing too strenuous —she's not an outdoorsy type. And, not too far a drive."

"Drive?" Everyone at once asked why you wouldn't be flying to your destination.

"She doesn't cotton to going up yonder in the old tin can," you said. "We'll be rocking the Mercedes."

Hodges Ringholder, whom you all call The Colonel, threw out white shining rock of Caesar's Head, situated up in the pie-crust corner of good old South Carolina. "You can be there in three hours. Two and a half if you take back roads and open up that 450SL of yours, Roy."

Luchok, scolding. "Or an hour if he shows her the statistics on auto crashes along two-lane country roads versus piloting personal aircraft like his Piper."

"Boy, I tell ya." The Colonel, shaking his jowls and stamping his cane, two round bandages covering spots of skin cancer he'd had removed earlier that week. A father figure to you. A grandfather figure. "What're ya gonna do? Women."

You admire the living shit out of the Colonel. Had been shot down over Vietnam by those yellow bastards, held in the Hanoi Hilton for seventy damn months, until early '73. Hurt bad, but made it through the injuries and the imprisonment. Lived to tell the tale. Flew again—not in combat, but as a teacher. The Colonel.

The Colonel, like his name suggests, holds a kind of seniority over this group, but it's voluntary and admiring: he's a POW, a hero. Piloting F-4s with the 8th Tactical fighter wing out of Uban in Thailand, the stout, tough codger had flown seventy-four combat missions over Southeast Asia, but on the seventy-fifth a lucky volley of Commie flak shredded the navigation system of his aircraft and he ejected, as he told it, with only a second or two left before the vehicle disintegrated underneath him; he extolled the notion of ejection being a state of mind less than a conscious decision. When a plane came apart at those velocities, you had one chance, and it was to get out.

"Eject. Deploy the chute. Pray. That was the scariest part—knowing the gooks in the jungle could see me floating down out of the sky. Waiting for the bullets to rip into my legs, my nuts, my ass. But boys, it didn't happen. And here we sit."

Real action movie stuff. Ron and Cal informed you in private that not a word of the story came exaggerated.

Nawalinski brought the matter at hand back to the fore: "Here's a good one: Lemon Gap to Max Patch, up in Western North Carolina. Hour outside Asheville."

"How far of a trudge?"

"It'd be—oh—about ten miles. A ten-miler."

"A ten-miler?" The Colonel, aghast. "No Sedge Island woman will agree to it. Oh, boy." He wrapped his cane. "You jackasses realize that's twenty miles round trip?"

"No, no. That's round trip. Ten—check—maybe eleven miles total. Hell, you can hump that before lunch."

"Oh, boy." The Colonel, apoplectic with disagreement and deaf to Ron's reassurances. "She'll never agree to twenty miles."

You were with him on this. Ten miles didn't faze you, but it did sound like a lot. She'd be like, WTF, boy? You'd have to slip into your superhero guise known as The Cajoler.

"You guys don't get it. The distance on this one goes by like a dream—it's a stroll more than a hike." With this part of the trail, as Nawalinski pontificated at length, you got a taste of alpine farmland covered in wildflowers that time of the year, which'd been late spring; you anticipated mountain brooks, scenic forest, whispering breezes, stunning long-range views of the Smokies.

"Ye-*eah*, about two-thousand foot incline, right, up to the summit of Max Patch. Passing by the Roaring Fork shelter, you might see a few through-hikers." Ron instructed that, as a day-hiker, one always stepped aside to let the through-hikers on their more serious way than yours.

"Will it be crowded with—real hikers?"

"Crowded? It better not be. Most northbound hikers, the smart ones, are already in Virginia by now. But the ones you do meet deserve respect and deference." How the return from Max Patch to Lemon Gap is almost all down-hill, so novice hikers won't be huffing and puffing too hard on the way back, not like on the approach to Max Patch. "Only steep right at the very end, and only for a couple hundred yards."

"Whole lotta scenery, eh?"

"Feels like top of the world. To put in terms a pup like you'd understand? Your mind will be blown, Royster. Blown."

"Boy," the Colonel says, dry. "Could I stand to be blown. I tell ya."

Guffaws and the slapping of knees.

You note the names Max Patch and Lemon Drop—no, Lemon Gap—on a scratch pad with the airfield logo and you try to get the wise old dude's atten-tion to ask where these colorfully named places might be, but he's moved on to a filthy joke with a punch line having to do with Phyllis Diller and a glory hole. Old dude jokes. You slap your knee right along with them. Your peers. Always stuck with these old-timers, aren't you. Seemingly from birth. You'll look it up later yourself.

⊛✻◉

Rain.

You and Creedence suffered two full days in a stuffy, rustic cabin at the Mineral Springs Resort and Spa waiting for the weather to clear. The French Broad River, turbid and unsettled, swelled and rose only yards away from your bed.

"Most rain I ever seen up here," the day clerk said in his hick accent. "Most anybody's seen." The young desk attendant, scratching behind his ear and adjusting his clip-on tie like Rodney Dangerfield. "Well—I don't know about anybody. Most I ever seen, though."

"Should we check out? Will there be a flood?"

"I ain't never seen her flood."

"So—it's not the most rain ever, I guess."

"Not unless this here's the end times getting underway, I reckon."

As the deluge continued, Creedence sat with long stems folded under reading a book you packed: a local novel from the 90s by Cort Beauchamp, a well-thumbed trade paperback called *Keys to the Rain*, its title offering an ironic commentary on your predicament.

"Haven't you already read that?"

"Not much else to do."

A complaint; a challenge.

Bored out of your minds, you did more than mull the literary legacies of Edgewater County figures—you also made sexy time, and it was hot, real hot. How by the third time Creedence got off good, best you could remember, her on top grinding away, into it. Your honey's back, arching, and fingernails digging into your forearms as she held you down and said UH UH UH, and god-damn, and holy crap; explosive, mutual, the energy rising and cresting along your cranium like a purple sunrise, a dizzying sense of unity and connection. What you two had been missing.

She lay sprawled across the bed like a damp dishrag, draping that long freckled leg you so love across your beefy body. This was before you lost the weight and got all toned up from the island walks. But chubby or not, you still had the steam to get it on a couple times with your sweet sexy mama, who relaxed and seemed to enjoy herself. Like the old Creedence.

"Gracious. Maybe this was a good idea after all."

"Yeah." But getting your priorities straight. "I need to see that mountain-top, though."

❁❋◉

DURING THE DRIVE UP into the mountains to take the rain-delay hike—further into the mountains, that is—Creedence, holding on for dear life. Fretting that the road had gotten too winding and narrow. Wanting you to turn around.

To give up short of the goal.

"Forget it. The sun's out. And look—here's the last turnoff."

A fork in the road. A faded sign:

MAX PATCH — 5

"And now it's gravel?" she hollered. "Five more miles of gravel?"

You hid from her your own discomfort about driving on what seemed like the next thing to off-road. Flying the plane was nothing compared to this wild card. The Torrences, driving to the haunted Overlook.

But revealing none of that uncertainty to her. "This's nothing. Relax."

"Easy for you to say." She'd been trying to read a magazine. "Did you know we were OINKs?"

"Do what, now?"

"One Income, No Kids."

"Oh—I get it. What are you reading?"

She showed you. Fortune Small Business. A complimentary subscription with your AMEX Platinum card. An article about the changing demographics of young urban professionals. "If I had my own money coming in, we would be DINKs."

"You have your own money."

She explained about earning versus being given, or inherited, her two sources. They had cleared almost a quarter mil in capital gains on the Rucker house in Pine Haven, abandoned after Devin left for good. Cowan, your money guy, doing some finagling with investments to avoid the tax bite.

"OINKs are fine. Is fine. Whichever."

"But I feel useless."

"You're not useless. The fortune I've made is ours."

"See—that 'you've' made."

"Well?"

"I helped."

"That's my point. You should share in the pride I feel. We're DINKs. Not OINKs. It's all us. Not me." You meant it. Even if it wasn't true.

At last, arrival at the parking area. Creedence, unbuckling, declared she'd already become "slap wore out" by the harrowing drive.

"I could live up here." Ignoring her complaints, you stood in the shady grove at Lemon Gap where a few other vehicles, mostly four-wheel-drive trucks and Subaru Outbacks, sat parked. "Listen to that silence."

"So I go from being Edgewater County white trash to Sedge Island gentry to Western NC hillbilly white trash? You gotta be kidding."

You were both wearing your Crocs for the hike which had been a good call, a super smart, thinking–ahead call, and she didn't even know how much yet. How easy the black mud would rinse off.

Black, thick, sucking mud, encountered within the first steps down the trail. As established, a wet season preceded your visit. Patches of deep mud, hidden under benign looking leaf cover. You remained bright and encouraging even as your Crocs squished down in the viscous dark brownie batter of the forest floor. "See, it's downhill already, not uphill."

A grunt from Creedence; a sigh. She belched—the winding roads and magazine reading had made her borderline carsick.

Checking out the flora, all brilliant and green and alive from the heavy rains. "This rhododendron's too much—it's like a weed." You suggested bringing in a vegetation management specialty firm for an assessment. See if this rhododendron ought to be eradicated and replaced.

Creedence, a dry wit, said you should run for president of the Appalachian Trail neighborhood ass-sociation.

You made fun of what few other day-hikers you passed on your bad-ass chunk of the AT you could soon say you had hiked. Those who were obviously through-hikers—huge backpacks, beards, dreadlocks, bandanas, weathered and durable boots, with chill but purposeful demeanors on their stilled and dignified faces—garnered your respect, your absolute hells-yeah high-fiving approbation: you recall the advice from Nawalinski to stand aside and let them through, that this was SOP on the trail, and if you didn't you risked appearing as the equivalent of the 'tourons,' as he called visitors to Sedge Island. "Those a-holes making wrong turns and getting stuck on the traffic circles and causing problems for the stakeholders, the year-rounders—that'll be you."

The through-hikers were the stakeholders, and this resonated with you like the bash of a gong. They enjoyed the right of way, on many levels. You stood aside for their big-dick asses, like when you and the other officers of the Downtown Business Alliance had walked into city council meetings en masse: The murmuring hushed. Acknowledgement. The faces, downcast and penitent. Knowing you da boss.

The smart ones, anyway.

With this in mind, you could dig the 'real' hikers who passed. You made eye contact. No small talk, though. These were important people. Busy.

As for the day-hikers, in their bright neon clothing and fancy walking sticks and shiny blue and yellow and much smaller backpacks and shoes that looked new, you held them only in disdain, even though you were but a half-assed version.

"Poseurs," as you put it to Creedence after passing a spry group of yellow slicker-wearing retirees, chattering and enjoying their group hike. "Amateurs."

"And we ain't?"

"Shoot, no—we're day-hikers."

"But—"

"We just don't need any specialty gear to prove our worth."

To demonstrate this, you found a massive walking stick you imagined as made of hickory and like that wielded by the justice-seeking, 1970s redneck movie sheriff Buford Pusser, portrayed first by the great Joe Don Baker but less memorably in sequels fronted by Bo Svenson. You stabbed the great piece of wood into the soaked and squishy ground; with it you found purchase. "See?"

"Gotcha."

But as the hike went on, the land now sloping upward by lengthy switchbacks that crossed and re-crossed the same gurgling mountain stream, the stick grew heavy, and you remembered seeing the day-hikers and their slender machine-made trekking poles with the rubber grips on the handles and the slight give as they supported the weight of their bearer, and oh how you resented your walking stick. Wanted to chuck it aside but not after you'd insisted it was the one, the best walking stick a flatlander could ever hope to find.

Wet bark, flaking off and making your soft pink hand grimy with peat. Your shoulder, aching. A good solid stick.

To take her mind off the fact that your wife trudged in ill-concealed boredom and misery, for miles you spun out ridiculous jokes and stories, outrageous exaggerations and lies and fibs designed to make Creedence giggle at the absurdity of your routine and the silliness of the voices you used in the telling. Here you expounded at length, challenging yourself to see how long you could keep going about the sad history of the Hungadunga Indian tribe that'd once inhabited these ancient mountains, these deep cut-in valleys and hollows, and how descended from human royalty—perhaps extraterrestrial in origin, as you speculated—the spirits of those Indians who suffered at the hands of disease and blight brought by the white settlers from across the pond still haunted these woods.

Your voice, echoing back from the mountainside: "The Hungadunga, they rode on the back of a mighty eagle from far away, their even mightier blue star around which their home world rotated, among all the mighty worlds which rotate always, yes, that first Hungadunga man." You made stupid bird calls you claimed were the mighty SKREE of the legendary interstellar eagle. "And upon seeing these woods proclaimed them to be good! And to be true! And that he would raise his sons here and they'd grow strong as the mighty trees before which he stood, an alien yet not. He'd come home."

Creedence, breathless, trying to keep up. "No daughters?"

"Seven—seven sisters as well."

"Thank goodness."

From that esoteric thread you rolled out a tangential legend about one particular Hungadungan tribesman haunted by the angry spirits of displaced forest dwellers and through whom attacks and other bloody acts of violence throughout the ages and dimensions have been enacted, a morbid, Stephen King-esque narrative that veered into gratuitous detail about the crimes of the modern people finding themselves possessed by this wicked spirit, all the horrid details cadged from Jasper Glasscock's Coy Wando interview book, the one by which everybody in Edgewater County had been rightfully sickened and horrified. Still in print, though. Folks ate up death porn like that.

Your murderous digression made Creedence finally say, "Jesus, baby— what are you planning to do with me out here? You that sick of my mess?"

"Aw, I'm just having some laughs. Doing schtick."

Her voice, tiny. "My feet are ruined. And you're making up stories."

You started to say, I told you stories were important. I told you I wanted to be a poet and short story writer. But you've forgotten. And maybe I have, too. But instead you asked about her feet, for which you had a plan.

◉✴◉

DOWN IN THE WOODS, no; you hadn't much enjoyed that part of the hike, but through the rolling grassy areas among the wildflowers and up the steep approach to Max Patch you felt alive and in control. Before, you'd spent too much time imagining how dark it would be in these woods at night. You knew unseen presences moved around in the murk the way fish swam in the rivers and the sea, that presences unknown used the inky black dark, a malevolent spiritual medium—the aether, they used to call it. Or so you'd always believed. Perhaps for this reason men had always feared the dark. You didn't know. Highfalutin' thoughts on this here hike, like back in college getting high with Dobbs and Devin, and dreaming of writing stories and poems.

Now the dreaming was over, and the being, the being was everything—the aircraft, the house on Sedge, the money, the dream girl, the fruitshakes. The fruitshake windfall.

Of the group of owners that comprised your company and several sub-companies in which you did not have an ownership stake except as originating trademark holder of the brand, you decided, for all of them—you, the progenitor—to take a sweet deal in cash and stock and simply sell your interest in the trademark to ConParAgCorp, and otherwise sign away all rights to your creation.

But oh, for a sweet fucking score. The goal. The prize. IT.

IT was, though, like one of those creatures moving in the darkness along the mountainside. You knew these things must be there, but you never saw them, not on your camping trips as a Scout, nor camping in the dark in the Glade back home with Devin and Dobbs. Just as you'd never seen IT. IT was something whose shape you could not define. IT could not have been fruitshake money. Or you'd know it by now.

The Spotted Banana™ Fruitshake Company®? Hell, you hadn't planned it to end up so cheesy, but the name had been perfect for corporate America, for its malls and food courts. Or would, you surmised, as ConParAgCorp rolled out the brand nationwide, for the most part in airports since all the malls were drying up. The checks would keep coming. You'd always get a taste of that growth. Cashing checks. Money for nothing. A new hobby. You'd sit on the board, if you wished. You had turned them down, leaving that role to two of your owner-managers, lifting them into wealth beyond their wildest dreams. Like you. The light-bearer.

At the Roaring Fork AT Shelter, an open-faced little log cabin with a large wooden platform for hikers to stretch out on and sleep, and deserted there on the deep-wooded mountainside, you suggested having a quickie.

"Pinch off a piece," as you put it, nuzzling her neck and holding her by the hipbones like you liked when you were giving it to her good. "Out here in front of the good lord."

Creedence, never much of an exhibitionist. "Have you gone nuts? We've seen a dozen people out here today."

Chastened, you lost the good energy surrounding the humor and sexual overtures, all subsumed by the endeavor of the march, which she asked you to continue—"get over with" might have been the words—before her feet hurt any worse.

You noticed the root bed of an overturned tree by the trail. It looked from one angle like a bear, roaring at the heavens with power, and you thought, *That it's, that's my spirit animal, that's my Hungadunga Indian spirit guide animal—that's my destiny, if in metaphor. The fearless grizzly ruling the forest.*

But you glanced back—you should never look back; the parables are clear on this—and the root bed, which could have passed for modern art in some place like New York, or even a mere black-and-white photograph of it hung on a gallery wall, now looked like an owl: a wise, ancient and massive owl, its brow turned toward you with two deep hollows for piercing and boundless depths of eyes. An owl, the wise owl, silent and taciturn and unknowable.

Is this my spirit animal instead? He who doesn't roar, but stands in stillness? Fudge if I know.

Cal Luchok had gotten himself a trophy bride who'd made him do yoga, meditation, all this shit, he said. But he told you how deep he'd gotten only by sitting still. By not-thinking. The idea had intrigued you, except for the sitting still and not-doing part. Doing was living.

Not-doing? That's what the beggars did in places like downtown Columbia or Charleston, hanging around slacking instead of working. Those assholes epitomized the concept of not-doing. And it sucked balls. No, no hippy-dippy sitting still crap for you. Endeavor is your meditation.

ONCE THE TREES fell away you gasped at the sight of Max Patch, not only the goal and the peak but also the turnaround on the disastrous hike, all the anxiety you'd been hiding melted away, because you now knew every blessed step of the trip back. You thought you'd known what to expect from the old dude's wisdom and the online searches, but in the doing it'd been less than your expectations and not much fun, not with Creedence griping the whole time.

But once you knew what to expect, you got this AUM sound in your throat and an assurance beyond feeling, and in wondering where the idea of AUM had come, a glimmer of light flashed from a mountaintop several peaks away, and you rued leaving the binoculars in the car.

At the notion of unpreparedness, your stomach, twisting into a knot. That damned anxiety—it sneaks up on you.

At one time you took pills for the condition, way back when you first bought Maxine's and were hemorrhaging money doing the build-out. You'd tried your best to keep the decor as Maxine had it for almost thirty years. You didn't want the renamed Carolina Beanery to scare off all her old customers, but you lay awake at night worrying because not only was the work costing too much and taking too long, but it became clear never to take contractors at their word on costs and schedules. In this period you learned how to threaten and cajole and influence such business associates into being your friend. Into being honest. Into getting the fudging job done, and getting it done fast, and not coming up with all sorts of delays and expenses and surprises. Which cause anxiety.

Surprises. Did you despise anything more?

The one surprise party Creedence had thrown for you, about a year after you'd gotten married, and for your thirty-eighth birthday pissed you off so much you drank ten heavy beers and got angry at her and yelled. After you saw how hurt she seemed, you almost quit drinking that next day.

All you did was cut back, though. While watching her drink more.

⊛⊛⊛

ATOP MAX PATCH, a steep but grassy climb compared to the rest of the journey, you spun around on the dewy Alpine bald and felt a rushing sense of A-L-L. Of freedom, and infinite possibility. The most amazing vista you'd ever experienced.

While awake, that is.

Right, the dream about the mountain bald, from back on your boyhood camping trip to NC. You'd hiked with the other scouts up to a small, cleared mountain a twentieth the size of this one. You'd lain on the day-lit long grasses and perceived wholeness and satisfaction while staring up into the sky. You were ready to do it again, for hours. A sense of "forever." Whatever that meant.

"This is my dream!" you shouted there on top of Max Patch, startling your po-faced wife. Damn if you didn't want to live there. You'd be able to see what was coming. In a heavenly idyll like this, a man could think his three moves ahead at his leisure, this far remove from the frisson of modern life making extra space in the noggin for healthful cogitation.

But Creedence, she displayed a set of feet rubbed raw by the new Crocs, pieces of crap which had begun to pull apart at the synthetic-rubber rivet points. You attended to her, gazing with pity and love at her red feet. The pads on her soles, inflamed, a stained rustiness deeper than her normal peach-colored hue. You rinsed them with water from your Camelbak bottle, which she said was cold, too cold, ouch ouch ouch, cold cold cold.

You felt like a heel—get it?

But looky-here, you said, this ain't no thang. Despite the forgotten binoculars, your ass is totes-all prepared. With a flourish designed to impress and relieve, you produced a fresh pair of Crocs from your pack. Maybe also exclaimed, "Voilà!" Kinda shit you do.

"Got ya covered, babygirl."

"Oh—good. Thanks."

"We'll just chuck these old one over the side. Or, wait—we'll return them to the outlet mall. Ought to hold up better than this."

Still, far from a triumph; she only gave you that sad, pitying smile of hers:

Aw. Look, everyone—chubby little Roy Earl's trying. Bless his heart.

Also having brought your own spares, you showed them to her to demonstrate how prepared you'd been for the hike, for this possible but unwelcome eventuality, in fact, because you knew how she was about her feet, which she thought were ugly, but seemed to you as normal and ordinary—even appealing, it could be said, in a sensual sense—as girlfeet were likely to appear.

To wit, with great reverence and care you dried them off and placed the fresh Crocs thereupon, stashing her filthy, ruined pair in a large Ziplock freezer bag you'd brought for this need. This exact need.

Mud, as you'd predicted. There will be mud.

Shoe crisis averted, you sat eating almond butter, honey, and banana sandwiches, fruit, and the chocolate-chip energy bars intended as a snack for the return hike.

Creedence, relaxed at last, sat soaking in the spectacular view, a three-sixty vista of rounded blue-green mountains stretching away into forever. She squeezed your hand. "The new Crocs—they fit better."

"And going back is mostly downhill."

"So it's all fine. Right?"

"Damn straight it's fine—we can see three states from here. We're brushing up against the underfloor of heaven itself. Couldn't be finer."

But at that moment you noted a creeping wall of gray approaching over the tops of the mountains to the west, and a sudden coolness to the air. You started to shiver in your thin T-shirt and mesh workout shorts.

Prepared? A joke. You cursed as you pictured, clear as day, the rain slickers you'd taken out of your pack to make room for the spare Crocs, as well as the hoody that made the backpack too bulky as you'd stood outside the bungalow at the resort and peered up to a brilliant sky filled with only a suggestion of wispy white clouds, like the brush strokes on the smooth blue canvas of a master painter wielding a subtle brush. You'd need no hoodies or slickers today.

And thus the hike back became an ordeal at which the first half only hinted, with soaking rain and fear and Creedence in distress for 5.4 miles of dreadful, squishy AT tromping, the trek broken up only by a sojourn under the Roaring

Fork Shelter with a few amateurs and two pissed-off through-hikers, all sitting huddled on a large wooden bench meant for overnight sleeping.

As two more through-hikers had come rushing under the shed, you grabbed Creedence by the arm and pushed her outside to press on. This despite the rain not letting up—but you weren't supposed to be in the shelter.

"What's wrong with you? It's pouring."

"That shelter is for the stakeholders—the real hikers. Not a couple of flat-land, coastal elites like us."

The rain let up after a few minutes, but the hike back had gone so wrong, in fact, that on the soaking wet, grim, white-knuckle drive back down the slippery and muddy mountain road, and the interminable creep through the small mountain towns back toward Asheville, Creedence sat shivering and swearing up and down and all around that she'd never set foot in North Carolina again; seemed furious over wasting a vacation on an activity she hadn't enjoyed. *Thok thok thok thok* went the wipers. A fresh downpour, sluicing. As fatigued as you were, now your vacation seemed dangerous for real. More hazardous than flying in the Piper. That much for sure.

No way you'd say it aloud, though. Not to her. Kept your eyes on the road instead.

◉❋◉

BY THE TIME you got to the high-rise downtown hotel you'd arranged in Asheville, the sun had come back out. You both showered, one at a time, and cruised downstairs to grab an early dinner, but Creedence, insisting upon breakfast food. One of her quirks—breakfast equalled comfort food. You didn't know why, nor did she.

"You think you can talk them into it?"

Your chuckle came malevolent. "I'll do more than talk."

You went to cajole the restaurant manager into making omelets and pancakes and skillet-fried potatoes; slipped him a C-note, you did, at the sight of which he snapped to, a marionette yanked to attention by its unseen puppeteer. Told him how upset and tired your wife felt, and how you would also dine in a private space away from other guests.

After a few minutes he seated you outside on a closed patio, the last of the sun sneaking over the mountains. Soon after, a server rolled out a cart with your food.

"Anything else folks? Understand this is a special occasion."

"Thanks. It's our fiftieth wedding anniversary."

The youthful male server, tan and trim underneath his starched white shirt and black trousers, wagged a finger. "No way. More like fifteenth, is my guess."

Creedence, sighing. "I need syrup for my pancakes."

"Right away, ma'am."

He brought over a decanter of syrup from a locked cabinet against the wall where the condiments for outdoor diners lived.

As the server smiled and disappeared inside the busy restaurant, Creedence poured the syrup over a stack of the most delicious and fresh and dripping with butter pancakes you recalled seeing outside one of those Charleston B&Bs y'all used to frequent before moving down there.

But the syrup, something wrong. "It's full of little specks. Little—raisins?"

"Currant syrup, maybe? This place is top-drawer, after all."

Inspecting a forkful of pancake by drawing it close to her face, Creedence screamed—not raisins, but ants. Dead ants.

"Ants have gotten to the outdoor syrup containers!" Your voice, rattling the glass of the inside dining room, caused heads to turn. You sat shocked at your frustration and volume, but look, you work in food service. You couldn't help but experience horror. "Help!"

Ants served as the last straw for Creedence. She bolted past the server and manager off the patio and through the restaurant, but only running the best she could—her feet, killing her. Bleeding from the hike, or so she revealed once you caught up to her, weeping and distraught, in the suite. Where you were having fresh plates of breakfast sent, which she wouldn't eat. Said she wanted to sleep, hitting the bed at 7pm.

You hated wasting the earlier pancakes—but that had been the ants' fault—so you ate every blessed bite of that second stack when it arrived, gratis, with a handwritten note from the hotel manager apologizing and pledging to fire the restaurant manager and anyone else involved in this fiasco.

You decided to make a stink. Maybe even yank back the C-note out of that feckless restaurant manager's pressed trouser pocket. *I'll put ants in your syrup, buddy, for how you've given my wife PTSD. I'll sue this dump over these dead insects.*

But you didn't do that. You're a freaking grownup, and as such, knew you had to play all this bad luck as it lay before you. That's what you told yourself. Helluva a note on which to end the romantic getaway you thought would strengthen your faltering bond with the woman of your dreams, though.

THAT NEXT WEEK, back home and miserable over the getaway going so remarkably bad, you saw the failed restaurant building for lease on the outparcel, a shell sitting fallow and empty and unprofitable on a prime piece of real estate in the Midtown Harbor Plaza—the top strip on Sedge Island, the top strip in three counties—hell, the top strip between Charleston and Savannah. And over a mile from the nearest Starbucks. To the residents of the nearby condo complexes and luxury vacation homes, domiciles from which thirsty coffee lovers would love to stroll for their morning fix, that corporate mermaid might as well have been washed up on the mainland.

Without consulting Creedence—she wasn't your business partner, after all —you called the realtor. Did a walk-through. Saw what needed doing to an iteration of about ten steps ahead.

After a brief negotiation in which you made clear that you held a straight to the ace, and would walk in a skinny minute to build your own structure elsewhere on the island, you got the price you had in mind per square foot, after which you signed the lease on what would become Carolina Beanery Sedge Island. And after talking to your grandmother about her conversations with Creedence, you now realize this had been the moment, the true beginning-beginning even more than the hike or buying the plane, of the coming dissolution of your marriage.

Nobody knew, especially not you; you were playing your role. Making scratch. Making money grow like weeds. What could be wrong with that?

RUMINATING on it all made you dread the day ahead, this meeting with Trudy and the rest of the staff of The Dixiana you've called. You're early, and not one employee has shown up yet, leaving you to reminisce alone out here on a hard bench that's put a strain on your lower back. If they didn't show soon, they'd have to find you elsewhere. Like the mountains.

But do it right this time. Get in control of crap like the rain. Who did the sky think it was, fouling up your marriage by ruining that hike? Who knows—if the mountains had worked out, she might never have met Estes Patel, the little bastard.

MANNY AND BECKY L

Manny, giving the bad news—it got to be over. Listening to her go off. Crying and hollering. Stomping round. Like pointing out the truth was saying something wrong.

Like she don't know what she gonna do. Hurt herself. Hurt somebody.

Yo, now. We got to chill that shit out.

Like so often all through this thang, Manny meet her ass up at Becky L's pad, what she calls the summer house, out on Jensen Pond. Old rich white people got houses back in the woods here, but not like no subdivision—oldschool shit. Secluded, this place. She says Jensen Pond was like a few of the prominent families' lake houses, back before they filled up the valley and made Lake Hollings with the power pant and the nuke station and all that hoodoo. The Masonic lodge had had a building on the other side of the pond too, as she reminisce. But it burned when she was little, and wa'n't never built back.

Neecie tell Manny one day how her people remember them days before the big lake. How there once was a town called Bertram Crossroads where the lake is now. That her mama and her granddaddy used to go and eat chicken at some joint down there. All that shit at the bottom of two-hundred-foot of water, now. Might as well be the floor of the ocean. New Orleans on it way, that much fo-sho. Manny seen on the History channel about how they got evidence of all kinda old-ass cities under the water, different places round the old rock, like a whole worldwide civilization don't nobody ever seem to want to talk about. You even found seashells in the sandy Edgewater County dirt sometime. Shit changes over the years.

A whole mess of years, a whole lotta change possible. Who know how long this shit been going on. And by who-all, and what-all.

Or what. That's right. Manny get home late, watch that *Ancient Aliens* mess. Shit give him dreams. Mo-fos with big heads and dark almond eyes peeping at him. Wake up sweating. Ain't good to fall asleep in front of no TV. That what his granny always said.

⊛⊛⊛

Manny stand his ass on the little fishing dock back here in the Edgewater County pines near where the national forest start and think, shit, man, this here more in the boonies than Neecie family place, that sharecropper shack stuck all the way back in the woods cross the county line, a part of her childhood—one that ain't underwater now, that is.

"Manny," Becky L call out from inside. "Come back. No more yelling."

Manny don't say shit. Keep smoking, deep and thoughtful. His ass got to be firm on this breakup.

But dude? When he bring it up, she crying and screaming. Grab round Manny neck like a wrestler, a wild-ass animal, a side of her he seen a good bit lately between the sheets. She like yelling, her voice echoing across the pond, you can't do this shit to me. I'm-a falling in love with your black ass. She ain't say it that way. But ya know. Climbed up over his shoulder with one of them long stems.

Manny push her off—hard, hard enough—and say, we got a durn problem.

She quiet down. Knows what that mean.

But she ain't know how bad.

When Manny tell her—that Neecie say she know what going on—Becky L like to shit herself. Run on them long legs of her'n back across that weedy lawn and up the steps onto the screen porch and inside into the dark of the old house. Porch sagging, roof too. Manny think, she better check for termites. They be eating it from the inside, and you not know it till they start coming out the walls.

And he stay out there, smoking and watching and seeing the water sit still as glass, so peaceful. From all her hollering you would think big waves be lapping, the pond blown all round like a nor-easter rolling through. He wait that shit out, though. Manny T ain't gonna run after no crying-ass woman. They just doing that shit to manipulate your ass, yo! Women ain't do nothing but scheme and plot to get what they want. They do it cause they know they got to let the mens get away with shit. Like a little tail on the side, among other hobbies. All a play everybody acting out.

Word. Manny ain't make this shit up. Ain't invent no wheels. He go along with what is. You fault his ass for that? Go on, now.

And look at Becky L's ass—she ain't married, but she half sneaking around by fucking Manny ass? Then sitting in that room looking at Neecie T with her big old dragon-gaze and them nails like to scratch eyes out if you not careful? That some crazy-ass shit there. Women. They ain't good for much but drama, but Manny love they asses, too.

He halfway love this crazy one, who ain't really crazy. He know this shit. You can tell when they ain't right. Becky L an awesome girl. She just scared. They got their asses carried away. Flirting, getting out of hand. Scared of consequences. And shit.

Like his ass is right now. But he ain't show it. Not even alone. Not even to that still lake. She call it an oxbow lake. Said the river used to run through here, eons ago, in her word. Some of it got left behind. A blackwater oxbow lake. The girl smart, smartest one Manny ever been with. Book smart, he mean. Cultivated.

"Manny," she holler again. "Please come inside."

"Why don't you come your ass back out here. We gonna be all right."

"*Manny*."

An order.

Goddurn, he ought'n've done this shit. Manny need to get his ass out—he got to host Blues Roundup tonight. He need to remember to keep his eye on the prize, whatever it is, and quit messing with pussy and letting pussy get all up in his shit. Manny jerk off for the rest of eternity, for all he care, to keep down this drama. He working with a two-hander, but shit yeah—he been taking care of that since his ass was eleven, that freaky-deaky day over at his grandmama's place in the projects when his cousin showed him stuff cousins ain't supposed to do.

Here on Becky L's dock looking down the barrel of all this mess, it occur to Manny how his ass been sneaking round with women since minute one. From the first night he got with Neecie, twenty years on now, he went off later and pinched off a piece with another'n he was seeing. Just Manny's thang.

Manny pitch his muh-fucken Kool out into the weeds and think, Becky L got cash from inheritance. She need to pay out some of that dusty old money and get this yard cut.

He steel himself and push in through the screen door, thinking, man, this place got a nice feel, rustic—old leather couches and fish mounted up and dark wood paneling and a bunch of old hardcover books on bookshelves. Doilies and lamps and kitchen appliances out of the 60s. A little musty.

But, tell truth? Manny could sit out here in the musty quiet beside the pond all day long. Just being. Playing the horn, maybe. Running scales and lines outta Manny's copy of Slonimsky's *Thesaurus of Scales and Melodic Patterns* to keep his chops up. Or maybe messing round with the guitar—more practice always good. Manny started playing a little rhythm some nights with the combo. Just for shits'n giggles. He hear hoots and hollers out in the house when he strap on that axe. He like it.

His eyes adjust. "Where you at, sugar? We got to talk this shit out."

"Back here."

Manny go into the dim bedroom. He draw in his breath.

Becky L on that bed, nekkid, one of them creamy white legs propped up showing that trimmed bush of her'n, and she wet down there, but also on her face: tears pouring down and shit. Barely keeping it together. Trying, though.

"Manny—please."

"Aw, baby. We c'ain't do this."

"Yes, we can. Come and make love with me. In case we never get the chance again."

Manny say, yo. Some real romance novel shit here. "This shit nuclear. You and me both know it."

"If it's that apocalyptic, all the more reason, then."

No question—his ass go and do it. And damn if it ain't the best yet, which wasn't gonna make nothing any easier. Slid into it like a frog between lily pads. If they had to cash in they chips and say, fuck this, we done—and Manny ass kinda knew they muh-fucken had to do that now—grabbing a piece of ass like hers was one hell of a way to go out, so much so he doze off after they finish with her draped all over him. A pale goddess. His love-muffin.

Her people came from Louisiana, too, she tell him one time. We fit together so well, she speculate, that maybe our asses been together in a past life and shit, but course she said it more elegant than that. Manny don't know about no voodoo mess like that. No Christianity, either. It all hooey, if you ask him.

Lord, but Manny ass in trouble, he say once he wake up. Sweaty skin sticking together, they pull apart as he roll over and sit up, go and get his pants.

Manny and Becky L look across the room at each other. He say, you keep chilling. "I'm-a settle her black ass down. We all gonna be cool."

Becky, all tore up again. "Bernice knows, and that means this is goodbye. There's no other way. Back to friends. I guess."

Manny hate to hear that shit. But it what need to happen.

Boohooing anew, she go, "I just want to die."

"Yo, now. Ain't no thang. What can Manny do to fix all this?"

Sniffling. "Nothing. I'm coming to terms with it all. Et cetera." She bite her lips the way people do when they holding something back. "I'm already failing to live up to my bargain by being with you today, in fact."

"Bargain? With who? My old lady?"

She nod.

"So you knew she knew already?"

She nod again.

"And them her terms? No booty, but we can still be friends?"

Her face tell him it's true.

He pissed, now. "Y'all talked? Behind my back?"

Becky L, all she can do is caterwaul again.

Manny try to get his head round Neecie and Becky L negotiating this arrangement. "Quit boohooing long enough to bring my ass up to speed here."

It all tumble out. Neecie know the shit going on. She say, Manny no stranger to this behavior nor was she, but she—Neecie—say she not gonna countenance such disrespect no-mo.

"I couldn't disagree with her about that part. Besides, as she said," trying not to cry, "'it ain't like he love your skinny white ass, bitch.' And by the way, I wish we'd get off the whole 'black and white' thing. If we could."

Manny say, wellsir, that sound like Neecie. Manny further say, it ain't about race. Now it all just description.

"Well, I be dog," he further-further say, musing and sighing and thinking, fuck this shit. Ain't no way no woman gonna decide—check; two women—what his deal be. He don't need Neecie, and Lillyanne bout half grown now, which mean she smart enough to say, oh, that all okay, daddy. You and mommy split up, word, cause all the parents do it.

Then Manny and Neecie got the business together—it might be Manny's on the Green, but it her money, too.

Shit shit shit. Ain't none of this good or right, and furthermore if he don't get out here, Manny gonna have to tap this beautiful baby again. That dick start twitching every time he get a whiff of her, or catch a glimpse of the shape of her long body, them legs and feet under the sheet, toes peeking out. Manny get into some feet, now. Hers pretty, and perfect. Neecie feet like these big old Fred Flintstone slabs. Da-yum.

Rest of her fine, of course. His old lady still got the fire. Was only that Manny don't feel it for her ass no more. Not exactly. Or maybe he do. Twenty years a long time with somebody.

Shit don't make no sense.

Instead of fucking again, Manny get up and shower, and now he got to have Blues Roundup at the club like nothing going on.

Becky L all cool to him as they both get they shit together and get in separate cars for the drive back into town. Manny and her, this could be the last time, he reckon. Dang it.

⊙ ❀ ⊙

As Neecie greet Manny ass at the door of his joint, which as established is their joint, she all smiles, looking fine as wine. It feel good to be welcomed by his old lady.

Manny play up his penitence. He put on a hang-dog face.

She ask: "Everything all right?"

Manny think about it. "Is what aw-ight?"

"That's more like it." A glimmer of frost, all crackly like on a winter windshield. "Now get on that stage and start honking that horn of yours before I find me a new bandleader."

Manny, giving her a kiss, which she let him do—cheek, not lips. "Yes'm."

It all an act. Ain't agreeing to nothing these two cook up. Manny the one who decide who his muh-fucken dick belong inside. Manny, his own man. He gonna show them all who's the boss.

ROY E. PETTUS AND THE STAFF OF
THE DIXIANA

While waiting for Trudy and the others, you indulge in a solitary walkaround, starting outside.

If you're a stakeholder, a partner in this town now—and you are—you'll soon make your feelings about every blessed problem known to all; you've been waiting years to force these podunk boogers to slurp a salty-sweet taste of your big swinging dingus, flopping it down on conference tables all over town and telling them to get a load of their futures tattooed in hieroglyphics along the pulsating purple shaft of your vision and leadership. Rest thy weary heads upon it, you'll say. Sense the heat of its infinite insight. Grab ahold the ridges, bumps, and veins, folks, of an anatomically correct future filled with a new prosperity, an economic reification long absent the lives of these poor fools trapped in financial and cultural stagnation. Absorb the wisdom borne on the feathery fluttering wings of your extreme personal financial success, all ye who seek who seek knowledge.

You've got the touch. Yeah—you've got the power.

Downtown, stretching a few blocks in all four cardinal directions, held many empty storefronts. Once a thriving retail area, but now only musty antique stores, if housing any businesses at all. As established, a nucleus of commerce remained in orbit around the green—if one could call a barbecue juke-joint, a honkytonk, and a freaking tattoo parlor 'commerce.'

The death knell came first with the interstate highway being built ten miles away from Tillman Falls, and later the downtown bypass so folks could easier and quicker get to the commercial corridor clustered near the freeway exit rather than in the old town.

No grocer. No bank branch. The insurance agency who once rented the office space at the other end of the block from The Dixiana entrance, your friend Devin's dad Mr. Rucker, long gone; after the State Farm shingle came down, a new tenant never moved in. Like the backyard area behind the honky-tonk, a former thriving insurance agency now sat filled with old junk, the windows covered with craft paper gone sun-faded and drooping, suspended by a few desiccated squares of masking tape.

In time it would all disappear—dust to dust, whole bit. You'd sweep away the chalky remains like a planetary magnetic pole shift, one that reshapes the topography of the world through the influence of epic weather events like earthquakes, tsunami, and volcanic eruptions. You are a force of nature; your will and acumen will reinvigorate the heart of this sleepy Southern county like the traumatic, transformative birth of a new universe.

Center of it all. That's what you, the bossman, got going on. And it's what will change all their lives. If they'll let you. And from your efforts, a kind of business-development gravity well will form around which other groups of partners may coalesce and invest, "all to the profit and to the profit of all," a cheer you used to lead at gatherings and meetings of the owners to whom you had franchised a few Spotted Banana™ Fruitshake Company® stores.

You flash on an image of yourself seated under a domed ceiling of cerulean, gold and blue, enthroned as if within a glimmering faceted sapphire or diamond and wearing a hood of heavy linen draped upon your furrowed brow, a dark blade held aloft above your head encircled by shimmering rings like the crown of Saturn.

In the recent past this daily affirmation-style vision would have included Creedence as a comely Venus swathed in gossamer linens and bearing an enormous bowl of glistening fruit and leaving a cascade of fragrant, vibrant lotus flower petals in her wake, her body dappled with dew, an alabaster epidermis whose freckles bespoke not of dermatological aberration, but rather erotic perfection. Now, of course, the vision required editing and reduction down to one you could maintain with enough will and sincerity to manifest in reality. And it didn't include your wife anymore. Only you. The you who stands here thinking all this up.

Leadership. They all needed your shimmering diamond, your blade stained dark. You'd give it to them.

In spades.

Once you set these wastrels straight about The Dixiana's fate, you'd go around to what appeared to be the other viable businesses—the barbecue restaurant, the tattoo and salon empire, Gooch Wimmel at the paper, Becky L at the Fine Arts Center, Jasper Glasscock, not as a musician but the last practicing lawyer in Tillman Falls proper, it seemed. Press the flesh. Let them know help had arrived.

Ambling around onto Common Street, you run your hand across the rough surface of the curved brick wall around to where the mural starts, the blessed General Reb mural you despise—it looks awful, faded and peeling and so last century the sight of the artwork makes you ill.

"Gather ye rosebuds, General. Know what I'm sayin'?"

The rooster, implacable, marches on.

For now.

Color it gone.

You peer over the back gate, see your granddaddy's old truck, which is where you will always park once they clean this mess out. You're an owner. The spaces out front are for customers.

The back area, stacked with junked kitchen equipment and other crap, like ancient appliances Uncle Burnie used to sell in his store down the street. Barrels. Tires. Crates. The grease-trap, grungy and brown with old fried chicken and still in use—if they bothered to change out the grease, that is. Weedy and overgrown, this space was once manicured and green, where your granddaddy held outdoor hootenannies, which happened before your time— to you, the back lawn, always a forgotten area, but never full of rusting, cast-off garbage like this. Once the hoots ended, the loading dock—the hundred-plus year-old building had once been the town dry goods and grocer—hadn't been used for much of anything in the 70s and 80s except as the employee lounge, a place for folks to do drugs, at least when Rabbit wasn't around.

You mosey back down the sidewalk and into The Dixiana, pardner. Inside, the odor of the cigarette smoke lingering in every nook and cranny further turns your stomach. The smoking ordinances in these small Carolina towns are still catching up, and in honkytonks like this one—the one you now own—a body could still light up. Mindblowing.

But wait—not residue. Fresh smoke.

Fury.

The music coming from the jukebox only adds to your distress: a piece of classic country called 'Waltz Across Texas' that you remember well. Good old Ernest Tubb. The jukebox, a Wurlitzer, a real jewel of a machine always stocked with the giants of country, at least back in your day. Songs like Hank Snow and Anita Carter, 'Bluebird Island'; Patsy Cline, 'Seven Lonely Days'; Tom T Hall, 'Old Dogs, Children and Watermelon Wine.' Grudgingly, you acknowledge your warm memories of those tunes.

Gag.

You can't get past it—a jukebox? How inefficient. How not-charming. How anti-charming, its cumbersome antiquity an embarrassment rather than an asset. Didn't she say they were paying for sat radio?

Gone.

A cold gully-washer of bracing acknowledgement sluices into your gut, filled as you already are with the gas and juices from all the down-home cooking you've been shoveling into your body. Stress eating. Would have to stop. You were about to be on the market again, romantically speaking. Now not the time to pork out again.

Ownership. New rules. Bringing it all up to speed.

You got this.

Trudy, dabbing at her eyes, comes out of the women's restroom. At the sight of you the grief on her face softens, and she gives you the most loving, sad smile.

Trudy's cancer stick smoldering in an ashtray on the bar, however, is like a stab wound to your gut, to your eyes, your respiratory system. Your lips pursed in distaste, you lock eyes with her and stub out the cigarette.

"Beau, I was smoking that. I mean, really digging on it, too."

Nonchalant, you shrug—you made your point. "I didn't realize."

Trudy, the defiant C-word, relights the damn thing. "They don't never taste right when you fire them back up after being stubbed out, though."

"I wouldn't know. Empires would rise and fall in the time I wouldn't have smoke passing my lips and going into my body. If I had any say about it."

"Hoo boy." Ambles behind her bar. Rolling the eyes. "You for real, son?"

You decide to show her by fishing around the back of the Wurlitzer and yanking out the plug. At the end of the couplet *My heartaches and troubles are just up and gone/the moment you come in view* Ernest Tubb and the Texas Troubadours go SCREECH, and all falls silent.

Trudy cusses up a storm. "You'll scratch the record doing that—!"

"One question: how much does it cost to keep this running? Replace records?"

"Like the one you just ruin't?"

"Hit me. Bottom line."

"It ain't cheap."

You give the machine the once-over. Fifty years old—more. No, no, about fifty. Red. Chrome. Like a muscle car of a jukebox. You recall how Rabbit would tell people he'd had a Seeburg back in the 50s when he first opened but upgraded in '63 to the red Wurlitzer, as he'd always say. You'll let her discover soon enough about the Wurlitzer appearing on eBay, an action-item for the master list.

But hey, you're not a monster; you'll send her a link. Give her a chance to bid, if the machine means that much.

You trace your finger along the triangular shaped plastic punch buttons. You note that the song inserts, the A and the B sides of the wheel of 45s inside, looked sharp and pristine, while you'd remembered them as faded and curled.

"Seems awfully fresh, like it's had a recent rehab. That invoice must've landed with a thud."

"Button made those inserts on her computer." Trudy comes over and stands beside you, your elbows brushing. "She made them look good as new."

"Superfluous, but a nice gesture."

"Superb flu—what?"

Subject change: "Button? Ain't seen that girl since she was a fat little Vietnamese chunk."

Trudy scoffs. "Like you wasn't."

"Vietnamese?"

"A chunk, dumb-dumb."

"Hah—not when you knew me."

"Naw, now. I remember the first time I ever seen you."

"Do tell."

"I'd gone outside after Rabbit interviewed me for the server job, and Miss Runelle was dropping you off after school—but you run across the green to the movie theatre instead of coming in here, though."

"Sounds right. I would've wanted to duck Pa-paw to keep from being told to swab the deck."

Wistfulness, like a cool breeze, seeps into her tone. "Seems like the next time I seen ya, you'd grown up a whole foot. And had lost that baby fat. Got so handsome."

Her chin quivers; you see the tears waiting to spill out. Rabbit's death, traumatic for Trudy. He'd always been so paternal to her. Maybe that'd been why she chose to break your heart—it felt like incest to boink you, with your cute sixteen-year-old boy self. Greek tragedy stuff brewing.

Maybe you'll go easy on her.

Or: maybe not.

A gentle, pleading whisper. "Sugar: I know you're hurting like the dickens. I am, too. But I wish you'd stop doing things like yanking the plug out the Wurlitzer and stubbing out my cig. Instead try to—to—"

"Two words: cool as this shiny hunk of metal seems, play your commercially licensed satellite freaking radio and forget the Wurlitzer. Satellite's cluttered with a dozen channels of this country crap. Enough to choke a hippopotamus."

"Well-now." A hand propped upon a jutting hipbone, she stubs out the remains of her stinking-ass Virginia Slim. "I'd like someone to explain how all that adds up to two words."

"Satellite radio. I mean."

"That's still four words."

"Hardy har." You adopt a mocking drawl that's close to how you spoke when you were a kid, later transmogrified more into flat, all-American homogeneity, like on a sitcom or the news. "But y'all, that old satellite radio's got it divided up into what the per-fessors over yonder in Columbia call sub-genres:

shit country, crap country, worthless country, cunt country," drawing that one out, leaning into it with a self aware wink toward an audience of one, "and dang if I don't think—wait, no, I'm right sure—both Willie Nelson and Garth effin' Brooks has both got their own dang channels. Like, twenty-four-seven, beau. Now look here, you c'ain't tell me. That ain't better. Than this old hunk of doo-doo." Giggling, guffawing, wiping away tears. "Mercy. But you get my drift."

Ashen, she's left mute by your speech. "—"

The afterglow of your laughter; the thrumming of the blade along your thigh. "So, day one, which is today, means you can color the jukebox gone. As well as lots of the other old ways." Grim. "Maybe all of them. Including that hex-thing above the stage," the painted mandala your grandfather had always insisted was important, for whatever vague reason—little horned, cartoon gargoyles arrayed around a doubled, encircled star. Your granddaddy always told you the hexes on the original Pettus house and the honkytonk were old country superstition from his own grandmother's time, and long before. That one day he'd explain it better, if he thought you'd understand. You'd never followed up. Just more corn-pone backwoods crud, like the music they force listeners to endure in this dusty dump.

"Day one."

"You heard me."

You stand duck-footed before the shrine to Hawg Hickens, an oil painting of the homegrown rockabilly one-hit wonder—'The Dixiana's Own,' as the now-tarnished plaque reads on the bottom of the frame. Garlands of plastic roses adorn the portrait, lit by an incandescent accent bulb in need of changing into an energy-efficient LED. Two framed record company promo shots sat to either side of the painting, one featuring Hawg's original backing band The Two-Tone Weejuns with everyone wearing early 1960s suits and ties, and the 70s version, his full-bore outlaw country persona with big beard, cowboy hat and biker vest.

All the portraiture, the walls lousy with it—everyone from country stars to movie actors to pro wrestlers like Wahoo McDaniel, Haystack Calhoun, Killer Kowalski and Gorgeous George—would soon find themselves in residence at the county dump.

"Probably ought to freshen up the decor around here as well. Get some new artwork." You launch into a practiced fit of mimicry of Buggin' Out from Spike Lee's seminal civil rights treatise *Do the Right Thing*: "Yo, Sal, when ya gonna put some pictures of the brothers on the walls all up in here, yo?"

Trudy stiffens, her face a mask of uncertainty, even fear. She grabs a rag, wiping the bar with furious abandon.

Ah—pleasure floods into your receptors. You have her now. She sees where this is going. Knows she needs to please the bossman, no matter how maniacal his nefarious plans. Heh heh heh.

"Soon as Fridge gets here, we do the full walkthrough. Until then I'll be outside. So I can breathe."

"Awesome, Roy Earl—Roy, I mean." Without making eye contact. "You do that. Wait outside my bar."

Her bar? You'll shut this mausoleum down first. Over your dead body. And so on. Cheery at the thought. "Will do—boss."

❂❂❂

COLD AND OFFICIOUS, you begin the walkthrough with Trudy and Fridge, at least once he rolls his fat ass through the door and comes over and gives you a big sweaty hug. Says how sorry he is.

In response, you manage a veneer best described as taciturn. "Appreciate it, beau. Now—let's get to work."

Trudy, defiant. "I dunno what we're doing."

"I told you once—this is the new owner's walkthrough."

"For what?"

"For you to give me the lay of the land. That's what."

Huffy, Trudy takes you around a space already familiar, but seen now through new eyes—owner's eyes. The filth you perceive on every surface and in every nook drives you mad; mad with the desire to clean.

No—not to clean.

To gut, like those river bream your Pa-paw used to make you clean.

To demolish.

And then? To dream anew.

You had the vision with your own eyes at a coffee shop you visited in Asheville on that hiking trip—third-wave coffee, the guy called it. Artisanal, slow food, that wheelhouse: each cup custom crafted by baristas swirling silver pots of steaming water over the grounds, drop by drop into a glass decanter looking like a beaker out of a science lab, their repetitive motion of their wrists graceful and deliberate. You sipped. You swooned. The coffee made your Carolina Beanery machine brew seem like over-roasted Starbucks swill.

You announced: "Dad-gummit."

"What's wrong, sir?"

"This here's the best darned coffee I ever had. That's what's wrong."

"Yep. That's black gold right there, our house blend," the barista said through his wispy, enormous beard. He fidgeted with his man-bun. "Next time try the Kenya," at an additional dollar. Brilliant and chill, this up-sell.

You brought the idea home, but not to the original Carolina Beanery™ in Columbia. That biz you long ago sold to a manager, while of course retaining ownership of the Carolina Beanery™ name and trademark. Rather, you introduced this slow-drip method at what you considered the new flagship store down on the island. The first of many.

Now? You will bring the concept to Edgewater County. Your investment in Carolina Beanery #2 will save the town.

BOOM.

It's as though you see a grid overlay, like the interior of The Dixiana has become the holodeck on the Enterprise-D from *Star Trek: The Next Generation*: you envision the gutting of the room. The tearing out of the L-shaped bar, the dismantling of the stage and the soundboard area and the floors. The floors—they would go. You will replace them with super strong faux-wood high density laminate that a team of three or four Mexican guys would put down in a day—the whole place. These floors would outlast the bricks in the walls. One thing you know is floors; how to put one in that's appropriate to the purpose. That will hold up.

None of this dump feels up to code. Maybe it is in a halfway legal sense? But not up to your code.

You go behind the bar. Trudy stiffens—this is her territory more than any other piece of ground in all of Edgewater County. You sense this more than know it. The grooves in the floor are from her boot heels.

Hell, you don't know Trudy Pirkle at all. You fucked her, once—several joyful times, actually—but as a human, she's more symbol than person. Your grandfather's go-to, right-hand gal.

And yours, now. If you're to keep the honkytonk as-is.

Which you ain't gonna do.

So—would Trudy manage your third-wave coffee shop? Would she, on the leeward side of fifty, stand polishing the imported Italian marble of your new countertops, which in your mind you're already measuring and preparing to order?

Trudy? Really?

No, afraid not—as difficult as this conversation was proving, you try not to imagine that one. That's a chore you wish to delay, and you are not a businessperson who puts off duties.

You pull out your penlight, a combo ballpoint, light and iPad stylus that is your go-to, right-hand gal—well, along with the iPad itself, which you've left in the car.

"Hold on. I need to take notes."

"There's scratch paper under the register."

You sneer at the suggestion. "Be right back."

You return with your iPad. Using the stylus tip of your pen—your magic wand—you make handwritten digital notes. This act resonates with happy college dorm room memories of watching first-run episodes of *Next Generation*.

You recall Dr. Crusher, tall Beverly Crusher with that red hair of hers, that angular dignified face, scribbling on the screen of her tablet computer. Fiction, become reality. In your hands.

A gorgeous face, that actress, Gates McFadden. Like Creedence.

Creedence, moaning and sweating with an assistant GM's dick inside her. Probably right now.

"Oh." You fall against the bar, clutching your side, and drop the iPad with a clunk. "Fudge factory."

Trudy's eyes have gone wide. "Sugar?"

"Don't tell me you having an M-I too, Roy Earl." Fridge says this biting into a Granny Smith apple he sauntered into the kitchen and procured for himself without noting the comp anywhere. "Mister Rabbit ain't even in the ground yet."

"He's not gonna be in the ground, you idiot." To you Trudy says, "You all right, honey?"

You assure her you're fine. "But this business is not. And I haven't even toured the kitchen yet."

"What's wrong?"

"We have issues. Serious issues."

Trudy, arms folded tight. "Such as?"

You try to hold back a hot jet of vitriol that threatens to vent like volcanic out-gassing. You walk around pointing with your combination pen and stylus and penlight to peer into crevices and flush out deficiencies.

Deficiencies in the details.

Corrections to be made.

Your gums flap: "The condition of what ought to be a duly regulated hospitality establishment, but clearly not recently inspected, is unacceptable." Rubbing it in. "When I used to keep this place clean, I kept it em-effing clean."

"You don't sound like the same person anymore."

"Oh? And what do I sound like?

"You sound like a robot."

"More like a member of the merchant class. That would be more accurate." You fix her with what you hope is a mechanical stare. "No—scratch that. How about simply a human being who holds himself, and those in his sphere, to certain modest standards of competence."

Fridge snorts and laughs. "Dang."

"You're next, friend-o. Let's go."

Fridge's smile fades. "You serious. Ain't you."

"As a heart attack." You regret this choice of words. "Serious as can be. C'mon."

Fridge trudges on through the swinging doors into the kitchen. You turn to Trudy. "Now, while he's in there, let's talk menu. Are you telling me that this is the same fucking burger or chicken basket deal? After all this time? Where's the vegetarian—rather, plant-based option?"

She's flustered and simmering, which makes you pleased and warm inside. "We sell good, Roy Earl. People, they come here just to eat. Don't much care about the music no more. But people love our burgers, still. Hell, and where else can you get broasted chicken? Not around here."

Bad taste: "What do you call it? The heart-attack special?"

Ignoring you. "Shit, beau—Dubya ate one. The President," Trudy whispers. "I shook his hand. And Roy Earl, do you know it had grease on it from the chicken basket that Fridge fixed him?"

"Tremendous. I hope you haven't washed that hand."

"Seriously. Our president, then anyway, set his butt right yonder! With his elbows on the bar! He called me sugar. He called me honey." Fury, bubbling over: *"There ain't nothing wrong with our chicken baskets—!"*

"Stop it." At the mention of George W. Bush your stomach becomes queasy. "Hate does not begin to describe how I feel about that feckless, retarded upper-class twit. Look at that misshapen head and those pig-eyes of his, set so close together. Fetal alcohol syndrome—the first fetal alcohol syndrome president. Now that, and," squinting up at the chalk menu board behind the bar, "eight bucks will get you a basket of broasted yard-bird at the ever-lovin' Dixiana."

"Hush your mouth."

Pushing her. "Now that, my friends, would be mission accomplished—wait. More like 'missing a conscience.' That's what I think of your phony, lying, fake-hero president who took the world to the brink. Who let those fudging terrorists fly planes into our towers. I wish he'd choked to death while he was eating my Pa-paw's chicken."

Her cheeks blaze. "You ain't supposed to talk about no president like that, even an ex-president—and you ain't supposed to hate nobody. Even if you're on the other side from them."

You grunt and snort. "Have you ever looked into 9/11?"

"What about it."

"The implications—they're monstrous."

"Oh, p'shaw."

It catches your eye on the wall, now, the largest of all the commemorative photos—Rabbit and Trudy and Dubya and worst of all, *Karl fudging Rove*. The two chubby miscreants sport those trademark leering frat-boy grins, as though they'd just chug-chug-chugged and exploded firecrackers inside a couple of frogs. You hold up your hand to block out the sight of the men, treasonous war criminals and possibly illicit, hypocritically bisexual lovers to boot.

A flash of you and Creedence watching the inauguration online, and crying as Obama'd been sworn in. A real president for the new century.

That little Muslim commie.

But sure—the sitting President, feckless or not, had broken bread here. You certainly remember the peppery flavor of your grandfather's special broasted chicken. Eating it so much you wanted to die.

You decide to ignore Trudy's obvious pride in what seemed from her emotive expression to have been the highlight of her life here in Edgewater County, meeting that bonehead. The notion makes you shake-your-head.

"One question—what year is it?"

"Do what?"

"Where are the veggie options? Not everybody eats meat anymore. You're alienating a huge potential market share."

She looks at you like you've suggested the moon landings had been faked. "Like what—collard greens? Green beans? Butter beans? You mean sides?" She's disgusted and sarcastic. "We talked about that one time. About freshening things up. Rabbit said you shouldn't never set to fixing what ain't broken. Roy Earl—he always said there wasn't nothing broken about us here at The Dixiana."

"That dried-up fart didn't know shit from shoe polish, the lazy old linthead. And, look—nobody calls me 'Roy Earl.' I'm just Roy, now. Or Mr. Pettus. Or bossman." You allow a little haughty scorn to creep in. "But you, Trudy? You get to pick which one of those three options you want to use in addressing me. I consider you a friend, you see. Nobody else gets the options. But you do."

"Oh-kay. Thanks. I guess."

"Choose—you must choose. Right now." You wrinkle your nose. "Let me hear it."

"Let you. Hear it."

"Sure—so I know where we stand."

Now she's close to tears, blinking as though slapped. When it finally comes, it does so in a voice so small it doesn't seem possible to have come from the brassy, bony redneck woman who'd bedded you so early and so well and good only to cut out your heart and leave it to leak viscous, unrequited love-juice onto this cursed bar. "Roy."

A sneer. "Excuse me?"

"Roy."

"Now that's too loud. I'm right here. You don't have to peel my paint. Which you're doing anyway with that sour nicotine breath."

In the kitchen, Trudy and Fridge stand mute on either side of the prep table as you explain the 'veggie option' idea, all while feeling an urgent low-simmer inside that could at any moment erupt through the crust of your mantle. "At the risk of over-explaining the obvious, I'm talking a proper vegetarian option, as though we woke up this morning and found ourselves in the actual freaking twenty-first century. A black bean burger. Hell, offer tofu-pups alongside those nasty fucking red meatsticks."

And they were disgusting, those hot dogs—disgusting, strange narrow tubes with a tough outer skin called snap-case franks. *Blech.* God knew what was in any wiener, but these seemed particularly savory and mysterious, and after you had a normal hot dog one afternoon over at the Congress Street Grille, you were forever after suspicious of your granddaddy's version. "You've gotta serve a wide variety of palettes these days, dearie. If you want to succeed."

"I thought we were succeeding. And we go to a lot of trouble to get them Sabrett weenies, still. They're a lot more expensive than they used to be."

"Granted, you don't keep a place going long as Pa-paw did without succeeding. I suppose. But it's all in how you define success. And he and I have very different ideas about what that means."

"Ain't always about money."

A veiled insult she doesn't believe in the first place, and that gets a snort out of you. "To've been still hanging around this mausoleum at his age, when he ought to be enjoying the autumn of life, smacks of travesty rather than success. If you ask me."

"He liked working. And he loved this old place." Fridge, quiet and chastened. "That what he always say when I ask him why he don't retire."

"You know what he told me? Huh?" Trudy says this in a confrontational, taunting schoolyard manner—she's had enough of you already. "That if he had somebody to leave it to—yeah—then he could retire."

You allow this remark to settle. Fridge's eyes have grown wide and fearful. He shuffles his enormous feet—you look at both their feet and think, why aren't they wearing Crocs, the shoe that's tailor made for the damp floors involved in food prep and other aspects of the hospitality trade? "Wait—what? Leave this dump to me?"

Trudy holds out her hands. "You little shit-ass. Who else?"

Pondering. As your grandmother had suggested, sure, but no more viable or real coming out of Trudy's mouth. "My dear, I wouldn't have it if you paid me. Or gave it to me as a gift."

Trudy, hushed with shock. "You profane your granddaddy's honkytonk."

"Now!" Your gunshot-sharp handclap, startling them both. You decide to explain yourself using a pop culture metaphor these fellow TV generation folk will perceive, process, and appreciate: "We are the Kirk, Spock and McCoy of this operation, and we've got to function together. So: let's get ourselves into sickbay, Bones, and see what how it stacks up against the science officer's substandard, demerit-worthy station, which is a blight on the whole command crew. Visiting commodore from Starbase Sedge Island included. And that's not gonna fly here on this heavy cruiser class rust bucket, the blessed war-torn old USS Dixiana."

Fridge laughs his easy old black man's laugh, which you note he's had ever since you were both kids. "Man—I dunno what all you talking about."

"I'm talking about the fact that this starship is chugging along in a dangerously low orbit." A lesson. "Y'all know how in *Star Wars* all the ships and space stations and planets were all used and dirty and worn looking, besides the Death Star, of course, which was new construction? In *Star Trek*, which is more our milieu, everything's all, oh, shoot, what's the word," snapping your fingers and squinting and marching around in a tight little circle, once, twice, thrice. "Utilitarian. Clean. Military-grade discipline and fitness.

"But look, I'm not just getting this from some TV show, folks. I got a friend back on the island—Sedge Island, where we've got a million-dollar house on the marsh that's all bad-ass and shit, and from where I just flew in my Piper Meridian—who's called The Colonel, and who had his ass in the Hanoi Hilton, that pit of hell, for six god-durn years. But he survived, and came home. He lived. And how? Discipline. Because you've got to have discipline to live. To live through the challenges and still do your best.

"That's it: not just living through, but excelling at the living. Thriving. Mustering the will to excel. That's his point, talking about having the discipline and will to persevere when you've been locked up for six years eating monkeyhead soup, tortured and hated because you were swooping around dropping fire out of the sky on the cowardly little commie fuckers, and now they have you. They have you, in their little POW camp. Can do anything to you. And would, absent the Geneva Convention. Now, to stay sane in a situation like that takes discipline. All you people have to do is manage and keep running and clean and ship-shape a tavern with a working kitchen, and from what I can tell neither of which are terribly sophisticated nor busy on a given day or night. That's all. That's all you got to do to attain discipline on this here starship—or maybe it's a concentration camp, depending on what your attitude's like when you come to work. Of course, it ain't a starship, or a death camp, it's just a lousy old honkytonk that somebody probably ought to reconsider his reluctant ownership of which. Now—if you please."

Dazed, confused, perplexed by and suspicious of you, your inept crew shuffles through the kitchen inspection, not as bad as you expected. Fridge, a lumbering, farting, middle-aged black man with wispy gray hair at his temples, has always been a pro. And you admit that his burgers have always had a good rep, going head to head with the Congress Street Grille's famous cheeseburgers found only two blocks away, behind the courthouse complex.

But there won't be any burgers at the third-wave coffee shop, no; as at your flagship store, the revised menu will feature gourmet sandwiches like the eggplant caprese with marinated olives on the side instead of potato salad;

house-baked deserts and breakfast breads and pastries. No broasted anything. You can already imagine kitchen equipment like the broaster being carried away on the back of a restaurant supply salvage operation truck.

Oh, ho, ho—you get a squirt of joy-juice in that good old boy gut. You have a control grid in place already. It's in your mind, yeah, but you're gonna make it real for them. You've got the holodeck switched on and humming and at the ready. Mercy, as folks like to say here in the EC. They don't have the first clue what's coming.

⊚⊛⊚

You gesture to your charges, who stand shuffling and anxious and unsure of what's coming.

"That a mighty suspicious smile playing round your lips, Mr. Roy Earl."

You're troubled—in your mind, you and Fridge have always been more like peers. This presents the first problem to the implementation of Third Wave Coffee Shop Expansion Project #1 a/k/a Carolina Beanery Tillman Falls, as you're mulling what you have in mind for this decrepit dump of an albatross hanging weighted around your magnificent and monied neck—these are people you know in various degrees of intimacy who now expect you to see to their gainful and ongoing employment.

Well—not Trudy. Not if she's smart. Poor dear's out of luck, but at least one bloodletting—a major one—to put the fear into the rest is a necessary evil.

And what kind of fear? The fear of failure, yes, but only in service to what's at meta-stake: *disappointing you*. That to *disappoint you* entails consequences. Consequences and repercussions. To set matters in motion—to impose the grid —you must first *establish this fear*.

This wasn't control or abuse, though—it's leadership, sayeth you.

"Let's go out back, if you please."

Trudy, a nervous dance from foot to foot. "What for?"

A stabbing, stiff arm directs them. "If you please."

"Damn," Fridge says. "His ass mad."

"NO," a vicious, cutting violence of sudden volume. "I'm not having an emotional reaction at all. And Fridge? Don't call me 'Mr. Roy Earl.' I am not Rabbit Pettus. I am nobody's mister. "

"Word." Fridge looks uncertain. "All right, Roy."

"There we go." You relax, give them a smile. You let out the rope, let their feet touch the grungy tile floor in the kitchen, which if you could you would rip out with your bare fingernails right now. "It's all good, y'all."

Flinging open the rusty screen door—and why the fudge hasn't this been replaced, the cost in time, labor and money negligible in comparison to the sanitary benefits of having a clean door for the egress of workers and delivery drivers—and drawing in a godlike, yogic breath, you rant without strong emotion about the junkyard in the back. You once wondered why Pa-paw had built the high wooden fence along Common Street, and now you know—to hide the what had piled up here, a place where folks once heard picking, seen grinning, and ate your grandfather's barbecue straight out of suckling pigs slow-smoked over hickory all day.

Through sense-memories of fragrant pulled pork so tender it melted in your mouth, you stammer, "How. Have. You people. Allowed this travesty. Back here. To happen."

Trudy, spitting mad. "You got any idea-r how many times I asked him if we couldn't clean out this mess? If it was once, it was a hundred. Nope. Wouldn't budge."

Your blue flame blooms in intensity; the pot on your stove is now roiling and boiling. Only on the inside.

Emotionless, you discover you've been gripping your right side as though having cracked a rib—to anyone who's worked for you it's an oh-shit sign, the rib clutch, like a live grenade tossed into the staff meeting. Until you took the anger management classes.

Your words, a breathless whistle. "How. Has the health. Department. Allowed this. To continue."

"Mister—I mean, Roy—you sound like a clock about to wind down."

You ignore the Fridge, sweep your gaze across the junk and pallets and weeds sticking up and the horrible ancient freezer replaced but not hauled off (excuse me?) any more than the old Ford pickup you used to drive, tables and chairs in various states of disrepair—beyond repair? then why keep them? out here?—and a general accumulation of detritus from the outside world that's made its way into what Rabbit used to call the back lawn, open to customers in the honkytonk's glory days and also where they used to roast the pigs for the famous barbecue they no longer serve.

The Ford junker pickup you drove throughout high school, its broken grill and fogged headlights like a sagging face that mocks your every move. You'd say it had been humiliating to drive a two-tone old man's truck, but half the student body had similar vehicles. Damn POS not reliable, not worth a toot, and now dead. Mocking you in its ultimate decrepitude.

Why didn't rednecks throw anything away? Southerners, suffering a senseless penchant for clutching onto past glories. It curdled your almond milk.

Overjoyed, however, to get out of the Ford for the brief time you drove a used Datsun that Uncle Burnie sold you, a red 1977 200sx, compact and full of zip and pep and with a cassette player, a crucial piece of gear, and only 95,000 miles and ten years of road-service on it. You all but cried as you counted out money you'd earned working at the Palmetto Grande for Mr. Sortwell.

Uncle Burnie had slid one of the hundreds back over to you. "You gave me one too many, son."

You protested—you'd counted it a dozen times. Most dough you'd ever seen.

He waved you off. "Take it. Ya never know what a used vehicle's gonna need done."

He'd been right. In less than a week you needed to get the alternator replaced, which with labor cost you ninety bucks. At the time you'd thought how lovely it had all worked out, but you never understood how Uncle Burnie knew a part was going bad. You suppose he knew enough about used cars to figure they could fall apart on you pretty quick, and this one would—many other repairs would ensue while you drove the vehicle. You loved it, but it soon died in a big way, the repair costing more than it was worth. Back to the Ford pickup, and right as you went off to college in Columbia, a final humiliation before escaping Edgewater County.

"Call them," you choke. Thick air in of your lungs like pudding instead of the Carolina autumn breeze tickling Trudy's bleach-blonde hair that, damn it all, looks sexy. "Call in the rest of the staff. If you please."

"If you say 'if you please' one more time, I swear I'm gonna have a conniption."

Black steel: "Call them—call them all." You check your phone. "Tell them we have a staff meeting—a mandatory one—at 3pm sharp. Not a second later. And I mean beginning with introductions and first order of business by 3pm and thirty-seconds. Not still settling down, shuffling around and chatting. Three o'clock EDT."

"I get it. We ain't a bunch of rugrats in school, son."

You let the impertinence slide, a choice based on intuition and the milk of human kindness that flows through your veins. "Any stragglers will be 86'd— in other words, shitcanned—on the spot. No exceptions. Not even you," you say to Trudy, and your glare is hard, your tone unforgiving and frozen like black ice. "Not even me."

"Why don't you kiss my lily white ass," she says, stomping inside. "'Not even me.' For god sakes. You are off your meds or some shit, beau."

Insubordination. Now you had her dead to rights.

Fired.

Sweet revenge. Under your breath: "Just be glad you've already been counted present, schoolgirl. All I can tell you."

Now you can bet your own chubby, pimpled pink booty she's gonna call everyone in, because you have shown her you-are-the-man. What she doesn't realize? After this weekend The Dixiana will close its effing nasty-ass, useless, outdated, stodgy, smoky, stale rotten doors. Forever.

But that eventuality ain't part of this meeting; they need not know. Not yet. Not until they've been made to clean.

THE ASSEMBLED FACES BEFORE YOU, pensive and innocent, have no idea what hell awaits them—the Black Blade. A slashing, razor-sharp symbol of your anger, a weapon you wield with impunity and without warning, the Blade is merciless, forever honed and at the ready and hungry for souls like the murderous evil servant-ruler sword of Elric of Melnibone, the conflicted fantasy anti-hero of a series of novels you read all in a row one dull summer thirty-five years ago. The good Elric, possessed by the evil sword, whose power only grows with every beheading. The Black Blade. After this meeting you'll be sure to blow off steam by cranking up the bombastic BÖC tune of the same name which happened to have a shared writing credit with Michael Moorcock, author of the Elric series. Cooler than cool, or else, epically nerdy; geek stuff that's stuck with you all these years.

Creedence had always just called you an asshole. She needed no further symbolization of how you treated her in your worst instances of rage, much of which you attributed to stress over money issues—loans, taxes, payrolls, maintenance, CAM fees, legal fees, licenses, insurances, graft, shrinkage. You've rolled the dice several times to get where you are. At one point you owed money "all over town," as folksy Uncle Burnie had cautioned you never to do. But the gamble had paid off. Only after nut-busting hard work, at least until the sell-out and cruising on auto-pilot ever since. In the old days you thought being in crazy debt gave you the right to show anger, and maybe such a burden did. All in the manifesting—abusing employees? Sure. But it's never all right taking it out on non-paid actors. Especially loved ones.

But sometimes not even employees: Once, after an appearance by the dreaded Blade over a weak health inspection report, one Spotted Banana™ manager, of Savannah #2, suggested with gentle, loving patience—another granola girl—that you try an anger management webinar she knew about. In doing so you learned much about yourself. About how it's better to keep the Blade sheathed. Keep the heads attached to the bodies.

All of this dwells in the back of your mind, however. Not the front. Thinking of these people assembling before you neither as employees nor loved ones. You can't.

You're overcome by the evil power offered by the Blade.

But heck, it's so much better than what you've been feeling—grief, despair, loss. So you allow the energy to flow. Quivering and thirsting for blood, hungering to kill. Killing, the Blade's food. Its manna, its fuel. Its raison d'être.

You know not for what it hungers, truly. Catharsis? One soaked in worthless Scots-Irish Edgewater County redneck blood? Yea, the blade, its thirst would be slaked upon this witless assemblage. Ye shall know.

Deep breath.

Not counting Trudy, a staff of a dozen—too many, far too many for the amount of business they seemed to do, driven by lunchtime hamburgers and chicken more than the nighttime honkytonkin'. You wonder if Uncle Burnie didn't drink up most of the profits—from what Trudy says, he sits in the bar every day from eleven until five. Your Pa-paw, letting his drunk friend finish himself off. Another issue falling under the aegis of what you're about to impose on them all: the control grid. A rubric of order. You will handle Uncle Burnie. In fact, you ought to be with him right now, as it comes to you. But you're hiding from him. Hiding from the grief. Another action-item.

"All right, all right." Everyone gets inside and stands around shuffling their feet, many wishing first to express condolences, which you accept but not without a fair amount of cursory and rushed gratitude. Also, you receive much mild consternation over the private nature of the memorial at the bluff, word of which seems to have gotten around already—the lack of security on this issue grates and unnerves you.

As a final prelude to your big speechmaking moment, you ask everyone, to the best of their gossipy small town abilities, to dispel the notion of persons aside from immediate family being welcome at the red clay fishing spot your Pa-paw so loved.

Now: "Much official business to discuss. And none of it good, I'm afraid."

Unease sweeps through the already grief-burdened room. Several dab at eyes.

"Button's not here," Trudy says. "Neither is Newbie Harrell."

"Button Sykes? Uncle Burnie's granddaughter?"

"She texted me to say she was on the way, but her mama was having one of her spells."

"And who the eff is Newbie Harrell?"

"He's maintenance—your old job," Trudy notes with acid. "Remember?"

You roll your eyes, an involuntary reaction you've tried to control, one Creedence claims, specious, you aim at everything she does or says.

Creedence. Probably right now conjoined with her lover, enjoying a vigorous sesh.

Stop it. Stop stop stop.

"And what the hell does Button Sykes do?"

"She runs front of house."

You don't know the term. "Explain."

"She run the soundboard." Fridge, pointing to the soundboard on the little platform tucked against the wall where folks step down to the floor area in front of the stage. "She make shit sound good in here."

You go *ah*, remembering the term from working on the St. Patrick's Day festival back in your civic leadership days in Columbia. The music, the PA, the sound guy, yadda yadda. You got it—somebody plugged in a couple of speakers and flipped a switch or three.

But wait—your grandfather, who used to do all that himself, really needed a full-time staff member for that now? A mental note: ask someone to give poor Button Sykes a ride to the employment office.

"Front of house." Your words, moist and discolored by skeptical disdain dripping like condensation from a rattling old rusted window unit. "I see. Let's add 'tardy' to that job description."

But when the door flies open and sunlight bleeds into the tavern, it's not Button Sykes but a stocky, short, bullet-headed nincompoop somehow looking both aggrieved and stupid, his eyes droopy and dim. "Hey, y'all. Sorry I'm—"

"What's your name? Do you work here? What are you doing?"

"Oh hey, Roy Earl. I sure am sorry—"

"Excuse me?" You charge over toward him. "You said what to who, now?"

"Roy Earl—I'm real sorry about—"

"And your name is what-now?"

"Roy," Trudy calls over. "Stop it and let him talk."

"I'm Newbie. Newbie Harrell."

"All right Newbie, Newbie Harrell. What are you, agent double-O tardy?"

Newbie laughs, realizes you are joshing. "Ha-ha, that's pretty good. I was gonna be here in time, but my truck—"

"It doesn't matter. Hey, Newbie, it's gonna be a short meeting for you."

"Oh. Well that's good. I reckon."

"Maybe. Long story short? You're fired. You're giving everyone a chance here, sacrificing so the others can live. So they can see how to live. And to die, Newbie, Newbie Harrell. If your truck breaks down, let me know. I'll arrange for a ride over to the job fair at the vocational school on Monday."

Newbie, guffawing. "Aw, dog. You got me. That's pretty funny—"

"STOP LAUGHING." Your voice slaps back in the silent space of the closed hospitality establishment, as they'd all better start thinking of this poop-hole.

Newbie stops laughing.

"Now. What part of you're 'fired' don't you understand?"

"For real? But Mr. Roy Earl—"

"Is that small cranium of yours capable of understanding speech? Get out, dingleberry."

Trudy, cussing under her breath. Your shooting glance silences her.

"Just go on, Newbie," Fridge says. "Roy Earl upset about his granddaddy."

"Don't you describe my state of mind to this non-entity. Don't you dare."

Newbie squawks and shakes his head and tears leap out of his eyes. "God dog, beau," he says with a breathless quaver. "I can't half believe this."

"And I can't 'half believe' you, or anyone else, would be so obtuse as to be late to such an important meeting." Gently. "Now go; go on and live your life. You are free, white bird. Fly away and let the grownups set to the business at hand."

To a new round of throat-clearing and shuffling, you hold up a finger and wait until Newbie goes, the door swishing shut in his wake, the tinkling of the bells ringing again into stillness.

Still holding up your finger for attention and silence, you begin examining the old curtains and acoustic foam and dust and think about the fire that burned up a rock club in Rhode Island that time. Horrors. That'd be the area over which Button, whom you haven't seen for decades, would be dressed down.

See? Order already.

All rather clear to you—everyone here had achieved a peter-principle level of general incompetence, a perverted balance to their lives and work that, trapped inside and unknowing, they misperceived as acceptable and normal. They could no longer see the filth.

Since the rest had not enjoyed the ass-kicking you delivered to Trudy and Fridge, you will next use Button as the example that puts the fear of god—of you—into all of them and establish good order in this professional business environment.

Button. You remember that sister of hers better. Thim, a beauty, an elegant Asian-eyed beauty you beat off to a few times in between thinking about Karen Black and her glorious eyes staring out of the movie screen. Button you recall as a little freak, a round, kinky-haired tribble with thick glasses. The last time you'd seen her had been when you came back for Aunt Henny's funeral, Button's grandmother, who knows how long ago—five, six years? You hadn't gone to Button's father's funeral, not even to comfort your Uncle Burnie. Too busy opening smoothie stands. Rolling the dice. Yelling at people. Banking the profit.

"So let's get down to the issue here," you announce in your loud, steady and penetrating owner's voice, which is a flatter and more shiny accent than your normal speaking voice, as though you're an announcer on *SportsCenter* or *Monday Night Football*: resonant. Cheery. Full of information. "Which isn't the past, or the future, but which involves present-moment change and growth."

"Such as?" Trudy, all wiseguy and shit. "We could bring back smoking."

Murmuring and laughter.

"Right on," from an emaciated white boy who'd been introduced as Skee-ball, the Fridge's kitchen assistant, and who said 'do-what' to your joke congratulating him on having become The Dixiana's 'sous chef' at such a young age, while you assess his discolored teeth for meth damage.

"Mr. Roy Earl...?" Etna Dixmont, a server. She's about a hundred pounds overweight, mid-50s. "Could we sit down, sugar?"

You make your speech about how we don't sit down on the clock, and that everyone's being paid for this meeting, and so by god you will stand, young people, you will stand straight and tall and proud and attentive and—but of course, this is not the college age staff of a Spotted Banana™ or Carolina Beanery®: the median age appears to be north of your own age, which in the last few days has seemed to be rapidly advancing.

"Normally, I'd say a roomful of heathy adults should be able to stand through a fifteen minute meeting. But in this case, and under the circumstances, I know everyone's still upset. So, I suppose we should sit," gesturing to the upturned chairs, which the employees remove from the table tops, a bustling cacophony that takes forever.

Trudy offers a seat to Etna, who waddles over and eases down, weary and burdened. "Oh, thank you, darlin'. This one bunion of mine hurt so bad I got to get surgery on it next month."

An idea pops: Right here, a stage. Use it.

"Let's try this—turn all those chairs around. Move them closer to the stage."

Everyone considers this, begins nodding and embarking on another bustle of shuffling and settling.

You mount the rickety wooden steps and stand looking down at them assembled in front of Button's soundboard area, at the light streaming in, at the history on the walls and the beer lights and the age of it all, a place unstuck in time, and in purpose.

You note the "Pennsylvania Hex" above the stage, as your grandfather called the colorful painted designs he always had tacked up different places, like on the outside of their houses both old and new, a variety of sizes and patterns, but always round. Another tradition that would be gone—the hex atop stage, with its little stars and devils, you'd pry it down yourself. Incongruous, these hexes. Some remnant of Pa-paw's youth in the West Virginia hollows and having to do with a kind of hoodoo his grandmother practiced, some kind of Appalachian mountain, Christian-based conjuring. Or so your grandmother had explained to you one time. You had shat a brick when coming home after building them the Victorian, and discovering the old man had gone and put up one of those fruity, tacky old eyesores, a round lotus mandala of twelve leaves with a stylized pineapple in the center, hammered into the expensive Hardiplank® Colorplus® lap siding designed with such care and quality to more than outlast the lives of the residents inside.

As you stand before the staff of The Dixiana, all chatting instead of turning their attention to the stage, you realize you possess an enormous well of sympathy for every grammar school teacher who ever lived—don't these people understand this is a work meeting? Trudy, whispering and gossiping, the worst offender.

If she had any sense, she'd have stood up there beside you, commander to your captain. Right? If she had anything at all on the ball, Trudy Pirkle would have understood that on the bridge, she should as First Officer take her place at your elbow—well, maybe a step back, whatever the protocol calls for—and assume the mantle of leadership that's yours to bestow on her anew. But she doesn't follow you onstage. She sits whispering and giggling with one of the other servers, another super-skinny redneck white girl with a big zit on her chin and skin so pale as to be gray, and while you're beaming Trudy to SHUT UP SHUT UP SHUT UP AND PULL YOUR ATTENTION TO ME, you scan the girl's legs and arms for bruises and needle marks, note to self to check teeth for signs of unusual decay.

"Everyone," you finally explode. "Please. If we could."

Trudy cuts her eyes, shimmering blue daggers. Her head bobs in that long-necked Pirkle way. She crosses her long legs and rocks her flip-flopped foot back and forth, long toes wiggling. You remember them well. Managed to memorize every inch of her, or so your memory has always led you to believe. Beliefs, as someone once said, though, are only thoughts you've practiced over and over.

You wish you could quell this animus inside and go back to that purely sexual and wondrous moment between the two of you, that you couldn't understand then why it couldn't go on, and don't understand now why it still consumes you so. Why you masturbate thinking of Trudy, Trudy, Trudy. You have a sexy wife, prettier than Trudy by far.

Had a wife, that is. She belongs to another, some Indian nitwit you should never have hired, or rather Sharolyn should never have hired, and all this does is dredge up thoughts of Sedge Island and the Beanery and whatever trouble Creedence is getting into now.

It strikes you: Perhaps you shouldn't have forbidden her to come up here. How she should have gotten in the Beemer and driven up and met you and reconciled. That would demonstrate she means how sorry she claims to be.

But she didn't come. She's down there right now screwing the guy. Doing it. Doing it in ways she didn't want to with you, because now you know she didn't love you, ever.

"Roy Earl." Trudy clears her throat.

"You all right, darling?" Etna asks.

All eyes lay upon the crown of shimmering anger you feel glowing from within the tight, thin skin of your skull. Everyone's been quiet and waiting for an indeterminate expanse of time. You find yourself standing with the heels of your hands turned inward and pressed against your throat. You relax this posture—you realize that this body language indicates high stress, and a desire to express your stress, though possessing a subconscious unwillingness to do so, the hands clutched around the tender neck-flesh an exoteric manifestation of an inner protection mechanism.

But protection for whom?

"Let's talk about right now," you say, picking it back up. You flutter your eyelids. "The past is the past. The future is coming and involves change. But right now? I suppose there's a honkytonk to run."

Everyone seems pleased. Trudy's glare softens.

This expression will not hold: "So let's work first on expectations."

You launch into the meat with a bright smile, phony but glowing with faux sincerity, the crinkled eyes and dimples and impish smirk you give to individuals as you speak; little winks, too, to put them at ease. "Here's the news: this isn't like the Eddie Murphy bit in *48 Hours*—there's a new sheriff in town, and his name is Roy Earl Pettus," you manage in a decent enough Eddie that makes everyone titter and chuckle. "But I reckon it is that. If there's any sense of ownership to be had, at least in the legal sense, it falls to me. I would say to me and Mama Runelle, but Rabbit Pettus did not leave the tavern to his spouse. He left it to yours truly."

"Tavern," Fridge says. "Ain't never heard it called that." Murmuring and chuckles.

You admonish him with a hard stop on the flow of your speech, all the crinkle gone from your eyes. You wait again. They settle.

Fridge holds your gaze. You blink twice, which releases him. He looks down to the tips of his filthy sneakers—the footwear on these people is appalling beyond reason.

What are they all thinking?

"And so," you go on, dredging up a strained smile, "with this new ownership comes a certain level of expectation that may or may not have been present here before. With this in mind I have one question, and it's rhetorical in a certain sense, but also one to which I want concrete answers— from each of you, sure, but also now as a group. And I want you to 'tell' me without opening a single one of your suppurating pie holes," said with sudden menace. "Which is what rhetorical question means. It means I will ask a question, and what you all need to do, is not answer this for me. Answer it for yourselves, on an intellectual level." This, the speech you had used the two times you had had to swoop in like the angel of death and clean house, dismissing entire staffs of Spotted Banana™ employees to start fresh with less incompetent and corrupt humans. "You need to answer this question in every sector of your mind and heart and life, much more than here at work. But as far as our relationship's concerned, you better spend time answering it regarding the quality and duration of your employment at The Dixiana.

"Now: The mysterious question I'd like to ask you all is: What. The fudge. Are you all thinking."

The interrogative you've left bereft of its signifying inflection doesn't so much hang as settle like a pall of dust from the rafters after an explosion outside some farmhouse in a World War II movie like your grandfather used to watch.

"Well?" you finally say.

A hand raises—Skee-ball.

"Speak."

"Thought you said we wasn't supposed to answer it."

Fridge is all like, "No, he said it was both."

"He's messing with our heads, is what," Trudy says.

Which makes your simmer boil over. Who did these little buttholes think they were? "Another word out of your mouth, Skeeter, and the answer you'll get is who's fastest in showing you the freaking exit."

Gazes lower, most of all Skee-ball's, whom you called 'Skeeter' as a gesture of genuine, heartfelt disrespect.

Trudy's face isn't downcast. She keeps staring right through you, hard. Now she knows where this is leading—yeah.

You get it—you get why she sat with them instead of stand with you: this way she can spread the blame around to the subordinates. The fish would not rot from the head, but there in the herring barrel alongside the rest. Sure, the staff might all be indolent nincompoops with a relaxed Edgewater County approach to a work ethic, but blame had to rest with the commanding officer. The troops, like a family of recalcitrant and misbehaved children, did not get this way on their own. They had help—from mommy.

You hurtle along into a dramatic recitation of the ills you've noticed, problems glaring and self-evident from your cursory walkthrough, which means that god only knows what your fine-grain, white-glove inspection will uncover. You point. You gesture. You smile your phony smile and dimple them cheeks, boy, and crinkle the eyes and sugarcoat your face while you deliver the kind of displeasure that only the *pater familias* can manage: deep disappointment, anger, befuddlement, bafflement, confusion at how it all could have gone to hell like this.

Stony silence. "And you all know why I get to say this to you cigarette-sucking, no-good, worthless, no-account Edgewater County pieces of trash? Do you?"

Trudy weeps, her face pinched and sour and hateful.

"*That's not a freaking rhetorical question.*" Your ejaculation makes them all jump.

Fridge says, "Roy Earl, c'mon, dog. You not only being mean, but you confusing us. Now I don't know if I should answer or not."

"The answer is this: *because I used to swab the deck of this listing, sinking ship myself*. You people understand? Eh? I don't just have legal ownership of this hospitality establishment—I have literal ownership. More over? I have sweat equity. And whether you know it or not, you all do as well—or at least the wise among you.

"Further, I stand before you a free man, remaining so no matter whose rules surround me, and if I find them tolerable I tolerate, if I find them unjust I break them," quoting a sci-fi novel you read thirty years ago, while sitting out in the shade of the pecan orchard on a summer afternoon. "What makes me free? Freedom is being morally responsible for everything you do in life. It's about knowing your responsibilities. And doing your best. So you can never, ever look in the mirror and say, I shirked. My responsibility is to The Dixiana and my grandfather's legacy, so you damn straight better understand I'm-a fixing to take a hard look at everything. Fine-tooth comb. And who knows what I'll suggest about how we're to do things around here going forward."

Deciding to let them off the hook, and not drop any big bombs about how you planned to gut this craphole to the bricks and do god knows what with it by the time you are done, you stand mute and allow the gravity of your words to settle.

"Now, that's all I have to say to you today, except this: get to work cleaning this filthy, broken-down, sorry excuse for a small business concern. NOW!" Again your voice echoes throughout The Dixiana. The word hath been given.

Etna raises her hand. Sounds sassy. "Well I ain't supposed to work tonight, and my foot hurts, and I'm going home. Ain't my job to clean."

"You and your hurt foot either stay and clean, or get another job. You hear me?"

Trudy, having had enough. "It ain't your job to hire and fire—it's mine."

"Folks," you say as everyone gets up and looking at one another trying to figure out what you want them to do. See? It looks clean to them already. No wonder. No wonder. "Whatever was before is no more. That's the way you should all be thinking."

You tell Trudy to hold up. To see you outside. And she knows that you're gonna fire her.

You feel pleased.

You have a kernel of fiery white-hot glowing power inside your body.

You give this dark energy an order, a focus: execute. You tell Etna, last check's in the mail, sister.

☾❁◉

But first, the sound of keys turning in the locked entrance door. A short woman with the most amazing head of dreadlocks enters, hair like nothing you've seen since those old Dead shows, like the one when they played South-eastern University one dreary October night, and you had gone with Devin and Billy and Libby, when those blessed friends had all been alive, now all gone from a variety of misadventures and tragedies; hell, Jerry Garcia himself now dead for twenty years.

This fascinating, petite woman's odd face comes to you out of the gloom, and as she smiles at you, this beauty—yeah; there's that stirring again, like with Trudy when you first flew in on the day granddaddy died—causes your heart to swap from coldhearted bastard to flirtatious charmer, a talent you'd cultivated as a barista to goose the tip jar. God, but you are horny.

"Gracious—who's this gorgeous presence we have here?"

Trudy throws up her hands. "That's Button, you big fat dummy."

Button seems taken aback by your velvety tone. "Hi, Roy Earl—remember me? I'm sorry. By the way. So sorry. About Uncle Rabbit."

"Button, my dear," feeling your nascent lust squelched and quelled like the campfire you'd quenched the time you and Devin and Dobbs had camped in the Glade, "appreciate the sentiment. Thanks; et cetera. But long story short? Everybody's in major trouble, including you. Being late to the meeting is an enormous problem, but it's more than that. But we'll get to the meat of your issues presently." Gesturing to a chair. "If you—"

Catching Trudy's eye.

"If you don't mind."

Button's nurturing and concerned expression for you melts into troubled consternation. "Whoa—and hello to you. What's going on here?"

"Roy Earl has his butt up on his shoulders, that's what." Trudy explains this with vicious snark, pulling out her cigarettes and sparking one up with hands that shake and almost fumble the pack. "He thinks his shit don't stink. And can tell us what to do. *Already.*"

"Outside." You brush by Button and poke Trudy in the skinny upper arm with a rigid, outstretched finger. Under your breath: "Trudy Pickle, former employee."

"Don't touch me."

"Dude." Button, from over your shoulder. "Let's take ourselves. A major chill-pill."

Insubordination. "Quoting myself: 'I will deal with you presently, Button Sykes.' Unquote."

❀❀❀

OUTSIDE THE DIXIANA, only feet from the spot where you once kissed this woman and felt a similar sense of power and happiness and joy, it is with a tone and words designed to hurt—no, lacerate—that you dismiss longtime general manager Trudy Pirkle. You tell her you're sorry, but that's it; her years of service entitle her to a severance package that's fair if modest, based upon salary and the general overall revenue trend of the establishment in her care for so long. In any case, her insubordination and disrespect leaves no choice but to ask for her keys. "No choice. Out of my hands."

"I don't want your fucking money."

"Goody. More for me to keep and spend."

Trudy beats you with sudden rage and horror, weeping and erupting in a manner so different from she had when you'd made love to her at sixteen, your goddess, your Karen Black made real. *"After Mr. Rabbit's funeral, I hope I never see your ass again."*

"There ain't gonna be no *god-durn funeral*," you boom out, sounding for all the world like your granddaddy. You only know this later, but you can see from Trudy's aghast look of shock—your voice sounded way weird, that's all you realized then—that it's as though a ghost has drifted languid across the town green of Tillman Falls. "How many times do you morons have to be told?"

"No funeral? What kind of asshole don't give his own granddaddy a service? Who does that?"

"No funeral; no freaking tombstone. If there's two bigger ripoffs these days than health care and funeral expenses, I'd like to hear what they are."

"You the worst son of a bitch I ever heard of. You ain't even gonna have nowhere for nobody to come on Decoration Day."

"Nobody with a clue cares about such ritualistic foolishness anymore. Nobody but you downmarket Pirkles and the rest of the redneck mothers in this damn—this freaking—this crappy—this—ah."

Shoving her away, you find yourself fighting back hot tears, which nevertheless burst open and flow like a rushing waterfall on a mountainside. Howling and sucking wind, you both stand facing away from the honkytonk.

Calming down. Hands on hips. Finding each other's face again, both swollen-eyed.

"Just go home," is all you can croak.

"Don't do this. Please."

"'Please.' You're lucky I don't call the law to take your ass in on an assault charge. You nitwit. You fucking asshole," falsetto, like a woman. Sounding like her. Crying again.

"You go and fuck yourself to death."

"No; and you can go suck a donkey dick," a ridiculous suggestion but made with a quavering, quiet menace.

Charged air. You both sound so stupid. Cursing like this is giving you a stomachache. But this rational thought, subsumed.

Submerged.

The Blade, heavy in your hands, warm, powerful, lending you strength. "Get out of my sight. 'See you next Tuesday'—get it?"

"What's on Tuesday?"

"Never mind."

Trudy whirls around and stomps off in a howling huff. You steal a glance long enough to watch her flip-flopping across the green, away from her Taurus and to a place you know not where; her body language, clenched and anguished. She had her chance to be your friend, and lover, and who knows what else. You could not have Creedence back then, nor Karen Black, but you had had Trudy, who'd seemed a trailer-park goddess, not trash, though one who had handed you off to your fate and destiny as an adult like so much garbage. That's the way you remember it, anyway. That's what you were crying over. No one, not even Trudy, would know this but you.

You collect yourself and cruise back inside to confront Button Sykes over her weak-sauce work ethic, or whatever the heck that weirdo chick's issue will turn out to be—and you'll find out. Oh, yeah. You always do with employees. You see through them. Their lies. Their excuses. Their rank and disgusting defensiveness. Her disguise, however it manifests, shall not resist your scrutiny.

BUTTON AND ROY EARL

From the moment she saw the man for whom she already felt such deep and abiding empathy, whom she regarded as a cousin, as family—Uncle Rabbit's boy—Button understood that Roy Earl Pettus needed help. Spiritual help, certainly. Perhaps other types as well. His megalomania on display a hallmark of run-amuck ego often found in the alcohol abuser, or even the untreated dry-drunk, a charge often leveled after an episode of George W. Bush's clear and present madness.

In fact, she suspected all this before getting out of the Baja; a suggestion more than a fact. The Dixiana, as she could see, had an etheric cloud hovering over it. Typically the bar didn't display much of an aura at all, only at night, and then, in a manufactured sense: it came from the pale glow of the sign's neon tubes, the ones still functioning, anyway. Here and now, though, the honkytonk itself appeared to grieve.

A lovely literary metaphor, but Button, her antennae super-attuned and third eye decalcified, knew this cloud, like a pall of fire-smoke, came not from a structure, but the souls inside. Stress had manifested here. Vibrations, pitched high.

And when she'd walked in to observe their faces, and gauge their energy, oh, how she suffered the shock of wading into a conflict scenario at its fullest flowering, its moment of apotheosis, as she intuited in what amounted to a precognitive instance of 'clairsentience' versus clairvoyance regarding the mood of the room; a feeling more than a vision.

As she waited for Roy Earl to return from whatever horrible transaction was due to conclude between him and Trudy, only the brief softening of his face at the recognition of her identity gave any hope she could assist him through the necessary strife and drama of this obvious emotional crisis. Otherwise, Roy's aura blazed in tones of ochre, like an ugly Sun Symbol of King-Philip II of Macedonia, undulating rays of blood-black emanating from a central singularity of deepest and unknowable infinity. He dwelled at the bottom of a spiritual well. That much came clear as day.

And she'd thought mere grief awaited here at The Dixiana. It would be interesting to discover what kind of syncs popped up.

BAD enough she had her grandfather's grief on her plate. Weak and tired after sitting up with him most of the night, she had given in and phoned Dr. Wise's office, the family GP, who knew Burnie Sykes's condition well, yet still prescribed Xanax and Wellbutrin. Pills to an alcoholic.

Guilty and conflicted, Button had gotten the scripts filled. Had stood in the cold white florescent light of the CVS pharmacy waiting area.

"I will look at my hands in my dreams tonight." Quiet, to herself, glancing down at her palms. A lucid dreaming technique. If one did that enough during the day, you'd do it in your dreams, and when you do, you realize that you're dreaming and can control the dream. Button, loving the idea of lucid dreaming; thinking much information might be gleaned from this aspect of consciousness, these sojourns on the astral plane. To fly. Take great leaps across wide rivers. Visit anyone you liked, anywhere. Like Heather Ponderview, for instance.

Trembling, all her mental discipline and personal ethics crumbling, Button rued purchasing this batch of pharmies from the man, man. The damn pills had been her own downfall. And yet she did it. Had paid in cash. Just like the old days in the Phish lot, scoring heady beans and rolls and whatnot.

The apple-cheeked, heavyset pharmacy assistant ringing up her order seemed to note the shaking hands that counted out the money, all fives and ones. "You need them meds, don't you," whispering with genuine concern. "Bless your soul."

"These little Luciferian hell rocks?"

"Do what, now?"

"The pills—they aren't going into my body. No way."

"Well, shut my mouth, Allyson Sykes. I mean—Button."

No one ever called Button by her first name. "Do we know each other?"

Disappointment emanated from the woman. "We was in school together, all the way from second grade."

How embarrassing. Button looked at the pharmacist's name tag, gleaned a glimmer of recognition. Sure. Now she remembered—Jouquoya. Jouquoya

Moulton. All those Us and Os, hard to forget. Said the name, hoped her pronunciation came close. "So sorry. It's been a long time. I remember you."

"You ain't remember my ass," more inward than as an accusation. "Don't pretend."

"No, I do. I wouldn't lie. About that."

"Folks call me Jackie. Folks who know me."

"Jackie. Now I remember."

"It's okay. It was a big class."

Button tried to smile but felt exhausted, and pushed to the point of almost wanting to gobble a couple of her grandpa's nerve pills—down the hatch they'd go, and then hard sleep, but, Lord, was she unwilling to go there. All would be lost. All she'd built up. In a pill-popping, ruinous incidence of weakness.

And backsliding.

Now?

No way. A spiritual blind spot she'd just as soon avoid, thank you.

"I'm sorry, but it's not like you remember me any better than I remember you. We're not—we weren't friends. Not that we. Couldn't have been." Button, dialing up her heart-light, projecting a warm, genuine smile. "Ya dig."

Shrugging. "You was one of the smart kids. You didn't pay no attention to nobody like me."

"Sister, I didn't pay attention to anyone. And they didn't. Pay attention to me. Now, I should get these. Back home. To my granddad." As a down-mouthed aside: "And I have a work thing."

"Bye, Button." Jackie, sad and frustrated, smoothed the front of her pastel pharmacy smock with big but feminine hands. A large girl, but attractive. "See you round. I reckon."

Only after pulling up in front of The Dixiana, and right before noticing the gloomy and forbidding aura, did it strike Button that, super-attuned antenna or not, her gaydar seemed to be spotty today: at last she realized Jouquoya had been vibing her. The fleeting, soft repose of that final expression on her face. Attraction.

A big, horny, beautiful black girl.

Huh.

A tingle. Whoa—how long had it been?

But: what would they have to discuss? Button had to admit that, at this point in her journey, difficult to imagine life with another person not at least kinda sorta leaning toward the spiritual, physical, and disciplined state of being to which she'd evolved.

More trouble than it was worth, a hookup. And then, only for a momentary burst of physicalized pleasure. Ephemeral; never the thing, the real thing. Not with anyone except Heather.

Nevertheless: Button, horny as fucking hell.

Also, Button had pledged to serve. Who could guess how opportunities for service might manifest—to give affection and pleasure to a lonely figure from her childhood, one not even remembered? Sure.

More like a rationalization to have oneself a good time—love the one you're with, eh? Clouds rise over the mountains, the moon resides in the heart of the waves. That's all Button knew.

◉◈◎

Roy Earl Pettus made it clear to her in an instant that Button's path lay in healing his grieving cracker ass, first by adding a little of her Saigon cinnamon to his recipe of angst and stress, which went far beyond the death of his grandfather and The Dixiana. She'd have to coax more out of him later, through means of as yet unknown complexity and duration.

First step, she decided, would be a copy of the Tao for him to study. The Mitchell translation. Accessible and cogent. Amazon.com called her name. Next: get him meditating. Get him off this ego stuff fueling the rage and the pronouncements and the separation.

Yeah—separation. His grandfather, dead. Wife, estranged, or so Button understood. Stress. Change. She got it.

Wait—how is this she understands he's having problems with his wife? No memory of anyone delivering such news.

Maybe Walfredo at work again? That rascal.

As Roy Earl came over to her inside the honkytonk, his eyes faraway and jaw set as though shattered and wired shut, Button generated the glowing heat of pure and unconditional love inside her solar plexus, prepared herself to give him biofeedback that might help the flow of his Q'i, which from this remove she could sense its flow blocked or occluded in some more particular and imbalanced fashion, due at least in part to the febrile, unbridled emotionality at work inside him.

Example: After making a vague threat, he shoved past and went outside with Trudy.

At his re-entrance everyone scurried and started grabbing cleaning equipment, with Fridge yelling at his prep cooks to do this and clean that by god, before he brought hellfire down upon the lot of their sorry asses; only Etna Dixmont, tears in her eyes, lingered as Roy made a quiet speech about the joys and advantages of early retirement.

Roy Earl Pettus! Button thought. Picking on poor Etna Dixmont? And what hath you wrought upon gentle, sweet Fridge?

Button shook off the shock and outrage. Breathed.

Her inner glow of love blossomed, an energetic salve both to assuage his pain and defend her own vibrational state of mind from the filth of his black bubble. She stood at the ready beside the soundboard platform, one New Balance up on the wood, stretching a calf that'd been tight all week, not to mention her back, which had been giving her trouble. After all her studious and disciplined refinements of the basic medicines, the three treasures of vitality, energy and spirit, yet here she suffered all these niggling aches and pains and it was driving her bat-crap cray-cray, truth be told.

Pain—deep and abiding. More like down in her side. Or her back. Or both. Weird.

"Hi, Roy Earl." Button, speaking with good cheer. "Everybody's really —busy."

"Damn straight they are."

She noted Roy Earl's words didn't seem his own. Demonic possession? Nah.

Grief. His eyes, swollen.

"Well. First, I'm so sorry about—"

"Now," tumbling over her words, a verbal bully, "about these areas: the stage, the backdrop, the acoustical foam, the general condition and appearance of all this. Long story short: it's far from ideal. More like deplorable." He stooped and bent down by her soundboard console. "It's beyond the pale. Look at this filth."

She foresaw his action. Mulled it over. Realized anew. "Oh, wait—!"

A giant breath, blown out under the soundboard. A cloud of dust going back eons billowed into her lungs. She ran, screaming and cursing, across the room toward the door. Outside, Button coughed until she thought she'd vomit.

Back inside, Roy Earl greeted her from behind the bar with an icy bottled water in his hand. "See what I mean? About the filth?"

She bloomed with gratitude. The dust-event had broken his trance; he retained a human side.

Her throat convulsing and painful, she reached for the water.

"Hold up," withdrawing the dripping bottle. "Where do we write down comp stuff? Inventory control, that's where."

"Please," she croaked.

"I presume there's a clipboard?"

"I think. There is. Somewhere."

"You think? So, is there a comp clipboard—*or not*?"

She couldn't believe his hateful withholding of the water. "Roy Earl. Please."

His eyes floated like two shiny marbles, like that of the cop who'd busted her and Heather Ponderview back on Phish tour in 1998, in Indiana trying to get around stalled traffic heading into the Deer Creek amphitheater on an alternate state road, an event Button had christened the Fort Benjamin Harrison

Gambit. It'd been a detour that landed them in the pokey facing serious effing drug charges, thanks to some fresh shrooms these cats had laid on them at the previous gig, Alpine Valley back in Wisconsin. They lost the Gambit; it caused them to miss the first of the two Deer Creek shows altogether, including a killer six-song second set.

The Midwest. Uptight mofos. And busted by some real assholes there in the Indiana countryside, a trooper who'd called in a special DEA unit in the area to 'service' all the tourheads coming through. Shorthaired bastards. Oy. At least the heady travelers had been at the end of their weed—for two days they'd been counting down the headstash by estimating how many 'stonings' they'd get out of the buds they had left. It was the shrooms that had gotten them in trouble—thirty-nine freaking grams, distribution weight. Damn things were still heavy and wet.

Thank god for Heather P's daddy, and daddy's money, and all that. Button's own Sykes family had pull, if only there in Tillman Falls; a mini-version of the Ponderview wealth and status, status bailing her out of legal difficulties at home once or twice, power now long faded away. Besides, though, by the time the Ziploc full of fungus made it to the crime lab, the wet mushrooms had molded over; the tech had refused to test for anything, much less psilocybin. Charges dismissed.

"Christ." Roy Earl, furious. "I want that clipboard." But handing over the water anyway, only after cracking the seal for her, an automatic action like an experienced bartender or server might make. "And I don't know this 'Roy Earl' everybody keeps referencing, but he's starting to piss me off."

"Piss you off?" Owing to the condition of her lungs and throat, this came out soft and slight. "You're the one. Who's on. A rampage."

This seemed to stop him in his tracks. "A rampage? Hah. You people have no idea," dropping into an affected European accent that came out of nowhere. "You've no idea of the powerful forces you're dealing with. Forces aligned with cleanliness and order and control. To anger them is to court destruction, *fräulein*."

"Why? Are you speaking? To us all? This way?"

Now he seemed embarrassed. Grumbling and mumbling.

She realized he was trying to apologize. "Look. This dust. It's killing me. Can we go outside? To talk?"

He sounded dejected, like a child caught in the act of premeditated wrong-doing. "Why not."

On the sidewalk Roy Earl seemed less angry than exhausted, out of gas. Brimming with tears, his slack gaze drifted over first to the corner with Manny T's place, then across the monuments of the green and over beyond the court-house and LaFreniere Square and finally, she could see, settling on the façade of the Palmetto Grande, a beautifully restored building. One of the few high points, sure. Gazing upon the old moviehouse seemed to quell his tortured spirits.

"My life is over." A sad confession. "Just so you know."

A flash came through her like lightning giving birth, a different warmth, a pulse of inner life as though cosmic meridians had crossed, and she couldn't know yet what this meant, only that what she had next to say would constitute neither bromide nor aphorism, but personal truth:

"No. The only rule in life is this: it begins."

At that he staggered across the street onto the green and collapsed onto the first bench he came to, steadying himself first on Button's silver, stubby Subaru Baja. A sign, she suspected. Not random it'd been her vehicle on which he'd leaned for support. Reality always operated also on the level of symbolism.

After his dark emotions and grief seemed to moderate, Button sat far from him on the bench, her small body—how many times in her life had she been able to say that?—perched birdlike and still so as not to disturb any settling of his energy now underway.

"Rampage—how accurate."

"I'm foresworn. To call it. Like I see it."

"How humiliating."

"Forget it, broheem." She scooted down and offered him a power fist he regarded with mild suspicion, what seemed like disappointment. Instead of bumping Button back, he reached over and enveloped her, burying his head in the dreads and pushing her face into his chest.

"God, you look so different," muffled by her hair.

"I lost a little weight."

He blurted, "I'm so lonely and sad."

She gave a giant, concluding squeeze to the hug that leaned more toward a passionate embrace between long-lost lovers; as in, how Button fantasized about hugging Heather when she got to see her again. "And listen. I'm so sorry about Uncle Rabbit."

Roy Earl broke the embrace and drew a deep breath through his nostrils, now sounding pissy and mean again. "It was that hound dog's time. Old piece of dirt."

"Hey," but backing off the aggression in her tone. "How old? Was he?"

"Haven't a clue. Same age as Uncle Burnie, probably."

That made him eighty-nine, which when she reported this to Roy Earl only made him seem disgusted.

"The scoundrels live the longest, don't they?"

A rhetorical question. "Couldn't say."

She sought to retrieve him from this emotional gravity well. But the closure and healing he required fell beyond her purview, not without a more intimate knowledge of his inner life, issues and general health.

"So what's going on with Trudy—if I may?"

He shook his head. Drew a finger across his throat.

"Meaning—?"

"Same thing it means for all of you, I'm afraid." He rested a warm palm on her knee. "May I share something?"

Button nodded, smiling but cautious. She sensed his energy shift from anger and grief to a more positive vibration, one she could not return except in the most platonic of manners: a sexual vibe. As Ficino put it, Venus soothes Mars as Jupiter soothes Saturn. She patted his hand, removed it. "Go ahead."

"Your hair—it's gorgeous. Along with the rest of you."

"If you say so."

"You don't look like the same girl."

"People change. You did, too. And I'm not a girl. I'm a woman."

"Sorry. Your dreads, they remind me of those beautiful hippy girls—women—I used to see twirling at Dead shows. You know, the Grateful Dead," he said, nodding. "I'm a Deadhead."

She toyed with identifying as a Phish acolyte and fellow jamband aficionado, decided it could wait. "I know a little about the Dead."

Now he became faraway again. Poor Roy Earl—his emotions, downright manic. "I only saw them a couple times. One special night in particular, over in Columbia."

Button remembered hearing about that concert, but had only been ten and nowhere close to being interested in rock music. "Heard it was a good one."

His eyes shimmering with fear, ghosts seemed to trammel across his future gravesite. "Like being in a temple of followers. It gave me goosebumps. Still does," displaying as evidence a stippled forearm.

"A power. From beyond the grave. Jerry."

"No doubt. I buy all the live show box sets. Well, the digital downloads of them."

Now for a misdirection designed to shake loose information: "Are you able to clarify 'same thing it means for all of us'?"

A blank stare. "Sure. But it's too soon."

But she already knew—every time his eyes fell on The Dixiana, he gave off a vibration of sweeping, angry contempt.

"Cleaning house, like a corporate hatchet man? Swooping in and lopping off heads?"

Offended, he snapped out of his reverie. "'Lopping off'? Like with a sword?"

Button, shrugging. "Figure of speech."

Emphatic. "No. I despise big corporations. I only incorporated twenty years ago myself because it served my ambition. And I only took money—oodles and oodles of money—from a mega-corp because they came waving it in my face."

"You didn't have to."

"It's what an American does. He makes money, waves it around. Otherwise, screw that whole corporate mindset. Personhood, my eye."

"Right on." She had no clue how to handle this case. Despite being in the thrall of filthy lucre, Roy Earl leaned toward wakefulness. "I don't much need the cash Rabbit pays me, but the others do."

"Goody for you."

"And Trudy?"

Another throat-slice. "Done deal."

"I hate to push, but: I feel like we're family. Like cousins."

"Permission to speak," getting her drift. "Say your piece."

"I realize you're the owner. Of this business. But so close after Uncle Rabbit's death? Seems too soon? To make all these decisions?"

"It's a time of transition. If not now, when?"

"Trudy runs this place fine, Roy Earl—wait. Roy. Right? That's what I should call you?"

"Roy is fine." He seemed to relax. "Button-Button."

"All right, now. If no Roy Earl. Then no Button-Button."

"Intended with all due affection. Allyson, then?"

"Button the singular. Is fine." She beamed him with love. "You never seemed. Um. To pay much attention," echoing the words of Jouquoya Moulton. "Always joking around with Thim. Ignoring me, like everyone did," she concluded. "Except the bullies."

"You were so much younger. Nothing to talk about." A brief shadow fell across them from above, a low-flying bird of prey blocking the sun. "But I hear ya on the bullies."

"How about now? That we're peers?"

At the remark he arched an eyebrow, canted his head, folded his arms, and affected body language suggesting discomfort leaning to effrontery at her suggestion of peerage. Eyelids fluttering: "How old are you now?"

"Since when do we ask ladies such a question?"

"You must be in your mid-thirties."

"On the nose. Why?"

Shaking his head. "Button—I'm a wreck."

Here we go, she said to herself. A reveal?

Need there be a catalyst?

Dead shows, eh?

"So listen here," she said, using a variety of euphemisms to ask if Roy Earl Pettus ever consumed cannabis.

Now both eyebrows shot up. "Not in a blue moon, as the yokels would say."

"Hey—I'm a yokel."

Sheepish, he apologized. "That would be—cool. I think."

"I have no doubt it would."

Conspiratorial: "Seriously?"

"C'mon. With me. Cousin."

⊚✷⊚

THEY TOOK a stroll around the corner and down Common Street beside the back lawn. Button led him into Forest Knoll Garden, one of the oldest cemeteries in settled South Carolina. Button, a deep connection here, as had Roy.

"Back in here? I don't know."

"Worried about Agatha of Aberdeen, aren't you."

"Agatha of Aberdeen. I remember my grandmother showing me that old gravestone and telling the story. Gave me goosebumps. I always hated being out behind the Dix at night, looking up here. But no, no. I ain't afraid of old Agatha. In fact, Pa-paw used to tell me to always make sure her grave was kept clean. Some kinda superstition. He had a bunch, ya know."

Agatha of Aberdeen had come over from the Scottish coastal city during the Revolutionary War. Heartsick with worry about her beau, a dashing British captain serving with honor in his majesty's army to put down the impertinence of the feckless, contumacious, rebellious colonists. The poor dear, stricken by visions of her great love's faraway death, searched for him throughout the rebellious colonies. Finally, she almost caught up to him in then-Breeley's Crossing, only to discover he died not of warfare, no, but of disease: a cholera picked up while trekking through the fetid blackwater swamps to the East in Beauchamp County, known then as Kennesaw District.

Where the story became horrifying: In a fit of extreme emotion, Agatha, howling mad with unrequited love, grief and shock, had self-immolated in the town square, located in those days much closer to the river. In the decades and now centuries since, not only had she been spotted strolling among the gravestones in the far, oldest corner of the cemetery, but accused of being a mystical cause behind several historic fires that in olden times burned the town center to the ground.

The worst Edgewater County fire, however, came in the form of the horrendous Sunbury School conflagration, in which scores perished during a school play performance. Two-thirds of the eighty victims lay buried together, unidentified, in a mass grave behind a nearby country church still receiving congregations every Sunday. The grave, a wide slab of granite inside a wrought-iron fence. Button had stood and felt the pain and death of the suffering emanating from across the lengthening expanse of time. Not only had the horrific magnitude and circumstances of the event overwhelmed the forensic capabilities of the rural county coroner's office, the coroner himself, Holland Leaphart, in attendance to see his daughter perform, also died. His body, identified, had its own place in Forest Knoll Garden cemetery.

Agatha's self-destructive pyromania kept manifesting as a lingering curse, as oldtimers claimed; her grief-stricken visage reported having been seen in the flames of those various fires, sorrowful and pining for her lost love to the point that her spirit continued to wreak havoc, manifesting as what the modern TV newsreaders might term significant fire-events. Or so the myth-makers would have ghost-hunters believe.

Button considered asking Jasper's older sister Letty about the Sunbury School Fire, but for the sake of decorum hadn't wished to broach the subject—the Glasscocks lost several family members that terrible night. Letty, only a baby. What little she remembered might remain better left undisturbed.

Button's concerns about the possibility of her magicking and various workings attracting a destructive entity like Agatha, however, chilled her blood. Gave her pause. Whole bit.

◉❀◉

THEY PAUSED AT THE HEAVY, ancient wrought-iron original gate, more narrow than the arched, ornate entrance, farther down the street, closer to Whaley Way and the modern grave sites.

Roy hesitated.

"Your dad's in here, right?"

Clearing his throat. "Yep."

"Mine, too."

"Oh—of course. I'm real sorry. Mee-maw told me Buddy was sick."

"You paid respects? Yet? On this visit home?"

"I haven't had time."

"Then let's go get high and do a little ghost walk. Uncle Rabbit—he's not gonna have a monument, right?"

"Right."

More love-beaming. "So let's think about him. While we visit your special marker. And mine."

Realization coursed across Roy's face. "I'm so sorry about your pop. I didn't even come home for his funeral, did I?"

"No."

Shamefaced. "What a cad I am. What a feckless, thoughtless, idiotic—"

She bade him to stop; assured him a fleeting sense of his absence had occurred to her only when Rabbit and Runelle paid their respects in the receiving line, saying Roy was sorry, but too busy to make it.

"Everything's in the past. And none of it matters. And it's all about right now. But I don't really. Want to go into the cemetery. Because we have people there."

"They why?"

"To keep from getting hassled for inhaling. Out on the town green."

Watchful slit-eyes swept all around. "Heard that—that'd be a helluva way to welcome me back to Tillman Falls."

Button dug in her small purse for the handheld vape she always kept charged and at the ready. "Are you back to stay?"

His chuckle came, bitter, clipped, and in seeming disbelief. "Button, believe it or not, but I'm afraid I might be."

"No kidding?"

"I'm a man without a rudder, so to speak. Without a safe and familiar port. Confused. I am wrath—and I don't know what to do with all these feelings."

"So I see." She dug for deets; the marriage, crumbling in a heap from infidelity. All very grim.

Further asking, "What caused all this?"

"We fell out of love with one another. One of us did, anyway."

"Happened all of a sudden?"

"Pretty much. Damn if it didn't."

No wonder he's so angry, she reasoned. Button, glowing with enormous empathy, attempted to magnetize the pocket of space around them with healing and loving energy.

They went in through the arched entrance to the cemetery, Button first. Roy E. Pettus, closing the iron gate behind them with a clangorous, portentous thud she knew well. Like many in Edgewater County, she'd been coming here to this graveyard as long as her memory allowed. And would keep on coming, it seemed.

At least getting high wasn't the same as watching your father cry at his old friend's grave—Roy's dad, as it happened. And of course, going to one's own father's funeral here not so long ago. That day still pulsed and resonated, f'sure f'sure it did.

But this moment held a different energetic charge, and felt more about being alive, being right now, than being dead. Button went with it. Heated the vape. And talked it out with her semi-cousin there among the enormous old oaks, their limbs reaching out low to the ground and beckoning like watchers over the stone monuments to the dead, whether grateful or otherwise.

CHRISTY BEAUDOCK AND NEWBIE HARRELL

With no plan as yet for the body, which lay stiller than still and remains in fact dead, Christy frets and fumes, and in a way gets madder than before he done what he done to his Daddy. And that don't feel too good.

He needs to do more than fume. But that's only part of the equation. Having the corpse at hand represents another whole mess to fume over.

Christy knows this and says, *Maybe Daddy will turn into dust really fast and blow away and won't none of it matter.*

A different voice in his head yells at Christy. He calls this the Ordering Voice, which sometimes makes him do things he don't want to do:

Little kids think that way! You will go to jail if you don't take care of your Daddy.

Christy, seeming like he never got to be no little kid. Wasn't nothing bad ever hid from him, not like you ought to do with young'uns. Or so Christy reckons.

Christy, he about shit his britches when he steps outside and sees two prowlers, Sheriff's deputies, parked a couple trailers away. Not that unusual—this black couple lived there, a man and a woman who would knock the crap out of each other, sometimes in the dirt driveway of the trailer park for all to see. You can hear them throwing stuff at each other from three mobile homes over. Earlier in the year that fat crazy lady had shot one of her boyfriends back in the other corner of the lot, and with all the cops running around, Christy's Daddy, with his pills and powders in the house, freaking out for over a day. Rock stars, he called the neighbors, which to Christy's daddy means crackheads.

Christy, still as a statue and watching until the cops leave. They only took the man into custody this time. Dude hollered the whole while the deputies, two big burly dudes with necks like linebackers, pushed down on the man's head and shoulders until they shoved him into the back seat.

Christy hoped the lady wasn't dead in there, because that would bring more cops.

Nope. They left. All quiet.

A relief.

But all of it underlines how Christy's got himself a problem. It already smelled funny in the trailer.

⊛⊛◉

WITHOUT A READY SOLUTION—NOT in broad daylight, anyway—Christy, catching a ride from an old black man in a pickup truck and hanging around the Gas Chief, and trying to think about anything but his Daddy laying dead.

Playing a few rounds of video games with his quarters and glancing into the back room, Christy, able to see old poker and three-card machines back there covered up, through a doorway after the glass case that has all the tobacco pipes, long skinny ones made of glass, and rolling papers and whatnot. Lord, but Christy could not abide smoking. Hated that mess worse than anything.

Christy wants to see if they have any other old arcade games under those tarps. That would be sweet. Original Donkey Kong. The hammer, beating holy hell out of those barrels. 'How High Can You Try?' Christy, reading on the net about Donkey Kong, and a documentary on YouTube featuring the occulted history of video games.

Aisha comes in, which means her homeschooling for the day must be done. She greets her father, cuts her eyes away from Christy, who stands staring.

At Christy's stupid school—Marion Simms High—he bets dollars to doughnuts nobody cares that Christy's ass ain't there.

"Hey now, girl."

"How are you, Christopher?"

"I been good. Real good."

Her smile, it's strained. She seems sick to Christy. Circles under her eyes. "That's—good."

Before he can ask if she feels well, though, her father tells Aisha to stop talking to the customers. She scurries behind the counter and disappears through a door marked **PRIVATE**.

Christy blazes hate at the father, whose gaze never wavers.

Going back to the video game, Christy tries now not to think about how he kinda loves Aisha, with her skin so different and coppery and eyes so green. She is a goddess descended unto Edgewater County, like how they would say such crap in the Holy Bible.

Christy, he don't know how on earth he could force her to love him, though. He's just too big. And kissing his cleft lip, the thought made him cringe. He couldn't stand to look at it himself.

Ain't too dumb. Everyone always got that part wrong, so wrong about Christy. He couldn't tell no one because they wouldn't believe him, but also because Christy didn't have all the words to explain why he wasn't Special Ed. Not yet. One day he'd march into the school and announce with his big voice that he was not Special Ed.

Or, he could quit school now if he wanted. Maybe he'd fly away, and none of it would matter.

That sounded like a plan, more than hanging around and seeing how nervous Aisha looks at the sight of him, as does her father behind the counter, stares wanting Christy to leave.

"You are not shopping today? Eh?"

"I reckon I ain't."

"Goodbye, then. Have a nice day," without sounding nice about it. Aisha's father picks up a clipboard and pen, counts cartons of cigarettes stacked up behind the plexiglass front counter.

Christy, lingering, taking his time on the way out. Touching and picking up merchandise. Pretending to look at candy bars and cell phone chargers and eyeglass cases. Holding the items close up to his face and going, Hm.

Senses the man watching him.

Eyes locking with the father, Christy feels saliva running from the corner of his mouth. He lets it drip. "Tell Aisha I'll see her around."

"I'll do no such thing," his foreign voice all clipped. "Now go and have a nice day."

"I feel ya. Ain't no need to get salty."

Now what. It's a long-ass walk all the way into town. Or to grandmama's house.

The Ordering Voice again? For real?!

You ain't got no choice. And besides, you been gone long enough it's like you been to school, and when, or if, one of your Daddy's friends finds him there, here's what they'll all say:

He must've up and died on everybody. Like we knew he would one day.

Christy, running with it on his own, now: His Daddy did drugs, as he would whine to the police. And beat him, his own son. All of which is true.

How smart are the local po-po? How much would they give a rip about Christy's Daddy?

Not much. But somewhat, I reckon.

But still—they wouldn't figure out Christy had smothered him, because no one would care enough to investigate how Christy's Daddy had died.

That's one blessed thing Christy is smart about—that people like his Daddy, and him too, he reckoned, didn't matter to nobody. Except to folks like Aisha's daddy, who take money. Otherwise, the Christies, and Christy's Daddies of the world, don't count for nothing.

If Christy mattered, maybe Aisha, or another friend, wouldn't be so afraid of him. If he wanted a girlfriend, he had to matter—he'd force it if he had to. But only after dealing with his Daddy.

⊙❀⊙

About the time Christy rolled outside the Gas Chief, feeling low and not at all happy about the walk he had in front of him, a muddy, beat-up Toyota 4-Runner pulled up next to the pumps. Maybe here was a solution.

A dude climbs out of the truck to gas it up. He stands short and stout and with a ball cap set way back on his melon head. Christy thinks the guy, who ain't a kid but looks like it, seems upset—a frown, while also carrying an open-mouthed gape of pleasant wonder, like a few of the dumb kids in Special Ed. Christy tried hard not to let his mouth hang open like that. When he did, like back inside, spit would run out like it done just now. *Christy, wipe your mouth* is probably the most common phrase folks have said to him throughout his life.

Putting a normal ordinary smile on his face—to seem friendly—he cruises over and sighs, heavy and loud. Standing by the pumps and peeping through his blonde curls at the guy gassing his Toyota, he's all like, "Hey."

"Yo," dude says, not changing his expression. "S'uh."

Christy, biting one of his nails. "N'uh. Yo."

Dude looks him over all suspicious. "You work here?"

"No."

"What you doing, then—acting like the Wally-world greeter?"

"I was just saying 'hey'."

"Well, 'hey''s for horses. Or ain't you ever heard that?" The guy laughs, hard and fast, his frown going away. He lifts his grungy ball cap straight up and back down on his head. "'Enjoy your pumpin' and shoppin' today at the Gas Chief, folks'." And going *haw-haw-haw* some more.

"Naw. It ain't like that."

Now the dude's turn to sigh. "Reckon that's what I'm-a gone do now."

"What?"

"Some dumb job, like at the Wally-world."

Christy, he goes, "Why?"

Dude says, because I got fired.

"What for?"

"For some dang reason. I dunno what."

"That's raw."

"I tell ya what." The handle goes ka-chunk, and he puts it back on the pump. Screws on his gas cap. "I'm of a mind to go and bless that butthole out. I didn't do nothing but come in late."

"That's harsh."

"So look here—you ain't no gay-boy, is you?"

Christy's like, whoa, what makes this guy think that? "Naw, bruh. It's totes legit."

"Whatcha want, then?"

"Nothing. Well—"

"You must want something."

"I was reckoning on wondering about asking if I could maybe get myself a ride somewhere."

The guy chews on it. Says, "What's your name, beau?"

Christy, saying, "Christopher."

"Newbie Harrell," sounding all proud.

"Newbie?"

"My name's Newton, like Isaac Newton. The smartest man ever. But they call me Newbie."

Newbie sounds flat and automatic like he's said all this the same way a bunch of times, like he's retarded. Christy, he knows you don't say that word, but it's what he's been called by his Daddy for so long it just slips out like that. Christy decides Newbie does belong in Special Ed, where Christy does not belong, but has been put because of a mistake.

Christy wonders if he really wants a ride with Newbie. But says, he says to himself, *Well, Newbie's not Special Ed enough to not have a license. He's okay to drive.*

Once Newbie pays and comes back and Christy works his bulk into the tight truck cab, he's asked where he wants to go. Christy tells Newbie where. In case of emergency, Christy, he has his Grandmama's address memorized.

"Whoa, dog—you know what that's right near?"

Christy, he don't know, and says so.

"Shoot. We could have us a good time out yonder."

Christy keeps saying, what, what, what.

Newbie gets all red. "You funnin' me? You really don't?"

"No—my granny lives out there. I ain't funnin' you."

Newbie snickers. "That's halfway round your hind end to bumfuck. And now I ain't got no job. You got to give me gas money."

"I ain't got much."

"Well you better. And, old Rabbit's dead," Newbie finishes with sudden wonder.

"Who?"

"The old man died. My old boss at The Dixiana."

"What happened?"

"Them old witches in the ELMS done something to him. It's what I heard."

"*Witches?*"

Newbie's like, naw, naw. "You know what I mean."

Christy does not, in fact, know what Newbie means. "My daddy's dead, too," he says in a blurt.

"He is?"

"Yeah, bruh. He's laying there right now. Dead."

"Aw." Newbie looks like he's gonna cry. "You ain't got to cough up no gas money. I sure am sorry, beau."

"For real?"

"Fuck it. It's like my daddy died too, now that Mr. Rabbit's gone." Newbie sucks snot and spits out the window, merging off the bypass onto the county road heading toward Red Mound. "Where's your'n laid out? Funeral home?"

More compelling to Christy than all this sudden sadness is Newbie's mysterious reaction from earlier about the address. "What you think's out there near my grandmama's house?"

"You must not have lived here long. If you don't know."

Christy says, he's lived here all his life.

"Pussy, beau," Newbie confides. "That's where you can get you some pussy. And I just might, one day. Maybe today—I deserve something nice."

He don't know why? But Christy, his stomach, it has filled up with cold ice.

"I ain't gonna have no more money soon. No matter what. Be worth it for some of that tail, though. I heard all kinda stories about what them girls will do. Course—it don't seem right, somehow."

Newbie, signaling and going to pass a logging truck and having to cut back over close to keep from going head-on into another car flashing its lights like crazy. The truck driver blows his horn, shaking his fist and which Newbie ignores, all going by in a blur.

"Your Daddy—what happened to him?"

Christy, panicked again. "He died, and didn't wake up."

"Was he sick?"

"Yes," and this seems like a true answer. His panic, subsiding. "Drugs."

"Dang." Newbie chewed his lip. "Sorry."

"Thanks. Thank you."

Newbie goes all twitchy. "You ain't got no Spice or K2, do ya?"

Christy, shaking his head. "Ain't that drugs?"

"Naw, that's the legal stuff. I wish these arabs would start selling it."

"Drugs is drugs."

"But like—what funeral home's your Daddy at? Karlaney?"

Christy, gulping. He might ought to tell Newbie what's what. But Grandmama's first. Figure out if Newbie's the right person to ask for help. Time, now short.

⚙⚙⚙

BUT THE THING with his Daddy, it's like this: one time Christy, he had gone with this Grandmama to put down a dog, one that had got a big growth on its neck, which she told Christy was cancer like people got sometimes, as if God were mad at them.

"In the old days, we'd take and shoot a dog like this," she said. "But we not mean and hard like them Macon boys," who were dogfighters up in the northeast corner of the county, near Parsons Hollow. "We humane. We got given the choice by God to be humane."

And that's how Christy behaved when it came to his Daddy, who before being put down was gonna end up one of two places: jail, or the hospital. Christy had done him a favor. No suffering. No more needing to get the five thousand dollars.

Maybe he would do Newbie Harrell a favor too if he wanted more gas money than Christy ought to pay—that might mean Newbie was on drugs. That wouldn't be fair to Christy in the least. He didn't get this whole pussy thing, which Christy didn't understand all that well to begin with, but he sure didn't see what the connection could be in his Grandmama's house, her house and the rooming house.

The girls.

Wait—Newbie's talking about the girls!

Now Christy goes, now he goes, I know why I kept thinking I might have to do to Newbie what I done to Daddy. Not to help him—to protect Grandmama's girls.

"Now I get it," Christy says aloud, before he could catch himself from doing so, which happened sometimes and embarrassed him, like now. "The girls."

"Get what? You want to get you some pussy?"

Christy, a lump, not believing this. He doesn't say yea, nay, or boo.

"Well if you do? You better have more than gas money on you. Real folding money. Or a credit card. I heard they take cards now too."

Newbie, merging onto Pisgette Forest Highway, the lonely two lane that went through Red Mound and the national forest all the way to the other north-south interstate over in the next county, but before that a road where you turned off to go to Grandmama Beaudock's place, set way back in the woods.

Christy never understood why she wanted to be back in yonder, but now he did: to protect them girls. To protect them from men. Men like Newbie.

Christy felt warm inside. God, showing him purpose. Day by day.

⊙⊛⊙

"So you really don't know where you are, Christopher?"

"Nuh-uh."

"Didn't you say your name was Beaudock?"

Christy nodded and insisted he did know, but it wasn't nothing but his grandmama's house. "This ain't 'Mama Beaudock's'. Whatever that is."

"The hell it ain't, beau."

"I can't figure out what you keep getting at," which was so many words it made Christy wheeze. The longer he took to say what he had to say, the less breath he could muster. "It ain't nothing but my grandmama's. And her boarding house."

"Boarding house? I reckon you could call it that. For people wanting to board up for fifteen minutes at a time." And that made him excited, going haw-haw and slapping his knee. "I been wanting to come out here all my life. I'm gonna do it, Christopher. This day don't feel so bad now. If I hadn't been driving around mad, I wouldn't've needed to get gas, or give you a ride, and or come here at all. I wouldn't've come today no more'n the man in the moon, Christopher. You brung me out here. To get me some pussy. I ain't never—I mean, I ain't had me no pussy since high school. I used to get it all the time back then. I was almost on the football team. You on the football team?"

Christy whined he didn't know what all this pussy talk was, but he couldn't hide no more. Couldn't hide from the fact that what his daddy had always said must be true. The cars parked around behind the dormitory house, as his granny always called it, were always different every time Christy had come here through the years, but he always figured his grandmama liked to change cars a lot.

As Newbie pulled in behind the house where people were always supposed to park, Christy gazed at the older farm house back behind the newer one. "I still think you talking about somewheres else."

"Well, you see your grandmama, and I'll go in here, and we'll meet back up and find out who was right. Deal?"

Newbie held out his hand. Christy reached over with his left hand to shake.

"Don't do it like that—somebody'll think we're faggots. If you don't shake right, there ain't no deal."

Ears still burning from Newbie's F-word, Christy shakes right and they part.

Winded and trudging, Christy, making his way down the gray concrete of the circular driveway to the main house and his grandmama's front porch, and the house dogs bark and Christy stands a-knocking for a long time before a man he's never seen answers the door.

TRUDY AND SAMSON

On the way home from getting reamed out and fired by Roy Earl Pettus, that son of a biscuit eater who, before he'd opened his smart mouth, she'd wanted to screw again—screw long and hard like back when they'd been kids—Trudy instead cussed him with such grief she about run off the river highway and wrecked her Taurus.

It happened right as she passed by the bar that represented the other pole of her existence, Ape Hangers, though she still thought of it as Fast Traxx. The biker bar. Where her husband had lived half his life. What a topper on the day —wrecking the car. Now that would've been her luck.

Maybe it wouldn't have been an accident. The way she'd been feeling.

Through misty vision she whipped into the dirt of the driveway in the woods to the house, a durn rotting old hellhole she lived in back here with Mickey Samuelson. She ain't had crap, Trudy. Not before, and not now.

Except for the honkytonk.

And what does that little stuck-up shit Roy Earl do? His granddaddy dies and then the little prince shows up waving a will, and takes it all away.

Took her job from her like it wasn't nothing.

Like she didn't mean nothing to him.

It couldn't be. Had to have meaning, after what they shared.

Thirty years ago.

She was the one giving the past meaning. Not him. Not with his money and pretty wife down on the island. Trudy, about as full of horseshit as they came.

Worse, as she sat stubbing out her cigarette in the filthy ashtray and checking her eyes to see how red they looked, Trudy knew she couldn't say nothing to Samson about the old-lovers part of today's drama, the history with Roy Earl that ought to've made a difference. She planned to keep all this to herself. Her husband, a jealous one, even about old boyfriends. One time he broke two of his own knuckles beating on one of her old BFs who got out of line at the bar. When pressed, Samson could still live up to his name.

⊙❀⊙

YEAH, she still thought of her husband by that nickname, as did everyone from what he called the old crew of proud, marauding Pagan Knights of Edgewater County. Trudy'd come along in his life long after those days of wild-ass riding on them choppers.

Samson—Mickey—fifteen years older than her, on social security. And her only in her early 50s. Didn't feel near as old as the way he done started acting.

At their height in the early '70s, brothers of the Pagan Knights biker club owned the two-lane blacktops all over the South Carolina midlands, but especially in Edgewater County. Tension came from encounters at rallies with members of Trinity, based in Camden and rivals by dint of proximity, and the Scarabs, out of North Carolina and threatened less by geography than the size of the PK tribe. Mickey cherished his big scrapbooks full of pictures of the custom bikes he worked on with his brother Rusty, an airbrush virtuoso who painted and finished teardrop tanks while his older brother handled the engines and the mechanics. The two of them customized them motherfucking hogs better than anyone in the county, or in Richland and Lexington Counties, for that matter.

To her eyes and ears, these days Mickey spent too much time still thinking about himself as Samson the Pagan Knight. Weepy and regretful. Filled with confessions about shit he pulled back in the day. And allusions to much worse, which creeped her out. Like beating people to death type stuff.

Facing it: Her hubby had turned into a creep in so many ways.

When he wasn't piss-drunk and crying, it was piss-angry, and sitting there smelling bad and with a black cloud all around him, an aura that Trudy swore she could half-see, not to sound like some hippy idiot like Button Sykes.

Samson always said he was always afraid of getting to where he couldn't ride, and with his lower back problems, that happened. Afterwards, about 1990, he come into Trudy' beloved honkytonk and scooped her up and carried her off to his house back in the woods—right here—and done her hard and long with that big pecker of his, and later that year made her his wife: the redneck trailer park biker trophy wife, leggy and blonde and ready to party. That's what Trudy Pirkle was to Mickey Samuelson.

"I always liked you Pirkle girls, with your blue eyes and them long old bodies," he told her on their wedding night in Myrtle Beach. They checked into in a fancy, fresh and modern condo set way up high, right there on the beach. Looking down from the balcony, she thought she could almost jump out into that green deep Atlantic Ocean.

How he made love to her so tender that night, the sliding door open and the sound of the wind and the surf whispering outside. Married. At last.

"I feel like I hit the jackpot," he whispered in her right ear as they lay together, still connected and damp in the aftermath of an explosive union, like nobody and nothing she'd ever had or felt. "My precious angel. "

"Stay inside me. Stay hard in me, Samson." And he had, moving on through another orgasm for both.

They'd gotten drunk, partying with some crank and a box of whippits, and sucked and fucked until both sore; she didn't half remember the rest of the weekend. A blur of beer and shots and smoking and loving and fucking, afterwards him laid out snoring like a gut-stuck hog.

What she complaining about? She still had all that shit. Well—not the loving and fucking part. But that wasn't supposed to stay, anyway.

Was it?

Samson, the old biker weaving tales about riding up to North Carolina and communing with other clubs. Raising hell and getting drunk and riding them hogs on mountain roads like it wasn't nothing to be hauling ass and laughing your way around those curves, and no Pagan Knight never ever had a wreck 'cause bikers were different, and lord but Trudy knew it was only looking back with rose-colored lenses.

Rusty Samuelson told her how many bad drugs there were, how many fights, the wrecks people had survived and the ones folks hadn't, too. Legs on the asphalt one time when this dude hit a concrete median and sent his girl flying across in front of a bus full of old people going to ride the Tweetsie Railroad. Legs on the road, he said, laughing. The girl died, he said, so she didn't suffer from not having them.

"Yeah, it was all fun and games, them days," as Rusty said, smoking and sitting in his truck. It was back around 2000 when they was sneaking around, which was awful and wonderful and awful again, and what did anyone want? Let anyone keen to judge try walking a mile in her boots. Like she heard someone say in a movie, a husband caught by his wife, 'it just happened.' Rusty was kind to her during a time when his brother wasn't, and so it happened. A bunch of times. For like, a year or more. Until Samson's brother had said, damn, we got to quit this mess; "I feel guilty."

And then she had, too. Awful, like she wanted to go back and jump off the balcony at her tall Myrtle Beach honeymoon hotel. Or else get throwed off the back of Samson's hog, have her legs split open on the road rather than laying sprawled in her brother-in-law's bed, him pumping away at her with a high, whining sound from deep inside his nose like a little kid worried about being caught doing something wrong. Which it was.

Karma. Like she feared back when she fucked her boss's grandson.

Samson didn't ride no more, even if his fat ass wanted to—he couldn't hardly get out of his chair no more, but when he did, he still stood half a head taller than her. Could still half kill her, if he wanted to.

He hadn't hit her in ten years now, not since the time she said, "If it happens again, I'm-a gonna leave your fat ass back in here," and he cried, cried like a baby—but it wasn't like he didn't do that anyhow when he was drunk. Squirted and begged like poor little Roy Earl did when she had told him, "No, angel. We can't do it no more. Mr. Rabbit—your Pa-paw, as you call him— he'll cut our asses. He'll fire me."

And now, after decades, Roy Earl finally made this terrible notion come true. Her worst fear, then or now.

She thought she was losing her mind. Now who couldn't stop crying, and who cracked open one of Mickey's tallboys, which made him holler, was that a beer for him he heard her opening?

Why put it off?

She took a slug, belched, and went to tell her husband what happened.

⊛⊛⊚

SHE SHOULDN'T NEVER HAVE SAID nothing. Oh, mercy. Lord, at the hollering and cussing.

"Mickey, calm down. You gonna have a thrombo."

"I'm-a gonna go shove his goddamn head down one of them shit toilets in that goddurn firetrap piece of shit honkytonk. Not worth a shit, son of a bitch Reynolds Pettus."

"Hush up, now. Rabbit didn't do nothing to us but be good."

Deaf with rage. "I'm gonna get my gun, Trudy. I'm gonna go and get my granddaddy's shotgun, load that motherscratcher and take it over and put a hole in that buttermilk-sucking, fat little bitch-ass motherfuckering Roy Earl. Show him he can't walk in there and fire you, not after all you done for them bastards—"

He twisted around like he meant for real to get a gun, but regretted it. Yelling at the pain, cursing his swollen foot. Trudy could only watch in horror as Samson hobbled down the cramped hallway of the old house, which had been his daddy's house, a ramshackle construction with additions built on it every which way and set back in the sandy woods off Highway 231, sand in which you would sometimes find seashells because durn if the ocean wasn't once all the way up here in Edgewater County, somehow. Every room and nook and cranny stacked with junk that'd accumulated across several generations of Samuelson men and their hobbies, she hated the house more with each passing decade.

Why not let Samson go and kill Roy Earl? *That a-hole done ruined my life.*

Yeah—Roy Earl ruined her life. Not by firing her. By not coming back for her after he got rich.

Shit. She was the one who had said "no" to him. But then, at the time he'd only been sixteen, and her a grown woman of twenty-one. These days? They'd put you in jail for what she done.

But all she said to her husband: "You ain't going nowhere. Not with that foot of your'n."

Like a specter of his former bad-ass self, Mickey sunk back into his own funk and down into his chair. He kept on cussing, but most of the fire had gone.

ABOUT THAT LIFE OF HERS, living stuck out in these haunted redneck woods, where old people said all manner of mess had gone on back in colonial times—witchcraft, weirdness, wickedness: Drinking three, three and a half cases a week of tallboys and a couple of bottles of Jack Daniels, smoking a carton of expensive-ass Marlboros; wanted hamburgers and fried steak or chicken every night, wouldn't budge on none of it. Ate and smoked and shit so much there wasn't no way she could keep up. Worked so much at The Dixiana, six nights a week, still, but still expected to cook and clean house, and damn if she didn't care what happened from here.

Roy Earl and Mickey would kill each other, for all she knew.

Maybe they'd all get Ebola and shit themselves bloody.

Maybe that son of a gun President Obola would make the world blow up. Michael Savage said on the radio every day that the boy-king wasn't worth a toot. Couldn't be trusted. That Pooty-Poot in Russia was laughing at us all.

Lord—when was this country gonna get a durn president to believe in again? She swore the more she considered it, not even Reagan with all that Iran-Contra mess. Not since JFK.

She fell across her stinky bed in the spare bedroom where she slept because of her husband's heinous sleep apnea, so bad she went online and googled Severe Snoring, and after which she knew he would one day wake up dead, and he'd be free of his heavy body and ailments.

Or rather: she'd be free. The thought of which made her feel guilty to beat the band.

After she wrestled him back in his chair and five or six beers down the hatch and tuned the DVR to last Sunday's NASCAR race, which he had not seen because he got up that day and started in on a bottle of Jack Daniels and passed out by lunchtime, she relaxed. Without the honkytonk to get open and running, she had the rest of the day to herself. When was the last time Trudy Pickle could say that?

She sat on the couch across from him. A flea jumped on her leg. She caught it, pinched it to death between her long, chipped fingernails she had been planning to work on at the bar the afternoon her sweet Mr. Rabbit passed away. "Don't do nothing, honey. We gonna be all right. Roy Earl don't know what he's saying. He's tore up over Rabbit. Over his granddaddy dying."

"I'm gonna whup his ass anyway."

"You ain't doing it tonight. Let's drink beer together. Party, and look at the race. C'mon, sugar."

"Still gonna beat his ass," he'd say now and then. Belching. Killing only his tallboys rather than rich Roy Earl.

She didn't really want anything bad to happen to Roy Earl. After screwing him back when he was a kid when she was a dumbass who ought to've known better, which she only done because she was drunk, she'd made the crucial mistake of feeling a spark there with that young'un. A baby-face, one she was only trying to show how he could make some other girl happy. Bad judgement all around.

But damn if she didn't get butterflies at thinking about doing it with him again. He seemed so smart, Rabbit's grandson. A pissant all full of himself. But successful and confident and handsome as hell. Look at what he went and done. Burnie Sykes said Roy Earl sold his company, the chain of smoothie stands, for a million dollars.

Trudy, admitting to herself that she stood there in that damn Dixiana for the last thirty-two years, and she'd be shit if two or three times a week, like clockwork, she'd remember the night she kissed Roy Earl, and screwed him and screwed him some more, coming with him hard, and loving him and his deep brown eyes, and she would catch herself drifting, fantasizing, looking right through Burnie's bald head nodding over his half-full mug. Saying to herself, what-if, what-if.

Maybe she and Roy would have owned The Dixiana together. And Rabbit would've retired and still be alive instead of keeling over in the street.

Damn that Roy Earl. Why hadn't he come back and gotten her!

As the years went on, she had grown so bitter, particularly when Rabbit would come in shaking his head and saying, that boy done opened another one of them Spotted Banana™ Fruitshake joints of his. "This time down in Savannah," or wherever. "He's gonna make him a mint. Boy, I musta done something right."

"You must've."

Faraway. And rueful, too: "My grandbaby's a good boy. Yes, he is."

Come back and get me, Roy Earl Pettus, as she prayed so often. Had sent the thoughts out to him. Only silence, and the turning of calendar pages, in return.

She knew it was stupid. Couldn't recall the last time she wished for him to come and get her. Probably after he got married to that stuck-up Rucker bitch.

Her brother Devin, a frequent presence at The Dixiana for a time, had been handsome like Roy Earl. She never knew what happened to Devin Rucker, though. A drunk, if memory served.

❁❖❁

MICKEY—THE mighty Samson—lay grinding his teeth and snoring in his chair, and so she put on *The Walking Dead* instead of the end of the race. Mickey, letting one of them awful old beer farts there in his sleep. He didn't know he was doing it, bless his heart. She lit a scented candle, patchouli rose, she bought over at the hippie shop in Columbia. It calmed her down.

His bad toenail was what she worried about, a thick one that had started running with pus. She would unwrap it in the morning and rinse it off again with peroxide. He couldn't hardly walk no more, what with the toe and his bad knees—they sounded like popcorn popping when he would stoop or try to squat or sit. She wanted to get some weight off him. He couldn't do it with a hurt toe and them knees of his, but one day soon, she needed to start him walking. The driveway was a quarter-mile off the road. He could go up to the highway and back a few times a day, and she bet the weight would come right off. When his toe was better.

Trudy, she hadn't never had an ounce of fat on her. Too skinny. Men liked meat on the bones. Not too much, but some. More than a lanky Pirkle girl from over in Red Mound. And yet, Mickey Samuelson loved her bony butt, though. Didn't he.

❁❖❁

TRUDY, leaving him in his chair to go to look through her old high school annuals, at the signatures of boyfriends and guys who'd had crushes on her long-legged Pirkle ass. She didn't cry or anything dramatic like that. You didn't cry over all such mess, not from that long ago, not in your 50s. That's what she'd learned. She wished she had realized about growing old back when she shacked up with Samson, so much older than her and married once before and with a kid by that one, and another'n had showed up one Thanksgiving saying, I believe you might remember my mama, sir.

Oh, mercy. If she had married Roy Earl, he would still be younger than her.

Still.

Trudy cussed and lit a cigarette and went to sit on the sagging porch, pine straw hanging off the tin roof. Crossing her legs, she slapped her flip-flop against a rough sole, rhythmic. Smoking and finally letting tears sneak out, hot and silent and tracking down her cheeks to drip onto the weathered wood, she hummed a Garth Brooks song popular back when Roy Earl was still a boy. Pretending she wasn't crying.

Moths, fluttering around the yellow light covered in cobwebs and with brittle brown oak leaves trapped inside the cracked, frosted glass alongside a few flies. Cicadas buzzed—still summer, it was hot today. Fall weather couldn't get here fast enough.

In a flash, she knew what to do. Soon, she would go and tell Samson everything—how she wasn't happy. That she loved somebody else even if she didn't know who, and as soon as his toe was better and his knees were right again, she'd go and be with that person. If he hit her, he'd hit her. With his bad toe, though, she could run. Run down the sandy driveway. Not look back.

Sighing and smoking, she figured it sounded like a plan. Enough of one for tonight, anyway.

GOOCH AND MAYOR HILL HAMPTON

After leaving the Nixon press conference, Gooch forgot to go to the office and work on the Pettus obit page. Instead, he took a notion and wandered around for a spell in rapt consideration of the dance of the sunlight dappling onto the gray sidewalks through the sheltering, gnarled limbs of elms and oaks, some as old as the town itself.

Older.

The trees, they seemed alive. Maybe because they were.

A peregrination, one that ended back at his car parked behind the row of storefronts that included the paper, the back alley with the dumpster and the slime on the asphalt from the hair chemicals at the salon. Tired, he didn't feel like going to his desk and writing up the story. Whatever it was.

Home. He ambled in and fixed a pimento cheese sandwich, turned on the History Channel, fell asleep on the couch with his gold-toe socks pointed heavenward.

About midnight he woke up with a start, confused at the time—early, sure, but since when was it too early to get down to the paper and begin news-gathering?

He showered, slipping on the tiles but not falling. Got dressed, prepared a scrambled egg and toast with a smear of peanut butter and fig preserves Letty Glasscock gave him last year for Christmas. As was his custom, he switched on HLN and observed the scroll and tried to listen and watch the anchor's face and lips, and then the footage cut in with A- and B-roll, and all terribly confusing, especially as it seemed the same as the news cycle he'd seen earlier, and worse, the time of day, or night, made little sense. Frames within frames, all moving. Tickers of information. His eyes didn't know where to settle, except on the news anchor's shining eyes and moving lips. Ebola, a big problem in the world. If the virus finally made it to Edgewater County from Dallas by way of Africa, Gooch would give a rip.

Flipping over to a documentary about the Korean War. The conflict had been going on since forever, or wait, hadn't it ended not so long ago? Had it? Maybe it'd been *M*A*S*H* being on TV for ages that confused him.

He flipped through the channel menu to FX, and there it was—*M*A*S*H*. Korea. The operating theater. The camp compound. The blood. The mud. The wisecracks.

Was the show still running? But how? Alan Alda must be eighty by now.

Unless it was still 1973.

How ridiculous. The war had not only never been declared, but never ended, either, and not only on some TV sitcom. A police action. A two-hundred episode, sixty year-long police action. These facts made for mind murk.

In reality, all the excitement occurred during three little old years. Gooch, a toddler then, remembered his parents talking about it better than what he had for lunch yesterday. In fact, such memories seemed like yesterday. As did watching *M*A*S*H* on Saturday nights with his mother, waiting for Carol Burnett.

He glanced at his Blackberry and saw it was 1am, but somehow his mind read this as 5am, and he said, *well the sun will be up soon, and old Dobbs will wheel in and see me banging out copy and think, maybe that Gooch Wimmel isn't so dried up and useless and ready to be put out to pasture.*

☉✳◎

Halfway to downtown, however, the old newspaperman realized he'd forgotten a crucial ablution. His bladder, aching—for how long?

Since the last time he noticed the pain.

Confused and desperate, he put the sedan in park; decided to get out in the middle of the street, which lay still and dark. The night—or morning, rather, any moment now—fell silent across Whaley Way, the grand old neighborhood adjacent to Common Street, the houses through which Gooch passed every day to work. Thick hedges would conceal his potty break here in the neighborhood of the local gentry; the old money, plus newcomers like the CFO of a mega-millions software company in Charlotte, who, being able to afford a driver, commuted to work from his restored antebellum mansion, Henley House, on the national register of historic places. Must be nice to have a driver, Gooch thought. Not his station in life. He unzipped his fly.

His home and station, fine enough—two-story, a good house for a family, one that'd never come. Not possible, but back then, you couldn't tell people the truth. Kids today had no idea. Nor did Dobbs. Son of a bitch went out on dates. With men. Openly. Not in Tillman Falls, but over in Columbia. A queer cripple living his life, getting to go out on dates with attractive young men. Scandalous. If Gooch had still been able to masturbate, he'd have done so thinking about Dobbs and his precious dates.

If not thinking about Dobbs himself.

But you couldn't talk about this stuff.

Feeling warmth, he glanced down to see urine squirting out of his penis in two directions, one of which ran down the leg of his khakis like a blood stain, as though he wore the fatigues of a foot soldier wounded in the groin or leg, a bleeder; triage, call Hawkeye and B. J. and Trapper and the rest. Gooch, unable to cease the flow of his urine—when he tried, it hurt. Like pissing razors. He did a mad little dance around in a circle, spraying like a horny tomcat.

Lights came on across the way, in Hill Hampton's ostentatious home, which sat surrounded by landscape lighting, a circular drive and a gurgling fountain topped by a welcoming pineapple sculpture.

Built to reflect a smaller version of the Henry Franklin Hendrix House, which Hill had seen as a boy on a trip with his daddy to a car auction over yonder near Batesburg-Leesville. Constructed in 1888 in the classical revival style, the actual Hendrix House featured a front-facing grand portico entrance, a dome, columns, red bricks and brilliant white trim. Hampton's version included a modern garage hidden away in the back, but you can bet the portico always sported whatever brand new model Hill was driving around at the time—the cars, an element of the design at least as crucial to the aesthetic as the general splendor of the home.

The mayor's dark silhouette, round of belly, appeared in a glowing upstairs window. "What's going on out yonder? Huh? Say."

Gooch waved while allowing his evacuation to complete. The pain now replaced by contentment, bliss, and a soaked left pants leg, he forgot to zip up as he saluted and climbed back into the car. Once the zipper's exposed teeth dragged across his scrotum and the underside of his shriveled little dick, however, he yowled in pain.

Fumbled at it, tore more tender flesh.

At last getting his privates free, Gooch gasped for air and lolled his head sideways and whimpered. He cupped his genitals; a flare of white-hot pain. Wetness.

Blood.

His call for help, a high, weak wisp of an old man's voice. "It's me, Mr. Mayor."

"Me who? I ain't got my eyes in. Looks like a late-model Civic." Hampton, the town's principal car dealer as well as current administrator, in his third term, a well-liked, seasoned campaigner not up for re-election this cycle. He used a personal mnemonic device for recognizing constituents: by the make and model they drove, as well from whom they had purchased or leased the vehicle. "What year?"

Gooch tried to remember his own name. "It's me—from the paper."

"*Wimmel?*"

The pain flared. "Yes-s-s," he hissed.

Bellowing across the lawn, the Mayor caused yellow light to blaze in other windows. "You got a story breaking here on Francis Marion Street? Now?"

"Just on my way into work?" Why it came out a question, he hadn't a clue. "Had to stop and—?"

Wait. He had been pissing in the street. He couldn't yell that.

Gooch moved to climb out, and the zipper bit again. Hard. He shrieked anew, clutched himself, collapsed back into the coffee-stained cloth driver's seat.

"If it ain't one thing, it's another'n." Hampton slammed shut the window.

The Mayor, billowing and robed, came marching across the dewy lawn in a hurried version of his rolling, side-to-side gate everyone knew from car shopping at Hampton Motors, which, back in the autumn of 2001 and after thirty-nine years in business, had been re-christened Hampton American Motors. "You staking me out? Ain't no story to break. If there was, I'd—oh, Bill. You're covered in blood."

"Nonsense. I needed to—stop and check tire pressure."

Hampton's tone softened. "Son: your tallywacker's bleeding."

"Oh, yes—it hurts quite a bit down there." His voice broke. "I'd forgotten."

The Mayor howled into the Edgewater County night. "One of you sons of guns watching us go and call nine-one-one—!"

✸❋✸

Woozy and lying prone in an emergency room stall, Gooch, listening to the Mayor shoot the shit with the duty doctor, young beyond measure. From the sound of it, the kid's first job had been working Hampton Motors wash rack one summer twenty years in the past.

Hill, apologizing for not remembering the boy. Laughter. Warmth. Golden memories of the early 90s.

"Mr. Mayor." Gooch, weak and thick of tongue. "A word, please."

"S'cuse me." the Mayor dismissed the doc, who went to see if Mr. Wimmel's test results were back. All the blood in the urine had prompted the physician to call for a late-night CT scan.

Yes: Gooch had heard the doctor saying the blood on his trousers wasn't from the zipper wound, painful, but minor. The doc said the pants-blood had come from the urine.

And Gooch said, oh that's right. "My pee, it's been like that. And hurting. Whenever I urinate."

"Why haven't you seen a urologist?"

"Keep forgetting."

"About the pink urine?"

"About all of it."

"I see."

Gooch shrugged. "It's a busy life keeping a newspaper running."

"Let's look into this blood. Try to relax."

And wouldn't it be perfect, Gooch pondered, that if he had cancer or other disease, it had to be an issue with his manhood, his useless old noodle nobody ever touched.

He rarely touched it himself, not after his mother walked in on him one time. He had been standing fresh out of a lukewarm bath and in front of the fan—nobody now knew how hot it could get in those days, those muggy summer nights—and the cool breeze caressed his tight scrotum and damp penis like tickling feathers, and a sudden swelling had occurred in a manner profound and glorious.

And she'd popped right in, hollering in shock and giving him that melodramatic horror-struck look of hers, the disappointed gaze that burned so. She'd floated over with a slow, malevolent head shake and red demon-eyes and slapped him hard, twice—across the face, and down there, too.

Had grabbed hold, in fact. She said, "Boy, don't you start messing with your body." His mother, a drunk and a smoker, had breathed through her sour mouth and squeezed on his dick till it hurt, and Gooch had screamed.

"Hush up," she said in releasing him. "You ain't nothing but a baby, still." He'd been twelve. "Leave it alone."

Other than the spell spent living in Atlanta, a few years, he would stay with her most of the next fifty-two autumns, never once masturbating in the house. Only down at the paper, or in public restrooms. When she died in her sleep two years ago, he danced a jig across the kitchen floor.

Gooch thought about the locked drawer in the old desk at the office. All the pornography, some of it he'd risked his freedom to get, back when being caught obtaining such material—men getting with men, the love that dare not speak its name—could come with legal ramifications. He couldn't help but still think this way. His, a public persona. He should clean out the stash of obscene paraphernalia. While he still remembered it existed.

❊❖❊

BUT MORE CRUCIALLY, Gooch, a newspaperman, had been hurrying into work—

it must be lunchtime now, and panic flooded in—to submit the information about Rabbit Pettus's memorial at the bluff.

What had been the crux, this information? A blank spot.

Not now, Gooch pled with himself. Tears, sneaking out of his eyes. Damn this hole in his mind. Damn it all to hell. Where was his notebook? He'd written the facts down.

No—Roy Earl had not allowed him to take notes. He'd have to remember.

How?

"What is it, old buddy?" The Mayor, trying to smile but stifling a yawn. "Figured you had nodded off."

"Hill—you need to help me."

"Again? Mercy. I know I got elected to serve, but—"

"What time is it?"

The Mayor checked his Galaxy. Squinting and wrinkling his nose, he swiped his finger around. "Five-thirty."

"Oh." Gooch, throwing his bare arm across his face, the paper ER gown flapping open under his arm. "It's too late. It's too late."

"Bubba, the sun ain't even up yet."

Confused, more so than ever. "I needed to get the notice into the paper for tomorrow. About Reynolds's—his funeral."

"Well, I can call Dobbs for you. That what you mean?"

"Yes, but—" He tried to quell the anxiety about missing a deadline. The pain in his side and bladder subsided. He calmed himself. Hill Hampton, concerned, put his beefy freckled paw on Gooch's leg, squeezed, then yanked it away as though fearing he'd hurt him, which he hadn't, leaving only a heat signature that felt like a miniature pulse down there. His dream for eons had been for a man to touch his thigh.

Not here.

Not him.

"I can't remember."

"You got to quit worrying about it for a minute—"

"—that's what I was trying to do—"

"—and start thinking about something else."

"Like what? Cutting off your own damn penis with a rusty zipper?"

Hampton snorted. "No. Forget that. Let's talk about politics. What's all this mess about Reverend Nixon wanting to change the name of my beloved Tillman Falls?"

Gooch, trying not to think, but thinking anyway. "Tillman's a controversial figure."

"Among the blacks."

Gooch shook his head. "Nixon's support, it's solid throughout the county on this. All demographics."

"Bill: you got polling already? From where?"

Gooch shrugged. Held close his cards.

And then caved. "No. Of course not. It was only yesterday. A feeling, though."

"Hard to imagine him having the votes. Let's let him get elected to council first. Then we'll get to work squelching that mess."

"I have bigger problems, anyway. I've got to deal with the Rabbit Pettus service."

"When is it supposed to be?"

Gooch, searching his mind. If the Nixon press conference had been a million millennia ago, the visit to the Pettus house and the conversation about the memorial closer to the big bang than his recent ride in the ambulance to the ER. He couldn't remember what Roy Earl said, like a scene cut from the movie of his mind and life. He couldn't grab hold. He saw the Reverend Nixon behind the podium, heard Burnham Sykes, could see the crowd, could feel the sun on his head; saw Roy Earl Pettus's face, standing on the porch at the Pettus's ostentatious modern house out on River Ridge Road. Could see the heir to The Dixiana legacy's lips moving—

Today. The word popped in. "Oh, lord, it's today. Rabbit's memorial is later today. They're scattering the ashes at the bluff down near Pike's."

One last detail. Searching.

A monitoring device. A glowing red number.

Eleven.

"That's it, today at eleven. The red clay bluff. The fishing spot."

Hampton seemed affected by this. "That Roy Earl. This's his idea, ain't it."

Gooch hadn't a clue. All the rest, slipping away, and wondering, in fact, why the scruff of skin below his penis felt as though he had a knot there. Where his pants and notebook were hiding. "I suppose it probably was. Him and his Daddy used to fish there all the time."

"You mean, Rabbit and Ronnie Ed used to."

Gooch, nodding, but not understanding to whom 'Ronnie Ed' referred. He'd better go over that obit some more.

"That boy loved his Pa-paw." Hampton's voice broke, and he sucked wind trying not to sob. "Didn't he."

"Anyway—Hill, I know it's not part of your normal duties, but you've got to propagate this news for me."

The Mayor snapped out of his grief reverie and into action mode. "We live to serve. I'm sending your boy at the paper a text right now to get the info up on the website, and I'll spread the word through my myriad channels of influence; I have the bully pulpit after all. Relax, buddy. They got you stitched up. You gonna be fine." Hampton paused. "Where's everybody gonna park?"

Gooch said, "Damned if I know. That's a soft shoulder along there down to that bluff."

"I know it. I know it." Hampton nodded. "Let me get Oakley on the horn. We'll get a few of his cruisers to act as shuttles, carry people down the dirt road. We can park vehicles in the empty field next to Pike's. Should be hard-packed instead of muddy, since we ain't had poop for rain lately."

"Why not use the prisoner van? It's a nine-seater, I believe."

"Shoot yeah. Good thinking, Gooch. You get better now."

"Feeling much better already."

"Super."

Gooch noted the Mayor's eyes betrayed a different emotion, but since this became forgotten within only a moment, it didn't matter. He lay back and let his mind meander through all manner of memories, until drifting off into a sleep that felt cold and dreamless and in which his bladder kept stinging him; he'd look down and see an enormous thistle or bramble sticking into his groin and try to pull it out, but when he did, the pain only flared worse.

WHEN HE AWOKE, the doctor had come back in and was all smiles, reporting only a bladder and kidney infection. Severe enough, but nothing dreadful like cancer. An afternoon spent on a powerful antibiotic drip, and he could go. Lots of water, rest. Not the crisis he'd expected.

Only one problem. "Doc, a question—how'd I get here?"

ROY

I n Forest Knoll Garden.
    With Button Sykes.
    Smoking dope amidst the tombstones.
Whoa.

Well, ingesting marijuana, anyway—maybe that's a better term. She manipulates a Star Trek-esque device called the VapeMaster Mark IV-XX, a small rectangle the size of a pack of cigarettes with a stem sticking up.

Button describes the device. How it works.

In her.

Halting.

Pattern of.

Speech.

That is.

Driving you.

Nuts.

"Man. Look at this thoroughfare." You take in tree-shaded Common Street sloping upward and out of downtown toward Whaley Way. "You guys gotta get all these power lines buried. Looks nineteenth century, all these poles and wires and crap."

Button, a hooded glance of bemusement. Of pity—like you're a child, wandering along, oblivious and dumb. You're not sure anyone's ever looked at you like this. "Don't you realize? The real power lines are buried already."

"Are they, now."

"It's always. Been. That way."

This, some kinda metaphor. Way too heady for you.

"Idea," she says. "Let's take off our shoes. Stand on the grass for a minute."

"On this grass?" You scrunch up your little piggies. "No telling how many teenagers have taken late-night pisses out here."

Button, saying, she doubted it. "Forest Knoll. It's a place of reverence. Don't you think?"

Reluctant, you slip off your sport sandals, and she her Birkenstocks. The blades of green, cool beneath soles thick and calloused from working on your feet for years. Your vibration settles.

"It does feel good."

"It helps to ground yourself. Literally. To the dirt."

"Ah—always thought it was a metaphor."

"Lots of things are metaphors."

"Metaphors be with you."

A wry chuckle from Button. "Clever."

On the grassy strip alongside the gravel road, your stroll pauses at the unmissable, mini-gated Topsham gravesite, surrounded by its own separate shin-high wrought-iron fencing. One of the oldest plots, the Topsham site found itself home to generations of a family name that, far as you know, has more or less died out in the county—they were big landowners who had not prospered following the war, nor treated their people well on either side of the conflict. And had since scattered. The latest entrants, from the 1940s, included a tragic family with multiple infant deaths—four small markers, all in a line—a young war hero gone at nineteen, a mother dead young from grief, and birthing dead babies. And a patriarch, buried within a coffin-shaped brick enclosure that looked like a most substantial place in which to rest, or else to keep a particularly malignant bastard. Like the descendants wanted to make sure the asshole stayed buried.

Yeesh. Gooseflesh. Getting paranoid already?

Thoughtful. Imaginative. That's all.

Once the first gentle waves of the high lap on the shell-strewn sandy shore of your conscious mind, you understand why: this raspberry kush, or whatever she calls it, presents as potent. The effects, different from the old toking days, persist on as you walk around the tombstones with her. The vapor, gentle on your mind. Your lips play with one another, trying to form what you believe to be a smile. The Black Blade, hot as coal only moments before, seems to quiet and cool against your muscular thigh.

"We should go behind a tree—we're right here. In the open."

"So what? I take this. To the movies sometimes. Put it inside. A drink cup. The tip," displaying the small mouthpiece sticking up, like from a juice box, "looks like a straw. To anyone. Taking the attention. To notice."

"What about the smell?"

Button, so unusual of skin tone and hair—a dorky kid grown into an exotic beauty—shrugs. "I don't go. When it's crowded. Nobody to notice. In the middle of the day."

"Guess I feel self-conscious."

"Who's gonna tell on us? The dead?"

Can't help shooting glances all around. "I feel exposed."

"It's like the Jedi mind trick? Nobody would believe. Their lying eyes. That type-deal."

"Huh?"

"That we're getting ripped. Out here. In broad daylight."

"I gotcha. 'These aren't the marijuana smokers you're looking for'."

She offers a fist that you bump. "But what we're really doing?"

A snap of your fingers. "Hiding in plain sight."

"Yes, but also—?"

You wait.

"Creating our own reality. I don't think I'm doing anything wrong. So, I'm not."

"Damn straight. We're doing what we want. It's not wrong."

"Freaking plant that grows in the ground. No human may tell us. We can't use it. However we please."

You dig this line of thinking, this reality-creation—that's the way your own life has felt. Of your own making.

Until Creedence.

That's the real crisis here.

You've been expecting Rabbit's crusty old Edgewater County ass to croak for the better part of two decades. Creedence's infidelity? A shock, hard, to the gut. To the nuts. And nothing else feels like that.

But to Button you only say, "Yeah, well, try telling all that to Sheriff Oakley right around the corner."

"Garen? Ah. He's down. I'm pretty sure."

"A cop? Bullcrap."

Shrugging. "Said he'd support de-crim. He'll be glad. When it happens."

"Fascinating. Good to know. Quite a change from fat old Sheriff Truluck."

"No doubt."

On the stroll around the burial plots you reminisce about the few common memories you share, that of long summer Sunday afternoons when the Pettuses, the Sykeses, and the Glasscocks would gather and grill steaks or barbecue chicken and make homemade ice cream in churns the men would take turns cranking. Jasper, like you, without parents, and in his way using your grandparents as substitutes. Surprised they didn't get worn out.

And of course musicians dropped in and played—nobody famous, only the local pickers who gigged on the venerable Dixiana stage or on the now-unused back porch, and Mama Runelle would sometimes sing, and everyone would always stop what they were doing and listen, like a rare bird whose song you only got to hear occasionally.

You admire the poetic nature of your characterization; you remember getting high in college, trying to write poetry and stories: 'Clouds on the Ground,' a title that came one night when it was foggy; 'Where the High Country Begins' another title you'd come up with after a few bong rips, giggling and thinking yourself witty, neither poem ever completed to any sense of satisfaction by the would-be author.

As for the Sunday jam sessions, you couldn't grasp why anyone wanted to hear more of that music, not with it going on all the time at the god-durn honkytonk over in town.

"But I remember you so well, you and Thim—what a beauty she turned into."

"Hah. Everybody says that. About her."

You mention that while it may be true enough, by the time she, and Button herself, had both grown into attractive young women, you emphasize how those cookouts seemed to peter out.

"Yep. Those family gatherings. They kinda. Went away."

"I grew up; I developed other interests," to which she can but shrug. "And everybody else—they got old on me so fast."

"They already were, though. Right?"

"Mee-maw and Pa-paw? Mercy. That they were."

"I always felt for you. Once my dad explained. About your dad. And Vietnam. And then your mom, too."

"A sad situation. No doubt. All I can remember about my mom is the smell of her hair. And the feel of this nightgown I guess she wore when she held me. All silky. I remember falling asleep with my face against it. So, yeah. Poor me. At least I didn't get to know them and then lose them, right?"

"Guess so. But still, a type of grief."

You observe as Button regards the field of tombstones—so much denser than back in the day, when old Rabbit would have his pickings out there on the old loading dock. With the shingled overhang Rabbit had added, you could never imagine the era when rumbling old trucks, if not horses and buggies, came and went delivering vegetables and dry goods.

Time turns elastic.

Tingling, along your scalp.

Every one of your fuzzy, tennis ball hairs start to stretch and move around. To grow, micrometer by micrometer.

Being high skews the normal facade of familiarity called perception, and as you consider your hands, you inventory the various pieces-parts of the human body, along with those of your fellow beings: sacks of gristle and fluid with bulging glassy orbs for eyes, pliant epidermis covered in stiff bristling hair, gangly stick-like appendages, and a variety of damp, pulsing holes that, if not shielded or otherwise cared for, could be prone to suppuration. Animated meat skeletons dancing on a spinning rock hurtling through the void of space.

Regarding your own feet, you begin to consider the concept of shoes, then of feet themselves.

Feet.

Hands.

Appendages.

Orbs.

Hair.

Growing.

"You good?" she asks, flashing the vape. "One more?"

"Shit no," your voice sounding resonant inside your own head. The act of blurting makes your heart flutter and voice seem loud, far too irreverently so here in the sacred holding place of the meat vessels heretofore bearing the bottled souls and spirits of departed loved ones. "I'm wasted."

"Okie-doke." She toots another 'toke,' if that's the right nomenclature. Sighs out the wispy vapor. Smiles at you.

You're troubled—your father's grave, yes, it's nearby. You want to see it.

Of course you want to. Right?

To what purpose? By now, not even his body remained. Much less his spirit. Your head, it's literally buzzing with questions and concerns and fresh doubts.

Boiling it down: You should get the gravestone visit out of the way—check it off. Chip away at the list. See the marker, pay respects, then you can float around stoned and relaxed. Get caught up with your cousin. Forget all that Dixiana drama—the staff is over there cleaning it top to bottom, or else their asses better be.

What a burden.

The burdensome heat rises inside you again, but seems to stop somewhere in the center of your chest. The high, which has settled around your neck and shoulders, pushing the rage down. Whoosh. Emotions = managable.

"Let's pay those respects."

"I'm ready."

On the walk deeper into the cemetery: "Question: did your father tell you about Vietnam?"

"Oh yes," Button says, smiling with a bliss you covet. "In great detail."

"Really? Deets and everything?"

Nodding. "I journaled it all."

Envy; a swelling of disappointment like a stomachache. "I never could get old Rabbit to talk about dubya-dubya-two. Mee-maw said he had nightmares for years afterwards. So I reckon he didn't much want to."

"Well then. That's. The reason."

"Yeah, yeah, yeah," with impatience. "I get it."

"You know actual combat's much worse. Than it even seems. In the movies."

"I get it, I said."

"Okay."

A vibration carries down your leg—the Blade.

Oh, how you were cheated, swindled and burdened by life. Dead parents. Old grandparents to whom you could never relate. Your dream girl, turning out to be an alcoholic like her brother—and worse.

A tightness in your chest—maybe Rabbit's heart attack gene is manifesting in you, only forty years too soon. And having never smoked so much as a single cigarette. "It might've helped him to unload on me."

"Men like him. No. They didn't—don't—talk about the war. My granddad doesn't like to either. He was an aviator, an engineer."

"Good-looking. I've seen pictures."

"There were girls in ports. Hubba-hubba. Acted like that was the biggest deal about it all."

"The sanitized, kid-friendly version."

"The sitcom version. But with my dad? Not so. He told me lots. But then again, he wasn't infrantry—*infantry*," she corrects, shaking her head at the insertion of the extra R. She clears her throat a few times. Spits over across the wrought-iron fence onto the sidewalk of Common Street, near some of the older graves in Forest Knoll Garden, going all the way back to the late 1700s—Agatha of Aberdeen territory. "I could use. An iced tea."

"You and me both, sister. Or maybe an iced mocha." Your words crackle—cotton mouth. Your tummy rumbles. All the clichés.

And, you love it. The very notion of walking around out here high and carefree delights you. You feel better than you have in weeks/months/years.

"One thing old Rabbit didn't mind telling was the after-the-war part. Charleston, where he fell in love with his Runelle. And North Dakota where they farmed for a few years. Then back here, and not long afterward, opening that dump," hooking your thumb at the honkytonk. "But the war, never a peep."

"North Dakota? Never heard about that."

You tell her about how your granddad's best buddy in the army, a kid named Schulein who came from Swedish immigrant stock, had told him how awesome it was in the Midwest, where land could be leased and even bought pretty cheap, too; a place where one could live as a farmer, a king in one's own little world. In touch with nature, and all that hooey.

"Granddaddy grew up in the mountains, in the hollers there in West Virginia. Coal miners. Deep, cold winters. Snow. Like a prison. He said he liked the idea of the Great Plains. That you could see forever, in every direction."

"See what?"

"See what was coming, from far off before it got there. He must've characterized life on the farm that way every time. You know how people do that? When telling their familiar stories?"

"Everybody has their routines. Their material."

"Especially old dogs like him and Uncle Burnie."

"He did tell me about. Opening The Dixiana. His reasons."

You know what she means—the legend says your Pa-paw opened the honkytonk so his bride Runelle would always have a place to sing her songs. "He always tells that part the same, too."

"It's so. Sweet."

"Yeah." And it is, and you consider all their years together, all the hardships, the loss, raising the grandbaby, and now her left alone without her Rabbit. But how well she'd taken it so far.

She needs you. Mama Runelle—the mother who gave you this life, far as reality is concerned—needs your ass. This is your charge; your debt to your Mee-maw.

Hell, your wife—with her skinny freckled feckless adulterous ass—has forsaken you. You aren't going back to Sedge Island at all. You'll hire a car service to deliver the Mercedes, placing it at your waiting feet. Or else fly back, crash the plane into the house on the marsh—you'll bail out at the last second, landing soft and easy in the water and pluff mud—and then drive the damn car back yourself.

A voice whispers, *Don't. Think. Such. Thoughts.*

At first you can swear that it's Button but you're looking right at her, smiling and silent, whom you can see has said nothing.

But you ask anyway. "Did you hear something?"

She shakes her head.

"Oh. Weird."

"Maybe there are. Spirits about."

"Whoa. I am super-stoned."

"In a good way?"

"I think so. It keeps changing."

"Go with it."

You arrive at the grave of her father. She kneels and places her hand on the grass, which is lush and full here—a patch of sun through the limbs of the old trees, enough of which have been cleared by the power company that this corner of the cemetery gets good light, as you surmise after a cursory survey.

You know landscaping issues. Your knowledge of community enhancements and livability features, honed from the years on the neighborhood council in the Old Market as well as being an engaged business owner, has made you an expert on issues of urban planning and development.

Build-outs.

Façades.

Landscaping.

Streetscaping.

Access.

Safety.

Aesthetic improvements.

Standards.

A vision, unfolding! It's all there—you foresee the future of The Dixiana, and the entire downtown area. Soon as you close the eyesore and run off a few other undesirable businesses, Tillman Falls would be primed anew for capitalistic liftoff.

You're not going back to the island; you have no more SBFCs to open or oversee; you couldn't give a crap if the CBSI shut its doors. Except for the folks like Sharolyn, on whom you depend, and who depend upon your bossman ass to pay them a modest living.

Ack.

In any case, yeah, you're thinking: *I'm here for a while. And when I leave again, it will be a different fudging Tillman Falls.*

"How different?" she asks. "Oh, look—it's right over there. Your dad."

You get chicken skin. Had you said all that aloud? Christ, this weed. This vaping. "Yeah, it's under that tree. And—how different, what?"

"Oh, nothing." She blinks a couple of times. "I sense change on the wind. Something big—it's coming."

"Are you reading my mind?"

Button Sykes, laughing and shrugging. "Not as a going concern. But if it happens, it happens. We're swimming in consciousness."

Suspicious, all this telekinesis. The potency and quality of weed—maybe that's what has changed. Perhaps raspberry kush unleashes heretofore unused mental faculties. "Gimme another vape."

⊛⊛⊛

YOUR FATHER'S GRAVESTONE, now decades old—as old as you are—sits weathered, faded and inconsequential, with its US Army logo and inlaid flag frozen mid-wave in its eternal stone breeze. The fact of Ronnie Ed Pettus's life being so short, so meaningless, so wasted, brings pain you haven't felt in a long time.

It occurs you couldn't care less about the past, or about right now. Being here. With Button. You've concerns, responsibilities and issues to dick around with. Looming crises. Retributions and revenge to plot and direct from afar.

Button notes how she can feel you vibrating at a low frequency.

"Yeah. I'm wired pretty tight at this point. Even with the dope."

"You ever meditate?"

"Shoot, no. My mind's too busy. I could never—"

"Everybody says that. Here's a quick. Lesson for you." Button describes a technique, a way of thinking about thoughts. Being in a room, when you're meditating, see, and you treat the thoughts that come like people walking into the room, and so what you do is let the people walk on through the room. Kinda being rude and ignoring them. Letting them go, one after another, until they slow to a trickle.

"Sounds like a good trick."

"I'll teach you. Some other. Concrete ways." Her smile, so lovely and warm. She coughs a few times. "Only if you want. Though."

"All right," slapping your hands together. "Enough. I have decisions to make."

"It's not the time." Shakes her head, voice soft and withdrawn and self-conscious. "But I can't make you see that. You have to. Come to it. On your own."

"This is why I like you, Button. You know the score."

"I don't. Know anything. Except this: Trudy—she loves the bar. Loved Uncle Rabbit. Loved him to death." Seems to regret the choice of words. "And she loves you."

You dispute this notion.

"Are you kidding? Trudy thinks you hung the moon."

You feel the blood draining into your feet. The blade, going still.

Then, more self-conscious stoner awareness, bubbling up among the headstones. Panic.

You've behaved like a boor.

What to do? What were you thinking?

Trudy, hurting because of you. All of them.

You son of a bitch.

Awareness.

And a notion.

Show them all the real face of who's now in charge—a benevolent despot. Get them to like you instead of fearing you.

And not just the staff. You mean the whole freaking town.

❂ ❂ ❂

REMEMBER SIMCITY™?

Of course you do.

Back in the 90s you'd get lost in that game on slow afternoons at the original Beanery, like when Southeastern University was out of session and the Old Market neighborhood barren of commerce, and well before you'd become consumed by fruitshake ambition. Building the virtual towns, the cities, the sprawling metropolitan areas. Growing these into Mega-SimCities. Planting the statue of yourself in the harbor, first using the landscaping tool to raise a small portion of seabed into a pyramid-shaped island, and erecting the monument to the creator. It was a tradition in every one of your SimCities, the construction and enshrinement of the Mayor Roy statue; you placed it only after the city had hit a reasonable benchmark of success, by SimCity™ measurement when the population surpassed a hundred-thousand Sims. You wished there'd been a feature to resize the statue so that in remarkably impressive cities you could digitally forge it on the scale of the Colossus of Rhodes, placing it astride the blue digital waters with its brass helmet of sunrays glimmering in artificial bits of Sim-sunlight, a mighty shadow cast upon ocean-going vessels, the statue's symbolic glory obscured in the longer game views only by the passing of transparent, gray animated clouds. You kept meaning to email or post on the SimCity™ Usenet message boards to suggest your customized mayoral statue idea. But never did. Decades ago, now. A lifetime.

Statues. Whether they one day replace old Pitchfork Ben with Roy E. Pettus doesn't much matter. Only the challenge ahead. Slicing people's heads off with the Blade, not the way. Why these thoughts of kindness come so easily now, you are at a loss.

Still, your inner drive shifts into high gear, your mouth crackling and dry and you're in the cemetery with this weirdo, and she appears she can talk to you without moving her lips, and you're going: whoa, that can't be true, and it's like:

I got to get out of here. Before I'm dead, too. And they put me under one of these slabs of granite.

Stammering, you tell her you gotta split. "I'm outta here. Now now now."

"Wait. But we—"

"Sorry," but you're already hoofing it through the tombstones, bobbing and weaving underneath low hanging live oak limbs, power-walking toward The Dixiana like on your workouts down on the island paths. "No time."

Button, calling after you in her halting, high manner. "I have. Much more to. Say..."

You squawk back over your shoulder, "It can wait"; that you've got shit to do, also thanking her for her contribution and how you feel better than you have in ten thousand years. Better than in an entire epoch of geologic time. "You rock, sister," giving her the heavy metal horns. "T-B-C."

Charging out of the cemetery and hurrying down the sidewalk, knocking knuckles on old General Reb hard enough to hurt, you blaze with ambition and inspiration.

Inside, you ignore the activity of the staff cleaning every dim crevice, their faces pinched and sad and resentful and grab scratch paper on which to scribble all the ideas racing through your mind like the rapids in the river in *Deliverance*, and if you aren't careful, if you don't slow down and catch your breath, you will have bones sticking out of your leg and have to be toted out by the rest of your canoeing party, whether sodomized or otherwise.

Eff.

That.

All these ideas allow you to shove out the awareness about right now, and people dying, and your wife fucking someone, and how all you have in your corner is your pile of money, and what will the P&L look like on the new venture here, which will be the crown jewel, the crystal cathedral of coffee shops, and it will wipe away the memory of the honkytonk and its drinking and smoking and hillbilly nonsense forever.

A new franchise. More millions. Untold glories to come.

No; or yes, rather: you are the bossman.

All their destinies, ready to sketch out on bar napkins, which don't even have The Dixiana logo on them. Generic, tissue-thin junk from the discount club.

Yes, there will be logos. But not for this old dump. For what it will become.

What felt like panic, now subsiding, only this laser-sharp focus and drive and immense, gratifying sense of inspiration, moving you brightly; you will obtain one of those vape devices and some of that raspberry jelly or whatever she called the goo inside. Heck yes, you will.

The control grid, descending like fine rain. Like manna, filling the belly.

Hummmmmmmmm.

When they see how much everyone'll prosper under your guidance, their current pain will be transmuted into the loving inner glow of gratitude, their eyes shining and hungry as you hand out the checks, more so at holiday or bonus time, oh, how then their happy faces glisten with desperate hope and relief when the bonuses come.

You: the job creator.

Big Daddy.

So, too, would these people give themselves over to you. Even Trudy Pirkle, who would come to see you as Daddy now, too, an idea promoting itself alongside a modicum of ickiness owing to the past sexual activity.

The future, beheld. And the fear, subsiding. A thousand important tasks ahead. The checklist, a stairway to the stars.

❁❁❁

BUTTON, bustling into the bar and shaking the sleigh bells. She startles you out of your skin. "Hey—what's with all this? Running off? On me?"

"Show me one decent trend this town's got going for it," ignoring her. "One."

Button tells you, sure; that you should meet her tomorrow morning down by the old mill building, at the trailhead of the Edgewater County Riverwalk, which it surprises you to hear even exists. "It's totes legit. All that undeveloped riverfront. Put to good use."

With gooseflesh breaking along your arms—you know the riverside well, from back when you and Devin and Dobbs used to hike and camp there—it's an easy decision to agree to meet her, at which time you'll fill her in on the rush of ideas. "There'll be significant physical changes around here. Mega-changes."

"Do tell."

Baked, you are. Like one of Letty Glasscock's famous peach pies. The words stumble out. Now you understand Button's deal. "You'll all. Um. Find out."

When you meet Button's eyes she's not so much stoned as super-pleased, beaming love and gratitude to you. You feel better. Relax.

Feel love and attraction for her.

Not a blood cousin. Don't forget that. Hook up well within the bounds. Another action item.

"You got it going on, Sykes. What's the secret? Oh, wait." You try to think up some clever stoner head trip shit. "Those who know, they don't talk. Right?"

"More like, if I knew the way, I would take you home. All I can do is, kinda point. That-a-way—or maybe that-a-way."

Your forearms grow a forest of little fuzzy trees. "I hear you. Well—looks like my path is here for now. So I'd better get to laying down the yellow bricks."

"That path is for—"

"—I get it; I get it—"

"—your steps alone."

Enough, you declare, with the Deadhead Easter eggs; Button, giggling and mischievous. A sprite; a spirit.

Feels like instant best buds. Like she's got your back: If you can't trust a gal that smokes you down, then whom might thouest trust?

"Say—could you sell me some of this pot?"

But before she can answer, you're again gripped by the sinister Big Idea, a wicked and pointed gesture designed to MAKE YOUR PRESENCE KNOWN here in the community, and in a way that goes beyond yelling at a bunch of dumb hicks who will have to face up to your management style in a way they never imagined under the gentle, cloudy eyes of your kindhearted old bastard of a granddaddy. Oh yeah. The color of your PRESENCE would not be black like that of your blade, but white.

White, solid and pure.

A whole motherfreaking wall full of white.

"Giving is better than selling. I'll sport you. No worries."

"You understand I've got plenty of money, don't you?"

Button, shrugging. "That's beside. The point."

"Appreciate the gesture, yes I do. That's right. We'll revisit this tomorrow."

Giving. That seems a Big Idea too, but stoned, they all seem that way, delicious, and compelling like the stale popcorn you eat by the fistful; it tastes like the best bar munchie since the Pilgrims and Natives popped corn as brothers to inaugurate the First Thanksgiving.

Buying stuff, however, it's gotta happen. But you have neither salted snack food nor a sack of dope in mind. Rather, your action-item shopping list comprises a bag of rags, a paint roller and a few gallons of primer.

CREEDENCE

Almost face planting, Creedence stumbled out of the cab into the gravel of the parking lot of the Sandflea, the island's longtime principal, if grungy, live music club. Twilight now, the sodium street lamps had begun glowing ochre. Like most buildings on the island, the music venue sat surrounded by moss-draped live oaks and spiny palmetto trees. It reminded her of The Dixiana—lots of pictures on the walls inside, many of famous bands who passed through on their way to stardom.

To be honest? She despised the dump, which Roy dragged her to every time this one Grateful Dead tribute band would come through. Gave her cover to get shitfaced. Both of them—finally about midnight her husband would get loose enough to start noodle dancing with the hippy kids. Creedence, the next morning always hung over as shit, saying, I'm done with that dump. It's beneath their class, now. Like going out for a nice drink back home in Edgewater County, but deciding on The Dixiana.

The Sandflea. The kids who went there. The bands who played.

She wanted no part.

And yet: here she stood.

The doorman watched her wobble on her chunky slides across the parking lot. Lidded eyes, rolls of fat around his neck, sweat on his brow. He held up his meathook and asked for ID, which she gave up only after saying "C'mon," and rolling her eyes.

His scrutiny of the license, with a frozen, impassive face, went on far too long for a patron like her, of obvious legal drinking age.

"How much?"

"You just here for happy hour? Ain't no cover until later." He passed back her license, which she had had to get renewed a few months ago. Her face, puffy—she'd been hurting like crazy that day, a hangover for the ages.

"I'm not here for the show, no. But I don't mind paying. To support the band."

His words, well considered, came breathy and calm. "In that case, it's twenty."

She dropped her purse, fumbled and picked it up and fished out an Andrew Jackson, which vanished into a pocket of his overstuffed jeans as though it had never been there.

The doorman slapped an over-21 wristband on her right arm, taped it down way too tight. "I'm here to make sure you're taken care of tonight, sugar. You need anything, ya come and get Sharaque. Ya dig?"

Creedence, understanding he'd taken advantage of her vulnerability, but thinking, well, now I guess this guy's got my back. "That's so very kind. Thank you."

Wincing, she adjusted the paper wristband that glowed under the black-lights inside the empty club—way too early for a rock show. The hairs on her forearm caught in the wristband, cinched and pulled. Ow. Like yanking off a bandage.

Hair. Mercy. Like an ape, these arms. She'd always hated her body and her hair and feet and hairy arms and freckles. What any of them saw in her—Dusty, Buddy Lawler, Billy Steeple, Roy Earl, and now Estes—she hadn't a clue.

She only knew Estes Patel, rock frontman, turned her inside out.

He'd better do more than that—all she had, now, was young Mr. Patel.

Shit-fire! Roy Earl, fixing to cut her off. She knew it was coming. He had a right to. He'd told her he copied all he read. "I copy-pasta'd it! I copy-pasta'd it all!"

She tried pleading. Sincerity. Atoning and apologizing—well, apologizing, anyway. Maybe not atoning. But willing. "Don't go. No."

But he had gone. No—she had run him off.

God, but she needed a drink.

Inside the club, deserted and dingy and the antithesis of her husband's fine coffee shop sitting two miles away through the cypress trees, tatted and tight T-shirted girls worked behind the bar stocking liquor and dumping chip-ice out of a plastic bin that looked less than sanitary. One customer, hunched at the bar in his board shorts and jersey, a sweating bottle of pale ale clutched in one hand and smartphone in the other. The drunk's busy eyes looked her over, not without appreciation, before going back to scrolling through the blue and white field of his shimmering Facebook feed.

The idea of social media filled her with revulsion.

The messages Roy had read.

How stupid of her. Not over leaving the laptop open. No. Also for pretending to have the feelings.

For having said she loved Estes.

For writing it. Which makes the unreal become real.

Small talk with the bored bartenders, both with substantial bra sizes with which to contend, thick eye makeup, going for the sexpot barmaid vibe to get those tips, honey. The island, she'd found, supported a young person's under-class of service industry types, most of whom lived on the mainland and commuted from as far away as Savannah, sometimes. Wasn't so crazy; servers and captains and bartenders did well in the fine dining places, at least if everyone tipped the way Roy E. Pettus did, which to her mind seemed exces-sive and often unearned. She just about couldn't stand those little resentful slit-eyed millennials. Well—not Estes. But some of those servers could kiss her foot.

And now here she was taking the Beanery deposits—Roy's money, that paid for his extravagant gratuities among all the amenities of their fine life—and giving them to the millennial to whom she'd also given her body. But this wasn't theft. She had to do it for Estes. It was she who'd caused all this, by responding to his innocent flirtation.

She could see clearly now—he'd only been nice, and she'd come on like a ravening wolf. What was a young, horny man to do? Estes deserved this money.

Over at the stage, the sound guy, hair swept up high like a 1950s greaser, squatted down futzing with pedals and cables. She asked where the band was.

The hipster squinted through the stage lights and picked at a thick mustache like so many of the young guys now sported. Seemed stoned. Every-body here did. "Green room, I suppose."

"Where's that? In the back?"

Long pause. Eyes glancing down to her breasts. "You on the list?"

"I'm—I'm yes."

Long pause. "You're yes?"

"I'm with. One of them."

Long pause.

"Dude, I'm the girlfriend. Of the singer."

"Course you are. I'm just messing with you, lady."

"'Lady'?"

"I thought y'all didn't like 'ma'am' anymore."

"Oh—that's right."

He stood up, flicked on a microphone. A brief burst of static through the PA made them both jump, and he switched it back off.

"Guess that cable's hot. Go through the tapestry," covering a doorway behind the stage. "Watch for the snakes."

"Snakes?"

He pointed at the thick black cables marked with yellow caution tape going across the floor to his sound platform back in a corner. "Yeah. The snakes."

She went through the Indian mandala print tapestry. It reminded her of one Roy Earl had hanging in his duplex back in Columbia back when they'd first fallen in love, when his home up the hill from the Old Market had still looked so much like a college apartment. It made sense; he'd still been more like one of the students, his customer base, than the grown man he would become with her. And if he hadn't been grown before, Creedence thought with a sick sense of shame, he was now. Again, thanks to her. An infamous gift.

Behind another curtain she found Estes's other bandmates and hangers-on lounging on a pair of filthy upholstered couches, the walls covered in graffiti and band stickers, a cooler of PBR tallboys iced down and glistening under a couple of bare bulbs hanging out of naked fixtures in the ceiling. The band, chilling and drinking beer with various young women, bare of shoulder and thigh, splayed all over in a variety of semi-casual poses. It made for quite the chattering tableaux, one that fell silent at her sudden entrance.

A greasy, thick guy with a yellow Security T-shirt slid off a stool and held up his paw. "Band and guests only."

"I'm with Estes—Patel," clarifying with embarrassment, clutching her purse to her body, feeling like somebody's aunt among these children. "Is he here?"

"Out back." This dude, skinny and freaky with a helmet of afro like out of the 70s and who she recognized as the drummer, nudged an elbow at an ugly green metal door with a broken emergency exit bar hanging down, itself a victim of some prior catastrophe. "Warming up his voice."

"Yeah, he was," one of the girls said to quiet titters.

She knew Meatbody by instrument if not name; it'd been after one of Estes's shows the first time they'd made love, the occasion when she'd lied to Roy that she was out doing the late night rehabilitated sea turtle release event, one of oh-so many lies and fibs and fudges so she could get diddled by her boytoy, and lucky her husband had scant interest in turtles. Roy, spending most of his time at home messing around on the internet with stocks and financial crud and the *Drudge Report*.

Didn't it come with the territory, a boytoy? Rich, bored island lady, husband busy all the time; a fine, familiar rationalization that flitted across her consciousness on more than one occasion.

"That's his sugar mama," she heard one of the tattooed, blue-haired groupies stage-whisper. "Cougartown to-night." Laughter, echoing after Creedence as she hurried out.

THE EMERGENCY DOOR, thumping behind her. Portentous and spooky out back. Deepening shadows; rich and horrid fragrance from the dumpster, the gray moss and the gnarled trees and that haunted Carolina low country twilight vibe. Southern gothic vampires, if they didn't stalk it already, would hunt well on this island.

It didn't take long to find Estes in the parking lot, behind a large step-van in which the guys hauled the gear, and where she'd first felt his tongue go into her mouth. Drunken, impulsive.

It just happened. Isn't that what people say?

Not impulsive. Premeditated. Had cooked up the whole affair. A construct. I'll show him, she had thought.

"Hey now." She startled her boytoy hitting a glowing glass pipe of 'nugs,' as he called pot. "That ought to warm up your voice."

Estes, leaning on the step-van and toking hard. "Hey—should you, like, even be here? Where's your—ya know—Mr. Pettus?"

"Not on the island."

"Ah-ha."

After a slight hesitation Estes put his hands on her, giving into the urge and sliding them around on her back and touching the sides of her breasts.

"I'm so sorry you're out of a job over me. That ain't fair."

"Who gives a shit? Worth it, yo." But his tone, sarcastic. "Not that I need to eat."

"I brought you some money."

"Money? For what?"

"You don't get severance pay from a job like yours, so—"

"I feel bad about the Beanery, mainly 'cause I don't want Sharolyn in trouble. She got kids and shit, yo."

He kissed her, snaking that tongue around. Her sex, dripping, and in a way that now felt so wrong.

Like this afternoon with him had been right?

This would not work. The money had to be the final gesture.

But the lovemaking—how to give it up. And here, where it'd begun, in the crappy band van, the choice seemed immediate and acute.

Yes.

Nothing left to lose. Creedence, having had several bracers at home before calling the cab, caved to her compulsions.

"Please." Glancing around at the deserted back parking lot, she reached down into his shorts. Reaching for the hot peterpiper, which hung flaccid and damp. "We got to quit this. But one more. To say goodbye."

"Right now?"

"Today wasn't enough for me."

"Damn, girl."

Wait—his dick. Hot. Sticky. Wet, almost. And not responding to her touch.
Like right after screwing.

"What's going on down here—?"

"Hold on, hold on," antsy and pushing back her hand. "Not. Not now."

The stench cut through the dumpster-funk even before she raised her
fingers to her nose. Pungent, rank and horrible—a sex-funk. The slime on her
hand, another woman's grease. Probably one of those little shit-asses inside!
No wonder they looked at her with such disdain and pity. Her in her T-shirt
and shorts and slides and big stupid purse—a middle-aged island lady old
enough to be, well, an aunt. A muffin top from all the boozing and wine
guzzling. Bags under her eyes. Hair a wreck. Toenails chipped. No makeup.
Looking every inch of her forty years.

Seething, unable to find the words. "You little butthole."

He pushed her back and shook his hands and waved it all away. "Nah, nah
—I didn't shower from earlier today, baby. That's all you."

Was he kidding? "You lying asshole. You don't love me. You're screwing
one of those groupies in there. That all you think of me?" She saw a black hole
opening in her vision; she shook inside like the paint mixer at Mr. Vincent's
hardware store back home in Tillman Falls, where her stupid first husband
Dusty had worked. And messed with a girl younger than her then, too.

A cycle, repeating.

Despair. "Oh, god—what did I throw my life away for?"

"Hey, yo, I don't know. You were the one talking about all that love shit."

"How can you say that?" Regret flooded in. Her heart raced. She gripped
her purse, thought of the money inside, a thousand dollars. Dug around for the
cash she'd pulled out of the deposit bags, so little to a man of means like Roy
Earl Pettus that he'd never miss it. "After what we've done. After all I risked—
after this—" She showed him the cash, a thick wad of fifties and twenties and
tens. Held it there.

"Yo, what's this—oh, hold on, hold on. You ain't got to give me no money,
girlfriend. I mean, I'll take it and shit," he said, laughing. "I thought you said
you didn't have none. That he didn't let you have any."

She yelled that these were the last few deposits from the coffee shop. That
she'd felt pity for him. That she'd gotten him fired, and had now just taken
money—stolen it—for him. "And got all guilty about it, too. Jesus."

"See, yo, that's what I'm saying—lady, you came on to my ass. For
real, now."

"I'm such an idiot," she blubbered. Her stomach convulsed. She needed a
drink. "And everybody's calling me 'lady'."

Estes, comforting her. "It's all good, angel-lady. We had a blast."

Creedence, a war cry: swinging her purse, whacking him against the shoulder.

He ducked, cringing against the side of the van. "You crazy, bitch."

"How could you do this to me—to us?"

Estes, a dark fury like she'd never seen. Like the night when Dusty had whipped her. All her men eventually despised her, for one reason or another.

"It was like, accruing personal mythology—my MILF-lady." He grasped his wounded bicep. "That hurt, yo."

She hit again with her purse, this time upside the head. He hollered and cussed and grabbed at her dress, but Creedence slipped free. She took off clip-clopping in her wedges through the dim alley beside the club. She heard voices —the rest of the band piling out the back door to see about all the shouting.

Creedence, lurching through the dark and ready to jump into her own vehicle to race away from this foolishness; hurry back down to the Beanery and crash through the plate-glass windows and the bookshelves and prop record albums and kill herself, burn it all, or else on down to Harbortown and off the pier and into the salty Atlantic to drown and die and end this life she'd squandered time and again. Only to remember she'd taken a cab, one long gone.

The doorman remained impassive like a statue even as she reappeared, breathless, in front of him. "Can you get that taxi back for me real quick, like? I shouldn't have come here."

"No refunds on the cover charge."

"I don't care!"

Without reacting otherwise, he touched a massive finger to the blinking bluetooth nestled in his ear. "Same fare," he mumbled to the dispatcher, "you just dropped off. Yeah. And she in some kinda hurry."

Creedence stood there, sick and shaking and holding herself, waiting. The cab wasn't long, and unlike her expectation, no one had followed her around. Maybe Estes had told the truth, which was that he'd taken advantage of a confused woman, and deserved pummeling with a heavy purse.

He hadn't seemed like an immature kid, not at first. That's what'd been so compelling and attractive about his attention. But to go and screw another woman today? This showed a lack of character on his part.

Said the hypocrite.

The cab reappeared, and once inside she boohooed, but only a little.

"You should have told me to just wait," the hack said in his Caribbean accent, probably a put-on for the tourons. "I woulda, ya know. I don't mind. Slow night."

"Take me home." Tearful, as though escaping a horrid date. "Please."

He asked where, and she said that she didn't know, but then she changed her mind and said to take her to the coffee shop, where she'd replace the deposits. That, Creedence hoped, might represent the first step in her rehabilitation, and return to her husband, which in the course of this reality wave—it'd been awhile since she'd had those bracers, and felt a modicum of clarity— she'd now decided with certainty. She only didn't know how, yet, to manifest forgiveness in him. But she'd try. The Sandflea receded behind her, and with it, Estes Patel, the biggest mistake of her life. One of the biggest, anyway. She had a whole list going.

⁕⁕⁕

"Oh, holy crap." Creedence panicked as the cabbie rounded the traffic circle and the outparcel containing the Carolina Beanery Sedge Island came into view: a cop car, sitting outside. "That pie-faced bitch called the police on me."

She'd been futzing in her purse for the fare, fixing up the deposit bags again, hoping she had divided the money correctly in the dark there in her lap. Now she shoved it all back in and clutched the sling bag to her chest.

"What's wrong?" Once into the deserted, expansive parking lot—only the 24 hour Publix down at the other end of the plaza had any customers—the cabbie jammed on the brakes and gave her a hard stare over his shoulder. "You not mixed up with the cops—?"

"The Beanery, that's my husband's business. My business."

"My shift's about over. No time for drama, lady."

No way out of this. She had to deal with the money. "Just drop me over there. I'll straight it all out."

Bad idea. After the cab driver drove off, too much on-the-spot explaining to the two skeptical people tumbled out of her; Sharolyn and the same fucking cop who'd pulled her last night for DUI glared with bug-eyes. Too much of what Creedence said made little sense. She stumbled over the words. Slurred like a drunk. She reminded herself of Devin, her dear sweet missing dead Devin.

"And so—wait. There's missing money, but we now have the money back. Correct?" The Island cop, hands hooked on his utility belt—Webhannet again. Contempt and pity in his eyes, which bore into hers.

Sharolyn shook her head. "I talked to Roy. He said she wasn't supposed to take any deposits."

Creedence, scoffing at her impertinence. "The money wasn't 'taken' like you make it sound. You gave it to me."

"Which I knew wasn't right."

"I wanted to help. By making the deposits in the morning. There's, that's the story," and now she felt herself losing control, verging on a crying jag or some other meltdown. "And like, there's no need to be calling the police on, on the husband's wife. I mean the owner's wife. Who's just trying to help."

She fixed both cop and manager with a wide-eyed stare she hoped looked menacing and powerful. "Call him. Tell him I'm putting it back."

Sharolyn, swinging her cornrows around. "Now I know it's none of my business, and maybe I shouldn't have called Roy, but with—with—with all this mess going on, and you getting in trouble last night, too, none of it seemed right. I had to call Mr. Roy and see about all this. He's the bossman here, not you. And my livelihood on the line." She lowered her voice, as though the cop couldn't hear, but of course he could. "Mr. Roy say his soul been poisoned by you, ma'am. I dunno what kinda hoodoo happening here, but—"

"I'm just glad to see you getting out of a taxi instead of pulling a Hollywood stop behind the wheel in that Beemer." Officer Webhannet, clear-eyed, straight of posture, clipped and officious from his time in the military. "But in any case, if the money's all there, and the manager over here's satisfied, I'd love to call it a night. All due respect to you both, and to Mr. Pettus," sounding like he meant it for real and not as sarcasm, "but I've had a long shift."

Creedence, staring down at his standard-issue cop shoes, steel-toed, heavy. Kevlar vest under his uniform. Robocop, weighed down. Poor boy. "Sounds like everybody has."

Sharolyn, refusing to meet Creedence's swollen eyes. "*Hrm.*"

"Here—!" She thrust the bank bag at the pissed off black lady Roy thought so much of, had hired away from a McDonald's, of all places, out by the Sedge Island freeway exit—he'd stopped there on the way out of town when they had gone on that stupid hiking trip that time, heard her dressing down two dudes for the quality and meticulousness of their work: now that was a manager, he said. She's preaching about white-glove stuff. She's talking my language, he said. "The deposits are all there."

Sharolyn took the bag, with a blue Carolina First Federal logo and dingy from use as a vessel for lucre. She unzipped and showed Webhannet and Creedence the space inside, quite devoid of cash. "Girl, you trippin'."

"Shut up. It's here." She fumbled in her bag, squatted down, poured out her purse junk. "Oh shit. Oh shit. Oh shit. This isn't happening. It was—it was just—the cab!"

She jumped up and turned as if to run after the taxi now long gone. "It must've fallen out just now." And boo-hoo-hoo, standing there in the nighttime and with two human beings looking at her like she was nuts.

Headlamps fell across them. Officer Webhannet, gesturing with his elbow. "Your lucky day."

The cab—thank god.

The cabbie rolled down his window. He handed her the plastic sleeves with the deposits that had fallen out of her purse.

"I get the honest man award for tonight? Yeah?" But he said it like he was more irritated than bemused. "Too much money to leave laying around places."

"Oh my god," all she could say. "You are my savior."

"Jesus is your savior. Not me." He saluted the cop and Sharolyn. "Good luck," he called out to them, miming the raising of the wrist. "Sleep it off, lady."

"Fuck you," she yelled, flooded with anger at this impertinence. She stomped back and thrust the deposits at Roy's manager. "You want to count it and make sure I'm ain't no thief from my own husband?"

"No."

"Well. I want you to. I want to show you it's all—"

"Mrs. Pettus," Sharolyn said, gentle. "It's all right, girlfriend. Let's all go home. I'll just go put these into the night deposit at the bank over yonder." She went to her car, a late model Cressida with a dented driver's side fender. "Y'all have a bless night."

"I'll follow you over, ma'am."

"Appreciate that, officer."

Webhannet looked to Creedence, who stood simmering, her emotions raging and roiling and rocking back and forth like the big pirate ship ride at the Myrtle Beach Pavilion she used to fear, a giant pendulum. It had once made her puke, Devin laughing the whole time. She verged on puking right now.

"And now," the cop said to her. "What about you?"

"I'm taking my Edgewater County ass back home," she said, bitter. "What else?"

"And how are we planning to get there?"

"I guess I'm walking," turning pitiful.

"Get in. Please."

Resigned. "You're arresting me anyway, aren't you—he told you to, didn't he."

"No, you're free to go." But the cop, polite and young, gestured to his cruiser and opened the back door not like an angry gendarme, rather, a gentleman. "He asked me to make sure you got home all right. Again."

"He did?"

"Mr. Pettus—he seemed—duly concerned."

She thought about it. That sounded positive. "Aw."

Driving out of the parking lot, they watched as Sharolyn night-deposited the recovered money at the bank, sitting on another outparcel in the next ritzy shopping strip hidden behind the hanging moss. Webhannet blipped his siren at her and signaled to merge onto the connector to the marsh side of the island. Creedence lay her head against the cool glass of the police car and wondered if she had anything left to drink in the house.

At the front door, to which Webhannet walked her on his heavy and tired cop-feet, she felt a need to connect. Show gratitude. Things were turning around. Roy was concerned. He would get over all this.

"You're really taking good care of me. Thanks."

"To serve and protect."

Creedence, going all warm and gooey. Horny. Roy had sent this man to protect her, maybe this his way of saying, if you want somebody, here, have this, a proper young man, upstanding and true of moral and character. Not some halfbreed aging rock singer with no money and no future.

She admired the cop accoutrements hanging from Webhannet's belt. Perceived a strong body underneath, muscular in a way Roy could never be, bless his heart. All this attraction made sense. Somehow.

"Officer? May I give you a hug?"

"Don't think so," dry as a good martini. "You get some rest, ma'am. I hope everything works out with you. For y'all."

Damn—he must know about Estes.

Shame and anger at Roy for spilling beans to strangers. "Sometimes I don't think nothing ever will. Anything ever will," correcting herself. When she drank she reverted to hillbilly Edgewater County patois, redneck as all get out. Weepy and pitiful, she croaked, "I got issues. All sorts of issues."

"Permission to speak freely?"

She waited.

"If you need help, or rather, if you even think you need help? Then you do. Like I said, Mr. Pettus, a man I admire, and that I've gotten to know and been fed by, and been counseled by at his place of business, has asked me to ensure your safety. And that's all I intend to do. Now, if you want help with the alcohol, I can look into that for you. But not tonight. Not unless you need help tonight, ma'am. You don't seem too intoxicated. But I will say this—there's a group that meets at my church. It's straight up AA, not affiliated with the church per se, they use one of our meeting rooms. And, I'm not proselytizing to you in any way, shape or form. Let me be clear," his professional neutrality blazing brighter than his need as a believer to witness. "If you need to talk to someone—somebody else who's had a problem—believe me, you won't have to look far. Nice people like you. Other Islanders. Who might have insight. Who might be able to help."

"That's so sweet. But, I don't got a drinking problem. It's—it's other stuff. Family stuff. That's just me being upset and drinking to try and deal with being upset. It ain't like no al-coholism or nothing. Anything. My brother, boy, now he was one. An alcoholic. There—I said it right that time."

"Did he get treatment?"

"For a while. It didn't take. He died."

"Well—there you go." Pitiless. "Good night to you, Mrs. Pettus." Leaving her with that, the young cop clomped in his heavy shoes down the mosaic stone walkway to the curved driveway of her mansion on the marsh.

⁕⁕⁕

ALONE. Her oasis. Her castle, a lonely and gothic hall of horrors to face all by herself. Like being dead.

But she could do what she wanted. No Roy. No hubbie.

Didn't take long to get into the secret-stash vodka she remembered shoved into an unused cabinet over the refrigerator, an unopened fifth of Stoli. She drank, hot, right out of the bottle, the way she recalled seeing Devin do it as a teenager. Seemed to channel him.

She sat down on the veranda with the laptop and the bottle, began to write. The vodka. The computer. Company to keep her through the night. Till she got the courage to kill herself.

Yeah. There's the idea, now.

She would take the Xanax she'd been prescribed, the pills she got when the affair started and the pressure of the secrecy, so delightful and amazing at first, had become a burden, and she had to look at his face every night, and she did not mean her lover; she meant the husband who'd made this life possible for her.

The Klonopin as well. That'd make the right cocktail.

She'd write the letter to Devin—the last one; an epilogue—and take the pills, drink all the vodka and go to sleep to finish off all this heartbreak forever. It wouldn't be so bad, going gently into that good night. Would it?

⁕⁕⁕

```
Dear Darling Devin:

You told me once, back when Libby had died in the
wreck, that it could not get worse if it tried.
You said you could not imagine nothing no worse
than what you had been through. You told me that
one night when I asked you how it had been in
the car.
    Now, I know no one's died, not like Libby, and
everyone can still walk on their two feet, unlike
Dobbs. But I have run headlong into my own
stupidity in a way I find hard to describe. Maybe
because I cannot look at myself the way I need to.
Maybe I am looking at myself the wrong way.
```

When he started flying, and opened that coffee shop he didn't need, I knew he didn't want me anymore—that he wasn't interested.

Well which is it? That's what you would ask. Is it the flying, or the coffee shop? Well, it's both. He done both for the same damn reason, and that's because I don't do nothing for him. And I used to, oh so much. But I know that is not something for a sister to write to a brother. Not that you will read it anyway.

But the crux of my shit is this, dude. I been rejected by both of them, now. Estes has already wicked his dip into another chick, or however y'all damn men would say it. Putting your peterpipers where you will.

A child. What was I thinking, Devin???! Estes is not a man. None of them are at that age anymore. Not like Daddy.

And not like you, the you who wasn't drunk. Not that I got to see you much. You were always...shit. My phone just chirped.

A TEXT FROM ESTES. "You asshole. I don't want nothing to do with you."
But the text—

pls we cant end like that, yo

—melted her heart. Made her ache. Made her go, "Aw," again.
Made her consider being alone, alone forever. Even if she got the house.
Alone here wasn't no fun. Her and the kitties.
Speaking of the cats, who mewled and cried and stretched and ran and knocked objects over and fought and otherwise tried to get her attention, she went into the kitchen and pulled out the cat-cart, a separate rolling island on which she prepared the cat dinners, cans of top-quality meat-blends and veggies and other healthy foods for their bodies. She arranged the twelve food bowls—she had a rotating system of twenty-four wet food bowls, with one set always in the cat-dishwasher, and how lucky it had been that this fabulous gourmet kitchen had already had a second dishwasher that Roy designated as 'hers,' meaning, for all the nasty cat stuff, the water fountains and dishes and dry food bowls.
But tonight she discovered she had not run the cat dishwasher. She cussed and went to collect all the dirty bowls from the floor, dropping them with a

clangorous racket into the sink, the big sink rather than the little one Roy prefers her to use to wash cat stuff, especially the cat food cans he can't stand the sight or smell of, because he's not used to it even after all this time.

After making a drink, a stiff one, and sipping it and crossing her arms and sighing and walking around, out onto the balcony and back, looking at the phone, starting to text Estes back but stopping, she arranged the dirty bowls on the cat-cart and started cracking open the cans and slopping the food with haphazard abandon, more concerned with keeping juices and bits of the food out of her cocktail than in the bowls. A wet, meaty mess all over the counter. For all she cared, the fur-babies could lick it clean in the night. She swept the empty cans into the main sink, a huge no-no, but who-the-fuck-gives-a-crap.

Drinks. Looks at the phone. Struggles to decide. Watches through blurry vision as her cat babies all mewl and swirl and wait, at least the eight who live in this part of the house.

Owing to various behavior issues, the 'lower four' remain sequestered—a house divided—in their own little separate fiefdoms, in the rec room and one of the bedrooms and the lower storage level. Roy doesn't even know about two of them. He never goes to the lower level anymore. Doesn't seem to ask why Creedence disappears down the stairs every night with two cat food bowls in her hands.

"Hold on, my precious angels. Let me finish this drinkie-drink and text back my shit-ass little boytoy. Tell him to go eff himself. How do y'all feel about that?" She spoke to them in the singsongy, *is everybody hungry* voice, driving the roiling mass of fur into a feline frenzy of mewling and reaching and hopeful rubbing against her bare shins. Her ginger tom, Mr. Peepers because of his enormous blue eyes, bit like a snapping turtle at her bare toes, his little affectation.

She texted that Estes was a shit and could jump off the cross island bridge.

He texted back super fast, a long one full of errors and thanks to autocorrect weird non-sequitur words, but she got it, she got the gist, replied, I will have to think about it. She put the outlying bowls in the various spots, petting each of the below-decks, sequestered kitties.

He said, think about it while I'm there with you, instead of here. Where we can talk.

She finally called. Fuck this texting.

"Man, you really chucked me upside the melon."

"You don't love me."

"Naw, naw. Wrong."

"No."

"C'mon, forgive and forget, and I'll forgive you for hitting my ass—girl, that's assault. Everybody told me to call the cops. But I said, yo. I can't. I love her! You hear that? And so, we can get on with shit."

A wall of silence.

"...yo?"

"It's late. I need to go to sleep. What about your gig?"

"We just came offstage. And the whole time, you were like, all I could think about."

She sighed and gazed down at the cat bowls on the kitchen floor slopped full of brown gravy and bits of shredded meat, the bobbing heads and smacking and the dance they all did, switching from bowl to bowl, sometimes resulting in minor altercations that sounded worse than they were. Poured another tall one. Checked out the vodka on the counter—she'd had a third of the bottle. Already. Maybe Roy was right, that she should cut back.

Huh.

"C'mon, girl."

"No. I got shit to do tomorrow, thanks to you not being employed at my husband's coffee shop." She belched and hoped she sounded mean. "And I don't take no sloppy seconds after some little cooze. You hear me?"

He did. Begging. Soft cooing and cajoling in her ear like she loved.

There wasn't no way Roy Earl could walk in on them. Wasn't that part of the deal? One more, and done? That way you could forget him.

Creedence, a knot in her stomach that made her drink more. Creedence, giving him the code to the gate to get into the Marshside community. They had to end this thing for real this time, and she didn't want to say goodbye that way, either. No sir.

⊗✳◎

TANGLED up in the Egyptian cotton sheets, the windows open and the vertical blinds moving and the sound of the marsh coming to her gentle and peaceful, Estes thrust inside her and licked her face. She hooked one leg around under his ass. He moaned and quickened his pace, bumping up into the special spot, but damn if she felt much of anything. He humped away, moaning and grunting like a pig.

And she lay there. Let her leg fall back. Sighed.

"Come on, girl. Fuck on it like you do. Where you at tonight?"

He thrust a few times. She started to cry.

She could smell him.

Not Estes. Roy. Her Roy. His pillow, under her head. Estes had grabbed for it to shove under and prop up her ass, she'd said no, no, use mine instead. He had not understood. And now defiling her, and she couldn't enjoy it, and my god. My god. She wiped her eyes. Felt her gorge rising.

"Well—all right, then," and he went at it hard and came, finally, arching his back and saying shit, shit, shit the way he did, which at first she'd loved and thought, how intense, but here sounded like, body function, body function, body function.

He rolled off. "Like, that's what I'm talking about, yo."

She gulped tepid water from a glass at the bedside table. Saw the digital alarm clock and iPhone base that Roy turned off in the morning, bounding out of bed to get started on one of his walks, or a project, or an airplane ride. By himself.

Her guts ran cold: a smartass voice came to her, Devin's: *a mess of your own making, dearheart.* Blowing cigarette smoke in her face. She should've kept writing to him instead of doing this with Estes. For no good reason other than she was drunk. And weak.

But she wanted to finish. One last time. Get to sleep. And start fresh tomorrow.

She wanted to gush and squirt and come and lose herself. If she'd gone this far with her lover—one more time, she kept saying, or rather, this was the one more time and Roy Earl would never know, he'd never know about any of it, one time was the truth and she believed it, she knew how to pretend, had done it for years with Roy Earl; no, with Dusty, she meant, and why would she think that?—it needed to be for both. To say goodbye right. "Do me, now. Make me feel like that. One more time."

Scratching himself. Yawning and afterglow-sleepy. "Raincheck. In the morning. Besides—you caught one, didn't you?"

Creedence, saying, no. Saying, I want.

"Well, go rinse it off, yo."

"No, please—I need this. Hurry."

"Like I said." He laughed. "I ain't gonna eat my own spooge, yo. Go Summer's Eve it. Naw naw, I'm just kidding."

Creedence, burning. She wanted another fucking drink. "Eat my pussy, boy."

Estes, laughing. "But like I told ya. Ain't gonna slurp up my own squirt."

"You afraid you gonna taste some other pussy down there?" Her words came thick and stumbling. "I can't believe I done this."

"Whoa, whoa." A pall in the room. He threw off the covers. "Cool out—I'll go get a washcloth. Where's the light?"

"Don't you turn that light on."

"I can't see."

"I don't want you to see my husband's things."

He staggered and barked his chin on the ottoman near her sitting spot by the other window, the neighborhood-facing view that got the morning sun. Goes into the bathroom. Voice comes back hollow. "God-damn that is a big tub. Shit, we got to get in that mo-fo before I go. Whoa, dog. What a bathroom. Man —let's fuck all in this shit."

Creedence, saying, I thought your mother was a doctor, and so surely you had nice bathrooms in your house back in Columbia; he says, no, they do have a big house, but in Indian culture the whole family lives there, and there's like the grandparents wing, and his older sister lives there with her husband. "By the time I left to go to school, man, I couldn't wait to get out. People on top of people. This is the shit, though. Big ass place like this."

Unceremonious, Estes, yanking off the sheet. Slapping the rough, cold washcloth between her legs. Rubbing it hard—too hard.

"Ow." Pushing his hand away. "Go easy."

"Sorry." Shoving two fingers inside. "Mm-boy. It's like hot grits in there."

It didn't feel good. No longer wanted it. Said so.

"Excuse me?" Estes, shaking his head, the large black plugs flopping back and forth. "Why don't you make up your mind?"

How Roy had hated those plugs in people's ears, how he would say, what the hell are they gonna do with their earlobes when the fad's over. Who's gonna pay the costs of the cosmetic reconstruction, he'd ask. Roy Earl, her husband, so smart about so much. So worried about everything. Lucky to have him.

Not worried enough about her. And neither was this one.

None of them had been.

She burned, now. But not sexually.

"Here," tossing the washcloth aside. "Now let's get some waterworks going."

He started in, licking and sucking.

Zing! That was better.

His tongue, though. It felt rough and scaly and hard against her clitoris. Images of Estes turning into a lizard, into the Creature from the Black Lagoon, filled her mind.

He swirled and slurped; she heard his gills sluicing and wet and working. He sucked. Hard. Harder. The way he did to get her to finish, but hurrying, too much, too fast, too hard, too much pressure—

"Stop! Stop! Stop!" She kicked at him, beat at his back with her heels. "You're doing it wrong. You're doing it wrong."

Estes, tumbling off the bed. Cursing, raving at her. Grabbing his pants. "You're fucking nuts. And I'm fucking nuts for, for screwing around with you. The boss's wife—the fucking cougar stalking me at my fucking job! This is your fault, and now I'm fucked. I'm fucked. I should've taken the money from you. I got shit for cash right now. My mom's—she won't give me any more money. I got to get another day job now, yo," his voice cracking.

"I don't give a flying fudge what you got to do. Get out of my husband's bedroom. And his house. You ain't worth nothing compared to him."

"Like I couldn't tell that already."

"You know what he calls you? Do you?"

"No. Tell me."

Considering it. Wanting to hurt him. "An n-word. That's what. And I don't know that he's wrong." Roy wouldn't use that word if his life depended on it. Lord, but she could lie when she needed to.

Quick as lightning, Estes, in her face. A fist drawn back.

Again, a voice booms. *A man will beat you.*

Creedence, shrieking and rolling away from him, tangled in the sheets, falling off, hitting the floor. "Get out," screeching and vowing never for any man to lay hands on her, not caring if she ever came again. They hollered and grappled throughout the house, pushing each other and shouting curses until she hustled him out the front door and off into the humid island night.

A crash; she staggered against the table in the foyer, toppling the vase.

A thump of the front door. Hearing his car crank. The squeal of the tires.

He would get pulled over. Maybe her cop benefactor would beat the shit out of him. She hoped so.

❂❀◉

CREEDENCE, nipping on the vodka, but almost puking from it. Running a tub of water. And feeling the emptiness wash over her for real, now, the sex-slick between her legs, the liquor sloshing in her empty stomach.

And soon, the pills. The pills in the cabinet.

Bony and sick and freckled, she thinks hard on it all, but definitely maybe knows she at least needs to have another drink. Bathe, get the stink of Devin off her, and finish the letter to Estes.

No—the other way around. Finish writing to Devin—the final one—and leave it out. For Roy Earl to read.

After she's gone.

She went to get the medications. All of them.

BOOK THREE
Doubtless the Sea

What you prepare for, confidently expect, and think about most, you get. It may be trouble, or it may be joy. It's up to you.

— CONSTANCE J. FOSTER

JASPER GLASSCOCK

Pulling into the parking lot of Pike's Bait & Pawn, Jasper recalled the dying words of his father, who'd been heretofore unwilling to play ball at the practice of dispensing wisdom.

His last thoughts to young Jasper came more enigmatic than pithy, however:

"You ain't who you think you are." This, uttered by the man right before his other child, Letty, came into the hospital room. "It ain't like we told you."

"What you talking about, Pappy?"

"Hush up now." Letty, barking from the doorway. "Damn you."

"Oh, mercy," grasping his midsection in agony. Being given another dose of morphine by a nurse. Breathing heavy and slow.

When Letty went out again—nothing else had been said; she wouldn't meet her little brother's eyes—and with the sharp smell of a dying body in his narrow boyhood nose, Jasper leaned over and whispered, "What you mean I ain't who I think I am?"

By then his father's eyes had gone all blue and rheumy, like a newborn puppy. "Let me sleep," slurring the way people did when they were drunk. "We'll sit. First, we'll set the table. And set ourselves. For dinner later. Just you and me."

"What did you mean?"

No answer. Dozing off, his lips trembling and body twitching as the cancer finished gnawing away at his gut. His daddy had eaten next to nothing for two months. Was but a skeleton. Jasper didn't know how a body could live without eating.

That night Jasper dreamed of sitting at that dinner table full of cobwebs and bones and his father's skinny emaciated beak dripping snot onto the dusty plate. Waking up sick to his stomach. Hollering for his half-sister Letty, who was all he had left: she told him the hospital called to say his father had passed on—forever.

Jasper never found out any more about the cryptic remark. Would have asked his mother, but she died before he knew her. It was only his sister and him, Letty from his first wife killed in the Sunbury School Fire, and him from the second, failed, brief remarriage. Or so he'd been informed.

At least his daddy left money, and the farm. And, Jasper had Mama Runelle and Rabbit across the pecan orchard. A new family, one forged over the decades here on the gentle, rolling hills of the Edgewater County river bluff.

A family that had lost a key member. A damnable shame, but inevitable. Probably overdue, at Rabbit's age. No doubt in his mind Jasper would never live to see ninety. Not in the cards. Only way to come to grips with mortality? Put it out of your mind best you can.

After the funeral, his sister p'shawed when Jasper asked what she thought Pappy meant. "People that close to the end? They ain't got the first clue what they're saying anymore."

End-of-life dementia? Thing was, Pappy had seemed pretty all-there, right until that last stage, anyway. An enduring mystery.

⊛⊛◉

JASPER SAT in his unwashed Accord in the shade of the prop monster truck outside "Money Man" Thurmond Pike's Bait & Pawn, a squat hodgepodge of a fabricated building fronted by an enormous facade covered in symbols—$$$— and messages. The current selection of pre-owned motorbikes all leaned in a long row across the front of the parking lot, rolled out ritually by Pike minions every morning from the garage, and locked up again at sunset.

On one side of the double glass door entrance it glowed:

MINNOWS * CRICKETS * LIVE HERRING

And on the other:

ESTATE JEWELRY * PREOWNED ROLEXES

MUSICAL INSTRUMENTS

With MOTORCYCLES and MOPEDS also in neon on the front windows, along with WE BUY GOLD. For miles in either direction on the interstate Pike had billboards all painted in the same hue of lemony yellow, looming above stands of loblolly pines. When you started seeing the Money Man signs, you knew you were getting close to Edgewater County. Iconic.

The bikes, a couple dozen, all leaned in a long line all across the front of the parking lot. They were rolled out every morning from the garage and put away again at sunset by Pike minions, an orderly ritual. Signage and product to beat the band. An institution here in the Tri-county area and beyond.

Jasper's interest lay in all the musical instruments, which Pike took as seriously as the motorcycles. Knew a good guitar when he saw one. Whatever else Pike might have been, Jasper had to respect a fellow human being who appreciated the finer points of a luthier's craftsmanship, and could even play a little, not that Thurmond ever sought to appear onstage at the Dixiana open mic night. A fan of music, not a maker. Nothing wrong with that. Some of those open mics had more musicians than listeners. Jasper tried not to think of those nights as circle jerks. But they kinda were.

After Pike had seen Rabbit Pettus's grandbaby's silly commercials for his yogurt shops on TV—must be twenty years ago, now—old Thurmond paid for his own local cable TV spot, one that ran late-night, and geared toward getting business from the capitol city thirty-odd miles to the south; Tillman Falls, situated in a far outer spiral arm of the midlands metro area. Pike's tagline, delivered dry and affectless and unquotable: *"Hurry on up past the lake country for deals that draw enough water to make your head swim."*

He didn't need to advertise. Thurmond Pike, rich as hell. Lived on a point at the lake, big ass house. Probably had more money in mattresses than over at the Wells Fargo. Never know it to look at him. Crusty stooped-over redneck with a bulbous nose glowing with rosacea, hair dyed shoe-polish black and swept up like a young Elvis. Had himself a trophy wife, if you could consider a woman with a backside wide as Chesnee Pike's being award-worthy.

All the real business of Edgewater County—the black market side, anyway —flowed through this building. Everyone knew it. Even the cops. But hey, everyone on both sides of the law makes money from vice—beat cops, captains, sheriffs, federal agents, judges, lawyers like Jasper. The way of the world. America didn't make much of anything but crime anymore, especially in a place like Edgewater County. What else was there to do but profit from sin? They sure as shit didn't manufacture bedsheets and pantyhose up at the mill anymore.

Jasper, belching hot gas and noting the vehicles parked outside Pike's; a major sit-around in the back room, with discussion of important local issues and plans and whatnot. He wanted no part of that shit. Of course, neither did the powerful participants inside wish his presence. Jezmund Rembert and his criminal bunch needed him when they needed him, and when they didn't, they weren't the type Jasper desired to maintain as chums. He saw them here, and at The Dixiana. No real way to avoid it.

The private VIP club area at Pike's; the balance to the stranglehold that the ELMS often seemed to have over Edgewater County matters and community standards. Pike's Bait, Pawn and Motorbike, where men like Rembert, the real pacesetters, met to counter all the foolishness of the female community power-brokers, whose own organization now admitted men, the times being what there were in terms of inclusiveness. Few applied.

But here at Pike's? A grand tradition, this club. Kind of an open secret more than a codified membership. No 501/c shit here. The progenitors of this bunch, the prior generation or three, they'd gathered for a spell in the old upstairs of The Dixiana, where all kinds of action used to go down, and now their children congregated here to turn cards and trade money and make deals. Movers and shakers, these men.

Or so they wanted to believe. A sub-group of men had their own places of meeting, rules of order, agendas. That club you didn't talk about. One could find charred remnants of their summertime ceremonies, a longstanding yet all but secret county tradition, out by Jenson's Pond, a circular area in front of owl rock. Jasper, at one time a future initiate of the order, knew enough of their ways and means to wish to avoid such a club, especially one who'd have a drunken reprobate like Jasper.

Jasper felt that all groups, official and otherwise, were delusional in their self-aggrandizement. Perhaps they should be set against one another, winner take all to the blessed death, using prison-yard rules and engagement and brutal weapons like shivs and broken bottles. And let the victors turn the implements upon themselves. The cycle, written in blood.

Mercy.

Ever since the heart trouble began and he had gotten the stent, Jasper had tried to keep a lid on the misanthropy, the arguments with his sister, the anxiety and existential dread. On the drinking and smoking. Least he wasn't out screwing. No chance of VD. Or other complications.

Instead of all that, Jasper sat doing what made him happiest: listening to music, in this case the pop-oldies channel on the satellite radio, a godsend, that played pop music from the 70s, a guilty pleasure—The Eagles, a longtime favorite, he didn't care what anybody said. He quaffed a good glug from the half-pint kept in the glove box, what in his mind he capped a nip, but was in fact a gulp. Remembered as a kid watching hard-boiled movie characters who did that: the brooding and troubled private eye or cop, let's say, who nips the flask and goes right out to where he's working on some investigation. Talking to witnesses. Colleagues. Victims. Superiors, even.

Thing was, they never showed them boys chewing up three Altoids, though, did they? Or in countless other scenes, the immortal line, "Would you like a drink?" and everybody knocking back measures of brown liquor and then going around conducting their business. Can't hardly get away with shit like that in real life. They smell it on you. Like his worrywart sister.

A 'nip' from the bottle, then cupping his hand in front of his face: Yep—he reeked. Using that as the excuse for another nip.

A drunk like Jasper—now, not near as bad as some he knew—kept on coming up with reasons. Doozies, as Letty would put it. *You come up with a doozy of a reason for drinking this time*, she'd say.

Did they sell Altoids back in the 1970s? Jasper thought they did.

Castigated himself for sitting in Pike's parking lot, sweating in the sun and smelling his own farts and thinking this useless shit. Started in on a nip, stopped himself. Wasn't close to lunchtime yet. Instead, he sipped tepid bottled water, the thin plastic crackling in the grip of his calloused fingers and refracting sunlight into tiny prisms.

He turned up the music, sang along to 'The Pina Colada Song' followed by 'Whatcha Gonna Do' by the inimitable Pablo Cruise. Jasper felt tears welling. Took another snort. He didn't want to go into the office anyway, shuffle briefs and talk on the phone, or be across at the courthouse messing around in that stuffy old mausoleum. Hated practicing law anymore. Always had, really.

Should have written another book or two.

Oh—maybe he still would.

Someday.

It was all Jasper could do to keep Coy Wando out of his head, even after all this time since he'd written the one book. Sick bastard. Kept on doing his dirty work after they caught him—did a number on the victims' families. On their heads. On the men who arrested him, too. On Jasper as well, the man's own chronicler—a deal with the devil, as it turned out—and by extension everyone who reads that durn book.

It still sold a few copies every year. Libraries. Serial killer fanatics. Made you wonder. Jasper had taken the last royalty check and bought himself a three-pack of fresh Fruit of the Loom, size XL. The big time. He should've put in less about the murders and more about the philosophical debates they also had along the way. Some of that made it in. Mainly the gruesome stuff. Still surprised it hadn't sold more. But sometimes these appealing qualities of the macabre are simply too much. Wando's story, sure. A lot like that. Unpleasant. Much Jasper left out, which caused a rift in their relationship—but then, Coy, long dead in the chair, one of the last to be executed in the state by that method, and no threat to Jasper.

On certain anniversaries, Jasper still got calls from the media to offer what he had to say about the infamous Wando child murders, and the mystery of whether the "confession" he'd dictated to Jasper held true-truth about all the other purported victims, accounted for and otherwise, he murdered over several decades—lots of quote-unquote accidental deaths in the South Carolina midlands, Wando claimed, had actually been his doing. Fascinating. Probably not all true, as Jasper always concluded. But the awfulness of the thought of all Wando professed to have wrought, and what he did get caught doing—the ritual torture and murder of three pubescent girls—you couldn't shake it, not once such horror burrowed into your mind, like hookworms way down in your gut feeding on blood.

Writing a book was supposed to have defined Jasper's life, as the music did now, but like many writers he'd become disillusioned by the process with the small publisher who had put out the book. They had paid for next to no promotion, and his royalties—well, it was embarrassing. No future in writing. Too much work, not enough return.

Being involved in the Wando case, as a journalist rather than attorney— back then, the 1980s, Jasper had been a PI and bail bondsman—was how Jasper ended up going to law school at thirty-five. Seeing the inner workings of the penal system, the justice system. Observing and interacting with victims on the inside and outside. Poor saps, most, who had gotten fouled up in a system that cared only about them as numbers and actors, statistics and metrics rather than human beings. He'd tried to represent those folks well as he could over the last two decades. Most of his business came from Easton. Destitute black folks, Latinos. He'd been brushing up on his Spanish.

Cash in hand. When he got paid. If at all.

If Jasper was anybody now, though, it wasn't a country lawyer—a picker. Sometimes a grinner. But most definitely a picker. Letty scoffed at it all, his little music hobby. At least he still had Mama Runelle around to encourage him. And Rabbit. Until a day ago. Damn.

❂❖❂

THE ANDROID VIBRATED against his leg. Still sitting with the seatbelt on—and the car running, and his foot jammed down on the brake, and who knew for how long—he fumbled out the phone in time to see it was Letty. What a shock. Always checking on him. Intuited that he hadn't made it into downtown Tillman Falls yet. Damn woman had radar.

He answered, trying to sound nonchalant instead of downtrodden. His heart fluttered. Knew he needed to make changes. To stay cool and even and eat better. Not drink so much. Letty'd been on him about the health stuff like stink on shit. "You checking up on me already?"

"I'll have you know Roy Earl called to confirm this little service they putting on for Rabbit. And that he'd like to talk to you in private about some-thing else."

"Now, old Rabbit said he didn't want nothing like that."

"You wrote his will, so you know it's not what he wanted, but you also understand how the doctrine and ritual surrounding the funeral service represents catharsis for the people left behind. This matters much more so than with the wishes of the loved ones who've passed on."

"I do believe you're right, sissy. But that's a helluva attitude."

"I didn't make up these rules. I can only interpret them as I'm challenged by their expression in day-to-day life. In any case, I wish to attend Rennie's service, such as it is."

"Well'm, I reckon I oughtn't go. Given I made sure it'd been put into writing that no such ceremony occur."

"Roy Earl's asked that you sing. That you and Runelle sing for his grand-daddy. And I think you should."

Jasper tingled in the left part of his chest. Thought about the sensation for a second, made himself quit. You had to make yourself quit thinking about what might happen, like a heart attack, or else you'd coax it into reality. "Then I'll accept your argument, counselor, that the wishes of the living outweigh the intention of the dead, who have ceded agency to those left behind. But, I'd like to know what Runelle has to say about it."

"I already know the answer—she said she'd be honored. But peeved, still, he hadn't asked her himself."

"Roy Earl?"

"Her husband of sixty-eight years, you ninny."

"Well'm, reckon I better warm up my vocal cords."

"They already sound warm enough." Smarmy. "If you ask me."

"Why, I dunno what you mean, Letty."

"Here, let me be clear, then—you're slurring your words, and it's not even eleven in the morning."

And so their conversations went. He agreed it was early for a bracer, reassured her for medicinal use only; she said, well now, I didn't say a word about drinking this early in the day, and how he must be projecting, and how if something's thought to be a problem, then it probably was. They rang off. A mind game.

Damn her hide.

If only Letty suspected how right she was about his health—Jasper had gotten himself a heart prognosis that'd made his asshole snap shut. Had surgery in his future. Just knew it. The full assessment from the cardiologist sealed the deal.

Sexiest damn cardiologist alive. A fringe benefit.

On one hand, the idea of heart issues scared him shitless; on the other, glad it wasn't cancer like Burnie's boy, Buddy Sykes. He'd come to Jasper for help with end-of-life documents, and had confessed to the severity of his condition only under the strictest of confidences that his lawyer tell no one.

Poor Buddy. Throat and tongue cancer. It robbed him of his life long before the Lord took him home. The docs had to take out all Buddy's teeth, and his neck swelled up like a frog, his pink tongue sticking out dry and scaly, those blue eyes getting bigger and glassier and it'd been a horrible traverse of suffering, bless his soul. And bless his family, in particular Button, dutiful and loyal and who seemed so damned unaffected by it all—placid, in fact. The girl floated still and untroubled like a calm lake next to a meadow of wildflowers, and he envied and admired the shit out of her. Coveted whatever inner peace she'd managed to maintain throughout a living hell like what she'd experienced as her father's caregiver.

What the hell gives you throat and tongue cancer? Nipping straight, hot liquor out of the bottle? Jesus.

⊛⊛⊛

Knuckles against glass. It startled the mess out of him. "Shit a goddamn."

Jezmund Rembert tipped back his fedora. Grinned a reptile smile. All slick and leathery and sunglasses and with a pair of chubby redneck goons looming over his shoulder, made the universal finger signal to roll it down, pardner.

"What up, beau?" Jasper, hoping his heart would slow down soon.

"Whatcha doing sitting out here like this?"

"Listening to the radio, taking a call. Dunno what to tell ya."

"You looking for me?"

"Should I be?"

"Naw. Not that I know of." Poking out his lip. "It's right nice to be thought of, but—whatever."

"Sorry my planet's not orbiting your star today."

Jez, a black-hearted, greasy redneck gangster, for lack of a less specific term, seemed disappointed. "All right, now. Ain't no call for such meanness."

Jasper sipped his crackling bottle of Aquafina. Rembert the lessor, as Jasper still considered the son of the former local crime boss, wanted small talk? Fine. "Everybody at home good?"

The legacy organized crime figure, this Michael Corleone of Edgewater County and his brave compatriots in vice and plunder, came out from behind a cloud and shone upon Jasper. "I appreciate you asking. Just this morning my old lady said, standing out on the veranda looking at the boat dock and the lake, 'Mercy, but if this ain't the best of all possible worlds, I'd like to know what is.' I found myself tending to agree." He elbowed one of his goons in the ribs. "Course, you don't agree with your old lady, then you got trouble."

All this banter made Jasper consider the possibility of possible worlds. Of alternatives. They called it the multiverse. Choose from a selection of doors, walk on through, and you had yourself a new reality. If only it were that easy.

"That's a real compelling thought exercise."

"What?"

"The possible possibles."

"Shit no, dog. Don't do that. Might-have-been and used-to-be? Forget it. Go with what ya know. Keep it on the DL in the right-now."

"I guess I'd feel that way too, if I could afford living out at the lake."

Jez, unimpressed. "Let us not bear ourselves beneath a covetous cloak. Besides, if you need big money, go into the Wally world, slip down on your ass and sue. Them bastards'll settle. Easy money. Wait—who the hell am I talking to? And Jasper—you should consider sucking on a few of them Altoids sitting on your seat there."

"Why's that?"

"Cause you smell like this little troll I know name of Jack Daniels pee-peed in your mouth last night. Or better yet, here—" Jez produced a small purple Tupperware container, a little cube he cracked open. "Try these."

Jasper opened his hand. Jez gave him a pile of fragrant, striped seeds smaller than grains of rice. "What the hell are these?"

"Fennel seeds. Chew 'em up instead of mints, which are slap-full of sugar, chemicals, gelatin—horse's hooves, all ground up. Since we went vegan, I don't touch no mints or gum, beau. No processed food at all."

"Bullshit." One of Jez's goons, milling around and smoking a few yards away "I want me a freaking steak *samwidge* for lunch."

Jez cut his eyes at the dude, six-three and three hundred pounds of good-old-boy with a head like a melon and a neck even wider. "You ain't getting it, son. We not gonna do this again today."

The young thug averted his own hard gaze; practiced, but yet to be perfected.

Jasper put the seeds into his shirt pocket. Said he'd try them later.

"Trust me—you need 'em now. So: what you heard about old Reynolds's funeral?"

"Ain't gonna be one. Private little ceremony only."

"My mind is like, blown. What a gyp."

"We're gonna put on a big to-do for him down at the old barn," a term of endearment Jasper and other regulars used for The Dixiana. "You can be sure. One day soon."

"Sounds good. Appreciate everything you've done for me, cuz."

"Appreciate you saying that."

Watching as Jez and his boys climbed into the black SUV that loomed over the other cars like a DEA undercover wagon. Once they pulled out of the lot

Jasper had another nip and chewed up the seeds—like licorice, sorta—and got out to go inside.

He sat for a spell and picked on Pike's pawn shop axes and tried not to think about how sexy his exotic Indian cardiologist looked and smelled, nor to ruminate on the pack of flavorless Marlboro Lights he'd switched to a couple years ago when he'd gotten bronchitis and it put him in the hospital for a day, and lucky he hadn't fallen ill with pneumonia. He missed his Marlboro reds. Cowboy killers. Would hate to end up like Buddy Sykes, however.

Wait—did Buddy Sykes smoke? Well, something gave him neck and throat cancer. That much for certain.

❉

JASPER RANG up the Pettus house. He didn't get Roy Earl but talked to Runelle, who hemmed and hawed until admitting she had ideas for appropriate songs.

Jasper made sure she felt up to it; she said, shit yes, least I can do for the old son of a whore, cackling and making him feel damn good about her sense of inner peace. Gave him a little of his own this time. Seemed less mysterious than Button's.

"What you got in mind?"

"I don't think he'd want one of mine." Jasper, laughing. "Not as many times as he sat there listening to me do the same tunes over and over. Until I finally learned how."

"Mercy, no. Not any more than he'd want to hear one of my silly little ditties from the old days. Poor Rennie. Bless his heart but he suffered through me learning to play and sing, pretending to love every minute. Worst liar you ever heard."

"If you ask me, ma'am, he wasn't acting. Not for a second."

"P'shaw."

Jasper propped his phone on his shoulder and tuned the Martin CEO8 cherry-burst Grand Jumbo he'd taken off the wall, an instrument Pike thought was worth five large but Jasper wouldn't have paid a nickel over four thousand. Not that he had the scratch to blow on another guitar.

Grief swept through him, that way it will after you've been trying to ignore reality and go on about your business. If he came home with a new guitar, Letty would know for sure he'd been drinking. "My heart just goes out to you and Roy Earl."

"We'd appreciate you joining us at the bluff," sounding curt and officious in the manner of one who wished to be done and on his way. "Roy Earl thinks eleven would be a good enough time. Just us, though."

"What about Burnie?"

Said, if he's up to it. She'd call, talk to that granddaughter of his.

"The bluff. No better place." Jasper, his left side tingling and twitching, tried not to start worrying himself to death about his heart. He put down the Martin and now held the phone, radiating heat, against his floppy earlobe. "That guitar of your'n still work?"

"Yes, sir. If I can tune the durn thing."

"I'll come round beforehand instead of meeting y'all over there, we can rehearse." The bluff wasn't far from where he now stood, only a half-mile down a bumpy, rock-pocked dirt road that forked off through an old cotton field and into the woods along the river. "Ride together over yonder."

"See you about ten."

Jasper dry-swallowed a Zantac. Thought about maybe scarfing half a Xanax after lunch. That'd be better than drinking any more today, least until beer o'clock, when he hoped The Dix would be open again. Yep. One more nip, and one only; his stomach would thank him later. Made sense. No reason to be hung over and belching acid at Rabbit's memorial.

At least the other day he'd held off on the bracers until after his doctor's appointment. He'd a-hated for her to've seen him, not to mention smelled his breath, in such condition. Not a looker like her. Married, of course. The ring on her brown, delicate finger had screamed, Just your luck!

Probably noticed his hands shaking. And how for a picker—a real one—he ought to have a better seasoned set of callouses. He'd work on it. He'd practice more. Rather than drinking.

Jasper pulled a capo out of his pants pocket. Clipped it to the seventh fret. Started picking and warbling 'Hotel California.' Didn't sound much like Don Henley. Nobody around to judge anyway, not unless the townsmen smoking in the back room could hear through the ducts.

⊛⊛⊚

"THINGS ARE CHANGING in this country, and in the world. We know it in our minds. We feel it in our hearts. Our bodies reflect these stresses in the form of disease manifestation. It's all really quite straightforward. And manageable. That is the sad part. Yes?"

"Reckon so. Heard it said the worst sin's the one you commit when you already know it's wrong."

"So you know this wisdom already, yes?"

"Yup."

"Well, I can only suggest you pay heed."

Dr. Kadambari Patel's accented English floated with a lilt that made Jasper burn inside in a manner different from his usual indigestion. "Not the first to tell me this."

"And I hope I am not the last!"

At a shade over five feet, the doctor's body seemed nestled within her button-tufted, mahogany-finish leather swivel chair while Jasper sat scolded in her spartan, tidy office; as well, the executive desk looked far too expansive for the diminutive, not unattractive woman—more bookish, perhaps, than erotically enticing. Or so he kept trying to tell the part of him that pulsed with far too much lust for a man brushing up against sixty.

Jasper had shifted in discomfort while she scrolled through his medical history, and he wondered if she couldn't just deliver the bad news without all the moralizing chitchat, which he received in sufficient quantity at home. Then again, bad news put off too long enough wasn't news at all anymore.

Hell, he wasn't worried. If he hadn't had a heart attack while interviewing that cold murderer Coy Wando twenty years before—child killer, no less— Jasper surely never would.

But still, he fretted and his back had suffered a twinge as he slumped across from her like a crumpled paper bag concealing a half-pint of Evan Williams shoved into the glove box. His khakis were wrinkled as was his plaid button-down, and the New Balance sneakers—he wore nothing else, except during court appearances—looked all road-worn and downright grungy from shuffling around on the old boards of The Dixiana and the grimy sidewalks of downtown Tillman Falls. The shoes stunk. Jasper, through the providence of proximity, realized this.

He straightened up and uncrossed his legs, trying to look dignified in the face of news about his incipient mortality. A fool for thinking, *Could she be into a haggard, trembling old country lawyer? Is she flirting?* That was rich. He needed a drink.

Patel considered Jasper over the tops of her round, tortoiseshell-rimmed glasses. "People are simply not taking care of themselves the way they should. Well, some people. Not all. But not enough. Not enough, I am telling you." She wagged a scolding, disappointed digit. "We have a veritable obesity epidemic among both young and old. This, I suspect, you also know already."

"See it every day. Buncha lard-asses."

"You should go to India, or South America. Come back here, and everybody fat! Even poor people."

He rested his hands on a belly attributed in his mind more to genetics than a lack of gustatory discipline. "Time to hit the treadmill. That's what you're saying."

"Sometimes I wonder what is going on with food and health and what-all. Very mysterious, the kinds of habits encouraged by corporations. But that? Oh, my. That is for another discussion."

"Well-now, I would be glad to sport you a cup of coffee if you're of a mind to chat outside of—"

Patel cut him off by waving her hand as if clearing smoke. "Now, we have gotten you fixed up five years ago, yes, with a stent? And your problem was not all your fault—some family history, yes?"

"Far as I know. Pappy died of cancer, but he also—"

"But the good news is from what I see, you have not suffered enough new scarring around the old stent to need additional catheterization at this time. So there's that. But I am recommending lifestyle changes, which from the data at hand you clearly need. In fact, that is the main recommendation, other than adjusting your cholesterol medication."

"I eat right good, all things considered." Jasper, protesting, albeit in the weak-voice of the liar. "I get salad bar twice a week like clockwork, and my sister's garden puts out like you wouldn't believe. Stowing away more roughage than Bugs Bunny. It's working, too. Ain't there another pill I just need to take?"

"I can give you a pill for anything. But Mr. Glasscock, change has to come from within. You should begin a meditation practice. Eat a vegetable diet only —plant-based foods. Drink only water. No alcohol. No caffeinated beverages. No sugary sodas—these are poisons. And if you modify your behavior in this manner, it is possible you will never need to see me again. So I am a bad businessperson, I guess, trying to run away all my customers." Her face, stern, cracked into a smile. "Yes?"

Sounded like Button Sykes with all that meditation talk. "Well, we sure as hell grew up eating a typical, old-school Southern diet: Fried thus and such, you know. Fatback in the beans." He coughed. "I may still have a soft spot for such cuisine. And I drink too many Coke-colas. Having said that, ought to be easy to fix. Just change the way I'm doing everything. Got it."

"Lucky for us, you enjoy the privilege of choosing for yourself the outcome —improved physical condition, or me poking around inside your body."

Jasper thought about how a wire going through his veins had unclogged the river of his heart, made him whole and hale again. Wasn't that easier than having to adjust his whole dang way of life/

But what, pray tell, was there to stay unplugged for anyhow? Open Mic night at The Dixiana?

Well, duh: for Jasper's open mic. He had a rep to protect and propagate. He'd become as legendary as the damn bar itself. Hadn't he?

In any case, Rabbit Pettus had still been alive then. But not now.

⊚✾⊚

Speaking of the old barn, what was Roy Earl going to do now? Run it from Sedge Island? That's what Jasper wanted to know. That, and what songs he and Runelle would warble at the service.

Right as he was fixing to head out from Pike's and drive into town, Jasper hung the Martin with reverence back up on the wall and smiled: besides employees only he could go behind the glass countertop display full of old capos and straps and pedals and cables and sound reinforcement doodads.

Thurmond's trophy spouse sauntered into the pawn shop showroom from down a hallway where the card playing and so much of Edgewater County's behind the scenes powerbrokering took place—like Jasper was certain was happening today, matter of fact. Probably talking about Roosevelt Nixon and his name-change BS, or else the mural controversy.

The boys in the back wanted it left the way it was, maybe spruced it up a bit, but it was sounding like the ELMS wanted to raise money to repaint it and get rid of the General Reb stars and bars chicken. Their argument—that Southeastern U itself had long updated its mascot and logo in favor of the modern Redtail Hawk, prideful and muscular, who sported talons and a beak and plumage fierce enough to frighten and empty backyards' worth of songbirds throughout the region covered by the SEC football conference—held merit. The mural, important to the lifeblood of the town. Its sense of history. Jasper didn't give a shit about some flag-waving chicken. But some did. Enough to get pissy about it, even. Jasper, he'd never believed the hoodoo about the images having a mystical quality, that luck somehow flowed through the chicken's paint strokes. Jasper, musing that The Dixiana still being in business after so long must constitute good fortune.

Chesnee, greeting him with a question, but not about the mural: "Roy Earl gonna let Trudy run The Dix for him?"

"Couldn't say."

"He won't close it down, or nothing. Will he?"

"I reckon he might."

"He c'ain't!"

Mulling. "I'd say he could."

Huffing and puffing and folding arms across fleshy boobs. "It's been there too long to shut down."

"They shut places down all the time, my darling."

"Lord knows that's true."

"So—who knows."

The phone rang in the pawn cage. Again.

"You gonna get that?"

"I'm not answering the phone like a receptionist—where's Kenny?"

"He stepped out, earlier. Might be something important."

In a sweeter tone, she went and answered. After a few seconds of listening, the call sounded like it was about the presentation of a motorcycle to Thurmond for consideration of purchase or trade-in. Typical of such calls, Chesnee answered with a rote-sounding pledge to pass on the seller's pertinent info to Mr. Pike, who would be in touch, or not.

As Jasper half-listened, he winced and felt a sharp pain in his back. Thought about what to eat for lunch. Thought about a nip and a light beer and a Xanax. Maybe see what's shaking over at Hermie's Hot Dog Shack, home of the seven immutable hot dog condiments—slaw, chili, pickle relish, diced sweet onions, mustard, ketchup, and mayonnaise—or else get the John Wayne Special, a double cheeseburger on a hoagie roll, at the Congress Street Grille. Anything was better than going into the office.

Well, a heart attack wouldn't be better, but he didn't feel one coming on, only stomach acid from nipping on that ethanol out in the car like an old alky, which he wasn't.

"Thing is, a man like Roy Earl's made his money. Shit, Trudy Footwater rules the roost as it is. He wouldn't need to do nothing."

"Shit. That witch?"

"I never understood what it was between you and her." Jasper ran back through in his mind all the times where he'd heard Chesnee make similar snide remarks behind Trudy's back. "She's bout as sweet and country's the day as long. Loves music."

"It ain't worth talking about." She sighed. "Maybe if he don't want to run it, somebody can buy it off him."

"I wish."

Chesnee lit a cigarette and said she had stuff on her plate. "I got payroll to run."

"Thought you didn't work here."

"Counting the money ain't working, sugar."

She went back to the office passing by Kenny, a skinny, tattooed redneck boy of a clerk who reappeared looking red-eyed. He got himself behind the wire cage that Thurmond had put in a while back.

The way Easton had grown over toward this side of the river—hell, it was part of the Tillman Falls municipality now—Thurmond felt like he needed to put in the cage, keep all the money and jewelry and valuables in there. Said it didn't used to be that way here in Edgewater County, not like down in Columbia with its high concentration of soldiers and greasers and negroes, or one of the port towns with its sailors coming and going from the freighters and shipyards into North Charleston. When he got on one of those rants Jasper always reminded Thurmond that most folks considered the county as the Columbia metro area, but he'd always scoff and say, bullcrud.

"Having to drive that far to go to a man's daily work is no way to live," said the man who drove more miles on motorcycles ever week than most commuters—probably an exaggeration, but true enough, especially in the spring and fall. Thurmond, Jasper knew, had always been a motorcycle aficionado. Sure, he had the Bait & Pawn, but over time he'd made his hobby into a side-business. Test-drove all them motorcycles he bought and took in trade—for jewelry, for guns, for other items off the books.

The pawn shop phone buzzed again right as Jasper was hitching up his trousers to get on his way. Kenny, whose bad teeth and skeletal countenance suggested substance abuse, answered with a succinct greeting: "Pike's."

Kenny, frozen in the act of scratching at a zit, listened for a few seconds. "You better not be kidding me." Another pause. "Well, I'll be shit. I better go tell Mr. Pike. I'll tell all of them."

With blooms of pink in his cheeks, the clerk hung up. "Now there's some news."

"You look like somebody walked across your mama's grave."

"My mama ain't dead, Mr. Glasscock. But somebody's gonna be."

"What you mean? Rabbit Pettus dying in the street wa'n't enough?"

"Some son of a bitch down painted over the mural on The Dixiana—*somebody covered up General Reb*," in a voice full of gossipy shock and awe. "Mr. Pike'll go apeshit. So will Jez Rembert. Jesus."

Jasper got a chill. Thought, well damn, Roy Earl, way to make your entrance. Way to make fast friends in your old hometown. "Somebody must've been pissed as hell at old Rabbit to do that right after he died."

"Beats all I ever heard." Kenny, on the verge of tears, went girly-running down the hallway to tell his boss and whatever other oldschool boys were in the back.

Jasper, his heart thudding in his chest, hurried to get in his Accord and spun out toward the Pettus place, desperate to warn Roy Earl Pettus that men like Jez Rembert would beat someone's ass bloody over this transgression. If not worse.

GOOCH AND DOBBS

ooch, woozy as hell after the hospital, thanked Dobbs for conveying him home in one piece. How ironic—a man himself in a wheelchair serving as Gooch's savior. That's how sickly Bill Wimmel realized he must be. They had kept him most of the next day. Dobbs had come and gotten him.

How low he'd gone. How pitiful his plight. Pissing himself in the street. Having his balls ravaged and handled. How Bill got into such messes, he hadn't a clue.

The clarity he'd felt in the hospital seemed to ebb and flow with the pain in his scrotum, now more of a nettlesome, stinging itch than the burning fire of the zipper teeth. But one troubling notion remained. He couldn't reconcile that he'd been in the middle of the road in the middle of the night when he'd thought it daybreak, and had been urinating, fumbling his privates into the teeth of the zipper and bleeding to death, all with the Mayor of Tillman Falls standing in his robe and slippers bellowing at the top of his bearlike lungs for all of Whaley Way to hear about it.

Bill, making the news instead of reporting.

But forget all that—it was the forgetting. He'd been forgetting things. Too much. This he knew to be the real issue.

The problem.

Like his grandfather.

His grandfather, who gone off his nut. Took and shot himself, finally, sitting out by the airstrip. But not before Grandpa Wimmel had gone on a spree of beating his loved ones, Bill included, and acting like the Wild Man of Borneo, all of which was chalked up to demonic possession or just 'meanness' which for unknown reasons had taken seventy years to manifest and exhibit itself in the formerly mild-mannered gent Gooch had known. And who'd given him his nickname—all that gooching Grandpa used to do, gooching and tickling.

"Gooch!" he'd holler, and Bill would holler it right back. It'd stuck. Maybe it made sense to still have his childhood nickname, from almost toddlerhood—it looked like he arrived back in that state of being.

And this person was responsible for the news around here? Tsk-tsk.

He hobbled into the kitchen to make tea, in doing so trying not to burn the house down. The black and white checkerboard tiles, filthy. Self-conscious about Dobbs seeing the mess. Black grime around the sink, and the bases of the toilets. That mother of Gooch's would die all over again. And wouldn't that be fun.

Dobbs, rolling out of the downstairs bathroom, no mean feat in his chair, which didn't fit as well in the narrow confines of old houses. "Why are you on your feet? For heaven's sake. Go and stretch out on the couch."

"Tea. If you were here and going to stay, I thought we'd have tea."

"Seems like you should sleep."

"Well, maybe I'll sleep. After the tea. But you can still stay. I want to talk about—about—" A wave of self consciousness washed over him. "Tea."

"Fancy man wants to talk about his fancy tea, eh?"

"I don't know what you mean."

Dobbs asked what he really wanted to talk about.

Gooch searched his mind. "A novel I want to write."

"Oh."

"I wanted to share this. With you. No one else."

Dobbs blinked a few times. Cleared his throat. "I see."

Wait—how tender had Gooch's words come? He'd already forgotten. But he'd wanted to say them for so long that in his convalescence he supposed he figured now was the time.

Wait—what had he actually said?

What had Dobbs's facial expression meant?

"I forgot what I was saying."

"About your novel, which sounds wonderful. But, please go sit down. Do you understand the irony? I normally love to see everyone wandering around of their own volition, but not this time."

"Now look, I'm not some invalid—"

"I'd like tea; I'll stay. Besides, if you're up to it, we should discuss a few other issues. Like getting the Pettus special section for Monday put to bed."

A standoff; Gooch forgot about what.

Dobbs thrust his arm toward the couch with such force his wheelchair rolled back.

Gooch snapped his fingers and remembered the issue at hand, shuffled over to the couch. "Kettle's on the stove."

"Duh."

Gooch listened to Dobbs opening cabinets. "Where's the—never mind."

"Can you reach it?" Gooch leaned forward, peering around but unable to see into the kitchen, only the yellow glow from the old globe lamp over the table, the light filtered dingy and xanthous by the dust, smoke stains, and insect bodies. "It's on the lowest shelf."

Dobbs grunted. "Yep. And clean mugs right here, too. Now, chill out."

Gooch tried to relax. His mind raced. Forget the big stuff—what did they need to discuss for the paper?

Christ—Dobbs would need to put it to be soon if to make the print run deadline later tonight. Like he said, he wanted to talk about his project. Envious upon hearing Cort Beauchamp had a big new novel coming out this fall, his first in many seasons; a historical romance set in Reconstruction era, fictionalized Edgewater County. The notion had lit a fire under Bill's literary tea kettle to write his own such literary achievement, a long-held desire from boyhood.

Novels. Pish-posh. No time for all that.

The paper. The paper. The paper.

It came to him: the Rabbit Pettus ceremony. "Oh—I know what needs to be added to tomorrow's edition. A notice that Roy Earl Pettus will scatter Reynolds's ashes."

Dobbs squeaked into the living room with a suddenness Gooch would've thought impossible. "The mayor texted me this news."

"I was trying to get into the paper and get it all written up when I had my —my accident."

Dobbs, troubled. "Just surprised I didn't hear this. From Roy Earl."

Gooch had heard it from him; and that'd have to be enough. Besides, he had the deets, as the youngsters would put it. He filled in said details, that it was to occur out at the fishing bluff.

"I know; I know. It's the public memorial part."

"Anyone welcome. Roy Earl's words. Call him if you don't believe me."

"No—that's okay. No way you could get that wrong. Right?"

Bill Wimmel, journalist, only reported the facts, and didn't mull over the nuances, not unless for an op-ed piece. Said so. "Anyway, you took care of it?"

"Tweeted. Facebooked. On the website proper. Working on my piece for the Monday special section, which we can push to next Friday if good material starts coming to the surface. As for the memorial, I don't know where every-one's gonna park."

"I hear you." Gooch ruminated and cogitated and fretted about what he had to say next. But say it he did. "I hope you didn't mind covering for me yesterday."

"I think I should just plan to handle everything for you. For a week. Or two. Whatever you feel like. It's clear you need a break. When was the last time you took a vacation?"

"To do what?"

"To keep from getting into these situations. Like last night."

"Dobbs."

"Yes, Mr. Wimmel?"

"I can't remember what we were talking about."

"When?"

"Always," Gooch said, his voice breaking. "Oh, now I remember. My book. We wanted to talk about that."

Dobbs got a look on his face not of concern or trouble or panic—all the emotions Bill had been feeling—but one of satisfaction. "I know what's been wrong."

"You do?"

"I think so. Now I can help you, Bill. If you'll let me."

Gooch cried, then. And said, yes. Please help me.

Right then Dobbs's cell rang, and he took it. His face dropped in amazement. "Ex-squeeze me? Oh, boy. Oh—holy crap."

Gooch's tears dried up. He sat, waiting. "What's 'holy crap'?"

Dobbs waved him off. "I'll get over there for a photo. Thanks."

"Who was it?"

"A news tip—a big one."

His newspaperman's blood, racing: "*Tell me.*"

"Somebody's vandalized the General Reb mural."

"Two days after Rabbit Pettus dies?" Stunning. "Dobbs, that's a helluva story. You've got to let me help report it. Please. I'm begging you."

"Only if you feel up to it."

"Son, what else do I have to live for? This is huge. Let's roll."

ROY EARL AND RUNELLE

Controversy settled.

A controlled operation in the wee-hours, your mission of mercy-killing. You rolled that rooster. Shoot yeah, you did, with sweat rolling down your ribs beneath your black T-shirt. A humid night. Fall couldn't get here soon enough. You policed the area, stowing your painting equipment behind the fence in the junkyard that had become the back lawn of The Dixiana.

Once back home and hopeful you won't wake up your grandmother, you grab an indulgent, lengthy shower in the upstairs guest bathroom. Using a long-unopened, crumbly bar of Lava found in your granddaddy's work shed out back, you rid yourself of the white paint speckling your forearms, scrubbing until the flesh is pink as a baby rabbit. At last you emerge from cascading jets of heated water courtesy the innovative tankless system installed when you built this house for your folks.

With neck and shoulders tight as springs, you walked away satisfied by a coat and a half of thick, white primer applied over two long and lonely hours deep in the Edgewater County night. Oh, how you giggled and snickered as that stupid rooster disappeared beneath methodical overlapping swaths, the clandestine operation cast in dim bronze light from a streetlamp down the block and unseen by anyone.

Far as you know. At one point you perceived yourself being watched. You paused in mid-roll, rivulets of primer running like tears. Only silence broken by the low hum from a nearby transformer. From toward the cemetery, the flapping of wings. A big owl.

What really tweaked you out there? Not a single appearance by a late-night patrolman or county cop. It's clear you will need to bend power-holding ears about the overnight downtown police coverage. Another mission for another time.

For now? Shuteye, drifting into a dream-ridden half-sleep that's over before it begins—at daybreak, your phone blows up.

Annoyed, you silence it and check the screen:

Dobbs V

So, they have seen your work.

Forget it, old pal. You'll give a statement to the press when it pleases your tired ass and not a second sooner. Not until you get some quality sleep, which you manage, but for only a couple of hours.

⚙❀◉

A FEW HOURS LATER, yawning and groggy, you join Runelle on the front porch for a morning that feels cool, like autumn creeping in, and if that's not a relief to a South Carolinian, you'd like to know what would be.

You find her sitting with iced tea in an oversized frosted blue plastic cup and an acoustic guitar across her lap, the old one she keeps in the case with the peeling strips of fabric, dry rotting. It sat in its corner of the living room for all those years in the old house, a part of the firmament and furniture. Never collecting dust, no; not in Mama Runelle's tidy house. But untouched.

"You remember going to the Opry that time?" she asks.

"And to see Conway and Loretta at Collegiate Coliseum. Mee-maw: could it really be forty years since those days?"

Faraway. "Remember how you used to want to fly away with Conway Twitty, on the Twitty Bird?"

"I thought him having his own plane was right cool, didn't I?"

"You kept asking in the car on the way over to the concert if you was gonna get to see the Twitty Bird parked outside. It was the cutest thing, my darling."

"How about that." You had dreamed of being a person who could have a plane, his own aircraft standing at the ready. And now look at you now, with your Piper Meridian.

Recalling how it used to sit on display in the old house, you wonder where she keeps her guitar these days. Not only had she been the lead singer of house band the Dixiana Darlings, but legend has it your grandmother enjoyed a transformation in the civil rights era into a folkie. Certain songs you remember her singing to you as a young child bear out this aspect of the Pettus family mythos—Peter, Paul & Mary, 'The Times They are A-Changin,' songs in that wheelhouse.

Gesturing with one of her gnarled old granny-hands at the battered, worn case, she sucks her dentures and says, "I told your Pa-paw thirty years ago to get me a new case for this old fiddle. Thurmond Pike's got a back room full just sitting there. But Rennie never got around to it."

"That old so-and-so."

"I finally quit asking."

"You think Pike has himself a storeroom full of empty guitar cases?" You smile at Mama Runelle's schtick: fibs, exaggerations, hyperbole.

"I tell you what, if he's got one, he's got a hundred. I ain't saying they's nice ones. But better'n this rotted thing."

You twinge at her mention of the man you call 'Buke.' You still suffer a proprietary sense of rivalry with him over Chesnee Campobello, until you remind yourself that holding such a mindset after lo, these many decades seems foolish. "I'll run and get you one tomorrow. Best he's got."

"What on earth for, now?"

You hate the downtrodden tone in her voice. "I'm only thinking of the guitar's wellbeing."

"I'll get Jasper to pick one out. He spends more time there than at his office."

"You always were sweet on him."

At this she starts strumming. Horrified and sour of expression, your Mee-maw tries to tune, but the knobs seem frozen—she can't even get them to turn without twisting so hard, as she notes, it feels like they'll snap right off.

"Maybe we need to get you a whole new axe."

Strums some more. "It don't matter—it's just me out here."

"I didn't even know you ever played that thing."

"I don't."

"Why not? Afraid Jasper will hear you across the pecan orchard? Or all the way down River Ridge Road to Buke's?"

"To—where?"

"Pike's, I mean. I call him Buke—he looks like this writer I dig. Bukowski."

"No one I know ever called Thurmond 'Buke.' That's a new one."

You tell her that to your knowledge, nobody else does. Feel silly about the whole idea of having a private nickname for some random dude.

Changing the subject, you wonder if she's got one more song in her, at least. "Play me one of yours. Pa-paw always says—said—you wrote the prettiest country songs he ever heard."

She pish-poshes, strums and hums, but no songs come. "I ain't got the air left in me to sing no more. And my songs—they wasn't nothing but me messing around."

"The heck they were. The hell you are."

"You'll know one day. You'll find out when you're stuck in a dried up old body."

"I might not—I ain't no cigarette-sucking piece of Edgewater County white trash."

She cackles. Having lasted to this ripe age, she knows she hasn't exactly smoked her life away. Her very presence belies this, as does her daily habit of three Virginia Slims, morning, noon and night, sitting here on the porch. After supper was her favorite. You've always heard nothing like a smoke after a good meal.

Not that you'd know. A lit cigarette wouldn't touch your lips. The planet itself—the entire galaxy, nay, the entirety of the multidimensional multiverse—would expire before you took up the habit.

"You never did smoke, did you, son?"

Whoa—the old bird way ahead of you, reading your mind. "No'm, I sure didn't. I hated it—hate it still. I'm one of the folks who forced council's hand down in Columbia a few years back on the smoking ordinance. Everybody said, but dude, you own the coffee shop, the hippest one in town, and you know coffee and cigarettes go together. But I declared that, to a drug addict like a smoker cigarettes are a necessary adjunct to any particular set of behaviors; but to a person who wishes to be smoke-free there ain't no amount of smoke they should be forced to put up with. Sovereignty over one's own flesh, as I put it. That's what I got up and said before council."

"Were they able to follow along all right?"

"I feel like it made an impression. A vote or two changed after my speech, let me tell you. I said, growing up the way I did, stuck breathing that —that stuff—"

"I always tell people you ought to come and run for mayor of this two-bit town."

"Hah. After my time on the Downtown Business Alliance—as you recall, for a time I was even its president—I said I'd never be a politician again, not even at that puny neighborhood level. Too many compromises to be made. Too much opportunity for corruption. Don't want any freaking part of it."

"That's like me and them ELMS, son. Did you see them all over here? Bunch of biddies pecking around. You know they want that corner, don't you —they'd love nothing more than to tear down The Dixiana. That's what I've always believed."

"Seems more like they want to preserve the place. The mural, especially," the words tasting like bitter medicine on your tongue, which feels furry, like when you get cotton mouth after smoking dope, which you wouldn't mind doing again soon. "Which is now a non-issue."

Weed. If you'd wanted, you probably could have gotten some back home from Estes, right? Hipster kid like that? In a rock band? Maybe you should call him up, or send a text: *Yo, hook a brotha up with a dime-bag, beau.* Least the boy ought to do for you. After banging Creedence.

Right?

A sound—*blargh*—clambers out of your dry, clicking throat-hole.

"Like I said before, it's up to you what happens downtown. But there's something I need to say to you, Roy Earl. That needs to be said."

Her voice has gone quavery. You prepare yourself; and already know:

The club.

Nobody in this house dared call it a honkytonk, a term of derision. You got told to watch your smart mouth that one time you said, hey granddaddy, I seen a poster at the Grande, and they up and named this here Clint Eastwood movie—*Honkytonk Man*—after you.

Pa-paw had ended up loving the movie, though, for the hot minute it had played at the theater. Dull, a story steeped in country music. A fake Hank Williams. Flop, said the critics. Clint, singing and playing a guitar? At least it wasn't another chimp movie. In any case, you'd dozed off, which in your little cinema church made for an act of heresy.

Mind racing with anticipation, you ask her to go on.

"You broke your Granddaddy's heart, you know. The way you done him. And me all these years. He could never say it to you. He could never say the way he felt about much of anything. And if you think it was easy, living seventy-odd years side-by-side with a man like that? Well, it wa'n't."

"He was a crusty old booger. No question."

"But don't forget, he give everything he had to take care of you. And he was so proud. So proud of all you done, because he taught you to work for what you wanted, and durn if you didn't go off and do that."

"Well—it all just seemed to happen. Truth be told."

"But it also disappointed him." She searches for the words. "You've just kept us at arm's length for so long now."

"Really now," glowering. "When was this? Sometime between buying the truck and building y'all the house? Somewhere in there?"

"Son—life is nicer when you have nice things. But things ain't the same as knowing your grandson loves you. Don't forget, you're all we had left after your daddy died in the war. And old Rennie Pettus, he risked everything to raise you. Sacrificed and paid so dearly. More than I can say."

Your Mee-maw begins to crumble into tears, and at the sight you damn near panic, take a step forward, but stern of expression, she beckons you to halt. "After a certain point, you never would let us inside your life anymore. It hurt him so. He couldn't never figure on why you stayed so distant from us."

"I was distant from you because I was distant. The generation gap."

"Yes. But it didn't have to be that way. Mothering is mothering."

"Suggesting I ain't shown you and granddaddy the love you deserve, that burns my butt, Mee-maw. I got to say."

She waves you away. "Said my peace. We can talk about whatever you want to now—about the club. About what you want to do."

You hide your anger at what's occurred here and tell her you won't make any changes without her say-so. Even if it isn't true.

Before you can go any further, she shushes you by strumming and giving a familiar recitation: how after Patsy Cline got killed in that damn plane crash, after which 'Mama Runelle' put away that guitar, which she shouldn't have bothered taking up, not to sing hillbilly music anyway. Not according to that self-satisfied dandy Ralph Peer, a story so ingrained as family lore your grandmother now elides most details, skipping ahead to the end of her brief reign as Tillman Falls's country crooning diva.

"Poor, poor Patsy. She had already done what I wanted to do better than I ever could—hers had been the voice I wished to've had. So I give up, son. I quit trying to write songs. I quit playing.

"Now, when Jasper was a young man, though, and he found out I had been a performer," she continues with a proud inflection, a hand over her bony chest, "he pestered me to pull out this instrument and sing, and I often would. He says I set him on his path, but to that I say, your path to what? Going to law school over in Columbia? Listening to that trash coming out of Coy Wando's filthy mouth?"

"Let Jasper thank you. You inspired him. He wrote some cool songs of his own," though you don't know this firsthand, but assume it because of his success as an open-mic impresario—the club's biggest night, apparently, both in attendance and cash flow. "Or so I've been told."

She's galled. "He'd already heard enough real country music without my help. What I played was only imitation."

You contemplate your grandmother's assertion, let notions of authenticity bob around in the stillness of your mind. Cicadas sing from the treetops; the air's warm and you've grown damp in your creases already for the long Indian summer day ahead. Your grandmother, eighty-eight years old, sits playing tunes you don't recognize, yet feel you do, somehow. Timeless melodies. A common language, music.

Except for country music. And hip-hop. And world beat. None of those genres set the twilight reeling inside you.

"You know something he told me one time?"

"Jasper?"

"Pa-paw. He said he opened The Dixiana for you."

"Not that wild claim again."

"He told me, 'I loved her so much, I wanted to make her own place where she could get up and sing whenever she took a notion.' Or, words to that effect."

Another Runelle cackle. "What a load of mule-hooey."

You're crushed. "*What?*"

"He seen how popular country music was getting. Seen a way to make money—or so Burnie put into his head. Either way, Pa-paw realized it was one of the few towns in South Carolina where he could get away with selling beer, too. Don't forget that part—that's where a club owner makes his living. Not off the music."

"So he always taught me." And how you wanted no part of it, selling booze, any more than the smoking. "Especially when you're booking touring musicians, with guarantees and all that. In any case, all this Scots-Irish mill trash never shied away from the raising of the wrist. That much I know about the history of this place."

"You better quit calling everyone around here trash."

"Call it like I see it."

Hands draped across the guitar, head bowed, her voice goes thin and fragile. "Be that as it may, but you're one of us. Not that there's much of an 'us' anymore."

You let this moment hang as she grieves for her husband. Fat tear drops dollop onto the scratched, butter-golden finish of her ancient acoustic guitar.

Your heart clenches and you place a gentle hand upon her knobby shoulder. Go to take the instrument from her.

She says, no, no, only grasps the neck of the guitar tighter. "Let me hold on for a bit longer."

"Hold on long as you need to—forever, if you want."

She smiles at you through fogged, oversized eyeglasses covering half her shriveled, puckered face. "I wa'n't that good a singer. Ralph Peer knew it. I mean—better than Kitty Wells. But not near as good as Patsy. Still—that's a sweet story your granddaddy used to tell. One that's partly true, partly fiction."

"Like all stories."

She wipes the tears from her guitar with her sleeve. "Let's go inside. Eat ourselves more of that dessert them fools all brung. One thing we never do around here is waste food."

"Dessert for breakfast?"

"Why on earth not?"

You consider the logic. "Good point."

You help her inside and go to put on a pot of consumer-grade bilge water, which makes the house at least smell a smidgen like the original Carolina Beanery, when you'd walk in on a sunny morning there in the Old Market and brew the first cup, and all had been right with your world, troubles and tragedies involving Devin and Billy Steeple and now Chelsea Colette "Creedence" Rucker lay far in the future, none of it yet on your radar.

How could disruption with your beloved not have been intuited by you? What had gone wrong?

It was over, you were beginning to realize, the day the dream of franchising the smoothie stand came to you, the first step on this lucrative but lumpy road. You said, I'm married now, the formula has proved itself profitable, let's do some magic and make ourselves a real nest egg. And you had.

But in the season of betrayal and what-now, what scant meaning behind this success?

At the end of your life in forty-odd years, what would you be clutching on your front porch that symbolized meaning and value and memory to you? Not an old guitar. Not your granddaddy's record collection, which you couldn't hold in your lap even if you were Superman or the Hulk. You haven't a blessed clue, and this upsets you while slurping up a slice of granny-smith apple pie, nuked and adorned with lo-fat vanilla ice 'dream,' a peach of a breakfast you both enjoy with genuine, fudge-all relish.

❀✾❀

Sipping her tea, Mee-maw's emotions seem to have modulated. Your granny sits beaming, with a look like getting another bout of weeping out of the way a task, a checklist item, now completed.

You can dig it. Your kinda method. Chipping away at it, as you like to say.

Or maybe what she feels is pleasure that a key destination, you soon understand, has been reached. "I need to tell you a few things. While I'm able. That your granddaddy wanted to be able to tell you himself."

"What kept him from doing so?"

"He couldn't say it aloud, son. No more'n he could tell anyone what he went through during the war."

You sit in stunned silence as she tells you the story of what happened to your mother: the circumstances behind her car accident, with the devastating and enormous reveal couched in euphemisms and evasive language that nonetheless ring out loud and clear to you. That a drunk driver hadn't caused it as they always told you, but by Pa-paw Pettus himself—by your own granddaddy.

Chasing them down. Them being you and your mother.

"The guilt liked to eat him alive." She exhales with the revelation of this long-held secret. Collapsing in her breakfast chair. "Ain't no one heard this. Not from my lips."

You finally realize you've been holding your breath for what feels like an hour. The shock of this news—your own grandfather seems to have killed your mother—settles in your gut like a tainted hamburger. "That's all good to know. That clears a lotta stuff up."

"I wouldn't blame you if you were mad. You should've been told sooner."

"Not at all. It might've changed how I felt about him."

"Don't hold it against us, son. Please. She was taking you away from us."

"What prompted this event?"

She considers her answer. "We couldn't lose another boy. You must understand."

Your mother had been absconding with you. "Clear as Luzianne tea."

But truly, nothing felt clear. Only more muddied. It'd been so hard for her to admit these truths you couldn't let her know you felt anything but relief, as well as welcome filial edification. Quelling your desire to ask for more deets. Putting this new knowledge into a box.

Letting it go.

Along with the breathtaking reveal comes an accompanying tidbit, however, a factoid, that puts everything else about your history and life in perspective:

How the baby version of you had also been in the car with her that terrible night; and it had to be God's hand, everyone said, allowing a delicate infant to survive a rollover wreck into a steep ditch off one of them damn River Ridge Road curves. This had been why they cherished and kept you close and safe; how you'd have been special no matter what, of course, but your unlikely survival—a rebirth, as you think to yourself, coming so soon on the heels of your difficult first-birth, a breech baby—only made your existence that much more precious.

"Our miracle baby. But we couldn't tell you why. I hope you can understand."

Special you are, sure. But the police car rolling into the yard has stolen your attention. Not any old cop, but Sheriff Garen Oakley himself.

Stout but in a muscular way, Oakley strides over flat and expressionless. About to deliver news which will not be news to you.

Awkward introductions. You admire his crisp uniform—you lack trust in Sheriffs who don't dress out. Badgeholders in suits equal inflated egos, in your mind.

Before you can complain about how none of his graveyard shift deputies patroled through downtown Tillman Falls for almost three hours in the night, however, the Sheriff removes his hat and delivers hushed, shocking news. The Dixiana, in particular its historic mural, has been vandalized.

"Well, I be dog." You strive to keep from chuckling. "Rolled it white, did they."

"Every inch, Mr. Pettus."

"If he said he was gonna do that once, he said it a thousand durn times."

Your grandmother, sucking her dentures. "He must've come back last night long enough to finally take care of it."

"Who said that, ma'am?"

"My dead husband."

Grinning. You can't help it. "This's just a travesty, Sheriff. Any leads?"

"If we had the security cameras installed like DHS recommends these days for all shared public spaces, we'd have ourselves a precise look at who did it. But council didn't allocate the money."

"Terribly shortsighted. When we put those in the Old Market in Columbia, the crime stats all trended downward."

He held out his hands. "Wish I'd had you here to tell them that."

"Oh—they'll hear it. Don't you worry."

Once you start the redevelopment plan for downtown, you'll be addressing all such security concerns. No need to discuss that with the head LEO of the area right now. Would take too much preamble and context, but when the time comes? You'll direct council to fund the money for extra deputies and military surplus gear; you will order them to fund cameras on every light pole, lenses streaming real-time video to police HQ and to the neighborhood associations. You'll see to it all, and oh, how his cop-eyes will light up, and cop-dick stretch into a nonsexual erection, when he sees you.

Money. Power. Influence. Who didn't get off on it?

"Sheriff, I should be straight with you. Unless you need to use this incident as a pretext to clean out a particular neighborhood, round up some thugs or run them out of town or whatever, call off the search for the vandals."

"Why's that?"

"It's an inside job."

Mee-maw cusses from the porch. "Roy Earl Pettus! Is that what you were off doing last night?"

"Yes'm. Naughty, naughty little me."

The Sheriff, suspicious as hell. "This was your doing?"

You explain how you'd always found the piece of art offensive, downmarket, and worse, divisive; and you'd been waiting for the day to come wherein it could be replaced, perhaps, by more aesthetically appropriate imagery. "The mural's useful public life has long ended, caused more trouble than it was worth—it ran off more business than it got us. A no-brainer."

"You sure about that, Mr. Pettus?"

"It's how I see things, yes. So that's how it is."

He raises his eyebrows at this assertion. "In any case, I suppose the mural question is settled."

Glowing with power, you all but shout, "Damn straight it is."

Mama Runelle, going inside the house to answer a ringing landline. "'More trouble than it was worth' is the right way to put it. Stirring up all kinda mess."

"Can't say I disagree." Oakley, smiling but serious. "The loser in a war between nations lowers its flag. End of story."

"I like your sense regarding the definitive nature of such matters," pumping his strong hand. "And I'm quite aware that a number of folks ain't gonna be happy. But you let me worry about them—part of rolling the mural is to demonstrate who'll be in charge of that block of downtown now. The heir to old Rabbit's honkytonk is here."

"Sounds pretty definitive."

"Around The Dixiana, I hear they're calling it Year Zero." Giggling and amused with yourself. "Now if ya don't mind, I'd like to get back to my breakfast. I've got a big chore to do later."

"I know you do." Tipping his hat. "My condolences."

"We'll holler if we need you."

Watching him drive off, you wonder: how did he know about your 'chore' later at the bluff? Nobody better be out there but your chosen few. And you mean, nobody. Too damn early to wield the Blade again.

CREEDENCE

Pain, the first sensation—a sharp stinging in the heel of her hand. And her throat striated and raw, naked skin dimpling against a dewy breeze from the marsh. Feeling paralyzed, she cracked open an eye. turned over her hand.

A jagged piece of seashell sticking out of the lifeline, a crease across her palm. The skin remained unbroken—the point of the shell had only made an amber pinprick.

Creedence, rolling over and coughing. Other bits of broken seashell clung to her damp naked skin, both knees torn bloody, the round patio table overturned and a huge mess over which Roy would have a freaking fit.

Ah—the bowl of decorative seashells. I busted it into a zillion pieces.

Her vision doubling, the taste in her mouth, and the smell of the drying vomit where her head had lain, made her dry-heave twice.

With nothing to do during her long days on the island but stare out at the marsh,or head to the beach, she'd worked so hard to collect the shells. At first they'd gone for long walks on the beach together, until he'd started the power-walking, the plane-flying, and the new Beanery.

Roy.

Estes.

The mess.

Shit—what happened last night? Her last memories were of...

Holy crap. Of doing it with Estes.

In the California king bed.

Hers and Roy's.

Her stomach, convulsing anew. Caked with vomit and seashells. Vomit in her hair.

Vomit.

Vodka.

The pills.

She'd tried to off herself.

Retching, coughing until her throat became shredded.

Staggering inside on bloodied knees, feet stinging from the gauntlet of broken seashells, Creedence, shaking, suffered a rush of clarity.

There—the laptop.

Open to the letter she'd left Roy.

The suicide note.

But the Macbook, dead—she'd forgotten to plug it in.

Remembering it all, now. Lying down and saying, yes, I want to die, taking the pills. Then, panicking and staggering downstairs onto the patio where she'd collapsed, puking. Puking up the pills she'd taken. *Thank god.*

Maybe it'd been more than a couple. Didn't want to know.

Heaving sputum into the downstairs guest toilet and splashing cold water on her face and abdomen, her heart went all flippy-floppy and she wondered if this was what having a heart attack felt like. She tried picking off seashells with trembling, nail-bitten fingertips. Her hands shook so bad she looked like a victim of Parkinson's Disease.

Screw the seashells—she fumbled a terrycloth robe off the hook off the door and hurried to make sure all the cats were safe and accounted for.

Satisfied with the headcount and having dumped out dry food for the mewling brood, she shuffled coughing and sniffling back out onto the marsh-side deck.

The sun, cresting the cypress trees. Its light tickled crusted, hung-over eyes.

As she hunched over sweeping up seashell fragments, tears dripped. Between her legs felt raw and dry, her stomach roiling and briny with acid backwash. Tasting the alcohol at the back of her teeth, a bitterness she supposed included a brackish remainder of the handful of Xanax.

Panic.

What if he came home? Saw this mess everywhere?

Creedence reached for one of the patio chairs, the first personal touch, purchased so the couple could sit side by side and watch the sunsets. Her vision so misty she misjudged the chair and lost her balance, collapsing with a yelp onto already injured knees.

And praying.

Praying for a solution.

For what they called salvation.

"Please, God. I can't go on. I almost done it last night—I almost killed myself. I don't want to do that. I don't want none of this no more. Wait. Yes I do: I want my husband to forgive me and take me back. I done him so wrong. Show me the way. Help me. Help me, lord. "

Breaking down sobbing she curled into a ball, but after a moment a warmth grew inside, and the nausea abated, her hands stopped shaking, the childish tears dried up, a feeling like the first breath of fall weather after a torpid, stagnant summer in Edgewater County came over her. All symptoms would return, but for this moment a peace settled inside, and an answer whispered on the wind.

She went and tried to call Roy Earl to tell him she would get his cop friend to take her to the hospital. To tell the doctor she had given herself alcohol poisoning, had also taken medication by mistake, and that she wanted to quit drinking.

But she couldn't get her husband—maybe for the best.

Called the cop, Webhannet; upon her report he insisted on sending an ambulance, which arrived in only five minutes.

After they collected her and put her on the stretcher—other residents in yoga outfits and bathrobes came out to their curbs to gawk—Creedence swore that the next time she saw her beautiful house on the marsh, she'd be sober. And would have her man, and her life, however unfulfilling, back to normal. She didn't know how. But in a sacred bargain made deep within her soul, she swore she would die trying. It's what her mother, who would be mortified by all this foolishness, would insist upon—normalcy in the face of dysfunction, whatever its disposition.

She'd make it all right again. Cover it all up. Make the truth go away. It's what mother Eileen had done best. Creedence, finally getting it.

BUTTON, MADDY, AND HEATHER

Getting her mother and grandfather ready for the surprise Rabbit memorial at the bluff: a nightmare, one making Button wish for her own early funeral. With both in states of declining mental acuity, getting them dressed could be like dealing with toddlers.

A house of sacrifice, this. Sacrifice and service given of free will to her faithful ones of Love.

The thought crept in: what if Button's magicking, benevolent in intention, had nonetheless attracted daemonic influences rather than angelic? A risk she hadn't considered at first, despite numerous warnings throughout both the literature and her dreams. Yes: The notion had come vivid in a dream. Soul-sucking entities, noticing a brilliant one below...and arriving to suck out her energy like crack hoes hungry to make their nightly nut. Battery packs for the archons. Maybe that's all people were. And people like Button, shining so bright, the most attractive prey of all.

No way. Button, too pure of heart. She blew up her magickal circle in the morning, sent off a shimmering frisson of sacred eternal light like a supernova. Elementals and imps and devils alike, black, smeary smudges glimpsed fluttery on the periphery of her astral vision, could be seen tumbling backwards from the spiritual shock wave of her banishing ceremony, if not hightailing it away fast as their dimensionality could transit them.

Putting the danger of interference from unseen actors out of her mind.

Removing the possibility from consideration.

Done.

Weaving her way around the stacks of books in her room, she sought to put together an outfit befitting the funeral of such a formidable figure in her life. Finally figured, who gives a crap, and slipped on stuff she'd normally wear, a pair of black jeans and her Keen hiking boots and a long-sleeved T-shirt, plain instead of emblazoned by a Phish logo, a powerful sigil, as she might so often choose to sport. Not a whisper of a flare of fashion sense. What a wretch. Fitting in so little around here, her whole damn life. But here she remained.

Ossifying.

Decaying.

No—quell that damnable negativity. Button, allowing herself to experience only the joy and reciprocally spiritual ennobling that comes with service to fellow incarnated souls.

⊛⊛⊛

THE COMPLAINTS from those souls began over being served scrambled tofu for breakfast, which her granddad couldn't stand, but her mom didn't seem to mind. Today's specific issue, however, involved the fact of the soy much being leftovers from yesterday.

"I'm hungry for a biscuit like my Henny used to make," her grandfather had wept from his bedroom, refusing to come to the table. "I ain't got no one left. My boy's dead. My wife's dead. Runelle won't have me. And my grandbaby's trying to feed me mush—I still got my lowers, you little shit-ass."

Button, shrugging and offering to make toast. "We have a funeral. To attend. Now is not. The time. For biscuits."

He shuffled into the kitchen. "I got to eat something."

She offered him the bowl of tofu. "Don't dump. Salt all over it. This time. Your blood pressure."

"I'll do as I please."

Tap-tap-tap-tap-tap around the rim of the bowl before the first bite; that, too, getting on everyone's nerves. Her grandfather rolled his eyes and mocked her by stomping around with his bowl clinking the spoon against it like a prisoner banging his metal cup during a nonviolent jailhouse protest.

Button's bowl tapping, a ritual; and duly important.

Rituals, crucial to the stability of the flow. Except, of course, when ritual decayed into the rote husk of true faith.

The point of her rituals? Conjuring the most benevolent of spirits.

To reside around her.

To aid and protect her.

To wit: Button, performing the banishing ceremony before her small, nondescript to the untrained eye and highly personal altar on which she lay symbolic totems representing her archangels. In paying daily veneration and calling for their assistance in pushing away the dark energy, she sought the stability of her bubble of glowing, etheric spiritual membrane for the remainder of the day, a barrier through which nefarious spirits attempted entrance at their own peril. Her ceremony, a standard lesser banishing ritual of the pentagram, a summoning of the archangels from their positions at the cardinal points of the four-winds, came complete with physical rotation and stations of the cross and specific throat vibrations. She could do it in her sleep —and often did.

But wherein the names of gods and angels had once been invoked, Button, in the grand tradition of the pagan and natural storytelling arts, had taken the ritual and the characters and made them her own; her instrument—her wand —was a pen with an LED light, given to her at a book festival she'd attended a couple of years ago, when she'd toyed with the long-held notion of becoming a writer and chronicling-slash-deconstructing her Phish journey, along with other relevant and interesting threads of her unfolding life. She clicked on the brilliant LED light and recited her modified prayer of the Qabalistic Cross, along with the appropriate gestures and tonalities, producing one or two of which made her throat itch and clench with pain.

With her lighted wand she made the sign of the pentagram, moving through each of the hard and true directions (determined courtesy of the compass app on her iPhone) and invoking not Yahweh, but vibrated the name 'Forbin.' Turning to the South, the same, but here she chanted 'Tela.' To the West, 'Rutherford,' its syllables more hummed than said. At last, to the north, true north, zero degrees, 'McGrupp.' These, the high, upper gods in her cosmology, less a beckoning than a show of acknowledgement and deference.

Next she chanted, smiled, glowed, and did a fluid, compact but swirling dance of arms and hands and feet and ankles and knees and elbows; traveling without moving. Now quieting her body, cultivating stillness in the womb of the banished circle, she held her arms cross-like, she invoked the personal archangels, who happened to share names with the Phish band members:

"Before me Ernest; on my right hand Michael; behind me Page; and on my left hand Jon. For about me flames the Pentagram, and within me shimmers the six-rayed Rhombus." And at last, a repeat of the initial blessing, which for whatever reason she had maintained from the original ceremony she'd been shown by Heather, the words more vibrated than spoken in the soft tissues of her throat: "Unto thee, the kingdom, and the power, and the glory; to the ages, ah-men."

And sighing; and feeling at peace.

For about ten seconds.

Next, meditation. Button, situating herself on the tattered plaid love seat cluttered with well-thumbed books festooned by innumerable colorful flags and Post-it notes, though not the most esoteric of her texts. Those she kept not so much concealed as simply not-noticeable, on a lower shelf of the bookcase beside her bed.

On the couch, trying for a meditation. Different chanting—her mantra. The syllables could not be revealed.

Quietude came quick; lasted all of a minute.

Voices, relentless. Her chattering monkey-mind.

No—calling from below. Calling calling calling through the heart-of-pine floors of the Sykes house, at one time one of the nicest and newest on Francis Marion Avenue here in Whaley Way, now a crumbling shadow of its former self—cluttered in every nook and cranny, overgrown yard, inhabitants dying off one by one. But with life left in them, no doubt, as their crying voiced declaimed.

A rushed moment of mental silence better than none, she supposed. Later, Button would have a proper sit, and during it, she'd find ample time—oceans and rivers of time. It was easy if one knew how to ride the waves.

Dutiful, she rose and adjusted her head-wrap, her hair pulled back into a manageable bun, cooler on the neck and upper body, but that caused people around here to stare much worse than if the dreads dangled. Around these parts, when somebody wraps their head up some funny way, folks get worried Button's already racially ambiguous ass could be some sort of Muslim.

Button, steeling herself: she missed Rabbit and grieved, and grieved for her grandfather and his grief, but she let herself realize this loss might finish him for good, which would be a net gain for her. She felt guilty, but also said, goodness' sake, he can't last much longer, not drinking the way he does. And remembering about Thim saying, he needs to rehab.

An old codger? Do they go to rehab?

This close to the end?

Granddaughter or not, who was she to decide? Button, not a fan of telling people what to do.

Ugh.

Why should she indulge that thinking anymore? Maybe her part to play was to get Grandpa Burnie into rehab. Tough as he seemed to be, maybe he had another few years in him—these days they were living to be centenarians. At the least, she'd get him back to the doctor. Not that the lecture last time did any good.

She shuddered. The realization settled over her—she was here in Edgewater County to stay. Wasn't she.

Newsflash: it'd been almost ten years.

And yet, less a voice than a notion seemed to say: *But you won't die here.*

Either way, it was fine. She loved her place here, accepted her service, blessed not only herself but her home. Cleaned it with respect. Smudged its doorways with white sage, chanted, arranged objects according to Feng Shui principles; but most of all felt gratitude. Came to her chores—her role—with a sense of positive intention.

Changing her sartorial mind, she pulled on a wrinkled black pants suit, the one she'd gotten at a thrift store to wear to her father's funeral. These, the first long trousers Button had worn since her jeans during the last cool snap back in April. The slacks hung loose. Over the summer, humid and hot, she'd gotten into the best shape of her life. Good on that.

She reminded herself again about all the positives and none of the negatives, put a smile on her face, generated light and warmth and love inside her body, and went to get her family together to go and say goodbye to Uncle Rabbit.

The shouting continued downstairs. Her grandfather, answering the phone and getting news that made him again lose his shit—as though his best friend had died anew.

"God have mercy!" Grandpa Burnie, cursing up a storm of aggrieved and unsettled energy. "*Some godforsaken cock-knocker's done whitewashed the mural.*"

Her intuition flashed: Roy Pettus. Oh, what an unnecessarily aggressive act on his part. More service ahead.

"Saturn on a sapphire. *Ay-yi-yi...*" Button, chanting her way down to the kitchen to calm her drunken, bereaved granddad. Again.

⁕

How she ended up back in South Carolina, after swearing never to return, following a lengthy sojourn on Phish tour and the aftermath, with Heather in San Diego:

Getting off a plane in Charlotte and being picked up by her dad, him being tearful at her announcement she'd rehabbed, of a sort, and presented herself to him broken, but sober.

The weeping came in a torrent from ruddy Buddy Sykes, who suffered a pasty cast to his features she'd find out had much to do with a precarious medical condition, one more acute than her more esoteric 'disease' of addiction.

Angry because she'd been out of communication so long, her comments insisting none of the problems had anything to do with Phish or the music or the amazing adventure her life had been set him off within the first five minutes.

"You put me out of touch. That one time. Didn't you. But it didn't seem to bother you then."

"I've done nothing but what we thought was best for you."

"I'm all. Screwed up for real, now. So maybe y'all's timing was off. On putting me in the nuthouse."

Truth: the Phish scene, mostly a happy and joyful, playful and creative space in which to dwell and dance and chase rainbow-farting unicorns in the form of rare tunes the band might play, or dope forty-minute funk jams they might throw down, had, through habits she'd gained along the way, all but eaten her alive and spit her back out.

Worse, or at least a piling-on of grimness, tour itself had forsaken her. That the band itself stopped playing soon after her personal collapse on the road had not been lost on her—everyone in rough shape, the lead guitarist phans called 'Big Red,' a ginger like Button Sykes, most of all.

A weighted, pop-cultural circus resting on his gentle artistic shoulders, Trey Anastasio emulated boyhood rock gods like Jerry and the Dead. But in becoming his own famous and successful version and vision of those icons, had withdrawn into substance abuse in much the same manner as Garcia suffered over being at the center of energetic focus for the expectations, criticisms and outright, unconditional love of so many untold, myriad other human souls. It's easy to see why one in such a position would turn to pills and alcohol and other emollients; easier still to understand taking a break from the rock-and-roll road, as Phish intended to do for several years, and which became a supposed permanent retirement. Or so Button would learn years later after Trey himself got sober and went around telling his story. And, thankfully, putting the band back together. Button didn't go much anymore, but damn it made her feel good for Phish to be onstage, still.

What about her excuse for the drugs? The recipient of nobody's love and attention, perhaps? Not even her own.

But blaming Phish tour? Nah. That would place blame upon external environments for a condition, addiction, which in reality dwelled within, and could be controlled from within, in varying circumstances and facing whatever triggers but remaining steadfast through the miracle of self awareness, the acquisition to the keys of higher consciousness and the wrangling of the beast-brain. It was working for this recovered addict, as she'd said to her father on the drive from the airport that day in 2001 she gave up and came crawling home to her old bedroom. A temporary situation. Sure.

TRYING at first to get a professional career going at least close to her field of study, Button worked a stint as a media librarian at the world-class library in downtown Columbia to which she commuted from Tillman Falls. This gig lasted a year and a half, a brutal and demoralizing experience with only one positive aspect: her breaks and free time hanging out around the huge Southeastern University campus and in coffee shops in search of bohemian brethren.

But without making new friends, and being an outcast at work, the search proved futile.

Work. Hah. A glorified DVD checkout clerk dealing with squalling kids and being gaslighted by the cliquish and snotty other staff members who seemed to have some secret club to which initiation went un-offered; removing objects and library materials from her workstation but insisting no one had touched her things. Whispering and disapproving body language. Egregious, aggressive and antisocial behavior, in other words.

A toxic environment, yet they made her feel like the weirdo. Never asking her to lunch. No one, not one fellow librarian. Maybe Button's attentiveness to detail and a tendency to point out inconsistencies in policy matters had irritated—no; threatened—her snobby colleagues. They hated her dreadlocks, her odd racial mix, her slow manner of speech—who knew? They never even gave her the chance to bore them with her Phish tour war stories. C'mon.

Suggestions of impropriety involving marijuana, however, made her exit from the library a fait accompli. Button admitted to puffing her herb, medicinal, in the car on the drive over, afterwards applying rich essential oils and chewing hot cinnamon gum to cover lingering odor. "This cannot persist," had been the mutual verdict.

A series of food service jobs followed, a desperation move designed to keep father-dear off her case, who by this point had endured treatment for lymphoma and seemed in remission. She also announced the intention to save money for an ostensible run at grad school, though the thought of doing so filled her with emptiness and ennui.

An attempt at fine dining service came first thanks to a tip from a library patron, in a classy Italian dump across the river in West Columbia with a view of the skyline. Her inability to remember the simplest of orders, which servers needed to be capable of doing rather than scratching onto tickets like at the diner, necessitated a change to a less fusty burger joint and bar in the Old Market near campus. Drinking held no interest, so the alcohol service presented no problem. Popped a Xanax here and there. Maybe a Klonopin. To help sleep through the daylight hours. She often worked vampire shifts that didn't begin until five in the afternoon.

This path, however, precipitated relapse: restaurant kitchens were petri dishes providing rich growth environments for alcohol and other drug abuse. A slippery slope. All too available, the pills. Everybody seemed to carry around little prescription bottles. Some actually had prescriptions. Doctors handed out drugs like clowns serving children's ice cream at a birthday party.

When she found herself having a Captain Morgan's and Coke one night after the shift, she said, I gotta stop this crap—if nothing else, having to drive all the way back to Edgewater County would cause her to get a DUI or crash or who knew what other vehicular-related ills. The tips sucked anyway, not coming from college students, the serving of whom accomplishing little but a stark reminder her of the passage of time. Of missed opportunities. Squandered ambition.

No; she needed solitude and routine more than a paycheck.

To stay sane and sober.

Practice.

Rituals.

Including, as discipline much later took hold, a revisiting of the Phish scene.

⊛⊛⊛

After ten years went by in a blur of failed writing attempts, lost jobs, relationships no deeper than those cultivated in chat rooms and on message boards, and family crises culminating with her father's fatal diagnosis and death from fresh cancer, for the first time in a geologic epoch Button Sykes traveled to see her favorite band. Phish stadium shows in weed-friendly Colorado had become the Labor Day capper on the end of their annual summer tour, and it was an easy call where she'd go on this self-help vacation.

But her trip, short compared to the years spent traipsing around all over the country behind the band, became more epiphanic than she expected: three dried grams of shrooms concealed in a chocolate candy, her entrée back into the world of mind expansion, would become one of the most therapeutic and profound experiences of her life.

She didn't consider her decision to trip as risky; Button's abused substances of choice, alcohol and pills, had nothing to do with psychedelics, which in this case precipitated a tubes-flushing instance of otherworldly, cleansing grace.

Best. Trip. Ever.

The next day had been the brightest and most beautiful of her adult life. And best of all there'd been one more show to go, by a band that'd returned from its own personal nadir to create some of the most profound music of its late era, right before her eyes, a fondest wish coming true.

The glow stick war seemed like spiraling self-replicating DNA strands exploding out of the soupy, swirling mass of humanity.

The brass ring.

Levitation.

With this mindset in place, and the band at a modern-era creative peak of health and happy energy, her concert mushroom experience had been a journey spinning her through one of those classic heady psychedelic traverses, from birth and ecstasy to fear and death to glorious rebirth, all in the course of a first set of classic tunes and then an exploratory, jammy five-song second set through which she twirled on the field at the back of the soccer stadium. The other two Colorado shows were hot, too, the best since Phish had reemerged from their supposed retirement; everyone seemed to agree, even online in the contentious message board forums. Who knew what the next year would hold. An artistic resurrection come to full fruition. Sweet.

Maybe that's why Button got back into Phish so hard, attending shows only so often, but in the internet age, never missing a note, streaming every concert and scrutinizing every live show vault release: doing so offered a glimpse of her youth, when all had been possible. Before it'd all gone wrong; before she became mired in Edgewater County; before Buddy Sykes retired from the plant and faced down a dire prognosis. Again.

Did it matter? Does it now?

Her father died. Phish came back. What did it have to do with anything?

Only as she'd walked around the lot scene outside the shows in Colorado checking out the itinerant hippy vendors did she get shudders of the old days, the bad days, the lost days spent as a helper on a chuckwagon during almost all of 1999 and 2000 Phish tour, including Big Cypress in the Florida everglades to ring in the new millennium, a fat trip of an all-night set, dusk to dawn, at which she'd had a less than mystical experience on Molly and shitty coke. But also damned hard work standing over a hot grill twisting eight-layer burritos all weekend, and for all the next year at shows by other bands too, like Widespread Panic and String Cheese Incident, the same druggy jam band demo as Deadheads, a tradition carried into the new age.

Her service back then all went to this flat-brim wearing dude named Sancho, the captain of the road crew, and his little assortment of crust-muffins, a mini-cult of girls with dirty feet and mildewy, unkempt dreadlocks. Button couldn't see what was happening, not for a long time. Too many good drugs and good times turned into indentured servitude, but hey, at first it seemed like a family, a road one to take the place of the real one in which she had no place. Sancho's real name was Scott McKendrick, another suburban middle class whiteboy, but he strutted around like a shaman. He talked the talk about spirituality, but in the end only about drugs and money. Slinging the burritos; slinging Molly. Gas to follow the band wasn't cheap. And tours back then could be long and arduous affairs.

Those last two years before her crash, Button hit pretty much all the shows, except the brief Japan tour and the last few, missed due to being left behind by her posse in Salt Lake City. Japan would've been the bomb; at least one show was now considered a classic. While on that side of the Pacific rim she could have gone to visit her mother's homeland, Vietnam. No one in her crew was flying across borders, though. Not with the habits they'd all acquired, Button included.

Pills and powders. Doses, Molly, speed, pills, coke, crank, crap like Special K. Garbage-pail partying: Trashy, sad, and untenable.

IN A PLACE FAR FROM HOME, her personal Phish hiatus began, in late 2000, only a week before the band's own self-imposed sojourn off the road, and precipitated by a trip to the hospital after a nitrous oxide binge. The hard-partying of the two Vegas shows and the hot ride down to Phoenix had weakened her system. That's all. Too much too fast. Next to no memory of the legendary Roses Are Free>Piper>Guy Forget>When the Circus Comes>Camel Walk sequence that comprised the meat of set two, but a vague recollection of her people discussing it in the RV while she puked and trembled, her extremities tingling and vision doubling long after the last balloon, a hot mess.

Dumped at a hospital. Unconscious in a wheelchair, covered in vomit, her feet black from the lot. Too much merchandise in the camper to risk the questions. She got it.

The medical personnel, their faces all blurry masks to her now, told Button she may have damaged internal organs like her kidneys and other 'vitals,' as the doctor explained to her like a child, because she looked like a kid, and it'd always been a goddamn problem, and here was this nice-looking young doctor treating her like twelve instead of twenty-three. Not good. But after some fluids and rest, her numbers bounced back and she felt better.

The gas episode had been the medical crisis that ended the good times—sucking on balloon after balloon in the Arizona heat outside the Desert Sky Pavilion, going out of her body several times and floating above the lot scene, asphalt poured over desert caliche and a phantom smell like sulphur or burning rubber as she teetered on an unconsciousness into which she ultimately fell, a deep well indeed. But being left behind by her crew had been the real reason tour ended for her. She'd never have left otherwise. She had nowhere else to go but with her road crew.

Lying there in a strange hospital bed sobering up, it struck her: two years out of Foothills State, the media arts degree worth nothing, at least to one who'd never bothered to pursue any film jobs beyond the student work she'd done. Ah, but the PA work on the Disney films that shot on campus the autumn before she got into Phish, an experience from which she'd been lucky enough to cultivate friendships with powerful and wealthy people, offered a hail-mary to keep from having to call her parents. One wealthy movie star in particular she called from the hospital.

"And, you're who, again?" World-famous Maddy Durango's assistant, incredulous. "'Button'? Is this a joke? Button calling on behalf of whom?"

"She said to call if I ever needed her," Button pled quite truthfully. "And I do."

"How did you get this number?"

Button, trying not to cry, telling the mean woman she'd been given the number. By Ms. Durango herself.

The gatekeeper made a sound like *Humpf* and put her on hold.

But yeah, the next voice on the line had been the movie star herself, half of the most famous twins on the globe, at one time anyway, the half who'd befriended Button during the location shoot of those Disney movies. The only movies on which Button would ever work.

Maddy, frantic, asking where Button was, and the nature of her condition. And where she'd been all this time, too. "I dreamed about you last night—I kid you not. Button. The campus of Foothills State. Karen Black. All in my dreams. And here you're calling today. In trouble."

"Are you serious? That's—that's." A blank spot. The words wouldn't come. A gear clicked into place. "That's wild, dude."

"There are no coincidences, Button. We made a special connection, the two of us. You've confirmed the magic. I am at your disposal."

Button wanted to say to the gatekeeper who'd been so disbelieving, see? It wasn't an empty promise, because damned if she and Maddy hadn't kept in touch for a year or more after the campus movie shoot, long emails that might have petered out, but for a time came with such regularity it was like a crazy dream that wouldn't end: the big-time celebrity with whom Button Sykes had a mad if ephemeral sexual affair, and which in her mind led to the ephemeral relationship with Heather Ponderview, once Button's door opened to her true carnal intentions, sapphic in nature.

Maddy Durango, Button began in that moment to figure out, released in her a spirit free enough to become the spun, weirdo crust-muffin who'd gotten into trouble on Phish tour, and so calling for a bailout made a symmetrical bit of cosmic sense. A lattice of coincidence, as the mystical, shamanistic character in *Repo Man* explained the mechanics of the universe? Or some wacky, intricate, magical cosmic plan? The eternal question. But that dream stuff, that was too much. Button, wondering if Maddy hadn't made it up.

❂❀◉

THE MADDY STORY: as Hollywood showed up in the spring of Button's junior year with the two of the biggest stars in the world, Maddy and Vangie Durango, to shoot scenes for not one but two movies, Foothills State became a bustling concrescence of opportunities for a media arts student—PA work, internships, academic credit, and as her instructors emphasized most of all, real-world experience no classroom environment or student project could replicate.

The pictures being shot back-to-back were modernized remakes of a series of late 1960s Disney programmers Button had never seen but looked up on a new at the time 'website' called the Internet Movie Database. It'd been easy enough by searching on the star of the series, a young, tan, all-American Kurt Russell. The young star, along with a troupe of other good looking kids, got up to shenanigans sounding from their plot summaries maybe one notch above Scooby Doo adventures, to be charitable.

The modernized version of two episodes from this ancient kid-friendly franchise chosen for corporate synergetic attention, *The Computer Wore Tennis Shoes* (a science experiment makes Russell gets super smart, leading to intrigue and shenanigans and chase scenes) and *Now You See Me, Now You Don't* (in which the discovery of an invisibility mist leads to yadda yadda more of the same), were to feature the Durango twins as a gender-switched re-imagining of the singular Kurt Russell character. An added wrinkle had these young women, one a brilliant and logical science whiz and the other a free-spirited, romantic philosopher, sparring with the long-suffering dean of the small college at which their episodes occur, a Dean who also happens to be... their own mother! Hijinks ensue as the twins become embroiled in similarly plotted adventuresome japes as in the Russell pictures, which to Button seemed like most Hollywood product, i.e., silly, inconsequential fluff. But what did anyone expect from Disney and the Durango twins?

But actual professional film work, right there on campus? This, an opportunity not to be missed. She checked with her academic advisor, a poet and media writer named Brenda LaRose. The professor, who liked Button, greased the wheels and got her name to the head of the list of students applying for the few course-credit crew positions not being filled by union folks from nearby metropolises Atlanta and Charlotte.

In any case, Foothills State, where Button studied toward a media arts degree after barely skirting out of Southeastern with a decent enough grade point average to get into the filmmaking track at F-U, as the student body waggishly called their beloved mountaintop college, had already been good to her: not only had she met and fallen in love—that is, become close friends— with Heather Ponderview, but thanks to Foothills's media college dean, who enjoyed deep and meaningful ties to the entertainment industry resulting in movies being made there in NC, Button's decision to transfer from Southeastern U appeared at that point to have been win-win-win.

Over her two semesters at F–U before the film shoot, Button had impressed her instructors and classmates by making her own well-received 16mm film, and writing a feature-length screenplay. Professor LaRose insisted Button ought to send out the script to competitions, but she couldn't bring herself to do so.

The work had been all so boring and messily, uncomfortably autobiographical—a mixed-up small woman from a rural small town without a clue who she is or from what blood her true nature and intellect flowed, her mother's

Asian DNA, or her father's redheaded, good old boy Edgewater County loud-mouth persona that'd so defined his personality. Echoes of each one—skin and hair pigmentation from him and diminutive size and Asian features from her mother Trinh, a tiny Vietnamese dormouse, the quivering, frightened woman with little English. The family called her Tinky. It suited her.

But Thim, she had gotten Daddy's long legs and broad shoulders, and the striking black hair of a Vietnamese girl, with eyes to match; a beauty queen to her little sister's mongrel.

But Button's time at Foothills, yeah, her brush with Hollywood, enough to put her off film work. Or so she claimed to herself after she later left ordinary life behind to go live on tour.

But in the heat of the moment as a student, she'd been thrilled by her proximity to A-list Hollywood moviemaking: after assuming she'd lose out on the PA positions to more experienced students, she'd lucked into one of the slots on the production. Yes, she got a break. But no way in hell did she plan to do below-the-line work on Hollywood shit like this. No way. Button would make incendiary documentary films that would light a fire under people's fat asses about the various issues at hand. A dumb teen comedy—starring a pair of vapid, millionaire nineteen-year-olds, no less—was, like, not Button's scene, man.

But her film teacher, another strong and talented woman named Hedda Garland, convinced her that, no matter which way her career might eventually go, the experience and contacts she'd make in those few weeks would prove invaluable.

"You'll find many committed artists working on this level of commercial filmmaking," Garland said. "It's not all pap like this Disney stuff. And you will need experience to pull off your cinematic statements, Ms. Sykes. So don't miss this chance to work in the business."

"I dunno. More of a writer. Maybe."

"Nonsense. You've got quite an eye for composition," making a thumb and forefinger frame in front of Button's face, which made her giggle. "Don't sleep on the chance at work, in whatever form it comes."

Button, taking the advice to heart. Before starting on the movies as an official production assistant she quit smoking herb and detoxed with a juice cleanse supervised by Heather, took Niacin and megadoses of multivitamins and hiked nearby steep trails every afternoon until drenched in sweat. By the time the crew showed and up and the production got underway, Button felt centered and certain all would work out.

✦❋◉

ONE MORNING on set she'd been given the task of beckoning the twins from their trailer, and on the walk over to the set, Maddy—the more friendly of the two celebrities—engaged Button in conversation. Within minutes, all three were squealing in delight at their mutual interest in issues such as the environment and energy and injustice.

Besides partying and getting laid with Maddy Durango—no fucking way; but yes, way, Button licking and fingering the worldwide movie star to orgasm, and being diddled and manipulated the same until climax and release, her most important experience of sexual awakening, like, ever— she loathed working on the movie shoot, rued her time on the set, had been treated in a shabby and dismissive by everyone on the crew. If this was film-making, you could keep it.

An example of this had been cinema icon Karen Black, late of such prestige Hollywood New Wave fare as *Easy Rider* and *Five Easy Pieces*. The method actress suffered having to play many over-the-top, histrionic scenes as the beleaguered dean forced to contend with the precocious and outlandish activities of her own daughters there on the picturesque campus of the fictionalized Middletown State College where the All-American, PG-rated pictures were set, and as a result the Hollywood veteran seemed out of sorts, forever suffering from an incipient migraine. Curt, rude, looking right through Button as though she were a vaporous reflection rather than a real human.

Inside the movie star's trailer, however, Black became motherly and confessional, chalking up her headaches to the "shit lines" her role forced through her white movie-star teeth. "But work is work."

Didn't a famous star like Karen Black have enough money? Button could only shrug. "You shouldn't do anything you don't want to."

"Honey, if you only knew what being a woman in this business entails."

Button asked what she meant. Black, a shadow crossing her features, said the ugly details were better left unspoken.

It'd been that day while Button acted as PA to Ms. Black when Maddy Durango, skeletal and hollow-eyed—the much more aloof Vangie looked so fresh-faced and healthy compared to her sister, who suffered anxiety and eating disorders—had blundered into the trailer, plopped down on Ms. Black's couch and burst into hysteric tears.

Ms. Black shooed Button toward the door, but Maddy smiled through her tears and said, no no no no, Button can stay. "I need a younger person's perspective, too," the red-nosed, famous face pled. "I want someone real to talk to. Who isn't in the business."

Black snorted. "It's like you anticipated what we were already talking about."

"Which was what?"

"That any woman getting into show business should prepare herself to eat shit."

Maddy grabbed Button, forcing her to drop her clipboard. "Sit down. I asked craft services prepare herbal tea for us—isn't that special?" And operatic tears again, flopping her bony frame onto the couch and covering her pale, pimply face, so different out of makeup, with a suspicious, bruised forearm.

At that point Karen Black, the famous actress, and Button Sykes, diminutive PA from Edgewater County, SC, exchanged a look of solidarity: *what on earth do we have on our hands here?*

The bonding Maddy and Button would achieve over the next few heady, drug-fueled days together—oh, how disappointed Black seemed when the truth came out, that Button had not been a helper but an enabler—would lead years later to the phone call from the hospital in Arizona where her so-called tour family dumped her, and the amazing instance of reverse servitorship that grew out of the swampy, foggy bottom into which Button had floated on a plume of cold nitrous oxide.

A helluva story, her Durango episode, but in the end important only because the experience had gotten her sober. Easy enough when one's status affords them a personal physician, privacy, and the wherewithal to cover the costs of such top-shelf healthcare.

⊛

ONCE MADDY HANDED the line back over that day Button lay bereft and sick in Phoenix at the hospital, the chastened Durango gatekeeper, Tiffani, said, "Everything's being arranged. Tell the nurse your ride will arrive in three hours. Assuming they're ready to release you."

"I think they are," Button had said through a tearful throat. "Thank you."

"I can't wait to meet you, dear. Have a nice flight."

Flight?

The details didn't matter: Someone had taken charge of her unmanageable life. A miracle. Button gave herself over to Maddy Durango's care.

She hadn't felt helped by any of her posse on Phish tour—only abandoned like an unwanted pet. Half of those poseurs didn't even go into the shows anyway—they were there to sling bunk doses and pharmies, grill burritos and chalupas and sling those, too. Button would always try to talk about the music, the jams, the possibility of a Gamehendge show or just epic jams, and the dudes would be like, whatever. Girls didn't know much about music, only how to sell dope and lot food and fuck, even though it hurt and she didn't want to, but only did because of being drunk and spun all the time. A graceless, antipodal contrast to the beauty and music coming from the stage inside, her life on the road—what had she been thinking?

⊛

HOURS LATER, Button watched with interest from the wheelchair as a black SUV with tinted windows pulled into the white-zone turnaround of the hospital.

"Looks like somebody important." The orderly waiting with Button noted this with remarkable boredom. "We had the governor here one time."

"What was wrong with him?"

The young Hispanic man sucked his teeth. "All I know is it was a rectal-object removal. But you didn't hear it from me."

Button managed to laugh through the shakes and queasy stomach.

The orderly stiffened as two men in black, looking and acting like cops—or rather, as it became apparent, bodyguards to the rich and famous—rolled with situational awareness out of the shiny SUV.

The leader of the men, with a brow looming heavy and straight across the top of two small, no-bullshit, piercing little cop-eyes—oh, had Button learned to detect those, in watching out for undercover narcs in the Phish lot!—greeted her with a cold smile: "Allyson B. Sykes?"

Button nodded, as did the orderly.

"Ms. Durango says you prefer—'Button'? Am I reading this right?"

"I—I suppose I do," in a voice she suspected sounded small and Southern. She might as well have said 'reckon.'

"Where you from?" the second security dude asked in his own lilt. "Birmingham, Alabama born and raised. Yes-sir."

The lead security agent, who introduced himself as Chamblee, assisted Button out of the wheelchair and toward the SUV's open back door. "This is a lovely little ma'am, Jenkins. Not a sir."

"I know that," Jenkins said. "It's a colloquial 'yes-sir.' Right, Ms. Sykes?"

Button, flattered. She could only imagine how rough she looked. She needed more than the sponge bath the nurse had given her. "Sure."

"Southerners have a particular way of communicating. A Yankee like you, Chamblee, wouldn't get it."

"Happy not to get it. The Yankees won."

"Where are we, like, going?" Button, still feeling spun from all the nitrous and the doses and the whatnot and thinking maybe she might be in a movie, in one of those Durango girls' movies, the more grownup features they were making by then instead of the Disney kid flicks. She hadn't had her own home for a long time. "I grew up back in South Carolina."

Jenkins, no nonsense: "Ms. Durango's flying you to New York."

"New York?" It'd been a dream of hers to go there. Her ideal would have been attending NYU for grad school, but too damned expensive. She'd asked so much of her parents already. They were middle-class people, and by then granddaddy lost all of his businesses he used to have, and wasn't anything but a drunk. "For real?"

"Appears that way. Where are your belongings?"

She thought hard about the last place she had seen her backpack and sling bag with her ID and credit cards and other clothes and her notebooks with the screenplay ideas she was supposed to be working on while out on tour all the time estranged from her family and away from everyone and everything she'd ever known and loved. "My stuff. The assholes who dumped me. Still have it."

Chamblee informed her Ms. Durango would take care of her, and any lost material objects could be replaced.

Jenkins, on the other hand, asked a series of questions about the whereabouts of her belongings, which had not accompanied her to the hospital; Button, giving him the names of her posse and the descriptions of their vehicles and furthermore, where the tour was going from there, only a few more shows before Phish began their indefinite hiatus, and who knew if they'd ever play again and she almost died and it felt like the end of history to her sitting outside a small, suburban Arizona hospital surrounded by strangers. The bodyguard jotted down the details in a pocket notebook.

Button's tears dropped onto her lap. "I wanted to say I had gone to the last shows."

"Why—because of all the dope?"

She was like, nah, *bruh*. "In case the band doesn't come back from the hiatus."

"Relax. Rock stars always return from these retirements," Jenkins drawled with reassuring sagacity. "Country singers, though, they ain't got the shame enough to do it that way. Make it so obvious. Naw. They just keep on year after year without all that retirement hooey, which ain't nothing but marketing. You ever been to Branson?" He twisted around in the front seat of the humming Escalade, its fat tires eating up the sunstruck shimmering concrete of the Phoenix freeway system. "I bet your hippie band don't play there. Not yet, anyway."

The thought was absurd. Branson? Phish, a force and culture unto itself. Maybe somebody would build a town around them one day, the way Bill Graham had built the Shoreline Amphitheater, where Phish would perform the final show of the 2000 tour, so that the Dead would have an outdoor hometown venue always waiting for their performing presence to appear. What a beautiful dream.

⊛⊛⊛

Days later, in the fabulous Central Park-facing New York apartment of Maddy Durango, Button found herself attended by the star's personal physician, a sweet-spoken African man, Dr. Abuto Olabode, who supervised an outpatient detox regimen prescribed at Ms. Durango's expense and direction, all while wearing a white suit and a red fez and speaking in circumspect, accented riddles Button could have sworn were hypnotizing her into not wanting to get high.

By then Maddy, who had taken a hiatus from acting, had been sober for a year, as she explained to Button. "In asking the Universe for help and strength, I bargained to serve and help others," she said, with Button representing the first person to come to her with a situation requiring assistance of this nature; that when she heard Button's pitiful voice, the word SERVE appeared to Madeline Durango—her preferred adult billing—with a brilliant bluish-white light pulsating behind enormous letters clamped onto the rails of a cosmic marquee. "A mission. To serve. That's you, honey. At least in this moment."

Button, pulsing with gratitude. "I don't know why. You would help. Someone like me."

"In olden times, it would have been called noblesse oblige," Maddy said, poised on the edge of a sofa in an expansive room with floor to ceiling windows, the park and the west side glowing ochre from an approaching sunset. "To me, it's only giving back."

Ten days into Button's stay, and with her feeling much better after a brutal detox, the doorman rang to say FedEx had delivered a package from the security company, and damned if it didn't turn out to be her sling bag and backpack!

A handwritten note in the box read:

Allyson,

Your friend 'Sancho' gave up your gear without too much of a fuss. I made him feel bad for ditching you like that, but I'm not sure he cared, so I think this all worked out for the best.

Went into the show there at Shoreline Amphitheater and thought it was weird but kinda good, to tell the truth. One of the Grateful Dead guys came out and played with them. Everybody acted like it was the Second Coming. I didn't even really care, but all my little hairs stood up anyway.

On the way out somebody told me the same thing you did. That now no one knew when Phish would come back, and again, I thought it sounded almost like Jesus, in a way. But my faith's not something I should discuss with you in this professional context, and I could probably get in trouble for writing any of this. But I wanted to witness in that small way to a fellow Southerner who seemed in distress. You take care, now. I hope all your stuff is there and accounted for. Peace and healing be with you.

Yours in Christ,
    Chip Jenkins

Button, tearful with relief at seeing her notebooks all still present, also that she missed the onstage appearance by Bob Weir, a real passing of the torch moment from the Dead to the Phish world. Her photos, the set lists she kept, the stickers she'd collected, a tattered friendship bracelet Heather tied on three years before, that had dry-rotted and come off but kept close ever since, a sacred memento.

The bracelet may have returned, but Heather had not.

Button would leave those belongings in their packaging to ship them a second time a month later, when she'd said to Maddy Durango, who had pointedly NOT wanted to continue their sexual relationship from the North Carolina movie shoot, that she felt well enough to start life anew on her own, to which Maddy agreed, and how their paths would cross again one day.

"You know I'll have my people look at any screenplays you've written." Maddy, reassuring Button during their long and warm goodbye hug. "Soon as you land an agent," she'd added. "My people, they could get in trouble otherwise."

Button understood. The last thing on her mind was writing screenplays. She had to be more realistic. If nothing else, there were no more Phish tours, so she couldn't hide there. No place left to hide—and sober, to boot.

Maybe she'd return to South Carolina for a few weeks or months. Work in Columbia. Save money. Her father paid for all the schooling—there weren't any loans, not in her name. Button Sykes, at that moment, presented to the world as tabular rasa, pretty healthy, in search of a path of her own choosing. The harm in going home to Edgewater County for a teensy bit of time seemed modest. Tillman Falls would not hold onto her any more than it had the first time she left.

But first, a decision to reconnect with Heather Ponderview, which she figured she could achieve by contacting the Ponderview Foundation that funded so many of their prior touring adventures. Speaking of missions, Button had one: to find the girl. To hold her again. Reconcile; have closure; some fucking outcome. Back when Button had been fixated on outcome. An unenlightened time.

◌⚛◯

KNOWING Heather had stayed out west in San Diego, Button made the first choice on her new journey: to reach out in person to her old friend, explain the situation, consent to a visit. No way could Button go home yet.

The Ponderview Foundation owned an Ocean Beach house, a Victorian family home. The property had come on her mother's side, from before a young woman of privilege married into the fortune as the trophy wife, siring Heather and extending the heirs by one. Heather's father, pushing sixty at the time of her conception, also made a son, a phantom half-brother to her, all the way back in 1950, but the adventuresome, unencumbered young man of means, a mountain climber, had perished in his twenties trying to scale the face of Mount Meru; dead before Heather ever knew him. TMI.

Embarrassed at never pursuing her media arts work, Button, leaning her head against the fogged plexiglass of a Greyhound bus window seat, rued the catch-up to come with Heather. Nothing to show. No degree—she'd never finished a thesis project. No documentaries, about Phish or any subject. No meaningful work except being a jamband lot lizard, getting used and abused and spun out in parking lots from coast to coast.

Does life experience count?

What a waste, as she would present herself to Heather after the bleak bus trek across the country from New York, a far remove from Maddy Durango's chartered Learjet, but a ride taken at Button's insistence, if paid for by money given out of Maddy's purse at the door to the fabulous apartment.

A thousand dollars in crisp Benjamins. Button, tearful, couldn't meet her benefactor's eyes. "You already. Saved my life. That's enough."

Maddy, so much healthier than on the shoot of the Disney movies, pulled Button close, but in a completely nonsexual manner. Like Heather, another dabbler in the sapphic arts: Maddy, of late seen dating a series of airbrushed Hollywood hunks. "I don't know how I feel about all this bus foolishness. You need further treatment and rest."

"Think of it like. A beat writer's journey." She'd write a screenplay about her experiences. Ring up Professor LaRose. Get feedback on some fresh pages. The story required the profundity and discomfort only a cross-country bus ride could afford, but yeah, maybe she'd already done that part; also had to be worth telling. "I'll send it to you—your people, I mean. My agent. When I get one."

"Okay, sweetie. You do that."

Before Button could ask if Maddy had any agents in mind for the as-yet unwritten screenplay, the celeb had been swept back into the modernist glass and steel of her exclusive apartment building by Tiffanie, who shot the quivering tour rat the saddest smile this side of Pity Avenue.

Alone, Button, an ant crawling on the sidewalk, walked down through Times Square, a gaudy theme park filled with characters in various stages of LARPing, to Port Authority bus station. Free of drugs and obligations and with cash in hand, she could go anywhere.

First thought?

Only thought?

Heather Ponderview.

❀❁❀

BOTH BODIES, filled with longing. Or so Button wanted to believe:

The hug with Heather lingered there on the sidewalk in front of the mini-estate, which sat nestled between two narrow apartment complexes replacing what at one time had almost certainly been similar homes to the Ponderview property. One of the few old structures left on the street stretching down toward the Pacific Ocean, on Pescadero off Sunset Cliffs Boulevard—Pescadero Avenue rather than Drive, a parallel street causing confusion on Button's cab ride from the bus station—Button would find out the house was built in the early 1900s in "the familiar Spanish Eclectic style," as Heather put it, and sat behind hedges and flanked by two more of the towering palms dotting the area, red shingles curved and bright in the sun, and Heather standing under the portico with open arms, waiting.

Heather gripped Button's round face in her loving hands. "Oh, sweetie—you look like you've been through a rough patch."

"My tour crew. They fucked me over. Left me. For dead."

Beaming, Heather—eyes: pale blue—now gripped Button by her fleshy biceps. "That will never happen to you here. Not as long as I'm in charge."

As she'd seemed back at Foothills five years earlier, Heather was head hippie and housemother to a revolving cast of faces Button grew to know, and partially despise, over the next six months of the rest, rehab, and spiritual cleansing Maddy's doctor had prescribed. Heather suffered lost puppy syndrome, attracting a scruffy, hapless entourage of tour rats and other kids like Button, it seemed, with their many difficulties and travails. Button would only be one more.

After only a few days, however, she grew weary of what she perceived as drugged out leeches, including herself to a certain extent, sucking off the Ponderview tit (oh—if only she had been so fortunate in that regard). Button might have been spun for the last few years, but she always paid her way, either in cash or in-kind. She tried to remind herself of the extraordinary circumstances of her recovery. No less than two benefactors with enormous sums of money energy at their disposal had taken her under their wing. Lucky. Many drug addicts ended up in jail, or dead. Enjoyed no advocates, no resources, no good fortune. Were treated like criminals, lepers, outcasts rather than human beings with a medical condition.

And after Ocean Beach, Button, too, found herself grappling with an altered view not only of herself, but of her role in this incarnation: Loyalty. Circumstance. Illness. Sometimes people needed help. Needed guidance and support in means and manners other than materialistic. Service as a goal, not accumulating wealth. "It's our truest self, the self in service," Heather said on more than one occasion.

True selves. Now this idea interested Button, who'd spent much of her life feeling untethered and untrue.

That's the real reason she'd come back to Edgewater County and stayed—because others had served and assisted her; a spiritual debt owed not to the individual actors, but to the world. Sure, to take care of her parents, but Thim and Grandpa Burnie could have handled matters, and in her continued absence no doubt would have; Button, no savior. But emulating the people who, without hesitation, helped when neither had any particular call to do so, at least aside from the notion of friendship. Beyond the service element, Button perceived an obligation to the necessity of relative solitude, if not in a rural environment per se, at least away from large cities. Also, not have to hold down a regular-type job, either. Having a job only for the sake of money? Might as well be in prison.

Rabbit Pettus felt sorry for her. That's how she landed the front of house gig at the honkytonk. Doing his best pal and her granddad a favor, yeah, for poor, shattered, drug-addled little Button.

What they didn't know? How it all fit in with her plan; that to achieve the level of non-doing and non-being she had in mind once her mother died, she lacked the time and proper motivation to hold down some stupid workaday job. She felt no need for possessions anymore, no need for money, really, which Button held in disdain as part of the prison-planet reality matrix imposed on the species by forces unknown. Money, the ultimate abstraction; money, the ultimate veil over the eyes of the world. Having so little desire for money and objects manifested inside her intellect and spirit as an opposing force to the abstraction presented by commerce: freedom, concrete and at hand. Present. Right now. The grandest gift; the plentitude of the multiverse available to anyone wise enough to open their consciousness to the inherent possibilities.

We all had to live, though, didn't we? Provide? And eat? We weren't all child movie stars or Ponderview Incorporated heirs. Plus, the initiate is wise to remember that earthly responsibilities must not be shirked, nor should powers used only for material gain, with desire-focused, outcome-based work for personal aggrandizement, glory, or physical sensation prohibited and danger-ous, in a karmic sense.

Like, say, casting a love-spell to make someone fall for you. As an experi-ment in human psychology. Not that Button would pull such a stunt on anyone like a callow, frightened new college roommate.

On same days she still considered writing that book or screenplay, in her weaker moments while cooking dinner for her family, cutting the grass, picking up prescriptions, doing laundry, searching for her grandfather's hidden liquor bottles, when she felt a dearth of accomplishment.

Stabs at it: A drug-addiction memoir, *The View from Point Loma*, had been started there on the beach in San Diego. Intended to track back through the era of her drug experimentation in college and on Phish tour, in the end the few chapters she completed came out too raw, personal, and inconsequential a story to continue. The latest idea for a novel, called *The Greening of Ponderview Alley* and subtitled 'A Sapphic Romance,' had stalled at the point of character creation: her first description of the obvious Heather persona left her shaken and in tears and wishing only to hold the real flesh and not that of her ghostly half-creation, a chimeric reflection of the real. A sad and shallow and useless one.

This wasn't art, it was a plea for Heather to love her again.

⊙❀◎

BUTTON HADN'T WRITTEN a word in weeks, now. Maybe she'd revisit one of her projects over the long and dreary-dull winter ahead, at least when she wasn't drumming up opposition to the billion-dollar Sugeree River Station reactor expansion project. Who knew what would be happening with The Dixiana? She supposed her job was kaput. Roy Earl, in his state of mind, liable to tear it all down. Plenty of time to write.

But San Diego with Heather had been different, way different than their old relationship at Foothills State and on tour, when it had seemed more like best-friendship than either love or what was to develop in Cali: a mentorship.

Button, not special; now only one more of the lost puppies, and given all due attention, but only a modicum. Heather had gone way out there, it seemed, in a way they'd never done on the drugs, and Button didn't know if her friend, with all the New Age stuff and chanting and meditation and rituals, didn't have herself a cult going.

Until Button grokked the vibe, one that's carried her this far.

Love—a cult of love, and service. Nothing sketchy. Altruistic. The way to live. Pledges and queries of occulted, spiritual entities, summoned to do works. No big whoop.

⊙❀◎

FOR MOST OF the first afternoon, Button released suppressed emotion in the form of tears saltier than the ocean by which her temporary home lay.

"Let me tell you about a vision I keep having." Heather, supportive and cheerful, held Button and let her dampen the pillows on the bed in the master suite where Button hoped and assumed and wished she could reside during her stay. That voice of Heather's, like cats purring. "Books."

"What—um—about them?"

"They're gonna be important, in a mission-critical kinda way."

"Like, in a way they're not now?"

"People are starting to think that books won't be around, with the internet and all. They say all of human knowledge will be on the net soon, in the hive mind." This was 2000, and what Heather described was already well under-way, not that Button had spent much time online, not since college when she had been a fixture on the alt.music.phish Usenet discussion group. "But a day will come when printed books will regain primacy as the principal instrument used in transmitting knowledge, sacred and otherwise. Or maybe, books will fall away, and information will be communicated through symbol and ritual. Maybe telekinetically as well."

"I've always felt connected to you. Like that. My mind to yours."

Heather, blushing. "That's so sweet. In any case, in these dreams—and today's dreams offer the answers to tomorrow's questions, as Edgar Cayce said —I keep seeing what I think is money, or sometimes food, and when I look again these objects have transformed into books. This is important. Books as money. Books as food."

"So we ought to? Stash away books?"

Heather nodded and stroked Button's nappy dreads, which Maddy's hair-stylist had trimmed and manicured to a more manageable mess from the rat's nest she'd presented. "There's more to it. I'm waiting for more visions. I also keep dreaming about plants—plants talking to me."

Button, a rushing sense memory of the taste of fresh bud sparked up in a clean glass bowl. "I know that feeling."

"The plant part's crucial as well. I don't know how yet. The dreams are always set in those old mountains. Back in North Carolina. I'm often stuck all night in traveler mode, trying to get back there, driving on streets that rain-slicked and shimmery-silver, like rivers of starlight..."

Button had stated her intent to never return to the Carolinas. Hah. How little she understood. A month clean, plus one day. Hah.

Heather shrugged. "The ultimate meaning of it all will reveal itself in due time. A golden age—that's what my dreams indicate is coming. People living in a small tribe on a mountain. Everybody happy and free; reading; living; loving. Time ceasing to have the same meaning it does for everyone here in this clusterfuck civilization of ours. Time, turning elastic."

Button, thinking, wow: Heather has really gone off the rails. "I'm going back to writing. Screenplays, I guess. Short stories."

"About—?"

"About being. On tour. And what happened."

"What did happen?"

Button, shrugging. "Maybe I'll find out."

"Movies, though? Finished, over, done. Same as every form of electronic media."

Button asked what Heather meant.

"When the power goes off? And like, doesn't come back on?"

Button, flashing on the plumes of the Sugeree River Nuclear Station back home. Such an outcome didn't seem possible.

"Books," she mused aloud. "I'll write one of those, too."

"There you go. Write it down. Make it real. Don't dream it—be it."

After that, she changed the subject to that of the lost Domes of Point Loma, the Theosophical Society, and a social worker and New Age thinker named Tingley who had built a special compound, "a white city in a golden land by the sundown sea," with buildings domed by amethyst and aquamarine and purple stained glass under which aspirants would practice yoga and study the works of Blavatsky. All Greek to Button then, but later she would understand all too much.

She longed to see these magnificent domes of the buildings with names like the Temple of Peace and the Raga Yoga Academy, as she recalled telling Heather, who only shook her heavy hair and smiled with knowing sadness. "Too late. Most are gone."

"'Most'?"

"The complex verges on being forgotten forever by the people who live here—its original purpose, that is." The finality of the statement felt leaden. Nothing lasts.

❂❉◉

BUTTON, spending hours alone on the beach, sunning and reading tomes from Heather's library and getting her mental processes under control. Dr. Olabode had written her a prescription for a mild, nonnarcotic anxiety medication to help with the sleeplessness, but that seemed a recipe for acquiring another pill addiction, with which Heather found agreement. "What was the point of sobering up if it's to be more pills? Herbal only, now. Melatonin tea. Let's see how that does."

The tea helped. She slept well, but had been suffering dreams epic and vivid in scope. Still, Button grappled with mania and panic. She'd been immersed in gauze for a couple of years. Clarity came with edges sharp enough to cut. At such, she felt uncomfortable amidst the others in the Ponderview house, and this despite—or perhaps because of—their general hippiness.

"And what on earth was it like—Maddy Durango's apartment?"

"I could see Central Park."

"That's the only way I'd live in New York—access to greenspace. I'm really getting sick of being here in San Diego, even with the beach right here."

"Why'd you come here?"

"To get in touch with my mother's past, not my father's."

"That's something. I should do. At some point."

Heather nodded in encouragement. "Go to Vietnam—yes."

Sober, the thought of encasing her consciousness in an aluminum tube and launching it through the air at five hundred miles per hour over the ocean provoked a stab of terror. "We'll have to see."

As though on a similar wavelength, Heather patted her on the hand and said, "But I'm not too sure anymore about air travel. What it does to our bodies, not to mention the environment."

Button shuddered. "Seems unnatural."

"Another discussion."

Off all toxic substances and glowing more with earth-goddess good health, Heather had become no less gorgeous to Button. Heather's magnificent, dreadlocked curls, her loving face draped by heavy royal curtains framing the infamously mysterious eyes, which in this light looked gray-green.

Heather Ponderview.

An angel.

A savior.

Dinner each night was communal, vegan, delicious and subtle, several gastronomic universes away from either lot food like she'd slung or the Edgewater County barbecue on which Button had been raised, chubby and unhealthy and still likely to die of cardiopulmonary disease, not only from the South Carolina diet but all the cigarette smoke she'd ingested living in tobacco country.

The faces around the long table, all young, felt like a true family of broken children and vagabond poets, multiracial, other mutts like her. Little hippies, broken and lost and in various states of either recovery or active usage; cannabis, Button noted with extreme discomfort, not included on the list of banned substances in the house, a facet of life discussed only after Button settled down from the emotional torrent Heather's embrace had released.

Helping to clean up the kitchen, a process directed by Heather herself, Button took a brief opportunity when the others all scurried away to connect with her 'old pal' in a more profound way, close like they'd once been. But here, she only meant as best friend. Deep inside, Button knew the rekindled romance, eh, didn't seem all that happening.

"Tell me what's. Going on here. Really."

Heather cocked her head, her curly macaroni hair dangling and bobbing, a loving spirit warming the air between them across the cluttered, working kitchen. She held out her hands. "What-what, my desolate angel. My old friend."

"You running? A halfway house?"

Heather laughed in a manner pitying—*oh, please.* "That sounds so institutional. This is a family situation."

Not another road family, Button thought.

NO, she seemed to hear Heather reply, who stood with a small frown and crossed arms.

"These people—yeah, even you—need a family. And you could say I'm here to provide some context. Not forever. But until they—you—can stand on two feet again, I'm at the ready to lend a hand or a hug. Let's call it big sis more than mother."

Sister? Mother? Nah. Button fought the urge to cross the room and grind her pelvis against Heather, hump her like a dog. "Where do you find them all? The bus station?"

"*Bus stay-shun?*" Heather, giggling and relaxed, seemed reminiscent of their old stoner sessions. "How long it's been since I've heard that charming *accent of your'n.*"

"But I tried so hard. To get rid of it."

"Back at F–U I used to notice how you would say things, and then adjust and flatten the next time. How you were trying to find your voice."

Button's face flashed white-hot. "I had no idea. You were even paying me. So much attention."

"You didn't say much, but when you did? I made sure to listen."

"You made me feel so—welcome. And loved." Here Button meant what she meant, and yes it included the lovemaking Heather had always been so easy to dismiss as teenage experimentation. "Right from the beginning," she added in a rush to emphasize the burgeoning friendship connotation of 'loved' rather than type that included having her pussy eaten and orgasming against Heather's moaning, joyfully full lips and probing tongue. Button's voice had come strained and tight: "And I've really missed you since tour."

"I actually went to Shoreline. Since that might be all she wrote on Phish."

No-shit, Button said, shaking her head. "If I hadn't been such a nitrous whore in Arizona, I'd-a been there."

"But you wouldn't be here now. If it hadn't happened."

"True story."

Button cringed at telling Heather the ugly details, like the memory of Sancho fucking her in the RV that last morning, rolling on and pushing himself inside and stroking to a brief, grunting climax without looking once into her eyes or saying a word. Rolling off. Farting. Talking about going inside the Walmart to buy tortillas for later in the lot.

And worst of all, not seeming to give a crap about Phish or the music. Only the drugs and money and grunting body functions. The nitrous episode? Easy—she'd wanted to feel nothing.

A revelation, the first of many: getting sick had made her free. "I suppose the universe wanted me here."

"Something did. And so, you are."

"Come here, Heather Ponderview."

She did so. Button enveloped her in another one of those special hugs, the swing-you-around style after not having seen each other in who knew how long. Button's legs tingled and she cleared her throat a few times. Tried not to cry again. Tried not to profess love.

They released each other. Heather said she had a few tasks ahead, journaling and meditation and so on, but in the morning wanted Button to walk along the shore and describe how it had all gone wrong, and how best Heather could now be of service.

⊛⊛⊛

On the beach in the glimmering California morning light, Heather demonstrated basic yoga poses she combined into a flowing, energy-clearing set of movements called a full sun salutation. Talked about kundalini energy, and the chakras; of a suppleness of body achieved first thing makes one ready for the endeavor of the day ahead.

Meanwhile, Button related the story of the Phish tours on which she'd all but lived after Foothills State. This had been the difficult part for Heather, hearing what had happened after they parted ways. Not that Button's touring days were all bad, like at the end. Fraught with a touch too much drug abuse— the bad ones. The refined stuff.

Powders.

Powerful pills.

Bathtub LSD and other concoctions, a far cry from the white-lightning purity of the Owsley days.

Heather took a deep breath, and in the style of a recovering 12-stepper, made amends by admitting to having abandoned Button in a most hurtful and selfish manner. Started her on a path, but left her to make her way.

"It's what you're supposed to do—set someone on a course and let them find their way. But I admit I suffered enormous guilt over leaving you the way I did. If it helps. And now I felt compelled to change the energies surrounding me—including yours, angel."

Button, gratified to hear the words but remaining nonchalant. She waved away the apologies by patting Heather on the forearm, and delving instead into some hot jams of the era like the Camden 'Chalkdust,' the epic 'Ghost' from Lakewood Amphitheater in Atlanta on July the fourth, the digital-delay looping of the '2001' that capped the Pyramid in Memphis. The lot life she'd lived with her new posse post-Heather. Eliding a few salacious details.

Heather, still shocked. "Can't believe how much you—changed."

"It was different. My crew. Not like us together. None of us had money. We would figure out—um—places to park and sleep for free. Like Wal-marts."

"Wal-marts," incredulous and sour. "Just say no."

"You can park there. Overnight. If you're driving an RV. They let travelers do it."

"Even vagabond wastrels on Phish tour?"

"It's mostly retirees. Sancho had a regular RV, his granddad's. No stickers or other stuff. So as. Not to attract. You know."

"I get it."

Heather, sounding trancelike, now soliloquized about Button seeking to find her true place in the world; how it probably wasn't here, but she could stay as long as needed. That the oversoul knows all, always, and does not keep time. But also that Heather, and the Ponderview Foundation, could only do so much to set Button's life right. Could only light the way.

"But that's what the master does, you know."

"What's that?"

"Point you in the direction of the path. But the further steps, those are yours alone."

"I understood the choices. I was making. I was depressed and lonely." Hint hint.

"So you're not looking to place blame outside yourself?"

"Like, no way, dude."

"Then you've made a good start."

Button left out the part about how she suffered at being left behind by Heather, which amounted to saying, hey, I'm not mail-ordering tickets for the next tour, sorry. Nothing like what Sancho pulled, a betrayal an order-of-magnitude worse—left for dead.

All Heather had said at the time? Look, I have my degree; I've done my Phish; I'm moving on. What had been so wounding to Button, as she'd learn, had only been selfishness, viewing Heather's decisions through the narcissistic lens of Button's own desire.

In retrospect, there on the beach the process of healing had truly begun.

Which left plenty of room for the old desire for Heather to bloom.

Which didn't seem tenable.

Fuck.

But Heather, Button understood, had only been honest. It was time for her two years before, and time now for Button—even Phish themselves—to get off tour and regroup. To seek answers elsewhere. Button could not fault her friend for having given good advice, only her own inability to see the truth.

"I missed you. I never made. Another friend like you."

"Same here. It's part of why this all feels so right."

Button broke like a dam again in expressing her feelings, a torrent of truth-telling emotion pouring out of her on the beach along with a gallon of snot and tears. More hugging, and tears, from Heather, too. A good sign.

"Hold me," Button had plead, their scratchy dreads bobbing and mingling together against damp cheeks. "Love me."

"I am, angel. I do. I never stopped."

Despite knowing in her heart this love wasn't as she most desired, Button let herself believe Heather's affection could grow into more than friendship. Sucked in some breath. Felt cleansed. And most of all, grateful. Her train of thought now running along unfettered: "I'm so thankful. To Maddy. And now to you. I'd forgotten what it was like to have real friends. Gotta relearn how to relate to the straight world."

A figure over Heather's shoulder startled Button, a boy from the house. "Has Kumari been sitting there the whole time?"

Kumari Kandam, a rangy, barefoot Indian dude, sat cross-legged on the warm, dry sand a few yards away. Chin dipped down toward his chest, the light breeze making the tendrils of his black curly hair dance all around a face round and open like the sky, he appeared in a state of remarkable bliss. His lips, moving in a silent chant. Higher than high.

Gulls called. Waves lapped in the languid Cali sun. Button envied him.

"He's a long way along his path."

"I'd love to catch up quick."

"Look at it this way: All spiritual growth involves reconstructing not what you never knew, only what you as a being of light have forgotten here in the material realm."

"So it's not learning—it's only remembering."

Heather beamed and glowed with affection. She put her arm around Button and left it there. "That's right, sweet Button."

While they sat on their yoga mats in silent contemplation of the foamy, green-gray Pacific lapping nearby, Button noticed Kumari had vanished. Gone on back up to the house. Or somewhere.

Weird thing? Kumari Kandam never returned that night, and wouldn't again during the few months Button remained there.

One day a week later she asked Heather about the missing Indian boy, as though he'd meditated his way into nothingness. Swallowed up by the sea and sand.

Heather's sanguinity fell like a shawl around Button's shoulders worn to cut the chill of a brisk breeze. "People, they come and go. Maybe Kumari dropped the body and ascended into fifth-dimensional consciousness."

Button snorted and scoffed. "He disappeared? That's what? You're saying?"

Vulnerable and self-effacing, Heather glanced down to her sandaled, tan feet on the mosaic tiles in the rear courtyard, a gurgling fountain amidst lush tropical greenery where they sat sipping tea. The Ponderview heir seemed less sure of herself than Button ever remembered. "Who knows? I certainly don't. He's not here, that's all I can tell you."

Button, sober, seemed to believe a little less in the magic of the world. "Seems like an extreme theory."

"As the Tao teaches, it's better to not-know than to be sure. Certitude leads to rigidity, and it is the supple reed that bends in the gusting, unpredictable wind who does not break. The mark of a moderate person is freedom from her own ideas. And so on."

Intrigued, later that same day Button picked up her own copy of a particular Tao translation Heather recommended, carried still and consulted daily, its spine held together by a piece of clear tape. She thumbed through its simple parables while sitting at a doctor's office to which Heather had sent her to be tested for HIV.

HEATHER, Button, and a couple of the others including a sensitive poet and a scruffy wastrel of a tour rat named Crunchy Cal, whom Button believed to be nothing more than a leech living off the good graces of the Ponderview Foundation—an energy vampire; a user; a whiner—saddled up one night to go to see music at a local club. Winston's, over on Bacon Boulevard, featured a newgrass act, up-and-comers Cal deemed "the next big name."

She'd heard the same discussion about myriad and supposed successors to the jamband kings since early 2000, when the rumors of a Phish hiatus circulated and the online meltdowns and debates began. In the lot some said the String Cheese Incident would now reign supreme, or by next summer Widespread Panic would fill stadiums the way Phish had blown up in the wake of Jerry Garcia's death. Maybe no one would be the next Phish. Lightning in a bottle. But Button knew everyone said that about the Dead, too, back in their heyday.

Button distrusted every inch of Cal, short and swarthy, a hustling little twerp like hundreds of others she'd encountered in the hardcore lot scene. Or maybe in his case, a skunk: in the Range Rover driving over to the club, Heather making everyone buckle up like a soccer mom, someone kept releasing plumes of acrid flatus, and Button knew it'd been him.

But Cal, no, he had denied, denied, denied from underneath his hair wraps and scruffy beard and stained patchwork pants. With his sour Birks ruined by foot-sweat, dribbled urine and the gravel and dust of myriad parking lot scenes, he had an air like that kid who'd hold in his farts, saving them for when he could do the most damage. Crusty little wook. Reminded her too much of dudes to whom she'd be slinging burritos in the lot, 'free-gans' who always wanted to get a deal, to pay less, or preferably nothing at all. Sancho himself was always on the hustle, even though the fucker had family money and credit cards. Wooks gonna wook.

What had she been thinking, letting that sketch-ball screw her? Jetting samples of his DNA inside her body. Made her want to shower. And shower some more.

Arrival at the venue, ringed by traffic; a sold-out show complete with fingers in the air.

"A hot ticket."

Cal mumbled from under his beard. "I'd sneak in for free."

"Or accept a free ticket from a benefactor." Heather, dry, staring at Cal in the rearview.

She bypassed the line of cars waiting to turn into the fenced parking lot next to the building, an old warehouse, and pulled up to the valet service.

Cal, snide. "Premium-style. Courtesy the Ponderview Foundation."

Heather, ignoring him, paid cash for the valet and ordered everyone out.

Standing on the sidewalk beaming her graceful and beatific motherly love down on Button, Heather cupped her chin and stroked her hair as though her charge a literal lost puppy. "Here we are at a show again together."

"Yeah. I don't know. If I should be doing this."

"Does the dancing make you happy?"

"Yes."

"Can you do it without the drinking and drugging?"

Lucidity, her mind sharpening day by day, Button abhorred the idea of partying. "I don't even want to get stoned anymore. And I don't mean like in some rehab, twelve-step, I think it's all bad type-deal. No judgment, of me or anyone else. So I need to try a different way into the groove."

"These are beautiful words."

Button, smiling. "I lost the thread. Maybe I can dance my way back to where I was when this all started."

Heather, considering all this. Waving and blowing kisses to people who recognized her like the queen of the scene, just like back at Foothills. "Or maybe someplace better."

"I dunno if there's anyplace better." Staring up into Heather's eyes, which had darkened along with the sunset. "Than where I've already been."

Button wrapped her arm around the waist of Heather's flowing, cotton-print Indian sundress. They cruised over and joined the restless, partying queue of freaks snaking along the blank wall of the former warehouse.

No cops around; plumes of kind lavender-sweet smoke wafted down the line. The hissing sound of an active nitrous oxide vendor issued from over in a dark corner of the parking lot of the club in a wharf-side, gentrified industrial district where now a mini-scene raged.

The sound of the tanks gave Button a sick, sinking feeling.

Heather wagged a finger. "Balloon-heads—see, that's deceptive magic. You think you're going through a doorway of perception and insight, but all you're really doing is depriving your brain of oxygen. Forget it."

"You never were much of a gas whore."

"Neither were you."

"No. Until I became one." Button's shame came rippling through her down-mouthed words. "I dunno what. I was doing. Or thinking."

"When the lights go down, we're both going to start spinning again, like before, in 1997, in the glory days of cow-funk and four song second sets, when the groove would go for twenty, thirty minutes—or more: a forty-five minute 'Tweezer,' the 'Runaway Jim' that went for almost an hour."

"Who needs drugs?"

"Or Phish, for that matter?"

Button, incredulous and intrigued. "Wait—are you saying these guys jam like that?"

Heather said, not yet. "But like, there's flow."

"Right on."

"These are the jam-flow men," Crunchy Cal called out to the line, which cheered in response.

Button, still committed to 'her' band, thought: *I'll be the judge of that.*

Inside, sure, the music had been decent—Americana and acoustic and blue-grassy and folky, but no way could Button get a true groove going. Didn't make her want to get fucked up at least, but shaking it down with Heather felt forced and bizarre and stupid.

Ruinous self consciousness.

No flow.

At that moment Button decided she was through with live music, with the scene which only made her feel depressed, she realized with the acuity of sobriety, even as brief a period as she'd had. She kept getting weird flashes of light in the periphery of her vision, suffered instances of auditory hallucinations, brief and shocking. Came out of sleep that way, sometimes, twitchy and halfway sick, she came to realize. She had detoxifying yet to go.

But at least she had a port in the storm. Heather, like Maddy, said, use me to heal. In a few months, she'd strike back out. Not on tour following a band, but on a course toward a meaningful life. Back home for a spell. And then, who knew where. Yeah. Diggity.

⊛⊛⊛

HEATHER, San Diego, her recovery, and the Phish tours: it all lay long in the past, and while she accomplished some writing in the years since getting straightened out, nothing in a professional sense had come of Button's intention to craft literary efforts. Her life became filled instead by a dying father, her devastated and bereaved grandfather, a still-grieving and helpless mother with barely any English, even after forty years here.

A problem with the mother-daughter relationship, the language thing: Button had learned so little Vietnamese. Her daddy forbade the speaking of Tinky's mother tongue, with its high, rising tones; he had his reasons. Said, the girls are American-born, and English is what we'll all be speaking. But Button's Daddy, forever frustrated by his wife's inability to learn except in the most rudimentary of ways, a case of instant karma blooming from the fertilizer of his cultural stridency, perhaps.

She'd have said, Mama, Mama, teach me anyway, but everyone too afraid of Daddy and his Irish temper. Not a beater, thank god. Thim, the only family member brave enough to stand up to him, but uninterested in learning Vietnamese, only in mastering the world as it lay before her—and succeeding. Thim Sykes had had more than one media profile suggesting her as a successor to previous South Carolina political operatives like Lee Atwater and Harry Dent. A kingmaker.

How Button envied her sister's poise and strength and courage, and from a young age. Winning speaking contests in the third grade, and so on until Button wanted to puke, finally. Worse, as she had started ninth grade chunky, zit-covered and socially awkward, Thim, top-five in her graduating class and senior orator, model UN delegate, a scholarship awardee, a crown-holding winner of the Miss Marion Sims High School beauty contest, a star of the campus. Everyone was like, that's your freaking sister? What's a Button? What happened there?

But what was happening a quarter-century ago meant nothing now. Not when you cared for a drunk granddaddy and a whack mother, day-in, day-out, a purgatory of loving service that often felt more dreamlike than real. Thank god for The Dixiana, at least. LARPing as a sound mixer offered a fine, if escapist, fantasy of creativity.

Maybe she could talk Roy Earl into putting some of that fruitshake money into rehabbing the honkytonk. Making it new again. She'd talked to Manny T about the idea after he'd voiced it himself. Team up with the rednecks to promote Tillman Falls into some kind of quote-unquote music town, he said. Manny loved Rabbit's open-air festival idea that'd never found favor with the power brokers. With the ELMS and their spring fest and fall harvest celebration and Independence Day craft fair and charity barbecue, no place left in the schedule of events for a music festival. In Manny's street parlance, least not one they wasn't gonna run they-selves.

Button had given Manny T the history of how the ELMS ruled around Tillman Falls on matters such as community festivals and other issues surrounding the lifeblood of the township. "They're secretive, though. Like Skull & Bones, or some shit."

"Skull and what-now?" Manny had said, scratching at his short, receding afro. Manny often wore a ball cap and one of those 70s T-shirts with the 3/4 sleeves, baseball cut or whatever they called it. Sunglasses. Toothpick always tucked in the crook of his mouth, from all that pulled pork on his buffet, she reckoned, but Manny was in good shape: Button could see he worked out; his muscles bulged. Referred to dudes 'champ,' and flirted with all the ladies. Blew a mean sax. Ran a nice joint. A real character.

"They have it all locked down."

"You think I don't know that? My old lady hip-deep in it all."

"Oh—how cool for her." Button Sykes would be invited to join such an exclusive club sometime around the 12th of Never.

"I reckon," Manny had said, shifting the wet toothpick from one side to the other. "Take up a lotta time. All I know."

Her stomach rumbled—maybe after this Rabbit ceremony she'd go to Manny's and chow down on some of that stringy, brown-crusted mac and cheese holding down one end of the buffet steam trays. Screw the vegan trip, just for the day. She hoped the gathering wouldn't be too crowded, and in fact had no idea how mourners were to access the riverfront. She hadn't been to that bluff, at the end of a rutted track through the trees, in years. Getting drunk and high out there with her misfit-freak adolescent friends, sure—she preferred the river to Jensen's Pond, another teen hangout that felt creepy to her, a weird vibration around Big Rock.

Fooled around once with a guy at the bluff, her only attempt in high school to forge a sexual relationship. Backing off after rounding a base or two frustrated the dude, Timmy Truesdale, a lunkhead who had gone on to become a cop, even presiding with a smirk over a weed bust during one of her visits home from Foothills State. So, like, no fond memories of the river bluff. Or Edgewater County at all. Joke.

Sigh. In college, though? Screwing around with Heather and with Maddy Durango? Those times represented a peak never revisited. How Button wished she could go back, try to hold onto those precious moments. She wondered if anyone else suffered with such longing and grief about past glory. Ever felt wistful. Kidding.

☉✹◉

"THEY KILL HIM ON PURPOSE. They give him the cancer because he bring Vietnam war bride home."

Not this—Tinky thought they were going to Daddy's funeral again. "Mama. No. Please."

Matter of fact. "They kill him."

"No, they didn't."

"I not go. I not go and see him."

"We need to do this for Grandpa."

"No no no."

Grandpa Burnie in no better shape. She found him in his downstairs bedroom, the one with its own door to the side porch where Thim's room had been and later Button's, after her sister had gone off to college.

In his graying, threadbare undershirt still, dress shirt wadded into a ball, sport jacket on the floor, he cussed and cried and wailed. "*Some dumbass done gone and rolled paint over my beloved mural down yonder.*"

"The confederate flag chicken?" Button, intuiting how this had been Roy Earl's big idea when they'd been at the cemetery getting baked together. "Thank freaking god."

"You watch that smart mouth—oh, lord." He clutched himself, with the other hand flinging slobber from his mouth. "The world's done turned upside down."

Button, delighted. Her least favorite part of The Dixiana's lore, that mural. She knew too much of its true history—some mystical hoodoo attached to it, or so the rednecks believed—to accept the painting as a mere tribute to a college sports mascot.

"I know that's awful for you. But to me. I'm like, glad."

A string of curses and epithets, grievance with her attitude.

"Be that. As it may. We need to go. To Rabbit's memorial. Hup hup, now."

"I can't see him all burnt up. I c'ain't go."

"But—he was your best friend."

Howling, her octogenarian forebear fell onto his side and wept the way Button had in her dorm room bed after Heather had told her she didn't love her, wasn't really a lesbian, it had all been a lark, experimenting with magic, et cetera. "And now they done killed General Reb, too. Lord have mercy on us all."

Button found an empty pint of Evan Williams, black label, shoved between the mattress and box springs. "No wonder. Here—we don't have to go after all."

Button rolled him over, stretched him out, took off his heavy dress shoes. She tossed them into the corner where they fell with heavy thumps. She filled up a glass of water from the downstairs bathroom, brought it back, tried to get him to sip, but he'd already drifted into a peaceful, morning-drunk sleep.

Button, thinking: *I should go anyway. But I can't leave them like this.*

Silently paying her respects to Uncle Rabbit, Aunt Runelle, Roy Earl, and everyone who loved the old honkytonk proprietor, Button went downstairs to attend to Tinky, who still seemed to think they'd decided to again stage her husband's funeral. This happened now and then, usually when Button tried to take her grocery shopping.

Thank god nobody would ever have to relive that funeral nightmare, though, right? That'd been the greatest test of Button's sobriety, that grim time, but not the funeral, no: while she'd watched him suffer. Losing his ability to speak, to eat, finally to see, in the last couple of weeks when her father's face and eyes swelled so, and he sat hunched and curved upon the fetid bedding, tubes running from his throat. And how the madness had overtaken her mother in the same time. A double whammy. But as she thought then, and knew now, the universe—the Tao—had made Button aware of tools and techniques to not only deal with all her threads, but to keep her sanity. Keep her strong.

Proof; pudding.

She called out to her mom, reassured her, said, they didn't give cancer to Daddy on purpose. Things just happened.

People—they came. They went. Like her Daddy; like Uncle Rabbit. They've all gone; we'll go, too.

None of that frightened Button, though. Death, she believed, represented only an end to physicality; 'twas but a transition. Near as she had figured out. Wasn't anything you could talk about to some like her grandfather. Or much of anyone here in Edgewater County. While Button may not have been washed in the blood, when the local church folks spoke of ascension to heaven, she understood that the faithful weren't wrong.

Our spirits are as water, returning to the eternal well.

If only she could explain all that to her grandfather. Give him some peace.Another chore; more sacred service. She bowed her head to the task, her calling, her speciality. She glowed inside.

ROY AND RICO

Shaken up both by the story about your mother and the errand you're about to run, you climb into Rabbit's Ford F-150 and crank her up. Engine purring, it's not only well-built, American-made solid as the neckless carved granite visage of Teddy Roosevelt tucked into the side of a South Dakota mountain, but maintained inside and out. Not to your taste, but in Pa-paw's absence, its cab feels comforting.

Off to collect your grandfather's ashes, the remnants of the body who'd fought in Europe.

Had seen horrors forever unspoken.

Run your mama off the road, he did—you and her both.

But you began working to put it out of your whirling, troubled mind. A few more complex emotional hits this week, hey, who knows, you might crumble into base elements and re-form as an entirely new entity to get out of the maze-like prison whose walls redouble and shift with each bracing revelation. Or maybe get your passport and drive to the airport in Charlotte. Disappear. Buy a cheap island somewhere. Pacific Ocean, not Atlantic. Away from all this.

Perhaps you haven't been tested enough. That's it. Your business success, it came easily. Lots of elbow grease, but that, mere labor, and the rest, gut-check courage and willingness to write the check. Testing one's mettle on the level of relationships? Real work. Losing people you love? Now this, a true test of a human being's maturity and personal growth.

Woof, comes the sound of the big dog from the backyard. *WOOF.*

Shoot—poor Rico thinks it's Rabbit cranking this truck. Goddamn it all. Your throat, closing like a vice. Already this morning.

YOU INSISTED on buying the truck, like the house, for the old man, who had cussed and spit and told you he could go to Hill Hampton any day of the week, including Sunday, to get himself a sign-and-drive deal on the fanciest hunk of junk they had sitting on that square of asphalt.

"Sign and drive." Your granddaddy slapped his leathery, thick hands together. "You want to ride over there in that piece of kraut plastic you parade around in and I'll show you?"

Back then you were driving a Mercedes, a 450SL. You'd wanted one ever since riding in your rich college pal Billy Steeple's midnight blue model. Said his grandparents, plastic-packaging millionaires, had given it to him on his sixteenth birthday. You liked yours better—you'd bought it used, cash in hand, boo-yow, from a friend up the hill from the Old Market, a professor who hung out in the original Beanery and graded papers and talked about movies with you. Said how much he admired your pluck, owning multiple businesses, in different towns. You moved to Charleston right after buying it. Had driven away from your old pad in Columbia for the last time in the Mercedes, your leggy redheaded girl at your side, a fat wallet, a future leading who knew where. Arrival; but also a beginning. Endless arrival. That's how it has felt. Until this week.

You went home, and saw your Pa-paw in that junker of his, the late 70s two-tone model you used to drive and which now rusts on the cluttered and junky back lawn of The Dixiana. No no no.

"How you liking that new F-150," you'd asked when calling a few months later to talk to your Mee-maw. If you even got Rabbit at all, he'd say, how you, how you, good, good, here's your grandmother, Roy Earl, good to speak with you.

He couldn't hear well on the phone. As Mee-maw always explained, the war, again, left him with ringing ears. "Gave him nightmares," as she told you one night, "and rendered him half-deaf. Now if that's not a raw deal for a man who loves music much as your granddaddy, I'd like to know what would be."

You'd always felt sorry for him, made sure the truck had the top add-on stereo sound system. You went to Best Buy in Dentsville and bought a bulging sack of CDs, classic country, some mellow modern stuff, some folk, some Bob Dylan, especially *Nashville Skyline* with Johnny Cash, on which you put a sticky post-it that read, *REMEMBER THESE GUYS???*

You turn on the truck radio, and it's still on the local country music station, way down on the AM band. The song that's playing is Vern Gosdin's 'Do You Believe Me Now,' a real heart-tugger.

God-dog, beau, but if you don't feel like you're gonna puke with pain and grief over your ruined marriage to your dream girl. Seriously. Puking hot, clabbered and black-clotted blood over her off fucking some young guy. God almighty, as your Pa-paw would put it. A million songs and stories about heartbreak and betrayal all made sense now. Whoopie-doo. Lucky you.

❀

YOU BLOW off steam by giving the F-150 a workout on the back roads. Truck handles well, hugging the twists and turns on which you zigzag around here in the north river area, putting off the duty in Chilton.

The southern end of the county near the lake is where the Karlaney Funeral Home has moved. Their original location, two hundred yards off the green in Tillman Falls and a block behind the County Library and Archives building in which you spent so much time as a kid, made them one of many legacy county businesses that had deserted the actual township for more suburban real estate.

How you had noticed those big hearses, and the lines of mourners, and the sheriff's deputies directing traffic and taking their hats off as the processional would pass, a slice of small-town life. You wonder if they still do that for funerals. If you're cheating your grandfather out of his due.

By upholding his wishes? From beyond the grave? Check.

Vroom vroom. Big. Sitting up high. Swapping out the country music for Jimmy Page, ripping off heavy, bombastic blues-rock licks. Should have brought the dog, taken him through the drive-through and gotten him a steak biscuit. Mee-maw says it's what your granddaddy would do on Saturdays. You make a plan to go through the Hardee's and grab a couple. Maybe eat one yourself.

Hoo-boy. Naughty. Creedence would kill you.

Screw her.

Steak fudging biscuit. Mustard. Your Pa-paw's dead—you're gonna splurge.

Before leaving to pick up the ashes, you went into the family room of the new house and dug through the shelves of old records, and the smaller bookcase with tapes, many of which you'd recorded from albums you'd borrowed from Dobbs or Devin, searching out a few CDs you'd left behind the last summer you came back home from Southeastern.

Led Zeppelin—why not? *Houses of the Holy.* Hells yeah. Blue Öyster Cult, *Agents of Fortune*, next in the CD changer. The thought of media is so retro— your iPod hard drive sits crammed full of all this music, but stuffing a disc into the dash feels comforting—a cassette would be even better. You'd rather have a Grateful Dead show to crank up, but all that bootleg stuff sits archived on a dusty shelf back on the Island.

You grunt in recognition—you'll need to retrieve the Dead tapes and CDs, a few other personal items. Sacred. All tied into Edgewater County, Devin and Libby, Billy. All the departed ones.

You remembered getting this CD from the folks one Christmas, maybe '89, from a list you had to make at birthday and holiday time. "We don't got no idea what a little boy these days would want," your sweet Mee-maw would always say, stroking your buzz-cut tennis ball head. "Make Mee-maw a list, now, and Granddaddy'll send it off to Santa for you."

You crank up 'The Rain Song,' ethereal, and find out what this F-150 you bought your granddaddy can do on the back stretches of River Ridge Road, the opposite direction from where you ought to be going. You go all the way to the Parsons Hollow turnoff. Here you backtrack the CD and listen to your fav tunes multiple times before continuing down a straight-shot two-lane, a tunnel of overhanging old-growth trees and only an occasional house way back in the woods. Hitting the ramp onto the freeway at the northern county line, you express the twenty miles back down toward the plumes of the nuclear plant, and the funeral home, and your Pa-paw's ashes waiting there.

As you park, you discover a fresh problem—a whiff of black, oily smoke puffs from the grill of the truck. You'll need to get that checked out. Another checklist item. Drop it off at Hampton Motors first thing. Whatever.

You notice your chin quivering. An emotional episode? No. That would throw you way off schedule, the notion of which prompts the incipient tears to retreat and regroup for deployment at a time more convenient for the owner of the swollen eyeballs.

⊚❋◎

THE GRAY BOX in the plastic sack, and the lovely envelope with the paperwork. You sit there across from the funeral director in the mood to negotiate. To say, *Pal, you're dealing with a bossman—a prime mover and eater of worlds. Let me get my little reading glasses out and scrutinize these here exorbitant charges of your'n, Mr. Fancy P. Pants Funeral Dee-rector out here in Podunk.*

Goes without saying they have beaucoup cash flow. Compared to the old Karlaney Funeral Home you remember, the smug opulence and sense of unearned privilege of this funerary superstore here in unremarkable suburban America stings your skeptical and jaundiced eyes and mucus membranes like when entering a nice, new doublewide mobile home, one of those like your Uncle Burnie used to sell side-by-side with a used car lot. You got your enterprising spirit from old Burnie, whom you need to check on, but can't yet. You don't have the juice to deal with another drunk. Not right now.

But no Walter Sobchak scene takes place. Other than the mild debate regarding the unadorned box you chose over a more elaborate vessel, there's been no haggling. Why bother—a game you're certain to win isn't half as interesting as a genuine challenge.

You fork over the AMEX. Its appearance forces the pallor of Mr. Karlaney's cheeks to flame with spidery red veins creeping down into his starched collar. "I'm terribly sorry. We don't accept American Express."

You mask your annoyance. "Don't blame you. Helluva a discount rate."

His smile, sad and unwavering. A small shrug using only the tips of his tented fingers on the desktop.

"Me? I cash in rewards points. I've got this coffeemaker at home—well. It's a doozy." You produce another card, the household discretionary VISA debit, probably eighty or ninety large in cash you keep lying around—mad money. "That painless enough?"

He nods, all but imperceptible. An air of contempt has settled in the room, coming more from him than you. Some 'comfort' from these moneygrubbing fools. What if AMEX were all you carried?

You can remember starting out trying to buy Maxine's, back when you didn't have crap regarding credit besides a single AMEX card Rabbit had gotten for you the semester you started at Southeastern. Starting with a five-hundred limit, you ran up the card in no time buying hot wings and pitchers of beer for the rest of the fellas in your crew, even got a cash advance you blew on a hundred-dollar ounce of pot to split with the guys. You pledged to send the proceeds from the weed as your next credit card payment, but frittered away the cash instead. Never repeated that mistake. No sir.

Despite needing help to retire that debt at the end of the school year—unanticipated late charges and an over-limit fee kept you scrambling to stay ahead—you worked extra shifts at the movie theater and later Maxine's, paid it down, paid it off. Over time the limit found itself raised, and raised again, and again, and six years later when you were ready to get money to buy the coffee shop and rehab it into your own vision, you'd acquired the credit history sufficient to secure modest financing at reasonable terms, as far as usuriousness went. So, you maintain a soft spot for AMEX. And so, too, for your granddaddy in this context, bless his cracker ass, who'd had the sense to get you building credit.

You hesitate, holding the Visa suspended between thumb and forefinger as though it stinks. "'Jesus, he was a handsome man.' You know that poem? e. e. cummings? Buffalo Bill is defunct?"

The funeral director shakes his head.

You only know it because you once took classes about poetry and writing and art, before commerce became your schtick. "If I were having a memorial, that's what I'd read for my grandfather. Nothing else. That'd say it all."

"Sorry, but I'm not familiar with it," Karlaney says. "I'm sure it's a lovely poem. But—you chose to hold no services here."

"True that." You flop down the premier edition Visa, heavy, a black-matte finish with a flecked gold patina one may discern only when the light catches the card in the right way. It clatters with reluctance to a settled stillness; you realize you've all but chucked it at the peckerhead. "Swipe away."

"Very good, Mr. Pettus."

You watch with amusement as he tries to pick up the VISA from the glass-topped desk, his fingertips struggling for purchase against the high-end beveled edge of the weighted crown account card. His humiliation and consternation assumes a satisfying consistency before lifting the corner with a manicured nail.

"Good for one of us, maybe. No points for this transaction. But, this coffeemaker?"

"Yes—?"

"A hundred and sixty thousand points. I call it our $160,000 coffeepot."

"Must make quite the cup of joe."

"It's remarkably ordinary, to tell the truth. But hell, I can make you top-shelf coffee all day long, freestyle, that'll put hair on your chest."

Ignoring what must seem an odd assertion—he has no idea about the CBSI and its method of slow-drip, pour-over coffee preparation—Karlaney clasps his hands to affect a studied air of condolence. "Again, please accept our sincere wishes for your family's peace during this difficult time. Please know you will always have friends who care here at Karlaney Funeral Home," the tag line, the stinger, the grace note signaling the close of the transaction.

"Appreciate your help with my Pa-paw."

"Keep us in mind for the future."

Which brings reality home; which makes you have to clear your throat forty times on the walk outside to keep from blubbering with grief for folks who haven't even passed on yet.

❀

ONCE BACK ON River Ridge Road the smell of the steak biscuits fills the cab, actually pork chops, a new addition to the Hardee's morning menu, but boneless. Round, gray pucks of mystery meat you gnaw and that your stomach receives by saying, yo, bro, WTF? Gurgle gurgle. The juicy flutter you get in that spot before having a lower GI episode. Gotta cool it on all this dirty eating.

You slow down passing Pike's Bait & Pawn, which seems to have an unusual amount of traffic around it, including a sheriff's deputy and several people standing in suits and ties, and at the turnoff to the road down to the bluff and the river, there's a dump truck full of gravel. You roll down your passenger window to hear a guy in an orange vest shouting at the cop, "*Just what y'all want done? We ain't been told nothing, beau...!*"

As you chew your rubbery biscuit, you sure hope this DOT clusterfuck clears out by the time you and your Mee-maw come back to scatter the ashes. Terrible timing, a-holes. You'll make a call. Get them to believe something important's at stake if they don't snap-to and do your bidding.

⊛❀⊚

BELCHING POKE CHOP BISCUIT, you hop out of the truck and go to Rico in the backyard. At the smell of the food, his ears form a different shape from that of boxy fear.

You shake the greasy sack and feed him meat out of the biscuit. "Hope this makes up for your daddy being dead."

Happy as a clam, Rico groans and does a slow-motion flop down onto your sandaled feet.

"Who's a good dog? Who wants to run over to the fishing bluff? Who wants to go catch him some fish? Huh? Huh?"

Rico, spittle running out of his fleshy pink and black lips like tiny mountain streams, rolls his eyes roll to gaze up at you. You offer him the biscuit-part, now soaked in fake pork chop grease.

The dog, chomping happily and drooling—ignorance is bliss. What do you think this industrial-grade food is made of? How do you think you lost all the weight, finally? By cutting out junk. It's not fit for this dog, this corporate food, much less you.

"Who wants the heart-attack special? Who's eatin' his biscuit? Good boy."

Rico lets go with an explosive sneeze, a spray of ropy sputum all over your bare shins and feet nestled like lovebirds inside their Keen sandals, formerly dry.

"God-durn it, you little fudge-pucker."

Rico yelps, and his ears go boxy.

"Roy Earl Pettus!" Mee-maw, standing with her hands on hips in a floral print dress and Sunday shoes—not that y'all had ever gone to church—calls you out from the deck: "If you don't hush that filthy mouth."

"Sorry."

You turn on the hose-pipe to rinse off your feet still in the sandals, after which you traipse around the yard squishing and cussing to yourself.

"What on earth are you doing?"

"Rico sneezed on my feet."

"That's all? The dog sneezed?"

You hold your arms out like, well? But you can't even see her up on the deck—a red veil has dropped. The black blade thrums against your leg. The dog eyes you with worry and distrust.

He senses your vibration: Fury.

His seeming acknowledgement of your state of mind allows you let it go. He sneezed. He's only a dog. These are only Keens. His spittle is only water—sugar water, in fact, if you love the animal in question.

The truth: "I just ain't used to dogs. And, I'm just upset in general."

"Son, we don't have to do this today. It ain't like time is running out on this chore."

"No, no, no." You go squishing across the lawn, giving big dog a cursory, apologetic scratch on head, and say to your grandmother, all but grabbing her by the forearms, "We're scheduled to get this squared away, it's next on our list, and if we're not chipping away at the list, we might as well be surfing the dirt like—like—"

"You better calm down. I told you not to make that coffee so durn strong. I must've watched you put in four scoops."

"We're gonna get you a better coffee maker. No more scooping. Beans—fresh roasted beans. You about ready?"

Your grandmother stops in her tracks and gives you a look up and down like you haven't got a lick of sense. "Yes; but you ain't even close to being ready."

"Par-don?"

"We ain't scattering your granddaddy's ashes with you looking like you're on the way to a durn camping trip."

Your uniform: black pocket T-shirt, cargo shorts full of stains and rips, and the outdoorsy sandals. The foyer coat closet at home is full. You keep the pairs after they wear out. Creedence, she's always trying to throw them away, and you're like, no no, those are the ones you wear cutting the grass, or the knock-around-the-island sandals and the everydays, or the nice new ones for going to the better restaurants on the Island, the top drawer style you can't get except at Keen outlets, like you have over on the mainland.

"I didn't bring any other clothes. Left in a hurry."

Aghast. "I sure didn't raise you to show such disrespect, but fine. He ain't gonna care. He wouldn't dress up for it, would he?"

"His own funeral? Probably not, ma'am."

"Don't you 'ma'am' me, you little smart-butt. Now come sit with me while I finish my face. I want to tell you a little tale."

This fills you with anticipation, not all bad, but a little trepidation-y—not another revealing story.

You apologize to the dog and go sit on the bed behind your grandmother at her old dresser, and while you're transported back forty years she has been at this routine since before then. Only the bedroom now is different but the dresser and the lacy doilies and the lamp the same, along with a lighted makeup mirror you have a vague sense Creedence must have given her one Christmas.

The makeup containers are mostly modern and fresh, but she also retains a collection of older ones so aged their caps sit crusted shut, and you suppose it's like a medicine chest with its old prescriptions filling up over time, like Creedence and her anxiety stuff and mood adjusters and elevators and managers. She'd gone through a half-dozen, had finally gotten weaned off the last couple after persuading the doc she felt better. That's when she'd started drinking. Said, I can't remember shit no more. I hate them damn pills. Let me drink a couple of glasses of wine at night instead.

"They say it's good for your heart," she explained sipping and nodding out on the patio overlooking the marsh, and you were like, right on, I hate all those pills; and you thought, this is getting better. Surely.

"Now, I know you always wanted to hear about Granddaddy and being in the war," Mee-maw says, and all at once you become one long, cold, hard goose pimple, stiff-haired from your toes to the tufts behind your jug ears. "But he didn't want to talk about it."

"I remember how I'd sit watching Combat reruns on Sunday afternoons with him. I'd always be like, 'Was that how it was for you'?" He'd get so mad. I never could understand why."

"He had his reasons."

You fondle your spongy wattle, which you didn't lose along with the weight. One of the old guys at the hanger had told you—in confidence, not in front of the rest of the men—how he'd had his wattle tightened up and it'd taken ten years off his appearance, not that you could calculate such a metric with specificity. Showed you the straight little cosmetic surgery scar, like a minor shaving nick. "Hell, Pettus, dye the hair and the goatee, too. Go to town."

You hadn't known what he meant—pursue younger women? It'd crossed your mind. Particularly after Creedence's drinking had gotten worse, and you'd retreated to the safety of the plane and the succor of the Carolina Beanery Sedge Island. Your baby.

"Did he ever tell you what all happened?"

"He didn't have to tell me. I slept in the bed next to him."

The nightmares. She'd told you that, lord, it must have gone on twenty years after he got back from the war, complete with screaming and hollering and kicking off the blankets and coverings. "It was real bad in North Dakota. When I always told you I up and said to him I wanted to come back to South Carolina, to home, it wasn't only because I was homesick. It was because I wanted to get away from him. And then I was carrying Ronnie, and that seemed to calm your Pa-paw down. Heal him. I wasn't having our baby there, I told him. And quick as he could, he moved us back here. Where we stayed. Where you come along."

You tell her you know that part. You lived it.

It hits you: "Dang—*you wanted to leave Pa-paw?*"

Ignoring the question. "But what I'm trying to say," going over to a closet, out of which she stoops and produces a box, the familiar Amazon logo, "is that he got this for you last Christmas. It's a TV show he watched that he said you ought to see. And I lost it. He was so mad at me. In all the wrapping I did for the twins, I misplaced this durn thing. He said, you stupid old bag of bones, you probably threw it away. He must've cussed me up and down until New Year's. Didn't come across it until a few weeks ago."

You remembered this. You had come home for about three hours that day, Christmas Day, to drop off gifts. Creedence had had to lie down instead of eating dinner. The night before you had gone to a holiday party, and she'd gotten screeching drunk, staggering around and spilling red wine on a couch and shushing you and covering it with a throw pillow real quick before the hostess saw. "He was ornery that day."

"That was the reason."

You open the box, and it's a DVD set—*Band of Brothers*, an HBO miniseries about D-Day and the rest of the European war from that point. "I saw one or two episodes. Didn't get hooked. That's the cool thing—nowadays you can get into a TV series, sit there and watch the whole thing through. Remember back when you had to just wait to see stuff when they showed it to you?"

"It's still that way for some of us."

"It'll be like when we used to watch Combat. Not like hearing it from his lips, though. Still only a TV show." You remember the incident at Wal-mart, the aborted TV purchases. Shake your head at suffering through this HD content displayed on those old standard definition Sonys.

"But the point of all this is that he never told me anything, either. Not really. Bless his heart."

She says this with sweet sadness, patting you on the knee and going to retrieve another box, a plain one, the waxed cardboard ancient and pliant in your hands. "But he always said that when he passed on, I should give you this. It's got most of his Army papers in it. That way, he said, you could finally look up what his unit did. He knew how curious you were—he told me you would get so red when he'd tell you 'no.' That you were about to bust to know what it was like to be overseas in that war. So, I don't what to say about that TV show. For someone who'd had nightmares like he done for all them years, you'd think he wouldn't want to look at war pictures no more than he did to talk about being in it. And, mercy me, the noise—he would crank up that volume. Yes, he would."

Stunned, you cradle the old box. Your eyes sting and your breath comes short. You feel immense gratitude. "How cool is this? Oh, man."

"I'm glad you're pleased, son."

You look at the digital bedside clock: 11:11. "Time to get these ashes scattered."

"Letty called earlier—she said they'd collect us. And Jasper and I need to rehearse real quick, if you don't mind."

Now you understand the importance of the makeup, of your clothing. Your grandmother Mama Runelle, the Darling of The Dixiana, had one last performance to give, even if there'd be no audience to appreciate it. "We've got nothing but time."

CHRISTY, HIS GRANDMAMA, AND NEWBIE

Getting told NO by his grandmama hurt Christy worse than anything he could have imagined. He would rather have had his Daddy alive again to push him and beat him and call him names.

Having his grandmama try to explain the men and the girls and the man with her in the back, drinking and smoking and doing what-all, only made it worse. Made what his Daddy, Newbie and other people said come true, all in a big rush. It felt like cold water pouring over Christy's fat head and down into his shoes, like he had peed himself. It used to happen all the time. His worst fear, peeing his pants in front of somebody.

"Christy, lord have mercy. Now, you know you ain't to show up here like this. What's wrong?"

Without waiting for an answer, Granny, wearing a shiny outfit, like fancy pajamas with black hose with red roses, went swishing back down the hall in her stocking feet. The man's voice, sharp like he was mad, came muffled through the walls.

He'll be gone in a minute; you settle down, Christy heard her say. *"Ain't nobody staying here tonight but you, sugar."*

Some stranger was more important than Christy.

To his own grandmama.

Well, dang.

He didn't want to pee in his britches. He wanted to cry.

Christy made a deal with himself that after getting his Daddy squared away, there'd be no more bawling, unless alone in his room where no one could see.

She came back now in a robe, a fuzzy one like she'd wear all normal-like.

"My friend Newbie brung me." He tried not to cry or whine, but his next words came out that way, like when he wanted her give him money for a new game. "I don't want to go back home tonight."

"Is that little shit-ass son of mine being mean to you again?"

"No'm."

"Is he feeding you, Christy? You looked peaked."

"No, ma'am."

Christy's granny looked mad enough to bite nails. She cussed his Daddy up and down. "I bet he took that last money I give him and pissed it away on— god knows what," she said real fast. "Told me he was buying a car so he could get a job and keep it, for once. Has your Daddy taught you to drive yet, son?"

Christy shook his head. "He ain't shown me how to drive yet. Said he had to get money to pay taxes."

"That fibbing little turd. And with you needing to get a job soon. A real job. Not like your Daddy. And not like me. I mean that, Christy—that's the most important thing right now. You learning to drive and getting a job. Granny'll help you get a car, or a little truck. Would you like that, sweetheart?"

Christy, blubbering with gratitude. He mumbled how he needed a Wi-fi enabled tablet, too, to use for his schoolwork.

"A tablet—like an Excedrin?"

She listened as Christy wheezed and whined all fast and excited about what a tablet was, but cussed him anew once she realized it was another computer doohickey, on which she said Christy had already spent too much of his Granny's money.

Christy, busting into a gale of tears. This ought to work.

"All right now. All right now. You come here."

He hugged her. Granny was so small and skinny, except for her boob-boobs, which were big and hard against his stomach. "I can't stay in a room? With them girls out yonder?"

His grandmama got mad again. "No, and no. Now, you and your friend get your asses on home. I don't got time for no surprise visits." She softened her tone again. "Just go on like Grandmama wants. You go on, learn to drive, and she'll get you a car from Mayor Hampton, who loves Christy's Grandmama, don't you worry none about that. Here, take this." She gave him two brand new twenty-dollar bills, so crisp they looked wet. "Maybe your friend can show you how to drive."

He shoved the money down into his pocket. "Yes'm."

She shooed him out, slamming the door.

Christy shuffled back down the driveway, reckoning he would ask Newbie to let him ride back into town with him. Stay in Newbie's house, wherever that was.

No way Christy was going back to the trailer.

Then he remembered how the trailer was all paid up for a while; recalled his Granny yelling about that to his Daddy just last month. That the trailer was paid up. And what more could she do? Mercy, how she yelled. "You gonna suck me dry, son."

"Sounds more like what you do for a living, Mama."

That had made Christy's granny cry, after which she slapped his Daddy across the face so hard it knocked him sideways.

That was the moment Christy'd decided to put his Daddy to sleep. That the business about robbing Aisha's Daddy's filling station gave Christy the juice and the reason to git'r done, finally. His Daddy's own fault, when one thunk of it that way.

It wasn't a problem. Christy needed to get rid of his Daddy's body, that was all. Driving, his grandmama being a whore, quitting school, going to work, finding a girl to love him—maybe another misfit like Christy; yeah—it could all wait. He would persuade Newbie to help with this one particular chore instead.

CHRISTY WAITED by Newbie's truck. After a couple of minutes, his new friend came bounding down the steps from the porch of the back house where the girls stayed.

"You're my best friend, Christopher. That's all I got to say." Newbie, dancing a jig in front of his truck. "I'm a man now. Again, I mean. I'm a man *again.*"

Christy said he was glad. He also said he needed a ride back into town. That he was sorry, but he would come and visit his granny another time. "I got gas money."

"That's good, cause I sure ain't got no more."

"You paid her. And she—she—!" His throat closed up.

"Yeah. But that girl, Christopher? I think she might've begun to fall in love with me. I know I give her money, and all? But she let me do it to her. And she was all moaning and fucking me right back." Newbie bent his knees and mimed three quick thrusts like a dog humping somebody's leg. "And I went like, ka-POW! I'm-a tell you what!"

"Ain't that what they supposed to do?"

"Man, this one sure did. I think she loved me like she ain't never loved them others."

Christy said he didn't know about all that. Inside his head, the wheels turned. On an idea.

All in a big breathy rush he told Newbie that not only did he have gas money, but a free place to live. If Newbie wanted it, at least until he got another job.

Newbie, real curious and halfway excited, but then, he was in a place where everything made him happy: a look of wonder, like he could see the world all shiny and new. Kinda like how Christy felt when he knew his Daddy wasn't gonna hit or cuss at him no more.

Aw, Newbie's only a baby inside, Christy thought. He needs someone like me, who's halfway got his mess together. These grownups, they knew nothing. If you could call Newbie, who said he was twenty-two, a grownup. Nope. Special Ed, all the way.

DRIVING BACK FROM RED MOUND, Newbie talked about how his granddaddy told stories about bones men had dug out of that hill of dirt way, way back. That the skeleton of an Indian nine feet tall, with a skull big as a basketball, had been found and shipped off to the Smithsonian. Last anyone heard from the Smithsonian about those Indian bones.

Christy grunted and said it sounded like a fairy tale. Wasn't nothing but a story. Newbie said, probably.

Also said he had half a mind to go take a big piss on the side of that shit-hole, The Dixiana. But he couldn't. Not on the mural. "I might piss yellow all over that smart-ass grandson of Mr. Rabbit's, but not General Reb."

Christy didn't know nothing about any of it—he hadn't worked. Didn't know how it felt to be fired. But his Granny sure thought he ought to get a job.

Special Ed or not, Newbie would help him figure out that part.

He needed Newbie to help him with multiple tasks. There wasn't no one else, as Christy fretted. He didn't think he could trust his Granny any more. Nothing more confusing than feeling that way.

Them twenties in his pocket said otherwise, a voice mused. A real grand-mother would let her grandbaby at least stay one night, though. It was hard to sort out what the different voices had to say about stuff Christy needed to decide, like whether to put his dog-Daddy to sleep, or how the world worked.

"There's just one thing." Christy, wheezing. "That I need help to do. To fix."

"You need tools?"

"No, but after you help me, the trailer will be ours. To do with like we want."

"Ours?" Newbie, again with his amaze-balls look. "I ain't never had nothing."

"This will be something, then."

He slapped his thigh. "Beau, I tell ya—I never dreamed that when I got fired from The Dixiana it would end up such a good day."

"Did you know you was gonna get fired?"

"Yeah. Just a notion that kept coming to me. But who cares? This might be the best day of my life. What you need me to help you with?"

As they headed onto the downtown bypass, Christy told Newbie what he needed, albeit in a roundabout way. Not so roundabout Newbie Harrell didn't get quiet, seemed nowhere near as happy as he'd been coming out of Christy's grandmama's cathouse. In fact, the more Christy got to the point of what this task entailed, Newbie looked like Christy tried not to feel: worried. Real worried.

MANNY AND NEECIE

Shit been real for a couple days now. All Manny wanna do is say, hey now, y'all: we got to dial back the drama. Or else this ain't gonna work.

The truth. His old lady demanding an update on where it stand. With the sidemeat.

And her? Becky L acting the fool. Changing up on him. Agreeing it over, saying, what a dumb mistake we done; saying it c'ain't be over, no way. That the universe don't make mistakes. How they was meant to find each other and all that. And how they got a mess, sure, but it c'ain't be swept up so easy as Manny trying to do it.

A side of her he ain't seen. So pissed, Becky L said, *I'll kill both our asses.* She don't say it like that. But ya know, ya know. Words to that effect.

In the back bar, Manny sit his ass on the edge of the stage with his white Chuck Taylors hanging off, while at a cleared off four-top, Neecie sit working on the books. She got her big beautiful legs crossed, patterned pantyhose and with a shoe-dangle, a tight skirt and blouse, long, straightened hair pulled back, makeup and smelling all perfect. Dressed to the nines, working away with her ledger and laptop open on the table.

Great god, son—your woman hotter than sin.

She glance up from her figures like she hear his thought. But it ain't that. "Are you gonna answer me?"

He try playing dumb. Absent-minded. All that dope he used to do. "Mm-hm?"

Puts down her pen. "What's this glassy-eyed, mealy-mouthed mess outta you?"

"I ain't know what you mean."

Devil eyes. "You lucky I ain't cut it off. Is what."

The kinda statement that settles in a room. Hard to respond.

"You know I ain't kidding this time, boy-o."

"Don't never call no man no boy-o. Not in his crib."

"Listen at you. Listen to you, rather. Tough man. You hiding behind that."

"You don't know what you talking bout."

"Hell I don't. *Boy.*"

Neecie, waiting.

Banging and noise from the back: Ahmad, calling out to the produce delivery driver, who from that aggravating beep-beep-beep Manny know he backing down the alley off Congress Street. "Uh oh—better go check on that."

"Ahmad got it under control."

She had his ass. This meeting, their business meeting, Manny hate it with a passion. Ain't no fun under ordinary circumstances. Cook food, blow his horn, hitting the pussy, Manny good on all that.

He never get off on this counting money part. She promised she'd never let him have to worry about it again, not once they got reestablished here in the EC. Now that babygirl older, Neecie said, more time for her to run that rest-runt for his ass so he's can play, and menu plan, and cook.

She done all that. And it going good. ELMS shit take up a shit-ton of her time, but ain't no thang.

And how he repay her for making their asses part of the movers and shakers in town? By hoglegging all up in one of the key women his wife got to run around with in her civic life. That's how she keep putting it to him, anyways—as in, Manny, you ain't got the sense not to shit where you eat?

She ain't wrong. But still. She rubbing it in.

"Y'all go and fuck one last time?"

"Whatcha mean, 'one last time?' They ain't no last time."

Recrossing both legs and arms. Demanding clarification.

Face get hot. "It—it already happen. A while back."

She don't look like she believe shit. "I'm getting some strange mother-fucking vibes over all this. That all I know."

"Girl, I done wrong. Said so. What more a nig—" The rule, no more n-word, not now, not ever. Manny broke it all the time. Who give a shit? Every-body all sissified anymore about words. Everybody tender nowadays, like Manny dick after slapping the ham all night. "What more a husband can say except, his ass fucked up."

"That cool and that real, y'know? I got the feels. But hold on here."

"Baby, what I'm saying is: I'm muh-fucken sorry as shit. Ain't got no explanation."

"Again: y'all squared away? Or what?"

What a red-handed nig—no—what a red-handed muh-fuh supposed to say? Hold out his hands like, *what what what?*

"How about this: Your ass gonna let me have my say out."

Aw shit. Manny don't say it aloud. But he know she see it on his face. "I reckon I got it coming."

Manny haul his ass up on the stage, get out a fresh Rico reed. He pace around and give it a good soak, which he do when he nervous. The taste of the wood and the texture of the ridges on his tongue calm him down. A sax man ain't getting nowhere without a good, wet reed.

She lean into it. "I'm telling you what—ain't nothing I ever wanted but to earn respect for the work I'm capable of doing, be a part of a community. Now, when we run our place back in the Ward, it was as a business owner, and so I got treated right sometimes. And sometimes not. But here, they embrace me from the git-go—both of us. Let me be in their durn club. And if you told me when I was a little girl I'd come back here and be one of the ELMS? I wouldn't have laughed at you—I wouldn't't've even known who they were."

"Yessir, that's a helluva club y'all got going." Manny get scared talking about them—every one of them ELMS got a way about them. Like, they could hear a muh-fuh badmouthing them from afar. And could make you regret it, if they took a notion. Manny, he ain't believe in no voodoo, and all? But still.

Them eyes on his old lady, flashing and shining—they always had a hold on Manny ass. And she ain't done yet:

"Them old and not so old white women make me feel like a sister in there —you hear how I put that? I got sisters there, yo. But you—you had to go and screw one. Didn't you."

Damn—this gone south quick. "I said it was stupid. You ain't got to shove the knife in deeper."

"Speaking of shoving, can't you put a double rubber on that thing and go on down to Mama Beaudock's like the rest around here do? Nobody bat an eye. Not even the sheriff." Pointed: "Not even me, if I ain't having my nose rubbed all in it like this. Having it shoved back in my damn face."

"Aw, baby, look here now—"

"I keep smelling her on you."

Lord, she always had a sniffer like a durn Sherlock Holmes basset hound.

Dang it—Manny done as bad before. Or worse. Probably ain't wise debating shit from that angle. "Told you, ain't happening no more. Your mind playing tricks."

"I said my ass was sorry."

"This behavior is egregious, Manny. Do you understand me?" Fired up, now, she come over to the lip of the stage and plant them stems. "Did you ever think once about me? And how it gonna look? You decided you wanted that one, so you just done it?"

"Takes two to tango. Don't forget that part."

"As for 'her,' I'm dealing with it on a different level," with blazing eyes that put the fear of God into Manny ass. Dragon lady time, the hot dragon's breath. Time to chill the fuck out.

"It just happen, yo. Don't mean nothing."

"You—you and Rebecca—you're both so full of—oh." Neecie break off, sputtering and slamming shut her durn laptop that musta cost a grand, easy. "I depended on you for everything back in Louisiana. Now that we're here, on my turf, I don't need you as much. And I think it's driving you stupid."

Manny plop down on his onstage stool where he rip off them runs and arpeggios and solos and act like a man. "Girl—you making shit too complicated."

"I'm making things complicated? Jesus God in Heaven."

"Hear me out. All my ass wanted was to pinch off some strange. Ain't got nothing to do with us."

"Respect, Manny. Just keep going back to that idea. And maybe try showing it one day."

"If I didn't still love and honor your ass, I'd-a hit the road long before now. But I feel ya. Word. Respect gonna be given."

This do the trick. She ain't got much else to say, because it the truth.

Except the part that ain't. Which is about how it more than pussy. And has been for awhile. Manny hiding, all right. That what a wife know. Manny telling the truth, but only on the inside: his stomach bunched up over Becky L. When he say he ain't in love, he only pretending. And Manny wondering how much more role-playing he got left.

Neecie don't wait to find out. Grab her laptop and ledger stomp out in them heels, but not before cinching the noose tighter: "We've still got to go over these numbers. But it can wait."

Manny reed wet enough, but now he don't got the pull to start playing. He got vegetables to go help his brother-in-law load in. Honest work, anyway. That much he got going for him.

But obviously, it ain't gonna be easy to walk away from this one. Not only do he think he love the girl—damn if he don't—but she might not be joking around about that threat of her'n, not after Becky L showed Manny the nickel plated .38 she carry in her purse. Like Manny say before, shit getting real, yo. He ain't kidding.

ROY AND HALF THE DANG TOWN

While you and Letty Glasscock stand chatting in the yard, Jasper and your grandmother sit on the porch and run through the song they planned to sing—'Beyond the Sunset,' a hymn recorded by both Hank Williams and Ernest Tubb, is her choice. Jasper's so pinched in the face and shooting you knowing glances that he must have heard about your paint-rolling stunt.

The tune is unfamiliar. "Did Pa-paw love that one?"

"I don't know if he did, but old Ernest sung it at the Opry when Hank passed away."

"They also did 'Peace in the Valley.'" Jasper, a country music pedant. "Red Foley got up and done that one. Was so broke up over Hank he barely got through it, or so they say."

"I'm having a hard time equating Granddaddy with Hank Williams. He never touched a guitar or sung a song, not that I know."

Mama Runelle says *p'shaw*, hollers for you to hush up so they can practice. "Don't you worry about this. You never could stand your granddaddy's country music, anyway. For some durn reason."

The statement sounds so caustic it embarrasses you. Crotchety old dame.

They sing the hymn. Jasper, picking a simple guitar line and sing-speaking the first two verses, with Mama Runelle harmonizing on the chorus:

Should you go first and I remain, one thing I'll have you do
Walk slowly down that long long path, for soon I'll follow you

While you dab at eyes gone misty, Letty Glasscock drapes a crooked old arm around your hunched shoulders. Comforting.

You tell her she's also invited to take part. "Anything you want to say?"

"Gracious and thank you but no, I shan't be eulogizing today. Particularly a man of your grandfather's esteemed stature."

Letty's Old South accent caresses your ears; along with Howdy Shull, she has the noblest and most antiquated brogue of anyone you've ever heard, regally melodious in both tone and cadence; Letty would sound equally at home on a Charleston veranda south of Broad as here in Edgewater County. "I believe it sufficient that people he loved sing their special songs for him."

"It ain't like a real funeral anyhow."

"No, well, I suppose it isn't, not like many of us are used to." A pitying sigh of disapproval. Her jowls shake in distaste like that bug-eyed 'dowager' on *Downton Abbey*, the third season of which you and Creedence were halfway through streaming when she started staying out late and going to various functions without you, and spending untold hours on her password-protected laptop, a development you'd praised in the name of cybersecurity. "Traditional decorum has withered on the vine like an unwatered garden."

"Reckon times change."

"The times must—the only other choice is brittle ossification. But still, when you get to my age, you realize that all you've followed and believed in may not be built to last. But nor are we."

She'd know—Letty, the last survivor of the Sunbury School Fire. She'd been only a toddler. You hope she holds no memory of that awful incident. Ancient history.

Jasper calls you over and asks if there's one you would want them to sing. You do, but feel stupid asking: You inquire if he knows any Grateful Dead. The thought of death and sadness always takes you back to Devin and Libby all those years ago, the Deadhead concert that should've been your first date with Creedence, but you fucked it up; another story. The car wreck months later that killed Libby, and that whole drama, hurt worse than memories of standing up your pal's little sister. She'd become yours after all, hadn't she? For a time.

OUCH.

You're relieved when Jasper says he knows him some Dead. Tells you which ones. "'Black Muddy River'—now that there's a good'un. It's real, what's the word. Elegiac."

You're pleased he knows an appropriate Jerry song, if a touch concerned that Jasper smells fresh off a sampling tour of a Kentucky distillery.

"It's what-now?" your grandmother asks. "Ella-what?"

Jasper clarifies: "Mournful."

Mama Runelle mirrors your earlier question: "Roy, you think your Pa-paw knew that song?"

Before you can answer 'probably not,' Jasper chimes in:

"I'm certain he did," tuning and strumming and going mm-hm, holding the pick in his mouth while he adjusts the strap, which props up the collar of his lime green polo shirt like one of those tanned tennis and golf pro types crawling all over Sedge Island. "I played that one quite a few times on the man's very own stage."

"Don't surprise me none. My husband used to say all the time, 'when that old Jasper gets ahold of one he likes, he blame near runs it into the ground'."

Jasper's cheeks, shot through with purple veins, turn outright rosy. His expression speaks less of embarrassment than a welling of grief and affection for your grandfather. "I'll bet that son of a gun did," sounding choked up. "I done open mic for years now. A lotta songs got played."

A twinge of your heartstrings as you realize you must tell Jasper your plans, soon, to tear that old building down. To foment a better class of trade than a decrepit, smelly honkytonk ruining that prime corner of a town in dire need of redevelopment. "Maybe the Dead song's for me, too. A little bit."

"Boys, y'all can sing all day out there in the hot sun, but one's all I'm gonna have in me." Mama Runelle, taking off her guitar. "Jasper can do your muddy river song solo."

"You all right, Mee-maw?"

"Yes yes yes; but let me run inside again for a moment. Then we can get this business done and come on back. Well—listen to me." Cursing under her breath. "So we can pay my husband his due. That's what I meant to say."

You and Jasper and Letty wave your hands around and tell her, it's okay, Runelle, sweetheart, bless your heart, it's okay it's okay. "You go on, and then we'll all ride over together in the truck." Your Pa-paw's F-150, an XLT Triton model, featured an extended cab with comfortable seating for four.

While you wait and Jasper hums his way through 'Black Muddy River,' Letty goes around the house to say hello to Rico, the backyard big dog, the master of his domain.

Left on the porch, you watch as Jasper fumbles around, trying to shove his guitar back into the case.

"You okay today, bud?"

When he straightens back up, he pretends not to have heard: "Well-sir, speaking of playing music. I guess at some point. We should—you know. Talk."

"About? Oh. You want to talk about open mic."

"Yeah. Open mic."

You stammer, equivocating, stalling. Jasper's always been like an elder to you, mainly because he is, by fifteen years. You man up and explain that you can't say what will happen with The Dixiana per se. "But you maybe should think about where else you're gonna do your open mic night. Eventually. Because I don't know. About going forward with it. The way it was."

Jasper, pale, his red nose shining bright as a beacon. "You mean, going forward with open mic?"

"I mean going forward, period."

"Are you shitting me?"

"I am not, sir."

He looks more grief-stricken now than over your dead Pa-paw. "That's how Runelle feels, too," he says with finality. "I'd bet money."

"Ain't discussed it in detail. But I don't believe she'll mind."

"Look here, Roy Earl—did you do what I think you done?"

"Last night?" You smile, big and broad. "Sorry. Had to be did."

Jasper, cussing and walking in a circle. "This's all too much for one week."

"Don't tell me you were in favor of keeping that stupid old Confederate chicken?"

"Well'm—a little, Roy Earl. I got to say."

You make a quiet and reasoned speech on the theme of change as the natural order of things; that the mural's time had passed decades ago, and how you could get good solid backup for your viewpoint anytime of the day or week by posting a social media poll using the warm mini-*2001* monolith resting in your pocket, information you could access even without a decent wifi signal. Good 3g network going here. Tower nearby. All set. "That rebel flag's used like a swastika these days. Besides—it's been decided. And executed. Case closed."

You observe Jasper's wheels turning. You wait. One must allow a person to come fully to their moment of telling you the contents of their mind and heart. "I'm just worried somebody's gonna whip your ass over it."

Your head flares hot as a pizza oven, a brick one such as where you and Creedence like to go on the Island, with flames licking and wood-smoke drifting hazy along the top of your cranium. The Black Blade, too, hot as an iron poker left to roast in hell's own wood stove, thrums along your leg and begs to be unsheathed. "I'd like somebody to raise a hand to me. Now that I'd like to see."

Wait—are you scared? You find have scant breath to make your threat.

You ain't scared of anything. Not with all your money.

Are you?

When was the last time somebody threatened to beat you up? As a little fat kid, it had happened so often you dared not count. Christ—maybe you *could* go home again.

"I'm just saying, beau." Jasper hitches up his seersucker pants and discovers his flipped collar. Fixes it, wipes his brow, licks his lips like he's thirsty. "That was mighty durn presumptuous. I hope nobody don't make no legal hay for you over it."

"Legal hay? Explain."

"Well, look. If anyone does, I'll help."

"Dude, I own the wall. Every brick, every piece of mortar."

Jasper, with his assertion of phantom assailants, seems like a doddering country bumpkin unversed in the ways of the greater world. You feel sorry for him—for all of them.

You check on your grandmother, who you find crying into a tissue, and at first you rush over, but back off. You're not sure you've ever seen this woman weep like this. She seems too frail, her once long and gamine frame now stooped and bony, hands likely aching from the effort of strumming her beloved instrument. You know she wants to get this nettlesome emoting out of the way while she's alone. You can dig it, easing on out of her bedroom. Never let them see you cry. You're down with it.

Before you even get over the big hill on River Ridge Road, you see dust in the air, shafts of sunlight. And a helicopter, circling.

"I saw DOT boys working up here earlier." Slowing down as the glimmer of sunstruck windshields along the roadside blind your eyes. "But what kinda chopper's that?"

Jasper, leaning out the window and squinting. "Might be one of them black ones."

"Looks to be a whirlybird," Letty calls out from her side. "With the propeller on top."

"Thanks. That narrows it down."

Closer, slowing, the stands of scrubby pines fall away and you encounter vehicles every which way you look. A sheriff's deputy in the middle of the road blowing a whistle. People in suits and Sunday dresses standing beside cars parked alongside the shoulder.

People dressed for a funeral.

Fudge.

As you approach the turnoff to the dirt road leading to the fishing bluff down from Pike's Bait & Pawn, every face turns, with expressions ranging from exasperated to imploring; every man takes off his hat; every woman holds prayerful hands in front of ample bosoms.

You pull up to the traffic cop, whom on close inspection you find is the sheriff. "What the freak is happening here."

"Mr. Pettus—at last. Afraid we've got ourselves a public safety situation. And I'm not sure how to handle this unorthodox funeral service of yours."

Rather unlike yourself, you cuss a blue streak.

Oakley snaps his eyes to yours with disapproval. "Thank god they got the gravel spread, but it's still not sufficient to support vehicular traffic."

A shimmering white Escalade appears. Out hops Mayor Hampton, with a scurrying, officious twit following who, from his gangly musculature and promontory of a beak, must suffer the presence of Pirkle DNA. "Sheriff, I'm gonna pile into the lead vehicle with Miss Runelle and her grandbaby and Jasper, and we'll start down to the bluff."

You've got to get in control. "Hill, there's been a misunderstanding."

"You can say that again," the Sheriff barks. "Who planned this debacle?"

"Now Oakley, this here boy's granddaddy just passed. And not just any granddaddy." Hampton has turned beet-red. "I'm in charge here. I say what's what."

From the other direction roars another SUV, barreling around the traffic still backing up along River Ridge Road toward the interstate. The sheriff goes karate-chopping his arms at the driver, as does another deputy who in the process shoots you a withering glance, his bulging uniform sweat-stained, a Kevlar® vest straining against every seam.

From inside this dark SUV, a tinted passenger window rolls down to reveal the enormous shimmering brown melon of your old pal, the Reverend Nixon. "Roy Earl," he hollers out in sonorous desperation. "I heard you needed someone to officiate, and so here I am. Sheriff: I'd like an escort to the river overlook for my mother, who is infirm."

"Reverend Nixon, that's not possible." Oakley takes off his trooper's hat and wipes a brow gone shiny and wet. "Now, see here, everyone—"

Another blaring horn, another truck weaving toward the growing knot of aggrieved motorists and Rabbit-mourners, accompanied by a coterie of rough looking bikers in full regalia. Revving engines. Jesus, but you hate that noisy crap. Horsepower standing in for modestly proportioned penises. If anyone asks you.

A tousled blonde head pops out of the driver's side, sputtering with indignation—Trudy. *You wasn't even gonna tell me about Mr. Rabbit's funeral?*

Out of the passenger side, a giant, hairy redneck; her husband, you surmise. "I'm-a kick your ass, boy. I don't give a squirrel's nuts if you's in mourning for that crusty old bastard or not. Just you wait."

Trudy shushes her aggrieved companion. "Where in the hell's everybody supposed to park, Sheriff?"

Oakley throws up his hands. Horns honk like a gaggle of southbound geese cruising high above the Sugeree. Voices calling, shouting, and arguing carry up and down the country road.

"Gentlemen: this service, it was never intended for—"

A throaty rumbling cuts you off and heralds the approach of Thurmond

Pike, weaving through traffic on his three-wheeler with fleshy bulk poured into a plaid suit like Charlton Heston might have worn in 1975, with a wide belt and white bucks instead of biker boots. Chesnee, Pike's rider, sports a hot pink suit and lacy pillbox hat like a chubby, bleach-blonde Jackie O.

"Where we gonna put all these *vee-hickles*, boy—I mean, beau?" Pike shouts at the sheriff with bilious disdain, a man you are sure a redneck bastard like old Pike mistrusts based on the color of skin, as well as Oakley's high position of power in a place like Edgewater County, itself lacking a stellar record on matters of race, labor, policing, and other human relations.

"Damned if I know." Oakley, answering a call on his radio. "Oh, shit."

All notions of restrained leadership desert you. You're THIS CLOSE to unleashing the full might and fury of the Black Blade, but even if you do, on whom? The Mayor and the Sheriff? You might have money and success, but you don't have that brand of pull here. Not yet. Not after being gone so long. "I told that nitwit Wimmel that it was to be a private ceremony. Don't you hayseeds know what private means?"

Mayor Hampton's blue eyes bulge. "Gooch musta got mixed up."

Now you're steamed like milk for one of your coffee drinks, one served with skull-and-crossbones latte art. "'Mixed up' offers a weak-sauce assessment, Mr. Mayor. This is an outrage, sir. Not only that, but a public safety issue."

Sheriff Oakley, his face running with sweat, surrounded by running engines and honking horns, seems close to furious. "You aren't wrong—look at this mess. Not to mention I've had DHS breathing down my neck all morning."

You're all like, do-what? "Homeland security?"

"Sir, it seems the Governor of the State is on her way to pay respects."

Before you can respond, your grandmother calls from inside the F-150. "Roy Earl—I think the truck's fixing to overheat."

That cursed puff of oily steam, seeping from the grill again. Your heart, palpitating. This cannot stand. None of it.

You lean in the driver's window of your Pa-paw's pickup. "We got to do this another time, Mee-maw. I sure am sorry."

Jasper: "But all these folks—they came to honor him."

Mee-maw, fanning herself. "Get this straightened out, son. I don't feel so good."

Panic.

That gives you cover; causes the Blade to glow black and warm and to thrum with a pleasant sense of inevitability.

"Mayor? Sheriff? I demand respect for my grandfather's wishes, here. And I want these—people—sent on their way. Not five minutes from now, I mean now-now. I want to blink my eyes a few times and have it come true."

"Well, wouldn't that be easy."

"All right, pal. If you can't manage traffic around here, I'm gonna buy me a sheriff who can—I'm not a visitor to your little county. I'm a legacy stakeholder." You blaze inside with personal power and integrity and hefty account balances that would make these ordinary folks poop themselves bloody with envy. "Is that understood?"

Oakley looks like he would enjoy grabbing your fuzzy noggin in a head-lock and throwing you in the back seat of his prowler and taking you back to the shed for a thorough going-over about who's in charge of what. He barks orders into his shoulder mic. "And so y'all would like me to inform Governor Three-Rivers she should turn around and go back to Columbia?"

"Damn straight." You puff out your chest. "This is our county, ain't it?"

As if on cue, a fresh cloud of sunlit dust and two more oversized, black SUVs pull as close as possible on the opposite shoulder. The Governor's entourage, led by Thim Sykes, has arrived; all now becomes complicated beyond anyone's immediate control. A shouting match ensues between Thim, the governor's security detail, the Sheriff, the Mayor, and many other voices from the growing throng, gums flapping out of automobile windows—a dreamlike vision of madness and stress threatening to overwhelm you. Voices, calling and arguing and shouting.

A warmth grows within. A vibration of fury. It blazes outward from you.

"ALL RIGHT." Your voice, resonant, carries. Everyone nearby takes an involuntary step back. All fall silent. Eyes bulge. Hampton clutches his side as though cramping. The silence rolls out like a ripple in Jensen's Pond, spreading over the heads of them all. A mockingbird, dead, falls out of the sky and lands in the dust on the shoulder of River Ridge Road with a muted thump.

Now that you have their attention: "Here's the news, folks—this ain't happening. Not today. Not ever. Now go back to your lives."

Hampton, chagrined, snaps out of the trance you've induced. He rests a meaty paw on your shoulder, pats it a few times, maybe a little too hard. "Oakley, if I could borrow a bullhorn—?"

You nod and let them know one more time to get their asses in gear and clear out this mess, after which you shove that F-150 into reverse.

"*Funeral service for Mr. Pettus is postponed*," Mayor Hampton says again and again, a droning cadence, rotating the bullhorn in all directions.

As you pull a difficult six-point turn, with folks glaring and confused and waving and shouting and shrugging and sweating in the September sun, a typical Carolina late summer morning good for sitting at the bluff by yourself fishing, you finally get it. No wonder your granddaddy hadn't wanted a public memorial. What a clusterfudge.

This chaotic crap doesn't happen to you. Not the bossman. You are playing 5-D chess with everyone, always. But here, in your old stomping grounds?

They would need vigorous and sustained seasoning to get used to your brand of discipline and unequivocal, clear communication skills. Mad skills.

Once clear and with the near-riot fallen behind, you gun the engine and cause straggling well-wishers still arriving to swerve along the shoulder from your fuming plume of irritated exhaust.

⊛⊛⊛

You don't get far. Yet another SUV, a spotless, Sopranos-Edition white Escalade with deep black tinted windows, approaches. As it draws near, it flashes its halogen headlamps at you.

Cold terror—it's DHS. The Feds can disappear someone in a heartbeat. Even a citizen, a card-carrying member of the merchant class like you. Post-9/11, they stripped away all the old constitutional safeguards. Most Americans don't even realize this.

"Everyone get their papers ready."

"Do what now, Roy?"

But it's not the Feds. As you pull to a stop in the middle of River Ridge Road, the window rolls down to reveal a skinny, pockmarked redneck with a mullet hanging from underneath a tragically hip, trilby-style fedora.

"Help you, pardner?"

"You Rabbit Pettus's boy?"

"Something like that."

"True what they saying?"

"Who's asking? Gawker? Vice? TMZ?"

He gives you an eat-shit look. Glares you down. "You know what I'm talking about."

Jasper's voice shakes. "That's Jezmund Rembert. You remember JW, his daddy. Don't you?"

You get it—a gangster. "Listen pal, if you're coming to pay respects, there ain't no event. Go back home."

"I ain't coming to no memorial. Not after what you done."

"I enjoy every right to do what I did, my friend. It's a new day around here. Better settle in."

Fury rolls across Rembert's hard, puckered face. "That codger put you up to it. Said, 'I'm too much of a coward to roll paint over our blessed General Reb'," his would-be mean voice shattering with emotion, "the way your ass did to us all last night."

You snort with merriment. "Your 'blessed' General Reb? In any case, a man who owns a wall may paint it any damn shade he pleases."

"You ain't got no respect for nothing, do you?"

"As if white trash like you'd know anything about respect."

"Whoa—you think you're better than me." Extending a shaking, stubby finger. "As if your granddaddy was pure as the driven snow."

"You hush up your mouth!" Runelle's shout comes as a shock from her small back window. "You greasy little wiseacre."

"Mama Runelle? All due respect, but this chubby little grandbaby of your'n don't got no clue about that old honkytonk. Does he."

A standoff. "He knows enough."

"Why don't you go stage a dogfight, or whatever you freaks around here do for a laugh." Without waiting for the inevitable retort, you roll up the window and haul ass.

"Damn you, son—you almost made me snap my durn neck," Mama Runelle hollers. "Slow down."

"Me, too," Letty says. "You're going to kill every one us."

"Nonsense. Settle down, ladies."

Jasper doesn't complain, for which you're glad. You roar down that road, adrenaline coursing through the bloodstream and making your eardrums bulge. You can't get over it—threatened by a passel of pussy-assed, superstitious goodfellas, all broken up over rolling primer upon bricks you now happen to own. It's so laughable you hope the Redtails—and this hurts you to wish—lose every game for the rest of the season. The team's already got a sorry enough head start: 0-2 against Georgia and East Carolina. Pitiful.

Not that you care about football anymore. That'd been the old you. The new you, a sports heretic, wishes with a fervor bordering on religious for the team to go on a massive and ruinous losing streak; as you do so, you can feel psycho-electricity pulsing out of the center of your brain, your will transmitted into an energetic reaction with the greater universe. An image on a wall? Forget it. It was nothing compared to the power of an indomitable mind such as yours.

⊙ ✹ ◉

BACK HOME, you put your grandmother, shaken and upset, to bed for a nap. She seems feel the full brunt of the grief, now. Good. Get that phase checked off the list.

With reverence you place your grandfather's ashes on the dining room table, which still has a variety of desserts covered in plastic food wrap and probably starting to produce the fruiting bodies leading to mold. You know an onslaught of people are certain to traipse down here again. Perhaps there's a chain you can stretch across the drive up by the highway.

While getting the Glasscock siblings on their way back toward the pecan orchard and their old farmhouse, decrepit compared to the pristine and still-fresh Victorian you built for your grandparents, you instruct Jasper not to worry about Jez Rembert, the now-obliterated mural, or singing for the old man.

"We're gonna have ourselves a whole festival in a few months. Multiple stages. And you're gonna program the entertainment."

His entire energetic signature changes. Jasper's spine seems to straighten before your eyes, adding inches to his height. "I am?"

"That's right. Your task is to come up with your dream music festival lineup, and we'll set to booking the acts."

"Dream lineup? You mean, anybody?"

"Anybody. We won't get them all, so why not shoot for the stars. You know what music he liked. Who all's still alive—Ralph Stanley? Earl Scruggs? I used to deal with this crap during the St. Pat's fest down in the Old Market. If we're doing this in the spring—that's my feeling, anyway—we need to get going on securing guarantees for the talent."

"Yes sir, Mr. Roy."

"Don't address me like that. Please. I am not he."

"I didn't call you 'Mr. Rabbit,' now did I?"

You shake your head.

"A sign of respect, m'boy. Just appreciate it instead of throwing it back in this old man's face."

Suitably chastened, you decide to call Dobbs and bless him out for allowing this debacle to happen, him and that blithering idiot Gooch Wimmel. You'll deal with him later. Jez Rembert, too. Two-bit thug. Laughable. You'll handle them all. Oh yes you will.

You fish out your phone, which you'd switched to silent before y'all left to discover a dozen missed calls from Creedence, as well as numbers you don't recognize but which feature the Sedge Island area code. "Da fuh?"

You listen in shock, finding out the messages regard the condition of your wife Chelsea Colette Rucker-Pettus. The saying of her name that way, by a stern-voiced official who isn't your buddy Phil Webhannet, fills you with a new wave of revulsion and terror.

What has she done now? God help me.

Once you find out, many of your own calls get made, including to the Edgewater County airfield to tell them you have a family emergency and are coming to fly your Piper out this afternoon, ASAP. Another mad dash in the air, this one back to the island to see about your unfaithful but precious wife, over whom you've all-but crapped yourself anew at the news she's attempted suicide there in your palatial Marshside home, where all should have been beautiful and perfect. Beats all you ever seen, beau, this mad maelstrom life has become. If only you knew how to step into another reality, you'd do it in a heartbeat.

GOOCH AND REYNOLDS

The words came fast and true and tumbling from beneath his pruned, knob-knuckled, clattering, arthritic fingers:

Reynolds Elder Pettus: He enjoyed himself a few nicknames—Rabbit to most, Rennie to his loved ones, or to his grandson Roy E. Pettus, 'Pa-paw'—but whatever you called him, everybody knew him in Edgewater County, because it seemed at some point everybody passed through his beloved, venerable honky-tonk The Dixiana. And when you came into those doors, you likely got your ID checked or paid your cover charge, if they had a hot combo picking bluegrass or modern country or what they used to call hillbilly music, to an old man in work pants and a plaid shirt and brogans, stooped but still taller than most everyone else. A man who'd been to war. A man who'd fought through D-Day and the European winter forest but lived to tell the tale, and more than that, survived to come back waving the flag and realize a slice of the American Dream that so defined what would come to be the height of the twentieth century, the American Century. His story is all our stories.

Gooch typed and typed, his best work in ages, until his noticed his hands beginning to ache, after which he felt confused and uncertain what is was he'd been writing.

His eyes puffy and sinuses plugged up, by the time he got settled into his jammies with his fancy-man tea, nursing a mysterious wound to his most tender yet gentlemanly of pieces-parts, he had no idea why he kept snif-fling; only the vaguest notion that Hill Hampton, the young black sheriff whose name kept escaping him, and finally Roy Earl Pettus had all called to bless him out for some dumb thing he did, the nature of which felt so nebulous and not-there that it didn't seem possible he'd been crying over a mere castigation by powerful men.

Tears? Really? He'd been yelled at by town fathers for forty years. Fifty. Even he didn't know how long anymore.

Scrutinizing the calendar: Still the mid-2010s. Good. Being in the twenty-first century seemed weird enough on its own terms, but at least the date felt familiar and right and not at all dreamlike.

His phone vibrated. His young protégé Dobbs, a text message, which Gooch barely understood how to compose, send, or respond to:

Hey there, my friend. Apologies for what happened today. That was my fault—I should have followed up like a good reporter, doubled checked the facts. Not that you didn't yourself. You just had a lot going on. I'll take care of the Mayor, Roy Earl, et al. Smooth everything over. Get some rest.

No idea. No idea what he was talking about.

Gooch fumbled a response—ok—and tossed the phone onto the cluttered desk with a clatter.

To get this obit written—he had a dozen audio files saved to his computer desktop that must be interviews that would need transcription, but already cooking with gas, best writing in ages—Gooch had a long night ahead of him. Rabbit Pettus deserved the best. The paper needed to be put to bed by midday tomorrow for distribution. That much he could remember.

A good newspaperman knows his trade. Or used to, anyway.

Did anything work the same as before?

Gooch didn't know. He couldn't remember how to work the TV remote, or his smartphone. Barely knew his way around a computer. If they had any sense down at that paper of his, the possessive feeling off and wrong in an obscure manner, they'd get rid of him.

CREEDENCE AND ROY

By the time her husband showed up, ashen and shaken and looking on the verge of his own heart attack, Creedence had slept and felt better, and now on her way to release. They didn't even put her in a room, only a curtained off area near the ER. Treated it more like a drunk than an OD. The fluids they've given her for dehydration, a whole bag's worth, perked her right up.

In time to receive judgement.

His judgement.

She needed a drink.

"This has been quite a few days." Roy, through clenched teeth. "Hasn't it?"

She pitied him. He looked exhausted. "Ain't been good."

"A bad run. For all of us."

"Seems that way." Pleading, but trying not to. "Please. I'm so—messed up."

"Do not say another word," in that cutting, diminishing way he had of talking to her like one of his employees. "Don't you dare. Not a whisper of a syllable. If you know what's good for you. Now, just like the other day, I've endured another difficult and dangerous flight because of you and your... antics. Do you want your husband to survive this ordeal to keep providing for your spoiled princess ass? Then stop giving me panic attacks and forcing me to get behind the controls of my aircraft. Do you understand me?"

Not 'Oh my god' or 'My sweet angel' or 'I love you.' He'd broken her, now.

She could halfway understand his stress and pain and upsettedness, which wasn't a word but seemed a good way to describe it when Roy's face turned red and he came at her furious. Not at her with a fist like Dusty had, no; Roy

Earl Pettus was good-hearted as could be and wasn't no hitter, but lord if he didn't still have a temper, a verbal bully.

And at the moment, his nastiness took away the good feelings about seeing him again. At first she had felt shame, but also relief at him popping his fuzzy round head around the curtain, and she had wanted to do one of her crazy spastic dances as she used to as an adolescent alone in her room, pent up with feelings she didn't understand and couldn't process worth a durn.

"That's all you got to say?"

"You're lucky we're speaking."

"You ain't worried about what's wrong with me?"

He plopped down, heavy, on the stool. "Don't you think I was debriefed by the doctor before I came blundering in here? You forget who you're dealing with."

"My husband. Who don't let nothing sneak up him."

"Damn straight." The words hung in the air like somebody had farted. "Hah. That's a good one."

Creedence, chin quivering. Penitent and raw. "I already talked to them about it. And the counselor, she said, from my condition," which she realized seemed twitchy, and how awful she must look. And how she must stink. She hadn't even had a sponge bath since before—oh, crap. Did she still smell of sex from last night?

"I need to go to rehab. I—need help." She broke down, but quietly.

"Help isn't for people who've done wrong." He leaned in, nose twitching, a snaky vein throbbing in his temple that popped out when there was a problem at any of the SBFCs or coffee shops. "Now you understand, young lady, that you gotta have punishment first. That we're gonna punish you?"

We?

But forget all that: if she stunk of Estes, what about the sheets at home?

Panicking and coming off the hospital bed and pawing at him, feral, with him pushing her away and going, get off, get off me you loon. "I want to go home. My kitties—*the kitties,*" straining her sore throat.

"I'll take care of the cats."

"I don't need no inpatient treatment. I changed my mind. Oh, lord help me, but I changed my mind." She shrieked for the nurse and the counselor again. "Let me go home with my husband! I got to clean up the house!"

"You're not allowed back in the house until you get a clean bill of mental health. We'll revisit you 'coming home' in twenty-eight days, my dear."

The duty nurse wobbled in on knees tired but dutiful. It must be hard work in healthcare. More like a perturbed schoolmarm than a caregiver: "What on earth going on here, honeychild?"

"My house is a mess. My kitties, they ain't been fed in hours. I got to get home. Here, here, here—*let me out so I can go clean.*"

Creedence rolled off the bed and yanked at her wristband, and Roy grabbed her and she struggled and pushed away, kicking and thrashing and afraid he would smell Estes' semen on her, and the nurse called for help and the tray by the bed with the water and a clipboard went over, CRASH, and people came running and Roy stepped aside and Creedence, screaming for her dead mama and daddy and brother, felt a needle jab into her arm like a bee sting.

The world, watery and distant, calmed down all around her. Okay. Okay. Okay. She didn't know if she were thinking it or speaking it, or who was there. One of those weird round lenses on her camera, out of focus around the edges.

"Baby?" she heard herself asking. "Let me go home now. Clean up for you… I'll make it all up to you."

In her mind, though, she continued her incessant shouting: that the sheets were dirty, house a mess, life a wreck, the kitties needed care and feeding and the litter boxes needed scooping, oh my god, I forgot to scoop the clumps; help, I'm drowning, his semen smells bad on me, I'm scared, the seashells are still stuck to my belly, now I'm covered in them, tingling and sharp and sticking all over and sinking; sinking down into a mass of broken seashells like quicksand, graying out the world, the shells covering my face and my head, I'm going to sleep.

ROY AND THE CATS

What an insane mess your ditz of a wife has gotten herself into this time. You kept her out of jail the other night only because of your exalted status in the community, and now in the hospital. Gracious sakes alive.

After you land and get the Piper squared away, you go into the hanger, but none of the old guys are here—at first you worry that the Colonel's died, but a field maintenance guy whose name you can't remember, Pedro or Paco, tells you it's only a quiet day.

Earlier in the year they finished building a glimmering jewel of a conference center over on the other side of the airport and named it for the Colonel, with a plush meeting room full of teak and captain's chairs and other amenities. Since the dedication ceremony, he's been spending time over there. You know this because you've a fixture around the hanger for the last few months.

Constantly.

Instead of being at home.

With your beloved life companion.

Check.

You recall sitting and listening to the Colonel, your personal, national hero, describe his experience in Vietnam. How the Vietcong tortured him.

"But they didn't break me up here." At this point in the telling, which you've heard several times, he always points to his temple. "My knees might be shot from the hard landing I took after my chute got tangled up in a tree and I had to cut myself loose. And my shoulder—boy, I tell ya. I still can't raise this arm over my head," demonstrating with a thick liver-spotted forearm lifted only to about the fourth rib. "That's from where they hauled me up with my arms pulled back, left me hanging like that for hours. They didn't get shit out of me. The rat-fuckers didn't get inside my mind, either."

"No?"

"Hell no, son—I walked out of that place with my shoulders back and head held high. It was February 1973, and I thought I might be dreaming. We were all standing on that transport in disbelief, laughing, crying, hugging, hooting, hollering. The pilot came on the intercom, 'Gentleman, please, sit down! We're going home!' That only got us more stirred up. Shit, all of it'd been a waking nightmare, full of soup with monkey heads bobbing around in it, and cold, and heat, and insects. That torture, they didn't bother with it for long. The rest of the time, we sat there. And maintained military decorum. And order. But most of all? Our dignity, Roy."

"Nobody's taking our dignity away. Are they, Colonel?"

He rapped his cane against the concrete floor. "I tell ya, they tried, though. Those commie bastards. They took time away from us. But they didn't strip of us of our patriotism, nor our sense of duty. They didn't get near that, the little rat-eating sons of bitches." His jowls jiggled and he lowered his voice. "Nixon, he should've dropped the bomb on them all. He would've, you know."

"Jesus—you think?"

"He told me so, standing right there in the Rose Garden. 'My hands were tied, boys, by all those hippie protesters in the streets, and by all the liberal cowards in the congress.' A raw deal, that man. But not us. No sir. Don't believe it for a minute."

"You didn't come home bitter?"

He scoffed, but his eyelids fluttered. "I would do it all again. And you would too, my boy, if the call to serve came your way."

"I'd like to think so," you tried to stammer.

"Of course you would. God bless our dear old country."

You wish more than anything to have a talk with this real man's man right now. But he ain't here. He ain't coming.

Or maybe he is, but you have pressing nonsense. Your own tortures to endure.

⊛⊛⊛

AT THE HOSPITAL, Creedence looks like a desiccated mud-sculpture of the spouse and best pal you used to know, an ancient monument built by enterprising ants and lashed by a vicious, searing desert wind, erosion whisking her away bit by freckled, wasted, drunken bit. In the ER, you feel her illness settling on your skin like the humid island air outside.

Maybe when everyone's finished dying and bottoming out, you can take a moment for yourself to grieve over these losses. Nope; too much to address.

Perhaps the strangest sensation throughout the ordeal, after talking to the counselor and the doctor and going through the recommendations—she needs alcohol treatment, duh; but to have tried to kill herself with pills indicates the possibility of deeper mental health issues than mere substance abuse—had been the notion of all these difficulties being put into good order. The woman under literal lock and key for the next month.

Getting fixed.

Getting squared away.

You said, right-o, then! Let's get her transferred into the dry-out place across the shimmering toll connector. The facility's a good one, classy, top-drawer, as one might reasonably expect in its proximity to prosperous, wealth-choked Sedge Island.

After her sedation they checked her into a proper room for rest and further observation; as arranged, you'd return tomorrow to take her to treatment over on the mainland.

Awesome. Steps toward a result. Tangible.

Sorta.

In the hospital parking lot waiting for Island Taxi, you call your grand-mother. She sounds weak but also relieved that you've checked in, and that Creedence is all right; you downplay the drama of it all.

"She mixed up some medication and suffered a reaction, that's all. She's sleeping it off and will be fine, fine as wine, by tomorrow," a turn of phrase in poor taste.

"You gonna stay with her? It's always so lonesome to wake up in a hospital bed at night by yourself, with no one but strangers looking down at you."

Your grandmother hadn't spent too many days in the hospital in her life, knock wood, so you don't know how she's aware of this, but it sounds right. Still, another part of you says, shoot, I don't plan to do anything except put Creedence's cheating ass into rehab, off my hands and in the care of the profes-sionals trained to peel away her layers and strip her varnish and refinish her, figure out what it is she isn't getting out of life, and the wealth and plenty you've cobbled together for her.

For you both.

Sure; but only after you got together with Creedence, ten magic years ago, did you feel the drive to excel, compete, fight and win, like you once cheered alongside 90,000 other Redtails football fanatics every fall over in the massive and magnificent concrete stadium near the Southeastern campus in down-town Columbia; but all that replaced, eventually, by your need to acquire capitalistic gains. Hell—you figured you had a family brewing. Would need to provide.

That hadn't worked out, a kid or three, but you'd never blamed her. One day it occurred to you the universe decided you were supposed to remain a solitary creature—he who had never known parents, and who would, in a cruel symmetry, also neither suffer nor revel in the throes of procreative parenthood. Would never know how it felt. Couldn't know. Perhaps because your parenting situation had been unusual, you stand at an awful, unnatural, somehow 'modern' remove from the whole process.

Sex-for-fun, however, has been so perfect with your gal; and she'd gotten off good with you, and so why, Chelsea Colette Rucker? Why?

Maybe the answer will come to you, like one of your Pa-paw's drunk regulars waking up from a screaming blue bender and recalling hazy versions of all went down the night before in the shadowy crevices of The Dixiana.

⊛⊛⊚

AFTER GETTING a detailed telephone report from Officer Webhannet—a recitation of foolishness on the part of your wife—you found Creedence hadn't been kidding about needing to feed the cats. The hungry felines made for a feral, swarming mass who all but climb your legs there in the foyer. Their faces, so hopeful and hungry.

The ammonia smell of cat urine and fresh feces hits you.

Your gut clenches: if Creedence has fucked up like this, with the care of her 'fur-babies' as she calls the brood, then the woman herself has to be broken for real. Broken and beaten and gone nucking futs.

A solution: You'll let them all out. You'll open the doors, front and patio alike. They will make their way out and find a new life here on the island, free amidst their natural habit.

"*Row-roo.*" The sweet tortie girl, Sissy, sings to you with her unusual voice. Your favorite, the one who sits at your feet while you're surfing the web, the kitty rubs against your bare shins, her thick coat of fur comforting and soft. The vibration of her purring, feeling much like love itself in a state of manifestation. You stoop to pick her up. Sissy wraps her paws around your shoulder. Purrs louder, an engine revving. Holds on.

All this love here. But Creedence, turning to Estes. Estes fucking Patel.

Really?

Why weren't you mad at that little half-breed son of a gun? You're ready to let your cats out into the cruel harsh unforgiving wilderness of Marshside, when it is not they who've done wrong. They're incapable of doing wrong. They are cats. Beloved pets.

Oh, boy. You will fix this; you will draw the Blade on Estes Patel.

Literally. An energetic correction to his whole mess. Unrepentant, watching him bleed out there in the plaza beneath the mossy limbs of the famous Sedge Island live oaks, some of which are said to be hundreds of years old.

But the result? Murder one. Jail, for the rest of your life.

Wait—no. The weapon you wield is rhetorical, not a literal broadsword. Fun as it all sounds, words will suffice.

Still, putting the fear of god into someone by making a personal appearance tickles your fancy, and you make a mental note to get Sharolyn to look up Patel's home address from the HR files, which in an operation as small as a single coffee shop, even a high volume and classy affair like the CBSI, mean a few folders in a filing cabinet.

Not even locked. You'll go look it up yourself. Later. Less of a trail of evidence that way. In case the verbal slicing and dicing doesn't go far enough.

Get these thoughts of violence out of your head, a voice whispers. *They are uncalled for, even in your upsetting situation.*

A calming sensation of relaxation comes over you. Let it go. You're not used to this voice, but you could stand more of its advice.

"C'mon, sweet Sissy. Let's see that you guys are fooded and watered. Mom didn't mean to forget you—she's not herself these days."

❁❁❁

AFTER GETTING THE CATS FED, sweeping, scooping clumps for a mind-bending twenty minutes and leaving behind several messes—the housekeeper would earn her pay tomorrow—you check in with Sharolyn; call your health insurance provider and ask about substance abuse coverage (you have it, in spades, and all fine and well there); call the airport and arrange service for the Piper; and, last, a petsitter you'll interview and retain, you desire only release and relaxation that can't possibly come. Maybe with some of Button's weed, which you don't have immediate access.

Or, get into the liquor cabinet. You'd rather not, for obvious reasons, and not because she drank it all. Had come close, as you discover.

I should crash tonight in my own bed. Healthy sleep. Try to pull myself together.

One look in the messy bedroom changes your mind—the sheets and bed all torn to shit, you supposed, from her thrashing around drunk. Again: housekeeper alert.

Instead, you stretch out across the untouched bed in the main guest bedroom, spotless and quiet and clean and un-lived in. It looks so safe and orderly it gives you a hard-on, and damn if you don't drift off to sleep, soon as you're done bawling your eyes out like a little kid, lost and scared and alone.

❁❁❁

LATER, a grocery run for a few items.

The Bi-Lo brand, often considered a downmarket choice in the regional grocery pecking order—Bi-Lo, Piggly Wiggly, Winn Dixie, Food Lion are all lower-tier redneck havens compared to Harris Teeters and Publixes, which you wish you had here on-island—but damn if this isn't the crystal palace of Bi-Lo supermarkets. Admiring the cleanliness and extensive selection of organic fruits and vegetables, you understand that the chain is successful, so it has to have smart dudes like you calling the shots, who know Sedge Island's consumer demographic and that they expect a grocery store to possess flair and sparkle and gilded edges.

You go down the colorful snack-food aisle looking for a can of Durkee brand potato sticks, but you find none. It's deserted as hell in here, and besides about a hundred dollars' worth of cat cans, you grab milk and bread as though there's a South Carolina snow warning in effect. Stand there with your mouth open thinking through what else you should buy, how long you'll stay, and all manner of other trivial nonsense—or not so trivial—that seems to keep you from making what ought to be easy decisions. Maybe gourmet chocolate and natural peanut butter would make for a treat. Comfort food.

You decide cat sustenance is the most important item. As you possess resources and free will, can scrounge and forage from any of the myriad fine dining establishments on the island, you will be fine.

Or eat at the CBSI, for that matter. Have them press one of your artisanal flatbread sandwiches, the turkey and brie and jam, or perhaps the grilled eggplant and sun-dried tomato caprese.

Sandwiches.

Time for you and Sharolyn to sit down and discuss switching over from the summer to the winter menu—which menu items to keep and which to eighty-six. Lunches, strong at the CBSI. The ladies who lunch.

"Ha—I got a sandwich for those lunching ladies."

"S'cuse me?" The off-island townie girl checking you out, and you do mean checking out with suspicion, glances from the depths of her item-scanning purgatory. "Find everything you need today, sir?"

"I did. Thank you." Small talk: what do you have to offer? There's only one question a business owner cares to ask anyone plying a retail trade: "How was the season? Solid?"

"Nope. Our managers," conspiratorially, scrunching her mouth over to the side, "are losing their minds."

You notice the small lip ring she wears, and know in your heart that, in an earlier time? The boss would have told the prospective Bi-Lo cashier to remove such a gaudy adornment. "Over what?"

"It never got busy-busy this summer. Not really."

"The numbers look good at my business, but I depend more on locals and regulars."

Bloop-bloop-bloop. She scans can after can of premium pet food and chucks them into the Stemplewicz Industries plastic grocery sack suspended in a rack. "On Saturdays we'd get a pop, from the vacationers coming in? But it would peter out during the week."

"Tourism—it hasn't recovered."

"Recovered from what?"

"The downturn—the economic crisis the last president caused."

She regards you like she doesn't know what you mean, says she hadn't heard about all that, and you think, mercy, the new normal's the new normal, now. This girl had been how old back in 2008? Thirteen? Jesus. It'd been so long since the Bush Crime Family® looted the treasury and said, dang, y'all, we're on the verge of a collapse that, to a youngster who'd never known another world, the ongoing, slow-rolling economic crisis which resulted—codified and approved by the current TelePrompTer-reader as well—seemed the everyday way of the modern world.

"To me it seemed busy enough." She punches up your total and asks if you want to use the coupons attached to a few of the cans. "If they want it any busier, they can keep this job, ya know?"

You tell her she need not scan the coupons; rue her ignorance about how it all works. "Busy means something different to your big boss. He's got to answer to the money."

"Glad I don't. I can barely handle counting down my drawer." A finger to her lips. "But don't tell my manager I said that."

Today's young—god forbid asking them to do simple math in their heads. Terrifying. What was that education legislation called? Every Child Left Behind?

◌◉◌

BACK HOME THE PETSITTER ARRIVES, a middle-aged woman named Maggie Passanant, stout of lower extremities and with a kind smile. You greet her in your most clipped and impersonal way; you're distant and distracted and down to business as you walk through and struggle to remember the names of them all, the cats; have to search to find Creedence's list of pet-sitting instructions, five typed pages, she produced when y'all went up to the mountains that time.

Passanant, who seems surprised by the number of furry bodies scurrying all around, pisses-and-moans about how her normal rate assumes fewer cats than you seem to have, which she also notes are all so precious and darling and cute and fuzzy, and how she already loves them so. Her fingertips held up to her mouth in a defensive body-language gesture, she explains how she must adjust her billing rate because of the extra time involved. "I have quite a few clients right now."

"What's the up-charge? It's not like you can give me sticker shock."

Taken aback. "A couple of dollars. Or so. Per visit."

"Couple dollars, eh?"

She shrugs and smiles. "Let's call it three."

"I see. Three bucks." You tell her to wait here. To get to know them. "Sissy's the alpha cat. We all defer to her."

"There's always one."

You come back and find Passanant standing stock-still, the more personable representatives of the brood swirling around her feet. "They're all so friendly and sweet."

"I can assure you of their pampering. Now. Payment: Let's get you caught up in advance. For a month. Plus 'a couple of dollars' for the extra trouble."

You scratch out a round sum on a check from the Crown account, the ones printed on a watermarked, heavy-bonded cloth-like paper, a regal and substantial document into which the ink from the gel pen sinks smeary and profane. You go to rip off the check, but then because of the weight and fine nature of the paper the check doesn't make a dramatic snapping sound like you'd hoped. Instead, it tears off with a near-silent swish, and you experience frustrated that the gesture lacks the aural punch you'd intended.

She examines the financial document. "Oh—my. This is too much."

"Too much is not enough for our feline family. And, I'd like, if we could, to make this an open-ended agreement. My wife—she could be gone longer than a month, but as of now it's twenty-eight days, if you get my drift. And I have business upstate that'll be taking up all my time. I'm giving you extra so you'll spend time with them. Quality time."

"I'll do my best, but—"

"I want to tell my wife someone's spending time her pets. But keep in mind that by accepting this check, you're not only agreeing in letter and spirit, but also with full knowledge that I may review security footage. Remotely. Not that I don't trust your professionalism."

She seems to understand on another level, now: a family crisis is unfolding. That your energy suggests discord and tragedy. Folds the check and pockets it. "I think I see now."

"I hope so, Maggie. I can't be any more clear than I've been."

On the walkaround, where you show her myriad light switches and points of egress and exit and the alarm system, she compliments the home you've made here on the marsh. "What's your business?"

You explain that you own the illustrious CBSI; she lights up and says, oh, my, how she loves that coffee and those sandwiches.

"Especially that grilled eggplant."

"The eggplant caprese?"

"That's the one. Best. Sandwich. Ever."

You beam with pride, note-to-self to inform Sharolyn: we're keeping the eggplant. "It's my own recipe."

You explain to the petsitter how you owned a coffee shop like it in Columbia that you sold to your manager, and while you'd been off earning your fortune in a different sort of food service venture (you don't describe the fruitshake empire, which despite its success feels meaningless to you compared to the Beanery), you never quite got coffee out of your blood. In fact, you tell her you're busy getting ready to open another coffee shop. In downtown Tillman Falls.

"Where's that?" Maggie asks. "I'm not from South Carolina."

"It's nowhere. But not for long, dear. We're gonna put the old girl back on the map again. You'll see."

⊙❋◎

Now in possession of your Mercedes, at last you cruise over to the Beanery. Oh, but this feels more painful than going to the house—who knew what had happened between them here in this building? Or in the parking lot.

The nights you came back from flying and she hadn't been home—how unusual. Creedence had been so content here alone with her kitties. You should have known! Where is your meticulous planning and foresight?

Who will lead yer people now, Moses? you think in your best Edward G. Robinson.

You get out and find the car filthy, embarrassingly so, and the parking lot equally dusty, detritus building in the crannies every which way you turned—it needs a good blowing, but at this point who didn't. In any case, you can spot a straw-paper or wadded up gum wrapper from fifty yards.

But see, your CAM fees—common area maintenance, part of any standard business lease in a plaza like this—are more than enough to cover a modicum of cleanliness. Check; more than a modicum. An assload of spotlessness. Sedge Island, and you, demand nothing less than perfection. Note to self: call the property manager. Bitch. Him. Out.

A deep breath.

Presence of mind.

Counting to ten.

Prayerful, you place your hands together in front of your face. You smile, hard and tight. Remnants of your anger management. Fragments, coming to the fore. Useful.

And so: You will put matters in a more gentle manner to the property manager. The Black Blade, thrumming and humming, but you persuade your inner warrior for justice it's not the way. Not the time. And not over this modest amount of debris that's drifted in from other sources than the fellow businesses in the plaza.

Trash. In the best parking lot on the island.

Fury.

Unacceptable.

You'll make that asshat PM sorry for this oversight. Yes; yes you will. But later.

⊛⊛⊛

A QUIET AFTERNOON INSIDE; the staff greets you with cautious warmth. Your proxy bossman Sharolyn's large and beautiful brown eyes brim with tears as she comforts you about various issues, spoken and unspoken. "I'm so sorry about your grandfather. And—everything."

"What a creeping clusterfudge of a trainwreck."

You whisper this behind the counter, smiling through your words at customers who wave to you from their tables set out amidst the warm and homey atmosphere you came up with for the CBSI: it's meant to be a boho coffeehouse like the original Beanery, which itself had been a re-branding and sprucing up of a legacy coffee shop there in the Southeastern University college ghetto.

Maxine's Koffee Klatch exuded a lived-in collegiate vibe, authentic and earned and appropriate; you remind yourself how the shelves of books and LPs lining the walls here, however, are mere decoration. How you bought them in bulk from various vendors and had your original staff load them onto the custom bookcases you had built high enough, all around the top one-third of the wall space, so that all but the tallest of customers would refrain from touching the objects.

If someone wanted to pull a book off and read it while they were having coffee, you wouldn't object. But know this, and know it well: these books and records are props. No turntable exists on which to play the albums, and upon closer inspection, anyone could see that most of the LPs are crap, worthless cast-off cutout bin junk like old Jackie Gleason records, Mantovani, those Firestone Christmas albums, Guy Lombardo, Jackson Browne. The record dealer who'd hooked you up must have had an entire shelf, over two dozen copies, of Herb Alpert's *Whipped Cream and Other Delights*, which the dude called the 'king daddy' of worth-free records he would find in his spelunking through collections at estate sales and from folks bringing in their dusty old music by the crate-load. You did him a favor. A big one.

YOU REMEMBER WELL the unusual transaction: "What if I take all these off your hands?"

"A take-all price? For this junk?"

You conducted negotiations in a musty anteroom at Primo Jazzman's Record Attic in downtown Charleston, which you remembered from your time living on the peninsula. You didn't much care whether the albums were Herb Alpert or Mantovani or Jimmy Nelson's 'Instant Ventriloquism' Lessons featuring Danny O'Day & Farfel; no one would ever play the LPs, as you explained. "I got a lot of shelf space to fill up."

"Shelf space?"

"I want to make my coffee shop feel like somebody's old college dorm room."

"I gotcha." Ruminating and tugging at his hipster beard, long and scraggly as so many young men now sported, as though a time machine had disgorged an entire generation of hibernating forty-niners from a snowed-in mining camp in the Klondike, the record merchant released a cloud of truth-telling: "You'd be doing me a favor, really, so I don't know what to ask."

A most unimpressive negotiating style. Probably loves the music more than the money he makes, the big dummy. That's what you thought.

"Make it worth your while," is all you said, tagging your statement with a brief coda: "For 'junk' like this, of course."

That had only made the record retailer look sad—even these LPs, you supposed, represented 'value' to him in a sense. Records were his life. And there you were treating these cultural artifacts with such disdain, like if someone came in and said, give me the shittiest instant coffee you got instead of that fancy-pants slow-food bullcrud you guys stay so busy dripping.

He named his price; you made him a counter offer, one designed to save you a few dollars, as well to demonstrate that you were no easy lay.

He shrugged. "Sounds fair. I wouldn't sell these records in the next ten years."

You shook on it and asked him about helping you load when you came back with a rental U-Haul for the drive back down to Sedge Island, and the owner of the record store had agreed.

In the course of wrangling this purchase—after you'd settled on a price, anyway—you revealed you were the Spotted Banana™ guy.

"Damn good smoothies, bro. Good product."

"Thanks. We try."

But compared to records or books, in that moment fruitshakes felt frightening in their ephemerality—you literally pissed them away. Herb Alpert whipped cream would live forever on these recordings, though. A legacy in which to hold a modicum of pride.

Yeah—whipped cream, sweet like the artificial sugars you slipped into your smoothie recipes. Part of their success. No one needed to know, only you and your fellow owners and a selected manager or two. "Delicious," had been the only feedback from customers. What they didn't know, et cetera and so on; few fruitshake buyers left your stores dissatisfied. You felt guilty sometimes, which had been part of your rationale, besides the millions, to take the ConParAgPro deal and sell out before the karma of your longstanding deception caught up with you.

Other than money and success, though, what will define your legacy? Sedge Island Cat Litter Consumer of the Year Award next spring? A shoo-in.

SHAROLYN HAS THE NEW GIRL, blonde and peppy and bright-eyed, drip you a delicious cup of Sumatra. Into the back office you sit down with your GM for a debrief, but as soon as you get started the barista appears with the coffee and you pause to make small talk. Ask her how she likes working at the CBSI, et cetera and so on.

"I wanted to thank you for opening this awesome place here on the island," she answers with maximum vocal fry, wrinkling her nose; name tag, Kaitlyn. "We didn't have anyplace as nice as this before."

"We sure didn't." Your smartass bossman persona sneaks out, your hubristic, know-it-all, I've-been-halfway-around-the-block rap you lay on young people to establish how you know they don't know their asses from a hole in the ground, and further, that any attempts to engage you on a meaningful level won't take hold, won't mean squat, not being of your exalted merchant class; it's your Daniel Plainview routine again. "That's why I went to the trouble of opening it, my dear."

Her sunny attitude flickers, a passing gray cloud. "Well I love it, even more now that I work here."

You detect a hint of flirtation, and my, how you love love love it so much you want to give this young girl the keys to the joint.

"Management material?" you ask Sharolyn in Kaitlyn's fragrant wake. Sipping your aromatic, custom-dripped cup of coffee, its complex finish with notes of cedar and spice tickling the back of your tongue, you start to feel almost normal for the first time in days.

"Maybe. These kids, they struggle with math so much, though. Blows my mind."

"A generational problem I was just considering."

"But we got to have someone, Roy. Eventually."

"Lord, don't I know it."

"I don't mind the extra work."

"The raise I'm gonna give you will take the sting out."

Her face brightens. "Really?"

"Next check. You'll see."

Her gratitude, palpable in the room.

You discuss more possibilities within the current staff, but it's the same conversation you had with her on the phone, and feels like tires spinning in mud. Ask if she knows anyone who needs work, but who also sports the gumption, the right stuff, to man the helm of the heavy cruiser-class starship USS CBSI.

"Lemme think about it. I know folks, but—"

"People who can live up to my standards?"

She gives you a flat smile that speaks volumes. "That's the problem."

"I hear you. But we can't just fumble along—without a plan—without—"

You stop yourself. You don't know what to say. You're busy flashing on all those faces at The Dixiana, which finally occurred to you had continued to enjoy employment by your grandfather not because he needed them, but because he wanted to help them.

A job creator. That's what Rabbit Pettus had been. That's what you are.

Every hair on your body stands up. Not about who you need to get to help Sharolyn run the CBSI, but about what needs doing back home in Edgewater County to keep those people whole.

Back.

Home.

In Edgewater County.

Your horripilation fades like the light leeching out of the sky that night you were trying to land the Piper.

⊙❀◎

After finishing with all manner of rigmarole at the CBSI and nearing sundown, you try to clear and banish the energy—the reality of it all—by going for one of your old power-walks. In your bedroom beforehand, though, you're shaking like a leaf; the second you get your shorts and exercise gear— iPod, kicks, terrycloth headband like McEnroe—you're overwhelmed with horrid nostalgia for better times.

Innocent times.

You stretch in the kitchen and pet cats. You drink water. Jiggle you gut, which feels soft and big.

You wonder how life could have turned out so wrong.

You wonder why you're bothering with wondering—this life is all over.

Gone. Marshside might as well have been nuked from orbit.

On the smooth, dark asphalt of the snaking traverse of the island walking path you get your pace up fast; your legs protest. You watch the clumps of Spanish moss swaying in the breeze like enormous gray horse's tails brushing away summertime flies. You pass two familiar faces, wave, holler, "How ya doing; I been real good."

It's hot and muggy and coastal; it's the low country, and it ain't autumn yet. Your body protests by dumping out a gallon of sweat in record time, far exceeding the wicking properties of your top-drawer workout togs. You'd note the brand and the fine weave of the garments, the price, the credit card you used to buy them at the Dick's Sporting Goods across the connector in the off-island commercial corridor, the place you'd considered opening another coffee shop, but only if you were Patrick Bateman.

You've always wondered why Creedence had gotten so mad when you'd suggested franchising the Carolina Beanery™ brand—how her eyes had filled with tears, or so you thought. She'd blamed it on allergies.

Bullshit.

At the bend near the highway connector crosswalk where you normally turn around, you keep going under the overpass and toward the beach. Walking. And feeling worse, not better. You get angry at the tour-ons on rented bikes, aging retirees going wobbly and slow along the winding black asphalt snake lying around the island, and if you do the entire course, it's like a marathon—twenty miles, eighteen clicks, something like that.

Twenty miles is nothing. You're the bossman. Gritting your teeth and walking faster and pumping your arms like an asshat making fun of another person powerwalking, you decide to go for it.

The path goes farther and farther, winding back into the trees and through the condo clusters and a shopping plaza—an old and crappy one; wherefore art thou, redevelopers and visionaries and investors?—and you perceive confirmation of what the girl at the Bi-Lo said: for this time of year, oughta be more visitors on this rock.

The world has changed.

The money's drying up.

Not yours, mind you. But everyone else's. You're a one percenter, now. But most of the rest? Fending for themselves.

But you earned it. Didn't you? The energy you put in had been returned to you tenfold. Rather—a million-fold, ten times over. There we go.

Sweat pours out of you. It runs into your eyes, stinging and burning, but still better than the tears you've been shedding.

You ease up, skitter across Oceanside Highway like a crab too far from the shore, which isn't too tough. Not much traffic. The pavement of the walking trail dead-ends at the gray and weathered beachfront roadway. Resurfacing lay in its future.

The shore. Shimmery, shell-strewn white sand, the ocean glowing beneath a risen, all-but full moon out over the horizon. A lilac band of light hangs on in the western sky behind you. Another day's end.

You take off your sneakers, peel and stuff the low-rise socks—power-walking socks you bought all specific-like. You had no idea they sold spinning socks, biking socks, running socks, yoga footies. What could be the difference? Socks equaled socks. File it under too many choices; capitalism has grown ever more rapacious; and so on.

The waves, small. Surfers along the Carolina coast are hearty and hopeful and always on the lookout for hurricanes and tropical waves to stir up the height and power and frequency. Here, tonight, the water at summer's end feels like a bathtub, and the swells lap gently against your shins.

You look down at your fruit-shaped body, your clothing sweat-wet and straining against your belly, your stomach that's growing back into its natural Edgewater County-fed state. Your pockets, bulging with keys and wallet and iPod and earbuds, Koss noise-canceling marvels that cost you a hundred bucks.

Distractions. Maybe the silence is better. Silence and stillness.

Stillness—the idea conjures an image of Button Sykes. Her stillwater pools of silence and presence and, yeah, stillness. Like her vibration is quieter than yours. Than anyone you've ever known. You want to stand next to her, she's so calm.

Button. You imagine her face, try to hold the image. She appears, smiling and beaming love to you.

But instead of happiness or tears, you feel nothing.

You keep walking, right through the hallucination.

Into the sea.

The waves, hitting you in the thighs. The iPod, ruined. Your wallet, soaked.

Trancelike, you go deeper, waves slapping you in the chest and face. Doubtless the sea remains unaware of your infinitesimal presence inside the watery currents of its vast body.

You remember the Grateful Dead and the music you'd heard at their concerts. You think about 'Dark Star' the night you saw them back at Southeastern, and how you'd looked over at your friends and felt so connected to them.

Billy Steeple. Libby Meade. And Devin.

But Devin, he'd left the concert by then, a precursor, you now understand, to the way he'd continue to disappear on all who loved him.

Devin. Why you thought about him, you know not.

Not because of Creedence. Because in your heart you know he is dead.

And you will join him.

The waves, up to your waist; the bigger swells, slapping salt into your mouth and knocking you back. Yet you press on. You've seen this in movies—the person walking into the sea. And being swallowed and consumed and made one with the enormous power of the water element; made one with all the universe.

Or, simply removed from its grand equation. An equation that no longer makes sense.

You start to swim. You're terrified of being out in the ocean—*Jaws*, remember? The Palmetto Grande? Almost forty years ago.

Your emptiness is filled with grief, now. And loss.

Creedence.

Your grandfather.

Your mother, whose eyes are alive but dead in her high school portrait.

Your father, like a character in a movie you heard about but never saw, a book they assigned you but never read, a famous personality that everyone knows but you.

And Button, again, who isn't dead. Her face, no longer smiling—distressed.

Ah, Button—we hardly got to know one another. Too bad.

You swim hard, hurling over the breakers, chopping at the roiling ocean. You've never been this far out. Not even before Jaws. Before the movie came out you weren't old enough to swim very far; your grandmother, overprotective and terrified of the outside world's influence on you, wouldn't let you go in over your knees. After Jaws, she needn't have worried.

A vision: the Coast Guard. Harbor Police. Thrumming helicopter blades. The brilliant arc of a flare over the inlet. The search for your body.

If only anyone had known you were coming out to the point.

No matter. A mystery for them to ponder, what became of Roy E. Pettus. Vanished. It happens, more often than people like to admit.

STOP. DON'T. COME BACK. COME BACK.

Button's voice. A siren song.

You snap out of your reverie. Terror fills you. You stop, bob, kick, dog paddle, turn around, see how far you've come. It isn't that far. The sea is calm.

You can make it back.

A sensation nearby. A nudge at your leg. The seafloor, sloping back up, probably.

No. Something bumped you. Breaking the surface, a slick gray body.

Choking on seawater, you shriek in terror. Your final fear, total and complete, surges into your gut. Paralysis as you await the clamping of the teeth; there is no going back. You are Captain Quint; you will die by that which you've always feared the most.

No—Quint had no fear of the sharks he hunted. Not until the last one.

The water, exploding nearby. Not sharks. Dolphins. You are surrounded by a pod of dolphins.

An assurance beyond feeling replaces the fear. You are whole and complete and alive and in the moment. The dolphins move through the water with grace and ease; the water shapes itself around them, allows their passage.

Allows your passage.

Back to shore.

You begin to kick back. Hard. The fear returns—you aren't home free, you've a hundred yards to swim. You can't see what's in the water beneath you.

The dolphins, gone.

On your own.

But the next solid surface your feet hit are the bottom.

Back onshore, you slither out as though from primordial slime and lie at water's edge, catching your breath. You start imagining, and imagining hard, a way for all this to work out. For all the pain not to throb anymore, for your heart to stitch itself back together. Think on it a good long while. Your exhaustion doesn't help matters. You haven't swum hard like that, um, ever.

After a while, you sit up. Evening beachcombers, you find, have turned flashlights in your direction.

"Say there, fella." A middle aged man wearing a red windbreaker, calling out in his upper Midwest accent. "There's a sign up the beach that says it's dangerous to swim here at the point."

After wiping the half of your face covered by sand, you shrug. "Danger's my middle name. Do it almost every night."

"You're nuts."

"Yeah," one of his kids adds, a smart-alecky eight-year-old boy. "Sharks are nocturnal feeders."

"Right you are. And maybe I am—nuts, that is. Not a shark."

The knot of evening beachcombers hurry away from the crazy man soaked to the skin and talking crazy.

Turning back to the turbid sea, moonlight glimmering like the lighted path ahead, you ask God—or the universe, or perhaps simply the You inside the ego-shell that one normally perceives as self—for guidance. For deliverance. For an answer regarding what you should do next.

And then you find yourself writing in the sand: a single word, a series of lines that are abstractions: language, mathematics, signs and symbols, all pitiful and artificial attempts by man to define the state of this odd, shared reality. A circle around it, waving over it with your open hand. Imagining the idea to be real.

Your word?

HOME

You wait and watch. If the waves come and take the word away—if the ocean accepts your idea, thereby answering your question—you'll know where you belong.

The wait is brief. The next, lapping, languid wave rolls unhurried toward your feet and the word in the sand, and with gentle grace the mighty Atlantic takes the idea of HOME. As a consequence, the concept now exists as huge as the ocean itself; your notion of solace and healing, growing with power and certainty.

In a flash it's the old you, capable and alert and bringing ten thousand percent to the effort. Bold, confident and wet, you rise and with your thighs sticking together, you're ready to stride back to your house: you will begin the process of returning to a state of mind in which none of this doubt and pain and fear dogging you, that still looms inexorable, will serve as motivating factors in how you'll live what remains of your life. You are reborn slick as one of those inlet dolphins, bearing you back to shore like waterborne angels. Saving your life.

A vow: You shall live up to their example.

You will save lives. Including your own.

Now there's a task befitting a bossman like you, a master of his place in the earthly firmament, in the noble, enveloping unfoldment of the spiraling universe, of the worlds which forever turn in their inexorable, graceful regularity.

Your world, still spinning backwards. But not for long. Not with you in charge.

CHRISTY, NEWBIE, AND HOWDY SHULL

Newbie, upon seeing the body, looked scared enough to poop himself. "This is crazy, Christopher. I can't believe I got mixed up in this."

"It wasn't nothing I did. He done this to himself."

"I don't care who done it, or how."

"Good. Cause it don't matter."

"Beau—the law's gonna think we both had something to do with it."

Christy feels like he's gonna mess himself all throughout this messed up mess they've gotten messed up in. Mess mess mess. His mind ain't been right, and at first, Newbie's panic only made it all the worser.

But then Christy's thoughts, they quit racing, and he had the idea about putting his Daddy's body in the river.

Didn't nobody ever go out to that walking path down there. It was too far from the town, and too close to the old rundown mill on one end, and the nuke plant on the other'n, and Christy knows this cause his Daddy, whose rotting, stiff corpse they had finally gotten wrapped up and shoved in the bed of Newbie's truck, said so all kinds of times. Went out there to make meth deals. Wasn't never cars in that parking lot. Not hardly ever.

"If it was me still in high school," his Daddy said, nodding and winking and smoking, "I'd-a been taking pussy down there while everyone else was in class. Like I done your mama at the old boat ramp under the river bridge, boy. But then, looking at you, maybe I ought better'n to've done it. Dumb and big as your ass turned out."

Christy remembers talk like this and says, Daddy got what was coming.

But now his Daddy, stinking up a storm. Foo-wee. And swelling around his lips and his eyelids, which had gone all gray, while the rest of him looked purple. Purple and puffing up.

⊙⊛◉

Upon entering the trailer Newbie had hollered out, hiding his face in his arm and leaning against the wall away from the body on the couch while Christy checked to make sure-sure his Daddy was still dead. Not that there was any durn question. Newbie run and puked into the sink, which made Christy holler about having to clean it up later. Christy, he was gonna start keeping this trailer neat as a pin.

But first: They didn't have no time to waste.

Newbie had been in a panic for too long last night. And had wanted to bail, until Christy pleaded in his whining voice and loomed over his friend like with his Granny, and Newbie looked scared in a different way. He settled down and declared, I reckon I'm in it now no matter what.

Christy said, "I bet we can figure something out together."

"I ain't figuring out nothing about this. This is murder, ain't it, Christy."

Christy motioned for his new friend—his partner—come and sit down at the table, making sure to place him in the chair facing away from the couch. Newbie sat shaking, like he was afraid he might wake Daddy, or the body would stand up and go BOO like on one of them zombie TV shows.

"Let's talk this through."

"I'm gagging. I'm gonna be sick again."

"I got something that will fix us up." Christy got two glasses and poured them each a drink of whiskey. To calm down.

He handed a glass to Newbie, who viewed the brown liquor with suspicion. "I dunno."

"A drink'll help us think straight. Like how people do in a movie."

"Booze ain't never helped nobody think. Not that I ever seen. That don't mean I don't take a taste of it, though, cause I do. But: ain't you got no Coke to pour in here?"

Christy didn't usually see people in movies bother to mix drinks—movie stars drank it hot and now like drive-through doughnuts, the thought of which made his stomach growl. They would have cereal after their drinks, and discussion of the body and its disposition. But Christy only said how he likes his liquor straight up. "Burns good going down."

Dang, Newbie said. He took a slug, grimacing and coughing, while Christy drank the rest down. Gulp.

"Beau, how long you been drinking? Thought you said you was only fifteen."

"Since the other day."

"Haw, haw." Newbie, sipping his drink and checking over his shoulder at the body. Drink or not, he still couldn't get over it. "Dang. This's a helluva thing, this body."

"We got to do something fast. Don't we."

"Yeah, you do. I don't know about no 'we'."

The liquor settling into Christy's stomach, he poured another for himself and knocked it back. Ever since the day Christy was born, or so it seems to him, he's had the word 'scared' inside his stomach and on the tip of his tongue, and it was cold and electric, that word, in the opposite way the liquor felt of fire and warmth. The drinks give him a sloshy-yet-settled, calm blue ocean floating in his belly.

His thoughts and words, coming easy now. He explained his Daddy wasn't nothing but a drug-head, and because of this, what happened wasn't murder: His Daddy, Christy reckoned, took too many drugs, finally, and had gone to sleep and not woke up. Which was true enough, and he felt good about what he had said. Christy helped his Daddy not wake up, but that part didn't matter, and might only make Newbie not trust him.

Pouring another swallow, Christy, he thinks he's been missing out. His Daddy should've stuck with liquor and not the drugs.

"Beau, why didn't you call the law? Or the EMTs?"

"Cause I was scared. I heard they put people in jail. That have drugs in the house. When someone dies."

"Is there drugs in the house?"

He don't know, but nods 'yeah,' figuring, sure, somewhere. "Probably."

"Where? What kind?"

Christy shrugs. "In his room. I dunno."

They went to look. Under the bed Newbie found an old metal box that had some money—not much, maybe fifty dollars in wrinkled up ones and fives and one mighty ten-spot standing tall. Underneath the money, a few folded glassine envelopes. He stuck his finger inside and licked.

"It's dope. Or was. But check out the money."

"Duh." Christy, snickering about the crisp twenties folded in his pocket. The worn-out play money of his Daddy's seemed meager and mediocre. It represented his no-good Daddy's whole sorry life, Christy thought.

Newbie, reluctant, handed him the bills. "I reckon this belongs to you, now."

Christy gave him back the sawbuck. "Gas money."

"That's your daddy's last money."

"It ain't no thang, dude."

"You alright, Christy."

Christy looked at the wrinkled money. Thought it didn't mean nothing. The liquor in his stomach felt warm and settled. It wasn't no drug, not like them powders and pills and pot.

In a dresser, inside a drawer full of old underwear and socks and bandanas, Christy scored another bundle of baggies that looked like they used to have meth in them. Newbie took and held one up to the light and said, yeah. "Crank. That'll make your eyes go crossed."

"We ain't doing none of that stuff. Ever."

"We better take this to the dumpster. Then we can call an ambulance, and you tell them all that like you told me. They won't take you to jail."

Christy had his doubts. He seen the way the cops did on TV. They could figure shit out. They might take his Daddy's body and put them CSI people on it. He worried about them taking a good long look and saying, it looks like somebody big and fat done smothered him.

Christy ain't dumb—he knows it wouldn't be the people on the TV. But the real cops did all that, too. That's what his Daddy always said, sitting there on the couch where his body lay. Them cops got ways of finding out shit nobody knows about. It they wanted to, they could put you in jail forever, he'd always say. If they took a notion.

"No," Christy ordered. "It's been too long. They gonna think I done something wrong for sure. Can't take no chance on calling the law."

"Man—I want out of this."

"Naw. You got to help me, now." Christy started whining. "Please please please Newbie. Please please please—"

"Shut up. Alright already." Newbie threw the baggies onto the messed up bedsheets all stained and torn, with Christy thinking he couldn't remember the last time he had been in his Daddy's room, all the way at the other end of the trailer. He wanted nothing to do with what went on in this room, and them baggies was the proof. They also found pill bottles in other drawers, but they was empty but for one or two little white pills half crushed and rattling around.

"I seen druggies lick inside these things. In the bathroom at The Dixiana. Yes I did. Till yesterday, anyways."

After another drink, and thinking about smells and nasty sheets and messes and trash and cleaning, Christy, he come up with his big idea. Newbie sat there bitching and moaning, saying that there wasn't no choice but to bury him somewhere, but Christy said nuh-uh. "The river. We'll put him in the river. And the waters, they'll take him home to the Lord."

"You believe that? About the Lord?"

Christy halfway did. He hadn't gone to no churches, but when he seen the people who did, they was usually clean and decent looking, and pink in the face and not a grungy little unshaven butthole doing drugs on a couch on which he would die one morning. "I done prayed on it," which was a lie, but one Christy figured on rectifying soon as they got squared away with this Daddy dead body mess. "And I think he wants to be put into the river."

"God wants it?"

"My Daddy, too."

Newbie said, but he'll bob up in the lake. Soon as the Sugeree carries him down there, he'll float up and that'll be that and won't none of it have been for anything. "They could put us away forever. The cops'll just make up shit, dude. Ain't you sees *Making a Murderer* on Netflix?"

But Christy, he knows better about the river idea—he had read in the library all about the dam and the hydro plant they built back in the 30s, way before the nuclear station, and the canal to divert the water from the rocks where it once flowed down near the walking path, and how the river was deep and cold in that narrow channel leading to the canal locks. Christy knew all this from looking at a book in the school library.

Christy was smarter than they realized, the big dummies running that sorry school. Every time he played one of his POV shooter games, it made him want to walk into Marion Sims High one Monday morning and give them all something else to study on, like picking hot lead out of their faces.

But for now, Christy had but this one task and duty to perform. He didn't know what he was gonna do about his Granny, but long as she kept giving him them twenties he figured he wouldn't do much of nothing. Have Newbie ride him out there now and then to get more twenties. Buy groceries from Aisha's Daddy's Gas Chief. And get by all right, all right. He could stock up on a good bit of cereal and milk with twenty bucks. Even more with forty.

Christy, he would figure out the steps, like a real pilot did when they were working through the checklist to get ready to fly a plane. Newbie would help get this body hustled down into the river, and then he'd show him how to fly the flight simulator. The thought of being able to play games all the time and not be bothered with anything else made Christy feel not anxious, but eager. Eager to get on with this mess.

"Let's buy us some big black trash bags." Christy, shoving the pill bottles and zippies into a plastic grocery sack; Christy, the boss of this operation. Telling Newbie what to do. No more pleading. "And a roll of duck tape. And there's some old bricks up under the trailer. Now c'mon."

❁

Passing near Pike's Bait & Pawn, all kinds of activity—cops, DOT guys, orange cones, traffic—gives them both a big fright, but nobody pays any attention to another old pickup truck with trash in the back, not with the county dump and recycling center a few miles across the bridge in Easton.

Dragging and carrying the body down the sloping river land after the end of the walking trail is rough, and a few times Christy, wheezing and winded, feels like giving up. But with all having gone good enough—like getting a dead person into the truck bed unseen and Newbie, shaking and half crazy with fear, covering it with a crackling green tarp with black mold they'd found under the trailer—ain't no stopping now.

Halfway down the embankment, the traverse of which has been tough carrying the body they can smell through the plastic, Newbie says, "I got to rest. My heart's bout to beat out of my chest."

"We can't wait," Christy says. "C'mon."

"You a durn slave driver. Hope I don't never have to work for you."

They struggle down out of the thick forest and scramble across a cascade of boulders, big and smooth like you see in the yards of the houses of the mill village farther back up the river. Lit from behind by the morning sun, the plumes of the nuclear plant downriver tower above the trees, and to Christy the river below looks silvery and mysterious.

"Water's deep and fast through here. Good place to put him in."

Newbie pulls his end around and goes down the embarkment first, standing up Christy's Daddy's body and holding the legs from behind him. "Hurry and push—my feet's sinking in."

Christy heaves forward with all his weight. The body rolls over him and Newbie topples into the mud, cussing up a storm as the corpse bounces down the embankment and splashes in the edge of the water.

They hurry, adding a few clay-colored rocks into the plastic shroud and then shove it further into the rushing river. Breathless, they both watch Christy's daddy go floating away.

"Oh shit, it ain't going down."

Christy, his own heart about to pound out of his chest. "Wait—hold on."

All at once a rush of bubbles like a dolphin clearing its blowhole, and the body, going under. They hustle along the soft embankment, following and watching.

"Now I can't see it at all." Newbie, covered in mud. "I think we done it."

Christy, relieved. "We make a good team."

"I reckon." Newbie splashes water on himself, but it will take more than a rinse to get him clean. "I got to change out of these wet drawers."

On the walk back out of the steep woods, which is uphill but so much easier without Christy's daddy's body, Christy thinks suddenly that his Daddy sure didn't get much of a funeral.

"Hold on," Christy says, right as they get back to the paved walking trail back to the parking lot.

"For what? We got to get on, now."

Christy turns back toward the river and kneels on one knee, saying a prayer about how he's sorry to his Daddy for the way this worked out.

"What, you praying?"

"Yes—I forgot back there."

Newbie, removing his dirty ball cap. "You was supposed to do that before we put him in. It don't work now."

"Shut up. It does too."

"Nuh-uh, Christy." Newbie could whine, too. "My butt's gonna get chapped."

Back at the truck Christy's heart jumps into his throat: a man there in shorts and a striped button-down shirt with the tail untucked and dirty high-top Converse sneakers, clutching a two-liter bottle of Canada Dry Ginger Ale. That crazy dude who walks all around. Howdy Shull.

Newbie's like, oh-no, not this weirdo. "I wish you'd get on away from my truck."

Without missing a beat or meeting either of their eyes, crazy old Mr. Shull starts yap-yapping: "—but as I was saying, the Great Cross of Hendaye and the French alchemist Fulcanelli, what he discovered and communicated appears to be describing not only the conclusion of the great four ages of the Hindu Yuga system, but also the four ages of alchemical chronological timekeeping," all in his froggy, old man's Southern voice.

Howdy opened the soda bottle, squeezing the plastic vessel and inhaling. He belches and slurs through the next few words. "The first age is the Satya Yuga, or the Golden Age. The Hindu texts tell us that this era lasts 1,728,000 years. This is an epoch of extreme splendor, when the beings on our planet appear to have lived much longer than they do now. In this age there are no wars, famines, strife or evil."

"S'cuse us, please." Christy, feeling fussy and annoyed by this unforeseen occurrence. "We got to go."

"Here's the thing. Here's the thing." Howdy Shull displays the bottom of one of his shoes, missing the sole—his foot inside, crusty and bleeding. "I was on my way to view the megalithic structures that predate history, predate their own history, so to speak, and this. This. This happened."

"Beau, that's one nasty foot."

Howdy, patting the truck hood. "Here's, here's, here's the thing."

"We get it, weirdo. You want a ride."

Christy, panicking. Saying no, no. "Step away from the vehicle," which Christy's heard a cop say on TV.

But Newbie's chill. "Howdy's all right. I bet he's got gas money."

Howdy, twitchy but smiling, reached into his pocket and showed Newbie a pair of wadded dollar bills. "Door to door? Door to door?"

Newbie says gimme the money, and Howdy does.

They pile into the truck, Howdy in the middle riding bitch. He crosses his legs and puts his bloody foot in Christy's lap, which makes Christy want to puke. Howdy smells like he's been working on engines all morning, but with no grease under his nails.

Before Newbie had even gets it into gear, Howdy launches back into his monologue: "The second age, you see, is called the Treta Yuga, or the Silver Age. As in the second law of thermodynamics, or entropy, things begin to slip in this period and the beings on Earth deteriorate. This slippage, at least during this second age, is the beginning of corruption, and evil is introduced into the planetary energetic sphere. According to the Vedic texts of India, this age lasts 1,296,000 years."

"That's a long old time."

"Oh, m'boy, it's all relative, time. It's metaphoric, however you measure it." Back into his trance: "The third age of this cycle is called the Dvapara, Dvapara, Dvapara Age. This is the 'fall' the 'fall' the 'fall' of humanity. In this era venality comes into full flower, evil evolves, and all falls into disharmony. This age lasts 864,000 years.

"Now: the final act of the cycle is called the Kali Yuga, or the Iron Age—this is the time we find ourselves in right now now now. Evil and corruption, these've become the driving force. Greed, wars, famine and disease spread, a tsunami of death and destruction. This period lasts, according to the Hindu texts, for a comparatively and thankfully brief 432,000 years."

"That's one mess of years," Christy whispers under his breath. "Too many."

"You can believe it. You can believe it." Howdy, picking at his scabby, bleeding foot. "Time runs through long cycles. Longer than we may fathom. But you go off this planet and time, what does it mean? It becomes relative, that's what. A million years here might be a day somewhere else."

Christy, sighing and realizing in a rush how bad Howdy smelled. His rap, it sounds like how his daddy used to bullshit.

Newbie shifts gears. "I c'ain't get my mind round how many years that is."

Howdy, energized by this news, blows his nasty breath into Christy's sweating face. "What this is, is a metaphor not for these millions' worth of years, but of the great year, which is only 25,000 years. The precession of the equinoxes through the zodiac. Twelve signs. Twelve ages within the great year, but four are the ones to watch. The transitions. The transitions."

"Them zodiac horoscopes ain't nothing but a bunch of foolishness. Now hush." Newbie pulls up to a stop sign. "So where are you getting out? You stink, beau."

"At the megalithic structures. The building wherein it rains. To the right, if you would. The right side of the rain."

"That don't go nowhere but through the old mill neighborhood."

"That is precisely where the megalithic structures are."

"He's talking about the mill," Christy says, just a feeling. "Ain't you, Howdy?"

"There ain't no reason to go there. It's closed down."

"Yes, that it is. Longer than most can imagine. Tens of thousands of years longer."

"Ain't been that long. I remember my granddaddy talking about working the graveyard shift at Gray-Peele," Newbie says. "He said there was this one bin full of this cotton stuff, big soft bales of it, and you could hide from the room boss there and sleep during your shift. Now that's a good job to have, where you can catch a nap and get paid."

Howdy's response: "Before the cataclysmic cometary impacts of 12,890 years ago that initiated the Holocene warming, sea levels were several hundred feet lower than those of today. Many pyramids besides those that we know, like Giza in Egypt, lie under the ocean, as in the form of the recently discovered Azores pyramid that's only 45 meters below sea. The pyramids we know, they're only part of a much larger story."

At the entrance to the mill Newbie pulls onto the shoulder and they make Howdy Shull get out of the truck. He stands at the chain-link fence around the enormous old factory to continue his discourse, babbling about this being part of a network of structures built for 'biorhythmic synchronization at precisely calibrated wavelengths that correspond to harmonics of planetary infrasound resonance,' whatever the eff that means.

With Howdy droning on, Christy cranes his neck and looks up at the looming red-brick edifice, understanding now that megalithic was another word for big. He sees how it fits in with Howdy Shull's mad rap—he was pretending this was his great pyramid. And maybe some of what the town crazy said is true—another feeling of Christy's—but they don't have time to figure it out. Still cleaning to do back home.

Christy wants to get done and sit for a spell all quiet. Think about what all had happened. It wasn't nothing, what had gone on. Christy knows that. But he can justify it all, if somebody down the line gets all salty and asks.

That's right—he works it all out in his head: People come around all the time, folks his Daddy owes money to. And who are mean as snakes, to both his Daddy and to Christy. Any policeman he tells that story will be like all, uh-oh, somebody whacked the druggie, like on *The Sopranos*. It was where Christy got the idea to wrap up his Daddy's body in the plastic—he remembered an episode where the gangsters had done that with somebody they whacked. Christy's Daddy messed around with Edgewater County's version of gangsters, the Rembert boys. That's who'll get blamed. If anyone cares enough to place blame.

They watch as Howdy ambles away from the padlocked gate to the mill and along the fence to where the overgrown woods lead down toward the river, waving his finger all the way, a mad prophet cradling the sloshing ginger ale in the crook of his elbow like a football. Howdy bends down and crawls through a break in the rusting chain-link fence surrounding the huge property.

"Wonder what he does up in there?"

Newbie, shrugging. "Don't know and don't care."

Christy, he halfway wants to go with Howdy. To hear more. Says so.

"Naw. I got to get outta these wet drawers."

Taking the long way through Chilton they make one last stop, but Newbie agrees it's necessary. Christy, running into the Walgreen's where they had gotten the trash bags and get air freshener, a whole bunch, to take back to the trailer.

As they finally park next to the trailer, Christy keeps thinking not about his Daddy but what Mr. Shull was talking about, this idea of a 'great year.' And a golden age. That all sounded cool, somehow. Now that he's free of his Daddy, like, for keeps and for reals, maybe this is the beginning of Christy's golden age. Who knows? Maybe Mr. Shull is onto something.

A LONG AFTERNOON, long and awful, cleaning the trailer, until Christy's finally had enough. Newbie too, who says he wants to live here, but only after it smells better from the Glade fragrance plug-ins, which they put into outlets all over the mobile home.

With Newbie gone to spend one last night in the room he rents and to get his stuff together, Christy goes for a walk to get some air. It ain't as hot outside as it's been all summer. Fall is coming. Change in the air. He thought he'd cut across the neighborhood to the westside highway, where he can cruise along a mile or two and arrive at the airfield. Look at the variety of shiny, single-engine aircraft sitting under their sheds.

Beside the airport now, a golden-colored pickup truck, barrels up behind and blows by him. The man dang near squeals the tires and whips in through the airfield gate.

Christy, startled, almost pees his pants. "Why don't you slow down, dumbass?"

After looking both ways, he heads across the road where he watches, fascinated. Christy, he hangs on the fence and wonders about the airfield, and the planes lined up. Pipers and other kinds.

All of this fitting together, now. Christy, feeling weird along the top of his skull. Tingling.

Sleepy, almost.

Like in a dream.

Inside the airfield, Christy sees a skinny old man come hobbling out of a building. There's all this back and forth with the dude from the pickup, talking and gesturing and pointing and nodding, and not one but two handshakes.

Christy gets bored enough he starts to walk away, but something says DON'T GO and STAY AND WATCH, and so he does.

And what he observes is damn-near amazing. He sees the truck man, who ain't nobody but some Edgewater County redneck riding in his Ford F-150, go to one of the planes, a Piper Meridian, a real beauty. The man in his T-shirt and shorts and sandals messes around with it, walking around and looking at stuff and finally getting in and... and...

Cranking the aircraft engine. Sitting there. And after a few moments, moving forward. Taxiing, as Christy knows it is called. And flying away.

Christy, staring until the Piper but a speck, and gone.

His mouth hanging open, Christy, saying to himself, I just seen a man come driving up in his truck and get into a real plane and fly it out of here. Like it wasn't nothing. Like he does it every day.

Okay.

Now he's got new stuff to talk about with his grandmama. A job. Money to be had. Chores to do. All so Christy, he can get done with all this mess here in Edgewater County. And fly away.

Christy, swinging his arms, walks fast as he can back home to see if the odor of his Daddy's dead body has gone away yet. He takes off the jacket he wears even when it's warm and ties it around his waist. He don't give a crap if anybody sees his big man-boobs bopping up and down. Don't care if some dude pokes fun at him. It was mostly his Daddy who bullied him, anyway. And that ain't gonna happen no more.

Christy, feeling free—or at least on the road to freedom. Soon as he gets his hands on a plane like the one that man flew off in. Then, nobody will make fun or stop him from doing anything—he'll be gone from Edgewater County forever. Yeah, he will.

BUTTON

Button, waking up from her first, best, and only successful attempt at astral projection; or maybe, she supposed, simply a dream; but then, the books she'd studied on the process all agreed that the dreamworld and the astral plane were likely one and the same.

Deciding beforehand to travel—to fly—and visit Heather Ponderview, instead her travel-slash-dream involved checking on Roy Earl Pettus. Having heard about the debacle on the river road, she knew his stress to be through the roof. Called to check on him in reality, in meatspace; found out an emergency had taken him back down to Sedge Island. The boy, not catching a break.

She had to help him. It's what she did for people. This decision, no dream.

But in her dream of astral night-flight, she glimpsed him on the island far below, a tiny human amidst crashing waves. Saw his face covered by tears. Saw him power-walking on the beach, but the wrong way—toward the briny foam.

Seeing his distress.

Feeling his existential despair.

Imagining he planned to kill himself.

Doing all she could to prevent it. Landing in front of him. Projecting not only her consciousness, but her love. All of it.

He strode right through her.

Calling for him to come back.

The sound of her voice. Snapping out of the dream, she awakened drenched in sweat—as though she'd been in the water with him.

She had more work to do. So much more.

Button hoped she would get the chance; that her dream was not true; and Roy Pettus would soon return to Edgewater County. Not like she needed a new project, not now that Mayor Hampton had agreed to letting her set up a free speech zone on the town green. She had fliers to print. Pamphlets to compose. Truth to spread.

A reason to live.

Not only that, but in glancing at her email, and seeing a note from Heather —HI THERE!!!! read the subject line—she experienced a blooming of warmth in her back and left side, a good one, indicating a possible shift in the frequencies on the way; a break in the case. Button Sykes didn't need to scrutinize the content of the email from her lost love to know she and Heather would again reunite, and soon. She didn't even need her future self, Walfredo, to visit and tell her so. Her fondest wish—it simply had to come true. End of discussion.

And while Button didn't remember closing her sacred circle earlier in the day—a huge mistake in performing a working, in this case a spicy little spell to ensure her no-nukes information clearinghouse would be noticed—she was sure spiritual muscle memory would have seen her through the completion of the ceremony. She hoped so, anyway. Otherwise, the consequences, like leaving open a gate wherein packs of ravenous wild demon-dogs could enter the material world, might be devastating, if not deadly.

ROY EARL PETTUS

Creedence in rehab, cats squared away, sand washed out of your navel; back home in the EC. On River Ridge Road.

Home. Yep. Call Tillman Falls home again. Why not?

And this act? Not like the mural.

This?

With your grandmother's permission.

At the red clay river bluff, standing in your sandals slapping at ants or no-see-ums biting around your ankles, you complete the deed they all stopped you from carrying out. When you want it done right, you not only complete a job yourself, but you might as well do it all by yourself, too. When have you ever needed helpers? You're the one making up this reality tunnel as you go.

Alone. That's where the magic happens.

Here.

Now.

Black as pitch.

Nah. Not really: Milky pale lunar light runs along the river's rippling surface, this channel that flows deep indigo with midnight mystery. The moon, high and centered and with a magnificent halo, lighting your way down the path that seems so much wider than back in your childhood. In your father's time of fishing alongside Rabbit, the trail must have been so narrow as to not exist at all. They must've hacked their way through the weeds.

They forged the path.

Enough with the poetry. You didn't stick with that English major crapola.

You sell adulterated fruit drinks and coffee so acidic and strong that stomachs from here to the coast are rotting.

The box under your arm; the corners, digging into your ribs. You set it down on the clay and fiddle with the lid, pull out the plastic bag of your grandfather's ashes. In the end, a grown man big as your Pa-paw ended up no more than a blamed morsel of matter.

A piffle.

Dust.

But this spoonful, weighing a ton.

You kept some ashes back home. Scooped them into a snack-size ziplock and tucked them into your overnight bag. Another time, maybe at the man's music festival on the green. These simpletons here, they would bend to your will on that deal. They will honor his wishes. Oh, yes; yes, they will.

Cash in hand.

Demands, agreed to and fulfilled.

Snap of a finger.

The plume of powdery dust, flung in a wide arc with nary a word of funerary ritual, drifted over the surface of the river, the wind picking up enough to send the cloudy ashes of the former human body swirling into the cooling night air.

Your gaze follows as your grandfather drifts toward the bath of artificial illumination spilling upwards from the campus of the Sugeree River Nuclear Station. The steam plume above the tree line given depth and definition by the hard orange light against an otherwise opaque, black sky, it seems to mix before your eyes with the remains of Reynolds Elder Pettus.

Blinking, you finally find a few words, and they are this:

"Now—enough of this sentimental foolishness. Let's start thinking about getting ourselves down to work. Much new reality to pound into shape. Everyone's counting on me to save them from themselves. And so I will, by God."

Musing and mulling all the way back to your Pa-paw's truck, you sort through myriad plans within plans. And when it all comes to fruition? Nothing here will ever be the same. This you swear. And one thing you've learned? Your wishes will manifest. Might not be this particular moment. But eventually.

The best part? Folks wouldn't know what had hit them until way too late to stop the process. You, the bossman, Roy Earl Pettus—yeah, baby, you heard that right—are back to stay.

The Story Continues

DOWN IN
Dixiana

CHARACTER GUIDE

POV Characters
(with supporting players)

ROY EARL PETTUS

Despite tremendous financial success, a lovely wife, and a wide-open future ahead for him, Roy suffers a midlife crisis of confidence and inwardly flails for purchase…but it's for good reason: When we meet him he's discovered his dream girl, Creedence, has been unfaithful. Not simply sexually—the letters he's read indicate more than a fling, rather a full-on love affair. At the same moment he gets news his grandfather has fallen ill, perhaps critically so. He flies home to Edgewater County, where he'll end up staying for some time and through quite a number of story lines, all of which revolve around his grandfather's honkytonk, The Dixiana, that Roy will find is now his to run. It's not a welcome inheritance — he blames The Dixiana for most of his childhood ills.

REYNOLDS ELDER 'RABBIT' PETTUS (also POV in *Dixiana* and *Dixiana Darling*) — 89, "father"/grandfather to Roy Earl, his presence hovers over the rest of the story, culminating as it does in a town music in his honor festival; 'Pa-Paw' to Roy

RUNELLE KITTERY PETTUS (POV in *Dixiana Darling*) — 88, "mother"/grandmother to Roy Earl, the Darling of The Dixiana, 'Mee-maw' to Roy. She calls her husband '**Rennie**'.

MERVIN PETTUS — a cousin, 40s, who attacks Roy over a dispute regarding Rabbit's estate (wife **CARLA MAE**, kids **DALE** and **DJ**). Grandson of Rabbit's brother Rutledge Pettus

RONALD EDWARD 'RONNIE ED' PETTUS — Roy Earl's father, long dead before the events of DIXIANA, a haunting presence: his father, like his grandfather in WW2, he served in war, Ronnie-Ed ends up giving his life in said service.

CLAUDIA BALLAHACK PETTUS — Roy Earl's mother, also deceased, a young waitress struggling along after the death of her equally young husband in Vietnam. Claudia, killed in what Roy Earl will find out was a car accident that also almost took his infant life.

ALLYSON BUTTON SYKES

Dreadlocked granddaughter of Burnham Sykes, this iconoclastic second principal character has already retreated to Tillman Falls well before the arrival of Roy E. Pettus, a family friend, obviously, owing to her grandfather's close friendship with Roy Earl. In her mid 30s and considering herself a failed writer, Button cares for her mother Tinky, left bereaved by the cancer-death of Button's father, as well as her grandfather. A new age devotee of the jam-band Phish, when we meet her Button has decided on a new mission in life: to protest the new nuclear reactors being built. Her plan of outreach? A good old fashioned American pamphleteering campaign on the town green. A lifelong outcast—a mix of ruddy Irish and Vietnamese, an odd physical combination—she is the story's heart, soul, and conscience.

BURNHAM 'BURNIE' SYKES (POV in *Dixiana Darling*) — 90, Rabbit Pettus's best friend for 75 years, a very important character to the overall arc of the story, and to Button and Roy personally. In the old days, Burnie's business success made much of everyone's reality possible

HENRIETTA 'HENNY' SYKES — Burnie's wife, dead for a number of years prior to present day narrative

THANH THI TRINH 'TINKY' SYKES — Vietnamese mother to Button and Thim, a nervous type, has panic, is medicated and near irrational, but as Button says, "she always was."

THIM SYKES — Button's older sister, and nothing like her boho younger sibling. An aide to Governor Sandra Three-Rivers, who has her eye on the U. S. Senate. Thim leaves the care of her mother and grandfather to Button.

BURTON 'BUDDY' SYKES (POV in *Dixiana Darling*) — father to Button, dead already prior to events of novel. The Vietnam vet who'd gone off to war with Ronnie Pettus, the one who'd returned sporting an Asian wife. He'd been a part of a unit that carried around the "backpack nuke" that could be used on short notice should President Nixon have wished to ramp up the firepower.

Buddy died of cancer, possibly from his service in Vietnam, but also possibly due to his long career as an engineer at the Sugeree River Station.

CHELSEA COLETTE 'CREEDENCE' RUCKER-PETTUS

Roy's wife Creedence, 40ish (childhood initials CCR, nicknamed by her beloved late father for the 60s rock band Creedence Clearwater Revival) is in crisis as well: in love with another man but not out of love with Roy Earl, alcoholic, confused, stuck. She writes her journal in the form of endless letters to her brother Devin, missing and unheard from for 10 years—an inveterate drunk, likely long dead. Once the affair is discovered by Roy, however, reality comes crashing down, and so does her alcoholism.

> **DEVIN RUCKER** — vanished older brother to Creedence, and to whom she writes epistolary-style letters that provide exposition along with raw inner monologue
> **LIBBY MEADE** — Devin's college love, referred to in flashback only
> **EILEEN RUCKER** — mother, deceased, referred to on occasion, a former esteemed member of the Edgewater Ladies Munificence Society (ELMS)
> **DWIGHT RUCKER** — father, deceased, a town father who appears in flashback

BILL 'GOOCH' WIMMEL

Gooch Wimmel, the publisher and editor of the *Edgewater Advocate*, a once thrice-weekly paper now reduced to a weekly, is an aging, closeted gay who is lonely and unhappy about his waning influence in the town. He'd been a reporter and editor in big city newspapers for years, but found that as he aged, he longed for a more quiet and peaceful life. Working the crime beat in Atlanta left him cynical and burned out at a young age, and now in his late 60s, he suffers from severe memory issues and dementia; he keeps forgetting that he's already retired, and only helping out at the paper. Another man's the publisher now, and Gooch is supposed to be following his dream to write a great novel.

CHRISTOPHER 'CHRISTY' BEAUDOCK

Christy Beaudock has a heart filled with pain and hatred. A fat, unattractive kid with a girlie name, bullied, unhappy, and hopeless. At 15, he's now a physical giant, if emotionally stunted. Special Ed classes. But there's a secret: Christy's much smarter than that. His quiet demeanor has been mistaken for mental deficiency. His father, a meth-head, and his grandmother, the madam of Edgewater County. Quite a troubled background, living in his trailer park and playing his flight simulator game, an obsession. When he decides he's had enough of his Daddy, then he has a new problem: what to do with the body.

> **CHRISTY'S DADDY** — Identified only in this manner, what happens with him sets this storyline in suspenseful motion.
>
> **MAMIE 'MAMA' BEAUDOCK** — The legacy madam of Edgewater County, she runs a brothel that's been around as long as The Dixiana. Mama Beaudock's is out near the bump in the road called Red Mound. Why she's still allowed to be in business—who doesn't know about Mama B's?—is something of a mystery.

JASPER ALVIN GLASSCOCK

A small-town, small-time attorney, Jasper mainly handles poor clients from "across the tracks," which in the case of Tillman Falls and Edgewater County means across the Sugeree River in recently-annexed Easton. Jasper, when we meet him, is in much worse spiritual and financial dire straits than Roy Earl: at 60, his practice is unfulfilling and barely pays the bills, he's moved back home with his sister Letty. A musician, he only wants to play guitar and sing, but how can an old Southern lawyer make a living doing that? In his younger years, Jasper had been a bail bondsman and PI, as well as a published author: he interviewed homegrown serial killer Coy Wando from death row about all the other heinous crimes the murderer committed. After Jasper finished that book, he swore he'd never want to write another.

> **LETTY GLASSCOCK (also POV in *Dixiana Darling*)**— Older sister to Jasper; they have a very close relationship, one that will be clarified by novel's end to reveal that she's actually Jasper's mother. The truth had been hidden from him because of family shame over her becoming pregnant at 14.
>
> **OLD MAN GLASSCOCK** — Letty and Jasper's widowed father, a farmer with a sordid family secret Jasper has never known

MANFRED 'MANNY' THEODORE

Manny Theodore, 50, an ex-pat New Orleans resident driven out by Hurricane Katrina, as well as his wife's desire to return to her roots in order to care for an aging set of parents. His wife Neecie thinks that, among its many possible meanings and causes, Katrina was a sign that they needed to get out. After moving to SC, money they received from an insurance payout was used to purchase Lucinda's, the dying lunch counter on the town green in Tillman Falls, which they remodel and re-christen as Manny's On The Green, a restaurant and music club that mainly features Manny himself on saxophone, as well as the occasional touring act and open blues jam night. Manny, when we meet him, is in deep trouble: he's been foolishly unfaithful with Rebecca LaFreniere, a town stakeholder and member of the venerable Edgewater Ladies' Munificence Society—as is Manny's wife Neecie.

> **LILLYANNE THEODORE, 13, daughter** — Lillyanne, a lovely, intelligent young woman who disapproves of her father's behavior
>
> **BERNICE 'NEECIE' (DUCKETT) THEODORE, 42, wife** — She handles the discovery of her husband's infidelity, a recurrence, with an unusual approach
>
> **AHMAD DUCKETT, 40, brother-in-law** — brother of Neecie, Ahmad is a troubled ex-addict from New Orleans that Manny's giving a second chance. They butt heads frequently, eventually become unwilling roommates mixed up in the discovery of a large amount of money

TRUDY (PIRKLE) SAMUELSON

Rabbit's longtime bartender and manger of The Dixiana, 51, a one time lover of Roy's, when she was twenty and he was only sixteen! A heartbreaking experience for him, she has watched through Rabbit's eyes as Roy became a millionaire. Married to an aging, sickly biker, Trudy is terribly conflicted and unhappy. The Dixiana is all she has. When Roy fires her in retribution for her rejection thirty years before, their reunion turns toxic.

> **MICKEY 'SAMSON' SAMUELSON** — Trudy's husband of twenty years, and nearly that much older than her. A former motorcycle mechanic and member of the Pagan Knights biker club, Samson has a bad toe and bad knees and a big alcohol problem.

NON-POV CHARACTERS
Note: listed in order of relevance to the plot

HEATHER PONDERVIEW — wealthy heir to the Ponderview Trucking Company fortune, owner of a magnificent estate in the Smoky Mountains of western NC. Button's one time lover and Phish fanatic on tour, Button still pines for her. She will prove crucial to Roy's development and to Button's redemption. Crucial flashback scenes with Heather take place in San Diego, at Foothills State, on Phish tour.

CAUGHMAN HOWARD 'HOWDY' SHULL — The town crazy, 60s, walking the streets with his two liter bottle of ginger ale and babbling about ancient history, secrets, esoteric knowledge, and generally being that afflicted soul that every small town seems to have. It's sad a bad acid trip did him in. He will make new friends in Christy and Newbie, with disastrous consequences for Howdy and his sister.

REBECCA LaFRENIERE — 40s, a legacy matron of Tillman Falls society; old money, the town green is named LaFreniere Square. She's having an affair with Manny Theodore. She's secretary of the ELMS, runs the Palmetto Grande Arts Center, located in the old town movie theater. She left Edgewater County to become a New York theater actress, failed, returned to her home.

DOBBS VANDEGRIFT — paraplegic reporter/writer/ad salesman for the *Edgewater Advocate* and close childhood friend of Roy Earl's. He was in a car accident with Creedence's brother Devin in college, leaving him in the wheelchair.

The REV. ROOSEVELT NIXON, PhD — a contemporary of Roy Earl, he's running for Town Council now that the formerly unincorporated and traditionally black area called Easton has been annexed into Tillman Falls. Nixon has a a mega-church, a significant force in the community, and his Sunday sermons are broadcast on WABA. He has a large family, including son and presumptive heir to the Nixon pulpit should the Rev. win election to public office. He's been agitating for more political clout from "across the river" ever since the town annexed Easton into the city limits, a move designed to capitalize on a huge project going into the impoverished county, a regional distribution center for a discount retail giant. A key plank of his platform is controversial—to remove the reference to Pitchfork Ben Tillman, Nixon wants to change the name of the town itself. A high school friend of Roy Earl's, Nixon is also an Egyptology scholar with four sons: **Denmark Vesey, Eusebius, Syncellus,** and **Hammurabi.**

NEWTON 'NEWBIE' HARRELL — a former custodian at The Dixiana, Roy's first act as new owner is to fire him. Newbie becomes fast friends with Christy Beaudock, who will get him mixed up in the disposal of the body of Christy's Daddy.

ESTES PATEL — Assistant GM of the Carolina Beanery Sedge Island, 30, Creedence's younger lover and lead singer of rap-metal band Megalith

PHIL WEBHANNET — a Sedge Island cop and Army veteran of Afghanistan whom Roy will pay to keep an eye on Creedence, which makes her think the guy has a crush on her

RICO — an enormous white dog, a Great Pyrenees, for whom Roy will take responsibility

JOUQUOYA MOULTON — a pharmacist who will become Button's friend and lover

JEZMUND 'JEZ' REMBERT — Edgewater County's chief crime kingpin, the Southern mafioso if there ever were one: his hands are filthy, into drugs, prostitution, gambling. His father and Rabbit Pettus were once partners in the underground economy. Rembert will be furious about Roy's decision regarding the mural on the side of The Dixiana, and the threat of violence from this quarter is possible throughout the story.

THURMOND PIKE — He owns Pike's Bait, Pawn, and Motorbike, whose billboards covered in dollar signs can be seen for miles on the interstate. More importantly, he has a series of 'back rooms' where organized crime figures gamble and politic among themselves, a power center to rival that of the ELMS on the legitimate side. Pike rides a motorcycle in and out of scenes but doesn't have much of a role to play in moving the story forward, but what's disturbing is that he's married now to a trophy wife, one who happens to be another unrequited childhood crush of Roy's. He's like the "tricycle man" character from Altman's *Nashville*.

AGATHA OF ABERDEEN — a pyromaniac of a spirit who stalks the town and may be the cause of a number of historical fires. Grief-stricken over the death of her handsome British captain, Agatha, who had traveled from Scotland during the Revolutionary War to be with her love, she self-immolated in the middle of then-McBreeley's Crossing, forever after haunting Edgewater County

TRAVIS 'LUCKY' LATHAM (POV in *Dixiana Darling*) — friend to Ronnie Ed Pettus and Buddy Sykes, the third friend who went off to Vietnam, who like Buddy returned safe and sound

CHESNEE CAMPOBELLO — wife of Thurmond Pike, at thirteen she broke Roy's heart: there's no way her father, a recovering alcoholic, would allow her to date the grandson of the man who owned The Dixiana.

SHAROLYN MONTINE — Roy's GM at the Carolina Beanery Sedge Island, with whom Creedence will bond as a co-worker and receive both wisdom and understanding

CECIL WAUGH — The owner of Head Trauma, a tattoo, piercing and hair salon that took the place of the old barber and beauty shop on the town green. A former football player like Roosevelt, Cecil and his brother Harlem bullied and tormented Roy Earl. Adult Roy wants to recruit Cecil (and others, like Manny, Becky L, etc) to become part of a new merchant's association to challenge the old order represented by the ELMS, especially after he finds out how much Cecil has changed.

GAREN OAKLEY — Sheriff of Edgewater County, Oakley is a tough as nails Marine and veteran of Desert Storm, an African-American authority figure, but no less corrupt than some old redneck like Whardell Truluck, the man he replaced.

TIMMY TRUESDALE — a police Lieutenant to whom Roy will be 'assigned' for special attention after bribing Oakley

YAZID OMAR JUBOURI — An Iraqi refugee family who have made their way to Tillman Falls, SC, based on Yazid's friendship with an American contractor from the area, and who have managed to become the proprietors of a convenience store called the Gas Chief. Christy Beaudock is obsessed for a time with his daughter Aisha, and a controversy over a vendor license for the Rabbit festival will cause tension. (**Fatima,** wife, **Aisha,** daughter)

MADELINE 'MADDY' DURANGO — Maddy, along with her child-star twin sister **Vangie**, are one-time America's Sweethearts: Twin actress/singer/entertainers/activists. Maddy is friends with Button Sykes, who as a student worked on a movie shoot on the campus of Button's college, a remake of Disney's *The Computer Wore Tennis Shoes*, a reboot that also starred Karen Black, for whom Button worked as a PA

COY WANDO — Edgewater County's most notorious murderer, a killer of children in the late 70s who Jasper Glasscock interviewed on death row and wrote about. Wando claimed to have killed 'hundreds' and provided gruesome detail about these other murders, including his involvement in the Tragedy of '77, the mysterious drownings of six high school seniors in the river the week before graduation

COLIN KWOTH — Roy's handsome, outdoorsy business partner in the fruit-shake empire, and a potential rival for Creedence's sexual attention while on vacation together

GOV. SANDRA 'SANDY' THREE-RIVERS — two term governor of the state and Thim Sykes's boss, she'll give some key advice to Button: cut off those dreads!

EVERLYNNE SHULL-SCHLOSSER, PhD — Howdy Shull's older sister. A confrontation between her and Christy Beaudock will turn deadly.

ARTHUR BEAUCHAMP — Roy goes looking for the writer Cort Beauchamp and finds his brother instead, who reveals an unknown corner of Edgewater County: a survivalist compound.

PASTOR DUSON MIRE — a corpulent Baptist preacher, part of a group who once used to street-preach on Friday nights outside The Dixiana.

JOSIAH 'J. W.' REMBERT — Father to Jez, Josiah will have to do prison time for a shooting he commits during a civil rights protest outside the Congress Street Grille

RON NAWALINSKI — one of Roy's buddies from down on Sedge Island at 'the hanger' where the hobby pilots hang out. He has two key roles to play in the story: he recommends a hike, and gives Roy and Button a ride

HODGES 'THE COLONEL' RINGHOLDER — A Vietnam POW war hero and former jet pilot, he's a mentor to Roy down on Sedge Island at the hanger where the other retired and hobby pilots gather for bull sessions

CAL LUCHOK — another hanger buddy of Roy's

RUSS WETHERELL — AA sponsor to Creedence, a wise figure for whom she struggles with attraction, a big no-no in recovery

KIP EPPERTON, DVM — a Sedge Island veterinarian who dispenses advice to Roy while caring for Creedence's kitties

SISSY — one of Creedence's cats on Sedge Island for which Roy holds great fondness

COLE BREEDLOVE — a deacon in Pastor Mire's church, he'll reinstate the oldschool street preaching outside The Dixiana, but against Button and her free-speech tent on the town green

NORRIE SORTWELL — the former owner of the Palmetto Grande movie theater and influential figure from Roy's childhood, to others as well

PORTER BUCKNAM — a former *Columbia Record* writer and editor, Gooch's successor and new publisher of the *Edgewater Advocate*, with Dobbs Vandegrift taking over as EIC

SHIGEHARU 'SHIGGY' HAMASAKI — another of Roy's business partners, while on a golf retreat together Shiggy will procure salacious entertainment

SAMMY MACKLIN — another of Roy's business partners, and partner in crime with Shiggy

HANK HALVORSIN — another movie theater manager, this one to Roy when he worked at the multiplex while in college

RIP SHORLEY — a dishonest usher at the multiplex where Roy works in college

MAGGIE PASSANANT — a petsitter on Sedge Island whom Roy will retain to deal with the cats

FRANKIE 'FRIDGE' WASHINGTON — longtime head line cook at The Dixiana

ETNA DIXMONT — one of the kitchen workers at The Dixiana

Dr. KADAMBARI PATEL — cardiologist to Jasper Glasscock and mother of Estes Patel

RUSTY NEDDICK — a contractor skeptical of Roy's desire to rebuild The Dixiana exactly as it is now, only with materials to insure that it will last 'a thousand years'

KALLEN SWYGERT — a stereo salesman who hooks up Roy with a turntable, amp, and speakers costing forty grand

Dr. DAHLONEGA — a d0c-in-the-box whose misdiagnosis of Button's throat condition reveals nothing about Button's true medical condition

RODNEY COWAN—Roy's financial adviser, assuring him that money will always grow, and his money in particular. He ain't wrong. Money is never an issue for Roy Pettus, so much so that it's both fraught with meaning and yet meaningless.

FELICITY BELINDA 'FEEBEE' ELMENDORF — a colleague of Roy's from his time as the president of the Downtown Business Alliance in Columbia

RUTH DeKALB — éminence grise of the ELMS, mother to a former governor and a Hollywood voice actor

MIRIAM VANDEGRIFT — Dobbs's mother, in the local nursing home where Bill Wimmel will consider placing himself

ALICE FAITH WESTMORELAND — member of the ELMS, more Edgewater County royalty

RUFUS BINDERNAGEL — the DHS rep to the Rabbit Music Festival, he expresses a number of security concerns, in particular the vendor license application from Yazid Jubouri, whose family back in Iraq has ties to terrorism

JEREMY CHIMIENTO — Button's college attempt at heterosexuality, he'll get arrested with her on a visit to Tillman Falls

DR. ABUTO OLABODE — Maddy Durango's private physician, who helps Button Sykes get through a rough patch

HERBIE BERTRAM — a fellow Boy Scout who introduces Roy to smoking weed

CARLOTTA MALDONADO — Edgewater County Memorial hospital counselor, she wrote a twice-monthly self help column for the paper and helps Gooch

JENKINS — a security agent who assists Button with the recovery of her personal items from Sancho

CHAMBLEE — with Jenkins, he accompanies Button to the New York apartment of Maddy Durango

CASSI — a barista whose tattoos—FORGIVE and FORGET—spur Roy toward action regarding his marital problems

KUMARI KANDAM — a hippy kid living in the Heather Ponderview house in San Diego

CRUNCHY CAL — a hippy kid living in the Heather Ponderview house in San Diego

JUDGE HAROLD HARTSOOK — a back room deal with Button's granddad will pull her and Jeremy's asses out of their hometown pot bust

JUDGE SHULL — Howdy's father and an old-line Edgewater County power broker

OTILYA DUCKETT — an Edgewater County civil rights pioneer

EVAN TYGH — the Roy of Independence, VA, he pulls the F-150 out of a ditch on the side of a mountain where Roy has gone for a retreat

LATRICIA THEODORE — a naughty cousin of Manny's who introduces him to sexuality

ENOCH ROYAL — a teenaged street preacher who taunts Button at her free speech tent on the town green

CORT BEAUCHAMP — Edgewater County's novelist of note, his book *The Diary of Anna Dixon* plays a role in Creedence and Roy's relationship

ANNA DIXON — protagonist of Cort Beauchamp's novel-within-the-novel *The Diary of Anna Dixon*

DURHAM DOVER — second protagonist of Cort Beauchamp's *The Diary of Anna Dixon*

TUCKER — a big box employee who assists Roy with a TV purchase

RODRIGO — a big box employee who assists Roy with a TV purchase

MR. KARLANEY — a funeral director who assists Roy

OFFICER HERTFORD — a highway patrolman who almost shoots Roy during Rico's crisis over failing to stop for his blue lights

SKEEBALL — a Dixiana kitchen employee

DICKIE GIUFRIDDA — a member of Roy's childhood baseball team

HARLEM WAUGH — Cecil's twin brother, tormentor of young Roy

SHERM WRIGHTSON — Roy's little league coach

TIMMY LATHAM — son of Lucky Latham, and a positive baseball team member to young Roy

MARLON KETCHAM — a little league player who taunts Roy

STONEY MARCHANT — another little league doofus, the only player more inept than Roy

KAITLYN — a barista at the Carolina Beanery Sedge Island

BRENDA LaROSE — college writing mentor to Button

MARGARET TUGGLE — Roy's middle school yearbook editor and crush

GREG RINKER — handsome jock and rival for Margaret's attention

GLORIA GRAYMONT — Roy's high school newspaper advisor

KITTY BERWICK — Roy's 1st Grade teacher

MRS. GARFINKLE — Roy's yearbook advisor

COACH PEMBROKE — Roy's physical science teacher

MR. HALSEY — Roy's childhood barber

MR. BATES — Christy's high school science teacher

MRS. DUNWOODY — Letty Glasscock's fifth grade teacher and fellow survivor of the Sunbury School fire

LOTTIE — a cashier at Roy's college multiplex job, a brief romantic relationship

BENJ — an usher at Roy's college multiplex job

LENZA SPINNOZI — stylist at Cecil Waugh's salon 'Head Trauma'

SCOTT 'SANCHO' McKENDRICK — the head of Button's Phish tour 'phamily'

SHARAQUE — Creedence interacts with this doorman at the Sandflea rock club

SEDGE ISLAND CABBIE — returns money Creedence left in the taxi

RAY DEKALB — Tillman Falls native and now Hollywood voice actor, a celeb who attends the festival at the (presumed) behest of his mother Ruth DeKalb.

Mr. DeKALB — a presumptive forebear of the DeKalbs, Ruth and Ray, the builder of the ill-fated Sunbury School

AVALON —a hippy chick Spotted Banana manager

SHELBY FORDHAM — Roy childhood crush

NATASHA PROTHRO — Roy childhood crush

BEV LeSAGE — Roy childhood crush and dance partner

LaVISTA TUCKER — friend of Sharolyn who bakes cakes and cookies for the CBSI

DAVIS MACON — a 1960s peer of Josiah Rembert, known as a dogfighter

IDAHLIA — kitchen worker at Manny's on the Green

OLD NEECIE — kitchen worker at Manny's on the Green

SEAN PAUL — a former coffee shop manager of Roy's to whom he sold the original Carolina Beanery

MAULDIN SAUGUS — US Representative from the district that includes Edgewater County

MOUSAM 'SAMMY' BEANHOPPER — longtime member of Tillman Falls Town Council, the first African-American member and a legacy figure

DUWAYNE DRIGGERS — an oldschool Dixiana bartender, drug dealer, and friend of Coy Wando

Lt. WETHERELL — an officer under whom Rabbit served in WW2, possibly Russ Wetherell's father or grandfather

Pvt. MAHONEY — a corpsman serving with Lucky Latham

MARTY HARRELL — Newbie Harrell's grandfather, a gas jockey at Pike's

CORDELIA KARLANEY — curator of the Edgewater County archives

UNCLE WALLY KITTERY — Runelle's uncle

CHESTER — a Dixiana bartender from Roy's youth

DR. WISE — town GP

Lance Cpl. LAWRENCE LAUTENSCHLAGER — the Sugeree River Memorial Bridge is named for this fallen highway patrolman

HISTORICAL OR LIVING FIGURES
WHO APPEAR IN THE TEXT

KAREN BLACK — Roy Earl has had a crush on her since adolescence. Along with a few other celebrities, she will be in Tillman Falls for the Rabbit Festival at the end of the third book.

GILLIAN WELCH — The musician plays the Rabbit Music Festival in Book Three

DAVID RAWLINGS — The musician plays the Rabbit Music Festival in Book Three

PAGE McCONNELL — Keyboardist for the band Phish with whom Button and Heather interact, albeit indirectly

GEORGE W. BUSH — After making a photo-op stop at a nearby US Army base, the President drops in on Trudy and Rabbit for The Dixiana's famous Broasted Chicken Basket

JOHNNY CASH — in 1969, on his way to a State Fair appearance, the country music icon stopped in and did a few tunes at The Dixiana, along with his wife and a friend

JUNE CARTER CASH — accompanying Johnny Cash

BOB DYLAN — accompanying Johnny Cash

GEORGE WALLACE — the presidential candidate makes a speech outside The Dixiana

JERRY GARICA — a pre-stardom Garcia and a friend attend a bluegrass jam at The Dixiana in 1962, where they get in trouble with Mr. Rabbit over recording

SANDY ROTHMAN — Garcia's friend and fellow bluegrass traveler

ABOUT THE AUTHOR

James D. McCallister is the author of five novels, two short story collections, and numerous other shorter pieces of fiction and creative nonfiction. A lifelong South Carolinian, he lives in West Columbia with his wife and beloved brood of cats, muses all.

CONTACT JAMES D McCALLISTER:
www.jamesdmccallister.com
editor@mindharvestpress.com

RETURN TO
James D. McCallister's
"EDGEWATER COUNTY, SC"

in

King's Highway
Fellow Traveler
Let the Glory Pass Away
The Year They Canceled Christmas
Dogs of Parsons Hollow

and

DOWN IN DIXIANA (2019)
DIXIANA DARLING (2020)
RECONSTRUCTION OF THE FABLES (2020)
MANSION OF HIGH GHOSTS (2021)
WANDO (2022)

MHP
Mind Harvest Press
COLUMBIA, SC

www.jamesdmccallister.com